MW01282452

THE HOLLOW EARTH
&
RETURN TO THE HOLLOW EARTH

TWO NARRATIVES OF
MASON ALGIERS REYNOLDS OF VIRGINIA

RUDY RUCKER

Transreal Books
Los Gatos, California

Cover design by Georgia Rucker.
Cover art by Rudy Rucker

Transreal Books
Los Gatos, California
www.transrealbooks.com

ALSO BY RUDY RUCKER

SF NOVELS

Juicy Ghosts
Million Mile Road Trip
Turing & Burroughs
Jim and the Flims
Hylozoic
Postsingular
Mathematicians in Love
Frek and the Elixir
Spaceland
The Hollow Earth
Master of Space and Time

TRANSREAL SF NOVELS

The Big Aha
Saucer Wisdom
The Hacker and the Ants
The Secret of Life
The Sex Sphere
White Light
Spacetime Donuts

THE WARE TETRALOGY

Realware
Freeware
Wetware
Software

HISTORICAL NOVEL

As Above, So Below: Peter Bruegel

For Martin Gardner,
My parents Embry & Marianne,
My wife Sylvia,
My children Georgia, Rudy & Isabel, and
My grandchildren Althea, Jasper, Zimry, Desmond & Calder

The Hollow Earth

Return to The Hollow Earth

THE HOLLOW EARTH

1. Leaving the Farm

I went to Poe's funeral yesterday. There was a minister, four mourners, and a grave digger. The grave digger called me a black bastard and chased me off. Otha should have been there to see.

Eddie wanted to write the account of our "unparalleled journey," but he's dead any way you look at it and Otha's in the Umpteen Seas. That leaves me and Seela living as penniless, free Baltimore Negroes, with the winter of 1849 coming soon. I'm writing as fast as I can.

My name is Mason Algiers Reynolds. I am a white man; I am a Virginia gentleman. My unparalleled journey started thirteen years ago, when I left my father's farm in Hardware, Virginia. There were five of us on the farm: Pa, me, Otha, Luke, and Turl.

I woke in the dark that last day at home. I'd been dreaming about being buried alive. The dream was tedious more than it was scary. In the dream I couldn't see anything; I could just hear and feel. First there was the noise of the folks praying over me, and then came the bumping of the coffin being carried out and lowered into the ground. There were some hymns, and then they shoveled the dirt in on me and it was nothing but black.

Right after I woke up, everything felt like a coffin—my bed, my room, Pa's farm. But then I got happy, remembering that I was fifteen and that tomorrow I would drive the wagon to town.

I got up to pee out the window. The moon was low, and the predawn breeze brought the smell of rainsoft fields. We'd made it through another winter, we Reynoldses, and tomorrow was today. Pa was sending me and Otha to Lynchburg to sell three barrels of whiskey. We needed seeds, a new plow, some books for me, and a wife for Otha if we could find one. All winter I'd had nothing but Euclid's *Elements*, a Latin primer, and our accumulated subscription copies of *The Southern Literary Messenger* to read, which is where, come to think of it, I'd gotten the idea of being buried alive: from Edgar Poe's tale "Loss of Breath."

Beneath the surface, my thoughts were still running down the tracks of that bad dream, wondering about the worms that eat corpses. Were corpse worms the same as the purple crawlers that Otha and I used for fishing? Or were corpse worms the fat white grubs with hard heads that bite? I'd once read in the *Messenger* that if an angel from another star were to come and do a census of Earth, she'd think this was a planet of worms, since there's more of them than of any other living creature. Beetles would come in second, as I recall.

In the barn, our new-farrowed sow was grunting, warm and slow. I said a prayer and went back to sleep.

Turl woke me up for real, yelling up the stairs that it was time for breakfast. She was a handsome yellow woman who never tired of telling all of us that she was too good to be a slave. According to Turl, her grandmother had been a Hottentot princess and her grandfather a Spanish buccaneer. It was no secret what she thought of the rest of us: Pa was a drunkard, I was a dreamer, Otha a baby, and Luke a mule. The only one of her relatives she ever said anything nice about was her sister's little son, Purly, at the Perrows in Lynchburg. We all put up with her because with Ma dead, Turl was the only woman to care for us men. When she was feeling sweet, she could cook and sew and clean to a fare-thee-well.

But today wasn't one of Turl's sweet days. Breakfast was a sloppy cold porridge of watery grits and rank fatback. Turl slapped some of it in bowls for me and Pa, and took the rest of it out to the slave cabin, holding her mouth stiff and stuck out. I was glad to be leaving today.

"How's the boy, Mason?" said Pa, coming in from the barn. He'd already been out to feed the stock. He was big and strong and he had a black beard. Sometimes I wondered how Ma could have stood to kiss him—in the picture we had of her, she looked so delicate that it seemed like a rough beard would have torn her face. I took after Ma; I was blond and short, with pale brown eyes. Ma'd died aborning me. Occasionally I worried that Pa hated me for it; not that he was ever harsh with me—far from it. Pa could be rough on other men, but he still had his gentleness to let out, and mostly it came to me.

He walked over and rested his callused hand on my neck. "Are you ready for the trip, son?"

"Lord yes, Pa! I've been packed for two days! Soon as we eat our breakfast, I'll help load the barrels into the wagon."

"Luke and Otha and I can do that, Mason. My boy's too fine to coarsen up his hands. He's going to be a university man!"

"Aw, Pa. You sit down and eat, too."

We sat and ate for a bit, and pretty soon Pa commenced to chuckle. "Tastes like Turl's upset."

I stuck my lips out to imitate Turl's mad face, and Pa laughed harder, making a deep rumbling sound like a bear. I set my dish down on the floor and let Arf finish it. He'd been lying under the table waiting, the way he always did.

"Looks like Turl'd want her son to have a wife," Pa said. "With her womb all dried up, that's the only way we're going to raise any more slaves."

"Otha's scared," I told Pa.

"He won't stay scared long, young buck like him." Pa wiped his mouth off and stared at me. "Would you be scared of a wife, Mason?"

"No sir. Leastways I don't think so. Not if she was as kind and beautiful as Ma."

"Be careful of the women in the Liberty Hotel, Mason. They beautiful, but they not kind. After you sell the whiskey to Mr. Sloat, go straight to Judge Perrow's and stay on there with his family. I'm putting a demijohn of my best mash on the wagon for him."

"Yessir. I'll give it to him." The good thing about Judge Perrow was his daughter, Lucy, a reckless blond girl several years my senior. Last year Pa'd brought me into town for Christmas, and Lucy had played a kissing game with me.

"Good. And, Mason, it might not be a bad idea to just buy Otha a gal from the judge's household, or from one of his friends. The ones you might see at auction, there's no telling what they been through. I recall the judge owns a nice gal called Wawona. Look at the Perrows' Wawona before going off half-cocked."

I winced at the thought of doing business with sour old Judge Perrow. It was no secret that he thought of me as an unmanly bookworm. Last Christmas dinner when I'd tried to talk about one of Edgar Poe's stories in the *Messenger*, the judge had launched into a long tirade against Poe's character and against literary thinking in general. I was already known to all our family and friends as a good reader and writer; indeed, whenever Pa or my uncle Tuck needed a letter written, they came to me. When I'd taken exception to the judge's remarks about literature, he compared me to a chicken-killing dog and asked if I'd eaten a dictionary. It was hard to see how he and a girl as nice as Lucy could even be in the same family. Pa saw my expression and sighed. "Just make sure the new girl is broad-hipped and healthy. Mason. And try not to pay more than sixty dollars. Don't give Otha too much say-so; he changes his mind every ten minutes anyhow."

There was a whoop out in the barnyard, and then Otha was at the door. "Lez go, Mist Mason! Lez go to town!" He was dressed in his Sunday clothes, Pa's castoffs carefully patched by Turl. Otha was three years older than me and a foot taller. He was lanky like Turl and coal-black like Luke. His head was small and round, and his big mouth went a third of the way around. Yesterday he'd been scared, but today he was raring to go.

Luke was out in the barnyard waiting with the wagon and the three barrels of whiskey that Pa'd distilled this winter. In the summers we grew corn, and in the winters Pa turned the corn into whiskey. It wasn't just that Pa liked whiskey; this was the handiest way of getting our crop to market. One barrel of whiskey was worth the same as five hundredweight of corn.

Otha helped Pa and Luke roll the barrels up some boards and onto the wagon. Arf got excited and started barking. He had the noble profile and the feathery legs of a retriever. His legs and ruff were white, but his head and body had the tawny coloring of a collie. I'd grown up talking to him like a person. He had a way of moving his eyebrows and his feathery tail so expressively that I often felt he understood me. Now in the farmyard, his tail and eyes were merry as he pumped his barks skyward, There was no sign of Turl. Pa went back in the house to get Judge Perrow's demijohn.

"Gonna get us a sweet gal, Mist Mase?" said Luke. He was a strong man with a dazed air about him. It was as if he'd given up thinking years ago.

"Ain't no *us*, Daddy," cried Otha. "Gonna get *me*! I'm the one fixin to jump over the broom with the new gal." In our part of Virginia, a master married slaves to each other by having them jump over a broom handle that was held a few feet off the ground.

"Sho you is!" said Luke. "Just like me an yo mam." He glanced back at the slave cabin and lowered his voice. "Don't bring back no thin mean yaller bitch, Marse Mase, I swear to God. Bring me a black gal with a big butt."

"Ain't gonna *be* yo gal, Daddy," said Otha one more time. He tried to laugh, but the sound came out all cracked. I knew he wanted to leave as bad as I did. Things were too tight on our little farm.

I went in the barn and got our mule. His name was Dammit. Pa'd given him a big breakfast of corn, and he was in a mood to ramble. Otha and I hitched Dammit to the wagon tongue and drove him forward a little, checking how the barrels rode. They were heavy enough so that Otha and I'd have to walk, but that was no matter. It was turning into a sunny April day and the mud had stiffened up pretty good.

Finally, Pa came out with the judge's demijohn. I could smell from Pa's breath that he'd sampled it. Without me there to watch over him, he'd probably stay drunk for a week, Poor Pa. I hugged him goodbye, and Otha started Dammit toward the gate. We all knew Turl still had her licks to get in, and now there she was in her cabin door with her face all wet.

"Otha!"

"Mam?"

"Otha, ain't you gonna say goodbye?"

"Goodbye, Mam." Otha looked desperately unhappy.

"Otha, why you wanna leave yo mam?" She started across the barnyard toward Otha. If I was man enough to take the wagon to town, I was man enough to stand up to Turl. I stepped in between her and Otha, blocking her way.

"We'll be back in a few days, Turl. Goodbye."

"Get outten my way, you whelp."

She raised her hand as if to slap me, and I wondered what I could do about it. Pa spoke up before it went that far, "Turl!"

She stood there a moment, a proud thin woman afraid of losing her son. Otha urged Dammit on through the gate, and then I was out of the barnyard, too. Arf slipped out the gate after us, his tail held demurely down. I scolded him, and he cringed, but he kept right on coming. Luke and Pa and Turl stood there watching us, Turl with her hand still up in the air. Finally, she started to wave. I prayed we wouldn't bog down in the muddy farm track that led over the hill to the highway—not that the highway was anything more than a dirt road three ruts wide. If we could only get out of the grown-ups' sight!

Otha was thinking just like me, and if Dammit had balked then, I think we would have stove in his ribs. But Dammit pulled and the wagon rolled and in just a few minutes we creaked up over the crest of the rise that separated our farm from the highway. We looked back and gave the parents a last wave, little realizing we'd never see them again, not that we would have stopped even if we'd known. We were right sick of life on that farm.

It was a fine day, the last day in April. There was enough wet in the ground so the sun had a weak, watery feel to it. The highway was muddier than I'd expected, and every so often Otha had to get behind the wagon and push while I urged Dammit from the front. Arf liked it best when Dammit would balk and I'd have to pull at the mule's bridle. Arf would help out then, barking and snapping and coming as close as possible to getting kicked, all the while glancing up at me for approval. Going down hills, Otha and I would hop on the wagon and drag the brake levers against the wheels. It was hard, muddy work, especially for Otha, but our spirits rose higher and higher as we neared Lynchburg. Otha began chaffing me about Lucy Perrow—I'd had no one else but Otha to confide in that time she'd kissed me—and I let him in on Pa's plans about Wawona.

"What she look like?" Otha wanted to know.

I only remembered pigtails and a wide smile, but I talked her up to Otha, secretly hoping we wouldn't have to go to the auction. There'd be ugly rednecks there, and I'd be cheated sure as night.

The green-hazed woods were full of blooming white dogwoods, peeping out at us like shy girls. There were bright red-buds, too, and best of all, the big purple bell-blossoms of the paulownia trees that only bloomed every few years.

I knew the way to Lynchburg from having made the trip with Pa before. The highway meanders along next to Rucker Run Creek for some eight miles, at which point you find yourself on a high bluff looking down at the James River and at the town of Lynchburg on the river's other side. The creek cascades right down the cliff, but a body has to drive left and loop all around to get past the bluffs to the James.

Before hopping on the wagon to ride the brakes down the loop, Otha and I paused a moment to rest. I unharnessed Dammit, and we led him over to the last pool of Rucker Run for a drink. He slurped for a bit and then began cropping at some of the early plants that stuck up green through the mud. Arf splashed across the creek and into the underbrush, in search of small critters. When Arf hunted, he flexed his ear muscles so that his flap ears would hang an extra half-inch farther out from his head. It gave him a harried, overalert look.

Otha and I washed some of the mud from the road off ourselves, and then we skirted around the edge of the pool, right out to the edge of the cliff where the creek went waterfalling down. It was a lovely view of Lynchburg from up there, all framed by the water and the flowering trees. The little town was on a hill that sloped down to the river.

"I'm a bird," sang Otha. "I sees everything, and when I poops, look out!" He pointed out across the river toward the top of the hill. "Looky there, Mase, see the carriage ridin over the hilltop with the two dogs runnin after? I bet that's Judge Perrow. Wawona, here I comes! And, Lordy Lord, see all the folks down to the market, Mase. You reckon it's Saturday? Whoooee! See there down in the river, they loadin up a boat! How about you send me and my new gal to Richmond for a honeymoon?"

The boat Otha was pointing to was the sort known as a bateau. The bateaus weren't cruise boats, they were flat-bottomed barges designed to carry tobacco down the shallow, rocky James to Richmond. They were rough and uncomfortable; crews of slaves poled them downstream and up.

The tobacco warehouses were on the first street up from the river, as were the cigar factories and the flour mill. The next street held the wholesale merchants: the feed stores, the slave traders, and the like. Another block up was Main Street, with its market square, its fancy stores, and the Liberty Hotel. Higher yet was the crest of the slope on which Lynchburg flourished, and on this crest was the great domed structure of the county courthouse, flanked by the offices of the bankers and lawyers who fattened on the city's trade.

We were brought back to the present by a howl from Arf. With great floundering and yelping, he came crashing toward us through the underbrush. His ears were flat to his head. Close behind him was a half-naked boy of ten.

"An issue!" exclaimed Otha—meaning the boy was the "free issue" of mixed slave, white, and/or native blood. A number of them lived wild in the woods.

Arf splashed across the pool and threw himself down at my side, panting with his mouth wide open. Now that he'd stopped running, he looked totally relaxed. Had the free issue boy threatened him? Or had it been the other way around?

"Hey," I called to the boy in the breechcloth. I'd thought he was splattered with mud, but the marks on his chest and face were regular stripes rather than random splotches. "Why you chasin my dog?"

The boy made a gesture and melted back into the underbrush. "An issue will eat a dog," said Otha. "Specially in the spring."

"What was that he did with his hand?" I asked. "Was he waving goodbye?"

"Maybe he puttin a hex on us. Lez move on, Mason." Otha didn't call me Mist or Marse when it was the two of us alone.

By the time Otha and I got down past the cliffs to the ferry, it was late afternoon. The ferry house was a wretched shack near the edge of the river. As the James flooded every few years, all the structures at its edge were temporary. I was glad to see that today the river was running clear and slow. I led Dammit and the wagon down onto the cobblestone apron that was the dock. The ferryman and his wife lived in the ramshackle ferry house; the wife sold biscuits and slices of ham.

"Buy us some food," urged Otha.

"Can't," I told him truly enough. "We don't have any money till we sell this whiskey to Mr. Sloat."

A hawser led across the river from a ring set into the cliff side. Its other end was similarly fastened: It served as a guide for the ferry. Right now the ferry was on the river's other side, just upstream from the bateau wharves, I waved to the ferryman and finally, slowly, he set his craft in motion. The ferryboat had hoops that hooked over the hawser, keeping it from drifting downstream. The ferryman had two slaves, each with long poling sticks.

As the ferryman drew near, his wife stumped out to the porch of the ferry house and began quizzing me. "Who you? I know I seen you befo, but you done growed!" She bent her mouth in a smile.

"I'm Mason Reynolds, from Hardware."

"I knowed it!" she shrilled. "Don't you and yo boy want some food, Mist Reynolds? I can give you a steam catfish on a naahce little loaf of bread."

"I don't have any money yet," I explained. "Until we sell these three barrels of whiskey."

"Lord! And how was you plannin to pay my husband?" There was nothing kind or gentle about this old woman. She reminded me of a splintered tree branch slimed over with river scum. She looked smooth, but she'd cut you fast. She was so excited about the fee, she took a step toward us, which set Arf to barking. He had a special deep-chested bark he used on strangers, a bark quite different from the tip-of-the-nose bark he did when he was simply excited.

"I'll pay him on our way back," I said. "Surely you trust a gentleman." Pa was fond of saying how he and I were gentlemen, but this old woman wasn't having any of it.

"Dirt-farmer whiskey-seller kind of gentleman! How about if you leave that demijohn with me for safekeepin?" The old bitch had spied out the extra wicker-covered whiskey bottle I had for Judge Perrow.

"You'd drink it dry," I exclaimed. "Two dollars," said the ferryman, who'd just stepped ashore. "Twenny-five cent each for the mule and the Negro, fifty cent for the young *gentleman*, and a dollar for the loaded wagon. Right this way, and set the brakes good for the ride."

"He says he don't have any money," cried the ferryman's wife. "His wagon's full of whiskey!"

The ferryman smiled broadly. "Fetch a jug, Helen, and the gentleman'll tap us off a gallon."

"We get three dollars a gallon for our whiskey," I protested.

"An I get three dollars for ferryin it," said the man calmly.

"I'm mighty hungry," Otha reminded me.

"Get us two fish breads," I called after the old woman, who was in her house looking, no doubt, for the world's largest jug. She reappeared presently with the food in one hand and the jug in the other. She'd brought us each a small loaf of bread split in two and with a whole catfish on it, still warm from the steamer, its eyes all white. I set mine down on the wagon, but Otha boned and ate his fish right away. I got the demijohn out of the wagon and trickled the ferryman's jug full. He watched with a pleased smile as his jug swallowed up about half of what the judge had coming. When I went to put the demijohn back in the wagon, my loaf and fish fell on the muddy ground. Arf bolted the slippery gray catfish with a nasty gasping sound. Nobody noticed, and I was too disgusted to say anything about it. I led Dammit onto the ferry, urging him to pull our wagon up the sloping planks that led aboard. Dammit couldn't quite make it, and when I asked Otha to push the wagon from behind, he was slow about it. Losing all patience, I cursed Otha for a lazy black fool. In truth, I suppose I was abusing my companion to look big to the ferryman and his wife. Slave master Mason Reynolds! Otha gave me a puzzled look and leaned his strength against the stalled wagon.

Finally we were all afloat, gliding across the green James River for Lynchburg. There were huge rapids upstream from us, and cooling bits of mist came drifting down on the early evening breeze. The ferryman pulled at his new-filled jug, sighing with pleasure and gazing up into the darkening sky.

"Do you like it out here on the river?" I asked Otha.

He eyed me suspiciously, still smarting from my harsh words of a minute ago. "We out here, Mase, and ain't neither one of us can swim." There were lights on in Lynchburg. The closer we got to the town, the bigger it looked.

"I'll act right by you, Otha, you can count on me. I was only yelling at you because Arf ate my fish."

"Arf ain't the fool," muttered Otha. "An neither is I. *You* the buttho." He swallowed the last word, but the ferryman's two slaves caught the tenor of his remark and grinned at me with expressions that dared me to object. I was just a fifteen-year-old country boy, and they were full-grown men of the city. I kept silent, stroking Arf and biting my lips. This was an example of what slave owners always said: Give the crow a kernel, and his flock will eat your field.

The ferry grounded on the Lynchburg landing ramp. I coaxed Dammit forward, Arf and Otha followed, and there we were, big as life, on the Lynchburg waterfront, six o'clock of a Saturday evening, April 30, 1836.

Otha came up next to me, and we stood there, the two of us, staring at all the people. There were heaps of darkies, whole crews of them, with their own black bosses. One gang was swarming over a bateau, loading it up with hogsheads of tobacco. Fussy little white bankers and merchants were dithering around, and knots of rednecks, too. It was more different people at once than I'd seen total all winter in Hardware. I stood goggling; breathing in the smells, mostly bad, and listening to the hubbub of the wharf, with its waves lapping, timbers creaking, and barrels rolling on beneath the noise of the wharfmen's hollers and farewells. Behind those noises I could hear the great hum of Lynchburg's thousand voices and the ceaseless grinding of her thousand wheels.

Someone tapped my hand. I glanced down to see a four-foot white man with a heavy pistol strapped around his waist.

"Hidee," said he. He had an upturned nose that showed the insides of his nostrils.

"How you," said I.

"What's your load?" asked the dwarf, as if he couldn't smell the sheen of good corn whiskey that had sprung through our barrels' dray-battered staves. I figured him for a damn thief. His gun meant that he worked for some one of the gangs of thieves that called themselves government. United States, Virginia Commonwealth, or Town of Lynchburg, they were all the same according to Pa—they all just wanted to drive the honest man down. Pa'd warned me not to answer any questions on the wharf or we'd end up giving out money to every thief who thought he had the right to ask for it.

"A gentleman's business is none of your affair," I said, calm-like. "My boy and I are heading into town. A good evening to you. Otha, get in back and mind the cargo." I hopped onto the seat of our wagon and flicked Dammit with the bridle. We clattered up the sloping cobblestone street. The dwarf yelled after us, but Arf barked and snarled so hard the little thief was scared to follow. Every now and then Arf did himself proud.

After the long day's haul, Dammit was inclined to slow down on the slope up to Main Street. I kept after him, now smacking him, now talking about oats. Fortunately enough, the Liberty Hotel was right at the corner where we crossed Main. We pulled around into the courtyard in back. A hostler came out of the stables, a sharp-faced blond boy not much taller than me. He seemed right watchful of things and even had a pistol to hand in a holster hanging on the wall. I asked him to give Dammit some water and a half pail of cracked com. Brushing down the mule could wait till we got to the Perrows'.

Otha went over to the kitchen shed and started chaffing with the cooks. To see him there so free and easy, you'd think he'd been hanging around Lynchburg all his life. For my part, I felt small and no-count. Standing in the courtyard, I could see through a small open window into the hotel saloon. There was a lively crowd in there, no doubt about it. Men were singing and cursing, with pretty women laughing loose and bold. The sight of them cheered me right up. They were the women Pa had warned me about! As soon as I could finish up my deal with Mr. Sloat, I hoped to get a closer look at some of those famous women. I lifted Arf up into the wagon bed to guard the whiskey, and went in the hotel back door.

The back door led into a dark wood-plank hall. There was a staircase on my left and some smoke-blackened frame paintings on the wall on my right. About ten paces in, the hall opened up into a lobby with stuffed chairs and a small Oriental rug on the floor. Pa'd never taken me here before, but he'd told me about that rug. It was marvelous, all red-and-blue-bordered, and with twelve squares marked off, each square with a different kind of zigzag explosion in it. I bent over to get a closer look at how it was made.

"Don't bed down just yet, country cousin," said a voice. "The rooms are upstairs. Would you care to register?"

I turned around, blushing, and saw there was a fat man at a desk in the rear corner of the lobby. He wore gray trousers and a shiny black tailcoat. I blushed harder, realizing that with my rough shoes, simple blue breeches, and loose white blouse I looked no better than the stableboy outside.

"Are...are you Mr. Sloat?"

"You have the advantage of me, sir." Sloat cocked his head questioningly. His eyes were dark and bright in the white dough of his face.

"I am Mason Algiers Reynolds of Hardware, Virginia."

Sloat picked up a pencil and chewed the tip. "The whiskey Reynoldses?" I'd expected him to be pleased, but he merely looked distracted.

"I have three twenty-gallon barrels on my wagon in the courtyard outside. Pa said you could pay four dollars a gallon, which would make two hundred forty dollars, would it not?"

"Would it not." Sloat shook his head and gave a short, mirthless laugh. "God save me from petty Virginia gentlemen with manure on their shoes. Come closer, son, and don't step on the rug." Pa'd warned me that Sloat was a sharp one. The rock bottom I could take for the whiskey was two dollars a gallon, though last year Sloat had paid two fifty and this year we were hoping for three.

"It's unusually good mash this year," I said. "Last summer's corn came in extra sweet." I thought of Judge Perrow's already opened demijohn. "Would you care for a taste, Mr. Sloat?"

"Your mash may be better than last year…Mason, is it?" I nodded, though I wished he'd call me Mr. Reynolds. "Your mash may be better, but my custom is worse. Prices are down. The very most I can pay per gallon is…" He stared at my eyes, and I could have sworn that he was reading my mind. "Two dollars a gallon." He knew he had me, and he pressed right on. "Let my men unload your wagon, and you can settle in here as my personal guest…Mr. Reynolds." Another sharp glance at my eyes. "For a valuable supplier like you, everything my hotel offers is free: room, board, and…" He rolled his bright little eyes toward the saloon door on the other side of the lobby. "And one night's companionship."

One of the women laughed again, long and wild, like there was no tomorrow. Nobody would have to know. I could go to the Perrows' tomorrow and say I'd just come into town. Otha would back me up if I…but where would Otha sleep? Not in my room, not with a woman there. "What about my manservant?" I asked Mr. Sloat.

He shrugged. "Have the hostler put fresh straw in your mule's stall. There'll be room enough for both of them."

I knew I couldn't do that to Otha. He was here to find a wife, and I was going to put him with a mule so I could bed a whore? He'd tell Pa for sure. I followed Mr. Sloat down the hall to the courtyard, still thinking.

Some of Mr. Sloat's men rolled our barrels down into the hotel cellar, and then Mr. Sloat took me back into his private office, a dark little room right behind his desk in the hotel lobby. It had a peephole in the door so Mr. Sloat could keep an eye on everything. There was another peephole set into the left-hand wall.

Mr. Sloat had a big rolltop desk and a metal safe with a lock on it. The safe door was ajar. He gave me a sharp look and then hunched over the safe till he'd found the $120 he owed me: six gold double-eagle coins. They were so heavy I worried they'd drop through my pocket.

"So," he said, pushing the safe door almost closed. "That's our business, and I thank you, Mr. Reynolds. Did you want to have supper in your room or at the bar?"

"I…" I'd been thinking about what to say, but it was hard getting it out. "I have to go on to Judge Perrow's tonight, Mr. Sloat. But if…if you really mean that about…companionship…" The women through the wall were laughing hard and high. "Just for an hour," I said finally. "Just to see what a woman is like."

Mr. Sloat smiled like I'd made him very happy. Perhaps it was his pleasure to mislead the young. "Go on into the bar and pick one," he said, leaning back and waving his fat hand at the door. "There's four of them there, fat and fresh and ready to go."

I scuffed my feet and shook my head. The women wouldn't believe I had Mr. Sloat's go-ahead, and the drunk men would laugh at me. They'd tell all their coarse friends. Pa and Judge Perrow would find out. *Lucy* would find out. I couldn't go in the bar and ask a woman to come upstairs.

"Look through the peephole if you're a-scared," said Mr. Sloat coaxingly. He gestured at the little glass bull's-eye set into his office wall. "Look in there and make your pick and I'll send her upstairs to you." He was uncommon keen on this. I was such a hayseed that I couldn't see why.

I stared through the peephole for a long time. At first it was hard to see, but then I got my vision and began picking them out. It was two older women and two younger, two of them blond and two of them dark-haired. I didn't want to choose the young blond one, on account of Lucy, so I told Mr. Sloat the young dark-haired girl would do. He sent me on up to room number three. It was a plain enough room, with a shuttered window that opened onto the courtyard. I sat on the bed for a while, and nothing happened. Finally, I cracked the shutters and peeked down in the courtyard. It was the last breath of twilight. Our wagon was right down there, with Arf lying on it licking his balls and Dammit standing next to one of the wheels, sleeping. I wondered where Otha had gotten to.

"Welcome to Lynchburg, Mason," said a sweet voice behind me.

I jerked back and the shutter slapped shut. It was the young dark-haired woman, sure enough, smiling at me and holding a candle. Seen up this close, her hair had some kink to it. A quadroon, I expect, but Lord knows she looked clean and she smelled sweet. She set the candle down and came right to me before I could start worrying about what to do. Her name was Sukie.

Pa'd never quite explained the details of sex to me, but at the end of an hour I knew all about making babies and I'd seen exactly where they come from—though it meant getting some candle wax on the sheet. I bounced with Sukie three times, just to make sure I understood. It tired me out so much I dropped right off to sleep. It was Otha yelling down in the courtyard that woke me up.

"Mist Maaaaason?"

The room was pitch-dark and the woman was gone. I got up and banged into things till I could get the shutter open.

"Mistuh Maaaaason?" I could see him as a dark patch against the courtyard's pale cobblestones. Off to the right, the kitchen fires were burning.

"Hsst, Otha, I'm coming."

"What you doin up there?" he said, all mock innocence until he burst out laughing. Darkies always knew everything that white folks did. I left the shutter open and dressed by the faint light of the town outside. I realized I should have hidden my gold, but—thank God—my pocket was still heavy with it. Next I started worrying that the Perrows would be able to smell the sticky perfume of Sukie's body on my loins, so I dropped my pants to splash myself off with the water in the basin. How late was it?

I hurried downstairs and found Otha lounging against the wagon. He looked more loose-limbed than usual and more content.

"What time is it, Otha?"

"I ain't got no clock, Mase. All I know is it be dinnertime come an gone. I traded a few pannikins of our whiskey to the cook for supper. Whoooee, it were good. Beefsteak from a cow, Mase, all fried up with taters an onions an washed down with city-made beer. I don't never wanna go back to no farm."

There was lots of noise from the hotel bar—I thought I could hear Sukie singing. Warm lights filled the windows in every direction. It couldn't be later than eight or nine. "We better head on to the Perrows', Otha. I'm all done here."

"I see you is." He grinned broadly. "Were she sweet?"

2. Murder

It wasn't till the next morning that I learned Sukie had replaced all my gold pieces with lead slugs.

I woke to the sound of church bells and rain. Lucy had said we'd be going to St. Paul's Episcopal Church downtown today. I knew the Perrows had a closed coach, so the rain didn't matter. The idea of taking Lucy to church touched something deep in me. I was a man now, no doubt about it, and before too many years I'd be getting married. First I'd go to the university, of course, but after that…

I lay in bed for half an hour, listening to the rain and running over the happy memories of my wonderful interlude with Sukie. I wondered if there was any chance of seeing her again. Already the exact sensations of the act were a bit a hard to recall. It had been smooth in her, smooth and warm.

The drive to the Perrows' had been easy—with his belly full and the wagon empty, Dammit hadn't minded a bit. Otha had thought to pour the judge's remaining whiskey into a tight small jug from the hotel kitchen. The judge had graciously accepted it, never knowing that twice as much had gotten away. Mrs. Perrow was fluttery and hostesslike as ever, happy for some distraction from the judge's endless talk of politics. The slave girl Wawona had been brought in for my inspection: She was firm and sassy and interested in Otha, who was bunking down with the rest of the Perrow slaves. The judge said we could have her for sixty dollars. Lucy above all had been thrilled to see me. She'd pressed more than one kiss on me out on the stairs before bed. I'd gone to bed happy and woken up the same. Everyone loved everyone.

"Oh, Maaason!" Lucy's voice came drifting up the kitchen stairs. "Get up, sleepyhead! It's May Day! You said you'd take Ma and me to church!" Judge Perrow was a freethinker, and the Perrow women were happy to have a man accompany them to church this once. I didn't have much religion, but I'd be glad for the outing.

"I'll be right down, sweet thing!" The gallant words sprang easily from my lips. What a change Sukie had wrought, quiet radiant Sukie, goddess of the night!

What a change indeed. After I'd washed up, I reached into the pocket of yesterday's muddy breeches and pulled out...six gray lead slugs.

The rain kept right on like nothing had happened, and Lucy called me again just the same as before. But I stood there thunderstruck, staring down at the gray metal in the window's gray Sunday light. Of course Sloat had wanted Sukie to come up to me. Sukie had robbed me, and she hadn't even done it for herself.

"Mason! Am I going to have to come up there and fetch you?"

Slowly, I took Pa's good clothes out of the portmanteau. It was a white linen shirt along with black trousers and a tailcoat. I'd looked forward to wearing these fancy clothes when Turl had hemmed up the sleeves and pant legs for me, but now it was all ashes. Even the bright red cravat Pa'd given me failed to lift my spirits. I shoved the lead coins into the right-hand pocket of my tailcoat and walked numbly down to the kitchen. Lucy was at the table, and Wawona's mother, Baistey, was at the stove.

"Some ham and eggs, Mason?" said Lucy. "You'd better eat fast, there's not much time. Walloon has blacked your shoes." She had a bossy edginess that I'd never seen before.

"Ham and grits," said I, still fingering the lead disks in my pocket. "When is the church service over?" I had to go see Sloat.

"It starts at ten," said Lucy, "and it's nine o'clock now. See my watch, Mason? Lieutenant Bustler gave it to me for

Christmas." She stretched out her arm to show me the little gold brooch watch she held clutched in her hand. It was the smallest watch I'd ever seen—no bigger than an inch across—and it even had a fast-moving thin hand that counted seconds. "Wasn't that dear of him?" went on Lucy, turning the watch over and opening its back, "See here? Lieutenant Bustler's picture." The cameo showed a pie-faced man with muttonchops and a high collar.

Baistey set my ham and grits down in front of me and filled me up a big glass of milk. There was butter and black-berry jam to put on the grits. For a few minutes I ate without thinking. When I noticed Lucy again, she was looking at Lieutenant Bustler's picture and now and then glancing over at me. I had the feeling I was supposed to ask her something, but I didn't know what.

"Will Bustler be at church?" I said finally.

"No," Lucy quavered. "Lieutenant Bustler is serving the naval department in Norfolk, Virginia. I'd thought, Mason, that he would take me with him, but the fates would have it not." She gave me a look that said she had much more to tell.

"I wouldn't trust him," I blurted out. The upset of losing all Pa's money had me on edge. "Your Lieutenant Bustler looks too flat-headed for anything *but* soldiering. What kind of a fool is a military man anyway, Lucy? A fool to fight other fools at the head fools' say-so." I'd heard Pa say this many times.

All of a sudden Lucy was in tears. "You're so right, dear Mason. I trusted him too much. He…he caused me to fall and, oh, Mason, *everyone knows!*" With her face red and twisted in the morning light, she looked less lovely than I can say. My heart went out to her.

"Hush that talk, Lucy. You'll find a husband soon enough. You just wait and see. Pshaw, if you last till I'm out of the university, I may come a-courting you myself." The implicit admission that I was not courting Lucy *right now* made things worse. She cried harder, and Baistey left the room, no doubt heading for the African Baptist Church with the rest of the slaves. I walked over to the kitchen door and stared through the glass at the rain. There went Turl's sister, Calla, carrying Turl's two-year-old nephew, Purly, a cute little boy with features as fine as a new-minted coin. The lead was heavy in my pocket.

Someone was scratching at the bottom of the door. I opened it a crack and Arf surged in, soaking wet. I caught him, but not before he'd executed a big shake, which showered Lucy's pale blue dress with muddy spots.

"Goddamn you," she screamed in sudden anger. "Stupid bookworm with a stupid dog. I don't need your pity. Mason Reynolds!" Before I could react, Lucy had stormed upstairs.

I fed Arf a big slice of ham, dried him with a kitchen towel, and snuck him up the back stairs to my bedroom. "Good dog," I told him. "You stay here." He stared up at me and blinked his eyes twice, the way he always did when he pretended he understood. I shoved him down on his side and hoped he'd go to sleep.

Was the trip to church still on? And what was I going to say to Sloat? Too bad I didn't have a gun. I thought of Judge Perrow's gun collection. I hurried back downstairs and through the kitchen to the gun cases in the den off the hall. They were locked, but as luck would have it, the key was right in the first desk drawer I tried. Wonderful. I got the case with pistols open and took myself a four-shot pepperbox pistol, small enough to fit in my tailcoat's inside pocket. There were rapid footsteps all through the house now; the women were almost ready to go. Working quickly on the floor, I got my pistol charged and loaded. I swept the spilled powder under a rug, locked the case, dropped the key back in the desk, and put the pistol in the left-hand pocket of my coat.

"There you are, Mason!" sang Mrs. Perrow, popping into the den. "Lucy's changed her dress and we're all ready to go! Get your shoes!"

The weight of the judge's pistol balanced out the weight of Sloat's lead. I sat through the church service with equanimity, enjoying the rare sensation of being part of a crowd.

St. Paul's Episcopal Church, Lynchburg, Virginia, had a minister called Spickett. He was an older man with thinning hair and a smarmy accent. His sermon was about our stewardship of the Negro race. It hadn't been so long since the black preacher Nat Turner and his followers had killed off some fifty white people, and folks were still buzzing about it. We all knew that if the slaves ever *really* revolted, there'd be hell to pay. Maybe we should free them first. But what would the blacks do then, and what would happen to the South? We looked up at Reverend Spickett, waiting for his answers.

Not that I expected much. We weren't big on religion in my family. Pa was known to say God was a hoax, and that ministers were thieves. Even so, it was a treat to be inside a church. I doubt if I'd been to church more than a dozen times in my life.

Reverend Spickett's text was the saying, "Suffer the little children to come unto me." The darkies, according to him, were our children, given by God unto the white race's care. We were to be firm yet gentle, ever mindful of the fact that the Negro was our ward, a subordinate human species whose ongoing growth must eternally trail the wake of the ever-wiser white race. Here the reverend got to his point: Although *someday* the time might come when it would be proper to teach certain Negroes to read, that time was not now. *No Negro should read, whether or not he knew how.* Nonetheless, it was fitting that all God's children should find Jesus Christ through the divinely inspired words of the Bible. Therefore, St. Paul's was adopting the African Baptist Church as a mission and had begun sending a deacon over to their Sunday services to act as a reader. Congregation members were urged to increase their offerings today to help with this holy work of stewardship.

There were a number of rich planters' families in the church, and they filled the plates right up. The unspoken point was that Nat Turner had been a Negro preacher who read books. My mind wandered, and I started thinking what it would be like to own Sukie. She was just about black anyway, wasn't she? But if I was so much wiser than her, how had she turned my gold into lead? And why could Otha beat me at checkers whenever he really wanted to? These vague thoughts damped down into a trance as I sat there staring at the pretty colors of the stained glass over the altar. It was a picture of Jesus standing on an orb, with clouds all around and a bright light overhead.

We took communion, and we sang some hymns. I had fun picking the different voices out of the singing and then looking around to see whose they were. I felt like I knew lots of the people by the service's end, not that anyone rushed up to say how-do. There seemed to be some truth to Lucy's belief that her affair with Lieutenant Bustler had made her a social outcast. But Mrs. Perrow was good friends with Reverend Spickett, and she dragged me over to meet him.

"This is Mason Reynolds from Hardware."

"Ah, yes. I know your father. A real man." Evidently Spickett didn't know the kinds of things Pa said about religion. The preacher peered at me like I wasn't much compared to Pa. I hadn't gotten my growth yet, you understand. "Is your father well?"

"I left him well. He had me bring our whiskey to town."

"I'm sure Lynchburg needs more whiskey!" said Spickett cheerfully, and turned to shake the next person's hand.

"That reminds me," I told Lucy and Mrs. Perrow on our way out of church. "I have to stop by the Liberty Hotel and speak to Mr. Sloat."

"You can't expect us to go in there!" exclaimed Lucy. She was all set to plunge into another of her snits. "Really, Mother, can you fathom Mason's manners?"

"Can your business wait till tomorrow, Mason?" said Mrs. Perrow.

"No ma'am, it honestly can't." I could see the hotel from the church steps. "Suppose I go over there alone and meet you all back at the house."

"And leave us unescorted?" wailed Lucy. I was liking her less all the time.

"If you'll be quick, Mason," suggested Mrs. Perrow, "we can take the carriage down to the market square and meet you there."

"Wonderful." I helped them into their carriage, which was driven by their black boy, Walloon. I rode up on the front bench as far as the hotel and jumped off there to see about my gold.

The lobby was empty. I went behind Mr. Sloat's desk and pushed his office door open. He was in there right enough.

His face was mean and startled, but he was quick to set it in a lecherous smile.

"What must of squoze my Sukie mighty hard, Mason. She's flown the coop! Did she say anything to you about leaving?"

"You're a damned liar, Sloat!" I pulled the lead coins out of my pocket and threw them on his desk. "Give me back my gold!"

His eyebrows went up and down a few times, and then he forced out a laugh. "She robbed you too, did she? She took a suitcase of my silverware! But we'll catch her, boy, don't you fret."

Sloat was a slippery one all right. He'd told Sukie to rob me and now she was lying low, I was willing to bet. But who would help me prove it? "Have you called in the law?" I said finally.

"Just on an informal basis. Sheriff Garmee's a friend of mine. I believe you know him too, Mason. Little fellow, wears a gun?" Sloat squinted his eyes at me and chuckled nastily. "Sheriff said you was right short with him down by the wharf yestidday."

I sighed so heavily it sounded like a groan. These city slickers had me coming and going. If I pulled my pistol on Sloat, I'd land in jail. It was no use standing there with him smirking at me, so I left his office.

Just on a hunch, I went out the hotel's back way quiet-like and stood in the courtyard staring up at the windows. Most of them were shuttered, but—by God, yes—two of the windows up on the top floor were open, and there sitting by one of them was Sukie, looking in a hand mirror and combing out her curly black hair. I hurried out to Main Street before she could catch sight of me.

There were upward of a dozen carriages driving slowly around the perimeter of the cobblestoned market square. The clouds had broken up, and the sun was gleaming on the puddles. All those fine horses and coaches made a brave sight. It looked like May Day after all. Lucy spotted me and waved laughingly from her carriage window. I sprinted over and sprang nimbly onto the little step by her door.

"Good afternoon, lady fair!" I was trying to make up for this morning. Soon I'd talk things over with Otha, and we'd do what we had to do. I already had the makings of a plan. Wasn't no way Sloat was getting away with the Reynoldses' whiskey money. Sloat didn't realize what he'd gotten himself into. No indeed.

"Are you talking to yourself, Mason?" said Lucy. "What's the matter?"

"Nothing a-tall." I plastered on a smile.

Otha, as it turned out, had taken quite a shine to Wawona. After Sunday dinner, I went back to the kitchen and asked him to come outside with me. The Perrow house was up at the top of a long sloping field leading down to the river. There were vegetable plots in the field and a few acres of tobacco. With the torn bits of gray clouds drifting across the pale blue sky, it made for a lovely view. Otha couldn't stop talking about "that little girl."

"I'll buy her for you," said I. "But you have to help me get the money,"

"Whuffo get what you done got, Mason? Wawona cost sixty dollar an Mist Sloat done give you one hunnert an twenty."

"I'm telling you. That girl last night, that Sukie, she took the gold out of my pocket and gave it to Mr. Sloat. I went and asked him about it today, and he pretended she'd run away. But she's still right there in the Liberty Hotel. I saw her through a window. More than likely our money's right back in Sloat's safe where he got it in the first place."

"Damn and *hell*." Otha's lanky frame twitched in horror. "You teasin me, Mason! Cause what was that you was jinglin in yo pocket last night?"

"Lead."

"Damn and *hell*. I want Wawona, Mason, you white folks owes me that. Ain't my fault you done lost the money to a fancy ho'. Tell the judge you gonna pay him on account. That little girl comin home with us tomorrow." His voice softened. "She sweet as can be. I held her hand in church."

"Was there a white man reading the Bible?"

"I ain't pay him no mind. Bible pages be white, but the ink be black. Nat Turner say God be black, what they say."

I glanced around uneasily. "That's no way to talk, Otha. We're not on the farm here. We're in Lynchburg, and if you think Judge Perrow got rich by selling slaves on credit, you're dreaming. You got to help me steal that money back."

"An get caught and whupped an sold at auction for to pay yo fine? You gonna be the one to tell Turl what happen to me, messymess?" This was a childhood nickname that Otha still mocked me with from time to time. I hated it, as well he knew.

So that I wouldn't be in the demeaning posture of looking up at Otha, I glared into the distance. "If you gonna mouth at me like that, bonebrain, we might as well take our losses and go on home. You and me and Dammit and Arf. I expect there's plowing to do."

Otha made a high keening noise in the back of his throat and peered down at me with his big eyes. "Tell me yo plan, damn fool."

The two of us walked downtown right around dusk. I still had Pa's trousers and tailcoat on. They were loose on me, but after yesterday I knew better than to play the rube in breeches. I still had Perrow's pistol in the coat's left pocket. Otha followed me by the customary three steps, and Arf hung close to Otha.

We loafed past the Liberty Hotel entrance, checking that Mr. Sloat was on duty at the desk in the lobby. And then Otha took Arf and rolled him around in a big mud puddle, making sure to get his own feet good and caked. I hurried around to the hotel's back courtyard entrance and slipped on in. By the time I got as far as the lobby, the excitement had already started.

"No suh," Otha was saying. "I ain't goin leave till I sees Mistuh Bustler." He and Arf were standing in the middle of the Oriental rug, Arf shaking and Otha scuffing his shoes. There was no Bustler here, of course, but it amused me to have Otha use Lucy's pie-faced seducer's name. "Miz Bustler's powerful upset. I'se real sorry to sturb you folks, but…"

"*Don't stand on the rug!*" Sloat screamed. "*Are you deaf!*"

"I'se mighty sorry, suh, but Miz Bustler done tole me as how she ain't goin…"

Sloat's chair smacked against the wall and he went puffing across the lobby. In his passion, he didn't see me waiting there at the head of the back hall. I darted around the corner and into his private office with my coattails flying. Out in the lobby, Sloat was screaming, Arf was barking, and Otha was still maundering on in stubborn slave talk.

I went right to the safe and yanked on the door—it was open. I tried drawer after drawer until I found the right one. A small metal drawer at the bottom held several handfuls of gold twenty-dollar pieces. Should I take them all? Frightful thought! Was I not a gentleman? I took the six coins due me and whipped back into the lobby, aiming for the safety of the dark back hall…

It would have gone off smooth as snot on a doorknob if Arf hadn't run over to dog my steps. Sloat was still busy trying to shove Otha off his precious rug, but Arf s excited rush for me made him look around. He turned just as I stepped into the hall—me with the gold coins glinting in my hand.

"Mr. Mason Reynolds," said Sloat, his voice calm even though his face was still red. "This is *your* boy here, I do believe." He raised his voice back to a scream. "Sheriff Garmee! Arrest these two!"

As soon as Sloat called him, the damn midget from yesterday was there in the saloon door, his upturned nostrils making black holes in his humorless little face. I took off down the hotel's back hall as fast as I could run. Arf and Otha followed close behind.

The blond stableboy in the courtyard got a hand on me, but Otha shoved him off. Glancing back, I saw the stableboy pull the gun out of the holster hung by the stalls. I reached my right hand across my body and drew my pistol from my coat. Not aiming any too precisely, I fired a shot back toward the hotel. At the same moment the stableboy fired a shot after me. His bullet whizzed past my head, making a tearing sound in the air. And with it came another sound. The stableboy's scream.

In that moment I had a guilty vision. I saw a fat demonic worm with writhing tendrils. It had taken hold of me, and was peeling me in two—as if seizing my damned soul. I lost my footing and nearly stumbled.

Otha caught me by the shoulder. With Arf at our heels we ran around the corner to Main Street and took the first alley down toward the river. Folks turned to watch us clatter by. We cut right on the next street and slowed to a walk so as to not attract any more notice. Another alley popped up, and we followed it the rest of the way to the river.

It was dark and quiet down there. Back up in the town, people were yelling…yelling more than seemed fitting for a reasonable settling of scores.

"You done messed up for true, Mason."

"We better cross the river and walk home. Do you think we should try to swim? Hell, dogs can swim, Otha. I bet we can too."

"What about the wagon an the mule?" said Otha, shaking his head. "What about my little Wawona?"

"We can't go back to the Perrows, Otha. Yesterday I told Sloat I was staying there. That's the first place they'll look for us."

"Yo pa gonna be bleak over this."

I knew just what Otha meant. When things went wrong, Pa'd be quiet for days on end, and usually drunk as well. But things could still work out!

"Listen, Otha, unless Sloat gets the law to seize our wagon, Walloon can drive it out to us. And Walloon can bring Wawona. There's none of this city law out on the farm. All we got to do is cross the river and walk home. I got the money back, didn't I?"

"I don't know, Mason. Did you?"

There was a sudden hubbub of voices nearby. Sheriff Garmee!

"This way, men," he called in his nasty tenor. "We're lookin for a blond little fellow, a long black, and a dog." They had torches, but they were still a few hundred feet away.

"Hsst!" said Otha. "Get in the bateau!"

The bateau that the slaves had been loading with tobacco was tied up right nearby. We slipped down into it, fast and bumpy.

Arf stood up on the wharf staring at us. "Come on," I hissed. "Come on down here, Arf." He snuffled and backed off. I lunged and got hold of the loose skin of his neck. Man's best friend had to let out a yelp, of course, which set off hallos from the sheriff's torch gang. I yanked Arf into the bateau, and a few seconds later the three of us were stuffed under a tarpaulin with some barrels of tobacco and bags of provisions. It was lumpy and close, but we didn't dare move. Two of the searchers came within an ace of lifting up our tarp, but then a noise up in Water Street led them uphill.

The tarpaulin smelled of pitch and the river, and the bateau rocked slowly in the current. Before too long, the three of us were asleep.

3. On the River

Feet. Someone stepped on my back, and I woke. The first thing I saw was Otha's muddy toes, right in my face. There were voices and footsteps all around: black voices and bare feet. Pinpoints of light showed through the tarp. It was dawn, and the bateau crew was setting out for Richmond.

I held myself still, bracing steady against the foot on my back. "C'mon now, Custa!" yelled someone. "Pick up yo pole and lean into it, son. This ain't no steamboat and we ain't bout to set no sail!" Grudgingly, the foot moved away. Arf pushed his snout forward and gave my mouth a lick. I shoved his head down against the bateau's wet planks. Otha and I had wedged ourselves in head to tail, with Arf in between us. It was hard to tell in the faint dotty light, and with just his foot to judge from, but Otha looked as if he were still asleep. He liked to sleep.

"Look out, Richmond, here come the Garlands again!" whooped the same voice as before. With great wallowing and splashing and banging of poles, our boat seemed to be making its way out into the James River's stream.

"Turn it, boys, and head it on down!" Feet ran back and forth along the two walkways built onto the bateau's gunnels. The hull groaned, turned, and picked up speed.

"Go left, go left, go leee—Custa, hang on!" We struck something with a heavy jarring crash. Another crash and another, and then shouts and laughter. Otha's foot twitched: I

39

pinched it hard. He thought for a while, and then his invisible hand gave my ankle a twist and a pat.

The hammering of the rocks lasted another few minutes, and then we were in a smooth stretch. The polers moved up and down the bateau with steady strides. When it seemed sure we must be out of sight of Lynchburg, I began struggling to sit up. It took a minute, what with Arf and my tailcoat and Otha's legs tangling me. I was a little dizzy from the strong smell of tobacco. By the time I finally wormed my head and shoulders out from under the heavy tarp, the whole bateau crew was pointing and jabbering. My collar was awry and my red cravat had come partly unwound.

"Lord help us," cried one of the crew, a chunky boy my age. "It's the bloody ghost of the stableboy!" Arf pushed his head out next to mine then, and the chunky boy let out a high scream. "It's the ghost an the devil!" With that, he fell overboard.

"Get holda Custa, Marcus!" cried a wiry little man standing by the steering sweep. His was the voice I'd heard before. He had high cheekbones and bright darting eyes. "He can't swim! Fetch the ax, Luther! This ain't no ghost, it's the murderer!"

A bulletheaded, barrel-chested blue-black man surged back from the bow, snatching up an ax from a toolbox. He yanked the tarp free, then crouched over me, weapon at the ready. Arf growled furiously.

"There's another one under there too," called the steersman. "I sees his feet! Come on out, long legs!"

While two of the crew members hauled plump Custa in over the gunnel, Otha extricated himself from the tarpaulin to sit at my side. I was glad to see his face. He'd be able to soothe these savages.

"Hush the dog, Mason," he said quietly. "I *knows* this man."

I threw an arm around Arf and squeezed him reassuringly. Arf yipped at my first touch, but then he settled down.

"We ain't no murder, Unc Tyree," said Otha, looking up at the steersman. Otha had that special honest look he always put on for talking to grown-ups. "You might not 'member me, but you be cousin to my ma, Turl, who work out at the Reynoldses in Hardware? This here Mist Mason Reynolds. We…"

"I knows you too, Otha," said Tyree, "Whole town knows bout you and yo young Marse robbin Mist Sloat and shootin his hostler dead. Sheriff Garmee, he got a hundred-dollar price on Mason's head, dead or alive."

"What about me?" asked Otha.

"You ain't worth nothin dead, long legs. With yo master a fugitive, you's a runaway up for auction, I speck. Less you goes back to yo farm."

"We both want to go back to the farm," I put in. "I didn't murder the stableboy. It was an accident. And that was *my* money I was taking from Mr. Sloat. Just set us ashore here, Tyree, and we'll make our way back to Hardware." I sat up straighter. "And tell your boy to put down the ax."

"Who you callin *boy*?" said the blue-black man named Luther. "Sheriff'll pay me hundred dollar to chop yo haid off. Nuff to buy me free, and my missus too."

"I seen him first," shouted Custa, soaking wet. "*I* gets the reward."

"Share and share alike," sang a deep-voiced man with a perfect physique. "Right, Moline?"

"I'll be the one to chop his head off," said the last of the five bateau-men. "Killin a white boy wouldn't bother me none at all." He looked like he meant it. He was as strong and well-formed as Marcus, but some mishap had removed his front teeth and left his nose smashed flat against his face. His eyes were small and angry. "Feed his body to the catfish and we got less weight to pole!"

Otha formed his face into an expression of exquisite contempt. "I may be country, but you boys is fools. You really speck some white sheriff to hand each of y'all a gold double-eagle? Without yo Marse Garland say nothin? You really speck to walk into Lynchburg carryin a white boy's head? They'd mess up yo faces as ugly as Moline's."

Everyone ruminated on that for a minute. The bateau continued drifting down the James. It was a bright day, with a few puffy clouds. The river's smooth green-brown water mirrored the clouds perfectly. The stream wasn't but twenty yards wide here, and it would have been easy to swim to shore had I known how to swim. But even if I got to shore, these Negroes would chase me down. And, I now realized, even if I could get away, even if I could get back to Pa's farm, there'd be bounty hunters coming after my head. My only hope was to enlist this crew's support.

I rose to my feet. Sensing that my sprung collar and wadded cravat detracted from my appearance, I tugged them off and shoved them into my soiled tailcoat's right pocket. I could still feel my pistol's weight in the left. Bullethead Luther made a menacing gesture with his ax, but I fixed him with a stare that rocked him back.

"I'll make you men an offer," I said, looking up and down the length of the bateau. Wiry Tyree, big Luther, puppyish Custa, handsome Marcus, and angry smash-faced Moline, "*I'll* pay you the hundred-dollar reward. Deliver me and my man Otha to Richmond, and the money shall be yours. I give you my word as a gentleman."

"Listen at him," said Tyree. He pursed up his thin-cheeked face and spat into the river.

"Y'all ain't gettin nothin if you pole back to Lynchburg, Unc Tyree," said Otha. "Nothin but sore backs. An trouble. Sheriff likely to think you took us on purpose and changed yo mind. Specially if that's what I tell him. But if you takes us to Richmond, you gets a gold double-eagle each. Mist Mason ain't no lie."

"Lez see the gold!" shouted Marcus.

I shoved my hand in my trouser pocket and fingered the six coins. I glanced questioningly at Otha. He nodded. Holding myself extra steady, I drew the coins out and displayed them in my cupped hands. They glinted wonderfully in the bright river sun. I turned this way and that so everyone could see them.

"Six coins," I said. "It's all I took. If I give one to each of you men. That'll leave one for Otha and me to share."

Luther set down his ax and reached up as if to take one of the gold pieces. He looked like a boy reaching for a beautiful butterfly.

"Not yet!" said Otha, slapping Luther's hand away. "Y'all gets the coins when we's in sight of Richmond!"

"Sloat and the sheriff sayin yo Marse stole a thousand dollar, Otha," complained Tyree. "Where the rest of it?"

"Oh, it were *ten* thousand dollar," said Otha. "And we spent it all to buy this here yaller dog. He be so smart he can say his own name." Arf stretched, bowed, and shook himself three times.

"His name is Arf," I said, putting the six coins back in my pocket. "Let's head for Richmond!"

"Lean into it, boys," sang out Tyree. "Lez get there early and claim our gold!"

The trip took five days, where usually it would have taken seven. Otha helped a bit with the poling, but that work wasn't my place. I spent the days sitting on a barrel in the middle of the boat, staring out at the gentle scenery of Virginia. The river was lined with big ashes and elms, thick-trunked giants that reached far out over the stream. There was tangled scrub behind the elms and on the river's many rocky little sandbars. The thickets were just starting to green up, and it was still easy to see the roll of the hilly land. Now and then we'd pass a plantation of great cleared fields surrounding a mansion. There were poorer farms, too; the white farm kids would hear us coming and come down to the river to wave. When that happened, I'd lie down flat in the bateau bottom with Arf.

Nights, we'd camp out at the river's edge in a clearing beneath the elm trees. There'd be a fire, and Moline would boil up a mess of pork and dried corn. The crew would fill up to busting, and then they'd sit around the fire talking and chewing tobacco before they dropped off to sleep. Arf and I ate the same food as them, though Moline always acted like he didn't want to give me any.

It was interesting for me to hear their songs and stories. I'd never been this close to a gang of slaves. One of the reasons Tyree was boss was that he knew a lot of chants and legends that went right back to Africa. According to Tyree, his father's father had been an African medicine man, and the power and the knowledge had been passed on down to him.

Every night, the first thing after eating, anyone who'd gotten a cut or a bruise or a sprain during the day would show it to Tyree, and he'd rub on some herbs, and chant in African. After watching him a few times, I let him work his magic on an elbow that I'd smashed against the hull. His spooking really did make the throbbing some better.

After Tyree's healing they'd sing a couple of spirituals—but with the words changed around so that the songs were about running off to the North instead of dying and going to heaven. And then they'd start in on the ghost stories. Custa knew dozens of tales about killings and ghosts. After listening to a few of his chillers, I'd spend the whole night with that poor dead stableboy's sharp little face hanging over me. We could have been friends, and I'd shot him without even needing to. I considered throwing my damn pistol away, but I couldn't quite turn loose of it. There was always the possibility one of the men might decide to take my money in the night.

The money was another big topic of conversation. Twenty dollars wasn't enough for any of the men to legally buy his freedom, which was something they all seemed to want, Luther most of all. By law, slaves weren't allowed to have money—any more than they were allowed to read—so by law, any sum short of the sixty to a hundred dollar slave price was only good for hoarding. But—though they avoided clearly saying so in my presence—if a slave were to run away and head North, twenty dollars could make a big difference in escaping the "paddy rollers"—the patrollers who hunted runaways.

And there were certainly pawnbrokers in Richmond willing to do trade with slaves. A house servant might bring a filched silver spoon to the back door of such a pawnshop and leave with a jackknife or a bolt of cloth or a box of peppermint candy. The crewmen spent a lot of time debating the merits of this and that shop, with the house of Abner Levy being mentioned most frequently.

Their chatter ran in various levels of comprehensibility. If they really didn't want me to understand, they could layer on so thick an accent that I might as well have been listening to the cawing of crows. I watched the scenery pass, now looking at the land, now at the river's sinuous flow. I couldn't bring myself to think about what lay ahead.

The whole afternoon of the fifth day, the men's talk was incomprehensible jabber. Something was up. That evening, we grounded the bateau on a sandbank just above the shallows and rapids of Goochland. Two other bateaus were already here.

"Tomorrow mornin we goes into the canal bout quarter mile up there, Mist Mason," Tyree told me. "And then it's twenty-some mile to Richmond." The James's flow was accelerating and there was a graveyard's worth of white-foamed rocks ahead, bright in the gathering dusk. Up to the left where Tyree pointed was the granite bulwark where the Kanawha Canal branched off from the river. There'd be toll takers up there, men likely to remember my passage if the sheriff eventually searched this far. "It be best for us if you an Arf stays under cover all day tomorrow."

"All right," said I. The thought of our trip ending made my stomach tighten in fear. I'd never been to Richmond.

"You might's well pay us now, Mist Mason," put in Luther. "Less there some confusion later on." He was smiling and happy about getting his money.

"Come on," put in Moline, pushing his ugly face toward mine. "Lez have that damn gold, white boy." No amount of money was going to make *him* happy.

"I said I'd pay you in Richmond," I said uncertainly. Were they planning to turn me in after all?

"You gonna pay us now," said Tyree. "Stead of slippin off in Richmond, like you might be fixin to do."

Didn't they trust me? They were all squeezed around me in the middle of the boat. I glanced at Otha, who gave me a shrug and a nod. I took the bitterly won gold coins out of my pocket and handed one each to Tyree, Luther, Custa, Marcus, and Moline. Five gone, and one coin left for me and Otha, He looked like he thought I ought to hand it over to him, but I shoved it back down in my pocket.

There was a regular beaten-down campground here; the two other bateau crews already had their fires going. They visited back and forth with plenty of that incomprehensible crow-cawing. I was the only white man in the campsite. After our fire was going, Moline put on the fatback and cracked corn. As usual, he served all the others first—only tonight there was no food left by the time he got to me.

"Too bad, Mase," he said jeeringly, and took his own big plateful of food off to eat. Although I was very hungry, I was damned if I was going to beg black men for food. Tomorrow I'd be shut of them. A few of them—Custa and Moline and Marcus—were grinning up at me, but I didn't give them the satisfaction of saying anything. Instead, I found a soft spot and lay down to sleep. Someone must have fed Arf, because after a while he came over and lay down with me. I half expected Otha to bring me some food, but he never did.

I woke up suddenly in the middle of the night. Arf was gone. The fires were burnt down to red glows, and the moon was high. My stomach was so empty I couldn't think about anything but filling it. I decided to get myself some corn from the supply sack and boil it up. I found the sack all right, over by the fire where Moline had left it. I carried the kettle down to the river and waded out to get a scoop of clear water. I stood out in the river for a minute, watching the moonlight quivering off the ripples and listening to the steady roar of the rapids coming from downstream. Standing there, I woke all the way up and realized there was something wrong.

What was wrong was that I was all alone. There were still some rags and wads of clothing lying around, but none of the crew was there by our fire. Peering over to where the other two crews had been, I could see that their campsites were deserted too. Yet all three bateaus were still on the sandbank—I'd just seen them.

I boiled a little corn, keeping my ears pricked all the while. Sure enough, I could hear something back in the woods, a steady humming that blended in with the river noise. Now and then the humming rose into a yell. I bolted down my half-cooked cracked corn and headed through the trees, turning my head this way and that to catch every noise. The ground turned swampy and the humming sound grew. There was an orange glow up ahead. I pushed twenty yards further, trying not to crackle the underbrush, and then, peering through the branches of a sassafras sapling, I could see.

There was a clearing of raised ground with a bonfire in the middle. All around the clearing, the wet ground sent back streaks and patches of the firelight. On the far side of the bonfire were a tent and a huge old oak tree, lightning-blasted and half rotted out. Perched inside the tree's hollow was a huge man with skin as white as paper. He had curly white hair and thick lips and he could have been an albino Negro. Yet his whiteness was so total and so extraordinary that he seemed, rather, a member of some different race.

Standing in a knot on the near side of the fire were fifteen or twenty slaves; among them were all of the six I'd been traveling with. They were chanting some repetitive phrase that I couldn't make out. Now and then the huge man in the tree would beckon, and one of the slaves would go up to him.

A man from one of the other bateaus took a bag of corn up; when he set down the bag, a big snow-white arm extended out of the tree and handed him a leather pouch on a thong. The man tied the thong around his waist and skipped back to the others with a smile on his face. He kept pressing the leather pouch down against his privates; I expect it was a spell for having children. Diverse exchanges occurred, turn by turn, and then came Tyree. He had a little bundle of tobacco that he must have filched out of one of the hogsheads on our bateau. The paper-white man's mouth made a big welcoming hole in his face when he saw Tyree, It seemed like they were old friends. In the firelight it looked as if the weird man had bright red teeth. He dug around in his tree for a bit and then gave Tyree three little sacks in trade for the tobacco.

I was just wondering if any of the boys would be bone-headed enough to give their medicine man one of my gold coins when Moline did it. He pulled out his coin, held it high in the firelight, and marched right up to the tree with that big white man lurking in it like a termite. Next thing I knew, Moline and the magic man were dancing around the fire together. They made a frightening sight: Moline with his dark, hating, smashed face, and the big treeman white as the inside of a toadstool. In the firelight I could see his face

47

more clearly than before. Though he had a Negro's big lips and kinky hair, his nose was thin and pointed and his forehead was flat and high. At first I'd thought he was fat, but now as he moved around, I could see all those bulges were muscle. He wore nothing but an oddly patterned loincloth. I wondered if he might be from the Feejee islands, perhaps come to America on a whaling ship. It was a strange thing seeing him.

He was working himself up into a frenzy, yelling something over and over—it sounded like "*Lamalama tekelili.*" His teeth really were red. The bateau-men were dancing and yelling "*Lamalama,*" too, and goddamn Arf was in there as well, I now noticed, frisking right along with the war dance, so excited that he was practically walking on his hind legs. After a little more dancing and yelling, Marcus got worked up enough to give his gold to the big albino too, and the massive man ran into his tent and fetched a sword for Marcus. They all cheered the big albino and called him Elijah, and he yelled something that, just this once, I could understand only too well,

"Kill the masters!"

As Elijah cried out, Arf sped away from the circle of men like a clot of mud thrown off a spinning wagon wheel. He bounded through the underbrush and ran right into me. I was glad he didn't bite me.

I decided to get back to the campsite. Arf showed no inclination to lead, but by using the moon and the sound of the river to guide me, I found my way back to where I'd been sleeping. After Arf and I'd been lying there a half hour, the men came traipsing back. I had my gun clenched in my hand, just in case Marcus decided to stick that big sword in me. But they dropped off to sleep without bothering me. I lay awake till dawn, wondering about what I'd seen.

The next morning Moline was missing and Marcus had the sword, but nobody offered to explain why. I didn't press them; I was ready for the trip to end. Arf and I got under the tarpaulin, and the men maneuvered the bateau into the canal. My mind had been blank during this whole river trip, but now it was teeming. Elijah, Pa, Sukie, Lucy, Sloat, and the dead hostler's faces all swam before me. Should I warn people about Elijah? How soon could I return to safe Hardware and to Pa's proud plans for my future? What would become of me in the big city? How could I live? I was only fifteen years old!

I dozed through most of that long last day. Over and over the stableboy showed me the hole in his forehead, over and over I used a candle to see between Sukie's legs, over and over Elijah screamed, "*Kill.*" The canal was busy, and each time I heard a strange voice I jerked awake, thinking it was the evil midget Sheriff Garmee. In my dreams he became small enough to crawl through a bunghole, and each of the roaches that crossed my face felt like him.

Finally, it was dusk and we were bumping into the canal basin. Once again Custa stepped on me, and once again Arf licked my face. "Right here's fine, Unc Tyree," I heard Otha say. And then, "Come on out, Mase."

I sprang out from under the tarp. The canal basin was a lagoon in the midst of Richmond. Up ahead of us was a wharf with some dozen bateaus in various stages of unlading. But right here on our left was a low stone embankment edging a nearly deserted square. Without a pause, I grabbed hold of the wall and swung myself onto land. Otha passed Arf up and then joined me on the canal side. The crew was eager to be off, lest they be seen with a fugitive. We bid them a hasty farewell, and they went poling off toward the bateau wharves.

"How about mine, Mason?" Otha held out his pale-palmed hand for the last double-eagle. Seeing all the other blacks get coins yesterday had been too much for him.

"*Mister* Mason, please, Otha. People might hear. Don't forget you're my slave. I'll keep the coin. You know that what's mine is yours."

"Sho. Do that make *me* mine? I believe I'm ready for that."

"Are you asking me to free you, Otha? Why in hell should I? Can't you see we'd do better to stick together?" This was no time to say so, but I had a half-formed plan of renting Otha out as a factory worker if need be.

"You the one messed up, Mase. You the one lost my bride money and killed that boy. I could still turn you in."

"Sure you could. Turn me in and get sold down the river by Sloat. Get sold down to 'Bam, where the masters whip instead of jawin!" I was getting really angry. I'd seen enough black faces in the last five days to last me a lifetime. Otha's expression was hard and dark. He stuck his hand out again.

"Gimme the money. Mason. We's splittin up."

Behind Otha I could see a street leading uphill several blocks to some kind of green field. The lower part of the street held offices, but higher up were beautiful homes with shiny brass doorplates and lace curtains in the windows. The whole big world was waiting for me. Would I never be free? In sudden revulsion, I drew the coin out of my pocket and slapped it into Otha's hand. "Go on then, bonehead. I'm dead sick of trying to boss you. Sign up with crazy Elijah for all I care."

Otha pocketed the coin without a smile. "Don't call me names, you white mess." He turned on his heel and marched across the square, heading toward the wharf where the bateaus were unloading. Arf trotted after him.

"Come here, Arfie," I called. "Come on, boy, you stay with me." Arf stopped and looked back at me, cocking an eyebrow. Otha kept walking. "Come on, Arfie!" I repeated. Arf flapped his tongue at me and scampered after Otha. I'd raised Arf white and now he'd turned into a black dog. Arf and Otha could both go straight to hell.

I stalked up that pretty street I'd had my eye on before. My heart was pounding so hard I could barely see. I hadn't gone but two blocks before I banged into somebody, a well-dressed man in one of the new-fashion frockcoats.

"Pardon *me*," he said sharply, raking me with a look that made me realize how unprepossessing I must appear. After he marched off, I crouched in front of one of the elegant houses' brass door-plates, using it for a mirror.

I still had Pa's tailcoat and trousers on, but after five days of riding the bateau, they were right motley. I was stained all over with mud and water. Dog hair, dead insects, and bits of vegetation were pasted to me. My shirt, socks, and underwear stank so that even I could smell them. My shoes were invisible beneath a layer of dried river slime, and more of the slime matted my hair. The only possession I had in my pockets besides my collar and cravat was that cursed pepperbox pistol, still loaded with three shots—though after the days on the river, the powder was surely too sodden to catch.

I needed to find lodging in an inn, where I could bathe and have my clothes laundered. Yet with my appearance like this, who would extend me credit? I wandered further uphill until my street butted into the big field I'd noticed before. The field covered the whole hilltop, and there was a low black iron fence all around it to keep livestock out. In the middle of the field, at the top of the hill, was an enormous white building with columns. I realized it had to be the state capitol, which Mr. Jefferson had modeled after a Roman temple he'd seen in France. I swung over the fence and sloped across the field to get a good look at the building. It was a simple design: a long rectangular box with a triangle roof on top and the big columns at either end. The columns were so tall that looking up at them made me catch my breath. Even if politics was all thievery and lies, those boys certainly had a grand stage to play it on. I went on across the rest of this field, which was Capitol Square, and went another block till I got to a street called Broad Street. There were all kinds of shops there, with lots of people and carriages moving around. It was close on to dusk on a Friday night. I needed to find lodging before the streets got dark.

Off to the right was a church called Monumental Episcopal. Despite what Pa would have said, I had some hope the preacher there might help me. I started up the church steps, but before I could even get to the door, a fine-dressed woman frowned out at me and asked me what I wanted. She had some cloths in her hands like she was there to fix the altar. I didn't feel I could introduce myself, so I simply said I was looking for a place to stay.

"Do you know horses?" she asked, looking me up and down. She had a hard little nose and a lot of rouge. "I believe my brother is looking for a stableboy."

Stableboy. The word made me run chills all over. "I'm sorry, ma'am," I informed her. "I'm a gentleman."

She let out a laugh and closed the door.

I walked another block down Broad Street. The boys on the bateau had said something about this street, and when I got to the next corner I remembered what. The pawnshops were supposed to be off Broad Street near the capitol. I could pawn my pistol and get cleaned up enough to find a position befitting my station.

I took an empty alley that went to the left behind the church, and then I took another alley off that to the right. Another left, and sure enough, there was a building with three gold balls hanging over the door. ABNER LEVY, read a small sign under the balls. I felt myself smiling for the first time in days.

There was a gaslight on in the shop and a man in there, a stocky fellow with dark hair and thick lips. He flashed me a ready smile.

"Good evening," said I. "Would you pawn a pistol?"

We were alone in the shop and the pistol part put him off a bit. But once I'd handed it to him butt first, he brightened up.

"Shouldn't leave these loads in here," he said, tapping the powder out on the counter. "Wet powder can go off unexpectedly when it dries. I didn't catch your name."

"Lieutenant Bustler," I said easy-like. "Of Norfolk, Virginia."

The dark-haired fellow raised his eyebrows at that, me being fifteen, fair, and five foot two. But there wasn't anyone else there to hear my lie, so he let it pass.

"I can let you have a month's loan of three dollars on it," he said presently. "If you come back before June sixth, you can redeem your pistol for four dollars."

"That's fine," I said, not wanting to fuss.

He wrote out a pawn ticket and counted the three dollars into my hand. When he leaned over to write the ticket, I noticed that he had a little round cap on the back of his head.

I went back to Broad Street and headed the way I'd come from. There was bound to be an inn somewhere near the capitol. There were all kinds of people on the sidewalk: gentlemen, ladies, farmers, slaves, and free blacks. In my tatty condition, I was ashamed to look any of them in the face lest they take me for a beggar or a drunk. A few more blocks and I saw the gold sign of the Swan Inn. I headed right in.

Fortunately it was murky in there, so the woman behind the counter couldn't make out just how shabby I was. With a minimum of conversation, I engaged her to give me a room, to send up supper and a bath, and to take my garments down for a wash. All this would cost me two and a half dollars, payable in advance. I paid her, and a serving girl escorted me upstairs. An hour later I was asleep in my bed, clean and well fed.

4. Eddie Poe

I woke up earlier than I wanted to. I tried to go back to sleep, but it was no use. Today was the start of my new life in Richmond; there was no shirking it. My clothes were in the hall outside my door: cleaned, pressed, and folded. My shoes sat next to them, freshly blacked. If I could find a position at all, I had better find it today.

I dressed with care, enjoying the touch of the clean cloth on my clean skin. My room had a fine looking-glass; I adjusted my cravat to cover the creases in my collar and then spent a few minutes regarding myself. My blond hair was clean and straight, my pale face had a bit of color from the days on the bateau, and my hazel-brown eyes were clear and rested. If only I were a bit taller and had hair on my face! I formed a smile—no, that looked too scampish. I tightened my thin lips in resolve—that was better. A competent, well-born young man, ready to succeed.

But at what? I walked downstairs and passed through the tavern, assuring the innkeeper that I would return. If I did the thing right, I might hope to spend another few days there on credit. My feet led me toward Capitol Square. Today I noticed that the templelike capitol was not the only building in the grassy field. There was a smaller domed building as well. A passerby told me the smaller building was the Richmond city hall. It occurred to me that I might find employment there. After all, I could read and write excellently, which was a skill our pastoral commonwealth could ill despise. If I were indeed a thief and a murderer, then might not the political arena be the place for me?

Only a few offices were open in the city hall, it being nine o'clock of a Saturday morning. In one office a red-faced man dozed, with his feet on his desk. Another room held a thin man scribbling furiously with a quill pen. In still another office a strapping young man in shirtsleeves tried to explain something about a certain street repair to an underling. The largest office held three men behind desks and five more men sitting on a bench, everyone in trousers and tailcoat. I slipped onto the left end of the bench, where there was space. The room had a pleasant smell of cigar smoke. I noticed that there was a fourth desk with no one at it. Maybe that was the spot for me!

Now and then, one of the men at the desks would look up and call, "Next." The rightmost man on the bench would get up and go sit in a chair by one of the desks, and then he and the deskman would shuffle through papers together. As time wore on, I scooted down closer to the business end of the bench, and a few new arrivals came and sat down to the left of me. Finally, it was my turn. "Next!"

I tightened my lips and marched over to the desk by the window, where the man was waiting. He was a baldpate, with a greasy fringe of gray over his ears. He wore spectacles that flashed in the sunlight. His mouth was much thinner and tighter than I could ever make mine.

"Is this a debenture or a deed in trust?" he asked me.

"I'm Mason, ah, Mason Bustler," I told him. "A gentleman."

"To be sure." He held out his hand. "To cede the notarized instrument of the parties in bailiwick?"

I made as if to feel in my pockets. "Suppose we use one of your papers. I can read and write. Better than that, I've got *literary style*." That's what my uncle Tuck had said about a ten-page letter I'd written for him, and it was true. With all the close reading I'd done, I could write as flowery as in a magazine.

The baldpate sat back like he didn't know what I was talking about. "You waive conveyance of the warranty?"

"I'm looking for a job." I hooked my thumb over at the empty desk. "Looks like you fellers could use an extra hand."

The baldpate took off his glasses to see me better. It didn't seem to help. "Affidavit of all property representation must be filed within ninety days," he told me. "In lieu of putative tenure."

"Can I start today?"

"Nincompoop." He put his glasses back on and made a shooing gesture with his hand. "Next!"

I knew what *nincompoop* meant all right. On my way out, I noticed what looked like a thick discarded newspaper on the floor; I scooped it up and took it with me.

It was a fine sunny May day, with weeds and clumps of grass pushing up shoots in every spare corner of Richmond's muddy lots and streets. I wondered if I might have better luck in the capitol building. Not likely. I set myself down on a clean patch of grass to read my paper.

I was pleased to see it was a copy of the April issue of *The Southern Literary Messenger.* That issue hadn't made it out to our farm yet. Scanning down the contents list, I saw an article called "Maelzel's Chess Player" by Edgar Poe. He was my favorite new writer; he had a horrifying or humorous tale in the *Messenger* almost every month. I read "Maelzel's Chess Player" straight through right then and there.

It was an essay rather than a chiller like I'd been expecting, an essay about a chess-playing machine that a Mr. Maelzel had been showing around the country. Edgar Poe argued that it couldn't really be a machine or *it would always win.* Instead, wrote he, there had to be a midget hidden inside the machine, and he had a diagram worked out to show how. I finished the article with a sense of satisfaction and sat there for a while thinking about how it would be to have a job hiding inside a chess machine. I didn't know how to play chess, but I did play a good game of checkers, if not quite so good as Otha's.

Flipping back to the front of *The Southern Literary Messenger,* I noticed that their editorial offices were at 1501 Main Street, Richmond. Reading the editorial matter (which I normally skipped over), I learned something I hadn't realized before: Edgar Poe was now the *Messenger's* editor! What luck! Edgar Poe would understand my predicament—he'd seen trouble himself. According to Judge Perrow, Poe had been kicked out of the university for gambling. I'd go and ask him for a job!

I made it to Fifteenth and Main without even having to get anyone's instructions. Like Edgar Poe says, man's highest ability is his power to ratiocinate.

When I came to the appointed street corner, it was a quiet dusty noon. A hog slept in a shallow wallow at one edge of the street. There were brick buildings all around; 1501's Main Street storefront held a shop selling jewelry and optical goods. A sign by the building's side entrance indicated that inside were the offices of *The Southern Literary Messenger*, T. W. White, Prop. Though no man was in sight, the door opened to my touch. I found myself in a large plank-floored room filled with ink-marked papers and printing equipment.

The printing press dominated the room; it was a ponderous black iron machine, wonderfully scrolled and ornamented, with powerful-looking screws and levers on every side. The far wall held a huge double door that I supposed gave onto a loading dock and an alley. Piled next to that door were stacks of newsprint and stacks of finished papers—issues of the May *Southern Literary Messenger*. The near wall, which ran along Fifteenth Street, was lined with tables lit by large windows to the street. Dust motes jigged in the steep-slanting light. It was so quiet that I could hear someone talking in the shop out front.

Some of the tables held ragged-edged printed sheets laid out for proofing, and some were strewn with bits of metal: letters and punctuation marks. There were sticks and trays with letters lined up into mirror sense, and pots of pitch for sticking the letters into place. A long, low case resting on the tables held scores of small drawers—one drawer for each version of each letter. As no one was about, I pocketed three handsome italic letters: *M*, *A*, and *R*.

To the left of the door I'd entered was a staircase with a pointing hand painted on the wall. I went up.

Upstairs I found a large, bright room with windows on two sides. There were masses of print stuffed into shelves and tottering in stacks: manuscripts, magazines, newspapers, and books. A single empty desk bore a sign reading T. W. White, Proprietor. Well-used sheets of flypaper hung from the ceiling. The whole building smelled of ink.

"Hello?" I called presently. "Is anyone here?"

I heard a dry, delicate cough.

There was a small square office jutting out into the room's space from the right rear corner. The office door was half open and on the door was written in gold leaf:

Edgar Allan Poe
Editor, Allopathist, and Poet
Abandon All Hope Ye Shams Who Ram Here

I peered in. A young man lay easily stretched out on a morocco divan. He looked up at me with no great interest.

"I assume you are Mr. Poe," said I. "I am Mason Algiers Reynolds of Hardware, Virginia." He nodded very slightly. As this was of all men the fantastic Edgar Poe, I felt I could speak honestly. "I have inadvertently killed my double. I am a fugitive, and I stand in need of employ."

He widened his eyes a bit, eyes that were deep pools of darkness set beneath a high and somewhat too prominent brow. Should I forget everything else about Edgar Poe, I will never lose the image of his eyes. Poe's eyes seemed to look in as well as out—at all times scrutinizing his mind's play of fantasies as keenly as the happenstances of the world without. His eyes were wondrous portals between two worlds. As for the rest of his face, he had a straight mouth, a pleasing aquiline nose, a small mustache, and wavy dark hair, already a bit thin at the temples. But his eyes were everything; they were lamps to my soul's fluttering moth.

"What is your age?" he said presently. His voice was low and clear, and as he spoke, the line of his mouth sketched a bewildering range of expressions: from contempt to boredom to amusement to interest to genuine concern. "And why do you speak of a double?"

"I am fifteen, Mr. Poe. I say double because the boy I shot—purely by accident, mind you—was blond like me and just my size. I feel terrible about it, and Sheriff Garmee wants me dead or alive. I was only getting Pa's whiskey money back from Mr. Sloat at the Liberty Hotel in Lynchburg. I was supposed to buy a wife for our slave Otha with the money, but one of Mr. Sloat's fancy women stole it from me."

"Whoring and killing at age fifteen," mused Poe. "A lively lad. A Virginian. You have not brought your African to my office, I trust?"

"No sir. Otha took off on his own when we got to Richmond yesterday. I've read your stories in the *Messenger*, Mr. Poe, and I like them enormously. I practically know 'Berenice' and 'A MS. Found in a Bottle' by heart. I read and write better than anyone in Hardware, or even Lynchburg. Do you think I could have a job? Only you mustn't tell anyone else my real name. Call me Mason Bustler."

"Come in then, little brother." He made a rapid gesture with his delicate white hand. "And close the door."

I stepped into his office and closed the door behind me. Besides the divan, the office held bookshelves, two straight wooden chairs, and a desk piled high with papers. More books were stacked here and there on the floor. There was a window in the wall behind Mr. Poe's desk. I took one of the wooden chairs and sat down. "I could help with the printing," I suggested.

"A very printer's devil," said Poe. "Your name is Mason? Does your father adhere to the Accepted Lodge?"

"The Freemasons? No sir. We are Episcopalians. Ma's dead and Pa drinks. All I own is fifty cents and a pawn ticket for my pistol."

"You forget your bucolic health," said Poe with a smile. "And the outsized raiment on your limbs. You've cast yourself adrift, Mason, and the tides of fate are sweeping you to sea. I know the feeling, I know it well." He paused and regarded me for a bit, his expression subtly changing with the rapid flow of his thought. "I will help you," he said presently. "Though first I must jot down my morning's musings. Today I've set aside my cursed book reviews to work on a new tale. Do you drink spirits?"

"No sir. I don't want to be like Pa."

"Nor do I wish to be a wild-eyed slaving farmer, Mason, but today is the biblical Sabbath and Mr. White is in Petersburg. Allow me, as I say, to preserve the fruits of my interrupted labors and then you and I shall off to the pothouse, young killer, young devil, young Mason *né* Reynolds *appellé* Bustler. *Bustler*—the name has the sound of an odious, sanctimonious fool. You would do better to keep your own name. I am close friends with one Jeremiah Reynolds, a brilliant man with a global mind. He will come here next week, perhaps to make my fortune. I have a wonderful plan for a trip of exploration. But now, silence!"

He swung his legs to the floor and moved nimbly to his desk. Taking pen in hand, he wrote rapidly for the better part of an hour. At no time during his steady penning did he so much as glance at me. Not wanting to disturb his labor, I passed the time by looking through the books stacked on the floor by my chair. I noticed a book of letters and recollections of the poet Coleridge, a pamphlet called "South Sea Expedition" by the Jeremiah Reynolds of whom Poe had just spoken, also some travel books on Switzerland, Spain, and Pennsylvania, and at the bottom of the stack a geographical treatise with the full title: *Symmes's Theory of Concentric Spheres; Demonstrating that the earth is hollow, habitable within, and widely open about the poles. By A Citizen of the United States.* This odd treatise caught my fancy, and I delved into it.

Symmes's Theory started out with a slew of prefaces, apologies, and advertisements to the effect that Captain John Cleves Symmes, "the Newton of the West," was a great genius whom the world did little appreciate. There was so much about Symmes that I soon reached the conclusion that he himself had written the book. Once all the strutting and throat clearing was over, it turned out that Symmes believed our planet is a huge hollow sphere with big open holes at the North and South poles. According to Symmes, each of these holes is at least two hundred miles across. Symmes held that it should be possible for a ship to sail over the lip of one of these holes and onto the Hollow Earth's inner surface. The inner surface was supposed to be covered with continents and oceans just like the outside. Symmes had some further theories about other hollow spheres concentric to the main one, but these extra spheres struck me as unnecessary garnishment to the inspired flapdoodle of his initial premise: a Hollow Earth.

The idea tickled me so much that I eagerly read further, forgetting all about Edgar Poe busy at his desk. Symmes, or his mouthpiece the Citizen of the United States, had a list of reasons why our planet is in fact a hollow crust. Centrifugal force tends to squeeze all of a spinning planet's matter out into a spherical shell. If you put the end of a magnet up to a sheet of paper with iron filings, the filings will naturally arrange themselves into a hollow ring. Wheat stalks and birds' feathers are hollow. Heavy mountains sit on top of light soil. The material around Saturn arranges itself into rings. The poles of Mars look dark because the poles are actually great openings to the hollow inside. A correct interpretation of the Hebrew words *theoo* and *beoo* shows that instead of starting out, "The earth was without form and void," the Bible actually reads, "The earth was without form and *hollow!*" And finally, as a clincher to it all, it makes sense for the planets to be hollow because "it displays *a great saving of stuff.*"

A great saving of stuff. I liked Symmes's thinking. I'd always had a yen to explore; what an adventure it would be to discover a whole new world, the world that lies inside! How would it feel to sail over that great thick lip to the interior? What would be the conditions inside the Hollow Earth? And why hadn't any travelers yet brought back reports of great continent-size holes in the arctic and antarctic seas? The Citizen of the United States had two answers. First of all, the earth's magnetic field reverses direction on the inside, which means that along the great round verges of the holes the field runs east/west, leading to a phenomenon that the Citizen termed "winding meridians." An explorer who tries to follow his compass toward the North or the South Pole will inevitably end up sailing east or west along the rim of one of the great verges. And even if the explorer eschews the use of compass measurements, and employs the more reliable methods of celestial navigation, his attempt to enter the hole will be gravely hampered by the "great walls of ice" that ring the holes both north and south. The battlements of these icy hoops have occasionally been sighted by storm-driven whalers and sealers, yet none *that we know of* has ever survived an attempt to venture beyond. Symmes felt that the best way to reach the Hollow Earth would be to head north over the ice fields from the northernmost shores of Siberia.

"It is well," said Poe, breaking into my dreams of exploration. "My hero is launched; I thirst and tremble. With bandy-legs White from the scene, I shall dare the forbidden precincts of Hogg's Tavern." Noticing the book I held, he smiled broadly. "How do you like Symmes's theory, Mason? He is a madder drunken farmer than your Pa."

That was typical of Eddie Poe, I would learn; typical of him to fasten on some one little thing you told him and to come back to it over and over. I was in no position to stick up for Pa right then, so I ignored the slight and spoke to the question.

"I wonder what it would be like inside the Hollow Earth. Do you think there might be a sun on the inside?"

"A sun! Interesting notion." While he spoke, Poe busied himself rolling his fresh-written sheets up into a scroll that he bound with a ribbon. "I had Symmes's theory in mind when I wrote my 'MS. Found in a Bottle.' Of course there, to end the thing, I filled the hole with a great black maelstrom. Have you ever seen a maelstrom?" He stared at me with his dark eyes.

"A giant whirlpool? No. Though there were plenty of little eddies in the James coming down. I rode here on a bateau with a crew of slaves."

"Did you converse with them?"

"Of course. You should hear the stories they tell around the fire at night, Mr. Poe. Some of the tales go right back to Africa."

"Absit omen," said Poe, making a two-fingered gesture at me. "Spare me the company of Pa and the slaves. And don't call me Mr. Poe, little brother, call me Eddie. I am no Mister Such-and-So, I am an international genius of twenty-five."

We headed out of the office, with Eddie going back twice to make sure he'd fastened the locks. Outside, we crossed Main Street catty-corner to Hogg's Tavern.

"I spent the night at the Swan," I told Eddie as we went in. "Maybe we should go there and if they see me with someone as important as you they'll give me credit."

Eddie was very cheerful now, and this supposition of mine made him shake with laughter. "Do you think writers are wealthy men, Mason? Pillars of society? I am penniless, though I despise to remain so." He said the last sentence in a whisper, as now we were in Hogg's Tavern. The place was nearly empty. Eddie made a commanding gesture and addressed the publican. "Ho, Hogg, two twists of tobacco, if you please."

Eddie examined his tobacco briefly and then placed it back on the counter. "I don't much like this tobacco, Hogg. Bring us rum and water in its stead." We found seats on a bench by the wall. The bench had horsehair cushions. It was nice being there. Hogg brought us a pitcher of water and a noggin of rum with two glasses. When Eddie lifted the noggin, I put my hand over my glass.

"Please," I told him. "No strong drink for me. I've tried my fill of Pa's whiskey a few times and I don't like it. It makes me dizzy and sick."

"Lucky lad," said Eddie. "Pedestrian carking farmer. You talk, then, while I imbibe. Tell me your misadventure in dramatic detail."

I told him the whole story of how I'd left the farm, made a mess in Lynchburg, and fled to Richmond. He was particularly taken by the fact that I still dreamed of the dead stableboy.

Eddie's behavior changed noticeably with each of the four toddies of rum that the noggin held. During the first drink he remained cheerful and cutting, with the second glass he became deep and thoughtful, with the third glass he grew fluttery and maudlin, and the fourth glass started him to speechifying on Symmes's Hollow-Earth theory. With his tongue loosened by the rum, Eddie freely confessed that he believed Symmes's theory from the bottom of his heart.

Just last month Eddie's friend Jeremiah Reynolds had delivered a speech to Congress in favor of a United States exploring expedition to the south polar regions. Although Reynolds had once been a follower of Symmes, he dared not speak to Congress of the Hollow Earth. Instead, he had urged polar exploration for such petty put-up reasons as better trade and better maps.

Eddie was disappointed that Reynolds had missed his opportunity to lecture Congress about the Hollow Earth, and the farrago he now poured out to me was what *he*, Edgar Allan Poe, felt Jeremiah Reynolds should have said. Eddie's reasons for believing the theory were not scientific at all. His reasons for belief had to do with what he termed poetic necessity.

"The womb and the skull," he intoned, sitting up straight and wagging his finger at me. "The womb, the skull, and the Hollow Earth. If a man's head be but a ball of empty bone, why not our world as well? And what is the womb but a cave of muscle and sinew? Is it not fitting that farmer Symmes makes our verdant orb a grinning *memento mori?* But who or what has eaten the moist brain or fetus that nestled once within? Some hero must drive to the Pole and seek out the worm that slumbers not! It may be, young Mason, that you are the one to carry it through." His dark eyes were magnetically fixed on me; their depths spun like whirlpools.

A moment passed. Eddie blinked and poured out the rest of the noggin. Only a few drops were left.

"The great wall of ice is the final barrier between us and the southern pole," he continued. "Like a virtuous woman, Earth hides her nether mystery behind a chaste and frozen corset. The frozen hoop lies between us and the hole, Mason, but is this not the age of aeronautics? Cannot a ballooning flight of fancy overspring the most beetling wall? I have written Reynolds all this, and next Saturday he comes to realize my plan. Some call me hoaxer, but I am in my way a man of science. Only science can save me from the melancholy similes which crowd my brain." He gazed gloomily at his last bit of rum.

"Foul," sighed Eddie then. "Birth and death are both foul beyond imagining—to be sealed up into the flesh of another, to be nailed into a box! I suffocate. I must have air!" Draining the last of the rum, he started to his feet and tottered toward the tavern door, with me dogging his steps.

"Sirs," called Hogg. "I believe you have forgotten to pay for your rum and water."

"Pay for my rum and water!" exclaimed Poe, his mouth set into a hard line of anger. All at once his fooling was quite steady. "Didn't I give you the tobacco for the rum and water? What more do you require?"

"But, sir," said Hogg, looking a bit uncertain. "I don't remember that you paid for the tobacco."

"What do you mean by that, you scoundrel? Isn't *that* your tobacco lying *there?* Am I supposed to pay for what I did not take?"

"But, sir—"

"Save your snares for the unwary!" snapped Eddie, and marched out into the street. He hurried off down the block so rapidly that I could barely keep up with him. His shoulders were shaking; when I finally fell into step with him, I saw that he was chuckling and talking to himself.

"...a most excellent diddle," he muttered. "Most capital diddle indeed. It is well that watchful White postponed my first visit to the Hogg. Today I wear the diddler's grin!" He spread his lips wide in an unnatural leer and turned his head to stare at me.

I was confused. "I...you didn't...I mean, Hogg was right! You owe him for the rum. The tobacco doesn't have anything to do with it."

"The tobacco has everything to do with it. Mason, as surely as a magician's hat has everything to do with his hares. Am I not penniless? Yet do I not thirst? I work, I am penniless, I thirst, *ergo* it is my right to diddle Hogg. Fix your mind on the first two premises of the syllogism: *I work; I am penniless.* Mr. White's magazine, Mason, the magazine where you seek employ, this same *Southern Literary Messenger* began with a circulation of five hundred and under my editorial hand has risen to a circulation of two thousand. *Yet I am penniless.* My best energies are wasted in the service of an illiterate and vulgar man who has neither the capacity to appreciate my labors nor the will to reward them. I wander drunk in the streets of pawky Richmond with none but a fifteen-year-old farmboy to witness my degradation."

Poe groaned theatrically and turned a corner that led down toward the James River. There was a harbor down there, with a steam packet-boat and several large sailing ships at anchor. A cool fresh breeze wafted up from the harbor. The day was still fair, with a warm afternoon sun. I'd never seen ships before; the sight of their gently swaying masts thrilled me to the core.

"The tavern at Rockett's Landing is our next stop," said Poe. His gait was unsteady, but he was nowhere near so intoxicated as he'd seemed when we left Hogg's. "They know me well, so the diddle is out. I must implore you for the loan of the half-dollar you mentioned. In return I promise you reasonable lodging and a position as printer's devil. I have not tasted drink in a fortnight, and now I would sup the Bacchic madness to its lees. Allopathy, young Mason, is the scientific treatment of plague by a poison whose symptoms counter those of the disease. Drink is the allopathic remedy for the maelstrom of madness whose watery slopes I ride. The long sea tale I began today…" He waved his scroll of papers in my face. "This tale should make my fortune, Mason, and if the fool publishers will not help me, I must find some other way to become a wealthy man. A bank note is but ink and paper."

I handed Eddie my half-dollar coin. If he was really going to lodge me and get me employment, the price was well worth it. But, why, on such a lovely day and in such an exciting city, why did he have to get drunk?

"I'll wait outside the tavern," I suggested. "I want to look at the ships."

"Wise lad," said Eddie. "Do this for me—come in and seek me out before sunset. See that I get home to Mrs. Yarrington's boardinghouse on Bank Street at Capitol Square. I lodge there with my dear aunt and sweet Sis. Should I sleep and wake in this tavern, my suicide could result."

"Can I stay at the boardinghouse, too?"

"You'll sleep beneath my eaves, small petrel." He gave me a final salute with his scroll of papers and disappeared into the Rockett's Landing Tavern.

I spent a pleasant few hours poking around the harbor. After watching the side-wheeler packet boat steam off down the James for Norfolk and Baltimore, I found out more about the sailing ships. There was a small schooner, a two-masted brig, and a slightly larger three-masted bark called the *Grampus*. I managed to get aboard the *Grampus*. The sailors were friendly, but they kept a close eye on me. They'd found a stowaway slave on board that morning. I helped a bit with some loading, and one of the men gave me a chunk of bread and salt pork. It was my first food of the day, and it came very welcome. I hoped Mrs. Yarrington set a good table; even more, I hoped she would take me in.

As I worked with the sailors, I thought of how Eddie had diddled Hogg out of the rum. If that was the way of the world, I was a fool to have not taken a few more gold pieces from Sloat's safe. To hear Eddie tell it, T. W. White was a niggard. Nevertheless, the prospect of being a printer's devil pleased me. I could master the printer's trade in a few years. A printer could go anywhere and find employ. If today I found Richmond wonderful, with its riverfront and its capitol on the hill above, nevertheless I'd want someday to move on, perhaps to Baltimore and New York, perhaps to Europe, or perhaps to some wild new lands on a bark like the *Grampus*.

The sailor who'd fed me took me below decks to see their forecastle. Their bunks were cramped as coffins. It seemed odd that to go the furthest you had to be hemmed in the most. I wanted to see the world, but now that I'd escaped Pa's farm, I wasn't yet ready to squeeze into a sailor's bunk.

When dusk fell, I went into the Rockett's Landing Tavern. I found Eddie pale-faced and clutching a half-empty glass of dark rum. I sat down next to him, but the liquor had really taken hold of him and he barely knew me. He was at a table with two other men, one of them a deeply tanned Scotsman who was the first mate of the *Grampus*. He'd been buying drinks all day.

"I took a twenty-dollar gold piece off a slave I found stowed away this mornin," the Scotsman told me. He had long hair and a ready smile. "The rascal wanted to pay his passage. Can you believe it? Would ye like a glass of rum then, young fellow?"

"No thank you," said I, feeling sick. "Which one was it? I mean, what was the slave's name?"

"He didn't want to tell us," laughed the mate. "A big man, full of fire. But we whipped the answer out of him right enough. His name was Luther Garland."

It put a heavy stone on my heart to hear this. I remembered Luther reaching up for the gold that first day on the river, reaching up with a human spirit's innocent desire to be free. Now he was whipped and shackled and on his way back to Lynchburg.

"Did he say where he got the money?" I heard myself asking.

"Didn't say a thing but his name," said the mate. "He was bawling so hard even that was hard to understand. Drink up there, Eddie, and make us another speech!"

"Eddie has to go home," I told the mate. "I'm to take him."

"He promised me a poem," said the mate, reaching across the table to poke Eddie in the chest. "He said he'd pay for his drinks with a poem written out for my wife, Helen."

"To Helen," muttered Eddie. "Copy it down."

At the mate's cry, the innkeeper brought pen and paper. Eddie recited a poem and I wrote it down. It was a fine piece, though as I copied it out, I remembered having read it before in the *Messenger*. The mate liked it, once I told him what all the words meant.

To Helen

Helen, thy beauty is to me
    Like those Nicean barks of yore,
That gently, o'er a perfumed sea,
    The weary, wayworn wanderer bore
    To his own native shore.

On desperate seas long wont to roam,
    Thy hyacinth hair, thy classic face,

Thy Naiad airs have brought me home
  To the glory that was Greece,
And the grandeur that was Rome.

Lo! in yon brilliant window niche,
  How statue-like I see thee stand,
  The agate lamp within thy hand!
Ah, Psyche, from the regions which
  Are Holy Land!

Eddie gulped the rest of his glass and shuddered. I got to work getting him home. I had to put my arms around him and dance him out of the tavern. On the street, I draped his arm across my shoulder and started up the long slope to Capitol Square. Eddie kept letting his head fall back so he could stare up at the sky. I think he could have walked better than he did, but he was content to let me do the work. He knew what was up all right, the hoaxer. He knew I needed his patronage, and he remembered our morning's conversation well enough to stick in a remark or two about "being drunk like Pa," though he wasn't. No matter how much Pa drank, he could always walk straight.

Finally, I found Bank Street at the edge of the hilltop field that was Capitol Square. Eddie began picking up his feet a little better, and we arrived at a boardinghouse door. As soon as we stepped into the hall, a door upstairs flew open.

"Eddie?" called a woman. "Is that you?"

"It is I, Aunt Maria," said Poe, his voice low and contrite. "In the arms of a devil. I've slipped. A wretched prodigal, I eat husks with swine." He shrugged himself free of me and stood there unsteadily. "Thank you for your aid, young man. Farewell."

"You promised me lodging!" I protested. "And a job!"

Footsteps came stitching down the stairs. A strong-looking woman with a moon face confronted me. "Go on then, you young imp. Haven't you done harm enough, getting poor Eddie drunk?"

"I didn't get him drunk," I protested. "I've been taking care of him. Let me introduce myself." I bowed and cleared my throat. "I am Mason Algiers…Bustler. I met Eddie at the offices of the *Messenger* and he told me…"

"Go on, devil," said Eddie, gesturing at me with his scroll of papers. He'd hung on to the scroll; at least he'd stuck to that. "Come back Monday."

"He owes me fifty cents, Aunt Maria," I told the woman.

"My name is Mrs. Clemm," she said tartly. "You were wrong to lend Eddie money for drink."

"Please," I told her. "Have pity on me. I need a place to sleep. Once Eddie comes back to himself, he'll remember that he promised…"

"We certainly don't have space for you in our rooms," said Mrs. Clemm. She leaned forward and sniffed at my breath. "At least you are sober. You could speak to Mrs. Yarrington."

While we were busy arguing, Eddie had stepped around us and started up the stairs. He was gripping the banister with both hands. Now the door upstairs opened again and a voice called out.

"Eddie! Mama sewed me a new dress! I'll sing for you in my new dress!" The voice was higher than high, and sickly sweet. I peered up past Poe's hunched form to get a look at the speaker. She had a round face like her mother, but where the mother was lankly muscled, the daughter was softly rounded. Now, taking in Eddie's condition, the girl cried out in a wordless torrent of liquid sound. I stared fascinated at her vibrating throat, wondering how she could produce such a noise. Eddie took his hands off the banister to reach up toward her. Right away he lost his footing and fell backward.

I surged forward in time to catch him, and now that I had hold of him again, I led him the rest of the way to his door.

The plump girl's keening accompanied our progress. It sounded like I imagined an opera would sound. She cut off her noise sharply when Eddie reached the door. She curtsied and favored me with a smile that pocked her cheeks and chin with a dozen dimples. "You're too good," she said as Eddie fell into her round, outstretched arms.

I turned to find Mrs. Clemm behind me. "Lay him out on the bed, Virginia," she told the girl. "Lay him out and put a basin handy for when he gets sick." Virginia bore Eddie away.

"I'm glad he's safe," said I to Mrs. Clemm. "Will you help me lodge here? Please understand that I am of good family, temperate in my habits, and am a great admirer of your nephew's writing. Where is the Mrs. Yarrington of whom you spoke?"

"Mrs. Yarrington does not live here. I run this house for her." She looked me up and down once more and reached her decision. "Very well then, Mr. Bustler. You may engage the garret room. The lodging and board is three dollars a week. You are too late for supper, but breakfast is at eight."

"Thank you, Mrs. Clemm," said I. "I'll pay you every Saturday at noon."

5. The Bank of Kentucky

My garret room was really just half of an attic. My part of the attic was separated from the storage part by a row of large upended trunks. The walls and ceilings were raw laths and rafters. My bed was a straw-stuffed tick on the dusty floor. Each morning I had to go down three flights of stairs to the courtyard to empty my slops and to fill my washbasin. But I was happy in that room.

Mrs. Clemm's food was nourishing, if plain, and the other boarders were decent folk. My room had a small gable window looking out over the Richmond roofs; at night it was a joy for me to gaze at the lit city. Best of all, instead of being knotted into Pa's farming and drinking and slaving, I was out in the world learning a modern skill.

Eddie stayed in bed all day that first Sunday. I had planned to accompany the Clemm ladies to church—just to get a look at the society folks in town—but at breakfast Mrs. Clemm informed me that they were not religious. With no one to escort, I gave up on church and spent the time till dinner wandering around Richmond. I went as far as Screamertown, the neighborhood where the free blacks lived. Many of them were craftsmen, working out of small shops in their tiny yards. I kept an eye out for Arf and Otha, but there was no such luck.

That afternoon, after we all shared a dinner of boiled ham and cabbage, Virginia played piano and sang in the boarding-house parlor. She had an exceptionally powerful voice for a girl of only fourteen. There was definitely something odd about the muscles of her throat. The noise made me think of hog slaughtering and of the big knife Luke used for cutting the throats of our hogs. Virginia had no inkling of my feelings; indeed she seemed to have taken a liking to me, and she favored me with many smiles during her pauses for breath. When she smiled, her full cheeks bulged up and squeezed her eyes into slits. The singing went on and on, but I felt it would be ungentlemanly to get up and leave. Finally, it was over. I went to bed with a headache.

Monday morning I was down to breakfast early lest Poe slip off to work without me. Breakfast was tea, warm milk, oatmeal, and molasses. I ate steadily till Eddie appeared. Though I was the only one left at the table, his glance slid past me as if I were just another boarder.

"Good morning, Eddie," said I. He twitched and spilled some tea on the table.

"You must call me Mr. Poe."

"You remember me, don't you, Mr. Poe? Mason Bustler?"

"I thought your name was Reynolds," he said, sullenly stirring a gout of molasses into his tea. "Jeremiah Reynolds is coming to visit next week. Are you related?"

I shook my head. Reynolds's South Seas pamphlet said he was from Pennsylvania, but my family had been in Hardware since 1710. "You mustn't call me Reynolds, Mr. Poe, because…" Not wanting to say it, I cocked my thumb and forefinger and pretended to shoot a gun. "My double?"

"Confused fancies," said he, drinking down his tea with a sick expression. "You are a nightmare come to roost."

"Please, Mr. Poe, you said you'd recommend me to Mr. White for a position as…"

"As a devil." He glared at me with his dark eyes snapping. "Have I not enough worries plaguing me?"

"I'm to pay your aunt three dollars a week," I offered. "And I'll do anything else I can to help you—errands, copying, anything."

He thought for a while and finally gave a curt, grim nod. "Very well then, Mason. You pester me till I am half-mad, and then offer to do anything? Indeed you shall do anything, and sooner than you think." He stared at me a bit longer and then rose to leave. "Run upstairs and tell my aunt to give you the scroll of papers I forgot."

At the *Messenger* offices, Eddie introduced me to Mr. White and to Glendon, their printer. White was red-faced and wobbly, while Glendon was a lean, long-haired man with a heavy mustache and a deep Southern drawl. As a test of my skills, White, Glendon, and Eddie watched me proofread a column and set a line of type. For some reason, getting the letters in the correct mirror order for typesetting came naturally to me. I was hired as Glendon's assistant at a salary of six dollars a week, with the understanding that I would also act as an office boy whenever Glendon didn't need me.

The first few days of work went by quickly. Glendon did most of the actual typesetting; I heated pitch and put used letters back into their little drawers. I also helped tend the big iron press, a beast of a machine balkier than Dammit had ever been.

It wasn't far to the boardinghouse, and I went back there for dinner at noon every day. Eddie tended to stay in the *Messenger* offices, busy with his new sea tale and with his editorial work of correspondence and reviews. Virginia always sat next to me during dinner; she'd gotten out of me that I'd grown up on a farm, and she loved to ask me questions about baby animals. I humored her, even though the squeaky voice that came out of her thick throat never failed to set my teeth on edge.

Saturday we got off for the day at noon. Glendon said I was working out fine, and Mr. White gave me six silver dollars. I felt wonderful. Just before I left, Eddie stuck his head out of his office and called me in. He held a handwritten letter in his hand. Something about it seemed to have upset him. Pacing back and forth, he demanded that I give him the three dollars' lodging I owed Mrs. Clemm.

"I'd rather not, Mr. Poe," I told him. "I'd feel better giving her the money myself."

"Aunt Maria trusts her affairs to me in every way," said Eddie, impatiently sticking out his hand. He'd been sober all week, but now I wondered if the fever for drink was on him again. Mr. White didn't pay him weekly like he did me. Eddie only got paid on the last Saturday of every month, which meant that right now he was as penniless as he'd been last week. If I gave him the three dollars, he would likely spend it in a tavern and blame me. I kept my money tight in my hand in my pocket.

"I'm going on back to the house right now," I said, backing out of the office. "It's dinnertime. Why don't you come on with me, Eddie. You don't want to end up like last Saturday."

With an ill will, he accompanied me back to the boarding-house. Mrs. Clemm had made a cabbage-and-cauliflower soup that you could smell from the sidewalk. I went into the dining room and sat down next to old Dr. Custer, a retired physician. Virginia scooted into the seat next to me and asked me how long it took tiny fuzzy baby chickies to peck their way out of the shell and if any of the sweet babies ever suffocated before breaking out. Eddie, seated at the end of the table, glared at the sight of us talking together. I wished he'd just trade places with me. Mrs. Clemm was at the other end of the table, and across from Virginia and me were the middle-aged widow Boggs and the two Reddle brothers. The Reddles were identical twins named Rice and Brownie. They both had jobs at the plug-tobacco factory. I'd known a few fellows like them back in Hardware.

As Mrs. Clemm was ladling out the soup, one of the Reddles rocked over to one side and let out a big fart. Quick as a whip, the other one said, "'Tain't no need to apologize, Brownie. Smells the same as our dinner anyhow." They laughed like hyenas and then Virginia started giggling, too. Nobody else thought it was funny, though, especially not Eddie. He jumped out of his chair so hard that it fell over backward. He took Virginia by the hand and led her out of the dining room and upstairs. I went ahead and ate my soup. It was a meal, and there was coarse bread for dipping in it.

After dinner, I gave Mrs. Clemm my three dollars' room and board and went out to sit on the porch. I had half a mind to go down to Screamertown and look for Otha or to go down to the canal basin and ask around about what had happened to the rest of the boys on the bateau. I couldn't stop thinking about them. Had they all cut and run like Luther? And was the word out about me fleeing to Richmond? How was Pa getting along without me? Maybe I should get some paper from Eddie and send Pa a letter.

Just as I was thinking of Eddie, he appeared. Before I could utter a word, he was standing over me, standing so close that I couldn't get out of my rocking chair. His face was twisted in spite and rage. "You are a sinuous, plausible weasel, are you not?" He gave me a poke that set my chair a-bucking. "You murderer. You drag me to taverns, you presume upon me in every way, you worm your viper self into my enchanted garden, and now you labor to turn my sweet Sissy against me." He raised his hand menacingly. "If you were not such a lowly stinking beast, I'd challenge you to the field of honor." He struck at my head, but I ducked the blow. This made him even angrier. He gave me another poke in the chest. "You need horsewhipping, foul country lout! Get to your feet if you dare!"

Eddie just wasn't the kind of person who could physically scare you, but even so there was no way I could get to my feet, what with the chair rocking back and forth so hard and with him standing so close that my knees bumped his. He took this for a victory and stalked off across the field of Capitol Square, casting a last gloating glance back at me. "Do your damnedest, fiend, yet *I* shall have her hand!"

I sat there wondering what was the matter. Something about Eddie's whole performance struck me as insincere. Mrs. Clemm appeared on the porch. "Is he gone?" she asked me.

"Yes, he headed off that way," I told her. "He's all het up."

Mrs. Clemm cocked her head and looked at me thoughtfully. "Are you sweet on my Virginia?" she asked me finally.

"No ma'am."

She sighed. "I didn't think so. Virginia likes talking to you, Mason, because you're a boy closer to her own age. But she's Eddie's. It was meant to be. I had my dreams of bringing Virginia out into society, but Eddie's a genius and he needs us so much. They're to be married right away. That's the only way he'll have it."

"They're getting married because of me? Believe me, Mrs. Clemm, I have no designs on Virginia."

"It's not just you, dear," said Mrs. Clemm. "I've always thought that Eddie and Virginia living in rooms together could cause talk. It's better all around to marry them, and with Eddie in such a passion, it might as well be today."

She went inside and Rice and Brownie Reddle came out, on their way to the taverns. They asked me if I wanted to come along, but I said no. Brownie gave me a plug of tobacco, and then they were on their way. Back in Hardware I'd gotten used to doing nothing, so I was comfortable just sitting on the porch with my chaw, enjoying the feel of the three silver dollars in my pocket.

"Pardon me, young fella, is this the home of Edgar Poe?"

A solid man of medium stature was looking at me. He had a short nose, a broad face, and skin that was deeply weathered and tanned. I knew Eddie still had some bad debts, so I didn't answer the man directly.

"What's your name, sir?" I asked him.

"Jeremiah Reynolds," said he. "Come to see Mr. Poe from Washington. I sent him a letter advising him of my arrival today."

I got to my feet and made him welcome. "Eddie's been talking about you. He went out, but I reckon he'll be back soon. My name's Mason Bustler, I...I know some Reynoldses in Hardware, Virginia."

"I'm from everywhere *but* Virginia," said Reynolds, setting down his travel case and taking a seat. When he smiled, which was often, his leathery skin creased in many wrinkles. "So, Mason, what is your trade? And what does Mr. Poe say about me? Good things, I trust?"

"Mr. Poe's taken me on as a printer's devil at the *Southern Literary Messenger*," I said. "And about you...he believes in the Symmes theory that there's big holes at the North and South poles leading to the inside of the earth. He was disappointed that you didn't tell Congress about the Hollow Earth in your speech last month."

"Ten years ago I was a firebrand like our Eddie," said Reynolds, chuckling a bit. "I traveled from city to city with Mr.

Symmes giving speeches. He was an odd duck, our Symmes. He's dead now, you know; his grave in Ohio is marked with a great hollow sphere. Symmes and I made some converts, and Congress approved an expedition, but nothing came of it. In the end I had to lead my own expedition to the high southern latitudes. We made sixty-seven degrees; a thousand miles south of the Falklands. Surely you've heard of the South Sea Fur Company and Exploring Expedition?"

"Was that trip the subject of your pamphlet?" I said politely.

"Indeed." Reynolds beamed. "It is a pleasure to meet a young lad of such erudition! You have profited from your association with Mr. Poe! Yes, I led my own expedition for the southern Hole, but very soon the crew—ignorant money-hungry sealers—rebelled and forced us to turn back. Rather than return empty-handed, I had the crew put me off in Chile, where I spent some years tramping about. It took me nearly five years to get back to what we call civilization. Civilization indeed, that pack of purple-bottomed Jacksonians that is our poor young nation's Congress. The Symmes Hole is real, young Mason. I have specimens and tales to prove it. What think you of this?"

He drew a thumb-size white lump out of his pocket and passed it to me. It was an animal's tooth, marked all over with lines into which some native craftsman had rubbed ink. Along the length of the tooth was a thin map—the map of Chile, with all its intricacies of islands. Carved in less detail was the eastern, Patagonian, coast of South America, and even more sketchily presented were the jagged battlements of the southern wall of ice. The striking thing about this crude globe was that a hole had been drilled in the tooth tip, and the tooth's interior had been to some degree hollowed out. Etched on the inside was a mythical landscape of fruits and great beasts.

"The natives speak of a Hollow Earth?" I said, handing the tooth back to Reynolds.

"Indeed." He nodded, his genial face grown solemn. "They call it the land of tekelili, and their gods are said to live there. When a volcano erupts, it is the gods reaching out from the Hollow Earth. I have more than the natives' reports, Mason, much more. I hesitate to speak openly of these things—I do not seek the ridicule of poor Symmes—but as you are a friend of Eddie's, you will understand. Did you know that in the southernmost climes of Chile the seals and migratory birds head *out across the water toward the Pole* when the season grows colder? And that there is a great white whale named Mocha Dick who turns his flukes, and sounds, and never resurfaces till three days have passed? He swims through a deep ocean hole to surface on the seas of the land of tekelili, Mason. Would that I could ride there in his belly."

"Isn't Congress going to vote for an exploring expedition?"

Reynolds laughed wearily. "I believe now that they will finally vote the money for a proper United States exploring expedition, but the expedition will be, as Mr. Poe fears, of little ultimate use. A scheming pock-faced poltroon named Captain Wilkes is even now machinating to take command of the expedition; there is no hope of his pushing past seventy degrees southern latitude to the eighties and on toward the final polar ninety, where the great mystery must be found. The high southern latitudes hold wonders beyond imagining. There is a whole new world there for the men with the courage to vault the walls of ice!" He paused and shook his head, and then he fixed me with his blue, twinkling eyes. "I'm past talking about it, Mason. The time has come to act. You say you are a printer?"

"Yes sir. I'm learning to be one. I want to be able to travel wherever I like. The *Messenger* has one of the new iron presses; it's quite a machine."

"Yes, yes, Mr. Poe wrote me of it." Reynolds's weathered cheeks grew flushed with excitement. "And you are quite in Mr. Poe's confidence? Do you know then why I have come?"

Before I could answer, Eddie reappeared, striding angrily across the sloping field of Capitol Square. It developed that in order to get a marriage license he had to post a temporary bond of $150—a bond that would be nullified as soon as the marriage was actually performed. But as there were a number of debtors' claims outstanding against Mr. Edgar Allan Poe, his signature was not sufficient for the posting of a bond. In order to get his marriage license, he would have to physically place gold or bank notes in the value of $150 in the court officer's hands, if only for twenty-four hours.

"That's more than miser White pays me in two months!" Eddie fumed. Now that his marriage plans were well under way, he'd set aside his supposition that I was his mortal rival. The court officer could serve as his new bugaboo. "The truly ludicrous aspect is that I am to receive the money back as soon as we are wed. To the meager sapience of this petty harassing mole of a bailiff, nothing but disks of rare ore or scraps of bank-printed paper can serve as a proper signifier of gentility and worth! Would it not be more fitting that I lend him the manuscript for my *Tales of the Folio Club?* I have the manuscript back from Harper and Brothers, Jeremiah. Every door is slammed in my face." Eddie moaned and threw himself into a chair. "Jeremiah, I know you have come to discuss my balloon plan, but whatever shall we do for money?"

"We shall print it," said Reynolds in a quiet tone. "I have followed your earlier suggestion."

Eddie jerked galvanically and glanced around. No one but he and I and Jeremiah Reynolds were on the porch. Inside the boardinghouse, Virginia was playing the piano and softly singing. She sounded lonely and scared. In front of us was Bank Street, with its steady traffic on foot and horse. Market was over and people were going home. Eddie hurried into the house and spoke briefly with Virginia, and then he was back out, all energy, leading us to the empty offices of the *Messenger.*

Once we were safely inside, the chuckling, leather-faced Reynolds opened his case and drew out two engraved-steel printing blocks that showed the front and back sides of a fifty-dollar gold certificate on the State Bank of Kentucky.

"How did you get these?" I asked Reynolds. "Are these stolen, or are they copies?"

"They are neither." Eddie grinned, picking up one of the blocks and peering at the finely detailed engraving. "There is no State Bank of Kentucky. It was my thought that we might diddle the Virginians out of some considerable stocks of goods ere they notice the lack of any such institution. But

I had little hope my plan would truly bear fruit. Jeremiah, these are capital specimens of the engraver's art!"

"Thank you, Edgar. James Eights has done them for me with the understanding that the money is to be used solely for the outfitting of the polar balloon expedition you have proposed."

"Stupendous," said Poe. "Can you mount them in the press, Mason?"

I took the blocks and examined them in the late afternoon light. They were quarter-inch-thick plates of fine hard steel, etched with a convincing amount of ornamentation and legalistic folderol. The main legends read STATE BANK KENTUCKY, and FIFTY DOLLARS, and GOLD COIN. One side of the bill bore a large picture of a frontiersman shooting a black bear with a long rifle; the other side showed a steamboat, a band of horses, and a field of hemp. The images were very plausible. They would print well.

"Have you any ink but black?" inquired Jeremiah Reynolds.

"Deuce!" exclaimed Poe. "We have not. Green or yellow would be the thing, eh? Mason! Run over to the Richmond *Whig* and see if John Pleasants can spare us some green ink. He inked his Christmas issue all in green this past year, I well recall."

"Stop right there," said I, handing the printing blocks back to Reynolds. "You want me to openly fetch the ink for printing these bills? If there is no State Bank of Kentucky, it will be less than a month before everyone knows the bills are false. The people at the *Whig* will remember me. And then what, Eddie?"

"You are already wanted for murder, Mason *Reynolds*," said Eddie coldly. "If you are to be a criminal, why not be a competent one? Give Pleasants another false name, dunderhead. Tell him you work for Thomas Ritchie at the *Enquirer*."

"What?" said Jeremiah Reynolds, staring at me in wonder.

I had been a fool to tell Eddie my bloody secret; silently, I vowed never to pass such confidences again. The dead stableboy was my weight to bear alone.

"Mason killed a boy during a bungled robbery in Lynch-burg," said Eddie coolly. "His true name is Reynolds, but he has changed it to Bustler. He lives in transit. He will print our bills for us, and then, to be perfectly safe, he will move on."

"Move on where?" I demanded. "I like my position here!"

"Mason," said Eddie quietly. "You are one of fate's chosen children. You are nimble. I think that you and Jeremiah shall ride our balloon over the walls of ice and into the Hollow Earth. I had planned to go, but"—his voice cracked momentarily—"I am soon to be married, and I have not the heart to leave a trembling new wife."

"No need to blush, Eddie," said Jeremiah. "It is enough to be a genius—you need not be an explorer as well. The young man will serve well in your place. And how apt that his true name is Reynolds! Surely we are related! It is a wondrous thing!" He drew a ten-dollar gold piece out of his pocket and handed it to me. "Go, cousin Mason, and fetch the ink. Edgar and I must talk."

The *Whig* offices were ten blocks away. I walked with a troubled mind. With my own money, I had thirteen dollars in my pocket. Whether I fetched the ink or not, Edgar Poe would have me out of Richmond in a week. I wondered if I oughtn't best go down to Rockett's Landing and get the packet boat for Norfolk right away. The stableboy's death had been an accident, but to print false bills was cold-minded crime!

Still I pressed my steps onward to the *Whig*. I was dazzled by the sheer effrontery of Eddie's plan. Counterfeiting the money of a nonexistent bank! How fitting a scheme this was for Edgar Allan Poe: Poe, the poor, half-educated orphan posing as an American man of letters; Poe, the sham priest of our nonexistent culture. Watching him work in the office this week, I'd quickly learned to see through him. The manuscripts he sent to New York publishers kept coming back rejected. The reviews he wrote for the *Messenger* were simple tirades butted in with generously scissored out excerpts of the pages in question. The multilingual sayings he set into his essays were culled wholesale from foreign phrase books. There wasn't an honest bone in his body, and he still owed me fifty cents.

When I got to the *Whig* building, I paused and glanced down toward the riverport. Dusk was starting to fall, but I could see that there was a new bark in the *Grampus's* place. The *Grampus* out to sea! I imagined the ship in New York, in the Marquesas, in the unknown cannibal islands of the far south. If I understood Eddie and Jeremiah aright, they planned to launch a balloon from near the great southern wall of ice. What an adventure *that* would be, especially if Symmes's theory was correct! First to sail and then to fly! The expedition would be dangerous, but it was in every way preferable to the stunted existence of Hardware and Lynchburg, preferable even to Richmond and my learning of the printer's trade. My heart leapt and I let out a shout as, once and for all, I resolved to go along.

At the sound of my voice, a dog came rushing out of the alley by the *Whig* building and jumped on me. He was white-legged with a tan head and body. He pushed his feet into my stomach and stretched his head up toward my face. His feathery tail was beating a mile a minute. It took me a minute to understand that it was my dear old Arf.

"Arfie! What are you doing here, Arfie boy?" Arf licked and whined and rolled on his back. I knelt down and petted him for a long time. He lay there squirming, with his front paws folded over like a dead rabbit's. When I stopped petting him, he sprang up and shook his head vigorously. The way he shook his head was to stick it far forward and then to rotate it back and forth so fast that his ears slapped like the wings of a pigeon taking flight. The head shake was Arf's way of punctuating his changes in moods. Now that we were through greeting, it was time for something else. He stood there next to me with his tongue lolling out.

I walked down the dark alley Arf had come from. The *Whig* building's big side doors were open there; the men were just loading a wagon with bales of tomorrow's Sunday edition. "Where's the boss?" I asked one of the men on the loading dock. The man hooked his thumb toward the doors. I lifted Arf up and went into the *Whig's* print room. A meaty, long-haired man with a twisting lip asked me my business. He was dressed for the evening and on his way out.

"Two things. I need some green ink, and"—I kept petting Arf so the man wouldn't get a good look at me—"I'd like to know more about this dog."

"An ingratiating cur, is he not? He is a canine eponym, this dog Arf, an animal of such sagacity that all his race must speak his name." He talked in an amused, patrician drawl. "I don't believe you and I have had the pleasure of meeting, young man. I'm John Pleasants."

"I'm Jeremiah Allan. I'm working for Mr. Ritchie over at the *Enquirer*. Mr. Ritchie needs the ink for a special pamphlet of poetry."

"Old driveling Ritchie print green poetry?" exclaimed Pleasants. "I believe I've heard everything now. Are they to be pastoral poems, then, and printed on paper of grass? Bovine rhymes to feed a bawling cow? Green ink! I paid three dollars a can for ours, so let's set it that your old dotard pays me ten. Don't neglect to tell your Mr. Ritchie that I'm diddling him, young Allan."

"All right," said I, still fondling the dog. I didn't care about any feud Pleasants had with Ritchie, and if I was going to be printing money, I certainly didn't care about ten dollars. But what was Arf doing here? "So this is *Arf*, eh? How'd you hit on a name like that, Mr. Pleasants?"

"Alas, so great a stroke of genius is too African for my pale mind. The noble Arf, complete with fleas and mange, was a love offering to that ebony Venus who dusts our rooms when there is no silver to steal. She is Juicita, he is Otha, and Arf the symbol of their tender bond. I hope he follows you home."

Arf did follow me, of course. By the time I got to the *Messenger*, it was too dark to work, and Eddie thought it unwise to attract attention by lighting the lamps. Reynolds and Eddie went down to the Rockett's Landing Tavern, and I took Arf home to Mrs. Clemm's. I fed him some scraps and let him share my straw tick bed. I asked him where he'd been, but he just sniffed my fingers and flapped his ears.

I spent all day Sunday printing up fifty-dollar gold certificates of the State Bank of Kentucky—ten thousand dollars' worth. We'd found a stock of rag paper at the *Messenger*, and the bills looked fine. Still drunk from the night before, Eddie put a red-ink "bank president's signature" on each bill with his own hand, each signature a different anagram of his name: Peale O. Garland; A. Prodegal Lane; Learn A. Godleap; E. Apalled Groan; Loan A. A. Pledger; Gaol Pan Dealer; and so on, through two hundred variations. Jeremiah, a bit of a scribbler himself, was amazed at how rapidly Eddie produced the anagrams; Eddie said it was a simple application of cryptographic principles. I thought Eddie was being needlessly brazen.

The better the bills looked, the more I worried. People would accept them, and we would be counterfeiters. Would it really be so difficult to trace the bills back to the green ink I'd borrowed, to the Edgar Allan Poe whose anagram stood on every bill, and to the presses of *The Southern Literary Messenger?* We agreed that it would be unwise to pass any of the bills in Richmond, where Eddie and I were known. Deciding who should carry the money was more difficult. In the end, we settled it by making three stacks of it and each pocketing a stack. As soon as Eddie had pocketed his share, he announced his intention to hand three of the bills to the Richmond City court officer tomorrow as his marriage bond. Jeremiah and I protested strongly, but Eddie insisted that although the main purpose of these bills was to finance a polar balloon expedition, it was equally important that he and Virginia be wed. *So you'll have an excuse for not going*, I couldn't help thinking.

"That fool of an official won't study the bills," said Eddie, sipping at a bottle he'd produced from somewhere. "He'll read the three number fifties, strain through a calculation, and be content. The clergyman Asa Converse will wed my Virginia to me Monday, and Tuesday morn the new husband and wife will set out on a honcymoon. Sweet words. I'll give out word that we are going by coach to Petersburg, but in fact we will take the packet boat to Norfolk. And of course I will redeem the bond before our departure."

"I'll leave for Norfolk today and rent our safehouse," said Jeremiah. "I'll use the last of my honest money for the rent. Mason, will you come with me?"

It was all happening so fast. Leave today?

"No, no," said Eddie rapidly. "Mason must stay close to the nuptial pair. He is our cocky bachelor; though small and young, our Mason is a man of the world. He starts the honeymoon with Virginia and me. Don't look distraught, young killer!" I was frowning and wondering what Eddie really had in mind. His true purposes were always hard to read. He jabbered on. "Jeremiah and I have the thing worked out in every detail. In Norfolk I will pose as…Colonel Embry, a Kentucky breeder of fine horses, and there I shall purchase all things necessary to our expedition—the silk, the caoutchouc gum, the wicker, the stove, the heavy garments, the instruments, et cetera. These things we shall privately convey to the safehouse which Jeremiah has honestly engaged, and before the false bank notes are found out, Colonel Embry will have melted into the pellucid sea air. *Il est disparu.*" Eddie paused and drank again from his bottle. "What's that beast doing in here?"

"That's my dog Arf. I found him yesterday."

Eddie stalked over to the corner where Arf lay. Arf flattened himself against the floor and rolled his eyes up, nervously watching Eddie's twitching face. Arf had been in the print shop with us all day, but Eddie had only now noticed him. It was the alcohol, I suppose, and the fact that he was so excited about his wedding and about all the money we'd printed. Several times today, Eddie had picked up big wads of our new bills and had rubbed them on his face, afterward insisting that he only did this so that the bills wouldn't look too new.

"Praise the gods it's not a cat," said Eddie, giving Arf's ribs a gingerly prod with his toe. "I can't stand a pussy—they scratch and they yowl. A cat attacked me once. I struck back, and the fiendish creature sank her teeth and claws so deeply into my hand that I could not get free." He lurched over to me, clenched his fist, and shoved his sleeve up to expose his forearm. "You see?" There were indeed some faint scars on the thin white tube of Eddie's arm. "I struck the monster against the pavement," continued Eddie, acting it out. "She screamed as her ribs cracked, and I laughed at the sound. I beat the ill-shapen bony mass till her blood ran and mingled with mine. Yet no release! Do what I would, the needle teeth and pinion talons stuck fast. Her body's knives were like stitches sutured into my flesh. Blessed cool rationality saved me, or I would bear the fiend on me to this day."

"What did you do?"

"I quenched my arm in a rain barrel. Ding dong dell, pussy's gone to hell."

Monday morning, Eddie was still in a state, though not quite so bad. I went to the *Messenger* office and told Mr. White that Eddie would be gone to Petersburg on honeymoon this week. White looked dubious and asked me if Eddie was drunk. I denied it, and mentioned that I too would need a few days' leave. I didn't like to quit the job outright, even though my return seemed unlikely. White granted my request offhandedly; he and everyone else at the *Messenger* was preoccupied by the day's news of a slave rebellion in Goochland County, west of Richmond.

While I was busy with Mr. White, Jeremiah Reynolds accompanied Eddie to city hall and gave false witness for a marriage bond certifying that fourteen-year-old Virginia was twenty-one. At noon, Jeremiah left for Norfolk on the steamer. In the afternoon, the Reverend Asa Converse came and married Eddie to Virginia. Eddie was obviously intoxicated, even though I'm sure he wished to be sober. He was in the midst of a bender like the ones that took Pa every so often, with no way out but a miracle or collapse. After the ceremony, we had a big dinner. At first I thought Virginia had no more idea of what a wedding really meant than would a child playing dolls. But there were looks she and Mrs. Clemm exchanged, and then, right after the cake, there was the kiss that she gave Eddie. She put the full strength of her oddly muscled neck into that kiss, pressing her face as tight against Eddie as a shoat against a sow. The kiss put cold sweat on Eddie's big brow.

I went to bed early, and I woke with Arf barking in my ear. The window was pitch-dark, but there was light from the attic stairs. I cuffed Arf and listened. A tiny noise came from the stairs, a high sound that made my skin crawl. Eddie was there, still fully dressed and taken very strange. The pupils of his eyes were huge and black. Somehow he was able to hold a lit candle in front of him. Close behind Eddie was... Virginia. She wore a white gown, and her loosened dark hair hung down to her shoulders. Her mouth was set in a bold, frightened smile.

Eddie marched up the stairs like an automaton; he did a slow tour about my room and then took a place by my bed tick. He stood frozen there, a human candelabrum. Finally, he nodded his head. Virginia, still smiling rigidly, pulled off her gown and lay down on her back on my bed.

It was clear what was expected of me. I, being fifteen, was randy enough to comply.

Throughout our congress, Virginia all but ignored me, so engrossed was she in staring up at Eddie's face. Finally, as I expired, Virginia heaved and shook. The candlelight trembled terribly; the candle clattered to the floor and all was dark.

6. Virginia Clemm

The fact that neither Eddie nor Virginia nor I spoke a word that night made a big difference. With no words to tether it, our strange, never-to-be-repeated orgy drifted to the border between reality and dream.

We greeted each other normally at breakfast, Eddie wobbly and Virginia gay. I had my tailcoat, collar, and cravat on for the trip. As no one else was present, Eddie instructed me to go down to Rockett's Landing and buy three five-dollar passages to Norfolk with a State Bank of Kentucky bill. It was safe enough, he insisted. I was, after all, a social nonentity. Meanwhile he would go to city hall and reclaim the three bills he'd left there yesterday. Virginia would pack. I was to hand them their two tickets as we boarded the boat, but we were not to converse. In Norfolk, Jeremiah would lead them to the safehouse, and I would follow.

"Why are there so many secrets, Eddie?" asked Virginia.

"Don't fret, Sissy. Wouldn't you like some new gowns? And a piano with candleholders? And a house and a garden all our own?"

"Oh yes!" She clapped her hands in delight.

"Well, then," said Eddie with a wan smile. "The secrets are because I made a lot of money, and the government men won't like me spending it. We're going to trick the old pinch-faces. Even though we're going to Norfolk with Mason, we'll tell everyone that you and I are going alone to Petersburg."

"I must never lie to Mama."

"Please lie just a little, Sissy."

She tossed her head and gave me a quick flash of that same fixed smile I'd seen last night. She was neither so dim nor so innocent as she behaved. "All right then, Eddie, but I want Mason to bring his nice hairy dog."

"You like Arfie, Virginia?" My voice caught in my dry throat. I was sorry I'd gotten involved with her at all. The pliant succubus of last night was swathed in Virginia's daytime persona of tight, greasy hair braids, spotted chalky skin, and strained high voice. Beneath the table Arfie started thumping his tail. He always noticed when someone said his name.

Virginia giggled shrilly. "Big noisy boy tail!"

It was raining outside, a steady spring drizzle. I took Dr. Custer's umbrella from its peg and left our house through the back door. Under Eddie's influence, all sense of ethics was leaving me. My thick wad of new bank notes rustled in the breast pocket against my heart. Arf trotted after me; he didn't mind the wet. The streets were full of men running this way and that. This seemed unusual for a Tuesday morning, and after a few blocks I noticed something else unusual: No blacks were to be seen. I stopped a hurrying ragged man and asked him the news.

"It's the blacks," he gasped, wiping the rain from his eyes. He was unshaven and had missing teeth. Ordinarily I wouldn't have spoken to him. "They've gone shit crazy! Butchered two families of whites in Goochland yesterday and kilt fifteen more in Richmond last night! Some of our boys strung up three of them at the edge of Screamertown this mornin and would of done more, only the damn soldiers come to stop us! Who the hell's side are they on, hey?"

"I don't understand. What were the killings about?"

"Rebellion! Those murderin savages want what *we* got! Want our houses and our clothes and our women and our smoked hams! It was a damn preacher set them off, a giant freak black man with white skin. Name of Elijah! Soldiers done caught him and his lieutenants; they bringin them to city hall! Come on, son, we gotta help git em!" He finished catching his breath and hurried on toward Capitol Square.

Elijah! Since coming to Richmond, I'd hardly thought about the strange firelit gathering I'd witnessed in Goochland. True enough, Elijah had yelled, "Kill the masters," but it had seemed like playacting more than a real plan, even if Moline had stayed with him. But now Elijah had gotten some of the slaves to rise up and kill, just like Nat Turner had done back in '31. The whole idea seemed as impossible as a dog attacking his master. Arfie poked my leg with his nose and I glanced down at him.

"You were dancing around Elijah's fire too, Arfie. You're a bad dog." He stared up at me with his dark eyes and nose like three black dots. We continued walking downhill.

There was a long line of people buying tickets for the noon packet steamer to Norfolk; they were worried the slave revolt would spread across all Richmond. With such excitement, the ticket agent didn't pay any mind to the unusual nature of my Kentucky bank note. He gave me thirty-five dollars' change in good solid-gold coin. No doubt about it, we'd done a profitable day's work on Sunday.

It was ten-thirty now, and I couldn't sit still. I kept thinking about weird white Elijah and about the feel of Virginia's pale, shuddering flesh. The memory of our congress was like a sore on my gum—unhealthy and painful, yet delicious to the touch.

I shoved my hand in my side pocket to see if the pawn ticket for my pistol was still there. It was. I resolved to run back into town to get my pistol from Abner Levy, and perhaps to catch a glimpse of Elijah on the city hall steps.

There was a good-size crowd in front of city hall, mostly riffraff like the fellow I'd spoken to. A double line of armed soldiers led from the city hall steps to Broad Street. I climbed into a tree so I could see. Before long, two wagons loaded with soldiers and black men came splashing up. Seemed like they'd arrested every loose Negro they'd set eyes on. The wet, ragged mob surged forward toward the wagons, but the soldiers held them back, and then here came two more wagons full of potential rebels. The mob stopped pushing entirely. Nobody wanted to tackle that many blacks at once. One last wagon arrived; this one held a bunch of soldiers and two men in chains. One was great big Elijah, standing straight up and yelling. The other was a dark man with a mashed face. It was Moline, wearing an army captain's coat. He yelled something that got both the slaves and the mob to hollering.

The soldiers started easing Elijah down off the wagon, and then all hell broke loose. I couldn't quite make it out, but it looked as if Elijah flat out busted the chains that manacled his feet and hands together. One minute he was being bundled up onto the city hall steps, and the next he was a pale angry pinwheel, kicking and hitting in every direction, his red teeth glittering like rubies. The mob went for him, some shots were fired, and then the wagons full of prisoners emptied. All at once, Capitol Square was like a dug-up anthill, with whites and blacks running every which way, slipping and sliding in the pouring rain. A black boy came scrambling up the same tree I was in. He saw me, glared, and climbed right on past me toward the top.

I couldn't see Elijah anymore for the mound of people on him, but it was pretty clear things were going to get worse. Time was running short, and I'd seen enough. Arf was waiting at the base of the tree. He followed me across Broad Street and down the alleys to Abner Levy's pawnshop.

Levy had just finished drawing his blinds—I could tell because they were still swinging. I knocked hard until he opened the door a crack. He was out of breath. I told him I had the money to redeem a pawn, and he let me come in. Arf pushed in with me.

I put my pawn ticket and a five-dollar gold piece on Levy's counter. "I left a four-shot pepperbox pistol with you," I reminded him. He picked up the money and the ticket and turned around to rummage in a cupboard.

Meanwhile, Arf gave himself a good shake and started sniffing around. The shop had a rack of fancy dress coats, cases with watches and jewelry, a variety of fine little tables, and several big trunks. One of the trunks caught Arf's interest in particular. He sniffed at it, gave it a good scratching, and then put his feet upon it and began to yelp.

"Get that dog out of here," yelled Levy angrily. "Why does everything have to happen at once? Shut him up, I tell you!"

I pulled Arf away from the trunk, but he leapt back at it, barking really hard. I noticed the lock was undone, so I decided to take a peek inside. Levy hollered at me to stop, but he was on the other side of the counter. I lifted up the top of the trunk, and there, curled up on his side, was Otha. He rolled his big eyes over my way and realized it was me.

"Marse Mase!" Otha sat up and threw out his long arms. "You looks mighty good indeed!" He jumped out of the trunk and did a little dance, unkinking his long limbs. His pockets rattled. Though he was soaking wet and a bit muddy, he was dressed fancy: yellow leather shoes, black velvet pants, an oddly cut purple jacket, and a watered silk shirt with a cravat of green brocade.

"Have you been in the trunk long, Otha?"

"No time a-tall. I only ran in here just befo you, Marse Mase. I'd a been here earlier, only I was delayed when some soldiers swept me up for bein loose an good-lookin without no mancipation paper." He threw his arms around me and hugged me. "But I don't need no paper if I got my little Marse!" I couldn't help but hug him back. There were lots of hard things in his pockets. Arf capered around us barking.

"You ran in here?" I said finally.

"Soldiers had me on a wagon by city hall, and when Lijah busted loose, I got away. Levy here done promise to send me to Baltimo in exchange for some goods." Otha sprang over to the counter. "I don't require freightin no more, Mist Levy, so I'll just have cash money for the silver teapot I done give you."

"I'm afraid that's impossible," said Levy, tightening his lips. "The risk on my part has already been undertaken. Your vacillation changes nothing."

"Is you gonna ship the empty trunk to Baltimo?" yelled Otha. "No you ain't. You owes me fifty dollar!" He'd certainly acquired a lot of city manners in the last eleven days. And where had he gotten the expensive clothes and the teapot he'd just given Levy? "I want my cash!" insisted Otha.

Levy addressed his attention to me. "Here is your pistol, Mr. Bustler. Thank you for your business. And…in the future, if you please, I prefer not to have slaves and animals in my shop." He handed me my pistol barrel first. It was unloaded. The clocks on Levy's wall said quarter to twelve.

Otha reached across the counter, grabbing for Levy's neck. I gave him a sharp poke in the side. "The money doesn't matter, Otha, believe me." I took Otha off to the side of the store and let him peek inside my breast pocket at the wad of bills.

"You stick with me," I told him with a certain amount of pride in my voice. "You've done well for yourself, but I've done better."

"If you done better, then do *me* some good. Tell Levy to give me a big ole bowie knife."

"Anything, if we can just get going." I gave Levy another five-dollar gold piece—it all was beginning to seem like play money—and he drew a hefty pig-sticker from his weapons cupboard. I handed Otha the blade as we left the shop.

We were down at Rockett's Landing a minute before noon. It was still drizzling. The wharf was crowded with people trying to get on the boat. All places were sold. I spotted Eddie and Virginia, him with his head up under an umbrella and her behind a thick pearly veil. I brushed up against them and passed Eddie his tickets. As we boarded, I tipped the purser five dollars to let me bring my slave and my dog.

Eddie and Virginia squeezed into the jam-packed passenger cabin, but Otha and I stayed on the deck. We found a dry spot under an overhang and leaned against the bulkhead, with Arf huddled in against our feet. The whistle shrieked, the paddles beat, and our steamer moved out into the rain-pocked James.

"Well, Otha, how'd you get so rich? You weren't in with Elijah, were you?"

He didn't answer me directly. "Moline joined Lijah in Goochland, and Marcus took word to the rebels in Richmond. Luther ran North. Custa lost his ten dollars gamblin, an Tyree drank his share up. They was the only two left to take Garland's bateau back to Lynchburg."

"Luther got caught," I told Otha. "Doesn't seem like those gold pieces did anyone much good."

"Did me plenty of good." said Otha, adjusting his cravat. "I bought me some fine clothes and started sparkin the help at rich folks' houses. Had me three gals on a string in no time, Mase. They'd sneak out for me to love em, and they'd bring me silver to save up to buy em free." He jingled his coat and then patted the rustling bulge over my heart. "Don't you call me crooked till you tell me how yo pocket got so full."

I glanced around. No one was near, but even so I stretched up on my toes to whisper in Otha's big ear. "I printed it, Otha. Thousands of dollars' worth. Two other men and I are going to spend it all in Norfolk."

"Whuffo?" His eyes were wide.

A crewman rounded the corner and leaned against the bulkhead to smoke a pipe. I gave Otha a smile and a quiet nod. It was good to have him back, and to have him wondering what *I* was doing. With a big smart slave like Otha. I didn't have to feel so small.

It was raining in sheets when we got to Norfolk. Reynolds was there on the dock all right. He, Eddie, and Virginia piled into a carriage, and I got into the next one with Arf and Otha. Our route lay along the waterfront. There were dozens of ships at anchor in the harbor, and scores of lighters and dories at the docks. We rounded a point and then, for the first time in our lives, Otha and I glimpsed the open sea.

There was a sand beach with rain running down it and the surf running up. I hadn't known that seafoam would be so white. The shapes of the waves fascinated me; I didn't see how they could lean over so far before they came apart.

"Don't they look like claws, Mase?" said Otha. "Draggin everything out to the deep?"

"They look like horses to me," I said. "Charging white horses that we can ride away."

"Where we goin, Mase?"

"The ends of the Earth."

Jeremiah Reynolds had rented us a barnlike wooden building in a sandy lot just around the point. Curved timbers lay scattered in the yard like the ribs of dead cattle. The weathered gray building bore a faded sign saying BURRIS BOATS—it had once housed a builder of dories and skiffs. The main floor of the building was a great empty room with a stove at one end. Stairs led up to a loft, which was fitted out with two bedrooms. Burris the boat builder had lived here with his family until cholera had wiped them out two years ago. The superstitious locals had left the building to stand empty, and Reynolds had been able to rent it very cheaply.

Blessedly, the iron stove was well stoked. Otha and I took off our jackets and began to dry ourselves. Arf flopped down on his side right next to the stove. For a moment there, it felt like we were back in the kitchen on our farm.

"Here now," exclaimed Eddie, coming down from the loft with Virginia close behind him. "This won't do! Who let you in, boy?"

"Don't talk to him that way," I cautioned Eddie. "His name is Otha. He's from Hardware. We came to Richmond together."

"He is your slave?" Eddie inquired.

"I expect so."

"Then tell him to remove himself to…" Eddie's voice trailed off as he glanced out through the back window. All but one of the sheds back there had collapsed; our little settlement's only standing outbuilding was a privy. "He can't stay in here with us," said Eddie. "There is a lady present."

That did it. Growing up on the farm with us, Otha'd never heard much abuse from whites. And now he'd tasted freedom in Richmond and seen Elijah's uprising. He grabbed a fistful of Eddie's shirtfront and began to shake him.

"I'm just as much a man as you, little bulgehead." *Shake.* "And if you's shittin yo pants so bad." *Shake.* "I'd say you the one belongs in the privy!"

I pushed in between them, but not before Eddie had drawn a tiny pistol from his waistband. "Put the gun away, Eddie," I cried, fumbling my own pistol out of my coat pocket and pushing its muzzle into his ribs. "Calm down!"

Eddie's face was corpse-white. There were beads of sweat on his brow. "Are you prepared to give me a gentleman's satisfaction, young Reynolds? Are you prepared to answer for your servant's vile abuse?" Though my pistol was in his ribs, his gun was jammed up under my chin. The big difference was that his weapon was loaded. Virginia watched us in tense silence. Must I promise to duel Eddie for what Otha had said?

Jeremiah broke the impasse. "Otha will sleep down here by the stove, Eddie, while you and Virginia will stay on upstairs. Mason and I'll take the other upstairs bedroom. I've laid in enough bedding for us all. Let's not lose sight of what we're here for, men! Just another few weeks and we'll be launching our trip to the Hollow Earth! Come, come— if two races can't get along here in Norfolk, how shall we manage in Tierra del Fuego and beyond? Apologize to Mr. Poe, Mason, there's a good lad."

Though *I* hadn't said anything to apologize for, I went ahead and did it. After what had happened last night, I owed Poe something. "I'm sorry Otha spoke roughly, Eddie. And, Otha, I'd appreciate it if you'd let me do the talking here."

Eddie postured a bit more, but the crisis was over. Otha went off to the big room's other end and began violently to practice throwing his bowie knife to stick in the heavy wooden door. I helped Jeremiah cook some of the provisions he'd laid in. He'd used his Bank of Kentucky bills, so we had quite a spread. There were cucumbers, tender new potatoes, slices of ham, and a bushel of live lobsters. Although Eddie pretended to know all about lobsters, I think only Jeremiah had cooked lobsters before. At his direction, I threw the big green seabugs into boiling water. Arf pricked his ears up, and it seemed to me I could hear the lobsters scream.

While they boiled, Virginia used a piece of coal to draw a rectangular tabletop on the main room's big wooden floor. When she'd finished with the table, she drew round circles for plates, and a big fluffy blob in the middle for a flower arrangement. She washed her hands in the tub of rainwater we'd brought in and stood back, beaming at her housekeeping.

Jeremiah fried up the potatoes and ham while I peeled the cucumbers. Eddie opened up a bottle from the case of champagne Jeremiah had brought. When Otha asked Eddie for a drink from his bottle, Eddie told him to open his own bottle, which he did. When Otha drew masses of stolen silver flatware from his pockets to set our places, Eddie began to laugh. Before long, the two were toasting each other.

The flesh of the lobsters was succulent and piping hot. With two candles on our "table" and the rain beating outside, I felt like a romantic prince in a gypsy band. Something of the same mood imbued the others. Jeremiah got himself a bottle of champagne as well. He, Eddie, and Otha grew very merry. The strange setting was to Virginia's liking; she sang for us after dinner, her face blooming with youth and beauty. Here at land's end, in our dim storm-whipped banquet hall, Virginia's voice, which had been so shrill and pinched in Mrs. Clemm's boardinghouse, was filled with grace and wonder. When she'd finished singing, she skipped outside to bathe herself in the rain. I resolved to make love to her once again, and fetched Eddie another bottle of champagne.

Before we went up to bed, Jeremiah Reynolds spoke a bit about the voyage he and Eddie had planned. The idea was that we should assemble a huge balloon that would be filled with an extraordinarily buoyant coal gas produced by a brazier of charcoal sprinkled with certain salts. The balloon, brazier, and balloon cabin were to be assembled to make a huge crate, which we would engage to carry by ship as far south as the wall of ice would allow.

"Who all goin in the balloon?" Otha asked. "Is you in, Mason?"

"I think I am."

Virginia darted in from her rainshower, loose wet dress flowing, and went tripping upstairs. I'd never seen her look so clean and fresh. She paused on the stairs to stare back at Eddie. He smiled and blew her a kiss, but made no effort to rise.

"Of course you'll go, young Reynolds," said Jeremiah, clapping me on the shoulder. "It's the opportunity of a life-time. You and I and Otha shall go. Eddie would have come, but his duties lie here with his writing and with his young wife. As wanted men, you and Otha are natural sailors." He stretched and rose to his feet. "You'll like the rough and tumble of shipboard life, Otha. All men are equal before the sea. You can help Mr. Poe purchase our equipment, and

Mason can help me assemble it. If you're truly a Reynolds, Mason, then once you see our cunning equipage, you'll jump at the chance to use it. Engineering has its own imperatives." He yawned again. "But now I'll off to bed."

Eddie gave me a sharp look just then. It struck me that he didn't want to go up to bed with Virginia. The tone of some remarks I'd heard him make—his fears of eyes, of mouths, of cats, of whirlpools—these remarks all suggested that he had a horror of a woman's most private part. It seemed unlikely that such a man would wish to crawl inside a great Symmes Hole in Mother Earth's nethermost clime. Perhaps Eddie's abrupt marriage to Virginia had been done not so much because he was jealous of me as because he needed an honorable excuse for backing out of the trip he'd promised Reynolds to undergo. First I was to explore Virginia, and then the Hollow Earth—all this in Eddie's stead.

Elaborately focusing his attention on me, Eddie drew out a metal pipe and a small glass vial. "Have you ever smoked opium, my young devil? It is most stimulating to the mind's eye."

"No thank you," said I. "I'm going to bed too." I wondered if Eddie could sense the pulse in my veins and the stiffening in my masculine member that came with night visions of Virginia. But no matter. If he was to spend the night down here drinking and smoking opium, Virginia and I would have free rein.

"Well then, black Otha," said Eddie, sending a thin blue coil of smoke up from his pipe. "How about you?"

Otha slowly nodded his head, a big loose smile on his lips. I knew from our experiments with Pa's whiskey that Otha had a stronger head for liquor than I. "I'se had me a full week, Mist Poe," said he. "Done took three girls in Richmond to see Lijah do his juju, done drank champagne with white folks tonight, so now I guess I be ready for yo sweet dreams." He rolled his eyes over at me and winked. "Didn't tell you about Lijah, did I, Marse Mase? Weren't just my good looks and promises that bound them three gals to me, it were that *I knew the prophet.* Our whole bateau crew got in with him, some for an arm and some for a toe."

"I saw you dance around the fire with him that night in Goochland," I said.

"I knows you did. Arf showed you to us. Lijah could juju the men an the beasts. He come from a long way away. Gimme that O, Mist Poe."

I left the two of them smoking together and went upstairs. Jeremiah was snoring, but Virginia had locked her door. I called to her as loud as I dared, but there was no response.

The next two weeks passed like an avalanche. Every day Eddie and Otha went out to buy more goods with Bank of Kentucky bills. Every day I worked with Jeremiah at assembling the exploring apparatus. Every evening we feasted, and every night I dreamed of sweet Virginia.

Posing as Kentucky Colonel Embry and his manservant Oscar, Eddie and Otha made a convincing pair, even when, as sometimes happened, they were glazed and vacant from poppy smoke or draughts of the opium tincture known as laudanum. Their initial antipathy had established a tone of mutual frankness between them; with the frankness and the drugs, they got along very well. Eddie rented them a room at the Hotel Norfolk and took all deliveries of goods at that address. Otha lugged the boxes and crates over to our boatyard after dark. Despite his fear of the sea, Otha was enthusiastic about the notion of exploring the Hollow Earth. He was of the opinion that his pale prophet Elijah might have come from there.

The equipage for our trip was elaborate. First we had to sew together our great silk balloon. The silk came in rolls that we stitched into long strips, half of them black and half of them white. The strips were trimmed into long, tapering gores, and then the gores were sewn together lengthwise to form a huge pear-shaped bag. Virginia was of much assistance in the sewing. When the great striped bag was completed, we painted its surface with four coats of the liquid rubber known as caoutchouc. Following this, we rigged a capacious network of silken ropes to contain the bag and to attach it to the cabin.

The cabin itself was of wickerwork. Of course no such thing as a ready-made wickerwork balloon cabin could be purchased; instead, we bought a number of large square wicker baskets (locally used for carrying catches of fish) and reassembled their sides into the big box that we required. Our cabin box had a swinging door, two shuttered windows, and a hole in its ceiling for our stove's flue. Fastened to the walls themselves were navigational instruments, most especially two highly sensitive chronometers: one with a pendulum, and one with a spring.

The stove was a lightweight affair fashioned from sheets of brass. A metalsmith constructed it for "Colonel Embry" to Jeremiah's specifications. The stove included a round chimney flue, which would lead up through our cabin roof to feed lighter-than-air gasses into our silk-and-rubber balloon. Packed in with the stove was a jar of the special salts that Eddie said would dramatically increase the lifting power of our stove's coal gas.

As this was to be an expedition that must initially pass across the antarctic wastes, we obtained a number of quilts and goose down feather-beds with which to line the cabin walls. Jeremiah showed us how to increase the quilts' insulating powers by opening their seams and padding them with goose down. As a precaution, we attached a pair of steel runners to the base of the cabin so that, should our balloon be downed, we could pull our cabin across the ice like a sled. Jeremiah went so far as to rig up silken traces with harnesses for the intended crew of him, me, Otha, and Arf.

Our dinners together were lavish affairs. Eddie was in a fever to spend or gamble away all of our remaining dollars before the counterfeit nature of the bills was found out. I tried to hold back some of my banknotes, but he took them all from me. Champagne we had always, and game, veal, seafood, and fruits of all sorts. Yet I had the feeling of a noose closing in on us. Norfolk was not so large a town that no one would connect Eddie's spending to the activity in our boatyard; nor was Kentucky so distant that its lack of a state bank would not be soon discovered.

I often sought to get Virginia alone and talk to her during those two weeks, but she was as elusive as a cat, now skipping up to her room, now running out to wander on the beach.

Even on the more and more frequent nights when Eddie did not come back to us at all, Virginia kept her door locked to me. As if to torment me further, she made much of Arf at all times, fondling him and feeding him bowls of delicacies. So lovesick did I become that I hoped Eddie might again have me mount Virginia in his stead. But Virginia's relations with Eddie were now minimal as well. Eddie was drinking much and gambling heavily.

Eddie's original justification for starting his now nightly gambling bouts had been to turn some of our Bank of Kentucky notes into gold coin. But here, as in everything else, he knew no moderation. In his first two days of gambling, he won enough so that Jeremiah could indeed set aside enough gold for three shipboard passages south. But then Eddie's runs of losses began. He was out all night, every night. Otha stopped going about with Eddie, and lent his energies to running out for this or that last item for our trip: shot and powder for my pistol, extra clothes, bottled juices, dried meat, and the like. Eddie slept alone in the Hotel Norfolk—if he slept at all—and in the afternoons he would appear in our workroom, pale and shaking, though trying to front a demeanor of nonchalance.

It was clear that the sight of his neglected Sissy filled Eddie with agonies of shame and self-loathing. So strong were these emotions that he often spoke sharply to her, sometimes even screaming with what seemed like hatred. Though his tirades were not wholly comprehensible, it was evident that Eddie regretted his decision to marry her—instead of traveling with us beyond the pole. Under the stress of his neglect and his attacks, Virginia once again took on the greasy, unattractive appearance that she'd had back at the boardinghouse. Once again her voice grew tense and shrill, and our boatyard echoed to the mournful mewling of her songs.

Finally, our preparations were done. We stowed hardtack, pemmican and bottled drinks in the wicker cabin with its instruments, stuffing the folded balloon in there as well. With its doors and shutters sealed, the cabin made a massive crate six feet by six feet by ten. Working together, Otha, Eddie, Jeremiah, and I were able to inch it across the big room's floor to the great side door. With the help of two more men and a wagon, we would be able to get it to our ship.

For our passage, Jeremiah Reynolds had chosen a fast-sailing schooner called the *Wasp*. Veteran of several trips to the antarctic seas, the *Wasp* was laying in provisions for a sealing voyage and would be leaving Norfolk on June first. Invoking the captain's duty to American science—and additionally promising to tell him first of any fine sealing islands we saw from the air—Jeremiah convinced him to transport the three of us and our wicker balloon box to the very edge of the antarctic wall of ice.

On Tuesday the thirty-first of May 1836, the day before the *Wasp* was to sail, Jeremiah, Otha, Arf, and I walked down on the docks of Norfolk to examine our ship. I asked Virginia to come with us, but she tearfully insisted she must wait in her room for Eddie. She said that he must take her home to her mother today. When I tried to comfort her, she said that I was a silly yokel and that she was sorry she'd ever let me touch her. She blamed me for her troubles with Eddie and said that if only she could be alone with him and her mama, then everything would be *arcadian* again.

It was a lovely day outside, with a clear sky and a light breeze. Jeremiah pointed out that the horizon was hazy; this meant, he said, that tomorrow the weather would be fine as well. We found a man willing to row us out to the *Wasp*, which was anchored in Norfolk harbor a few hundred yards west of Town Point. Arf liked the boat ride, but Otha was in an agony of fear.

"We got to learn how to swim, Mase!"

"Praying's more help than swimming if the *Wasp* goes down at sea," laughed Jeremiah. "Hellfire, man, we're going in a balloon later on, even though we don't know how to *fly!*"

The *Wasp's* Captain Guy was too busy to see us, but one of the mates, a tall, well-formed Virginian named Bulkington, advised us that the *Wasp* would be sailing on tomorrow's ebb tide, half an hour before dawn. We and our cargo had best come on board today. Yes, the dog was welcome, especially if he could kill rats. Bulkington lent us three crew members and the ship's heavy sealing yawl, which rowed back to the dock behind us.

While Jeremiah, Otha, and the three crewmen rode a flat freight wagon to our lodgings, I stopped by the Hotel Norfolk to rouse Eddie. In keeping with our plan of keeping Eddie's Kentucky colonel persona distinct from our expedition's outfitting, I had not yet visited the hotel. It was a comely sandstone structure, several blocks from the wharf. When I told the man at the desk I had an account to settle with Colonel Embry, the clerk gave a little whoop.

"You a card player, too? You'd better throw in with Lieutenant Bustler; he's already gone upstairs. One flight and then to the right."

I went up the hotel's richly carpeted stairs and took the hall to the right. A hubbub of sound drifted from an open door. Inside, I found three men in naval dress. One of them had the muttonchops and pie face that I remembered from the locket portrait Lucy Perrow had shown me…how long ago? Only a month? I resisted a crazy impulse to introduce myself as Lieutenant Bustler.

"I'm Mason Bulkington," said I. "Where's Colonel Embry?"

"Are you a friend of his?" demanded Bustler, too pig-arrogant to introduce himself. I resolved to rag him.

"Everyone honors the colonel," said I. "Though I don't have the breeding to call him a friend. I'm here from the confectioner's to present a bill. The colonel had me take a pound of chocolates to a lady this morning."

"What lady?" demanded one of the navy men. "Where?"

"A belle named Lucy Perrow," said I glibly. "She's here in this very hotel with her father. Touchy man, Judge Perrow. When I delivered the chocolates just now, he said he'd horsewhip the colonel as soon as he got through taking the starch out of some damn ponce called Lieutenant Bustler." I laughed easily, pretending not to notice the cloud on Bustler's face. "The judge meant business, too, I can tell you. He had a brace of pistols on, and a big black whip slung over his shoulder. Do you fellows know any Lieutenant Bustler?"

"Don't you be asking us questions, boy," blustered Bustler. "Your fine colonel cheats at cards!" The next minute, he and his friends had hurried off down the hall and out of the hotel.

I looked around Eddie's room. There were a few empty bottles, but the carpetbag he'd kept here was gone. I hoped with all my might that Eddie had taken Bustler for plenty of gold and that he and Virginia were safe on their way back to Richmond. Bustler wasn't in the lobby, but the sheriff was. He was deep in conversation with the clerk; they were leaning over a couple of Bank of Kentucky bills and jabbing at them.

"Counterfeit?" said the clerk unbelievingly. "Counterfeit?"

"No such bank!" said the sheriff. "We just found out!" Eddie'd cut his departure mighty fine.

I ran all the way to our boatyard. Otha, Jeremiah, and the three crewmen were struggling to get our wicker box up onto the wagon, while Arf barked furiously. I added my strength to the task, and the drayman got down off his wagon seat and joined us as well. The box was heavier than I'd expected, but finally we had it on the dray.

I whispered to Jeremiah that things were unraveling, and ran into our home of two weeks to see if Virginia or Eddie were there. The big room was empty, and the rooms upstairs were empty of life as well. Virginia's things were still lying about. I cast about for some message from her, but there was nothing. Perhaps she'd been too rushed to pack. I prayed she and Eddie were well on their way, and hurried after our slow-moving dray.

7. Aboard the Wasp

Writing this account of my adventures is slower work than I expected. If it weren't for all the tekelili I shared with Eddie Poe down in the Hollow Earth, I don't think I'd be able to do it at all.

I first set pen to paper on October 10, the day after Eddie's funeral, and here it is Christmas Day, 1849. My skin remains very dark; I've found work as a waiter in a Negro restaurant. Seela and I have a Christmas bird and a hot stove to roast it in. We have much to be grateful for.

When I began this narrative, I supposed it possible to produce a simple consecutive listing of one's memories, but I find, in the writing, that memory is a feathery branching tree. The dray that bore our box—should I mention that its wheels were hooped in iron, that these wheels clattered terribly on the street's cobbles, and that the sound reminded me of the first machine I ever saw: a crank-operated corn shucker belonging to Cornelius Rucker, owner of the farm next to ours in Hardware? Do I have time to mention the walk Otha and I took on the beach one day earlier, and to tell of the segmented leathery object we found, a mollusk's egg case, with scores of perfect tiny shells in each of its membranous disks? Can I mention that Virginia's last words to me were *I'm just a girl?*

I must prune and press forward.

On board the *Wasp*, our balloon box was stowed down in the hold, Jeremiah and I were shown to a cabin, Otha was lodged with the crew, and Arf was given the run of the ship. We set sail at dawn, June 1, 1836.

Given the prevailing trade winds, the natural course for a ship running for the South Seas is to sail southeast to cross the equator near Africa, and then to sail southwest to hit South America near Rio de Janeiro. This is what we did. The *Wasp* crossed the equator on the twelfth of July in longitude 26° W and we reached Rio on the fourth day of August. Rio was a revelation, a truly interracial city. I slept with another prostitute there, also wrote Pa a letter telling him I'd gone to sea. Though it was winter in Rio, flowers were blooming; more than anything, I was struck by the sight of the hummingbirds feeding on the blossoms. Otha and I took advantage of the good weather and calm waters by finally learning how to swim.

We replenished our stores and traveled down the coast past the Rio Negro, crossing 40° southern latitude. The wild South American coast of this region is known as Patagonia and is inhabited by a shy, gray-skinned race of men. Our sealing yawl landed in several of the bays, taking a few score of sealskins.

These takes were by no means satisfactory, as several thousand sealskins were needed for the *Wasp's* voyage to be a success. Bulkington told me that Captain Guy had plans to eventually shape our course in search of untouched sealing islands presumed to exist beyond 65° S, the antarctic circle.

For those as ignorant of navigation as I was at the start of the *Wasp's* journey, I should explain that every point on the equator has 0° latitude, and that the southern pole is the unique point with 90° southern latitude. The 90° symbolizes the fact that from the center of the Earth, there is a ninety-degree angle between a line to the equator and a line to the South Pole. A drive for the Pole is a drive for higher and higher latitudes.

Longitude, I may as well add, is a measure of one's angular deviation east or west from the prime 0° meridian, which runs north-south through Greenwich, England. South America lies in western longitude; most of Africa is in eastern longitude. Near the Poles, the longitude lines get so bunched together that one can effect large changes of longitude rather easily. But changing one's latitude stays just as hard.

On September 19 we reached the Falkland Islands, at lat. 52° S, long. 57° W, near the tip of South America. The Falklands are of good soil, with luxuriant meadows and many head of wild cattle. Though there are no trees, the lowlands supply an excellent peat or turf for burning. No humans live here, but the feathered tribes are very numerous, particularly the penguin and the albatross.

These two dissimilar birds form huge rookeries together—temporary camps for hatching their young. The chief rookery on the Falklands was nearly bigger than our farm back in Hardware. It was set on the rocky shore by the water. The birds had smoothed out their settlement by moving all the loose rocks out to form the walls of three sides of a square. The big square was divided up like a checkerboard, with alternating nests of penguins and albatrosses. The arrangement struck me as a symbol of how the two races, black and white, lived together in the south.

We stayed in the Falklands till September 26: overhauling our sails and rigging, obtaining a new supply of fresh water, and taking on board twenty-eight barrels of albatross eggs packed in salt. The plan was to run southeastward before the prevailing winds until crossing the latitude of 60°, and then to head back westward, beating our way as far south as the ice would allow. Captain Weddell of the English navy had achieved a latitude of 74° S in February 1822, and Captain Guy felt we might be able to do as well. If we could find a new, untouched seal rookery, we could well harvest as many as five thousand pelts.

Though Jeremiah was a pleasant, good-humored cabin mate, he had an annoying tendency to give me advice. I soon wearied of his homilies. I think he felt I was a bit of a criminal, not quite worthy of bearing the Reynolds name. He dined each day with Captain Guy, leaving me to share the mates' mess. Of all the mates, I got on with Stuart Bulkington the best.

Like me, Bulkington had grown up on a farm between Lynchburg and Charlottesville. He had a deeply tanned face and brilliant white teeth; it was a joy to see him laugh. For reasons he was unwilling to divulge, Bulkington had been steadily at sea for seven years now. He filled me with tales of the lands he'd seen, and though I had few adventures to reciprocate with, he seemed satisfied by my willingness to listen and to comment. We were kindred spirits, I felt: two men with troubled pasts.

Since Otha was not strictly bound to work, he stood somewhat apart from the crewmen. And in any case the handful of black crew members were near savages: Tasmanians and Feejee islanders with sharpened teeth and tattoos on their faces. Otha's best friend on the *Wasp* was a mixed-race fellow called Dirk Peters, son of a native woman and a fur trapper. When Otha was not with me, he was likely to be practicing knife throwing with Peters, who was a great one for whipping a bowie knife out of his boot top and flinging it at his target. He'd killed a penguin on the Falklands this way, sticking him right through the heart, which feat had impressed Otha mightily.

This Dirk Peters was short and ferocious-looking, with snaggleteeth that peeked out through thin, unbending lips. The straight mouth gave him an air of sadness, while the dancing teeth suggested he was merry. In truth he was, so far as I could tell, an empty-headed drifter who lived only for the moment. Not only Otha but Arf as well took a liking to Peters, who liked to pull the dog's ears and talk to him in a dialect he said came from the Missourian tribe of the Upsaroka, a part of the Crow Nation. Over my great protests, Peters and Otha passed one idle afternoon by tattooing a spiral Upsaroka good-luck symbol around Arf s navel, that is, on his belly just above the tip of his penis sheath. Tranced by Peters's chants, or by some of the opium that Otha still seemed to have about him, Arf endured the ordeal with no complaint.

We spent a week sailing about southeast of the Falklands in search of the missing Aurora islands. These small, round islands had been sighted in 1774, 1779, and in 1794, but no one had been able to find them since. We were unsuccessful, and on October 18 we made South Georgia island in lat. 53° S. long. 38° W. This is a steeply mountainous island, with its peaks perpetually snow covered and its valleys overgrown with strong-bladed grass. Captain Guy sent the yawl and two boats ashore in search of seal, but after three days they returned empty-handed. We circumnavigated the whole island without spotting a single pinniped.

We continued our course due east, driven by the powerful prevailing westerlies, with strong wind and much heavy weather, including snow and hail. We often spotted the free-floating islands of ice that are known as icebergs. On October 24 we reached Bouvet's Island, in lat. 54° S, long. 3° E. A boat went ashore and returned the next day with eighty fur-seal skins. The sailors had clubbed twice as many to death but had not had the time to skin them all. Arf and I rode to shore with Bulkington's boat the next day to watch the men taking the skins off the remaining seals. The procedure was to cut off the flippers and tail, make an incision around the neck and along the belly, and then to peel the skin off like a jacket. Arf nosed the fresh carcasses with interest, but he was not bold or hungry enough to tear off a piece.

It was a melancholy view on the beach there, two thousand miles from Cape Horn and a thousand from the Cape of Good Hope. I felt dizzy and unsteady on the unrocking land. The raw red flesh of the flayed seal carcasses was the only vivid color in sight. The sky and sea were gray, and the island was a mass of glassy blue-gray lava. The beach was of pale, crumbling pumice stone.

Out past our ship were scores of antarctic ice islands that had come aground in the shallows around Bouvet Island. Some of these huge icebergs were as much as a mile in circumference. In the slow spring warming (remember that seasons are reversed in the southern hemisphere, so that their October, November, December, January, and February are as our April, May, June, July, and August), pieces of the ice islands were occasionally dropping off and crashing into the sea with eerie roars that mixed with the cries of the seafowl feeding on the dead seals' flesh.

It seemed strange and cruel for men to come all this way and slaughter wantonly. Even if it were possible to reach the Hollow Earth, would it be right for us to pave the way for our civilization's further depredations? Or, more horribly, what if those inside the Hollow Earth were to come out and treat us the way we treated seals? I spoke with Jeremiah about these questions that evening, but he seemed not to take them seriously.

"This is a pretty fair sort of world, Mason, if you don't expect too much. There are a great many good fellows about. Captain Guy, for one, is a brick and a jolly toper. And your friend Bulkington seems right enough. Quit your vaporing! Don't you think those seals' jackets will look better on the pretty Knickerbocker ladies in the city of the Manhattoes? And as for Hollow Earthlings coming out after us—I wouldn't worry. It's likely as not to be dark in there, with nothing but mushrooms."

"I thought Symmes said there's a sun inside," I protested. "Right in the center."

"Yes, but our Newton of the West hadn't much of a head for mathematics." Reynolds grinned. "I have it on the authority of a professor from Johns Hopkins that there's no weight on the inside of a hollow sphere. If we could get past the ice and sail over the South Hole's lip into the Hollow Earth, we'd soon enough float off the ocean's surface in there. And if there was a sun in the middle, we'd fall into it and burn, and so would anyone on the inside who didn't cling fast."

There was a half-gale blowing outside and our porthole was battened shut. A flickering light of seal oil lit our little cabin with its table, chair, and two bunk beds. Arf lay sleeping on the floor. Puzzled by what Jeremiah said, I drew a diagram on the flyleaf of the atlas he'd brought along. The picture I drew was what you'd see if you could take a thin vertical slice right through our Hollow Earth. You'd see a big ring of matter, broken by two holes at the bottom and top: the North and South holes that Symmes postulated. My picture showed two thick semicircles on the left and right, like parentheses not quite meeting at the bottom and the top.

"Symmes said a ship could sail over the edge and then sail around on the inside," I said, drawing three ships, one on the outside, one on the southern lip, and one on the inside.

"Yes," said Jeremiah. "But the *real* Newton's integral calculus proves him wrong." He put his blunt finger on the ship inside the Hollow Earth. "Sure enough, the ocean and dirt right under that ship attract it." Now he swept his finger over the whole rest of the Hollow Earth's great rind. "But all this matter is, so to speak, *overhead*. It pulls the ship up. It's far away, but there's a lot of it. My Professor Stokes tells me that Newton's integrals balance it all out." He sketched a fourth ship, floating free in the Hollow Earth's airy interior. "*This* is what happens. And if there were a heavy little sun in the center, it would pull all loose things down into it. Pfft! Too bad!"

"But if there *is* a sun and we go in, then…"

"*We'll be safe*. That's another reason why we're going there in a balloon instead of a ship. As long as the Hollow Earth is full of air, a lighter-than-air balloon will float up *away* from any central sun. We'll let out gas to go down through the Hole, and we'll toss ballast to get back out. If there is an Inner Sun, then as long as we're inside the Hole, we'll float around and the Hollow Earth'll just be like a kind of roof. There may be birds nesting on it, or apes in hanging-down trees—who knows?"

I tried to imagine it and gave up. "But you think there might not *be* an Inner Sun, Jeremiah?"

"The Hollow Earth could be black and empty, with rocks drifting around like the small planets called asteroids. Some little light would come in the Holes." Jeremiah shrugged and gave me his bluff, honest grin. "Thunderation, Mason, I don't know *what* to expect. That's why I want to go in there! Man gets to be my age, he'll go a long way for a surprise."

There was a great roar outside and then, a moment later, our ship pitched horribly. One of the giant ice islands nearby had shifted its center of balance and spun over. I slept uneasily that night, dreaming of a ship that fell up through a crowded sky toward the sun.

The next day we sailed around Bouvet Island looking for more seal rookeries, but so steep were the cliffs that not another spot could be found where a seal might land. We put out to sea and ran southeast before the squalling west wind.

On November 13 we crossed 60° S latitude. The wind moderated, the weather cleared, and we found ourselves in a vast field of drifting ice. Most of the pieces were rounded pancakelike floes, but many were heaped up like crystal fairy castles or like mountains of glass. The brilliant morning sun reflected off the myriad angles and sent out rays of every color. We were dazzled by the brilliant beauty, but our wonder soon changed to alarm. Huge chunks of ice and snow were irregularly falling from the floating ice mountains. If one of those chunks landed on or near us, we'd sink like a toy paper boat. Providentially, we were not very near any of the icebergs.

The weather was mild and pleasant, with not enough wind for us to make any rapid headway. Pieces of ice kept seizing up around our ship's hull, which made our progress that much slower. But onward we moved.

Vast numbers of sea birds flew from one ice mountain to the other—albatrosses, petrels, ice birds, and many other strange species that no one had ever seen. I wondered if they roosted inside the Hollow Earth and migrated out here through the South Hole. Swimming about and clambering on and off the icebergs were also penguins in great numbers. To complete the lively scene, a great number of right whales and porpoises showed themselves in the clear water south of the crystal field we found ourselves in. The whales were leaping wholly out of the water and shaking themselves for joy.

On the third day, we awoke to find that the sheets of ice had parted, and we found our way into clear water south of the icy drift. The water was teeming with shrimp and squid. The wind shifted around to the northeast now, so we resolved to sail back to the westward, holding a southern course so long as it would be practicable. We passed through several huge bands of ice, yet each time we were frozen in, the ice loosened back up. Captain Guy had a genius for finding more clear water. With the lengthening of the days it seemed, perhaps paradoxically, that the farther south we got, the more open space there was. Despite the warming temperature, the weather remained highly variable, with frequent hail squalls from the west. The greatest fear at all times was that our small wooden ship might fetch up against an iceberg hundreds of times our size.

On December 1 we crossed the antarctic circle at lat. 65° S, long. 15° E. In this latitude there was no field-ice, though there were many icebergs. Captain Guy was still enjoying the challenge of picking his way farther and farther south, but now the crew members were beginning to grumble. We had taken no seals for over a month and were in daily risk of losing our lives. Fresh water we had plenty, but other provisions were running low. Taking all this into account, Jeremiah concluded that we had best bring our balloon box up on deck, so that we could leave whenever the captain judged it prudent to head back north. There seemed to be no sign of the new sealing islands that Captain Guy had hoped to find. He told us that if we found nothing soon, he would shape a northwest path toward the seal-rich archipelago of islands lying between us and Tierra del Fuego.

The balloon box was wedged into a wholly inaccessible recess of the hull. To make things worse, three boatloads of extra provisions had arrived on the evening of the last day, and these had all been packed in around the balloon box. It was the work of a full day for Otha, Jeremiah, Peters, Bulkington, and me to haul the boxes and barrels out of the way, and to wrestle our great wicker box up onto the deck. It was difficult work in the hold, suffused as it was with a vile smell of decay that I supposed came from the sealskins. Our box had an extremely foul stench of its own, and we wondered if our provisions had spoiled. Imagine my horror when, on grasping the stinking box, I heard a weak voice from its inside.

"Get me out," said the voice. "For the love of God."

In a minute we had torn the box's door open. I staggered back and vomited. Eddie and Virginia had been sealed in the box all these months, and one of them had long been dead.

With a superhuman effort, we lugged the box to a position near the hold and winched it up onto the deck. What a contrast between that box and the clean antarctic air! So smeared and tangled were the two lovers' bodies that it had been hard to tell who was who, but now I could see that it was Eddie who had survived and Virginia who had rotted into bones and black grease. Eddie's eyes were quite mad; Bulkington drew up bucket after bucket from the sea and dashed the cold water in Eddie's livid, twitching face.

Jeremiah pulled out the balloon bag and let the breeze into the box's interior. All our bottled juices and spirits were gone; also the dried meats and the hardtack. Evidently, Eddie'd had room to squirm about in the cabin. Yet we'd found him in the arms of dead, rotting Virginia. It was a horrible thing to imagine a man seeking out so macabre an embrace.

The whole ship's crew was in a furor of excitement and disgust. I think they might well have thrown Eddie overboard with Virginia's remains had not Jeremiah intervened. He carried the weeping Eddie into our cabin and began nursing him. Otha and I set to work putting the balloon cabin to rights, and Bulkington helped us lash it to the deck. This last step was important as now a sudden gale was rising from the north.

For the next three weeks we were driven southward. Over and over. Captain Guy tried to beat his way to the north, but a powerful current joined forces with the winds and the drifting fields of ice. We passed 70° S latitude, and then 72°, and finally, on Christmas Day of 1836, we reached a latitude of 75° S, closer to the Pole than any men had ever been before. Birds filled the southern sky, which was brilliant with the reflection of some vast unseen snowfield. There seemed little doubt that a landfall was imminent.

With the antarctic summer at its peak, we had sunlight all day and night long. It was a striking thing, leaning on the rail that Christmas Day, to see the sun and moon both above the horizon, each shedding its light. Our provisions were all but exhausted; our holiday repast had consisted of fish we'd caught, and fresh water that one of our boats had gathered from a pool in a melting iceberg. Nevertheless, all were ready for the new land to the south. We had two sails set square to let the gentle north wind blow us thither.

During our three weeks' southward progress, the icebergs had become ever more huge and fantastic. Some were vast, uniform rectangles, but others had sides that were smoothly carved by the water, with indentations that had become stupendous, arching caves. These caverns were at water level, so that the swell of the sea sloshed in and out of the ice mountains. In the fog, when it was the most dangerous, you'd hear the icebergs by the thundering of the water in their caves.

Christmas Day was fair, and land was near. Eddie was up and about for the first time. I'd been bunking with Bulkington, leaving Eddie completely in Jeremiah's care. Eddie's quivering had gone, and his ghastly pallor had abated. As he and I stood leaning over the ship's rail, staring at the icebergs, I sought to engage him in conversation.

"Look how the sun lights one side of that ice mountain and the moon the other," I said to Eddie, hoping to stimulate his love of beauty. "And see the white petrels flying in and out of that cavern! It's like a ruined alabaster abbey, is it not?"

"It is like teeth," whispered Eddie. He had his hand shoved deep into the pocket of his trousers. He looked at me oddly and then he drew his hand out of his pocket and showed the delicate ivory objects that lay in his palm. A chill crept down my spine.

"Virginia's teeth," said Eddie. His voice was fainter than the most distant cries of the birds.

I glared at Eddie till he put the teeth back in his pocket. "Tell me how she died," said I.

He stared out at the iceberg moving slowly toward our stern. His bulging white forehead was pathetically furrowed, and his mouth was pursed smaller than his little mustache. I felt some pity for him, and some rage. I nudged him. "I loved Virginia too, Eddie. You have to tell me."

He glanced over at me and shook his head. Still I insisted. "Why did you kill her, Eddie? Why?"

He shuddered and sighed, as if relieved I knew, and then at last he began to talk. His voice was weak and hoarse, but as he went on, some of its old melodious power returned. "The last night there, the Imp of the Perverse possessed me. What good were all our pawky careful plans? The end result of my machinations was that I'd alienated the affections of my beloved Virginia for an exploring expedition which I was not to make. Nothing waited for me back in Richmond but Mrs. Clemm's boardinghouse and the slow dungbeetle ball-rolling of my inevitable literary fame. The Imp of the Perverse, do you know him, Mason?"

"Not really," said I, eager to keep Eddie's voice flowing. "Go on."

"That last night I cheated a Lieutenant Bustler at cards and won a small fortune in gold. The Imp wished Bustler to be *sure* I'd diddled him, so I left an extra ace in the lieutenant's deck of cards. I made it back to my hotel in the early hours. I was out of opium. I could have waited till the shops opened, but the Imp would have it not. I took a crowbar from the tool shed behind the hotel and prized open the back door of the nearest apothecary. I found a ball of opium and a bottle of laudanum and stepped safely out. The Imp of the Perverse took it ill that things went so well. At his bidding, I stood there smoking pipes till a constable happened by. When he asked me about the open door, I said he insulted me and then I bribed him with a Bank of Kentucky bill. 'Be sure to check if this is good,' I told him. 'And if not, seek Colonel Embry at the Hotel Norfolk.'"

A chunk fell off a cathedral-size iceberg nearby. The birds screamed, and the spreading circle of waves rocked our ship. "Go on, Eddie. Tell it all."

"I went back to the hotel and slept. When I woke it was midmorning. As soon as I remembered all that the Imp and I had wrought, I packed my bag and left the hotel by the back door. I hurried to the boatyard. Nobody was there but Virginia. She was sitting alone upstairs. I told her we had to depart immediately and that I didn't want to go back to Richmond. I told her we should go to Baltimore on the eleven o'clock packet, and then on to New York. She said I was hateful to her and that—"

Eddie stopped and gazed at me. His eyes were darker and more whirlpool-like than ever before. I was a bit frightened, for all that any threat he projected was not so much physical as it was spiritual. "She said she wished she had married you, Mason. You did it. I remember what you did. You and I and the Imp—we brought poor Virginia low."

"Go on, Eddie, go on."

"Virginia said she was not leaving the boatyard until she'd asked you what to do. She said she'd been scared to talk to you, but that now the time had come. I resolved to drug her and to bodily take her away. I made her some tea, dark and sweet and strong, and I laced it with two hundred drops of laudanum, four times my normal dose. I watched her drink it, and then I watched the rapid waning of her sweet moon face. She slumbered. I hurried downstairs with an eye to going out for a carriage—I would tell the driver Virginia was drunk, I would tell the packet-boat captain she was sick, I would lie our way to a new life. But as soon as I came downstairs, I heard a heavy wagon coming. I couldn't let you and Jeremiah find us!"

Arf appeared between us now, wriggling and cheerful. He was a great pet among the sailors and had gotten holiday scraps from almost everyone. In that strange half-human way he had sometimes, he put his feet up on the ship railing between Eddie and me. Eddie glanced distractedly at Arf and went on.

"I hurried upstairs. She was so still, so soft, so warm! I had the strength of a maniac, Mason, I picked her up and raced to the balloon box. We'd hide in there, sail out from Norfolk, announce ourselves, and be set ashore in Charleston or Savannah. I had money enough to ask the captain favors. I had gold!"

Arf licked Eddie's face, and for an instant it was as if Eddie mistook the dog for Virginia.

"Oh my darling," he moaned. "My dark new moon! Are you awake?" He clutched at Arf and then, suddenly realizing his mistake, grabbed tight hold and tried to throw Arf over the railing into the still, deep waters we were gliding through. Arf squealed; I stopped Eddie with a sharp blow to his shoulder; Arf dropped to the deck and hurriedly skulked away.

"We were quiet in the box. I had always loved it when Virginia lay very still with me. I was in paradise, pressed up against her in there, so still and quiet, with the satiny balloon cloth padding us all around like …"

"Like a coffin," I said. "Like a womb. You killed her with the opium?"

"They loaded us into the ship's hold and went away and came back with more boxes, and they *would* bustle about until the time for waking up had passed. I slept, and nestled against Virginia, and waited till the ship should sail." Eddie's voice had grown whispery again. There was a sudden cry from one of the mastheads.

"Land ho!"

I snapped my head to the left and, yes! There, beyond a long perspective of scattered icebergs, was a jagged line of white and, ah!, a line of green!

"When the ship moved, Virginia was stiff and cold." Eddie's hand crept into his pants pocket to fondle her teeth. "I meant to die with her. That's why I never cried out. But I was weak. I crawled to the provisions, and fed, and crawled back to her. Over and over. Jeremiah says six months have passed, yet for me…"

"Look, Eddie! Land!"

He swooned and fell to the deck. Eddie was guilty of Virginia's death, yet he was not, in any clear-cut way, a murderer. This set my mind at ease. Only God could decide if Eddie had suffered enough for his sins. I dragged him back to the bunk he'd taken over from me and joined the excited crew.

We picked our way among the icebergs and came into a bay of smooth water, filled with floating sea plants and fish. Bulkington stood in the bow, taking soundings. For the longest time, the bottom remained too deep to find, and then, a mere fifty yards from the grassy shore, we were over a shelf but three fathoms deep. This bottom was covered with thick ropes and sheets of an orange seaweed too tough to pull up. We dug in tight anchors fore and aft.

The view of the shore was as follows. There was a smooth beach of black sand, a meadow of grass and flowers, some green hillocks, rocks beyond them and, further back, a towering wall of ice. Beyond the wall of ice was a lifeless plain of snow that rose toward a range of jagged mountains. The beach curved around a half-mile to the right, eventually being pinched off by the wall of ice. The beach went on somewhat further to the left, ending in an area where a plumelike gray cloud hung over the water. Nothing could be seen beyond this smoky veil. As we anchored, several of us saw smooth black knobs sticking out of the ocean, like bollards or overgrown walrus heads—but these objects failed to reappear. Though one might have expected to find seals and penguins in great numbers here, there were seemingly none.

Three boats were sent ashore; Otha, Arf, and I managed to get into the last one with Bulkington and the crewmen Sam Stretch, Isaac Green, and Jasper Cropsey. Jeremiah would have come too, yet at the last minute Dirk Peters shouldered him aside and jumped in.

We rowed like men possessed, then beached and jumped out. Otha ran across the beach and threw himself face down in the thick grass. I followed along and joined him. The grass blades were thin and wiry, with some stalks crowned by small, sweet-smelling yellow flowers. A hill lay ahead of us, and a stream trickled by on our left.

"Don't never want to go back on no ship." Otha sighed, digging his fingers into the black soil. Arf danced around us sniffing wildly. Something like a mouse scurried into a hole, and Arf began to dig. "Could grow yams here," said Otha.

"I wonder what we should name it," I mused.

"Don't need to name it no white name," said Otha. "It be."

The men still on the ship were crying out, so Captain Guy sent two of the boats back to pick up more. Soon all but a skeleton crew were on shore, scores of us, running and skipping and laughing with joy. Though there was of course no wood to be found, some men with spades dug up bricks of the thick grassy turf and made a brisk fire of them. Not that we needed the heat; Captain Guy ascertained the air temperature to be 54° F. The water was anomalously warm: 67° F! This unusual heat confirmed our suspicion that the bank of smoke or fog off to the east was of volcanic origin. It seemed that we had stumbled on a geothermal antarctic oasis.

Some large lobsterlike crustaceans were to be seen on the ocean bottom, which was covered right up to the shore with thick cables and mats of the ropy orange seaweed we'd seen before. Sam Stretch and a Feejee islander named Taggoo waded into the warm waters to try to catch some of the lobsters. The lobsters were fast and wary, but the men did catch hold of several melon-size creatures that they found swimming about. These curious animals were something like squid stuffed into snail shells. They had the surprising ability to either crawl on the bottom or to dart about through the water. They were carnivorous, preying upon fish, and upon the nervous lobsters. Far from being afraid of men, the shellsquid (as we came to call them) swam right up to investigate anyone in the water and were exceedingly easy to catch. They pressed so close to us that it seemed they took us for edible carrion. The *Wasp's* mate Joseph Couthouy, a conchologist, pronounced them to be a species of ammonoid, cousin to the nautilus, and he told us something of their habits.

The shellsquid's eyes, feelers, scullers, and ninety tentacles jut out from its open end in a writhing orange bunch centered around a fleshy flap, which conceals a strong and razor-sharp beak—as Isaac Green would soon learn.

A strong tubular nozzle projects from beneath the shellsquid's beakflap. This organ, Couthouy told us, performs a remarkable function: the creature propels itself horizontally by using the nozzle to slowly draw water into an inner pouch and to then forcibly squirt the water from the same nozzle.

The shellsquid has a separate, balloonistlike mode for vertical motion: There is just enough air sealed in the shell's chambers so that the shellsquid's net weight in water is but a fraction of an ounce. By filling an inner pouch with water or with air, it can tune its buoyancy to any desired degree. This means that the creatures can float on the surface, hover at any given thermocline, or contract their pouch to squeeze out all water and sink to the seafloor beneath. Once at the bottom, the shellsquid can swim back to the surface, squirting itself this way and that.

These were singular creatures—and far more sinister than we realized. But the most immediately striking thing about them was the incredible beauty of their silvery, logarithmically spiraling shells. It was immediately clear to all of us that these shells could make the ship's fortune. The shells were brilliant and rainbow-reflecting like thick mother of pearl, yet possessing in certain lights a haunting, nacreous translucency. Every woman in the world would want a shellsquid brooch. The hunt was soon on, and the men caught nearly a hundred of them.

The easiest method for catching shellsquid was to wriggle one's fingers wormlike in the water. Invariably, a shellsquid would jerkily squirt its way over and begin to attach its tentacles to one's hand. One then had but to snatch the shell from behind and fling the beast out of the water and onto shore. This was of course an operation that had to be done nimbly. Isaac Green was too slow about it, and one of the shellsquid managed to snip off the first joint of his forefinger with its powerful beak. Green screamed terribly, but the other sailors—hardened characters all—laughingly assured Green we could best revenge him by having a shellsquid "clambake." Our Christmas dinner of fish and water had left us hungry.

While a boat raced back to the ship to fetch a kettle, Otha and I wandered up to the top of the nearest hillock. Small, thick-furred rodents darted in and out of the flowery grasses underfoot, shying from our approach. At the top of the hill, Otha and I found a stand of bushy, thick-leaved plants that Otha thought looked like kale. Starved for any fresh vegetable, we sampled the leaves and found them edible, though somewhat thistly. We gathered two bushels of them in our shirts and carried them down to steam with the shellsquid. Some other men had found potatolike tubers beneath the swampy stands of pink flowers that grew on the borders of the freshwater streams that trickled down from the wall of ice; still others had gathered baskets full of eggs from the nests that covered one of the hillsides.

Jeremiah and Eddie were ashore now too. Eddie was once again his old self, strutting about, observing things, making remarks. He took me aside.

"I'm coming on the balloon," said he. "Otherwise it's all for naught."

"All for naught that you brought Virginia," said I. "You should have left her alone."

"I'm damned," Eddie softly said. "I know this to the depths of my soul." He looked into my eyes. "I beg you, Mason, be my friend nonetheless. Lend your support to my plea to join the expedition. I, of all men, am the one to witness the Hollow Earth."

"Fine," said I, my heart softening. "If there's room, then of course you should come."

Eddie beckoned Jeremiah over, and we quickly agreed that Eddie would travel with us.

To complete our feast, Captain Guy sent one last boat back to the ship for the last of the crew and a barrel of rum. We ate and drank for hours. With the sun and moon rolling along the horizon face to face, there was no feeling of time past or time to come, there was only the joy of our feast at the end of the world, with no witnesses but the ammonoids and the wheeling flocks of birds.

The shellsquid's bodies were muscular and tough. Although they were not large, a single one of the creatures was more than any man would normally feel like chewing down at one go. Yet the flesh was sweet and nourishing, and we all kept gnawing away at our victims. The scores of small orange tentacles were particularly easy to eat. And Arf was partial to a rank congelation that was found in the furthest recesses of the ammonoids' large, translucent shells.

At Jeremiah's suggestion, we began drying the bodies of the uneaten shellsquid over the fire. They would make an excellent pemmican. Moreover, according to Bulkington, there was a brisk Chinese market for exotic dried sea creatures of every kind. Captain Guy confirmed that members of the holothurian family—the sea cucumbers, the *bêches-de-mer*, and the trepang—fetched exceedingly high prices in Hong Kong. He expressed a hope that we might find *bêches-de-mer* in the waters that lay closer to the volcanic vent.

After eating and resting and eating some more, the members of our impending balloon expedition found themselves together: Eddie, Otha, Jeremiah, Arf and me. At the last minute, Dirk Peters attached himself to our group. We wandered slowly down the black sand beach toward the volcanic steam plume. The orange seaweed-covered shelf gave out quickly, and the water was very deep right off shore. Though as usual I had taken no rum, the others were in varying degrees of intoxication. Behind us were the crewmen, and their fire and their boats. It was midnight. Left to right we were the moon, the sea, Jeremiah, Eddie, myself, Otha, Dirk Peters, the antarctic land and, above its mountains, the sun, with Arf always somewhere in between.

"We'll set off from here," said Jeremiah. "We'll restock the cabin and leave as soon as tomorrow. Who knows how long this fine weather will last!"

"Where we supposed to be end up in that balloon?" asked Otha.

"Over those mountains," said Jeremiah, pointing. "Or around them. Once past them, we'll most likely see the great South Hole."

"I see it," said Eddie slowly. "My imagination used to rebel at the great Hole. I was too frightened of it. But now…" Here he glanced around at us in search of forgiveness and comprehension. "What has a man who's been buried alive with a corpse have to fear of a Hole? My mind's eye can finally see it. After the mountains, we'll glimpse a miragelike far horizon above a near horizon. These will be the two limbs of the mighty circle that rounds the South Hole. If the Hole is clear, our eyes will trace the paths of the sun's rays pouring into the vast Hollow Earth-egg. Or, more likely, the Hole will be filled with a great vortex of golden gauzy mist. We'll float down through the haze; living in the sky like angels! Angels! And perhaps…"

"I took the trouble to stoke the stove and put the balloon's lines in readiness," interrupted Jeremiah. "Just in case."

"Just in case what?" said Otha.

"Mutiny," said Dirk Peters. "Plague. Cannibals."

"There certainly don't seem to be any natives about," said I.

There was a sudden flash of white and a small, shrill scream. Arf was off like a shot and managed to head off the creature, which had just seized a mouse. It ran back toward us. With a slow, oiled motion, Dirk Peters threw his knife and nailed the creature to the turf. It shrieked once and died. It was all white, with hair that lay backward, that is, the hairs of its pelt ran along its body from the tail toward the head. Its claws and teeth were a deep garnet in hue. This color was not the stain of mouse blood; the teeth and claws were a glassy red all the way through. More ornaments for the city women, thought I with a slight shudder of disgust. The creatures in this small volcanic bay were unique, and it was disturbing to think that two or three ships like the *Wasp* might wholly annihilate them.

Peters gutted the red-clawed beast with quick, efficient motions and threw the offal into the sea. There were fewer shellsquid here than near our landing site, but seemingly all that were present sped over to tear at the fresh guts Peter had thrown them. The water fairly boiled for a minute as several dozen ammonoids devoured the red-clawed beast's lights and liver.

Peters hung the cleaned animal from his belt, and we wandered on along the beach toward the volcanic plume. Staring at the animal's teeth, I remembered the mysterious Elijah. His teeth had been red, too.

As we walked, Jeremiah told Otha more about the Hollow Earth, with Eddie adding fanciful word pictures and crack-brained hints that we might happen on the angel of Virginia. There seemed no special reason to go back to the crew; it was pleasant to be stretching our legs.

The seawater grew warmer and more choked with floating plants; there was no trace of the orange seaweed that so completely covered the shelf between our ship and our landing spot. The lobsters here were more plentiful, crawling about at the very edge of the sand and sunning themselves on clumps of seaweed. There were also great numbers of fish. Had we not been too full to care, we might easily have caught some.

Now we could see the volcano—a low cone jutting out from the edge of the land. The air had grown uncomfortably hot. An eerie flickering light filled the damp smoke that came from the low, whispering vent. Fluffy ash and pumice covered the beach. The drifting sulfurous steam made it impossible to see more than a hundred feet in any direction.

"How do I get back?" asked Peters, interrupting our continuing discussion of the Hollow Earth.

"Just turn around and follow the sea," said Eddie. "We have no special need of you."

"No," said Peters, drawing his stiff lips a bit back from his heavy, crooked teeth. "How do I get back from the Hollow Earth?"

"I don't think you're coming there at all," said I. "The balloon's lifting power isn't strong enough for five, is it, Jeremiah?"

"How anyone gets back from the Hollow Earth was the gentleman's question," said politic Jeremiah. "I think it's likely there's wood enough growing inside the Hollow Earth to restock the balloon's supply of charcoal and to float our way back. With any luck, we could make New Zealand, Cape Horn, or Tierra del Fuego. Or mayhap there are folk in the Hollow Earth who know other ways out to the surface—perhaps there's spots where the ocean goes all the way through. Or could be it's so paradisiacal in there we'll want to stay forever. Those of us that come."

"This world's been up with me for years," said Dirk Peters. "I'm ready for your new one." His voice betrayed a longing that his hard, expressionless face concealed. He flipped his knife in the air and caught it by its handle, very near my neck. He did this several times.

"Maybe the balloon *can* lift five," said I presently

"I can't decide which is worst," put in Otha. "Gettin back in that ship, stayin here with no women, or flyin up in the sky on some striped bag. Don't spook my man Mason that way, Dirk."

"Peters can always take my place," said Eddie, making one of his unexpected swings. "I've been through the crucible; there's no longer any terror that can hobble my talent. My greatest works lie ahead of me, ripe golden fruits that will find place in the granary, nay the treasury, of American letters. Ought I not best sail back to New York?"

"Let's just wait and see if we can get the balloon full," said Jeremiah. "First things first."

8. Antarctica

Our discussion was broken off by a series of odd noises in the distance. First there was great splashing, as of whales breaching repeatedly, and then there were shrill sounds that I initially took to be cries of creatures like the white animal Dirk Peters had killed. The distant furor went on and on. We hurried back through the volcano smoke, straining our smarting eyes to see.

When we reached clear air, we saw that the empty *Wasp* was still there. The distance was as yet too great to make out anything of the men. The splashing and the shrieks had stopped. I ran down the beach. It seemed for an instant that I saw a series of humps, as of several men rapidly crawling back and forth near our distant kettle…but why would they do so? The waves near our little feast site were fiercely agitated. I ran all the way there, with Arf and Peters close behind.

The tipped-over kettle marked the spot where we had left our fellow crew members. The fire was splashed out. The men had stacked the marvelous shells we'd harvested into a square pyramid six tiers high. The bodies of half-dried shellsquid were lying about as well, also our three boats, the rum barrel, and a few scattered shoes and coats. But there was no other trace of the fifty-some men with whom we'd celebrated, less than an hour before.

I halloed the ship, with no response. The ocean was bubbling violently in two spots, and the thick orange stalks of seaweed seemed to writhe with a purpose…writhe and splash closer.

Arf's ruff rose straight up. Sensing something truly evil, I ran with all my might for the same hillock Otha and I had climbed before. But Peters, savage Peters, grasped his knife and stepped to the ocean's edge to peer at the odd movements within the waves. And then suddenly—*a cablelike orange tentacle lashed out and wrapped around his neck!*

Like the stalk of a giant sea kelp, the suckerless tentacle was utterly smooth and flexible. It looked somehow familiar.

Unlike the fifty-odd victims before him, Peters was a man of such brutal speed and craft that he was able to slice off the giant tentacle tip that held him, jump over the next one that whipped out, and in one smooth gesture slash through a third tentacle that wrapped around his waist. The feeler-things were everywhere up and down a thirty-yard stretch of beach, lashing about in snaky figure eights. Arf and I were already high up on the hillock. Our three companions were still some distance down the beach. Small, mighty Peters came running up the hillock toward me, whooping and triumphantly waving a ham-size piece of giant shellsquid… for that is what his attacker was.

From the hilltop we could see clearly. The very large patches of orange seaweed between us and the ship were in fact the facial squidbunches of two giant ammonoids that were most likely the parents of the small creatures whose shells we had been stockpiling! Of *course* I'd seen tentacles like that before; I'd eaten about eighty small copies of them for supper! If each of these giant shellsquid had, in this phase of its life, a shell like the small shellsquid's…what an incredibly valuable thing a shell like that would be. You could *live* in one! And that much meat…

But this kind of thinking was foolishness. How were we ever going to get back to the ship? The most direct path lay right between the two giant ammonoids nestled against our shore. As it happened, each of our ship's two anchors was snagged into one of the creatures' flesh. They would part the cables or drag the ship under if they should swim down into the deep. I recalled that Bulkington's soundings had found no bottom. Poor Bulkington!

Otha, Eddie, and Jeremiah joined Peters, Arf, and me on top of our hillock. I pointed out to them that the orange "seaweed" patches formed two huge ammonoids. It seemed clear that they had temporarily moored themselves here to breed, and that the small shellsquid were indeed their offspring.

"Perhaps they are from the Hollow Earth," said Jeremiah, wonderingly. "Perhaps there is no ocean bottom here at all. Just think, we could be at the edge of a sinkhole that leads all the way through!"

"See," said Eddie, shuddering. "They see us."

Indeed, each of the creatures had lifted two vast eyestalks above the water. Thick and gray, the stalks stuck up like wharf pilings, and each of these slowly swaying columns was capped with a glistening black eyebulb two yards across. These were the same black knobs I'd seen briefly when we anchored. It was a horrible feeling to have them watch us.

"Ate all those men, and wants to eat us too," said Otha slowly. "I'm gettin out of sight."

Beyond our hillock was a stream-crossed vale and, beyond the vale, a talus of loose rock leading up to a forbidding battlement of ice. We threw ourselves down by a stream and tried to think.

"The balloon's the only way out," said Jeremiah.

"Or the ship," said Eddie. "Couldn't we still sail back?"

"Five men sail the *Wasp*?" said Peters. "And three of us *gentlemen!* Not likely, Mr. Poe."

"We still have the boats," said I. "We'll row out around the monsters and get on the *Wasp* from behind. We have to. That's where the balloon is."

"Bravely spoken," said Jeremiah.

"I ain't gettin back in no boat," said Otha.

"We have to stick with Mason and Jeremiah," Peters told Otha. "If they launch the balloon without us, they might not pick us up. Remember, we're just *coons*."

"Don't forget I'm coming on the balloon too," said Eddie.

"And you'll row like the rest of us," said Jeremiah. "It's high time you begin again to be of use, Edgar. We'll start at noon, when the sun is in the north. That's the time of day the ship landed. The monsters were quiet then."

We slept a bit, and passed the rest of the time in killing four more of the red-clawed white beasts. Peters squatted in the bottom of the valley behind our hillock and the rest of us acted as beaters, shaking every bush and poking into every hole. We skinned the beasts and saved the meat, also the pelts with paws and heads intact.

Finally the sun was out over the ocean. We put Arf, our five redclaws, and ten of our hard-won shells into our chosen boat and eased it quietly into the sea two hundred yards up the beach from the monsters. With many a sideways glance toward the orange-glinting patch to port, Jeremiah, Peters, Otha, and I rowed with a will, while Eddie in the stern pointed out our course. Every second, I expected to see one of those huge eyestalks break the calm sea's surface, but for now all was still.

Once we were out past the *Wasp*, we turned and slowly stroked over to it, and then we were bumping up against its familiar wood flank. Our boat held a rope and a grappling hook, which we flipped ever so gently over the taffrail. Peters was up first, and I was last. Before I went up, I tied the rope around Arf's middle and Peters pulled him up, and then finally I was safe on board as well. Safe? I was too well aware that either of the ammonoids could pull our ship under or scour the decks with its tentacles.

"Peters, you must cut the anchor cables almost all the way through," hissed Jeremiah. "Mason, you and Otha go to the galley and take all the food and water you can carry. Eddie, you and I shall start the balloon's stove."

Otha and I went belowdecks and fetched a large sack of hardtack, a box of recently salted fish, and two demijohns of fresh water. Jeremiah filled our light brass stove with charcoal soaked in seal oil; it began to burn briskly. Now Eddie sprinkled his special salts from the jar we'd packed with the stove. The fire flared up and stank. Eddie snugged the stove's flue into the neck of our great rubberized silk balloon. Slowly, slowly, its flanks began to swell.

Peters busied himself charging and loading five muskets from the ship's supply. Seeing this, I remembered my pepper-box pistol and went back belowdecks privily to fetch it. I'd loaded it long before. If—horrible thought—the balloon was unable to lift all five of us, a hidden gun might stand me in good stead. Sensing that some great departure was imminent, Arf stuck close to my heels.

A half hour passed till the great balloon sluggishly lifted itself off the deck. A mild ocean breeze was blowing, so the balloon hung out over the ammonoids. Were they sleeping? Eddie and Jeremiah loaded more charcoal and salts onto the fire, and now the balloon began gently to tug its wicker cabin across the deck. We hurried on tiptoe this way and that, making sure none of the ropes fouled. A single thick rope attached the balloon cabin to a boss on the ship's deck.

The balloon grew strong and plump; the cabin jittered on and off the deck, its steel runners clattering. Jeremiah fetched a last few scientific instruments, and then Arf and we five men squeezed into the jiggling wicker box. For an anxious ten minutes we held it heavy on the deck. The crowded cabin was hot and close from the blazing stove, especially hot because our walls were padded with down-stuffed quilts in anticipation of the severe cold we would encounter above the antarctic ice. Outside the open window-holes we could see the sea, the patch of orange, the antarctic continent, and the mountains far away. I kept my hand on the pistol in my pocket. My pistol would be handier in these close quarters than the musket that each of us had, thought I, but now, finally, our box began to rise, slowly at first, and then in a quick rush of speed that stretched our tether to strumming tautness.

The sudden jolt snapped the ship's anchor cables, which Peters had weakened, and all at once our balloon was dragging the *Wasp* across the monstrous patch of orange tentacles. The giants awoke and lashed two, six, twenty thick feelers across the *Wasp's* deck. Four horrible eyes lifted out of the water and gazed up.

Even as the orange tentacles began to stretch toward us, Peters reached out our cabin door and slashed through the rope that tethered us to the ship. Our balloon sprang into the air, racing up with a speed that pressed us against the cabin's creaking floor. We cheered until our throats cracked.

"My salts create a gas lighter than air," cried Eddie. "My theories are vindicated!"

The ocean breeze wafted us landward. As we drifted over the first great battlement of ice, the air temperature dropped and our balloon went even higher. I took what I thought was a last glance back at the giant ammonoids and saw something horrible. *One of them was still busy with the* Wasp, *but the other was floating up out of the sea!* I screamed and pointed as the monstrous shell rose into the air, righted itself, and began—with thunderous spewings of gas and liquid—to speed toward us.

"The shell is full of naturally secreted hydrogen," said Eddie, his voice oddly calm. "Air is a fluid like water, you understand. We see a demonstration of the solution to a rather pretty problem in hydrostatics." He sank slowly to a corner of the box and curled himself up there next to Arf. "Virginia," he said, stroking the dog. "Virginia."

"We'll shoot the damned mollusk down," said Peters, grimly shouldering his musket. "Aim carefully, men, and wait until it's close by."

We were a thousand feet up in the air now, with the icy antarctic waste sweeping by beneath us. It was easy to see it through the wicker cracks of our cabin floor. Otha and I aimed our muskets out one window, Peters and Jeremiah out the other.

"How do this thing work?" Otha murmured to me. As a slave, he'd never been allowed to handle a gun.

"Look down along it and squeeze the trigger when I do," I told him. "Hold your shoulder loose for the kick. Use your arms like a spring to gentle it." The vengeful ammonoid surged suddenly closer, its vast shell shining like a polished cloud. Still closer it came…and then with a great crash we all fired.

The guns kicked very powerfully. The cabin rocked so sharply that Arf and Eddie skidded across the floor. Arf hit a wall, but Eddie slid out the door. His frantic cries were drowned by the high shrieking of gas rushing from the giant ammonoid's punctured shell; it zigzagged wildly and went screaming down to smash into a smudge of orange and mother-of-pearl on the undulating white plain far below. There was no sign of Eddie.

Otha held my legs, and I leaned out the door to see beneath the balloon box. Sure enough, Eddie was there, dangling upside down, with one foot caught in a bight of rope. He gazed silently up at me, his face gone bright red. I was so shocked by the last few minutes' rapid changes that I burst out laughing at his awkward plight. I laughed so hard—if laughter it was—that I wet my pants.

Presently, Peters contrived to pull Eddie in. We battened the door's shutter closed and then, finally, we were fairly launched. The other giant shellsquid showed no signs of coming after us. Still speechless, Eddie produced a flask and drank all but the single gulp of it that Peters was able to claim. Meanwhile, Jeremiah got out a sextant and took a reading.

"How long do you think it will take?" I asked him.

"We're at seventy-seven degrees latitude," said he. "I think it likely that the South Hole's rim lies all along the eighty-five-degree latitude line. A degree of latitude is sixty miles, which makes it four hundred eighty miles due south to eighty-five degrees, and seven hundred eighty to the Pole. I measure our present speed some twenty miles an hour; that makes four hundred eighty miles in a day, and seven hundred eighty in a day and a half. It's one P.M. now. If the wind keeps up from the north, we should see the Hole sometime between noon and midnight tomorrow. Maybe sooner, if the wind increases."

"How you know there *is* a hole?" asked Otha.

"I'd wondered that myself," said Peters.

"Every animal has a hole at each end," said Eddie, lying on his back in the corner where Virginia had died. "And is not Earth a creature that lives and moves?"

"Mr. Symmes had many arguments for the Hollow Earth," said Jeremiah. "But the time for argument is long past. Right now we need to stoke the stove powerfully enough to lift our craft over the mountains."

As no one else offered to, I took charge of the stove first. We had two big burlap sacks of charcoal aboard, and every few minutes I eased another piece of it in through the stove's grating. After about an hour had passed, I was hot from the fire, but the others—who had been resting or sleeping—were cold in the thin high-altitude antarctic air. Otha was only too glad to spell me at the stove. I stood up and looked out the cabin window to the south.

For a moment I had trouble making sense of what I saw. The upper half of the window showed deep blue sky with a full moon in it, but the lower half of the window was simply white. For a second I thought it was glassed in and frosted over. But the window was a hole, and the white I saw was the inhuman landscape below. Refocusing my eyes, I could make out crevasses and wind-carved mounds—so prominent that for a moment I thought the ground was quite close below. Had I stoked the oven for nothing? Just then I glimpsed far ahead of us a small blue blot racing across the snow—our shadow, impossibly elongated, impossibly far. The space around me began to stretch and tremble as my mind labored to understand. I held tight to the wicker windowsill, fearing the great empty whiteness would somehow suck me out. We were over a thousand feet high, and those mounds and cracks I saw were mighty hills and canyons!

For half an hour I watched our distant shadow race and ripple ever higher—the foothills beneath us were piling up to a turreted mountain range ahead. With luck we would clear it.

Now Dirk Peters took his turn at stoking the stove, while Otha came to look out the window with me. Eddie was unconscious from the liquor he'd guzzled, and Jeremiah was constantly busy taking sightings, making notes, and adjusting the balloon bag.

"Where the jungle?" Otha asked me.

"What jungle?"

"Lijah talk about a big wet jungle down in Mama Earth's genitive parts. He say that's where he come from."

"He said that? Why didn't you tell me?"

"Maybe Lijah from the Hollow Earth, Mason. Maybe black folks is king of that world."

"Elijah wasn't really black. He was white. He was an albino."

"White *color*, but he were a slave. If he a slave, he *black*."

Peters glanced up at Jeremiah. "Are we going to make it?"

"It's hard to get a steady sighting," said old Reynolds, lowering his telescope with a sigh. "But since the sun is virtually on the horizon, our shadow on any vertical wall must be at the same altitude we are. One might think of the mountain ahead as an eroded wall. If our shadow gets over it, then we will. If not, then not."

We four watched as our shadow moved up the great slope ahead. We were close enough that we could see shadings in the ice, see caves and overhangs fit for beast or hermit, but all was empty. Our shadow was like a footprint—the big ellipse of balloon over the trapezoid of basket—man's first footprint here, wriggling toward the sky.

But not fast enough. We were still well below the great white mountain's ragged upper rim. Eddie slumbered. I took it on myself to go through his clothes and find his jar of salts. The jar was wedged into his trouser pocket, and beneath it was a rattling clutch of small pebbles that only belatedly did I understand to be Virginia's teeth. I snatched the jar out, Jeremiah prized the stove's top plate off, and I emptied in all the crystals that would come loose. The fire consumed them in bursts of color, and dizzying fumes filled the cabin. The fire sang, our great balloon bag creaked and swelled, and just as we were about to meet our shadow footprint, it slid over the mountain ridge and sprang away. We followed after; I turned and stared back.

I will not soon forget the sight of that eroded razor ridge. The others were looking ahead, so only I saw it—only I, of all men ever to live, have seen that ridge, its bare gray rocks touched by the western sun's gold glints and blue shadows, lit as so many million times before. This one time in all history

I was there to see it for all mankind, and I felt that the ridge knew—knew me as a human, and knew me as motherless Mason from Virginia. Sensing my passage, the ridge sent out long windblown streamers of snow, icedust fingers calling me back to the world of my birth. But no return is possible. That scoured antarctic spine was the final edge of a world I shall never see again.

The high mountain wind caught us, filling the flanks of our swollen black-and-white balloon with chaotic thrumming. For a few minutes, it was all we could do to hang tight and to keep our instruments and provisions from shifting too wildly. Eddie woke, stood up, fell down.

Finally, we gained our feet and stared southward. There was nothing but an endless expanse of white ahead of us as far as the eye could see.

"Where the hole?" asked Otha once agin. "An the jungle?"

"Where?" echoed Peters.

Eddie, still sitting on the floor, gazed up at us, an odd grin on his face. "Let me describe what you should see," he said slowly. "Undoubtedly you do see it, but are too narrow-visioned to *know*. The near edge of the great Hole is like a depression in the horizon. Above the depression are swirling fogbanks crowned by Jovian thunderheads flickering with planetary energies. Arching above the great atmospheric maelstrom is a second horizon line, the Hole's far lip. Surely you do make it out! Mason! Jeremiah?"

"Not yet," said Jeremiah softly. "Calm yourself. I said it would take at least twenty-four hours. Wait until the sun has gone full circle. We'll see the Hole soon."

But we did not. The wind held from the north, driving us along at a ground speed nearing thirty miles per hour, yet we continued to see nothing but unbroken white waste. We slept in shifts, keeping the stove stoked with our ominously diminishing stock of fuel. The sun rolled past the west to glare at us from the north at midnight; it arced through the east and on to the south for noon again and still we saw nothing; and still the sun rolled; and then it was three in the afternoon of our second day in the balloon.

The air temperature was thirty degrees below zero. Blessedly, the skies were clear and the wind was still from the north. Arf and we five men sat huddled together for warmth near our stove. We had pulled the quilts off the walls to wrap around ourselves, but it was not enough.

"Eighty-nine degrees and forty minutes of latitude," said Jeremiah, peering up through his sextant at the sky. "Twenty miles to the South Pole." He fell silent and began fiddling with his two delicate clocks, one run by a spring, one run by a pendulum. He expected the presence of Earth's Hole to show itself as a difference in the clocks' rates.

"There's no more charcoal," announced Peters. His voice was muffled because his mouth was full of dried shellsquid. We were eating almost continuously in an effort to keep up our body temperatures in the face of the nightmarish cold.

"We can break off pieces of the cabin to burn," said Jeremiah, trying to keep his voice calm. "Mason!"

I felt dumb and tired. Pretty soon we would all be dead. I hugged Arf and pressed against Otha.

"Do you hear, Mason?" said Eddie. "You and Otha break up the shutters and put them in the stove."

He was glaring at me imperiously from beneath his high, pale brow. A spasm of hatred went through me. Eddie Poe's mad notions were to be the death of us all, and still he struck his charlatan poses. I wanted to smite him, but any movement would let in more cold, so I tried to spit at him. The spit froze to my face. "Go to hell," I hissed. "You damned crazy hoaxing killer."

"Come, come. Mason," said Jeremiah, struggling to his feet. "Perhaps the Hole is very small! In less than an hour we'll be at the Pole! And the clocks…it's hard to be sure with the cabin's motion, but my clocks show certain —"

"In less than an hour the balloon will crash," said Peters. "Look how soft and wrinkled the bag is. Look how near we are to the ground."

"I'm *cold*," said Otha. "Do somethin, Mason!"

I moved Arf to Otha's lap and wrapped my arms around them. The cold was astonishing. Jeremiah and Peters broke up the balloon box's shutters and began feeding the scraps into the little brass stove. Out the door I could see the ground, only a hundred feet below. Once we landed, it would be all over.

"Where are my salts?" demanded Eddie.

The jar was in my pocket, but I didn't want to give him the satisfaction of an answer. Instead I lurched over to the stove, loosened the few remaining crystals with my finger, and tossed them onto the flaming wicker. The balloon puffed up feebly, and we limped a little higher.

Before four o'clock we'd fed the stove the cabin's ceiling and most of the wall that held our door. We hoped the door's joists and the other walls would hold our floor in place. But this was not to be. The walls' connections to our floor were giving way. The floor began to creak out from under us like a slow-opening trapdoor.

"We're landing now!" cried Jeremiah, yanking on the cord that led to our balloon's upper vent. If I hadn't held Arf under one arm, the dog would have skidded out through the gaping crack between the partially demolished wall and our sloping floor. We men clung to the window and doorframes like monkeys, peering and jabbering as the ever-blank white ground came up at us too fast.

We landed with such a jolt that the cabin fell over onto one side. The stiff wind plucked at the half-empty balloon, dragging us across the wind-polished snow and ice. Now the hot stove came into contact with one of the quilts and the cabin filled with smoke. To make things worse, it was the open-door side of the cabin that was facedown. We left the cabin in chaos, fighting our way out of the three windows. Peters and Otha were out first, I believe, then Jeremiah, and finally it was my turn. I thrust Arf out; he thudded to the ground with a yelp; we were really gathering speed. In the dense smoke I could see next to nothing, but when I lunged forward to roll out the window, something caught my ankle. Eddie.

I kicked out at him, but he clung with the strength of the damned. There was nothing for it but to reach down, get hold of him, and push him out the window before me. I followed close after. The rushing ice slapped my face violently.

I rolled twenty yards and came to a rest, aware again of how very cold it was.

The sun and moon gazed down blankly. The wind whistled, and from downwind came the crashing and bumping of our cabin being dragged further by the nearly flat balloon. Dotted out behind me were Arf and my four fellow explorers. I called Arf, and he ran to me, glad and barking to be on firm ground. When he got to me he shook vigorously, always his way of punctuating a new paragraph of activity.

All the others, save Eddie, were standing and straggling toward me, wanting to catch up with our cabin. A number of our possessions had been scattered about. Jeremiah and Peters were gathering things up as they came. Noticing Jeremiah wrap some rope around his waist, I picked up a nearby coil of strong silk cord and did the same. Arf shook again and stood there panting, fully at ease with the few hours of life that were left us. I wished I could share his sense of the eternal now.

The three others leaned over Eddie. Loud words and gesticulations, then finally the great man rose to his feet as well. Perhaps he'd hoped they'd carry him.

How strange it was to be here, so far from everything, beneath a sky so big and empty. There were no birds, no clouds. I felt this oddly wrong: Earth's farthest corner should be dark and packed, not bright and blank.

"...the pendulum clock was running noticeably slower than the spring clock toward the end," Jeremiah was saying as they approached. "That implies there is less gravity here, which means the Earth's crust is quite thin."

Otha and Peters said nothing, simply slogged along unlistening. But where Peters was grim, Otha was solemnly gay. I think he was very happy to be out of the balloon alive. Eddie seemed dazzled by the fantastic vast waste around us. His lips worked silently, as if he were framing verses. He kept his hands shoved deep into his trouser pockets.

"Are we at the Pole, Jeremiah?" asked I.

He drew his sextant; sighted the sun, the moon. "To a hair."

"Where is it?" said Otha. "I don't see no axle stickin up."

"It's just a spot like any other," said Peters bitterly. "Just a spot to die."

The wind dropped. Some distance ahead, the cabin and balloon stopped moving. The cabin was marked by a plume of fire and smoke.

"Let's go there and get warm," said I.

We walked slowly, for we knew that once we reached the burning cabin, there'd be nothing else to do. Each time I took my eyes off the smoke plume, I got dizzy and confused from the blank white everywhere. Then, seeing something red in the snow, I thought it was the stableboy I'd killed, sent by God to haunt me. But it was only one of our redclaw carcasses. I picked it up and shoved it into my pocket.

Eddie was a killer too, and certainly Peters as well. Probably, Jeremiah had done in an islander or two during his travels, which left only Otha and Arf as the innocent ones.

"I'm sorry, Otha."

He was right beside me, with Arf at our heels. Unlike me, Otha still had his quilt; he had it wrapped tight around him. King Otha of the South Pole. He glanced down. "You not as sorry as I is. You the same color as the snow. You fit. I'm gonna be whited to death here. Do you wish we was back on the farm?"

"We had some fun on the way."

"I had me a gal called Juicita in Richmond. If she with child, then I left somethin back there. Maybe that's the most a man can hope to do."

When we got to the cabin, it was burning pretty briskly. I'd had some thoughts of wrapping myself up in the balloon silk, but as we stood there warming our hands, the silk caught fire too. The liquid caoutchouc rubber we'd varnished it with was quite flammable; Jeremiah had been careful to put several layers of spark screens in the stove's chimney. But now a piece of flaming wicker fell onto the balloon and the whole thing flared up at once in a quick puffball of heat. It swelled like an earthbound sun, rose a bit, then burst and fluttered down in ashes on the dampened snow.

The contents of our cabin were pretty much gone, including our stores of saltfish, shellsquid, and biscuits. We drank from the puddles the fire had made, privily nibbled up whatever food scraps we had in our pockets, and then there was nothing left to eat at all. Peters seemed the most desperate, and began to talk of eating Arf. To placate him, I stripped the meat out of the redclaw pelt I'd found and shared that around for each of us to roast in strips over the dwindling flames. The meat tasted so odd that I let Peters have my share. By six in the evening, the cabin fire was down to coals and ashes. The wind rose and began to blow the ashes away.

"I *will* have that dog!" cried Peters suddenly. He drew out his knife and lunged toward Arf. Arf yelped, and circled round to the other side of the embers. Peters circled after him, and I started after Peters. Now the three of us were running around the burnt ruins of the cabin—Arf in front, his eyes rolling, followed by Peters with knife held high, followed by me not really wanting to catch him. I called to Otha, and he joined with me. Eddie had been sunk in thought but then, on our third circuit around the coals, he noticed Peters and the dog, felt threatened, and began running too, just in front of Arf. Jeremiah, feeling a need to calm our mad antics, leaped up and began chasing after me and Otha. I think we all felt it was nice to be doing something, utterly pointless though it was. Ten, twenty, perhaps a hundred times, we circled the dully glowing cabin ashes, speeding up, slowing down, stamping our feet and yelling. Only Peters seemed serious about it. Over and over he lunged at Arf, over and over Arf pranced away. The rhythm of our running began to set off a kind of cracking noise in the ice; we ran harder. More cracking. "Keep it up," called Jeremiah. "Something's happening!" Three more circuits we ran, with more and more noise from the ground below, and then, all at once, the ice gave way and we fell through.

9. Symmes's Hole

At first I thought we were falling into a crevasse. The ice gnashed, and big blocks and chunks fell every which way. Our screams were faint in the cracking roar. I was yelling, "Mother," and Otha was crying for Turl. Each instant I expected to be dashed senseless. The strong light through the ice and snow bathed everything in brilliant blue—all was bright confusion.

Arf and the men were near me, though I could only see bits and pieces of them. We were packed all around by a free-falling clutter of ice fragments. Above us were great creakings and thunderings; more and more of the ice was breaking free—monstrous tumbling chunks larger than the biggest icebergs seen at sea. We had started an ice avalanche into some incredibly vast cave or crevasse and—

Now there came a hideous shriek. "Help me, for the love of God!"

It was Peters. His body had gotten pinned between two flat-faced ice boulders. Peters's head and feet stuck out like the head and tail of a steamed catfish on one of the loaves the James River ferry woman had given us. Now a small, dense chunk of ice caromed off several others and cracked spinning into the boulders squeezing Peters. There was a shriek beyond anything that had gone before. Peters was crushed and mangled like a beetle in a mill, like a grape in a winepress. The whole blood of his body stained the giant crystal masses, and he was quite still.

Arf and Otha were somewhere above me; Jeremiah and Eddie, somewhere below. Still we fell. The light remained strong. There seemed to be no walls enclosing us at all. Bit by bit, the jostling ice chunks dispersed themselves. Even though more ice was still coming loose high above us, we were falling at the leading edge of the onrushing masses. There seemed no reason we could not safely fall onward in this wise—until, that is, such a time as we hit bottom, if bottom there was. We were falling at speeds no humans had ever known before, perhaps as much as a hundred and ten miles per hour. The buffeting air had turned me so I was on my back, facing up toward the ice.

What lay behind me, down toward the Earth's center? I knew better than to crane my head back and have my neck broken by the wind's savage force. Instead, I rolled sideways so I was falling facedown. This was a bad position, for now my legs tipped up and I began planing rapidly to one side, moving so fast that I couldn't breathe. The air at my mouth was a heavy stone pillow smothering me. Instinctively, I spread my legs and dug in my feet, making an air anchor. This slowed me, and tilted me downward. I managed to mask my face with my hands. I gulped air and stared through slit fingers into the dim pit.

Even had the wind not hindered me, my eyes were all but blinded from the pitiless light of our thirty hours on the iceplain. Yet I could see something below, a green disk with blue spots and washes of pink light. An inner orb? The tunnel's other end? Far away, but not infinitely so. Holding my breath and squinting, I stretched out my arms toward the disk. My hands just covered it; from here the disk was the size of a woman's round face. Tired of fighting the wind, I rolled onto my back to stare again at the spreading avalanche above us.

The falling ice islands had spaced themselves out nicely, and I could get a good clear view of the land overhead. It was an immense blue and white glazed boss of ice; the central antarctic plain, seen from beneath, lit by the sun and moon on its other side. It was a bumpy, gelid landscape, with a spreading puncture that we'd made. We were flying down this tunnel away from it.

143

It wasn't quite like we were flying, though. With all the ice tumbling right behind us, it was more as if we were riding the crest of a black powder explosion. I remembered once Ma's brother, Tuck Tingley, had packed black powder under a big stump at the edge of our barnyard. The stump had ridden skyward on a spreading dome of dust and rubble till all collapsed.

But we weren't going to fall back. With luck, we would fall all the way to the Hollow Earth. The air was thick but breathable, and as the time passed, we seemed to be falling slightly slower than before. The air temperature was becoming more comfortable every minute. It occurred to me the ice avalanche would melt and turn into friendly water before it could ever reach us. I spotted Otha crouched on a huge iceberg far above me. I wouldn't have wanted to be so near that unstable mass, but I suppose he found it soothing, with his love of solid ground. I waved, and he waved back almost cheerfully. Arf was a wriggling black dot in the bright blue distance. This was working out wonderfully.

The farther we fell, the more of the underside of the antarctic icescape became visible, its distant stretches fading into dim hallucinatory curved crests of antediluvian ice. Compared to the vast, crumbling ice-dome we were as dust motes, and the greatest of the tumbling ice islands were as fretful gnats.

Perhaps the ridge we'd flown over yesterday had been the outflung upper lip of this vast shaft. If so, the whole central antarctic iceshield was a plug, an accretion whose irregular eons-long growth had filled in the upper end of Symmes's Hole! And soon this plug would be no more.

Like a lever whose movement sets off the linked workings of some vast mechanism, the jarring of our footsteps had set the great plug to breaking up completely. The huge iceplain was shattering and falling after us. And the tumbling ice was melting as it fell.

A few fat water globs were starting to rain down past us. I caught a gout of water in my cupped hands and sucked at it. The water was fresh, it was clean, it was millions of years old.

Yes, Symmes was right. Mother Earth had a big South Hole, a shaft that tunneled straight down from the surface to…to what? I covered my eyes for ten minutes to drive the light from them, and then I got into facedown position to stare down again.

A quarter mile ahead were Eddie and Jeremiah, falling arm in arm. At the edges of my vision I saw dim hints of the shaft's incredibly distant walls, perhaps a hundred miles away from us on every side. The walls glowed faintly nearby, and more brightly further down. The far end of the shaft had waxed to something like the size of a porthole or a dinner plate held at arm's length. The disk was mostly green, but in its center was a bright pink spot, and flowing out from the bright spot were shifting pink lines. Clustered around the central spot were tiny blue-green jewels. I was looking through our great tunnel's other end, and seeing into the Hollow Earth. It seemed we must fall many more hours to get there. The air was so thick and heavy that I felt giddy. I stared down, musing, for quite some time.

Something thudded into me. I screamed, but it was only Arf. Last time I'd noticed him he'd been a dot far above me. Apparently, he'd tucked his legs up and pointed his nose out to fall fast enough to catch me. I spreadeagled myself on my back so I could put Arf on my chest and pet him and talk to him.

"Yes, Arfie. *Poor* Arfie. Peters want eat Arf and Arf ran away! Arf break through! Good boy. Good smart Arfie baby. Him sooo fluffy!"

Arf smacked his lips a few times as he did when uncertain, and then he attempted one of his new-paragraph ear-flapping body shakes.

He lost his footing, and the rushing wind tore him back away from me. Seized with a spirit of hilarious deviltry, I rolled facedown and began moving my arms and legs to dart this way and that. Our overall speed was less than it had been, and I was able to breathe, though each slow thick breath made me dizzier. Arf flew after me, steering himself with small movements of his head and tail. We played tag for about ten minutes, finally coming together in a crash that dazed both of us.

We fell quietly through the heavy, stupefying air for an hour or more. Finally the air began to thin, and with the lessening of the atmospheric pressure, my alertness returned. It was getting very hot, and there was rain all around us. Our speed had diminished to less than half of what it had been before. Peering through the rain, I could see the distant cliffs glowing dark red. Down below, there were white-hot seams and patches in the cliffs and shapes like huge stone terraces jutting out from the shaft's walls. Half a mile behind us was Otha on his big iceberg. I resolved to fly up there with Arf to escape the increasing heat. I hoped Jeremiah and Eddie would have the sense to do likewise.

By dint of much flapping of my arms and legs, I was able to make my way slowly up to Otha's great ice island. It was a strange experience to see the huge white mass loom closer and closer. I kept hold of Arf s leg to make sure he came too. His hair was very fluffy from the hot breeze, and the spiral tattoo Peters had put on his belly showed clearly.

Otha was squatting in the middle of a soggy icefield about the size of our Hardware farm. He looked cold and wary, reminding me all at once of the Christmas three or four years ago when Pa had gotten drunk and had raped Turl. I hadn't thought about that night in a long time.

All five of us had been in the house that Christmas Day—I guess it was 1832—eating and drinking, white just the same as black, or so Pa and I liked to think. Luke polished off half a ham and a jug of whiskey and fell blissfully asleep on the rag rug on the smooth boards before the hearth. Otha and I were happily playing with a polished beechwood skittles game Uncle Tuck had made for me. He'd dropped it off Christmas morning on his way in to the annual party at the Perrows. Otha and I had never seen a game like it before and we were enthralled. To complete our joy, Uncle Tuck had brought us a whole bushel of oranges!

A skittles game, I should explain, is a hollow box six inches deep with a bottom two foot by four. There are slender pins standing inside the box. The box has wooden baffles in it; it's like a roofless house with walls breaking it up into rooms, and the pins are like people in the house, with the more isolated pins counting more. The player whose turn it is winds a string around a tall wooden top and sets the top spinning inside the box, and the score is based on which pins are knocked down. The skittles-top is a spindle-shaped piece of wood consisting of a five-inch shaft with a thin disk at the upper end. Balancing on its long narrow shaft, the top must spin rapidly to remain upright. It moves about the skittles-house slowly, tremblingly, feelingly—until it hits a wall or a pin and trips or darts off on a tangent. The top's motions are quite unpredictable, and therein lies the fascination of the game.

The rape took place silently in the kitchen, where Pa and Turl had been drinking and playing dominoes, and we never looked up from our skittles or even knew, until 'round midnight Turl came into the big room with her face crooked and told Otha he ought to go in there and kill Pa. She started shaking Luke and screaming. Pa got his arm under mumbling Luke's armpit and waltzed him out to the slave cabin, with Turl behind them railing. Otha jumped on Pa's back and started choking him. I pulled him off, and Pa slapped him. Otha ran back in our house and broke up my skittles game—snapped the top and jumped up and down on the box till it was kindling—and then he ran off into the pasture. It was a warm Christmas, with a few inches of rained-on snow. Pa passed out, and I lay in bed crying over the broken game. Finally, I went out to find Otha. He was squatting in the pasture holding the broken skittles-top and looking like he wanted to freeze to death. I told him it was safe to come home; he said it wasn't safe anywhere. I said we'd make a new skittles game; he said he wanted a new ma.

It took the better part of a year till things settled down. At first Turl acted like it was forgotten, and then that spring she started flaring up and crying and yelling all the time. She wore more clothes than usual. I remember her standing in rags, hollering in the rain outside the farmhouse one April day. I didn't make out what she said, but Pa agreed to let her return to visit with her sister in Lynchburg for as many months as she wanted. Her sister belonged to the Perrows. Turl hadn't returned till harvest time, and from then on she'd chattered about her nice little nephew down to the Perrows' and how he reminded her of Mason.

Now I touched down from the air right in front of Otha. I was holding Arf under one arm. My feet dug into the iceberg's slush and held me still against the wind. Otha stared at me blankly. The chill of the ice and the narcosis of the high-pressure region we'd been through had quite numbed him. I talked to him and shook him till he stood up. It was cold next to the ice, but as soon as you stood up, you could feel the heat of the scorching wind. Otha looked around, slowly coming to his senses.

"Is we dead in hell, Mason?"

The cliffs were yellow-hot, and closer than before. Even though there was rain all around us, we could see pretty clearly. Vast cataracts of lava were gushing out of holes in the cliffsides and drizzling down into lakes of fire. There were a few falls of water, too, immense surging gushers that issued, I supposed, from maelstroms or from undersea caves. As the water hit the lava, it would steam up, with some of the vapor being sucked into other holes in the giant honeycomb structure of Mother Earth's steaming innermost flesh.

A distant iceberg tumbled into one of the lava lakes, releasing a titanic storm of steam. As more ice and rain bumped into the hot cliffs, the tunnel grew filled with clouds. Just before the fog grew too dense to see, Otha pointed out something moving out of one of the distant waterfalls: a giant spiral shell with a trembling fringe—a shellsquid!

I heard deep roars and explosive cracks as more and more ice crashed into the hot cliffs, chipping off chattering chunks of stone. Now the clouds grew quite black, and bolts of lightning began to flicker. The walls gleamed through the growing tempest. The air was witheringly hot, and now the cooling rain had turned into vapor. We crouched down against the surface of the iceberg.

"Can you see the others, Otha? Can you see Eddie and Jeremiah?"

As I said this, Eddie came planing up toward us, riding piggyback on unconscious Jeremiah's back. I signaled to him, and he managed to land near us. Eddie's eyes were blazing with excitement; he said that he'd seen shapes moving in the fire of the cliffs, great demons of the molten core. Though there were no signs of Virginia's ghost, this once the waking world had trumped Eddie's wildest dreams.

We dragged Jeremiah over and revived him from his heat prostration. He was feeble and confused. Arf and we four men laid ourselves down in a hollow of melted icewater like hogs in a wallow. As fast as the wind could evaporate the water from around us, the ice melted more. A full-blown squall was raging, and the hellish cliffs were racing past—though not nearly as rapidly as I would have wished them to. Every now and then, a lightning bolt would flash into our dwindling ice island and a tingle would surge into me. Jeremiah was moaning, and Eddie was chanting blank-verse descriptions of the fiery beings he thought he'd seen.

Finally, the air began to cool. The cliffs dimmed to red and then to black. We were falling much slower than before. Our vast ice island was shrunken to the size of a drifting, creaky ship.

"How far we've come!" exclaimed Jeremiah, fully recovered. With our reduced speed, we no longer had to yell to be heard over the beating wind. "The pressure, the heat—did you save me, Eddie?"

"I am not wholly a villain and a wretch," said Eddie. "And our Symmes was not utterly a fool. But why do we fall so slowly?"

"It's as I told Mason," said Jeremiah. "Newton's calculus demonstrates that there is no net gravitational force within a spherical shell. Although the matter below us still draws us down, all the matter above us is pulling us up. When we reach this tunnel's end, the forces will balance."

"Ah, but what of the masses at the Earth's very center?" said Eddie. "See them, pink and blue? They will pull us further."

"So they may," said Jeremiah. "I wonder—"

There was a great shuddering crack, and the ice island we were on broke in two, with Eddie and Jeremiah on one half and Arf, Otha, and me on the other.

"Jump free of the ice!" I urged Otha. "Remember Peters!"

"When we gonna see real solid ground?" demanded Otha. "I've done had it with water and air."

"I'll help you to the ground," I told him. "Come on, we'll fly arm in arm." Eddie and Jeremiah had already launched themselves together; Otha and I followed suit. Agile Arf flew alone, darting among us.

Glancing back at our shattering iceberg, I saw something extraordinary: A large flattened ball—approximately a hemisphere—had been frozen into the ice's core, and now the half-ball was tumbling back toward the clouds and cliffs. It was of a shiny substance a bit like metal, although it might have been gilded leather. It even crossed my mind that it might be some kind of preserved or mummified animal, quite frozen and still. It was some thirty feet in diameter, and with a slanting flange or ring projecting out along its base, giving it a shape something like a fried egg. Before I could point it out to Otha, the gleaming entity had vanished into the glowing haze behind us. Months later, at the very center of the Hollow Earth, we would find another one like it, but just now, not knowing what to think of it, I put it out of my mind.

Soon we were falling still more slowly than before. As we drifted down, the air grew caressingly pleasant. The disk of the tunnel's lower end was bright and big—when I stretched out my arms and held my hands on either side of the disk, my hands were four feet apart. Behind us I could see nothing of the tunnel's upper end, nothing but the continuing storm of fire and ice. We were ahead of what little rain made it through the hot storm zone, and there were only a few chunks of ice remaining. More worrisome were the numerous rocks that were falling after us.

"This been some wild ride, Mase! Smell the jungle?" Though Otha kept cautious hold of some part of me at all times, he was beginning to enjoy himself. I sniffed the gentle breeze; there was indeed a faint rank smell of vegetation.

I gestured at the disk ahead of us. "The Hollow Earth!"

"We gonna walk around on the inside?"

"Or fall clear to the middle. Can you make out what's there?" I knew his eyes were keener than mine. Otha put his hand to his brow and peered ahead.

"It be a spider," he said. "A pink light spider with blue-green eggs shiverin all around it, about to hatch. We don't wanna go way down there, Mason!"

"Can you see anything at the edge? At the lip of the tunnel? The edge looks fuzzy to me. Do you see trees?"

As we peered downward, a huge irregular branch of pink light sprouted out from the disk's tangled center. It was a river of light connecting the Hollow Earth's core to its inner surface, somewhere near the mouth of our tunnel. The pink glow filled our disk of vision—and now it was easier for Otha to see the disk's edge.

"There's a tree line alright," he said. "With vines." I could see it too. The lip's outline had the roughness of a wooded mountain ridge in the blue hills of Virginia. And here and there I could see twinkles of pink light through the tangle, like sunlight through bushes.

The light stream shifted so as to fill the tunnel around us with a pink glow. I felt a throbbing and heard a hum. My hair stood on end. Windblown Arf looked like a dandelion seed. The pink energy bath brought no extra heat. It lingered and buzzed, and then it moved on. While it was filling our tunnel, I got a good look at the walls. The tunnel sides were of mixed stone and soil, glinting with streams and bedecked with verdure. A few miles farther ahead, the walls ended, giving way to a formidable tangle of giant plants.

That we were quite near the tunnel's end was evidenced by the fact that the mouth's apparent size was growing so rapidly, even though by now we could not have been falling more than thirty miles per hour. We folded in our arms and caught up with Jeremiah and Eddie. I latched on to Jeremiah, and we all bounced around awkwardly as if we were playing crack the whip. Then Arf slammed into us and made it worse. Finally, we settled down: Otha, me, Jeremiah, and Eddie Poe falling arm in arm, with Arf in Otha's grasp.

"Let's plane over to the side while we're still moving fast enough," I suggested. "Otherwise we'll be stuck in the middle."

"We wants somethin to eat," put in Otha. "And some solid ground."

"Faint heart," said Eddie. "Would it not be nobler to fall on and on toward the light?"

"Not without provisions," said Jeremiah. "And who knows how long it would take? We didn't come all this way just to die, Eddie."

We angled ourselves like a great wing, and slowly, the nearer side of the shaft approached. So fissured and over-grown was the wall that it soon took on the appearance of a rural landscape; it was hard to remember this was the wall of a huge mossy well we were emerging from. What with our sideways motion, many of the lava rocks were passing us, and other debris as well—clods of dirt, loose tree branches, a few dead birds, and some shattered bits of a giant nautilus shell.

I kept glancing back to make sure nothing would hit us, not that a simple collision would have mattered at the slow speed we were moving. Once, a rock came close enough for me to touch. I caught hold of it and hefted it. It was very much more massive than any stone I'd ever held, quite outstandingly so. It was, I would hazard, five or perhaps even ten times as massive as lead or gold. Presumably it was from the inner layers of the great crust of the Hollow Earth.

Ordinarily I would have kept so remarkable a talisman, but now I threw it as hard as I could, in the hope it would drive us closer to the cliff. This helped a bit, but the slight impetus was soon vitiated by the natural friction of the air. We were still a few miles from land.

The appearance of the sphere's very center was as puz-zling as before. All lines of sight near the center were warped and distorted, surrounding the center's blobs of blue with weird halos and mirages. The light there was bright and chaotic and lacked all coherence. Central Sun? Perhaps not. I resolved to call it the Central Anomaly. Earth's interior was illuminated not so much by the Central Anomaly proper as by the branching pink streamers of light that stretched outward from that zone to the inner surface of the great planetary rind we'd fallen through. So important is this rind that hereafter I will capitalize it as *Rind*.

Slower and slower we fell, and then we were wholly becalmed. The great Hole stretched around us on every side, the nearest edge at least two miles away. Though we were even with the bottom end of the hole, the giant trees which clung to Earth's inner surface reached some five or ten miles farther inward, with fresh stands of trees growing upon them so that the jungle was at least thirty miles high.

How far had we fallen? Hard to be sure, but it might have been a thousand miles. Was our long voyage to end with us slowly desiccating in this balmy pink-lit air? We waved our arms and legs till we were exhausted, but no closer to solid ground did we get. One by one, we dropped off to sleep.

I woke with a start. Had I heard the cries of birds? It felt like hours later, but we were in the same spot, utterly and totally motionless. When our fall ended, we'd fetched up in midair, on a level with the inner edge of Earth's crust. Except for the dryness, it was like floating in water near land.

Whatever faint forces drew us inward toward the Hollow Earth's Central Anomaly were being counterbalanced, I suppose, by the very slight outward force induced by the Earth's spinning.

The tangled green band of the thirty-mile-thick jungle framed my view down into the Earth's vast interior. It was pink and teeming with life, shading into mist in the distance. Flying creatures filled the air like schools of fish; here and there, larger creatures preyed on them. I could see three huge shellsquid in the distance, also a large, flapping animal resembling a sea-skate or a ray.

Despite the mist, I could see a good way along the curves of the Hollow Earth's inner surface—perhaps as far as two hundred miles. This region was, as I said, covered with bright green jungle several miles deep. The jungle was dotted with great jiggling ponds of water like giant dewdrops. Here and there, drops were breaking free. The freed drops at to our level hung more or less motionless. But those drops near the top of the jungle inevitably tended, if let wholly free, to fall in toward the Hollow Earth's center. And, as the drops got farther from us, they seemed to fall faster. Newton or no, there was some force that drew matter past the Rind and on toward the center. Apparently the Central Anomaly drew things to it more powerfully the closer they got.

In any case, I repeat that there was no gravitational push or pull whatsoever to be felt in the aerial Sargasso sea where we now languished, dead even with the base of the jungle and with the inner surface of the Hollow Earth's Rind. This region was a kind of gravitational shelf between the zone of Earth's influence and the zone influenced by the Central Anomaly.

In the distance, above the trees, the curved landscape of the Hollow Earth rose higher and higher, growing ever paler, till it was lost in distant mists. This inner landscape was all in patches. Parts of it were nubby deep green jungle, parts of it were smooth and a lighter green, and here and there were bare gray rocks. One small region was a charred dead black—the site of a fire, I assumed, noticing a glowing line along the black patch's edge. And just beyond the nearest part of the jungle, I could make out a pale blue sea that shaded to green and blue-black. Perhaps there were deep marine holes in the Hollow Earth's Rind, places where the inner seas connected to those upon the outside.

The jungly edge of the tunnel mouth was over a mile away. Rocks from the tunnel and various-size drops of water floated around us. Though Arf had clung to my pant leg by his teeth while I slept, vagrant breezes had wafted the others away. We were situated at the vertices of a rough equilateral triangle fifty feet on an edge; Arf and I at one vertex, Eddie and Otha at another, and Jeremiah at a third.

Raucous cracking cries broke out. Quite near us two stub-winged white birds were tearing at a piece of food. At first I did not realize how large they were. I thought them near us, and I took the disputed morsel to be something like a fish or a rat. But then a human leg came loose, and I realized their food was the mangled corpse of poor Peters. Each of the birds was as big as two horses. The one holding Peters's severed leg flew off toward the cliff, and the one with the bulk of Peters shook its head briskly, working at tearing the body into bits.

The bird was roughly the shape of a penguin, though its small wings moved in a blur like those of a hummingbird. The bird's yellow, tapering beak was disproportionately large in comparison with its snowy head. The eyes were bright blue beads set into protective feather ruffs. Its claws were rather small—more like a songbird's than like the talons of a predator. Perhaps it was but a scavenger and we were safe.

More squawks rang out. Three more of the beasts were winging toward us. Arf pressed against me in fear. I took out my pistol and examined it. The powder was wet; certainly the gun would not fire. What else did I have on my person? A tinderbox, a handkerchief, fifty feet of silk rope around my waist, and the pelt and head of a redclaw. The birds drew closer. I resolved to sacrifice Arf, if need be.

The bird with Peters shook its head sharply, still not quite able to get its own piece of meat free. It was horrible to see the corpse dance to the rapid vibrations of the bird's head. The other men were awake and yelling to each other; for now, I paid them no mind.

Now something shone and flew toward me—Peters's knife! I stretched my arm to the limit, and the big knife's haft plopped into my open hand—a tangible sign of good fortune. I slid the long strong blade into my boot top. Arf's presence had brought me luck; I'd been mad to think of buying time by feeding him to the birds. But yet...

A fresh plan formed in my mind.

"Good boy, Arfie!" I unwound the rope from my waist and put a tight loop of it around Arf s chest, right behind his front legs. One of the dense boulders was near us, a big one the size of a slave cabin. I wrapped the free end of the rope tightly around my wrist and paid out the rest of the rope into loose bights. I threw Arf away from the boulder, and the reaction sent me tumbling toward my goal. But before I could reach the big rock, the fully extended rope twanged, and pulled me and Arf tumbling back together.

"Sorry, boy. Let's try again." There were four of the monster birds pulling at Peters's corpse now; unless they were solely carrion feeders, it would not be long until they set upon us. I threw Arf again, at a slightly better angle, and this time I caught hold of a ledge of the heavy boulder before the rope reached full extension. Arf yelped, the snap jolted my arm in its socket, but I hung fast. Arf tumbled back to me and the boulder. Now I had bait, and I had something to hide behind.

"All right, Arfie, pretty soon now we're going to fish for a bird."

"Mase! Hey, Mason, here I comes!" It was Otha. While I had been busy with Arf, Jeremiah had thrown his own rope to Eddie and Otha. The three of them were together, and now Otha braced himself against the two men's chests and sprang toward me, Jeremiah's rope uncoiling behind him. I held tight to my rock and reached out to catch Otha's hand. We connected on the first try. We four men hauled on the rope till we were all clustered together on one side of the massive cabin-size boulder.

"What a vista." Jeremiah puffed. "See how the land tilts up and away—I feel like we're in the Garden of Eden! And, ah, the glints of water everywhere! Surely we will find men in these plains and jungles. Kind men and lovely women."

"How we gonna get over there?" asked Otha.

"What of those birds nearby?" exclaimed Eddie, peeking around our rock's edge. "Do they feed on—"

"It is the corpse of Peters," said I, drawing his knife out of my boot top. "See."

"Hideous fowl," murmured Eddie, his eyes glinting. "Those small claws—almost like hands. I dub them *harpies*."

We all peeped around the rock's edges, staring at the harpies. Now a harpy flew close by, carrying one of Peters's arms away. Its small, active wings made a deep buzz. Three other harpies remained, wielding their beaks to open up the corpse's abdomen. Three more approached.

"Here is my plan," I told the others. "I throw Arf out as bait. When one of the harpies comes for him, I pull Arf back to us. We grab hold of the harpy, and in its fear it flies back to land, towing us with it."

"How about that beak?" said Otha. "How about them claws?" He had taken out his own bowie knife. "We gonna cut em off?"

"Better not to bloody the beast," said Jeremiah. "Lest its ravening fellows attack." His hands were nimbly working at his coil of cord. "Here is a noose to hold the beak," he said, holding it up. "And two others to bunch the claws."

"What if someone gets left behind?" asked Eddie.

"We'll bind ourselves together like mountaineers," said Jeremiah, fashioning four firm loops into the rest of his rope. Each of us slipped a loop around his waist.

There was a flurry of squawking around the grisly remains of Peters, and then one of the harpies came buzzing our way. The others had driven it off.

"All right, Arfie," I said. "Play dead." I gave him a gentle push, and he went drifting out to the rope's full extent. The harpy spotted him. Arf began to struggle fruitlessly; the harpy buzzed closer, darting its head this way and that.

I began slowly reeling Arf back, and when I saw the harpy cock its head for a deathblow, I gave the cord a sharp jerk. The huge white bird zipped around the rock's edge after Arf, and then we four men were upon it. I stunned it by slamming the butt of Peters's knife into its head. Jeremiah got his noose tight around its beak and then helped Otha fasten the two other loops around its claws. Eddie scrambled onto its back and sank his hands into its feathers. I snugged Arf under Eddie's arm. The next instant the beast was struggling and striking out at us. Finding myself at its breast, I locked my arms around its neck to hold it still. Otha and Jeremiah had light hold of its bound feet down below. My knife was still in one hand. I pressed the blade tip against the creature's throat, ready to kill. Sensing the danger, it stopped trying to peck me. One of its huge blue eyes was inches from my face.

"Don't fight," I said aloud, as if the bird could understand. "Just fly home. Over there." I jerked my head toward the jungle.

The harpy's wings were beating in fury, and we were already a hundred feet away from the rock.

"Land," I said soothingly, though not letting up the pressure of my knife. "Fly us to the jungle, big bird."

Slowly, erratically, it did. First it flew perhaps two miles in toward the Earth's center—and then it angled over toward the middle of the giant jungle wall. At first it felt to me as if the bird were flying up toward a huge green ceiling; and then my sense of up and down shifted, and I felt the bird to be flying upside down toward a wooded floor.

The jungle was a tangle of vines and branches, brightened with the shimmer of huge globules of water. Some immense flowers bloomed. Two harpies flew out to greet our carrier and then, seeing us, flew off uttering harsh caws of fear.

We circled a huge leafless tree trunk with branches stained white from bird droppings. The harpies' roost. A dozen of them flew off as we landed—or, that is, tried to land. I heard thuds and a curse as Jeremiah and Otha smacked into one of the tree branches, and then came Jeremiah's cry, "Let go!"

I unclasped my arms, slipped the noose off the bird's beak, and pushed my feet hard against its chest to get free. There was a jerk at my waist as my ropes pulled Arf and Eddie off the bird's back. And then our harpy screamed and flew away, leaving us five and our ropes tangled in the branches of the harpies' home tree. Slowly, Jeremiah and I got our ropes unknotted and fastened them back around our waists.

"Let's climb down," said Otha. "Fore they comes back."

"Up," said Eddie. "You mean climb *up*. See the loose twigs out there, see them falling toward the center? The center is down, the land is up."

"I ain't no fly on no ceilin," said Otha. "When I climbs off a tree, I climbs *down*. Come on, Mase, let's find us somethin to eat."

"I'll come, Otha, but I think Eddie is right. *Down* is toward the center; it's the way things fall. And *up* is the other way. We have to keep a common tongue."

"Sho," said Otha with a sour laugh. "Then tell me which way be north." He gave himself a shove that sent him up—or down—to the tree's next branch.

"Let's call it *out*," said Jeremiah, "*In* is toward the center, and *out* is back toward where we came from. Toward the crust. Agreed?"

"Agreed."

I pushed off after Otha. I floated easily through the empty air, steadied myself on the next branch, and pushed farther. Jeremiah was behind me, and Eddie took up the rear—the most *inward* of all.

Our progress was easy. Rather than heading straight back out toward Earth's crust, we chose to go deeper into the jungle, angling crossways. In the all but weightless surroundings, we could hop from branch to branch like squirrels—although it took some bone-shaking crashes till we learned not to jump too hard. It was so strange to be living with practically no gravity. How odd and how wonderful that the attraction of the Hollow Earth's great domed crust exactly balanced the pull of the nearby Rind.

Soon we were in the midst of foliage. Although no solid ground was visible, the fluttering pink light from the "sky" provided a steady reminder of which way was which. Birdsong sounded on every side of us, also the rustlings and cries of other animals.

There were large droplets of water everywhere—some as big as peaches, some as big as pumpkins. In the moist air, they condensed like dew. In these near-weightless conditions, the water drops were free to merge and grow to unearthly size. I drank several of the smaller ones. The bigger, head-size drops held tiny fish with stubby fins like legs. Our passage knocked the drops loose, and they slid inward to merge with drops closer to the jungle's edge, with the largest drops slipping into the sky and falling all the way to the center, and there—I supposed—to be cooked to vapor and sent back toward the Rind.

All the trees and vines had extra tendrils at their forks, tendrils designed to hold the waterglobs. Additionally, small parasitic plants had taken root in the tree trunks' crotches and flaws; these orchidlike plants bore flowers of an over-whelming intricacy. Small-winged dragonflies darted from plant to plant; there were also gnats, beetles, oversize aphids, and enormous pale ants that would have been unable to walk in normal gravity. Mist and fine rain from our tunnel's great icefall was drifting through the trees, swelling the bulging water globs.

After ten minutes of swinging through the wet branches, we found our first food: a vine covered with red berries the size of apples. Otha bit into one and smiled; the rest of us followed suit. The berries were sweet and juicy, each holding a single big seed. I ate three. Dragonflies buzzed around our discarded seeds; a thing like a thick eel stuck its head out of a hole in a tree branch and caught one of them. I wondered if the eel would be good to eat, but then it had writhed back into hiding.

A bit further on we found some fruits like bananas; these were filling, though somewhat bitter. A large, hairy spider leapt from one of the banana plant's white flowers and hurried away. A green-throated bird the size of a partridge caught the spider and began to devour it. Otha drew out his knife and threw it Peters-style, pinning the plump bird to a branch. It screamed terribly till Otha cut its throat and gutted it. Great scuttlings filled the branches where Otha threw the innards.

"Let's keep moving," I said. I was in no rush to meet this jungle's scavengers.

"Once we gets nuff food, we can build a fire and cook," said Otha. "You kill somethin, too. Mason. You got a knife, Eddie?"

"I do not," said Eddie. "I think it unwise to inaugurate our stay with wholesale slaughter."

As we went deeper into this Hollow Earth jungle, the light grew dimmer and the chatter of animal life swelled. I saw several small, furry creatures with long arms, but they were too fast to kill—not that I really wanted to. Something like a pig was what I was hungry for, or a fish.

My wishes were in part answered when we came on the biggest waterball yet—a monstrous trembling sphere the size of a barn, hemmed in on the upward side by vines and tendrils and cradled on the inward side by the crotch where a huge dead branch stuck out of a living tree. Peering into the water, I could make out some of those stubby-legged fish I'd seen before, only these fish were plump and a foot long. I slipped out of my clothes and pushed into the water, my new knife in one hand. The fish scattered. I swam across the waterball, stuck my head out for air, then swam back. One of the fish got right in front of me. I swam at it, trapping it against the surface, but just as I lunged with my knife, the fish jumped out of the water. I came out after it only to see the fish flopping its way up through the air, using its little finlegs to push off from every branch it passed. Maybe later it would creep back into this big glob, or maybe it would find another. Let it be. I rested.

The warm, humid air felt good on my bare skin. I sat on the dead branch's outward side, lightly anchored down by the faint gravitational tug. Arf was near me, now and then starting into midair and bouncing from vine to vine, propelled by the beating of his tail. The others poked around, looking at this and that. We all agreed that if we could catch some more food, this would be a good spot to camp. The ground or crust was at least a half mile further out, but there seemed no special reason to push that far; the jungle would only get darker and wetter and more filled with death.

"Let's try this," said Jeremiah, producing a fishhook and line from inside his coat. He pried some loose bark off the dead branch and found a fat grubworm to bait his hook with. My direct attack had left the fish too skittish to take the bait immediately, but after ten minutes' time, Jeremiah caught one, and then another. I found a strong hollow stick like a bamboo shoot and used a few feet of rope to lash my new knife to it. I'd planned to spear a fish, but just then another bird chanced past and I managed to hit it with my first throw. Otha and I set to work plucking feathers.

"How about a fire, Mason?"

"A fire by all means," said Eddie. "This jungle gloom oppresses my spirit. Why are we here? How will we ever get back? I should be busy *writing* about strange worlds, not exploring them. Jungles are rather beyond my purview."

"As for getting back, later we can build a new balloon," said Jeremiah. "Thanks to us, the Symmes Hole is wide open. In due time we'll balloon out and return to America. You'll write an expedition report, Eddie."

"Indeed," said Eddie. "A fabulous prose narrative. Or perhaps an epic poem. What to it?" For a moment he stared up through the jungle toward the flickering inner sky, and then he held up a finger. "*Htrae*," intoned Eddie. "The reverse of Earth. *Full fathoms they fell / To the land of Htrae / Within mother Earth's warm Rind.*"

"Capital!" exclaimed Reynolds. "You'll create a furor, and I'll garner funding for a full and properly equipped—"

There was a coughing roar in the distance.

"Build that fire," repeated Otha.

I took out my tinderbox. The branch whose outer side we rested on was perhaps ten yards in diameter, and the verdant tree it connected to was easily fifty yards through. Though our dead branch was rather damp on the surface, its pithy inner layers were dry and corky. I used my knife to chip out a pile of the punky stuff. There was no obvious place to put a fire, so I tried building it in midair. The pith caught fire properly, but the flames didn't seem to know which way to go, and soon the scraps I'd assembled drifted apart and died into sparks. I tried again, this time starting my fire right inside the depression I'd chipped out in the branch. With no real down or up, the flames couldn't rise properly, but eventually I'd ignited a stable, good-size glow.

Each of us skewered a fish or a bird on a green branch and held it to the coals. The hanging, weightless smoke made our eyes smart, but the sizzling of the meat was wonderful to hear. As we cooked, I poked and stoked the fire until it had spread all the way to the inside of the branch, which seemed to be hollow. We could see wisps of smoke coming out of knotholes for quite some distance away, and the huge tree stem was filled with the scrabblings of small creatures fleeing the fumes. A family of disgustingly jiggly flesh-colored salamanders squirmed out of a knothole nearby and flopped themselves away. One of them brushed against my neck, and I shuddered. What if some really big creatures showed up?

We crouched over the fire, turning our sticks till our food was ready. Otha and Eddie each ate a bird, Jeremiah and I a fish. We traded off bits of our meats; they were all quite good, though the fowl were somewhat underdone, or even bloody. By the time we were through, the fire had opened a three-foot-wide hole in the tree. The bright blaze heartened us.

Numerous grubworms and small transparent scorpions were squirming out of the hot wood; we used them to bait the fishhook and catch four more of the legfin fish. Once we'd roasted these, and had eaten some juicy purple fruits, we were full and ready for sleep—but by now our fire had spread so much smoke that the air was not easily breathable. By judiciously cutting a few vines, we managed to tease the great trapped waterball over a few yards to quench the flames. As the air cleared, we tethered ourselves to a thick vine that embraced the tree trunk. Hanging there like strange fruits, we chatted softly, drifting toward sleep.

"A balloon's the thing," said Eddie. "We can make one of gum and giant leaves."

"But how to heat it?" I queried. "We have no stove."

"Why not use them giant shellsquid," put in Otha. "We could catch one and ride it away. I seen some of them in the tunnel and more down there in the sky."

"Surely there are people here," mused Jeremiah. "If not in this jungle, then further along the curve, in the rocky zone, or at the jungle's edge where it meets the sea. We should find them."

"I saw something like a metal ship in the tunnel," I said. "It was frozen inside Otha's ice island. I think it was an airship."

"Infernal machines," said Eddie drowsily. "Can we trust hell-creatures for aid? If it's exalted adventure we want, we should press inward, down through the sky to the center. Angels may live there, sweet white angels with wings..."

10. Seela

It took me a while to fall asleep. Down in the center of the planet, huge vague fingers of energy wandered and branched, filling our deep jungle with shaking light. To my solitary fancy, the flickers came in rhythm with the sounds: the buzzings of insects, the stealthy rustles of unseen crawling things, and—most unsettling of all—the plops and wallowings of great creatures slipping in and out of the ponds. Now and then would come a distant howl or shriek to set my hair on end. So wet was the air that jiggling gobbets of water kept landing on my face and oozing into my nose. I tossed this way and that, fretting at my tether while Arf and the three men snored.

I thought of Virginia. It was incredible that Eddie's possessiveness and folly had killed her. Sis had been an odd duck, but I felt I'd loved her. The remembered feel of her chalky flesh up in Mrs. Clemm's dark garret haunted me in complex ways. More purely pleasant were my memories of Sukie, and of my two visits to a woman named Lupe in Rio. Sukie, Virginia, Lupe. Would I ever meet a girl to truly love? Love…love was a maze, a heavenly city…

Otha woke me, who knows how many hours later. "Hsst, Mason! I hears somethin!" I rubbed the sleep out of my eyes and tried to listen. The cries and rustles of the jungle beasts were unchanged but, yes, there was something new—a roaring, almost human sound, oddly warped and amplified.

"You think there be giants here?" asked Otha. The far-off garbled yelling went on and on. "Sounds like he hungry!"

Flesh-eating giants? I woke Eddie and Jeremiah. "There's some kind of monster," I told them. "Over there!"

Jeremiah cocked his head as alertly as Arf. "Let's go investigate!" said he.

"What if he eats us?"

"We'll sneak and mayhap steal his treasures. Stout heart now, Mason!"

So sneak we did. The direction of our travel lay crosswise rather than inward or outward. Along the way we passed a gnarled trunk that bore thorns the length of my arm. It struck me that such a thorn could serve as a capital weapon. But I didn't stop to harvest one. I wanted to press on and find the source of that giant voice we were hearing—and surely it was indeed a human voice—occasionally pausing in its droning blabber, but never for long, and as we progressed it grew ever louder. As the end of an hour approached, the light became brighter, and then we found ourselves at the jungle's far edge, peeping out of the immense thicket like anxious wrens.

A huge ocean lay spread across the Earth's inner curve here, rising in the distance like a great, never-breaking wave. The jungle's edge was like the face of a thirty-mile-high hedge. The tangled wall started by the edge of the sea and towered toward the center of the Hollow Earth. Great vines thrust immense flowers out into the free, light-filled air above the sea. Rather than facing inward toward the Earth's center, the flowers pointed out toward the sea, and many of the blossoms cradled nourishing globs of water. The blossom's centers were yellow or blue. The voice was now clear enough so that we could make out individual nonsense words—yet no giant was to be seen.

Turning our heads this way and that we finally deter-mined that the voice came from a flower just inward from us. This vast blossom was like a two-mile-wide sunflower, with a great yellow center and a ruff of lazily undulating white petals. There was a dark green spot near one edge of the flower's surface, roughly hexagonal, and lying near the spot was a long, straight tube—seemingly a section of plant-stem.

Otha, whose hearing was the sharpest, reckoned that the giant voice was coming from the tube. Some pale figures—people, insects, worms?—moved about in the flaw near the tube.

Jeremiah tossed a fat berry toward the flower. The berry coasted inward and dwindled to a speck, bound for the jewellike lake that rested in the blossom's center. After a brief consultation, we jumped after the berry. Midway during our approach, the owner of the giant voice noticed us and cried out an alarm. The green spot's infestation of pale figures dispersed. I prayed that we weren't making a fatal mistake.

We fell for two more minutes and then, ever so gently, we touched down beside the lake. All was calm. The yellow field of the flower's surface was smooth and leathery, filled with the buzz of large insects and the cries of the small animals that preyed on them. A regular pattern of raised welts marked the surface, dividing it into hexagonal plots or cells. Each cell was roughly the size of our barnyard; each of them formed a smooth depression with a hole in its center. The air near the surface was filled with a sweet smell. The central lake's near-weightless waterball bulged out sharply.

I tore off a piece of the yellow flower and chewed it. It was good, like a sun-dried peach or apple. A jewellike beetle with small wings landed to gnaw at the hole I'd made in the flower; I shooed it, and it flew off, glinting gorgeously in the light. After the dank, thicketed jungle, this was paradise. Slowly we gathered around a small, secondary pool of water which had collected in the center of one of the hexagons. The hexagons' central holes were ringed by stubby tubular petals of an especial toughness. There was still no sign of the pale figures, and no hint of the giant voice. We ate and drank and rested, Otha yodeled, and poor drawn Eddie's limbs began gaily to wave.

We'd all been eating at the same part of the flower, and now there was a hole big enough for me to stick my head in through the surface and look. It was like peering into a yellow room the size of a house. A thick column was in the room's center, stretching from floor to ceiling—terminating in the hexagon's central hole. Three embryonic seeds nestled against the central tube, connected to it by thick tendrils, the seeds the size of watermelons. Each of the big flower-cell's six walls had a triangular gap in its bottom, a kind of door through which I could see into neighboring cells, each with its own central pillar and a trio of seed embryos. For a moment I saw a pale shape moving in the next cell over—who lived here?

Suddenly, my legs and arms were seized from behind and I was yanked out of my peephole. A horde of pale-skinned men and women surrounded us. Their clothing was, as I say, of white and yellow petals, and they bore sharp rapiers fashioned from thorns. Their hair was red and blond; their eyes were green and blue. Many of them wore necklaces of heavy trinkets. My three companions had already been overcome, and one of the pale attackers held Arf tight in his arms. Before I could think of struggling, my hands were lashed behind me and my ankles were bound together. My captors, two pink-clad women, bodily picked me up. As they carried me, they chattered excitedly to each other and to me, but I could understand nothing of what they said—it might as well have been birdsong. They laid me down next to my companions, also bound.

"Yes, we are your friends!" Jeremiah was shouting in hearty tones. This having no effect, he switched to one of the Polynesian tongues he knew. "*Nui-nui lama-lama papeete nami-lo!*"

"They're angels!" raved Eddie. "They flew from the sky!" Our captors—there were perhaps thirty of them—paid little attention to our expostulations. Most of the pale people clustered around Otha, staring at him in solemn wonder, haltingly reaching out to touch his skin. One of them put her necklace around Otha's neck. Several of them made as if to kiss Otha's hands and feet; others began to chant.

Had they never seen a Negro before? Even more ridiculous, those few not worshiping Otha were enthralled by Arf. Ever in the present moment, Arf had stopped barking and was now wagging his tail and licking the face of the youth who held him. The youth simpered and began to lick Arf back. Several others pressed forward and licked Arf s nose as well.

While these odd displays continued. I had ample opportunity to examine our captors. They were so pale-skinned that their veins showed. Each of them had a thick shock of fair hair cut bowl-style. Their features were delicate, even beautiful, their teeth regular and white. They were short and slender, with the exception of their legs, which were thick and heavily muscled. Their necklaces held crystals, shells, and carved bits of wood. Some were also clothed in fluttering togas made of fresh flower petals, yellow and white, and each of them wore strapped to their legs some oddly shaped spats, evidently trimmed from the tubular bases of the petals. I grasped the purpose of these leathery tubes when I saw a girl hop up into the air and kick her way outward from the giant flower. Each time she kicked backward, the fin above her foot caught the air, driving her forward. Airfins! Wings!

"Ahnaa bogbog du smeeepy flan? Mii'iim doc janjee?" One of the pink-dressed girls was standing over me.

"Set me free," I begged her, raising my bound ankles.

She laughed and made a dismissive gesture. *"Ah'mbaa na toloo klick gorwaay,"* said she. Her voice was calm and musical, and she lingered over the long vowels, singing each of them through a tone or two. She and her companion took hold of my arms and, with a sudden spring, launched us into the sky. They kicked their legs in steady rhythm, popping the strong petal fins against the air. The rest of them followed us, bearing Otha, Eddie, Jeremiah, and Arf.

We worked our way around the giant waterdrop that occupied our flower's center and flew toward the great yellow disk's edge. There, in the surface of the vast sunflower, was a large ragged hole, and lying next to it was the great noise-tube we'd seen from afar. All the yellow cells with their seeds had been cleared away here—perhaps for food—leaving an open hexagon a hundred yards wide. My bearers kickpopped down to land us in the hexagon. The ground here was tough dark green vegetable matter, presumably the same material as our huge flower's vines and leaves. The wall openings in the cells facing the open space had been widened, so that the effect was of a village green surrounded by stores and houses. Numerous faces peeped from the cells.

Seeing their defenders land with all intruders tightly bound, the fair flowerpeople came surging into the green.

When they glimpsed black Otha and hairy Arf, their excitement knew no limits. It was only a moment till they were all around us, shouting in nasal singsong. Everyone wore the petal leggings; many wore nothing else.

Several of them began to beat on big hollow pods, now a slender, long-haired youth flew to the big tube that had attracted us and began chanting into one end. The tube's ends were covered over with tight-stretched membranes (one with a small central hole), thus turning the tube into a long reverberator. Giants indeed! The listeners called out words of praise to the performer who was chanting into the reverberator. Evidently his name was Yurgen.

Meanwhile flat leaves bearing slices of those melon-like seeds appeared, and the flowerpeople began celebrating in earnest. As the drone of reverb tube continued, it began to take on a hypnotic quality, like a primeval sacred chant. In my head I saw the notes as long, wiggling curves, glowing with strange hues. And all of this was coming from Yurgen's amplified voice. The man was something of a magician. Even though I was captive and bound, I was relishing his performance.

As always here, the sky was filled with pink flickers; it was, on the average, like late afternoon on a pleasant summer day. We four were propped up together in the green's center. Otha and I were side to side, with Eddie and Jeremiah behind us leaning against our backs. Arf, who'd been set free, lay at my side, alertly watching the noisy crowd.

"Maybe they cannibals, Mase?" said Otha. "Some do have a nasty look."

"You're right. See how that one has his teeth sharpened? And the woman over there...see the way she's painted her body? These are real savages, Otha. It's strange because they're so—"

"They be so white. They look too good to talk to the like of me, Mase, they look like the first families of Virginia. And then they carry on this-a-way. Looky!"

Yurgen's resonant chant and the drumming on the gourds grew ever more compelling. Meanwhile the dancers threw themselves about with ever greater abandon, emitting fearful whoops and making hideous grimaces. Several couples even progressed to public embraces of an ultimate intimacy. And those who had to relieve themselves did so quite openly. It was unpleasant and singular to see such fine-looking people exhibit this bestial behavior.

Just when the orgy had reached fever pitch, the drumming and the roar of the reverb tube broke off. All began crooning a single utterance: *Quaihlaihle*! They pronounced the far-fetched name much as we would say *"quite likely."*

A lone figure appeared from one of the empty seedcells: a tall bejeweled woman, with skin as white as the inside of a puffball mushroom. Her scalp was shaved and painted black. This was Quaihlaihle, the queen of the flowerpeople. She walked slowly toward us, ignoring the filth that had been scattered by the dancers. She was clothed in dyed and lacquered plant parts that fit her like armor. The bright plates of her equipage were spangled with glittering bits of stone and shell. Unlike the other flowerpeople, Quaihlaihle had the thick lips and dark eyes of a Negro. Yet her skin was, as I say, utterly white. When her gaze lighted on Otha, her face split in a fierce smile. Her glistening teeth were a bloody ruby-red.

"She look just like Lijah," Otha breathed.

"And like the redclaws," I added. I still had the head and pelt of one of the red-toothed antarctic beasts—not to mention my gun and Peter's knife. Our savage captors had not thought to search us.

"*Lamalama tekelili*?" said Quaihlaihle to Otha. Noticing Arf, she stooped to pet him, long and slow.

"Yes ma'am," said Otha. "I'm the boss of this party, sho. That's my dog, too. I hope you treat us nice. How about you unties us to start with, Quaihlaihle?" He raised up his bound feet and hands.

"*Bogbog doc janjee!*" exclaimed Quaihlaihle. "*Ombondoohoo!*" One of the men sprang forward and used a dagger of sharpened shell to cut Otha's bonds.

"Me, too," I urged, holding up my hands. "Untie me, too."

"Yes," said Otha, standing and rubbing his wrists. "Untie all of us, Quaihlaihle."

She stepped forward, took Otha's head in her hands, and licked him all over his face. Though Otha was tall, the flowerpeople's queen was every bit as big as him. As she greeted Otha in this singular fashion, the flowerpeople began again to chant. Quaihlaihle gave a command, and the man with the shell knife moved around the three of us, cutting the tight vines that bound our hands and feet.

"That's a relief," said Jeremiah. "We should present them with a gift. What do you have in your pockets, Eddie?"

"An empty flask," said Eddie. "A pocketknife. A twist of tobacco. Virginia's tee—" He cut the word short and hastily continued. "Paper with a few verses and—deuce take it! My pen and ink are lost."

"What do you have, Mason?"

I didn't want to mention my gun. "How about a redclaw pelt? I've still got one. The queen should like that; it has red teeth like hers. Maybe she can wear it for a hat."

"Excellent," said Jeremiah. "Give it to me."

"To you?"

"I'm the leader, Mason. I've dealt with savages before. Trust me."

So I pulled the wadded up redclaw pelt out of my pocket and slipped it to Jeremiah. The scabby skin was wrapped around the red-toothed head. With a flourish, Jeremiah arranged the pelt and head upon his two flattened hands, then stepped forward and crouched before Queen Quaihlaihle, making his offering. He was the very image of a humble subject.

The turmoil that ensued is hard to describe. The queen began to scream most terribly, and a second later a woman with a long thorn-rapier had darted forward and plunged her point through Jeremiah's heart. He gave a terrible groan and fell sideways. The man with the shell knife darted forward and sawed open the dying Jeremiah's throat, sawed as if to cut off his head. Great quantities of blood gushed forth, some of it floating off in bright globules. Still screaming, Quaihlaihle snatched up the offending redclaw and crammed it down into the yawning hole that the man had cut in Jeremiah's neck.

I drew out the big knife I'd gotten from Peters and took off running, making ten or twenty feet with each bound. I heard someone close behind me. If I went up to the flower's surface or into the sky, I wouldn't have a chance. Instead, I dove into one of the open cell doors and raced through to the next and the next and the next. All the cells I entered were empty save for seeds and central pillars. Most of the seeds were hard and dry, fully ripened and ready to drift away. Someone was still close behind me. I blundered on for ages and finally, out of breath, I caught hold of a cell's central tube and hid behind it. When my follower entered the cell, I leaped out roaring with my blade raised high.

"Don't, Mason, don't kill me!" shrieked Eddie, for it was only he.

"Thank God it's you," I told him. I could have kissed him. "Let's go deeper into the maze until they calm down. We'll escape when…"

"When it gets dark?" Eddie smiled.

"Escape somehow. What happened just now?"

"I surmise that the redclaws are viewed as sacred beasts and that Jeremiah has borne Peters's punishment for having killed one. Note that the queen has red teeth as well. Did you see how quick she was to push the redclaw into Jeremiah's gullet?"

"I saw it."

"Quite extraordinary. It was as if she meant to plant the slain beast's *mana* in poor Reynolds's hale frame. As if he were a sarcophagus and the pelt a pharaoh. I wish I had my pen! I need to write! So many choice happenings are flitting by. We must find a way back to Earth, Mason. My narrative of this trip could make my fortune. Make *our* fortune. Promise me that you will cast your lot with mine, Mason. I…" Eddie's voice faltered. "I know that you think ill of me. No man is a hero to his valet, but—"

"I'm not your valet, Eddie."

"If Otha is your slave, then you are my valet and Arf is Otha's dog. Arf and Otha are ensconced in the camp of the flowerpeople. You and I must stand together or die, young Reynolds. You know this, yet you find our union onerous.

You despise me, do you not? You think me a cold-blooded murderer. You do not forgive me for the death of Virginia."

"You poisoned her, and I do not doubt that you violated her dead body. It is a certainty that you pulled out her teeth; you bear the teeth with you still. You killed Virginia and you defiled her corpse. She deserved better, Eddie. She was only a child."

We were wandering side by side through the cells. Each cell was a hexagon in floor plan, with six rectangular walls ten to fifteen feet in height. As we moved away from the flower's edge and toward its center, the cells grew larger. Every wall had a small tentlike rent at its base. Wishing to ensure that Quaihlaihle's folk did not follow us, we moved rapidly through the rooms as we argued. When I threw my indictment at Eddie, we were near the center of a cell.

The sky sputtered to bright; Eddie blanched pale and dour. "Forgive me, Mason. I am three parts mad, this is no secret—but, pray, I am no fiend! The teeth…the teeth were my only violation. I had no thought of killing Sis. Truly, Mason, you do me grave dishonor. Were we in the real world and I in my right mind, I would horsewhip you or challenge you to a duel! But this is not Earth but Htrae, to be followed, I conjecture, by a MirrorHtrae and a MirrorEarth. I've had visions of the rest of our journey, Mason. We'll travel on through the center—"

"The Central Anomaly, I call it," said I as we pushed into another cell. The three seeds in this cell were full and turgid.

"How apt, my boy, how scientific! Through the Central Anomaly we shall go, and then—I do not quite grasp what I have forseen—we'll reach a layer of space that has a Hollow MirrorEarth and a MirrorEarth surface to tunnel up to. Believe of me what you will, I do not trouble to deny it. I am marked for torment and death, but also am I marked for greatness. I am not like other men! Do say now that you throw in your lot with mine."

"Eddie, I—"

"Hsst!"

He cut me off with a quick light touch. There was some-one in the next cell! Once again, I drew my knife and crouched behind the room's central pillar. Eddie got close behind me. The plant parts whispered as the person pushed through the dividing wall's rent. Delicate footfalls. A light rasping noise and then faint slurping. Ever so slowly, I eased my head out from around the pillar. A beautiful blond maiden was there, pressing her mouth to one of the seeds. She was naked save for her legfins, a loincloth, and an elaborately patterned necklace.

"Seize her," hissed Eddie, peering out from behind me. Even as she looked up, I sprang forward and clamped my left arm around her waist. She screamed but struggled little. I sheathed my knife and pressed my right hand gently to her mouth. Her mouth was slick with the seed's albuminous juices.

"Don't be frightened. I'm Mason, and that's Eddie. We want to be friends. Yes, we want to be friends." Her rolling eyes fastened on my face. Such bright, intelligent features she had. Her eyes were a shade between brown and green. Hazel. Her nose was somewhat flat. Her lips were full, with her upper lip like a smooth, kissable band, with only the smallest of indentations at its top. I smiled and nodded. "If I let you go, do you promise not to scream?"

She regarded me calmly. I smiled once more, and slowly I took my hand off her mouth. Her mouth moved slightly—I made a small cry and cut it off by slapping my hand over my own mouth. The smell of her saliva was wonderful. My arm around her waist held her body tight against me. She was marvelously supple and alive. I pretended to struggle at the hand over my mouth, popping my eyes and blowing my cheeks out. She stared, understood, giggled. I dropped my hand from my mouth and put it around her waist to meet my other. Everything about her looked and felt right. I almost blurted out that I loved her, but settled for staring into her alert, unafraid eyes.

"*Emthonjeni womculo*," she said presently. "*Thul'ulale*."

"Dear girl," put in Eddie, striding forward and startling her. "Be assured that Mason and Eddie are kind and funny men. I am Mason's master." Fixing an impudent simper on his face, he drew out a handkerchief and deftly knotted it into the shape of a rabbit. The girl stared at him in puzzlement that changed to fear as Eddie waggled the rabbit's ears and began to dart the head oddly,

"Stop it, Eddie," said I. "Sit down and be quiet or, better yet, go away for an hour. I saw this girl first. She's mine."

For a wonder, he left quietly.

"*Sini lindile*," said the girl. "*Nansi Seela.*" She made a graceful gesture at herself and then at me. "*Gooba'am?*"

"Mason," said I, tapping my chest. I was wearing trousers, boots, a collarless shirt, and a jacket. She wore but her leggings and her breechcloth, both made of white flowerpetal. "I'm Mason and you are Seela?"

"Seeylaaah," she said, imitating my voice. "*Nansi Seela. Ma'aassong?*"

"Mason," I said, correcting her. After a few more tries, I could say her name the way she wanted me to. She taught me that the large, embryonic seeds were called *juube*, and she showed me how to bite off a piece of a *juube's* skin and lap up the thick clear juice. The juice was something like sweetened eggwhite, with a bitter aftertaste. It was invigorating, and a bit dizzying. As we taught each other our names for this and that, I grew warmer and warmer. My feet were uncomfortable in my wet boots, so I took them off, also my jacket, also my shirt.

Seela plucked at my trousers. "*Nicabange orlooah?*" She stood and fluttered her legs. Her petal leggings popped against the air and drove her up the cell's leathery yellow ceiling. She drifted back down. "*Gooba'am?*"

I kicked my legs, but of course my trousers did nothing for me. Seela plucked at my trousers again, talking volubly. I went ahead and took them off. I was not to wear a full suit of clothes again for the next nine months.

So there we were, nearly naked in our yellow cell, Seela and I. Her hair was yellow-blond. Her face was neat and fine, with a firm round jaw. Her eyes were greenish-brown, her teeth strong and white. Her limbs were pleasingly proportioned, and her body a wonderland of young womanly curves. Did she mean for us to make love? Suddenly, she picked up my big knife, lying by my boot. From everything I'd seen so far, metal was unknown to the flowerpeople.

I took the knife from her and stabbed it into one of the *juube* seeds, showing her how sharp it was. Then I turned it sideways and let her look into it as if into a mirror. She was briefly fascinated. She stared at her own eyes for a minute, then put the knife between us and moved it up and down, swapping her view of my eyes with her view of her own reflected eyes. Our eyes were remarkably similar. More and more, I felt this woman was meant for me.

Just as I was about to kiss her, she leapt up the ceiling and made a big slash in it with my knife. She did this two more times till she'd cut out a triangular hole. She pulled herself out through the hole and beckoned to me. Before following, I rolled all my clothes together into a bundle and stashed them under the curve of a *juube*. Seela called to me from above; I crouched, then leapt with all my strength. In the low gravity, my leap was enough to shoot me right through the hole. Seela caught hold of my bare foot as I flew past her.

"*Nicabange smeeepy doolango*," she said.

I sat on the flower's cut edge and peered around. The village hexagon was far off, although closer to us than I had hoped. I could make out a few figures moving in the air over the hexagon. At this distance they looked like large insects. Instinctively I flattened myself against the flower's surface. Seela looked at me curiously. I pointed over to the hexagon and made a stabbing gesture at my throat. "They don't like me," I told her. "Quaihlaihle killed one of us already."

"*Quaihlaihle shange yejazi*," said Seela, making a sour face. Now she turned her attention to the center of the hexagonal flower dimple we were in. The big flower-cell's central column met the surface here in a hole which was surrounded by a cluster of tubular petals. Using my knife with growing skill, Seela cut off two of the tubular petals and trimmed away most of the material from one side of each, leaving a big concave fin with a ring at one end. She slipped the rings over my feet and then I was wearing petal airfins like her. She called them *pulpuls*. She was eager to give me a flight lesson. I hesitated; she grabbed my hand and kicked us up into the air.

When I tried a kick, my *pulpuls* fluttered uselessly. Seela turned around and showed me how to slip my toes and the front of my foot through a slit she'd made near the petal's end. Now, with the *pulpul* held by the ring around my shin and by the slit at the end, I could kick and catch the air just as Seela did. Even so, my first attempts at flight were anything but smooth. I kept kicking too hard or too soft and sending myself cartwheeling. Every so often my toes would slip out of one of the slits and the *pulpul* would go flapping. Seela was all around me, laughing and helping, and finally we managed to fly all the way to the flower's great central waterglob and back.

There were other isolated fliers here and there on the flower-surface, so there really was not so much to fear from the villagers' seeing us in motion. As we came back near our starting point, Seela began kicking outward toward the Rind. I flew at her side. Now that we were farther from the flower, I could see around it to the Central Anomaly at the Hollow Earth's core—the source of the soft pink lightning that pulsed and branched to fill this whole huge hollow world. We stopped kicking and began to coast back inward to the flower, and now Seela's arms were around me, and we kissed.

This was a moment I shall never forget—the two of us drifting through the mild, sweetly scented pink-lit air, only we two, nearly naked, clasped tight to each other, Seela and Mason, our mouths pressed together—ah, the feel of her bold tongue, the taste of her smooth lips—it was then, at that moment, that Seela became forever my bride. All my nearly sixteen years of life I'd felt incomplete, not fully real, but now, with Seela, some profound lack in me was filled, some parched longing was finally watered.

"Seela."

"Mason."

We kissed most of the way back down and landed on the cell where Seela had cut out the triangular hole. My knife was still lying there, stuck into the flowerstuff. It occurred to me to wonder what Eddie was up to.

There was no sign of him in our cell or in any of the six neighboring cells. We circled out to search the ring of twelve next-closer cells and the ring of eighteen next-closer cells after that. Halfway through the third ring, I noticed something:

There was a pool of juice by one of the *juubes*, and scratched on to the cell wall near it were words. I recognized Eddie's writing. He'd been here, drinking *juube* juice and etching words into the flower, perhaps with his pocketknife: "ICHOR. AN ANT I. SWEET CONFUSION. ANGELS CROWD MY HEAD."

There was more, not all legible. Evidently, he'd drunk enough of the *juube* juice to become intoxicated. The last words were, "I FEAR NOT!" Perhaps, emboldened by the *juube*, he'd gone to rejoin the flowerpeople.

Seela gave me a calming pat and motioned for me to follow her. First we went back to the starting cell and got my clothes. Seela used my knife to cut out a quarter of the watermelon-sized *juube* seed that she'd been drinking from earlier, and she gave me this large slippery segment to carry. Then we set off from the flower's center, going in the opposite direction from the village.

Within half an hour we'd reached a cell that Seela seemingly used for her home. This cell was on the flower's very edge, but not near the village. It had a round window cut in one wall. I was frightened to hear someone in the next cell over, but she drew me in there and introduced me to an old man she called Ogger. Although I initially assumed he was her father, I would later learn that the flowerpeople were somewhat cavalier about paternity. It may only have been that Ogger was an occasional companion of Seela's mother. In any case, he and Seela had at this point grouped themselves together for mutual support.

Old Ogger brightened at the sight of our *juube* seed, and Seela cut him a slice. He wolfed it down, smacked his lips, and fell into a reverie. I realized how very tired I myself was. I followed Seela back into her own room, with its view out into the Hollow Earth. I ate some *juube*, too, and, soothed by its effects, dropped off to sleep.

11. Inward!

Much later, I woke alone, feeling wonderfully rested. From where I lay, I could see out the window to the sea. Seela's room was the first safe haven I'd known since debarking from the *Wasp* for the antarctic coast on Christmas, how many days ago? I'd passed a day on the beach and a day in the balloon, nearly two more days falling through the hole, another day getting down into the jungle, and a day getting out to the edge of this flower. If I'd slept as long as it felt like, today was likely New Year's Day, 1837.

Here in Baltimore, as I write this narrative in a rented room, it is my birthday, the second of February, 1850. We've had a bitter cold winter of it, Seela and I. We are very much in love. It's dawn; quite soon I must go to Ben's Good Eats to wait the breakfast shift. I'll be on duty till after dark. I long for a better life. My skin is paling steadily, so there is hope.

Though I was born in 1821, I am seventeen today, not twenty-nine. The cause of this discrepancy is that twelve years passed during the few minutes that Seela and I were in the heart of the Central Anomaly. Looking out from that frenzied zone, I saw the South Hole dim and brighten a full dozen times. For me, the New Year's Day of 1837 is as one day, one month and one year ago.

When I woke that New Year's Day, a melonlike drop of water, a square of flowerleather, and a slice of *juube* lay nearby. I drank the water and ate the flowerleather but forbore from eating of the slippery *juube*. Its effects were too enervating. Instead, I took advantage of my isolation to get out my pistol and unload its four chambers, crumbling up the caked powder and spreading it out so that it might thoroughly dry. If I needed to free Otha and Eddie, I might have to kill someone. While the powder dried, I leaned out the room's round window, looking things over.

I had a clear view inward to the core. I could see the green curve of our flower's underside, tessellated with rhomboidal green plates. The air was adrift with fruits, leaves, and twigs from the jungle, falling slowly inward toward the core. Swarms of airshrimp fed upon the bounty, with insects in the mix as well.

Several miles further toward the center from us was a different vine, with a flower that was blue with orange petals. Like ours did, the blue flower faced toward the Rind, and it held a vast waterball cupped in its center. I wondered if people lived on that one, too.

Beyond the other flower, the jungle wall stretched still further toward the core, then gave way to sky. With so much life about, I could barely see the Central Anomaly, let alone the Hollow Earth's other side. This land's essential concavity was, however, apparent if I turned my gaze away from the jungle and gazed out across the stupendous ocean, perhaps a match for our Atlantic.

Clouds drifted outward from the center to sink into the sea—parts of it were covered by great fogbanks—while various-size drops of water came loose from the sea and the jungle and fell inward with the jungle's steady drizzle of debris.

Looking outward toward the ocean, I saw something that, by its very familiarity, surprised me most of all: a whale breaching. Due to the distance, I was not at first sure of what I saw. But yes, it was a pod of whales, four huge right whales like the ones we'd seen cavorting south of Bouvet Island. Instead of falling back into the ocean, the whales beat their flukes against the air and made a slow progress inward, their great mouths spread wide to take in airshrimp, insects, and whatever other small fry they met. The whales were perfectly comfortable in the Hollow Earth's low gravity, and as mammals, they had no pressing need for water.

I watched fascinated as the whales cleared out a volume of air that had earlier been hazy with life. They ventured inward almost as far as I was—to the zone where the Central Anomaly's slight attraction began to be somewhat too insistent—and then they turned flukes and beat their way back to sea.

My powder being now quite dry, I reloaded my gun and stuck it in my jacket, which I donned. I decided not to bother with my shirt, boots, or trousers, pulling on instead my *pulpuls*. I had underwear, I may add, to cover my privates. Seela had made off with my knife. Yesterday she'd been deeply impressed by the ease with which the steel blade could cut the *juube* seeds into manageable pieces.

I poked my head into the next cell to see what the old man who lived with Seela was doing, but he too was gone. Neatly arranged in one corner were the sum total of the pair's possessions: a few score small seashells, gnarled bits of wood, crystals, and the domed carapaces of what might have been a tiny lobsters. Each of these trinkets had a hole in it, natural or drilled, and they were threaded onto limp slender cords woven of plant fibers. The fibers crossed each other to form a mesh that held one of the baubles at each vertex. The joint treasury was like a net woven from of the necklaces the flowerpeople wore.

With the soft cell floor to sit or lie on, there was no need of furniture; and with food ready to hand, no cooking or eating utensils were required. I'd noticed two thorn-rapiers in here yesterday, but those were gone. Perhaps the two had gone to the village together.

I resolved to follow. Rather than blundering through the cells again, I would fly. Not letting myself worry about it too much, I donned my airfins and pushed out through the round window. My legs were sore from yesterday's exertions, but after a few kicks they felt right.

I flew out along the vast curve of our flower's outer white petals, then over the petals, and across the flower's yellow center to the village. Striving to be inconspicuous without actively skulking, I landed a hundred feet from the village hexagon's edge and crept forward to peer down.

Blessedly, Jeremiah's corpse was gone. Later I would learn the villagers had spun it off into the sky with no funeral rites at all, and that one of those huge, tentacled nautilus-shell monsters had eaten it. Today the villagers were wandering around sluggishly and at random, feeding on big slices of *juube* they'd gotten from…Seela.

She and old Ogger had set up a business at the edge of the hexagon; using my knife, she'd sectioned and brought in a number of quartered *juubes*, and now she was providing villagers with unlimited *juube* in exchange for the kinds of shells, crystals, and nuts that the flowerpeople prized. As I watched, a grinning man clumsily unknotted his necklace and drew off a large, exotic seed—bright red in color—which he gave Seela in exchange for a fresh slice. Ogger busied his fingers knotting the profits into the nodes of an intricate money net, a smaller version of the one I'd seen in his bedroom.

The powerful *juube* intoxication had calmed the villagers, and they seemed nowhere near so fearsome as yesterday. Yet the memory of Jeremiah's fate made their calm a bit terrible to me. Across the hexagon, I could see Quaihlaihle and Otha sitting face to face in a decorated cell. Eddie mingled freely with the villagers. He was reeling drunk, constantly in danger of drifting off into the sky. Arf was sleeping on the ground near where I lay. The flowerpeople were terrible, but could there not be a place for me among them?

Just then I saw something that fired my will. The slender, agile youth whom I'd seen playing the resonator tube last night—the one whom the crowd had called Yurgen—he was hanging in the air by Seela's booth, talking to her at some length, gesturing with his hands, effusively smiling, and singing to her in a sweet, melodious voice that echoed the enchantment as his performance on the reverb tube. It was time for me to act.

"Ssst. Arfie!"

The dog sat up, sniffed, and looked my way. It was a joy to see his long, toothy grin. I hopped down and embraced him. If I stuck close to Arf, then surely the flowerpeople would do me no harm.

This hope proved all too true. For the next four months I became, in effect, Arf's servant. I was expected always to be near him, and if I were seen to neglect petting and cozening him for any significant length of time, I would be bullied and poked. I came to know the dog's body as well as my own, and his smell became so much a part of my hands that it was unpleasant to bring them near my face. The noise Arf made when drinking water was a particular wonder to the flower-people. During their frequent feasts, they would serve Arf a water glob upon a stretched petal, it being my job to keep the petal tight. The taut membrane amplified the sound of the dog's slurping. Everyone would listen raptly. When Arf finished drinking, Quaihlaihle would drink, and then Otha, and then the rest of us.

Otha of course found our role reversal vastly amusing. "Curry that dog, Marse Mase," he'd call to me with a chuckle. "An be quick about it. Seem like there be some muck down on his foot. Brush that off, boy!" Otha was a royal consort; I was a dog's groom. The sheer absurdity of the situation kept me from taking it much to heart. The overriding fact that I was living with the woman I loved made everything easy.

Yurgen was aware of my blossoming relationship with Seela, and he was jealous. He made a point of mocking my ministrations to Arf. And if Yurgen and I happened to be kicking about in the air at the same time, he always managed to jolt me with his elbow or knee. But if I directly challenged him to a round of fisticuffs, he'd back away, as if our disagreement was a misunderstanding. He wasn't one for a fair fight. At times I even worried my sly rival might find an underhanded way to take my life.

Meanwhile, Seela herself seemed to find Yurgen tiresome. Not that I tried to discuss these issues with her. There were more important things to do when we were alone together.

For his part, Eddie Poe got on well enough among the flowerpeople. Now and then some of the women would force him to engage in sex with them, though he misliked it greatly. His very reluctance served to goad these savage women to take ever more scandalous liberties.

Aside from that, Eddie's life was peaceful. Like me, he abandoned all clothing but jacket and breechcloth, using the jacket to hold those few possessions he still had—paramount among them Virginia's teeth.

He drugged himself regularly with *juube* and, sober or not, passed much of his time writing. Ink and paper had he none: He wrote by scratching with a thorn on the flower walls. The impermanence of this medium troubled him not, for once he'd achieved some lines that he deemed impeccable, he memorized them. His work in progress was to be his epic poem *Htrae*, describing our journey, with meter and rhyme for ease of recall. He recited it to me from the start once every few days, and I confess that some of his felicitous phrasings have found their way into this, my own narrative.

I found myself getting to like Eddie as a friend. Eddie, Otha, and I were all learning a few words of the flowerpeople's tongue, but anything like a long conversation with, say, Seela was impossible. Instead of an elegant flow, communication with a flowerperson was like the passing back and forth of small smudged tokens. Water, Arf, Shellsquid, Me, Flower-leather, *Juube*, You, Fly, Hungry, Queen, Love—the same simple images over and over. In contrast to this, Eddie's speech was, as always, a fount of elegant expression and bold ideas.

He spoke to me often of his distress that he was not back on Earth's surface consolidating his literary reputation. The theme of the double obsessed him, and he had a notion (quite accurately prescient, as events would prove) that there existed some MirrorEddie who even now was taking advantage of all the groundwork Eddie had laid. "My style is his," Eddie said. "And more than that, my myth and my legend. After my work at *The Southern Literary Messenger*, are not my name and character familiar to every cultured American? Have I not made myself into an elemental force of our national literature? And now here am I, living among analphabetic savages with no intellectual companion but a farmboy!"

I attacked him on the last point, and he grudgingly allowed that due to my innate literary gifts and to my habit of wide reading from earliest childhood on, I am nothing like what the word *farmboy* suggests. I reminded him that

I'd studied my uncle's copies of Euclid's *Elements* Kennedy's *Revised Latin Primer*. And to lift Eddie's spirits, I suggested flatteringly that due to my association with him, I was in fact becoming an ever more highly educated man.

Eddie was above all interested in what lay inside the Central Anomaly. The more we stared at it, the more confusing to us it became. The huge pink sparks or discharges that lit up the Hollow Earth all ran through the Central Anomaly, and the air there was filled with glinting blue lights. Otha told us that Quaihlaihle said she had come from this zone, and that she referred to the Central Anomaly as the Gate.

Quaihlaihle's origin was one of the reasons the flowerpeople honored her so. For them, the Hollow Earth's center was a region of terrible awe, a land for the gods and for the dead. Quaihlaihle said she came from a tribe of black gods near the center; she said she'd been carried outward to us by some huge creature, which she called a *koladull*. Supposedly, she'd originally been black-skinned, but out here she'd faded to white. Otha was eager to meet the black tribe in the Hollow Earth's sky, and he supported Eddie's plans to journey to the core.

The flowerpeople's fears of the sky were not unfounded. A major sticking point in any plan to go further inward was the great danger of being eaten by a shellsquid during the long fall to the center. During the four months we spent on the flower, several flowerpeople fell prey to the marauding ammonoids, or *ballula*, as they were called. At unpredictable intervals, one of the great nautilus-like creatures would appear and drag its tentacles over the flower, feeling for prey. As it was easy to see and hear the monsters coming, those who fell prey were generally ill or intoxicated. Of course, one always took care not to sleep in the open. But what could we do if a shellsquid appeared during our proposed tumble to the Central Anomaly? No immediate answer presented itself, and so we lingered on.

Other than chanting and drumming, the only creative activity the flowerpeople engaged in was the weaving of nets. Some of these creations were quite remarkable. Made of long fibers from the stem of our flower, they grew irregularly to immense size, with individually designed patches branching off here and there. Sometimes these nets were left undecorated, to be used as seines to trap a school of airshrimp, which were then eaten raw. Other times the giant weaves were decorated with organic trinkets and set floating as airy ballrooms in which the tribe would dance. And, as I've mentioned, each individual or living group had its own treasure net or money net, to which they attached the bits of shell, bone, plant, or mineral that they particularly valued.

As on Earth, the most acute source of danger was other people.

My biggest source of peril was perhaps the increasingly resentful Yurgen, who became more unpleasant to me every day. And all the while he continued to enthrall the flower-people with his reverb tube. I feared Yurgen might turn the mass of them against me—perhaps to the point of lynching me. My saving grace thus far was that Queen Quaihlaihle valued my role as Arf's groom.

But there were other enemies as well. I'm speaking of the nearest tribe to our flower. They lived on the blue-centered, orange-petalled flower that I'd noticed New Year's Day, some five or ten miles closer to the Hollow Earth's center than us. The blueflower people were in every respect similar to the yellowflower folk, save that their garments were orange and blue rather than white and yellow.

Now and then, a few people would flap from one flower to the other to exchange flower-leather and *juube*, also to swap baubles and to look for mates. Generally, only the unhappiest and least attractive members of our tribe consented to join the blueflowers. Our tribe took great pride in having Quaihlaihle as queen, black Otha as royal consort, and Arf as mascot. The blueflowers had nothing so grand, so I suppose that a conflict was inevitable.

The war started quite suddenly. We were sitting around the hexagon talking and eating. I'd just held the taut petal for Arf to drink, and Quaihlaihle was feeding the dog some airshrimp. With the queen present, Yurgen was holding back from taunting me, instead he was playing a soothing drone upon the great, reverberant tube. Everyone was in a bit of a trance.

Suddenly we heard a discordant noise from above. A party of twenty blue-clad men and women flew down, long thorns at the ready. Before I could really do anything, someone had kicked me in the head and seized Arf. Two others got hold of Otha, who was sluggish from *juube*. Quaihlaihle quickly killed one of her attackers, but then, terribly, someone stabbed her in the neck.

"Run!" screamed Eddie, tugging at me. I hesitated, but Seela was running too, so I took shelter with them in the cells. A minute later the raid was over. Arf and Otha were gone; Quaihlaihle lay dead.

Our flowerpeople began a feverish process of mummification and sky burial. They wrapped Quaihlaihle from head to toe in a money net, and then in petals, sealing them tight with a strong-smelling mixture of nectar and sap. The idea seemed to be that by working quickly enough, they could pass her body off as some kind of seedpod; the plant juices would cover any carrion smell that might lead the harpies or shellsquid to eat her. Two hours after Quaihlaihle died, she was launched. Four of her most faithful subjects flew her so far inward that they shrank to dots; they released her and flew slowly back to our flower, where Yurgen was chanting a hypnotic dirge through his reverb tube.

"*Ahmani tekelili embogolo,*" said Seela. *She returns to the black gods.*

The funeral over, it was time for revenge. We cut ourselves strong fresh *pulpul* fins and picked out the sharpest thorn-rapiers we had in our armory. I drew my gun and checked my powder by firing a test shot into the air. Seela and the flowerpeople were mightily impressed; I would be an important member of our war party.

The reader may wonder at my willingness to risk my life in a dispute among savages, but you must realize how deeply the life on the flower had begun to bore me. *Juube* intoxication was an ever-present temptation, and I had to struggle to keep from falling into the bad habits of Eddie and Pa. I'd already examined and categorized all the dozens of creatures that lived here; I'd tasted the delights of love to satiation; and I'd worn out my brain with facts from Eddie. Now I was happy to have something exciting to do.

As one of the more agile flowerpeople, Seela was in the war party, too. It was to be expected that the pusillanimous Yurgen chose to remain our flower. But I was surprised when Eddie Poe insisted he join our foray. Was it his hunger for experience to write about? In a way, yes: I would soon see that Eddie's aim was to turn our attack on the blueflowers into a safe passage to the Anomaly at the Hollow Earth's core. But for the moment he told us only that he had an idea for an ingenious engine of war.

At Eddie's direction, we gathered fifty of the flower-people's sharpened shell knives and knotted them into one of our precious silk ropes. The flowerpeople were clever at weaving; in a short time, the knives were arranged in a tight spiral along the rope's axis, blades angling out. Eddie now revealed the elegance of his plan, and we cheered.

Two score flowerpeople set off with Seela, Eddie, and me, kicking across the sky toward the hated blue flower. Yurgen, safe in our village green, chanted a march. I was glad to be distancing myself from him.

As it happened, Yurgen had tried to sabotage me as our war party left. He'd darted over to me carrying an extra-large pair of pulpul fins, offering them as if they were a special boon. I'd been about to accept them and use them in place of my regular fins. But Seela struck Yurgen's gift fins from his hands. As they tumbled off, I could see what she'd already noticed. Yurgen had slit the backs of these fins halfway through—so that they'd fall to pieces when I was out on my own in the sky. As always when caught in one of his underhanded tricks, Yurgen had made as if it were a joke. And then, unsmiling, Seela and I launched off.

The flowerpeople in our party were highly animated, roused by the rush to battle. I had a moment of vertigo when we were midway between flowers—what if a shellsquid should come for us here? But I had little time to worry, for the blueflowers saw us coming and a squad of them came rapidly kicking to meet us.

I fired a gunshot to frighten the blueflower party, and then, while our rapiers engaged theirs, Eddie, Seela, and I flew inward past the blue blossom and lighted on the vine upon which the flower grew. No one bothered us. We found the thinnest part of the flower's stem and set to work pulling our bladed rope back and forth, like a team of loggers manning a double-handled saw. The plant stuff was tough, but slowly we made progress. Great quantities of sap oozed forth, lubricating our cut.

In the distance, the air battle raged on with screams and savage yells. As the stem weakened, the great blue flower gradually nodded away from the ocean and toward the planet's center. Massive globs of water were sliding off the blue blossom's surface, gleaming like gems in the air. We sawed like possessed souls. The flower turned more and then, with a great, leisurely rending, tore free. Slowly, slowly, it began drifting away from the vine and inward toward the core of the Hollow Earth!

We caught our breath, abandoned the bladed rope, and flew out to where the battle had been. Disheartened by seeing disaster overcome their home, the blueflower warriors were in full rout. Our rapiers surged after them, stabbing and killing, and taking the dead warriors' necklaces. Figure after figure came swarming out of the blue flower, looking for a place to go. Back on our flower, a battalion of defenders stood ready to demand fealty of all who came to beg for mercy.

"Quick," said Eddie to me. "Let's get inside the blue flower and ride it all the way to the center of the Earth!"

"That's why you had us saw it off!" I gasped.

"Of course. We can't hang here forever, Mason. We've got to press on! My dreams have told me. And remember that Quaihlaihle called the Anomaly the *Gate*. We'll go through the Gate, and back to Earth...or to MirrorEarth. Come!"

"All right," I assented. In the fever of the moment, I was ready for any adventure. "Let's get aboard. Come with us, Seela."

The open skies of the Hollow Earth held such terror for the flowerpeople that none of them wanted to ride the falling blue flower. Scores of the blueflower tribespeople kicked up past us as we made for their home. Seela seemed unsure what we were doing, but I urged her on. We wriggled through the falling flower's ruff of orange petals and kicked across its blue face. A last few stragglers were leaving. The flower would have been wholly deserted, but there, tied to the ground of the empty village hexagon, were two lone figures: Otha and Arf.

We touched down next to them. With the flower in free fall, there was no force to hold us to it; indeed, given that the fluttering blue flower fell through the air a bit more slowly than a compact person, one had to keep kicking upward to remain upon its surface. Once we'd cut Arf and Otha free, we made our way into one of the flower's cells. We drifted about and grabbed hold of some ridges on the soft leathery ceiling of the cell. Arf had grown very fond of me during my period of servitude to him, and he was inordinately glad to see me.

Otha immediately understood Eddie's plan: We'd ride the flower all the way to the center, with the flower a ship to keep us safe from shellsquid. Otha was eager to meet the fabled black folk who lived in what Eddie called the Htraean sky. But Seela was in a frenzy to escape the falling flower and return to the zone she came from. Falling into the empty sky filled her with a terror as great as what we'd felt when the antarctic plain gave way beneath us. I held her tight, trying to calm her. She clawed my face and got loose. Before she was out of reach, I tore off her *pulpuls* to keep her from flying away. A tyrannical act, I admit, but I was desperate to keep her.

Seela ripped a section from the wall that separated our cell from the hexagon, wriggled out the hole, and tried to flap her way toward the Rind by using the scrap of flower-leather she held. All she managed to do was to fall a small distance inward from us. I stuck my head out the hole she'd made and stared up at her. Her smooth face was wet with tears, and she was screaming about *ballula*. A melancholy sight. I ached to help her, but for the nonce she waved off my attempts to fetch her.

After we'd fallen another half hour, Seela seemed to accept that there could be no escaping, although she made it clear that she was furious at me. Otha kicked after her and brought her back aboard. The flower fell and fell, the air beating hard against us. Although the central attractive force within the Hollow Earth was rather feeble, our enormous blossom was massive enough to continue gaining speed in the face of the air's drag. Eddie estimated we'd level out at a speed of a hundred miles per hour, although there was no knowing how he produced a fantastical figure like that. He was a great one for playing the savant.

But even more, Eddie was one for playing the bard. He found our party's plight to be deeply romantic, and he wandered feverishly among the blueflowers' nearby deserted dwelling cells, declaiming new lines for his ever-growing epic poem, *Htrae*. Frequently he'd stop, amend a few of the lines, and start his performance afresh from the top. This grew tedious, and I bade him to stop. Too stimulated to fall silent, he then regaled us with a long tale about the legendary abandoned ship *The Flying Dutchman*, taking a ghoulish necrophiliac pleasure in his detailed evocation of a lifeless, floating ship.

Meanwhile we each ate several big slices of a *juube* that Seela found. I tried half-heartedly to interest her in sex, but she spurned me. Depressed and worried, I ate still more *juube* and sank into a daze. And this we passed some thirty hours of our trip.

I was brought to sensibility by Seela's cries of warning. Just as we'd feared, a giant *ballula* shellsquid was about to attack. The *ballula* was a large one, easily a quarter the size of the blue blossom we hid in. Having expelled enough hydrogen to ballast itself to our speed, it rapidly fastened its whole mass of tentacles to our flower's hexagonal clearing. I should have fled with the others into the flower's far recesses, but the *ballula* so fascinated me that I stayed glued to my spot on the ceiling of the ripped cell at the hexagon's edge, air whistling in at me. The effects of the treacherous *juube* made my plight seem comfortable and interesting, and to be honest, I felt a perverse and haughty pride in refusing Seela's tearful entreaties that I flee to the distant reaches of the flower with her, Otha, Eddie, and Arf.

Intoxicated and alone in my cell, I could see the *ballula's* basilisk eye on a stalk not ten yards distant, but for now it didn't notice me. Between its eyestalks was a long, tapering fleshflap, a kind of nose one might say. Beneath the noseflap was the inhuman beak. Quantities of saliva streamed from the beak's serrations. Ranged tight around the beak were ruffled palps, and beyond the palps were the ninety-odd orange tentacles, smooth as kelp stems, some of them two hundred feet long. The sensitive tentacles whipped and fumbled, forcing their way into cell after cell, feeling and tasting for human flesh. In due time, a tentacle entered my cell. I lay motionless, dully staring as the tapering fleshy limb palpated floor, walls, and finally ceiling.

When the feeler slapped across my face my trance broke. The grooves and ridges of the limb sensed me, and the tip of the feeler began to wrap around my neck. Remembering how Peters had saved himself, I took out his knife and cut off a yard of the feeler tip. The whole tentacle jerked back sharply, and there was a greedy, rapid beating as the *ballula's* beak tore through the thin flowerleather of my cell. The monster's cruel gleaming eye fixated upon me. Fully galvanized, I screamed floridly and dove for one of the cell's exit holes. A tentacle caught my ankle, but I cut that one off too. Moving as fast as I could, I hurried through a random succession of two dozen cells, and found myself with Eddie, Otha, Seela, and Arf, who were huddled in a cell further within. Seela grabbed me and gave me a fierce kiss.

"Mason done made that *ballula* hungry," said Otha.

"Hssst," said Eddie, white with fear. "The utmost silence is required."

The *ballula* tore at our flower for a few more minutes, randomly ripping out the ceilings of cells. Not finding us, it backed off and sped at our flower, ramming it heavily. The shock split our cell's ceiling and the wind sent us flying out like salt crystals from a shaker, one dog and four people, tumbling in concert with the huge blue flower. There would be no time to airfin ourselves to safety. The great nautilus was too close, its tentacles too numerous. Otha flung his bowie knife at the creature—to no effect. Remembering my gun, I drew it and fired its last two shots at the *ballula*, but managed neither to puncture its shell nor to hit any spot that was vital. The bullets disappeared into its furious orange flesh like stones into water.

My mind raced through memories as the great beak approached. I'd stolen this pistol from Lucy Perrow's father in Lynchburg, shot the stableboy with it at the Liberty Hotel, pawned and redeemed it with Abner Levy in Richmond, threatened Eddie with it in Norfolk, recharged it on the *Wasp*, dried the powder in Seela's flowercell, and now all in one day I'd used up its last four shots…for nothing. Cursed weapon!

I flung it into the *ballula's* maw with all my strength, giving the beast a moment's pause. And that would have been the end of me, only now there came a roaring noise as of a huge bonfire. By the time I'd turned to look for the source of the noise, it was upon us, a huge dark shape with flame trailing from it. A beast of some kind, with an upturned mouth wide open in rage—or was it joy? The vast *ballula* twitched galvanically at the sight of the thing and drew in its tentacles preparatory to jetting away. But before it could escape, its giant enemy was upon it. Borne on a flaming jet of gas, the intruding creature flashed forward, seized the *ballula's* bunched soft parts, and yanked the struggling cephalopod right out of its shell. And a moment later the flaming interloper was gone, carrying the doomed *ballula's* body along.

The fleeting glance I had of the attacker gave me the impression of a giant pig's head mounted on a body curved and segmented like a shrimp's. To have a name for it, I called it a shrig, even after Seela told me that her tribe called it a *koladull*. Normally the shrigs fed upon garbage, but they made an exception for *ballulas*, and were known for attacking them and eating them whole.

I would have liked to examine the empty *ballula* shell, but it was quite some distance from us, propelled by leaking gas. We got back into the shelter of our battered blossom and fell uneventfully for another few hours, now and then sticking out our heads to look around.

And what did we see? Though the air of the Hollow Earth is speckled with life, and cloudy in spots, we could discern a great deal. Behind us was the South Hole we'd come through, and the hole's surrounding jungle, and that great inner sea that stretched nearly a third of the way around the inner surface of the Rind. At the edges of the sea were two huge continents, and beyond these continents another ocean. All lines of sight that passed too close to the center of the Hollow Earth were warped, but it looked as if the over-all arrangement of land and water bore a rough and ready resemblance to the patterning of Earth's outer surface.

From our vantage point, we couldn't see directly through the South Hole. It occurred to me to try and see if there was a North Hole, but the confusion at the planet's center obstructed my view.

As we neared the twenty-fourth hour of our fall, the appearance of the planet's center changed drastically. Though we were falling more slowly than before, the center seemed to grow faster than ever, swollen by some miragelike trick of space and light

The blue dots near the center could now be seen to be immense floating waterglobs, jiggling irregularly, about fifteen of them. Otha dubbed them the Umpteen Seas. The seas were arranged as if upon a sphere around the center, a zone in which gravitational equilibrium apparently obtained. The average Umpteen Sea held the volume of one of our Great Lakes or perhaps Lake Geneva.

The region beyond the Umpteen Seas remained visually indecipherable. It was brightly lit, with some stable dark objects and a curious lensing effect about the center, as if a spherical mirror were located there. This was the region whence the continual pink light-tendrils emanated. Something in the tight wrapping of the space near here made me think of a skittles spindle. Seen from the inner surface of the Rind, the view of the Hollow Earth was clear, yet here, near the Central Anomaly, things were as tight and warped as on the girth of a spinning spindle's stuttering tip. As we fell closer to the Umpteen Seas, the inner anomalous zone began looming so insanely large that most of the Hollow Earth's surface was eclipsed. Whichever way I looked, save directly outward, I saw nothing but the jiggling seas, the blotched inner region, and the rubbish around us.

This near to the center, the pink lightstreamers were as all-pervasive as waves in the sea. Each of the streamers heated its own river of air, creating winds that buffeted our blossom this way and that. The air around was filled with other items that had fallen inward from the Rind—stones, twigs, bits of earth, dead animals, excrement. Flocks of birds were feeding indiscriminately on the objects that fell in. Most of the birds were like fist-size hummingbirds, colorful and harmless. There were also a few larger creatures that were not quite birds. These beasts, which Eddie told me resembled Earth's extinct pterodactyls, had scaly skin instead of feathers and huge serrated beaks that were balanced by conelike projections from the back of their heads.

Largest of all were the shrigs, present in great numbers. The youngsters could be as small as a pig or a cow, but the full-grown shrigs were twice the size of whales. Shrigbirds like small terns hopped around on their hides, pecking at parasites. Some of the lice were the size of saucers, and it took several shrigbirds to devour them.

Beating their fantails and their tiny winged legs, the shrigs themselves fed continually, not hesitating to gulp in boulders as well. Their mouths were long, lipless slits—toothless snouts that seemed, as I may have mentioned, always to be smiling.

It was hard to identify these pacific feeders with the creature who'd so savagely devoured the *ballula*. Their segmented, hollow bodies grew more distended as they ate. They ate not by chewing but by engulfing things whole. They made a resonant grunting sound as they swallowed. I later learned that when a shrig was quite full, it would convert much of its food to flaming methane, which it would spew forth in order to fly, cometlike, up to one of the rookeries upon the inside surface of the Rind, which is where the shrigs roosted.

A horde of shrigs fell upon our flower and began chewing it to bits. Inevitably, one of their snouts appeared in our cell. Seela poked it with her thorn and it moved away. Even so, after another half hour, the shrigs had so thoroughly eaten into our flower that they became a menace. A large shrig actually bit onto Eddie's legs, but we were able to pull him from the shrig's toothless maw before its powerful peristalsis had moved the great man into the shrigian gut.

We decided to abandon the blue flower and kick off for the Umpteen Seas on our own. We checked our *pulpuls* and flew out into the air. As long as we remained quite strenuously active, the grazing shrigs were unlikely to eat us. As omnivores, they generally preferred the simplicity of ingesting inert things. But this meant that if we were to sleep while falling through their zone, they would surely eat us. The lion-size pterodactyls were also a cause for some worry. We turned ourselves head inward and began kicking in gravity's aid. Without the great mass of the flower beneath us, we were falling slower than before.

A particularly powerful lightriver flowed past, bouncing me off the hairy, parasite-ridden hide of a nearby shrig. The creature twitched irritably and snapped its tail to move away. Eddie and Seela were nearby, as was Otha, who carried Arf in his arms. I regained my equilibrium, and we continued toward the Umpteen Seas. The gravity gradient was as gentle as it had been in the stagnant zone near the end of the South Hole. It took real work to keep moving inward, but at least the shrigs were thinning out.

As we progressed the air grew brighter and clearer, and I began to feel a rising sense of joy, coupled with an intense sense of affection for my companions. Quite spontaneously we broke into song—a familiar song of the flowerpeople. I'd never been able to get the words straight, but now, all of a sudden, the lyrics poured out of my mouth as if Seela herself were moving my lips. Singing her words, I understood Seela better than ever before. She was more than a beautiful, exotic female, she was a person just like me.

We sang on, and now our words were Otha's; we were singing a lullaby that Turl had used to sing. I felt a deep union with Otha, and then, as the song changed into Eddie's epic poem *Htrae* about our trip, I felt an acceptance and love for him that I'd never had before. I could tell him anything, and indeed I did, letting my thoughts race out into my *own* song that somehow all the others could sing just as fast and as feelingly as I.

Even Arf shared in this mysterious mental union; looking at him, I could actually sense the thoughts and emotions of the dog—the worshipful friendliness he felt toward me, his interest in our flight, his hunger for the meat of a shrig, and under it all, a boundless volume of what can only be called *slack*. No carking, swinking workaday worries for Arf the slacker, who was most truly himself when asleep in a patch of sun.

The streamers coming out from behind the seas were narrow and strong, leaving sharp wakes of heated air. The nearest sea had a big island in it, a turfy ball of dirt whose volume was perhaps one fourth that of the water. I could see small, dark figures where the island met its sea. The black gods. They spotted us, and one of them came moving up.

He had *pulpuls*, but he also had a shiny platform to stand upon. It was like a rounded-off plank or board. The purpose of the board became clear when he managed to station himself in the moving forked crotch of one of the pink lightstreamers passing by. The slightly cupped underside of his board caught the hot airwave, and the black god rode up at us like a man in a lift. He leaned back on his board, deftly exiting the wave a hundred feet from us. It was easy to identify with his movements; it was as if his mind grew clearer to me as he approached.

There were to be none of the communication difficulties we'd had with Seela's flowerpeople—for the boardrider seemed to address us in perfect English. This said—and perhaps it was just an odd trick of my mind—I tended always to hear the speech of the black gods as if they had a Southern black accent like Otha's.

"Welcome there," he said civilly, kicking his way over to us. His *pulpuls* were wider than ours and seemed to be made of leather. The lightriding board, which he now carried like a shield, was of polished shell. "Congratulations for completing your journey! We are honored to have so brilliant a guest as an Edgar Allan Poe. And, Mason Reynolds, we salute your efforts in bringing your party here. Seela, *dmbagolo laaa nuinullee orbaahm.* And, Otha, bro, we be hopin you stay here for good."

It was peculiar how understandably he could speak to each of us—even more peculiar was the fact that when he talked, his face and lips did not move.

"Yeah, Mason," said he, catching my thought. "We black gods are mindreaders. The Great Old Ones got it set up this way. Come on down to where we live, and be our guests." The words came as a silent flow borne on his gaze, and colored, as I say with a black accent.

"Do you hear too, Eddie?" I asked.

Eddie nodded. "What do you call yourself?" he called to the black figure.

The answering syllables formed themselves full-grown in my mind. "We are all one. We are tekelili."

12. Tekelili

We are tekelili. This was the constant theme of our time in the region of the Umpteen Seas. So long as any person is at the core of the Hollow Earth, that person has tekelili. And to experience tekelili is to be imbued with a mental and emotional state of the utmost compassion and understanding. If I can tell you truly that I have tekelili, then I can read your mind.

The tekelili flows from the mighty creatures who live in the zone of the Central Anomaly—which the black gods call the Gate. These wondrous creatures around the Gate are known as the *woomo* or the Great Old Ones. At times the black gods call themselves the people of tekelili. They do this in the same heraldic way that a tribe of snake handlers might call itself the people of the *hiss*.

While I had tekelili, I could sense directly the thoughts of all beings around me—aphids, shrigs, people, black gods, Arf, the Great Old Ones themselves. In immediate practice it meant that I was ever aware of each nuance of everyone's feelings. Note well that this tekelili sensitivity worked not merely on the emotive level but also on the abstract and purely intellectual levels, even to the point where if someone happened to think of a number, I would know what the number was…and they would know that I knew, and I would know *this*, on and on to the point where, as the black gods said, *"We are all one."*

We were all tekelili, living there at the very throat of the maelstrom, between the twin worlds, surrounded by the vasty mentation of the Great Old Ones whose cosmic thought stream flowed profound and unquenchable as a river upon which our thoughts were small eddies.

Our Eddie Poe talked to them most of all; it is thanks only to having absorbed the conversations between him and the *woomo* that I understand the geography of the Umpteen Seas and the Central Anomaly sufficiently well to attempt describing it here.

Suppose that at the Hollow Earth's center there were a large shiny ball. Outside this mirrorball would be the Umpteen Seas, the Inner Sky, then the seas and forests upon the inner surface of the Rind, then the thick crust of the Rind, and then the outer surface of the Earth I came from. Suppose that all of this were imaged within the central mirrorball, so that staring into the mirror one could see Umpteen MirrorSeas, an Inner MirrorSky, a MirrorRind and, beyond the MirrorRind (were the MirrorRind transparent), a MirrorEarth. Imagine all this and then imagine that the central ball is no mirror at all but simply a window between two worlds—an open airy window. This is what is true.

Or again, compare the human race to a race of water-striders darting about on the surface of a sea. Suppose that the striders cannot dive; nor can they jump off the surface any more than we can leave our space. Now suppose that on the sea's surface is a floating wooden Ring. Hydrologic tension makes it easy for the striders to cling to the Ring's outer edge. They find food on the Ring; also do they lay their eggs there. We are like them, living in comfort on our Earth, that is, upon the outer part of the hollow sphere that is our planet.

Drawing the simile further, suppose that a group of striders finds a small gap in the Ring; they wriggle through and explore the Ring's inner edge, which they call their Rind. Understand that these striders are like our party, pushing through Symmes's Hole to reach what we too call our inner Rind.

Were our Hollow Earth to hold nothing but empty air, it would be as if the waterstriders' Ring held simple flat water. But what if the Ring's center holds a maelstrom—a cylindrical tapering vortex tube on whose walls the spiders can move about? And what if, like a cake of ice, the water has a lower surface as well as an upper surface; that is, what if the space in the zone of their Ring has two sides? And be these hypotheses allowed, what follows?

For the waterstriders, the lower surface is an unattainable sheet of space that is parallel and distinct from their own. I say unattainable? Not quite. It is a law of nature that any vortex pushes on till it meets a boundary. Therefore, the Ring's central maelstrom leads down through the cosmic waters, opening out to blend smoothly with the lower surface. To complete the analogy, one must only imagine that on the other surface there floats a circular MirrorRing upon whose inner Rind our intrepid waterstriders may rest themselves before finding their way out through the Ring to its surface.

I fix the image and draw a first conclusion. The waterstriders live as two-dimensional beings—that is, for them space is like a surface. But their space has two zones, an upper surface and a lower surface. The space of the Ring, and the space of the MirrorRing. These two spaces are connected by a vortex. And the boundary between the space of Ring and the space of the MirrorRing is a circle around the narrowest point of the connecting vortex's throat.

We three-dimensional beings live in a world of space. But our space has two zones—one zone contains Earth, and the other contains MirrorEarth. These two Earths are hollow, and a higher-dimensional maelstrom connects their centers. At the midpoint of this higher maelstrom lies the boundary between the space of Earth and the space of MirrorEarth. And rather than being a mere circle, this boundary is a *sphere*. This curious sphere is what the black gods call the Gate, and which I have been calling the Central Anomaly.

Very well then. The Central Anomaly is a sphere at the core of the Hollow Earth. On the outside of this sphere lies my Earth, and on inside of the sphere lies the MirrorEarth. As one might expect, the black gods on the MirrorEarth side have quite the opposite view. They feel the MirrorEarth is *outside* the spherical Gate, and that our Earth is on the *inside*. Which view is correct? Both and neither.

The reconciliation of the paradox lies in the fact that, for a being directly on the surface of that spherical Gate or Anomaly, the sphere looks flat, that is, like a plane, with the jiggling Umpteen Seas and Umpteen MirrorSeas respectively above it and below it, and with Earth's inner Rind above, and the inner Rind of MirrorEarth below. I know, for I passed through that uncanny Gate. And when I so did, my point of view turned inside-out.

Let me give off theorizing and describe the events. As I said, we were greeted by a black god who rode a light tube's energy wave up to us, and when Eddie asked him what he called himself, he replied, "We are all one. We are tekelili."

"Sho," said Otha. "But what you *name*?"

Instead of giving us a word, the man gave us a personal totem image, a stylized picture of himself on his board riding a giant forked lightstream. From then on, when I wanted to refer to him, I had only to think of this image and all the tekelili people there would know whom I meant. To write of him here, I'll say his name was Lightrider.

Lightrider came closer to us, radiating interest and goodwill. He was naked, save for his leather *pulpuls* and a woven leather thong wound around his narrow waist. A dagger of polished shell was clipped to the plait. He had long limbs, and his skin was coal-black from head to toe. He had a straight nose, thin lips, and large gleaming eyes. His teeth were red, like Elijah's and Quaihlaihle's. He reached out and touched each of us in turn: Eddie, Otha, Seela, Arf, and me. He wanted to know our names. Feeling his query, each of us said our name and thought an image that, thanks to tekelili, all could perceive.

Eddie's picture was of himself standing, holding a sheaf of handwritten papers and reading aloud. Writer.

Otha's image was of himself in good clothes with an admiring woman (Juicita?) pressed up against him. Lover.

Seela's picture showed her back home, getting the flowerpeople to give her trinkets for *juube*. Trader.

Arf's image was non-visual; it was a simple distillation of his smell and his bark. Arf!

I hesitated before saying my name and forming a picture of myself. What, after all, was I? A bookworm? A farmboy? An explorer? Seela's man? As I said, "Mason," a terrible image appeared quite unbidden: the image of me in Lynchburg, gold in one hand, gun in the other, turning to fire back toward the stableboy. Killer-thief.

There was no use to try and change it. The whole story was written on my brain for all to see. While I still agonized, Lightrider showed us an image of his home, a green land mass stuck to one of the Umpteen Seas. He set off toward it, bidding us follow him. Kicking with a will, the others flew after him, silently chattering and marveling at the portals that tekelili had opened. Sensing my hesitation, Seela beamed love and forgiveness back to me. I followed.

The closer we got to the Umpteen Seas, the deeper did we venture into the spindle or throat of the spacebridge that stretches between the worlds. Earlier I'd been able to see Htrae—that is, the inner surface of the Rind—in every direction, but now, unless I looked back outward over my shoulder, most lines of sight led to a jiggling sea. The seas danced like slowed-down versions of the bucketsful of water that, on idle boyhood afternoons, Otha and I sometimes used to slop high into the sunny air to watch. Straight inward, past the seas, was the Central Anomaly, a mystery of dark shapes and pink light.

The sea that Lightrider steered us toward must have been fifteen miles long. Just now it was shaped more or less like a giant foot, oblong and somewhat flattened, with a round grassy chunk of island stuck to one end like a heel. But no configuration of an Umpteen Sea lasted long. As we approached, the watery foot stretched, pinched off a toe-glob as big as a city, and then rebounded, forming a kind of huge eyeball with the island as pupil. A little later, another sea's cast-off waterglob splashed into Lightrider's sea and set it shivering from side to side. Washes of water swept across the green island.

"How can you live there without drowning?" Eddie asked Lightrider.

"We sleep in the air, mostly," he said (or thought), forming an image of black gods hanging in midair with their slack arms in front of them like rabbits' paws. "Land's just a place to meet."

The closer to the island we got, the harder we had to kick. Though the gravitational gradient still pointed inward, it was weakening greatly. Evidently, the seas rolled about in a gravitational trough just this side of the Central Anomaly which, once again, the black gods call the Gate. The spherical surface of the Gate was clearer now, by the way. It was tiled with huge, slipperlike dark shapes dotted with points from whence the pink lightstreamers issued. Streamers must have extended to the Gate's interior as well, because the cracks between the dark shapes were very bright.

But again, unless I looked directly inward or directly outward, I saw nothing but Umpteen Seas, the real ones nearby and mirages of them more distant. Two black figures flew up from Lightrider's home island. Like him, they were naked and tekelili, and like him they were glad to see us. One, a woman, imaged herself as Shrighunter. Her totem showed her grinning by the huge dead body of a throatless shrig.

I might interject here that the only natural enemies of the shrigs are the black gods, the flowerpeople, and the *ballula*, who relentlessly prey upon young shrigs in their communal roosts, as if in revenge for the adult shrigs' zest in eating them.

Answering our questioning thoughts, Shrighunter explained that when searching for meat and skins, the black gods would fly or ride out to the zone of the shrigs and kill one. There was less tekelili at that distance from the great *woomo*, so killing a shrig did not cause a hunter the intense mental agony that it might down in the Umpteen Seas, where catching and killing even a fish was rackingly unpleasant.

Shrighunter's method for killing a shrig was ingenious. Holding her knife at the ready, she would draw a big breath and lie still in the path of one of the indiscriminately omnivorous beasts. Likely as not, the creature would gum her down into its maw. Once she was there, she'd cut her way out, severing the shrig's throat as she did so. Shrig meat was very good, she assured us, and all the black gods' *pulpuls* and braided ropes were made of shrigskin.

The second black god was a man whose personal totem was hard to decipher. It showed him surrounded by pink light and by irregular green-brown bulks, still and calm, with the distant Umpteen Seas whirling around at insane speed. One might call him Watcher. He was an imposing man. In strong gravity he might have seemed stubby-limbed and overly fat, but floating here, he looked solid and magnificent.

Lightrider and Shrighunter were in awe of Watcher—in the tribe of the black gods, he was a legendary figure, with them but rarely, bearing firsthand knowledge of the history of the race. He told me that he'd been living in this region for three thousand years.

At first I suspected that Watcher's notion of a year was not the same as ours, which is, of course, a surface-dweller's image of a planet circling a distant sun. But soon I would learn that the black gods' operative definition of a year was equivalent to our own, in that they based it on the annual summer brightening of an open hole at the North Pole. And, still on the subject of age, if the black gods were to be believed, their typical lifespans were three hundred years—so salubrious was the effect of a continual immersion in the aura of *woomo* tekelili.

But how, then, could Watcher claim an age of three *thousand*? He'd achieved his great age by periodically entering a curious zone of slow time near the Central Anomaly. Each generation of black gods had Watcher among them for but a few days. During his last twenty years at the Central Anomaly, and with his mental processes drastically enhanced by full *woomo* tekelili, Watcher had observed a growing lack of balance between Earth and MirrorEarth—and he'd deduced that, by way of capping the lack of balance, a party was coming from the Earth. He'd emerged today to witness our arrival.

Shrighunter was well proportioned, and as we kicked along behind her, Otha stared at her buttocks and formed lustful thoughts that all of us could see. Here was an embarrassing aspect of mindreading. Feeling as if Otha had said something rude, I began thinking apology thoughts over Otha's passionate ones, even though I myself kept shooting glances at Shrighunter as well. Eddie's reaction to these emotions was curiosity and a kind of contempt at the idea of black people having sex. And Seela wondered why I wasn't looking at *her*. The black gods laughed.

"Maybe later," Shrighunter thought to Otha. "You looks long and strong."

"Relax," Lightrider seemed to say to me. "Ain't no use trying to cover things up."

"Being black is a blessing," Watcher said to Eddie. "If you linger, you'll be black, too." He had a grave, erudite style of speech.

Their sea was slowly stretching back into a foot shape, leaving the grassy ball they called home mostly uncovered. We touched down on it where a flock of other black gods rested. A few of the region's iridescent hummingbirds hovered nearby. The island grass was waist-high and tangled, and bore small kernels of grain. It was relaxing to jam oneself into the grass and not always be floating away. The air was perpetually filled with pink streamers here, and their breezes dried the grass where the sea had wet it. Just as I landed, a lightstreamer ran right into me. Although it buffeted me about and made me feel hot and tingly, it did me no harm. The black gods thought welcoming thoughts and said that the light was a good omen.

Within five minutes of landing, I knew the members of the tribe of black gods a hundred times better than I'd gotten to know the flowerpeople during four months. How crude and brutal that old life seemed. I tried to keep this thought from Seela, but of course she saw it. Trying to cover a thought never had any effect but calling attention to it.

Coming to sit by me, Seela explained that I had never gotten to understand the flowerpeople's culture. Looking from inside her mind, I could see that their language had myriads of poetic nuances I'd been deaf to. And the huge, useless trinket-bedecked nets they were forever knotting together—these, I now grasped, these were the flowerpeople's art and literature. To my shock I next learned that till now, for her part, Seela had thought me a poor deprived savage from a distant small flower. Why else would I have known so little of knotting nets? All her friends had mocked her, she now told me, for taking a lowly captive slave as lover simply because she liked my looks. Yet all along she'd known I was good. And now she knew that I was smart. Her only surprise, she told me, was that Arf was so much less intelligent than I. Finally she could see the oddity of my four months' indenture to Arf, which all the flowerpeople had taken as being so obviously a matter of course.

"Dear Mason, you were very patient!"

"It was worth it, Seela, to be near you. Anyway, I like Arf."

Wedged into the grass at our feet, Arf grinned up at me, his light brown eyes mild and lively. "This is fun," he thought to me. "I'm glad. Is there food?"

The black gods had been listening in with interest, and now one of them sent Arf the image of a meaty baglike creature in the grass beneath his paws. Now that it was brought to our attention, we all could sense the thing. It was similar to the sea cucumbers or trepangs which are gathered in the South Pacific for the China trade. And thanks to the strong tekelili here, we could sense that the trepang was sensing us. Arf began to dig, and soon he had it. The tiny terror that the dripping leather bag gave off was no worse, I suppose, than the screeches of a chicken on the chopping block. But the powerful tekelili at Hollow Earth's core made the intimacy of this sensation unnerving. Arf dropped the sea cucumber and took a step back.

"Here," called a black god who lounged near us. I'd already noticed his intense interest in Seela. His icon image showed him riding a light tube and dipping a rack full of dead creatures' flesh into the heat. Smoker. He had a woven basket filled with dried meat, some of it shrig and some of it from these little trepangs. He gave Arf several pieces, laughing to share in Arf's doggy joy. Seela and I received some of the meat as well, as did Eddie and Otha. The shrig was like sweet pemmican, with the meat of the small trepang both tougher and more jellylike. *"Trepang koladull tana'a gooba'am!"* exulted Seela. She recognized both foods, from legend if not from actual contact. She said that the flowerpeople regarded them as the highest and rarest of delicacies: the equivalent, if you will, of our ambrosia. We ate the meats with the grasses' ripe grain, now and then tossing a scrap to the greedy hummingbirds.

I felt like a hero in heaven there, sitting with my loved one. The Sphere of the Central Anomaly loomed nearby like a giant sun. It no longer pulled at us, we were in a gravitational equilibrium whence every direction was up. Here at this balance point I began to feel as if I could sense the very mind of God: intricate, calm, and all-loving.

How was Eddie taking all this? He was overcome with a profound joy far beyond any mad ecstasy he'd ever dreamed to attain. By the time I contacted him, he knew so very much already. It was he who showed me the vast organ-chords of thought streaming from the Great Old Ones who made their home on the sphere of the Central Anomaly. Sensing Eddie's appreciation, the great beings had directed a blazing bright river of pink light directly onto him. Of us explorers, only Eddie had the black gods' ability to channel the tekelili beings' output into imaginable dimensions. Unaided, the complexity of their reality would have left me looking at my hand or wondering what there was to eat. With Eddie I could *see*, I could draw mentally near to the beings of the Central Anomaly, all the while taking in Eddie's commentary as directly as if he were whispering in my ear.

So what are they like, those buried Titans, those gods within the Earth? The answer is at first a surprise, almost cynically ridiculous, though Eddie explained to me that their appearance is a confirmation of what modern paleontological science might have predicted.

In fine, the Great Old Ones are huge versions—remote cousins if you will—of the sea cucumbers we'd noticed earlier. That is, the mighty, tekelili-emanating, light-stream-wielding *woomo* at the Hollow Earth's core are warty, watery bags similar that sailors call trepangs or *bêche-de-mer*. A zoologist would place them in the class Holothurioidea of the phylum Echinodermata, which means that the barrel-shaped holothurians are cousin to such echinoderms as the starfish and the sea urchin.

So humble to see are the Lords of Creation.

I remembered hearing Bulkington and Captain Guy talking of *bêche-de-mer*, telling of how the earliest cruises to the Feejees had gathered hundreds of the creatures, which had then been dried in the sun or smoked over open fires on the beach. Sold in Canton, the best quality *bêche-de-mer* fetches ninety dollars a hundredweight. Their purchasers are voluptuaries who use the *bêche-de-mer* as a tonic and as an exotic delicacy, akin to birds'-nest soup. Bulkington had asserted that when set into hot water, a dried *bêche-de-mer* will permeate the fluid with so marvelous and slippery an edibility that a woman treated to a private dinner of such wonder will surely—but I lose my train of thought, I shy away from our universe's humble mystery: the Titans at world's end are graven not in Man's image, nay, nay, the Great Old Ones are ludicrous slippery sacks. Even so, let me now stress, their minds are clear, wise, and beautiful. Indeed, it was their minds whose emanations I had thought to be from God Almighty!

Examining three Great Old Ones in detail with Eddie, I found them to be enormous thick-walled meatbags proportioned, severally, like a rolling pin, like a Turkish hassock, and like a gourd. All three had flexible bodies that were deeply striated as a sea urchin's shell. The five longitudinal stripes that run along their bodies consist of warty bumps in double rows, the warts the size of small mountains. These warts resemble a starfish's tube-feet and are flexible and roughly cylindrical, with somewhat concave tops. The extremities of the great sea cucumbers' bodies are as two poles: cloacal and ingestive. The cloaca is a thick turned-in pucker, but from their ingestive ends the trepangs evert ten branching treelike limbs of enormous intricacy. The flexible branchings give them an appearance like sprouting yams. The oral fans are used for seining food from the air; each *woomo* periodically drawing its branchings back into its mouth, there to consume what has accreted. The ten fans are taken in turn—as a child would suck its fingers.

More significantly, the branching arms are also used for sensing and for communication. The Great Old Ones' major sensory mode, other than tekelili union, is *electric*. Each of the trees of light that flows out in any direction from the Central Anomaly emanates from one of their mobile tendrils. When I watched attentively, I could readily see that the skeins of light darting through the inner sky were giant ghostly versions of the tekelili beings' fans, which transitioned smoothly from the material to the aethereal.

Eddie Poe reasoned that the dual, mirrored spinning of Earth vis-a-vis MirrorEarth makes the Central Anomaly an endless source of electric fluid. The fluid is absorbed by the swaying mesas of the tube feet on the giant holothurians' sides, and it is released in a continual discharge via their tendrils. Before he changed his mind about the Great Old Ones, Eddie took this to mean that our planet is a giant body, with the *woomo* comprising a galvanically active central brain that benevolently works for the greater good of the whole.

Of the Great Old Ones' inner nature I can give little more than my initial impression: They were serene, active, and filled, I would say, with love for the world and for all the living things in it. And they are not so numerous as one might suppose. The Anomaly is inhabited by at most two or three score of the *woomo*.

Regarding any further understanding of the phenomena we observed, I might suggest that their tekelili mindreading ability may take its physical cause from the higher dimensional nature of the Central Anomaly. An equally odd physical effect obtaining at the throat of the bridge between the worlds is *timelessness*. Relative to a mind on the Central Anomaly, Earth and its Rind are moving with immense speed. But so strong is the central tekelili that nothing on Earth goes unnoticed.

I recall the words of a hymn: "A thousand ages in Thy sight, are like an evening gone." How to fit such majesty into my small mind…and how to tell of it?

At the very peak of our first union with the great *woomo* at the Hollow Earth's core, Eddie and I were able to see out through them. That is, I could see out through the Great Old Ones' all-probing eyes of light, and into all of Earth, MirrorEarth, and their paired Hollow interiors. I could sense each sentient creature.

And as I groped for someone who thought of *me*, I came in contact with dear Pa.

Pa was drunk. It was evening; he was standing in a Lynchburg graveyard, very sad. Through his eyes I could see the hills that held the Perrows' house, St. Paul's spire, and Sloat's Liberty Hotel. That was in the background, but in the foreground was a gravestone that said:

MASON ALGIERS REYNOLDS
FEBRUARY 2, 1821 - MAY 1, 1836
"WHAT LAUGHING HEART HAS DIED IN VAIN"

Before the picture wholly dissolved in Pa's helpless tears, I called Eddie to share and verify the melancholy epitaph. Me dead on May 1, 1836, the very night I'd robbed Sloat and shot the stableboy? How, then, had I died?

Another mystery followed right away, for now Eddie drew me to a vision of his own: of himself and Virginia settled in New York City in a small house with Mrs. Clemm and two boarders. We saw through Eddie's eyes; we saw his delicate, ink-stained hands working at the ending of his novel-length sea-adventure. Now he squared together the manuscript and we could see the title page, which read: *The Narrative of Arthur Gordon Pym of Nantucket.* This other Eddie's gaze lifted from the paper to rest on happy Virginia, sitting by the window, singing a lullaby to a kitten in her lap. A gentle spring sunset was in progress outside.

Me dead and Virginia alive? Yes, yes, but it was MirrorPa at MirrorMason's grave and MirrorEddie dreamily admiring his MirrorVirginia. These images came not from Earth but from MirrorEarth! Working together, Eddie and I moved our concentration to the line of force in the lightstream issuing from the tubefoot radially opposite from the one that had led us to MirrorLynchburg and MirrorGotham. Back, back, back to Earth.

Here things were very different. Pa thought of me still, but with disappointment and loathing. I was the killer-thief ne'er-do-well who had forever left town. After stealing the gold, murdering the stableboy, and becoming involved in

211

a slave rebellion, I had counterfeited bank notes and taken refuge on the high seas. Pa was sitting on his porch at home. It was dusk, Luke and Turl were with him, and they were slowly talking about the lien on Pa's property and about the good times before the boys had gone.

I showed this to Eddie, too, and he showed me that on our native Earth Mrs. Clemm was still in Baltimore, alone to wonder and to grieve.

If we'd ever supposed that Earth and MirrorEarth might be identically the same, we were quite wrong. Indeed, our journeys and investigations made it impossible for the two worlds to match.

While the tekelili beings revealed these things, I was still sitting on the grass with Seela. Following my thread of attention, she could see the Great Old Ones too. She found them grotesque and menacing. Giving me a poke and a shake, she brought my attention back to the grassy field we sat in. Eddie wandered out of sight over a hillock, a stream of light still flowing down on him. Arf remained at my feet, still grinning—in his own way just as wise as any giant holothurian.

Before retrieving me, Seela had been in contact with a black god. This slender woman—we called her Jewel—bore the mental icon of a complex, glittering crystal floating in black night. She wore numerous lovely necklaces featuring large, brilliant, pentagon-faceted gems, unnaturally heavy, and the size of grapes. She was interested in trading a necklace with Seela. She was also offering Seela some special dye for coloring her teeth red. For the decorations on Seela's necklace were not all that the delicate Jewel was after—but here modesty must draw a veil.

§

"This be the best, huh, Mason?" said Otha when our ensuing revel with the black gods was done.

We were lying on our backs side to side: Shrighunter, Otha, Jewel, Mason, Seela, and Smoker. Seela now wore one of Jewel's necklaces in place of hers—and her teeth were ruby red. The long-lasting dye was squeezed from a musky ambergris found within the bodies of shrigs, and was a key tribal marker for the black gods. Jewel had dyed Otha's teeth red as well, but I'd declined the honor. Arf had wandered off while we disported ourselves, and Eddie remained out of view, in lonely mystic communion with the giant sea cucumbers.

"It's very nice indeed," I agreed. "Do you miss Quaihlaihle, Otha?"

"Quaihlaihle bossy and she too white," said Otha, his newly reddened teeth flashing. "Give me a black woman any day. Say black—you lookin kind of dusky, Mason. You and Seela both."

Earlier my skin had looked pale, or even paper-white, in the bright pink light, but it was indeed beginning to appear… dusky. I held up my arm and stared at it. Could the energetic Jewel's color have rubbed off on me? Of course not. Was it just that my eyes were tired from the glare? Why *must* the trepangs train the lightstream on us so?

"The *woomo* always shine the light on us when we make love," Jewel told me via the tekelili channels of thought. "Be glad. The light is good; it makes your skin dark and strong. You look better already. You sure you won't let me dye your teeth? The shrigs refine out a juice from the fangs and claws of those redclaw beasts—its dye, and we find it stored up in lump in the middle of a shrig's brain."

"Only gods are fit to touch the redclaws," thought Seela to me, smiling and feeling her teeth. "I am highly honored."

"Beautiful," I said courteously. "But not for me."

I now understood why Elijah and Quaihlaihle had looked white. The black gods were, strictly speaking, as white a race as the flowerpeople. It was only their constant exposure to the intense light of the Central Anomaly that kept them black! Or, it now occurred to me, one might equally well say that that the flowerpeople were, strictly speaking, black, except that they faded to white when they stayed away from the pink light.

Something amusing occurred to me.

"Eddie!" I called. "Are you nearby? Come here so we can see you."

The grasses shook, and a small man appeared, black as a raisin. Solitary Eddie had absorbed more of the light than any of us. Indeed, a steady stream of pink light was still cascading down over him, fluttering his fine hair. Eddie Poe! With his delicate features, he looked for all the world like a gentleman's personal manservant.

Seeing me see him, Eddie saw himself and screamed in horror. "Oh no!" cried he. "I won't be made into a Hottentot! We've got to get out of here, Mason! We've got to get white!" The depth of his anguish was easily apparent. Edgar Poe feared entombment and heights and women's genitals—all these he'd had to face during our journey, and he'd borne it. But his fear of blackness and of slavery was even greater. Being turned black was driving him into a frenzy unlike any I'd seen before.

Seela and the black gods were wholly unable to understand Eddie's passionate aversion to what they considered a simple state of good health. I could understand, but—to tell the truth—as a farmboy I'd never felt as fully white as city folk like Eddie. If being in heaven meant being black, then so what? At least we were here. Rather than gloating extravagantly, Otha contented himself with a few simple witticisms at Eddie's expense.

"Now you black, you be dumb too, hey Mist Poe? You gonna forget how to write? Gonna have white folks read you the Bible?"

"Don't, Otha," I murmured.

Eddie screamed curses at the Great Old Ones till they took the light off him, and then he floundered past us and dove into the Umpteen Seas. He stayed in the water a long time, swimming about and rubbing himself, his mind a frozen blank. The black gods giggled and began to chat.

Smoker and Shrighunter told Otha about how they'd caught their last shrig, while Seela and Jewel discussed their new necklaces. Seela explained what each of her threaded trinkets denoted—each stood for a state of mind or for a historical moment. Jewel began showing Seela how she wove plant fibers into little nets to attach her oversized gems to the necklace cord without having to drill holes in them.

"Where do the crystals come from?" I asked the trim and lovely Jewel.

"They're shit from the *woomo* eating shrigshit after they eat our shit," she responded—an answer rude and confusing until she showed me the images to explain.

The explanation involved another geography lesson.

The Central Anomaly is gravitationally "uphill" from the Umpteen Seas, as is the Rind. The Seas form a kind of gutter around the Central Anomaly; they lie at the very bottom of every unimpeded fall. Therefore nature would seem to dictate that it is the Seas' natural state to be choked with crustal debris. But in fact the Seas are as clear as spring water. This is due partly to the alchemy of the Seas' delicate plant and animal life, partly to the Great Old Ones' judiciously aimed light rays, and in no small measure to the efforts of the black gods, who haul debris from their seas as punctiliously as any farmer expunges stones and brush from his laboriously fructified terrain. If it had not been for the traditionally practiced custom of shrigshitting, as Jewel called it, the Umpteen Seas would have been foul puddles, dangerously jostling with muddy rocks.

For untold thousands of years, the black gods and their progenitors have been hauling rubbish out of the Umpteen Seas. A few choice tidbits are carried in to the Great Old Ones, but most of the debris is ported back outward to the zone of the shrigs. The omnivorous shrigs who frequent this zone will eat anything they can swallow: animal, mineral, or vegetable, living or dead.

The shrigs alternate between vacationing amid the Umpteen Seas, feeding in the jungles near the South Hole, and mating in their roosts upon the northern zone of the Rind, there giving birth and raising their young. These huge rookeries consist of caves in the walls of volcanic cliffs. The shrigs have no fixed migration schedule, that is, individuals come and go as they please, all year long.

How do shrigs travel? I think I mentioned earlier that, as a shrig eats, its gut cooks some of the food into methane gas. When the beast is full, it releases the gas, striking flints to set the gas aflame. The flints are gripped by prehensile extrusions of the shrig's muscular anus. As the shrig rides its flaming jet outward to its nest, a certain amount of debris escapes with the gas.

"So your jewels fly out of the shrigs' butts with the flaming gas?" I asked. It was wonderful to be sharing thoughts with these two beautiful women, even though the thoughts be of excrement. A huge Umpteen Sea hovered near ours, and the light from the Central Anomaly was strong and pleasant.

"More circling around than that," said Jewel thoughtfully. "More odd." She showed us further images. A certain proportion of the particles that leave the shrig have sufficient velocity to shoot past the zone of the Umpteen Seas and into the Central Anomaly. These remnants contain compounds of the incredibly dense matter found within the Hollow Earth's crust. It is primarily for these dense nuggets that the Great Old Ones comb the air with their vast fans. And when a *woomo's* slow bodily processes have fully processed such a nugget, it has been transmuted into the rare and potent gem which the black gods name a *rumby*. The process is perhaps analogous to the way in which geological forces squeeze jungle wrack into coal, and coal into diamonds.

"So they're not really shit at all," I said to Jewel.

She laughed. "I ain't sure *what* they are. They pretty, and they got power, and the *woomo* make them. Nobody knows exactly why."

"What kind of power?" I asked.

"Tekelili," said Jewel concisely. "Better than that, if you got a rumby, you can make a shrig or a ballula obey."

"And you fly near the Central Anomaly to look for the rumbies?" I asked Jewel. "Is it dangerous to go in there?"

The graceful, acrobatic Jewel smiled. "First of all, I don't find the rumbies. The rumbies find me. Like I said, they got tekelili. Deep down, they alive. And we don't call that spot no Central Anomaly. We call it the Gate. Some people go in there and they don't come back. Maybe they on the other side."

"Do the Great Old Ones eat people?" I asked.

"Naw," said Jewel. "The tekelili of you dying would hurt them to much if they killed you. They even more sensitive than we are, cause the tekelili is stronger near the Gate. We do carry some dead things up for them to eat. They like the food, but they don't like us to stay in there. They'll grab you with their branches and throw you out."

"What's it like near the Gate?"

"You can get real confused, and you can get stuck. When I go in there prospecting for rumbies, I move *fast*. But no matter how fast I go, my friends out here think I'm gone a year, or even five or ten. Watcher likes doing that. He goes in and he balances on the exact middle of the Gate till the Great Old Ones throw him out. He says he was born three thousand years ago."

"What's a year again?" asked Seela, quite unclear on this notion.

"Look," said Jewel, pointing out toward the Rind. Due to the odd spindling of space near the Central Anomaly, our view of the planet's inner surface was quite distorted. It was as if I was looking through a large lens that squeezed the whole planetary surface into a broad disk over my head. The edges of the disk were fuzzy, with faint mirage images beyond them. What we saw was like a round flat map of the Earth's interior, the land that Eddie called Htrae. I'd had occasion to look at it earlier, of course, and I noticed now that the disk had rotated from its original position. Listening in on my thoughts, Jewel explained that the Htrae disk rotated roughly once per full period of sleep and wakefulness, that is, once per day.

Seela had the flowerpeople's wholly chaotic notion of time, and found even the idea of a day confusing. Jewel went on to explain that a year was made of 365 days and that one could tell what time of year it was by looking at the North or the South Hole.

The North Hole! Though I'd often wondered if such a thing existed, till now I'd been unable to look for it, what with the Central Anomaly being in the way. But now, down in this space spindle that bent light rays like a lens, I could see our Hollow Earth's entire inner surface, and sure enough, it had two holes in it, each about the size of a silver dollar held at arm's length.

The South Hole was a clearly demarcated circle set into a big patch of green jungle—this was the opening that my party had made. As the time of year was now, so far as I could reckon, early May (I believe now that the date must have been May 1, 1837, the anniversary of MirrorMason's death on MirrorEarth), this meant that the antarctic day had shrunk to only a few hours of sunlight. It was not surprising therefore that the South Hole was quite dark, with only a faint reddish glow from its walls' molten falls of lava.

The North Hole was to be found in the midst of a great blue sea on the Rind's inner surface. As it was approaching summer in the north, the hole was lit with bluish light— seemingly from the open sky. The water around the hole glowed blue-green with light as well. The North Hole was a vast maelstrom, faintly dotted with bits of pack ice sucked in from Earth's outer surface. Another great discovery! And none of our explorers had known of this polar maelstrom, no more than they'd known of the hole beneath the antarctic ice.

I strained my eyes, trying to confirm that one really could see clear through. Was that not a bit of the sun's disk that I saw through the North Hole? Had we but known! With the northern hole wide open, our trip into the Hollow Earth would might have been easier, had we taken our balloon north instead of south…and had we been able to cross the arctic pack ice around the pole, and had we been willing to endure the terror of floating down the wind-torn throat of the North Hole's maelstrom vortex. Food for thought.

Making out the details was complicated by the fact that at all times the great *woomo* kept a steady barrage of pink lightstreamers going, with a special concentration of the streamers precisely at the North Hole. I am sure that some of the streamers went clear through to join the shimmering curtain of celestial light that the Esquimeaux term Oomoora's Veil. By sending lightstreams out through the North Hole (and, now that my party has reopened it, the South Hole as well), the Hollow Earth's Great Old Ones put themselves in touch with the solar system at large.

By way of answering Seela's question of what is a year, Jewel now spoke of how brightness moves back and forth between the two great holes. Seela, who had never seen either hole from her flower, found this quite amazing and wondered what lay outside the holes.

"My friends and I come from the outside," I announced. Perhaps with the North and South holes visible before us, Seela could now understand what I'd unsuccessfully tried to tell her several times before. There was some kelplike seaweed stuck in the grass near us, and the leaves bore hollow, round flotation bladders. I fetched one of the pods and showed it to my two female friends. "The planet is like this hollow ball," I said. "I come from the outside, and now we are inside." Using the tip of Peters's knife, I cut north and south holes in the bladder. "This is where we came in." Holding the ball in one hand, I made a fist of my other hand and put it out at arm's length. "Imagine light coming from this hand. Sometimes the hole points toward the light, and sometimes it tilts away. Back and forth. That's what makes a year."

Neither of them truly understood, but before I could go on, we were interrupted by the return of Eddie Poe, naked save for a breechcloth and still completely black.

"It won't wash off," he complained. "Realizing that, I half hoped to drown myself, but I am too exceptional a swimmer to stay under. And with those evil giant trepangs gloating over us—no, it cannot be endured. Mason, we must press *onward*." I knew that *onward to MirrorEarth* was what he meant.

"I like it here," said Otha. "I plannin to stay. Gonna go hunt us some shrig."

"I like it too," I told Eddie. "Can't you see that this is heaven? Even if I were willing to leave, which I'm not, I don't see how we could ever fight the gravity all the way back out. It's at least three thousand miles back up. And even if we were going to try to go to MirrorEarth, which we aren't going to, we'd have to start by finding a way through the Central Anomaly." Poor MirrorPa. I wondered how exactly MirrorMason had died. Nobly, I hoped. Surely MirrorPa would recognize me, and toast my resurrection if I made it to his farm. And what a thing it would be to see MirrorVirginia, and to watch Eddie hatch schemes with his double!

"Aha," said Eddie, sensing my interest. "Let me show you what I found!" Eddie fed me an image of a shining object, shaped like a fried egg, drifting beneath the waters of our Umpteen Sea. The entire disk-shaped object was no more than forty feet across. The egg's central "yolk" was a hemisphere some fifteen feet in diameter, and the surrounding disk of "eggwhite" added perhaps twelve feet on every side. It seemed a bit like the thing I'd seen when our iceberg broke up as we fell through the hot center of Symmes's Hole. Or maybe not. When I sought to peer deeper into Eddie's mind, I was blocked by his inner voice chanting verses from a poem he called "The City in the Sea."

> No rays from the holy Heaven come down
> On the long night-time of that town;
> But light from out the lurid sea
> Streams up the turrets silently—

My impression was that Eddie had been driven into a fugue state by the shock of his mad mood swings—from the pantheistic ecstasy of union with the Great Old Ones to the shocked despair of learning he was black. In any case, the black gods recognized his image of a skirted metal hemisphere; they knew the object well.

Cheerfully acquiescent to Eddie's desire to salvage the shiny fried egg, they accompanied Eddie, Seela, Otha, and me as we flew out over their sea and dove into the water some distance from their island. I made sure I knew which way the surface was, and then I kicked down into the clear water, keeping my eyes wide open. Refracted pink light filled the water; fish swam this way and that. Further down I could see something glinting—a craft shaped like a round cup turned over on a saucer. Then I was out of breath and had to kick for the surface.

Due to its weight, the fried egg tended to drift to the sea's center, but it developed that the black gods occasionally made a sport of hauling it up. They called it a *veem*. It seemed utterly impervious to rust or to erosion. I might have thought it was some unkown metal alloy, but it felt a bit too slippery for that. Could it possibly be a shell of some kind, or a seed pod, or some curious enchanted animal in a state of hibernation? But it showed no responsiveness at all, nor did I sensed any tekelili from it.

The black gods said it had been here for centuries, and that each time they fetched it out of the water, it was as bright as ever before. Seeing our continued interest in it, they contrived to get some of their braided ropes fastened to holes in the "white" of the fried egg, and they pulled it to the water's surface.

As the fried egg rose, Eddie told me it was his opinion that the Great Old Ones had ridden the egg here from some distant star. Now that they'd turned him black, he thought of them as malign and evil, so it was therefore comfortable for him to regard them as something external to the order of nature as it should be. The egg broke free of the water.

Eddie and I splashed over and tied my silk rope through holes in the egg's rim to help the black gods pull it free of hydrologic tension. As I say, although it had the gleam of metal, the rim's substance had the slippery feel of oilcloth. Etched onto the rim was a filigree of hieroglyphs too odd to decipher. Or perhaps the patterns weren't etched on. Perhaps they were spots within the substance of the rim—like the dots on some seashells. I couldn't decide if they were meant to be images or not.

The whole group of us pulled the gleaming fried egg through the air to a spot comfortably near the island's grassy ground. The craft had thickly glassed portholes and a hatch that stood open—although once again, it wasn't certain that the portholes were in fact filled with glass. In all of its aspects, the fried egg—or *veem*, as the locals called it—had an ambiguous quality of possibly being a naturally grown form rather than being a crafted artifact.

The hatch had straight sides and a rounded top, like the arched entrance to a companionway. There was no door or hatch-cover to be seen. A great amount of water was still lodged within the egg. The black gods showed us how to coax the water out and how to tether the thing to the grasses. As I said, they hauled the thing from the water once or twice a year for idle entertainment.

The inside of the ship was fully gutted. There was a shattered stand that must have held a seat; also, there was an alcove that could have housed bunk beds like those on the *Wasp*. Behind the alcove was a bulkhead sealing off a third of the craft's hemispherical bulge—I imagined that within the sealed compartment there might be a stove to produce hot air. The craft had a porthole on either side and a long, transparent view port right in front of where the seat had been. Beneath the view port was a slanting panel with the broken-off stub of what must once have been a control, perhaps akin to a tiller. Watcher said that the black gods' ancestors had broken off any pieces they could use for ornaments.

The cabin was adorned with numerous patterns, or pictograms, or hieroglyphs—as, for the sake of simplicity, I'll call them. A circular frieze of them wound around the walls, and hieroglyphs were also embossed beside the single vandalized control. The images showed the fan-capped barrels of miniature Great Old Ones, and exemplars fo that poor forked radish, Man. Had humans and the Great Old Ones used the *veem* craft together in ancient times?

Eddie was enchanted. "What an incredible sense of antiquity," he mused, running his black finger over the slippery walls that weren't quite metal. "Do you feel the hush, Mason? It's like the crypt of a cathedral, or a tomb in the heart of the great pyramid. The profaned temple of an unknown, raving god. Plato's myth of Atlantis—perhaps it is no myth at all."

In a fever of curiosity, Eddie began peering at the hieroglyphs and muttering to himself, his mind seething with symbols and theories. After a half hour of this, the black gods grew bored and drifted away. I stayed with Eddie, curious to see where his investigations would lead. Arf was here too, though Seela was off with the gods.

I dozed off, and when I awoke, Eddie was on tiptoes by the open hatch.

"See, Mason, see!" He dragged his fingers along the ceiling with a swift, hooking motion and the walls around the hatch grew together, covering over the hole. Another movement of Eddie's hand, and the door was back open.

"I triumph!" cried Eddie. "I care not whether my impostor's work be read instead of mine. I have stolen the golden secret of the Egyptians. This door shall take us to the MirrorEarth and to the charlatan MirrorPoe. I will indulge my sacred fury!"

13. Through the Spindle

Eddie spent the next six weeks in the fried egg. He was fascinated by the continuing puzzles of the hieroglyphs, and the larger question of what manner of artifact or fossil or seedpod the fried egg *was*. He also liked being set apart from the rest of us. Initially he might have had the notion that staying in the fried egg would help him get white again, but in fact the pink light could always find its way in through the ship's windows and branch into every crevice of the cabin. Tired of having to drift off into the sky and be brought back to ground, Arf spent much of his time in Eddie's egg or in the tangled grasses beneath it. Now and then an unexpected surge of water would wash over the land, and Eddie and Arf would dog-paddle above their home until the water sloshed away. So far the egg's tethers had held.

Occasionally I visited with Eddie, but most of the time Seela, Otha, and I were having fun playing with the black gods. We shared thoughts, we made love, we dove and swam in the lovely clear seas, Lightrider gave us lessons in riding the heated light tubes, and we helped with the endless task of hauling debris up to feed to the shrigs. The next stage of my journey began late in the month of September, 1837.

Seela and I had just shared a particularly romantic interlude, and had then fallen into that delicious slumber that is the consequence of passion well spent. We woke to find that as a result of a tekelili agreement, our close friends among the black gods had gathered to take us shrighunting. As the supplies of leather and dried meat were down, it was decided that we'd try to kill two shrigs if we could—though killing more than one per day was difficult. Usually, the first scent of blood sent the herd fleeing halfway around the Umpteen Seas.

We gathered to bathe ourselves and to eat some of the sweet, chewy grain from the grasses. Shrighunter had been schooling Otha in her craft's minor arcana, and he was ready to put his new knowledge to the test. He asked for the loan of the big knife I'd gotten from Peters, and I gave it. We all joined hands then, and Watcher put himself in contact with the network of the Great Old Ones. More so than the other black gods, Watcher had Eddie's heightened ability to channel the thoughts of the mighty *woomo*. Sputtery pink light played over his patrician features, and the knowledge flowed among us. There was a herd of twenty shrig fifteen miles out from us in the direction of the North Hole.

As well as shrigskin *pulpuls*, we each had a thorn-rapier and a polished piece of *ballula* shell. Despite the continual foraging of the shrigs, all kinds of debris falls into the seas. *Ballula* shells are deemed to be the best material for making what the black gods call lightboards, these being the little platforms on which they ride the spreading heat of the branching tubes of pink light. The cupped, pearly inner surface of a *ballula* shell is ideal for catching the pressure of the heated air. Each lightboard has a footstrap and is shaped like a lozenge bounded by two circular arcs. Even a small *ballula* shell can be cut up into as many as fifty lightboards.

Usually, it took a little time for each member of a hunting party to catch a good lightstream, but with Watcher here, the Great Old Ones were unusually helpful. Tube after tube of hot, forking light washed past our island, strong and steady as ocean waves.

Seela and I kicked up and caught a tube together. Under Lightrider and Smoker's tutelage, we'd gained skill, though I still knelt on my lightboard rather than standing on it. Seela hooked her foot into her strap and slid this way and that, carving airy curlicues around me.

Soon the shrigs were visible in the distance as distended larval forms with busy heads. We rode a little closer and joined the other hunters waiting there. Shrighunter and Otha had swathed their bodies in thick layers of damp kelp. Our hunting strategy was simply to kick our way close to the shrigs and there to leave Otha and Shrighunter like ordinary rubbish bundles. If all went well, a pair of shrigs would swallow them whole and they'd cut their way out.

"I knows where, but how do I knows *when* to cut the shrig's neck?" Otha was asking Shrighunter when I arrived. At this distance from the Central Anomaly, the tekelili min-dreading ability was terribly weak. We had to put our heads right by the black gods' heads to be able to understand them.

"Do it as soon as you can," said Shrighunter. "If you wait and I cut first, your shrig's gonna panic and fly away. Some of us get lost for good that way. If you do get swallowed all the way down, you cut yourself an airhole in the shrig's side as quick as you can. Make it a small hole. And squeeze yourself out fast."

Seela, Watcher, and I bore the wrapped Shrighunter while Lightrider, Jewel, and Smoker handled Otha. Watcher was in rollicking good spirits; it was rare for him to spend this much time outside of the Central Anomaly.

"Your visit is signal event," he said, pushing his head against mine. "You've put the torch to symmetry. You're dead on one Earth, and alive on the other." With MirrorMason dead, I, like a vampire, had no reflection. And somehow this was opening new possibilities for the dwellers of the Hollow Earth.

"Are there two of you?" I asked Watcher.

"Indeed there are," he said. "Today, the other Watcher, like me, is out hunting shrigs. But he doesn't have, the companionship of you and Seela." Watcher ran his thick, stubby hand across my shoulders and grinned at Seela's. He was admiring us. "Steadily the twinned worlds diverge. You'll build up the effect when you go to MirrorEarth with Eddie. The *woomo* feel your actions will eventually bring on a long-awaited blooming."

By then our powers of tekelili had faded too much for me to query further. This far from the Central Anomaly's influence, space opened back up, and I could see out toward the Rind in every direction except for the inward one. It was marvelous to be floating in this huge round sky, with the great North Hole maelstrom high above me like a distant navel of the world and the gleaming Umpteen Seas beneath my feet.

Three shrigs were nearby, watching us like cows waiting for crabapples. Cows twice the size of whales. From long habit, they were eager for the tasty dense waste the black gods brought them. One of them beat its tail to come closer, all the while eying our heavy kelp bundle with interest.

Watcher said something to Shrighunter in their own tongue, and then we flung her free.

Off to my right, the other party released Otha, who was wrapped like Shrighunter. We kicked back a few hundred yards; a shrig's death throes were said to be dangerously violent, similar in nature, I presumed, to a harpooned whale's flurry. Otha disappeared down the first shrig's maw, and the second shrig ate Shrighunter. The unfed third shrig sounded a grating oink of disappointment.

All at once, the second shrig's tiny winged legs began fluttering in spasmodic agony. It snapped its body, slapping its fan-tail against its underside with a sound like an iceberg falling into the sea. The force of its tailsnap drove it away from us. Its gaping mouth was bellowing a hideous cry of anguish that stopped—all at once. A balloon of blood appeared at the doomed beast's slit throat and then the powerfully kicking body of Shrighunter could be seen heading out into safe air. The dying shrig lashed its body this way and that, its opened windpipe whistling a cracked shrill tune.

I looked for Otha's shrig, but it was gone. Otha had been too slow! The other hunters were pointing outward toward a dwindling black speck whose vibrating tail suddenly blossomed with bright flame. Otha's panicked shrig was going to jet its way clear back to the shrig-nests on the Rind's inner surface.!

Moving quickly, Lightrider got on a lightstream and shot out after the fleeing shrig. It was pulling steadily ahead of him, but then, all at once, the flame-tipped black dot exploded in a great puff of fire. Shortly there came the boom of the blast and a shockwave carrying chunks of debris.

With the lack of tekelili, nobody could tell me what was going on—and then they'd all headed outward on their boards. Unsteadily, I mounted my curved shield of *ballula* shell and tried to ride out too, but I kept losing control and falling off. Finally, I put the board on my back and furiously kicked my *pulpuls*. I had to save Otha!

Just when I thought my heart would burst from exertion, I heard laughter above me. Looking up, I saw Seela, the black gods, and Otha—a bald Otha, with his hair and eyebrows singed off. Lightrider, Watcher, and Jewel had the blasted carcass of Otha's shrig in tow. About a third of it had been lost in the explosion.

This far from the Central Anomaly I could no longer sense the mentations of the black gods at all. Without tekelili, their spoken speech seemed an arbitrary system of grunts and squeals, like any human language. But Otha and I knew the same tongue.

"I seen a ghost in there, Mason," called Otha. "I seen Quaihlaihle inside of that shrig! Listen here, cause can't none of these others understand me. First that shrig swaller me and I get all twisted around, and then afore I can cut its throat, it done swaller me *all the way down*. It was all full of fart an rocks an rotten junk in there, Mason, and worst of all, I done rubbed up against Quaihlaihle. Don't ask me how I knowed it was her, but I did. She was rotted and dried up like she been in there for weeks. That perfume the flowerpeople put on her didn't keep no shrig away at all. It was nasty. Quick as I could, I cut a big hole in the side of that shrig. And then, oh Lord, all that fart from inside went on fire and the shrig blew up like a bomb!"

"Good God, Otha! I thought you were done for!"

"I was safe in the center of the blast. Like a lamb of god. And look here, I still got yo knife!"

I began to laugh, and bloody Shrighunter whooped for joy. We'd slain two leviathans today.

It was easy towing the carcasses down to the Umpteen Seas, as they were falling thither anyhow. Quantities of ptero-dactyls and hummingbirds shrieked about, snatching off scraps of flesh. The hummingbirds had iridescent blue bodies, with red markings at the throat. The pterodactyls were brown-ish-green. The tekelili intensity of the birds' small-brained greed was in some way amusing. On our approach, scores of black gods arrived to help skin and butcher the shrigs in midair at a spot near the watery end of our sea. Eddie ventured out of his fried egg to look and listen, while Arf gorged himself on offal from the shrig. Otha told everyone his adventure in full tekelili detail. Shrighunter couldn't get over the way Otha had made his shrig explode. She'd had no idea our metal knife could cut so big an escape vent in a shrig's body.

To round things out, Otha's tale of encountering Quai-hlaihle was quickly confirmed when a black god known as Offerer told us he'd just now found the partially unwrapped body drifting in the air near our sea. Offerer's function was to take certain special kinds of debris inward to the Great Old Ones instead of outward to the shrigs. He and a few others fed human corpses to the mighty *woomo*; also they hauled in the offal left over from the butchering of the shrigs. With a mortician's affinity for cadavers, Offerer had come upon Quaihlaihle's body soon after the shrig's explosion sent it to the Umpteen Seas.

When he picked up the tekelili of Otha's story, Offerer contacted Otha to say he'd found the dead queen a mile or two from where we'd brought the bodies of the shrigs. He asked if we wanted to see her before he fed her to the giant sea cucumbers.

"Ain't no way I go near that body again," vowed Otha.

"Quaihlaihle a mummy!" exclaimed Eddie. "She was in that shrig for—has it been two months? Come, Mason, we must investigate!"

Watcher and Shrighunter accompanied us. We followed Offerer's mind signals through the mazy congeries of great jiggling waterballs, and finally there Offerer was, with a surprisingly small object at his side—the mummy of Queen Quaihlaihle.

Much of the sappy glue had come loose, and some of the ceremonial money net was hanging free. Quaihlaihle's face was visible. Her lips had writhed away from her red teeth, which were pushed apart by her swollen black tongue. The air near her was pungent with decay. Eddie's eyes grew wide in fascination.

"Do you know her?" I asked Offerer, who was in the process of lashing a rope around the softened body's waist. "Is she of your tribe?"

He was unsure, but Shrighunter said that many years ago a woman had been caught like Otha in a fleeing shrig. The woman's tribal name had been Strutter. Our dead Quaihlaihle resembled Strutter enough so that Shrighunter deemed it likely that after being trapped in her shrig, Strutter had made a small enough airhole to ride all to the inner surface of the Rind.

Suddenly remembering Elijah, I asked Shrighunter if a *man* had ever left their tribe in the same way. I showed her my mental images of Elijah. Her reaction was immediate and intense.

"FarMan! You done seen FarMan? Then you really truly from the outside! Are you listening up, Watcher?"

Watcher blended his mind with ours and showed us the story of how the one they called FarMan had left.

A few of the black gods were natural explorers. Though the Umpteen Seas themselves were large and various as a small nation, some of the natives were not content. One possibility for breaking out was to try and travel all the way through the Central Anomaly. Watcher's images of this zone showed the Umpteen Seas spinning past with insanely mounting rapidity. Time slowed down at the Gate between worlds, and it became difficult to make progress, but once one could get in deep enough, the mighty *woomo* would assist. They disliked the presence of other living creatures in their realm and would catch hold of an interloper with one of their huge fans and fling him either through the inconceivable Gate or back whence he came.

According to Watcher, the world beyond the Gate is in some sense a reflection of our side and—this I find hard to understand—when you pass fully through the Central Anomaly you are smoothly transformed into a mirror-image, so as to match the MirrorEarth side. Setting aside these subtle points of higher geometry, when you visit the MirrorEarth, it looks normal to you, and your MirrorSelf there resembles an identical twin, and is apt to behave just like you.

In the past the Earth and MirrorEarth had been quite closely matched. When a black god presented himself to be taken through the Gate between worlds, then without fail his MirrorSelf would be on the other side—and they'd trade places. So it had gone for centuries or even millennia. Watcher had traded places with himself any number of times.

The transition was interesting and stimulating, said he. And the other side was so much like ours that, by now, he was no longer sure if he was Watcher or MirrorWatcher. But as of our arrival an asymmetry had arisen. My party had removed the ice plug from the South Hole on Earth—but for some reason our MirrorSelves on MirrorEarth had not emulated this activity. On MirrorEarth, the ice plug in the South Hole remained. And thus, given that Eddie and I were a source of unprecedented asymmetry, we should not expect to find our MirrorSelves passing through the Gate when we did.

A maze of thought, with much to ponder and to analyze! Setting these complications aside, I was on the point of asking Watcher about the status of the North Hole maelstrom on MirrorEarth, but then Eddie interrupted with his own query.

"How did Elijah get to the surface?"

"Going from the core to the Rind—a more difficult task than coasting through the Gate," Watcher told us. Not really an answer.

As we'd been discussing, Strutter had made the trip and become Queen Quaihlaihle of the flowerpeople. And Watcher knew of others who'd journeyed out, but this wasn't common. The black gods had a low opinion of those who hung and dangled from the roof of the planet's crust, and they had little desire to go there. In their view, everything from up there would eventually drift down to the seas anyway, so why make the trip at all?

It was Elijah, or FarMan, who'd accomplished the greatest exploration of all. After many trips outward to the far reaches of the shrigs' central feeding zone, FarMan had formed the idea that the space he inhabited was like a hollow bladder. This, Watcher remarked an aside, was the same idea

231

that Otha, Eddie, and I advocated. Reasoning patiently and at length, FarMan had concluded that there must be people out on the "egg's surface" beyond the North and the South holes. Most of the black gods had doubted him, for surely there could be no air out there.

FarMan had insisted that he could break out, as a chicken from its egg.

"How?" interrupted Eddie's. "How did he do it?"

Watcher said that the Great Old Ones had borne FarMan away on a beam of pink light. First he'd built himself a tight-hatched traveling cabin out of a whole *ballula* shell, and then the black gods had towed the shell far out toward the Rind. FarMan had selected the spot on the basis of visions the Great Old Ones had granted him. Once the shell was in place—with the determined FarMan safe inside—a tremendous lightriver had appeared to push the shell all the way to the Rind's inner surface.

But how an empty *ballula* shell could then have carried him through the Rind was unclear. Perhaps he'd floated out through the great open maelstrom of the North Hole? Or perhaps he'd emerged from the obscure channel that allowed *ballulas* to mate in the antarctic bay where our ship, the *Wasp*, had landed? But in either case, how would FarMan have made his way from the poles to Virginia?

"Eureka," said Eddie quite suddenly. "All the pieces are in place."

"How do you mean?"

"I know how to get us to the MirrorBaltimore," said Eddie. "Offerer, can we be the ones to haul up Quaihlaihle's corpse?"

"You can come along with me if you wish."

"We'll be taking the old metal ship up there, too," Eddie formed a quick image of Quaihlaihle resting on the *veem's* rim like a sardine on a dinner plate. He visioned himself inside the cabin, with Arf and me at his side. He had the idea that the Great Old Ones would snatch us to eat Quaihlaihle and then cast us away because they didn't like the fried egg.

"What about Seela?" I protested. "And Otha?"

"They may come if they wish," said Eddie. "Though I doubt Otha will choose to. Who would willingly change from god to slave?" There were many more thoughts in Eddie's head, but he obscured them from me by a full-length incanting of the new poem I'd earlier heard him reciting from. A fine bit of fustian.

THE CITY IN THE SEA

Lo! Death has reared himself a throne
In a strange city lying alone
Far down within the dim West,
Where the good and the bad and the worst and
    the best
Have gone to their eternal rest.
There shrines and palaces and towers
(Time-eaten towers that tremble not!)
Resemble nothing that is ours.
Around, by lifting winds forgot,
Resignedly beneath the sky
The melancholy waters lie.

No rays from the holy Heaven come down
On the long night-time of that town;
But light from out the lurid sea
Streams up the turrets silently—
Gleams up the pinnacles far and free—
Up domes—up spires—up kindly halls—
Up fanes—up Babylon-like walls—
Up shadowy long-forgotten bowers
Of sculptured ivy and stone flowers—
Up many and many a marvellous shrine
Whose wreathed friezes intertwine

The viol, the violet, and the vine.
Resignedly beneath the sky
The melancholy waters lie.
So blend the turrets and shadows there
That all seem pendulous in air,
While from a proud tower in the town
Death looks gigantically down.

There open fanes and gaping graves
Yawn level with the luminous waves;
But not the riches there that lie
In each idol's diamond eye—
Not the gaily-jewelled dead
Tempt the waters from their bed;
For no ripples curl, alas!
Along that wilderness of glass—
No swellings tell that winds may be
Upon some far-off happier sea—
No heavings hint that winds have been
On seas less hideously serene.

But lo, a stir is in the air!
The wave—there is a movement there!
As if the towers had thrust aside,
In slightly sinking, the dull tide—
As if their tops had feebly given
A void within the filmy Heaven.
The waves have now a redder glow—
The hours are breathing faint and low—
And when, amid no earthly moans,
Down, down that town shall settle hence,
Hell, rising from a thousand thrones,

Shall do it reverence.

"What that got to do with me, Mase?" demanded Otha, impatiently chewing on a chunk of shrigmeat with his red-dyed teeth. The great fart blast had flash-cooked a half acre of the second shrig. Though gamey and exceedingly fat, the meat was toothsome.

I had just finished telling Otha that Eddie and I planned to haul the shiny fried egg inward. We would carry in the mummy of Quaihlaihle with us to make sure that the forty or fifty Great Old Ones would not mind our intrusion. Our hope was that the Great Old Ones would hurl us through the Central Anomaly, that is, through the Gate that divides Earth from MirrorEarth. With luck we would eventually penetrate to the MirrorEarth's surface, and perhaps even reach MirrorBaltimore, where Eddie would help us to a good new start in life.

"Whuffo I go back be an be no runaway slave? An first haul that fried-egg shit all the way up to them giant *woomo*? *An* carry the mummy? Fuck that shit, Mase. Ain't no way." Otha's mode of addressing me had become even more familiar.

I'd found Otha floating near a large glob of pure water in which bobbed two women called Tigra and Bunny. They'd come from halfway around the Umpteen Seas, drawn by the explosion of Otha's shrig.

"We like the shrig that went boom." Tigra laughed. My Lord, she was beautiful. Being there in tekelili contact with her was as wonderful an experience as I'd ever had. There was something enticingly sinuous and loose about her mentation.

Bunny was rounder and still more sensuous, with a sunnier, more direct way of viewing things. Looking through her eyes via tekelili, the full wonder of our surroundings was borne in on me once again.

The filigreed pink light sent highlights off the lovely clear waterglobs on every side. Over our heads was the mighty canopy of the Inner Sky and the land of Htrae upon the inner Rind. The North Hole was near the center. As it was late September, the hole was fully illumined, with its great watery vortex gilded by the hidden sun. Beneath our feet, the Great

Old Ones were closer and larger than I'd ever seen them, for the chaotic peregrinations of the Umpteen Seas had brought us near the inner perimeter of the waterglob zone.

"Virginia's still alive in the MirrorEarth," I told Otha. "And I'm dead there."

"That still ain't got nothin to do with me. I'm stayin here, Mase. Even someone as white and dumb as you is gotta be able to see why."

"Mason's not white," put in Tigra.

"He use to be, but yeah, he black now. You done think about that yet, Mase, that you goin back as a black man?"

"It'll wear off. Eddie is already lighter from spending so much time in the fried egg. Now that he's learned how to close the door."

"Sho. Is Seela goin with you?"

"I think so." Recently, our mutual passion had tempered. We'd grown used to one kind of relationship—me as speechless slave—and now here in the Umpteen Seas everything was different. We'd each had several lovers among the black gods, and our mutual bond no longer seemed quite so absolute. Yet for me, Seela was still the special one. "She'll come with me. I aim to marry her."

"Wish I could be there to see, Mase."

The farewell emotions swelled around us, while Tigra and Bunny kept a tactful silence. If our partnership had been unjustly unequal, Otha and I still had shared much joy. Building dams, catching fish, playing in the corn crib. The sickness of thinking him an inferior slave had not come over me till puberty. "I'm sorry," I told Otha as he watched my thoughts. "I was wrong." The memory of the night Pa had raped Turl came welling up. Otha shared it, and in the sharing of our memories something new emerged, something that neither of us had admitted to ourselves.

"Purly!" exclaimed Otha. "He's yo pa's son!"

"With Turl!" I said. "That's why she went away that summer."

"And why she always talked about him," said Otha. "My baby bro."

"Mine too!"

Otha and I shared the same blood brother. We were kin. We wrapped our arms around each other and embraced.

§

I found Seela with Smoker and a score of other black gods, all of them busy tying chunks of raw shrigmeat into bundles for curing. They were working hard, concerned that the meat might spoil before they could dry it in the streams of pink light.

Seela's drifting blond hair made a striking contrast to her dark skin. She was laughing, and her full upper lip crinkled enticingly. At least on Seela, red teeth looked wonderful. And the two large rumbies that she'd gotten from Jewel sparkled against her skin like diamonds. Better than diamonds. Brighter, clearer, the size of marbles, and with a curious shifting energy, as if they were in motion even when they were still. Seela tekelili-saw me seeing her and turned with a ready smile.

She handed me her necklace, with the two big rumbies dangling in little hand-woven nets. "Feel how heavy, Mason. Magic stones. We have legends about them. They give you power over *ballulas* and shrigs."

In addition to their other qualities, the large, oddly faceted rumby gems were quite dense. I recalled the stone I'd found floating in the air at the bottom of the South Hole tunnel on our first day. It wasn't that a rumby had the weight of an equally sized globule of lead or gold. No, they were several times more massive than that. Deeply strange objects, and beyond the ordinary order of things. And they felt wonderful in my hands, so much so that it was hard to stop fondling them. I liked to shine them up with the oil from the side of my nose, and then polish them against whatever came to hand.

"Treasure," I thought appreciatively to Seela. "And you're treasure, too. Will you travel on with me?"

"But it's wonderful here! The gems, the dancing seas, the rivers of light, the handsome black gods. And look how much *koladull* meat we have!"

"It's wonderful in the world I come from, too." I imaged a moonlit night, a rainy day, and the flowers of spring. Buildings, machinery, and books. Oysters, champagne, and stuffed turkey. Us in a well-appointed city apartment, and us visiting Pa on the farm. A wedding at St. Paul's in Lynchburg, with Seela all in white. Seela pregnant, and Seela suckling our child.

The idea of night intrigued Seela mightily, but the inanimate buildings frightened her, and the concepts of marriage and family were—as I'd briefly forgotten—quite alien to her tribe. My suggestion that I might father her child struck her as something like blasphemy. The flowerpeople believed that women were made pregnant by the pink light from the Earth's center.

"But think of marriage," I thought to Seela. "Marriage means we can be together always. Only you and I."

Her reaction was anything but what I'd hoped. Was I then a spoilsport and a tyrant? A selfish self-deluding fool? A slave master intent on forcing her through the insane rituals of my barbaric tribe?

I abandoned this line of persuasion and told her more about the trip Eddie planned. "We'll get inside the metal egg with Arf and Eddie."

"I don't like Eddie."

"And the black gods will tow us up to the Central Anomaly."

"The what?"

"The Gate between the worlds. It's a spherical zone where the Great Old Ones live. We'll go right to the source, Seela, whence the holy pink light streams. The path to the MirrorEarth. The giant *woomo* will throw us through, all the way to the MirrorRind. We'll find our way through the crust, and be out on the surface of MirrorEarth before you know it. The nights are lovely, Seela. Imagine what it would be like with no light. And snow, let me show you about snow." I showed her memories of Otha and me sliding down a hill on our wooden sled, with the fluffy white flakes drifting out of the endless sky. Seela liked it.

"But what if you fall up into the sky?"

"You can't. Things fall toward the ground on Earth and MirrorEarth. If something's on the ground, it just stays there."

That was the best news Seela had heard yet. If there was anything about the Umpteen Seas she disliked, it was the lack of any stable place of rest. The flowerpeople had a deeply ingrained fear of falling. Pressing my advantage, I drew her close and caressed her. "Please come with me, Seela."

"Maybe."

The next problem was to convince a squad of the black gods to haul the fried egg. An inspiration struck me. What better way to quickly cure a great amount of the shrigmeat than to bear it up to the very source of the sovereign pink light?

Smoker, who had been following our conversation, showed me an image of the meat bundles sticking together and not getting fully dry. I replied with an image of the meats hung from the holes around the fried egg's rim—like tassels around the brim of a gaucho's hat. Whatever else it might be, the *veem* was the perfect rack for mass drying of meat! Smoker came back with an image of a Great Old One darting out a sticky fan-limb that absorbed all our plunder. I wondered if we might hold the fried egg back, just out of the Great Old One's reach. Now Watcher entered the discussion. He of all men knew the capabilities of the *woomo* and the topography around the Gate.

"The *woomo* move slowly," Watcher told me. "But their pink beams of light are rapid—as are their thoughts. It's nonsense to imagine tricking them. They know all. Simply ask them to smoke the meat, and they will. And were they planning to steal he meat, they'd inform you. There are no secrets amid the tekelili of the *woomo*."

As always, the mighty chords of the Great Old Ones' thoughts pervaded the background. For the moment they seemed unconcerned with our discussion.

A few beams of pink light had been idly playing over the dead shrigs, probing and feeling them. The light tubes had the shape of knobby tree branches, twigging out at irregular intervals. Eddie and I had come to realize that these tubes were more than mere light, for they were in no wise bound to the rectilinear urgencies of a lantern's ray. Eddie said that the tubes contained a heated vortical plasma of what he called latent motive craft. As this plasma turned and bent, so moved the light, growing as organically as a vine, as sinuously as the funnel of a tornado, and as palpably as a mounded row of eddies in a rain-swollen stream.

When Watcher suggested we talk directly to the Great Old Ones, Lightrider fin-kicked his way over to the nearest column of light and began skittering his board against it until he had its attention. The light bulged out at him, then split off streamers that played over his head. The vast beings the Hollow Earth's core were noticing Lightrider. I peered toward them. Inward from us, the dozen light tubes that had been fondling the shrig found their source in a bigger tube, which was itself the daughter of a nearby lightstream whose main flow continued forking out past us all the way to the Rind.

In its own aethereal way, the lightstream's plasma was like a rushing river, and I thought of the spring when the James River had run full flood, forty feet above normal water level. We'd gone to see it—Pa, Luke, Otha, Turl, and me. It had been too wet for a wagon, so we'd walked. The water had been an ugly light brown color, with hungrily sucking whirlpools. We'd seen trees go past, then two dead mules, and finally a whole house. A house floating down the river, with all its carpentered right angles flexing. The sight of it had given me nightmares about our own unsteady home.

As if piqued by Lightrider's actions, the big lightstream sent out a thick gout of warmly wafting light that blanketed all of us. Watcher silently spoke, telling the Great Old Ones that Eddie and I wanted them to throw the metal ship through the Gate that was the heart of the Central Anomaly and thus into the hollow interior of the MirrorEarth. He showed them our plan to hang the shrigmeat on the ship's rim to dry. The Great Old Ones were interested in moving our party through the Gate—they echoed Watcher's idea that the asymmetry of our actions was a good thing. And they reminded Watcher of their fondness for shrig innards. He promised that we would bring much to eat, and a mummy as well.

So now we went to get the trusty fried egg so as to load it up. We found it with the door closed, and Offerer nearby, playing with Arf.

Offerer informed us that Eddie had locked himself inside the cabin with Quaihlaihle's mummy. It had been half an hour. Soon he would have to open the door for fresh air. We waited.

Presently, the door opened and a stained and disheveled Eddie appeared, a ghastly grin on his lips. I was struck once again by how oddly Eddie's skull was shaped; flat on the top and with bulging brow and temples. The wild pungent stench of Quaihlaihle's dissolution floated out of the fried egg. Eddie's hands were wedged deep into his coat pockets, fondling something. Tentatively, I reached out toward his mind...but he was silently quoting himself again, quoting from his "Berenice," a gothic tale I remembered reading in *The Southern Literary Messenger* of March 1835.

And why did Eddie recite? I suppose he had some idea of obscuring his deeds and plans behind a hebephrenic torrent of inner speech, but knowing him as I did, it was all too obvious what he had done. Obvious? Far more than *obvious*, Eddie's newest outrage was made *ludicrously patent* by his selection of *which* passages to recite.

"'The eyes were lifeless, and lustreless, and seemingly pupilless, and I shrank involuntarily from their glassy stare to the contemplation of the thin and shrunken lips. They parted; and in a smile of peculiar meaning, the teeth of the changed Berenice disclosed themselves slowly to my view. Would to God that I had never beheld them, or that, having done so, I had died!'"

"What have you been doing in there, Eddie? As if I didn't know. What do you have in your pockets?"

"'The shutting of a door disturbed me, and looking up, I found that my cousin had departed from the chamber. But from the disordered chamber of my brain had not, alas!, departed, and would not be driven away, the white and ghastly *spectrum* of the teeth.'"

"You pulled Quaihlaihle's teeth too, didn't you Eddie?"

"'The teeth!—the teeth!—they were here, and there, and everywhere, and visibly and palpably before me; long, narrow, and excessively white, with the pale lips writhing about them, as in the very moment of their first terrible development. Then came the full fury of my *monomania*...'"

"Stop reciting, Eddie. There aren't any secrets to hide. Everyone knows you pulled the teeth, and everyone knows we're going through the center. The Great Old Ones already said they'd throw us through. And all they want for helping us is a mess of shrig guts."

This last was a real surprise to Eddie. He'd fancied the Great Old Ones to be evil schemers, so cut off from their supernal mentations had he become. Now he left off his inner speech and let me into his mind. He had Quaihlaihle's ruby teeth in his right pocket and Virgina's ivory teeth in his left pocket...nearer to his heart.

But this was nothing after all I'd already done and seen. "I don't care about the teeth," I thought to him. "Just so I can go back to the surface. But tell me. How will we get out through the MirrorRind?"

Watcher, Seela, Lightrider, Jewel, Smoker, and Offerer were gathered nearby, all of us in contact. They were listening with quiet interest. "You'll want to weave a necklace around those teeth, Eddie," thought Jewel. She was a regular visitor to Eddie's *veem*, and there was a certain affinity between the two. The teeth were no surprise to her. "Seela can show you how to do it," she added.

When Eddie stepped out of the fried egg, his mindset had been that of a criminal and a cringer. But now, to his tremulous delight, we were smilingly accepting him...just the way he was. *And* we were ready to help haul the fried egg to where the *woomo* were.

Flustered and smiling, Eddie pushed himself down from the *veem's* rim to where a large ball of water nestled in the grass. He took off his coat, carefully knotting its sleeves around one of the fried egg's retaining ropes, and began meticulously washing himself. As he washed, he tekelili-chattered to us, presenting his conclusions and his plans.

From his studies of the *veem* hieroglyphs, Eddie had concluded that humans and the Great Old Ones had come to earth together in the fried-egg ships. Young *woomo* were not greatly larger than humans—and they could easily travel in a fried-egg with humans. Eddie called our attention to one of the hieroglyphic drawings that showed a circle with a line across it. This, said Eddie, was a pair of *veem*, joined to make a circular craft. Within it were elliptical forms with branching ends—obviously *woomo*. The craft also contained stick figures, who were clearly people. Eddie believed that either (a) men and women had piloted the ships in the service of the Great Old Ones; or (b) the *woomo* had come to Earth as the slaves of Man. Vain as he was, Eddie thought (b) to be, on the whole, the more likely alternative. The *woomo* were upstart livestock.

Watcher objected, showing us a mental image of men, women, and *woomo* together in an airship, friendly and working in harmony. *Woomos* and humans had been, said Watcher, partner races since time immemorial. He stressed the point that humans have a special skill that makes them indispensible for journeying from star to star.

"What skill?" I asked.

"Yearning," said Watcher. "Pushing."

"Born to dream," said Eddie, liking this notion. "Yes, I suppose a human-*woomo* alliance is possible. If so, then perhaps those Great Old Dogs will, as Mason has proposed, throw us all the way to MirrorHtrae for the mere gift of a mess of shrig guts. In my fear, I had planned a less open solicitation."

Eddie now showed us that he'd meant to smear mummy flesh all over the slippery exterior of the fried egg so that one of the Great Old Ones would try to swallow it whole. Eddie imagined that, finding the carrion-scented object indigestible, the giant *woomo* would examine it and recognize it as the fearsome chariot of the old human masters and then, stricken with hatred, or with terror, the creature would fling the *veem* very far indeed.

Thus had Eddie reasoned, having wholly lost sight of the fact that the Great Old Ones could read our minds—and were in fact reading them right now, as attested to by the hairlike bright pink streamers that veined the space around us like root hairs in a flower pot, or capillaries within flesh.

Evidently Eddie thought the best way to get through the MirrorRind would be to float up through the sea. Yes, this was an option. If whales could swim all the way through, then why not we? Given that Eddie could open and shut the fried egg's door, we could use it like a diving bell. But what about air? And could we manage to emerge somewhere other than in the antarctic?

"As for air, Watcher knows of a plant we can use," came Eddie's voice in my head, in answer to my thoughts. "He pictured it when he was telling us about FarMan—the one whom you and Otha called Elijah. In examining Watcher's mental images, I noticed that FarMan took some odd plants in the *ballula* shell with him. So I deduced that FarMan floated up through the sea, and that the plants gave him air." Having finished his ablutions, Eddie turned and faced Watcher, addressing him via tekelili. "Can I get some pounds of the radially spiked vegetable which you helped load into FarMan's *ballula* shell four years ago?"

Watcher had a noble, arching nose that curved back on itself like a snail shell. He was quite bald. His mouth was broad and mobile, and his figure generously formed. He was nude now, having removed his *pulpuls* so as better to dabble in the water and the grass, and he looked for all the world like a black Roman senator in the baths. Yes, he could help us get the plant, it was called air-weed. It grew "uphill inward." Lightrider could easily get some on our way in. No difficulties were forseen. Hail and farewell.

Over us hung the saucerlike underside of the fried egg. All about us were man-size, house-size, and dog-size gobbets of clear Umpteen Sea water. A sweet-smelling fresh breeze was in the air. Rivulets of pink light played over us all.

"Eddie," said I.

"Yes, Mason?" His dark eyes were clear beneath his overdeveloped forehead.

"The mummy. You forgot to get the mummy out of the ship."

"Very well. Offerer, can you help?"

A short while later, we'd lashed Quaihlaihle, along with must have been a shrig's liver, to the flat underside of the fried egg, using festoons of shrig intestines as the ropes. Some eighty bundles of cleaned shrigmeat were roped to the holes around the fried egg's rim, and four long leather ropes led from the rim to the eight of us—Watcher, Seela, Lightrider,

Jewel, Smoker, Offerer, Eddie, and me—two of us to a rope. Arf sat inside the *veem's* cabin, which we'd rinsed out with a ball of water.

We kicked our *pulpuls* and slowly, slowly, the fried egg began moving away from the Umpteen Seas and further inward. The gravitational pull back toward the Seas seemed weaker moving in this direction than it had seemed when I'd kicked my way outward for the shrighunt.

In half an hour's time we'd progressed far enough so that I could glance back and see the Umpteen Seas spread out like gems on a jeweler's counter. The space here was warped and stretched in such a way that the zone of the Seas looked flat rather than spherical. It was impossible to see out to the Rind except in the radial direction that went directly outward from the Earth's center. The Central Anomaly looked more and more like a plane and less like a sphere. We were close enough to it so that I could clearly distinguish the two or three score Great Old Ones upon the seeming plane, although the view was a bit obscured by some gauzy green clouds.

These clouds were the airweed plants that Watcher had spoken of. Like a kelp, the airweed plants had flotation bladders whose slight buoyancy kept them here, "uphill inward" from the Umpteen Seas. Each plant consisted of some hundred leathery blades growing outward from its center. The blades were four or five feet long and were densely set with fist-size airbladders that held a breathable gas that was lighter than air—Eddie supposed it to be a mixture of helium and oxygen. With Lightrider's help, we gathered a dozen of the plants and squeezed them into the fried-egg cabin with Arf.

As we pushed further on, the tekelili mind-contact grew ever stronger. Pulling on our rope with Seela, I could actually forget which of us was me and which was her. Strong, happy Seela! It was wonderful to be so close to her. Ever since we'd passed the zone of the airweed, the gravitational attraction of the Umpteen Seas had grown weaker, so now we were practically in free fall. Looking back at the Seas, I noticed something strange: They were moving much faster than before.

I caught Eddie's attention and got him to look as well. The Seas were racing by like panicked buffalo on the Great Plain, merging into multiple images in the distance, and then miraculously returning from the direction opposite to the one they disappeared in. The directional confusion was the effect of the spindling of space near Earth's center…but why did the Seas move so rapidly?

"Time dilation," said Eddie. "Watcher spoke of it. The closer we get to the center, the slower our time goes. This is lotus land, Mason!"

Watcher confirmed Eddie's answer, and I was seized with a panicky desire to hurry. Redoubling our kickings, we carried the fried egg closer to the Great Old Ones. As I said, due to the space spindling, they looked as if they were laid out on a plane rather than on the surface of a spherical zone. One of them in particular caught my attention—the closest one of all—a *woomo* as big as the whole town of Lynchburg. Her name was Uxa. Her antediluvian hide was marked with great rows of flat-topped hills. The nearer end of this vast trepang bore ten enormous, branching fans. Flowing out from these tendrils were the vast streamers of pink light that played around us. Sensing our approach, the giant sea cucumber slowly, hugely, swung one of her branches our way.

"*Feed her*," thought Offerer, and we unlashed the mummy, the shrig liver, and the intestinal strips, pushing these offerings inward. With a massive, writhing movement, the Great Old One's fan caught all we gave it. In gratitude, she steered an intense river of light along the edges of our fried egg, soon drying all our bundles of meat. Smoker cut the bundles of shrigmeat free and fastened them to a series of loops on a long towrope he had ready. And then he and the others were heading outward and away. Everything seemed to be happening very quickly, although, compared to the outer world, we were moving terribly slowly. The high-speed jiggling of the Umpteen Seas was hideous to behold. Only Watcher was still with us.

Eddie, Seela, and I squeezed into the fried egg with Arf and the airweed. Arf was very agitated—yelping and whining. He was scared of the *woomo*. Eddie quickly got the door closed, lest one of us tumble out when the Great Old One threw us. Watcher shoved our craft further inward and took his leave as well. As the inward-falling *veem* spun, I could see out to the departing black gods. The further from us they got, the faster they seemed to move.

Now there came a great, sucking slap as Uxa took hold of our fried egg ship with her sticky fan. Arf gave a woeful howl. A terrifyingly powerful motion drew us down. With every fathom that we moved inward, the mad jostling of the distant Seas increased. I could see through the zone of the Great Old Ones now, seeing through the Gate between the worlds and into the Hollow MirrorEarth. It's Mirror Umpteen Seas were storming past with bewildering rapidity but in the opposite direction from our Umpteen Seas. Behind us I could see the distant Rind, steadily turning, with the seasonal light pulsing on and off in the North and South holes. Whole years were passing!

Now the mountainous bodies of the divine *woomo* were all about, great warty barrel shapes bedizened with suckers, puckers, and subbranching fans. They lay in the plane between the two worlds, half here and half there, each of them slowly and steadily rolling over and over, like basking whales, and with their tendrils moving from one side to the other.

This close to the dividing plane, it was very clear that the rotation of the Earth and the MirrorEarth are in opposite directions, This counterrotation is the source, I would suggest, of the biplanetary *vis viva* that powers the plasmic lightstreamers that the *woomo* manipulate with their preternaturally mobile appendages. I believe that the jittering of their undulating and microscopically pileated fronds is ever in complete synchronization with the whole of the biplanetary tree of pink light that grows from the center out to the Rind and to the MirrorRind, and that the tiniest tendril of the smallest subbranch cannot brush a feather without the Great Old Ones knowing it.

Now our host Uxa made a huge, wallowing motion, and we moved through the Gate at the center of the Hollow Earth, and for a heartbeat, *time was not*. The fried egg's cabin was suffused with total Light. All was One, and the One knew

All. Uxa was two hundred million years old, as man reckons time. Arf was about to vomit. For Uxa and the other *woomo*, the Earth was a kind of vehicle. And our fried egg, or *veem*? Man and *woomo* had come to Earth in the fried egg ship at the instigation of some other planet's *woomo*.

I also knew that Seela was pregnant. I could sense the day-old foetus in her womb, a boy, my own child, magically engendered by our lovemaking of the day before. Seela was frightened at the thought of something living within her. Eddie was planning to kill his double, his MirrorEddie. Uxa was pregnant as well, that is, she carried in her mantle the seeds for scores of more *woomo*, ready for the next iteration of the cosmic spawning that they called *woomo* blooming. And all the while the great *woomo* ship that we called our Hollow Earth continued on its way to its eventual destination, an inconceivably huge space spindle somewhere among the stars, mayhap at the very center of our Milky Way nebula.

A long-buried image of my mother's face flared up in my mind. Though she'd died when I was born, I knew her from within. There, at Earth's center, I could see my mother's lined, snub-featured face, her tentative smile, her strawy pale brown hair. It was as if Uxa were my mother's head, and seeing this, I worshiped her.

Uxa said we'd lost six years on the way in, and we'd lose six more on the way out. She would throw us to land on the MirrorRind surface of a great ocean hole. Arf made heaving noises. Eddie was racing up mental staircases of piled concepts, shaky idea edifices propped upon mighty teachings from the unimpeachable Uxa. Via my tekelili, I listened in.

Most planets are solid. Only a very few are hollow. It is only the hollow planets that have mirror counterparts. Each mirrored pair of hollow planets is umbilically connected, navel to navel, by a Gate at their shared cores.

The space zone of each pair of hollow planets is delaminated into two sheets, like a blister, with the planet on one layer, and the mirrorplanet on the other. These blistered pairs of hollow planets are interstellar spacecraft for the Great Old Ones. The mature *woomo* ride among the stars within linked pairs of hollow worlds like Earth and MirrorEarth.

As a matter of husbandry, the *woomo* populate their doubled planets with humans—just as a farmer might import earthworms to freshen their soil…or like another might grow milkweed to attract the lovely monarch butterflies. Our small thoughts, particularly Eddie's, were beautiful to Uxa.

Moreover, while on their great journey toward that inconceivably vast space spindle afar, the Great Old Ones would periodically cause their planetary craft to bloom, that is, they would send out seeds for fresh colonies of humans and *woomo*.

All this, and more, I knew in the timeless moment that we passed through the interface between Earth and MirrorEarth. Uxa rolled slowly over, and now a violent, lashing movement of her fan snapped us spinning outward.

The centrifugal force pressed us heavily against the cabin wall. Staring out the thick-glassed view port that was over the ship's worn control panel, I could see, in rapid succession, views of the giant *woomo* dwindling behind us and a view of the approaching MirrorSeas. Arf stretched his head forward, retchingly emptying his full stomach. The foul smell of the half-digested shrig offal set Seela, then Eddie, and then me to vomiting as well.

As we drew closer to the MirrorSeas, their nauseatingly reckless slewings relented; we were getting back into normal time. In her godlike wisdom, the great *woomo* Uxa had thrown us so as to miss the great waterglobs. We sailed past them handily, with barely enough time to glimpse the black Mirrorgods who lived there. We were still whirling too fast to dare reopening the door. I pressed my face down into the mound of airweed and knifed open one of the bladders. The gas within was under high pressure; a vivifying burst of oxygen and helium filled the cabin and our voices grew oddly shrill.

A persistent river of pink light flowed with us, pushing us ever outward. The MirrorSeas dwindled behind us, great lumps of water arranged as on a sphere. As space opened back up, MirrorHtrae—that is, the inner surface of the Mirror-Rind—became widely visible. The question I'd meant to ask Watcher was now answered. The MirrorEarth had a North Hole maelstrom, and an ice-plugged South Hole.

By now, the spinning of the fried egg had abated. We were drifting about within the free-falling saucer as if at random. Eddie managed to open the door and to shove out the vomit and to let fresh air in. We sailed past a herd of shrigs and sent a flock of pterodactyls scattering. Further out, we glimpsed a *ballula*, a possible threat.

Due to the effects of the Gate upon us, the inner surface of the MirrorRind appeared the same to us as had the inner surface of the Rind. Moreover, my companions looked the same to me as before, as did our *veem* or fried egg, and its inscriptions. Bodies, fried egg and the Hollow Earth remained, one could say, in the same relative relationships to each other on this side of the Gate.

Having closely studied the topography of the lands upon the inner Rind, Eddie felt that he knew the precise location of America's underside. He had directed Uxa to throw us into an ocean that he deemed to lie beneath the MirrorEarth version of the Chesapeake Bay. Precisely here, Eddie believed, there was a great hole in the planetary crust, allowing water to flow *all the way through*.

A point I failed to mention earlier is that, if there is indeed a hole in the ocean floor, one might naively expect the water to drain from the Earth into the interior of the Hollow Earth. But this expectation is quite fallacious—for at the inner edge of the Rind there is no gravitational pull to drag the water further. Eddie's conviction, based on his conjectures about Elijah and on his tekelili contacts with the Great Old Ones, was that we could splash into the ocean near such a hole and be lifted through the sea by the buoyancy of our sealed *veem*.

With the steady pressure of Uxa's light behind us, we made the sea in one day, although not without the eventual attentions of the vagrant *ballula* and of a land-based flock of harpy birds. But, encapsulated in the adamantine hull of our ancient skyship, we had nothing to fear.

During our passage, Seela helped pass the time by finger-weaving with string, a practice which the French term *macramé*. First her agile fingers unraveled some stout thread from my tattered coat, and then she took apart her necklace and reassembled it into two. Each of the two had one of

Jewel's stunning and eerie rumbies in its center and a variety of Seela's collected shells and seeds on the rest of it. Rather than making the necklaces decorative, Seela wove her *macramé* so thickly that hardly anything but the string showed. Using the tongue of the flowerpeople, I asked her why. She explained to me that Jewel's rumbies were our only treasure, and then she gave me one of the necklaces, with its fat, dense rumby hidden in wrappings of thread. More than ever did I feel myself her husband.

Seeing our matched necklaces, Eddie recalled Jewel's earlier suggestion. "Look you," he said, holding out his hands to Seela. "Can you weave these into a necklace for me?" He held fifty or sixty teeth, half of them white and half of them red. Virginia's and Quaihlaihle's.

After an initial exclamation of disgust, Seela knotted a tight-meshed little net around each of the teeth and ranged them on a dense plait, packed together like shrouded pearls. Eddie gladly tied the band around his neck. And now Eddie revealed that he too had gotten a plump rumby from the gracious Jewel. There was, I sensed, a certain attraction between those two, perhaps even a touch of romantic love. Jewel was, in her way, as wraith-like and strange as the maidens in Eddie's poems. Seela knotted Eddie's big rumby into a separate necklace for him. A memento, an amulet.

We had a bad moment when we passed close to a giant flower on a mighty vine that stretched up from the land near our targeted MirrorRind sea. There were flowerpeople on the blossom, small as aphids in the distance. Seela was on the point of jumping out to fly thither, and only my most heartfelt entreaties kept her aboard.

Eddie closed the door for the last time, and our fried egg cut edgewise into the water. Due to the singular nature of the gravitational potential here, the buoyancy of our sealed ship had the effect of moving us not toward the water's inner MirrorRind surface, but rather toward the distant MirrorEarth sea surface, which I judged to be a thousand miles outward. For us it was as if, instead of floating, the fried egg sank and—which was most unsettling—sank with a speed that ever grew.

Of all of my journey's stages, this was the most terrifying. Picture yourself sealed in a hemispherical room with a dog, a man, and a woman; and remember that your room is a tight-sealed capsule rushing through a thousand miles of water. The pressure grew greater than could be borne, and then grew twice as great again. We were constantly short of breath, and I sliced open a new air bladder every few minutes, hideously aware that I might use them all up too soon. The heavy weight of the air filled my ears with noises and my eyes with fog. The noises—each tiny sound was amplified and left to reverberate like the last scream of a dying demon in the nethermost hopeless hell, and no sound could finish its chiming before a new one set in. With all tekelili gone, Seela and I again had no more than a few hundred words in common, although her cries and sobbings spoke for themselves. Far from being joyful at the success of his plans thus far, Eddie was grimly brooding over the twelve years it had taken us to move through the slow time zone at the center of the worlds. Again and again, he called out for Virginia. Even noble Arf whinged and whined. It was bedlam.

As the pressure reached its maximum, I thought surely the portholes would burst—indeed, I half prayed they would, and put an end to our agony. Yet still the ancient metal ship held tight.

Throughout all this, nothing was still in the cabin; as we raced up through the water like an air bubble of swamp gas, our *veem* wagged like a fool's mocking head.

Outside our windows all had been utterly dark, but I now began to glimpse some luminous writhing forms: fishy denizens of the watery night. A few swam at us, but we waggled upward unarrested. Now, finally, the nightmare pressure on my ears began to slacken. Up and up we rushed, the water gurgling around us, and slowly, slowly, the inky water began to be tinged with brown, with blue, with green…

In a final great rush, our sealed ship shot high into the air, crashed joltingly back down, bobbed up again, and then finally settled itself, rocking on the surface of an unquiet autumnal sea.

14. MirrorEarth

Eddie opened the fried egg's door wide. Right away, two waves came crashing in, scuttling our ship. We barely got free before it sank. The situation was grim.

It was late afternoon and rapidly growing dark. Though not frigid, the air and water were cold. We'd all learned to swim in the Umpteen Seas, but I wondered how long we could stay afloat. Our clothes were dragging us down; we shed them all. Arf whimpered and tried to climb onto me.

Eddie kicked himself up high in the water, craning to make out which way land lay. But in the gathering dusk and the choppy water, what could he see? Lacking any better plan, we paddled slowly toward the dying sunset. If all was not wholly reversed, then MirrorAmerica lay in that direction.

Night fell, and we struggled on. I kept hoping to hear the sound of breakers. Arf stayed at my side, resting his head on my shoulder as we slowly swam. Seela and Eddie were a bit ahead of me. We splashed fruitlessly onward. Time passed… perhaps an hour.

Something in the sound around us had slowly been changing, and now there grew into audibility a low rhythmic thudding. Eddie kicked himself up high and looked.

"Over here!" he shrieked. "Help us!"

I pushed Arf aside and rose up to see as well. It was a steamship—a great two-paddle side-wheeler all lit up like a Christmas tree!

"Help!" cried I. "Help! Man overboard! Save us! *Heeeelp!*"

Seela joined her cries to ours, and some of the ship's sea-gazing passengers happened to hear us. An alarm went up, and minutes later the ship had lowered a boat with two oarsmen and a man with a lantern.

"Save us!" cried Eddie. "Save us, for the love of God!"

Presently, a shaft of lantern light fell upon us.

"My word! It's three blacks and a dog! Ship oars, boys, till I pull them in."

The speaker set down his lantern and stretched his arms down to Seela. "Ladies first," he said. "What plantation are you all from?"

"*Oonafoonah boolo*," said Seela. "*Klee ba'am.*" Her wet blond hair clung to her black skin, and when she talked, her teeth shone like rubies in the lantern light.

"Would you listen at her!" exclaimed the man. "Blond hair and red teeth? Can't say as I understand this a-tall." Now he reached down for Eddie. "How about you, boy, can you talk white?"

"I am not a Negro," said Eddie intently.

"What's your name?"

"Edgar Allan Poe."

"You hear that, Henry?" The man whooped, picking up his lantern and surveying the dripping Eddie, who now lay exhausted in the bottom of the boat. "Bill? This here's Edgar Allan Poe."

"Edgar Allan Poe's the name of the little fellow on our ship," answered a voice from the dark. "The poet. Got on board in Richmond, slept all afternoon, and now he's been in the first-class lounge ever since dinner."

"Holding court and charming the ladies," came a second voice. "But I'll be dang if this castaway don't look just like him. Only black and a little younger. Can you read, boy?"

"Hey," I shouted. I was hanging on to the side of the boat, too weak to pull myself in. "Don't forget me. And the dog."

"Here I am saving a black man's dog," said the man, setting down the lantern again. "That'll be a fine thing to tell the ladies. You speck I'll get a medal, Henry?"

I handed Arf over the gunwale, and then finally I was pulled in, too.

"Hello," said I. "I am Mason Algiers Reynolds of Virginia. My companions are Edgar Allan Poe of Richmond, and Seela Flower from Htrae. None of us is Negro."

"Especially not him," said the man, giving Arf a pat. The man had a slow, kind voice that held a hint of laughter in the background. His eyes were piercing, though hooded by puffy lids. He had a full shock of fine brown hair, an aquiline nose, and thin, mobile lips. The general effect was of cheerful dissolution. "I'm Dick Carrington, chief mate of the *Pocahontas*, and these here are officers Henry Langhorne and Bill Baldwin. Are you from the Reynolds plantation on the York River? Don't you know there's no free territory anywhere around here? Maryland's a slave state, same as Virginia. Old Marse pretty rough on you all? We're gonna have to send you back just the same."

"Wait a minute, Dick," put in Henry, a lean man with a small mustache. "We're on the high seas. Practically speaking, it's the same as if we'd caught these blacks in Africa ourselves. We can take them to the market in Baltimore and sell them. That girl with the blond hair...why, she could bring a thousand dollars. What do you think, Bill?"

"Too dodgy," said Bill. He had bony features and wore his long hair in a ponytail. When he talked, his prominent Adam's apple bobbed. "This ain't nothin like the high seas, Henry. This here's the Chesapeake Bay. By the Fugitive Slave Law, we're bound to return them to their master."

"Dammit, we're not slaves," I interrupted. "Check as you will, you won't find a runaway slave report on any of us. We're free men!"

"If that's really true, then we're legally bound to let them off in Baltimore town," said Bill. "On account of the Personal Liberty Act."

"Not that they *are* free men," harrumphed Henry. "Or why the hell would they be paddlin around here ten miles from land?" He unlimbered his oar and dug it into the water. "I say return em to their owners. Could be a few hundred dollars in it for us."

"*Wamgoolo oo'ka tekelili*," said Seela. She was complaining that there was no tekelili.

"You'll have to learn English, Seela," I told her, placing my arms around her. And then I whispered to her in the language of the flowerpeople. It felt good to hold her. We were chilled through and through.

"Wh-what's the date?" asked Eddie through chattering teeth. "Mr. Cuh-Carrington?"

"Thursday," said Dick Carrington easily. "Straight and steady there, Henry and Bill. Prepare to cast on."

We were at the stern of the steamship *Pocahontas*. She was a goodly schooner, with two narrow paddle wheels set amidships, one on either side. She carried some canvas as well, though the sail had been struck for the rescue. Crewmen winched down a sling. Dick and Bill made it fast, then we were lifted up and set aboard, nude and trembling. There was quite a press of passengers there to greet us.

"Runaway slaves!" cried a red-faced man. "Give them the lash!"

"We're not slaves," announced Eddie. "We are gentlemen born and raised." That's what he tried to say, but he was chattering so badly that few understood him.

"Shackle them," said another man. "Shackle them!"

"I'll take the girl in my cabin," offered another.

"I'll pay three hundred for her," yelled someone else. "Five hundred for the whole set."

"Bill," said Dick Carrington. "Take them down to the stokers' mess."

Thank God, thought I, for I knew the stokers would be black.

Bill Baldwin led us shaking and stumbling down steps and companionways to a low-ceilinged room in the belly of the ship. It was hot as blazes here, and the ship's engine gave a mighty thrum. A wizened black man stirred porridge in a pot. The voices of the black stokers came drifting in. They were shoveling and talking while they worked.

"Ayrab, we picked up these three,'" said Bill. "Let them warm up and give them a sup. Find some clothes if you can. I'll be back directly."

Ayrab set down his stirring spoon and gave us a long look. He was mocha-colored, where we three were ebony-black. He had small reddened eyes and only a few teeth. The sight of us seemed to fill him with glee, especially the sight of Seela, with her incongruously blond hair.

"Set ye down," cackled Ayrab. He stepped to the mess hall's other door and hollered down the hall. "Luther! Stop shovelin and come see!"

The blue-black, bulletheaded, powerful man who appeared was none other than MirrorLuther, the MirrorEarth copy of the Luther who'd gone down the river from Lynchburg to Richmond with me. He showed his age by a papery quality of his skin.

"Luther," I exclaimed. "It's Mason!"

"Mason what?"

"Mason Reynolds. From Hardware, Virginia. I knew you when you were working with the Garlands, poling that bateau down the river."

MirrorLuther narrowed his eyes. "Sho...I worked that boat befo I bought myself free. Can't say I reckernize you. Mason Reynolds, you say? There were a white boy of that name got shot in Lynchburg, I recall. Who you really be and whar you from? You be a runaway?"

"We are not slaves," insisted Eddie.

"But they think we are," said I. "There's no runaway slave bills out on us, I swear it."

"Till someone write one up," said Ayrab. "What you needs to do is get clear of the ship fast and lively once we land."

"I'll let you out the coal chute," said MirrorLuther. "An then you go to Jilly Tackler's rooming house down to Greene Street where it cross the National Road west of town. Jilly take you in. Now, whuffo this girl got blond ha'ar? What you name, darlin?"

"Her name is Seela," I said. "She doesn't speak English."

"She new from Africa? Is that why you run away, Mason? She come in new and you decide to make her all you own?"

"She's mine, yes, as a wife. But I tell you, Luther, she is a free woman and Eddie and I are free men."

"What's the date?" asked Eddie again.

"Thursday," said Ayrab. "Did Carrington say if he fixin to give you all over to the paddy rollers?"

"What?" asked Eddie.

"Patrollers," said I. "I'm not sure what the officers plan to do. One of them said that if we weren't runaways, they should take us to the market and sell us."

"You be slippin out the coal chute for sho," said Mirror-Luther.

"I know it's Thursday," said Eddie. "I mean what month is it, Ayrab? And what year?"

"This still be September, I speck. An the year? Dang if I know. How that African girl get her ha'ar look so white?" He ladled out three bowls of hot porridge and set them down in front of us. "Hyar."

"The year's eighteen forty-nine," stuck in MirrorLuther. "Have you been out to sea? You been over to Africa?"

"Twelve years!" cried Eddie. "It is as Uxa said. We have lost twelve years!" He shoved his plate aside, put his head on his arms, and began sobbing. Before we traveled through the Central Anomaly, Eddie had seen a tekelili vision of a living MirrorVirginia, happy with MirrorPoe. Now he feared we'd come too late.

"Don't mind him," said I, and started eating my porridge. Seela ate as well, but Eddie had no appetite. When his porridge had cooled, I gave it to Arf.

Though the stokers were all free men, they lived in the ship much of the time, so we were able to piece together enough clothing to be decent. Eddie and I each got a pair of trousers, and Seela a long shirt. Ayrab and the stokers were curious about our necklaces, but, as I mentioned, Seela had woven them over so thickly that the teeth, the trinkets, and the three rumbies were unprepossessing string-covered lumps. I fluffed and petted Arf until he was quite dry. He curled up in a corner and fell asleep.

After a while, Bill Baldwin reappeared. "Feeling chipper? Captain Parrish would like to see you three." Up the stairs and down the corridors we went, then up a final flight of stairs to a mahogany door. Bill Baldwin rapped briskly and showed us in.

There were two men in the comfortably appointed cabin: an erect, gray-bearded man, clearly the captain, and—

"The MirrorPoe," breathed Eddie.

The MirrorPoe had Eddie's odd high brow and the same large, dark-lashed eyes set in a pallid face that bespoke chivalry and refinement. Every particle of his clothing was black; and a black cane leaned against the arm of his chair. His upper lip twitched slightly beneath his mustache as he regarded us. He seemed careworn and haggard. Before saying anything, he reached a tremulous hand out for his cup of tea and drank deeply of it. He really seemed quite unwell; knowing Eddie as I did, I surmised that MirrorPoe was recovering from a spree.

"Is she still alive?" demanded Eddie. "Virginia. Is she well?"

"It is not your place to interrogate us," said Captain Parrish. His eyes were blue and sober, his face was strong and tan. He sat behind a desk on which were laid out navigational charts, dividers, and a heavy metal ruler. "Which of you calls yourself Edgar Allan Poe? You?"

"Of course me," said Eddie. "Are you then blind? I am Edgar Allan Poe and this wasted relic is but my double, the vile MirrorPoe."

"You ask of Virginia," said MirrorPoe slowly. "Are you straight from hell? Black Imp. Virginia is safe from you." He passed his shaking hand across his brow. "Do you have a past at all, or has my evil fancy invented you whole?" Perhaps he took us for unpleasant hallucinations.

"Safe where?" cried Eddie. "I must make amends to her!"

"Safe in the grave," snarled MirrorPoe. "And before you violate it, foul ghoul, I'll send you back to the Father of Lies!" In a sudden passion of loathing, MirrorPoe rose to his feet. He grabbed for his cane, but it fell to the floor and rolled away. Rather than bowing to pick it up, he snatched up the stout bronze measuring stick that lay on the captain's desk. "Imp of the Perverse, at last I see you face to face!" He strode forward, bringing down the heavy stick with all his might.

Eddie shrieked and cringed, but I had enough presence of mind to dart forward and catch MirrorPoe's wrist. The ruler clattered to the floor. Seela picked it up and held it at the ready, in case we were again attacked.

"Please, Mr. Poe," said I. "Compose yourself. This man is indeed your double, or you his, but there is nothing of the satanic in this. We come not from hell but from another Earth, from the real Earth, as we think of it. For us, your world is as a MirrorEarth. You can believe me when I say that our journey has been fantastical in the highest degree. Only calm yourself and let us tell you of it."

"Virginia dead," sobbed my Eddie, who had fallen to the ground. "A wretched sinner am I."

MirrorPoe took a stiff step back and regarded us three: beautiful red-toothed, blond-haired, black-skinned Seela, with her strong hand now gripping the bronze ruler; I, in form a fine-featured, smallish black youth of sixteen, exceedingly well-spoken; and unhappy ink-dipped Eddie, so obviously a tortured artist, so recognizably a carbon copy of the younger MirrorPoe. Slowly, MirrorPoe picked up his cane and fondled its handle. I noticed a joint six inches below the handle. Perhaps it pulled out to reveal a sword?

"It is as one of your tales come to life, Mr. Poe," said the captain soothingly. "Perhaps you should write their story! It would be a fine serial for the new magazine you were telling me of… *The Stylus*! Tell me truly, you three, how came ye here?"

"We are not slaves," said I. "You must understand that we are not runaway slaves."

"And if I grant you that?" said the captain. "Whence come ye?"

"We…we came up through the sea," said I. "From inside the Hollow Earth."

With Eddie on the floor so defenseless and pitiful, MirrorPoe's expression had already softened. My mention of the Hollow Earth won his interest. The faintest of smiles played over his pallid features, and he perched himself back in his chair, propping the cane against the chair's arm once again.

"Then narrate," said he. "I have no hope of sleep tonight. Pass the hours and tell me your story, young…"

"My name is Mason Algiers Reynolds. I am a white man, I am a gentleman. My unparalleled journey started thirteen years ago, when I left my father's farm in Hardware, Virginia."

"Don't tell him," said Eddie on the floor. "He only wants to steal the glory. If anyone writes our story, it shall be me!"

Seela, unaccustomed to MirrorEarth's heavy gravity, had seated herself on the floor as well,

"Let's hear the tale," said Captain Parrish, ringing a bell. The ponytailed Bill Baldwin popped back in. "Bill, can ye get us three chairs?"

"And some rum and hot water," croaked my Eddie. "I've been a year with no drink."

"It is better so," said MirrorPoe earnestly. "Alcohol is death. Bring no rum; bring us more tea." He had the abnegatory urgency of one who has but recently escaped from the pit.

Bill and a cabin boy had soon brought chairs and tea. I started talking at ten in the evening, by the captain's clock, and when fatigue forced me to stop at four in the morning, I was still not done. So weary was he from our voyage that Eddie dozed through much of my narration. The account I delivered was nothing like so complete as what you have read in the chapters printed here—salient omissions were all the events touching on Virginia, from the particulars of the Poes' wedding night to the state in which we'd found stowed-away Eddie upon the *Wasp*. With his threatening cane ready by his side, MirrorPoe's condition was far too volatile for such revelations.

He took in my narrative with every outward sign of interest and wonder, yet while I talked, I often had the feeling that he was not really there. He seemed like a hollow tree inhabited by small birds that only rarely peep out the knotholes. One could easily see that he had many sorrows upon his heart—and that he had tasted true madness. He welcomed the flow of my long tale's diversions, but he took them in as a man in a dream, with no real questioning or conviction. Still, the last thing he said to us before we went down to the stokers' mess gave me hope of some further contact.

"I am not quite myself tonight. Your tale…if only I could focus on it more acutely…" He sighed deeply. "Perhaps we will talk again after I have journeyed to Philadelphia. Pray tell me your name once more?"

"Mason Reynolds," said I. Remembering our plan to slip off the ship unobserved, I leaned close to him and whispered, "You may seek us at Jilly Tackler's rooming house at Greene Street where it crosses the National Road."

"I know the district well," said MirrorPoe.

"Don't tell him the secrets," murmured sleepy black Eddie, touching his two necklaces. "Don't tell him yet."

We bedded down for a few hours' rest under Ayrab's dozing eye. Shortly after dawn, MirrorLuther woke us.

"We gonna dock in one hour," he whispered to me, his black face huge over mine. "I'll show you the coal chute."

Eddie awakened heavily and with difficulty. He was more shattered by the death of MirrorVirginia than I could have expected, and beyond that, he was unnerved by the evident stature of the MirrorPoe.

Though blasted and broken, MirrorPoe had the aura of a great man, and all the remarks of Captain Parrish and the other officers had strongly confirmed this impression. Unlike Eddie, MirrorEddie had stayed and labored in the literary vineyards, building himself an international reputation as poet, author, and man of letters. Eddie was still free to try and do the same—if that were at all possible, with, one imagined, much of his work old news, here twelve years into the future. And where had MirrorPoe found the will for his adamant sobriety? My Eddie, for one, was ready to drink himself into a stupor. All his plaints and worries he poured out to me.

Meanwhile, MirrorLuther had installed the three of us with Arf at the back of the ship's large coal room, directly beneath a funneled tube that led, MirrorLuther said, to a hatch in the *Pocahontas's* side. When I could get Eddie to stop talking, I explained our situation to Seela as best I could. So far she did not like MirrorEarth very well.

Somewhat later there was a hubbub in the stoker's mess—an officer had come down looking for us, whether to free us or to shackle us, I do not know. Captain Parrish had given every sign of believing us to be free men, yet perhaps he craftily schemed against us. Certainly, he had stolen many long looks at Seela. It seemed best to hold by MirrorLuther's superior wisdom and to leave covertly.

The search for us was interrupted by the tumult of docking: crewmen's feet pounding around the deck, the roar of the steam engine powering us through tight spots, the clatter of the halyards, and the thudding of the sails. The passengers left as noisily as a herd of cows, and then the stevedores set to work, rolling barrels of tobacco out of the *Pocahontas's* hold. Reasoning that if we waited too long we might be found—or buried under tons of new coal—I wormed my way up the chute. Some good soul had already removed the hatch cover and I could stick my head right out of the side of the ship. The stones of the wharf lay four feet below! I called back to Eddie to hand Arf up to me. I put Arf through the hole and then scrambled out and dropped to MirrorEarth's solid ground. Eddie and Seela followed after. A few Negroes witnessed our arrival, but they said nothing. Moving quickly, we crossed the wharf area and found our way into a side street. We paused there while Arf shook and shook himself until he had the coal dust off. I wished I could get my proper color back so easily.

"Where did Luther tell you to go?" asked Eddie.

"He said to go to Jilly Tackler's rooming house," said I. "On Greene Street where it crosses the National Road?"

"The western slum!" exclaimed Eddie. "I used to live there with Virginia and Mrs. Clemm." His brow darkened again. "That is to say, the famous MirrorPoe used to live there. Where I lived, ah Mason, where you and I lived is a world and a world away."

We walked the mile or two to Jilly Tackler's with no great difficulty. To be sure we were only half dressed, but as we were black, no one cared. Jilly's establishment was a rickety three-story wooden house with five rooms on each of the upper two floors. The first floor held kitchen, common room, Jilly's own quarters, and one more rentable room. The basement was the domain of Mr. Turkle, Jilly's factotum, handyman, and (the roomers said) paramour.

Jilly was an ample woman with quantities of costume jewelry. Her skin was mid-tan, and she wore bright red lip-coloring. She had a pink turban on her head. I introduced our party and requested a large room. Jilly was willing enough to rent us a room, but she wanted her money in advance. Speaking in the tongue of the flowerpeople, I asked Seela if I could sell Jilly the rumby on my necklace. Seela wondered if I might sacrifice a seed or a shell instead. I didn't think this would cut any ice with Jilly, and after further discussion, Seela gave me permission to sell the precious jewel from the Hollow Earth. Borrowing a penknife from Jilly, I cut off my nuptial necklace and shaved away the fibers that covered my large, dense, sparkling stone. Jilly was enchanted by the rumby's radiance, and by its psychic aura. It was a jewel of limpid transparency, as large as a grape, and with a peculiar pattern of pentagonal faces. It rendered light into rainbows with the savage efficiency of a diamond. It gave off a faint five of that tekelili sensation we'd experienced among the woomo. Add—which struck Jilly the most—the rumby was so heavy that it made a little thud when she lifted it and set it down.

"Some *kind* of jewel," said the wondering Jilly. She turned and gave me a sharp look. "Where you get that, Mason?" She more than half thought us to be runaway slaves. "You steal that from yo Marse?"

"It is not stolen," I promised her. "Although we have no papers, we are not runaway slaves. This gem was mined in a strange and distant land."

"Mother Africa! Is that whar Seela from? How do she make her ha'ar so white?"

"It is an oddity of her tribe," said I. "Yes, I suppose you could say that Eddie and I are sailors who met Seela in Africa."

"A dark continent indeed," put in Eddie. "Madam Tackler, I can see that you desire the jewel exceedingly, and quite rightly so. This is a so-called rumby, worn by the most exalted of black queens. If we give it to you, will you let us live here for…"

Thinking of Seela's pregnancy, I named the figure. "Nine months?"

"Nine month?" Jilly picked up the strange jewel and tested it with her teeth. "If the jeweler say this be real…"

"Perhaps it is best if we take it to a jeweler ourselves," said Eddie, reaching for the gem. "Can you recommend one?"

"Six month," said Jilly, staring into the sparkling gem. "Don't need no jeweler. I got a nice big room on the third flo'. Number eleven. You go on up while I shows this to Mr. Turkle. If he think highly of it, you gets free rent for six month."

"With board?" asked Eddie, veteran of many rooming houses. "And can we have ten dollars?"

"I gives dinner, but I ain't got me no ten dollar. You bettah go find you a job, Eddie. What else you got in the necklaces?"

I sawed some more of my necklace threads away. Jilly's fancy was caught by an unearthly cowrie and by a lustrously red seed.

"Can we have *five* dollars?" I asked.

"Get on with you." She handed me four dollar bills. "Yo room's on the third flo' in the back. Number eleven, one-one. Spell good luck. There's a water pump down to the street corner if you wants to wash. You gets coal for the stove from Mr. Turkle downstairs."

"Thank you."

"That dog of yourn...is he housebroke? Do he bite?"

"He'll be no trouble. His name is Arf." I trotted out my old witticism. "He's so smart he knows his own name, and he's so famous all the other dogs talk about him."

Jilly chuckled politely and went back to gazing at her rumby, enchanted by its beauty and by its tekelili vibrations.

The room had two beds; pallets on the floor, actually. One for Seela and me, one for Eddie and Arf. The room was very dirty. What a place to bring Seela! Eddie was depressed to find himself in a Negro rooming house with a dog for his bedmate. He badgered me until I gave him one of our dollars and a cowrie shell. He went out. I took our pitcher down to the corner and got water. And then before doing anything else, I scrubbed down the walls and cleaned the dried spit off our stove. After getting a broom from Mr. Turkle—a bald brown man with almost no chin—I threw the rest of the water on the floor and swept much of the filth into the hall.

Now I lit the stove and put our basin on it to warm. Three trips to the fountain and I'd fetched enough to fill the pan. Seela and I bathed. She enjoyed it. The way water behaved in our gravity delighted her—just as the weightless waterballs of the Hollow Earth had delighted me. For Seela, trickling water from the pitcher into the basin was a fascinating novelty.

Once we'd washed the trip off ourselves, we went out to buy clothes, Arf at our heels. The shirt and trousers we had were little more than rags. There was a street of Negro shops not far from Jilly's. I got myself a linen shirt and a suit of worsted. Seela was ready to wear the same...until she noticed that the other women wore dresses. She picked herself a beautiful yellow dress, with a color like her home flower; and I got her a sturdy blue jacket to wear over it. Shoes, socks, and undergarments we purchased as well. Then we went for a little walk.

Back in the Hollow Earth, Seela had never worn shoes, or really walked for that matter, and her feet pained her considerably. We found a square with some benches and sat down there. The day had started out cloudy, but now it was sunny, though cool. Bright autumn leaves littered the green grass. Arf lay down and regarded us with alert eyes. After so much tekelili with him, I felt like he was a real person.

"*Oofanah goolu.*" I said to Seela, pointing to a red maple leaf drifting by. To help her learn English I had adopted the custom of saying everything twice, once in my broken flower-language and then in English. "The leaf is pretty." I wanted her to like it here.

"*Goolu,*" agreed Seela, smiling. Her blond hair and red teeth had attracted a lot of notice in the shops, but I'd settled on the story that she was an African princess from an unknown tribe. People liked the story.

But now suddenly someone was poking me with a stick. A policeman.

"Move along there, boy," he told me. "And take your fancy woman with you. The benches are for whites."

As we walked back to Jilly's rooming house, I tried to explain this to Seela. Given her tribe's worshipful attitude toward the black gods, she was having trouble understanding that here on MirrorEarth, white skin was deemed better than black. For my part, I wondered how many weeks or months it would take us to fade to white.

Jilly and Mr. Turkle served up a greasy dinner of greens, sidemeat, cornbread, and beans. It was filling, if not particularly fine. There was no sign of Eddie. After dinner, Seela and I went to our room and made love. Eddie came in shortly after dark, fiercely exultant. Instead of getting drunk, as I'd expected, he'd purchased pen and paper and had spent his day writing! No white public house would admit him, and the Negro establishments repelled him. He'd passed the day in the back pew of a church, no less a church than Mirror-Baltimore's great Basilica of the Assumption. Touched by the half-clothed black man's earnest scribings, a verger had given Eddie shirt and shoes and had provided him a dinner as well. And what had Eddie written? He lit a candle that he'd abstracted from a side altar and handed me two closely written sheets of paper.

I had expected the beginnings of a narrative about our journey, but instead I found that Eddie had penned a long, intricately rhythmic poem entitled "The Raven." I read it twice through silently, and then I prevailed on Eddie to read it aloud. Even though Seela could not understand its words, she too was spellbound by the poem's melancholy music.

Even now I find myself quite overwhelmed by the power of the last three verses of Eddie's "The Raven." Whipped into mad imaginings by the strange bird, the poet bares the hope closest to his heart and is rebuffed utterly. Next, he strikes a defiant posture as answer, but quickly the defiance fades to a desperate plea that the bird "take thy beak from out my heart." And then, in the heartbreaking last verse, comes the collapse into a nightmare stasis of oppression.

> "Prophet!" said I, "thing of evil—prophet
>   still, if bird or devil!
> By that Heaven that bends above us—by that
>   God we both adore—
> Tell this soul with sorrow laden if, within the
>   distant Aidenn,

I shall clasp a sainted maiden whom the angels
    name Lenore—
Clasp a rare and radiant maiden whom the
    angels name Lenore."
Quoth the Raven, "Nevermore."

"Be that word our sign of parting, bird or
    fiend!" I shrieked, upstarting—
"Get thee back into the tempest and the Night's
    Plutonian shore!
Leave no black plume as a token of that lie thy
    soul hath spoken!
Leave my loneliness unbroken!—quit the bust
    above my door!
Take thy beak from out my heart, and take thy
    form from off my door!"
Quoth the Raven, "Nevermore."

And the Raven, never flitting, still is sitting,
    still is sitting
On the pallid bust of Pallas just above my
    chamber door;
And his eyes have all the seeming of a demon's
    that is dreaming,
And the lamp-light o'er him streaming throws
    his shadow on the floor;
And my soul from out that shadow that lies
    floating on the floor
Shall be lifted—nevermore!

For all the poem's sadness, Eddie the man was uplifted
by having accomplished this wonderful creation. He went
to bed almost happy.

Saturday morning, the weather turned bitterly cold, with sprinkles of rain. Eddie proposed that Seela and I accompany him to the offices of the MirrorEarth version of the *Baltimore Saturday Visiter*, a magazine that on Earth had been the first to publish one of Eddie's stories: his "MS. Found in a Bottle." I had planned to spend the morning looking for work, but Eddie's enthusiasm won me over.

"And who knows, Mason," he continued. "Once we tell them of our adventures, they may engage to publish them as a serial. You've an itch to write too, haven't you, boy? Mayhap we'll work together—you can do the rough draft, and I'll polish it! In view of the fact that the MirrorPoe has used up my name, perhaps we'd best publish under your cognomen, at least until the true facts of our journey have been widely disseminated. 'The Raven' and *The Hollow Earth*…by Mason Reynolds! Remember, I will do the speaking. I have a long familiarity with the ways of journalism."

Arf and we three were admitted into the office of the *Saturday Visiter* with considerable difficulty, despite Eddie's insistence that he knew the editor, John Hewitt. Hewitt looked up at us with a complete lack of recognition, and when Eddie introduced himself, stubbornly using his real name, Hewitt's bafflement turned to truculence.

"Yes, and I'm Washington Irving," said he. "What is your business here? We have no present need for servants."

"Behold," said Eddie, and handed him the manuscript of "The Raven."

Hewitt read briefly, then threw back his head and gave an angry guffaw. "You dunces," said he. "Have you no concept at all? Is a poem, then, a shiny trinket to pass from hand to hand like a stolen watch?"

"But it's a wonderful poem!" I interposed. "Why don't you read it through?"

"Because I've already read it a dozen times!" shouted Hewitt, throwing the papers at my feet. "The real Edgar Allan Poe published 'The Raven' nearly five years ago. Do you ignorant wretches really think you can copy out a great work of literature word for word and pass it off as your own? Out! Get out of my sight!"

Eddie gave only a strangled sob. I pocketed the manuscript, and we left. Back on the wet, blustery street, I tried to cheer Eddie with the thought of writing *The Hollow Earth*, but he no longer wished to hear anything of it. Walking rapidly, he led us to a bookstore and hurried in. There we found four volumes by the MirrorPoe: *The Narrative of Arthur Gordon Pym of Nantucket, Tales, The Raven and Other Poems,* and *Eureka.* The Pym narrative was the completion of the sea story that Eddie had been working on before we left. The *Tales* included twelve stories, all of them new. The poetry collection held not only a word-for-word copy of Eddie's "Raven" but also the text of his "The City in the Sea." Reading through the printed "Raven," I was struck by how weak a poem it seemed if I thought of it as written by the effete and condescending MirrorPoe. From Eddie it was (and still is) pure magic, but from MirrorPoe it is plodding doggerel. *Eureka*, as far as I could gather from a hasty glance through it, was a rambling farrago about the nature of the universe. If this was MirrorPoe's latest, the man was in very poor condition indeed. How could he write of the world's structure without mentioning the central fact that *all celestial bodies are hollow!* Old fool.

Eddie struck up a conversation with the bookseller, a common-looking man wearing a green coat and a gray cravat with a stickpin. "You are a friend of Edgar Allan Poe's, are you not?" said Eddie.

The bookseller regarded Eddie with puzzlement. "You are a reader?"

"Yes, I read, Mr. Coale. I am an author. Things are not always what they seem. If you take me and my companions for Negroes, you err severely. We have traveled here by way of the Hollow Earth, and the pink light at Earth's center has burned us black."

"Indeed!" A smile played over Coale's fleshy lips. "To whom do I have the honor of speaking?"

"My name is Edgar Allan Poe." Eddie held up his hand for silence. "I come from an Earth that is a copy of your MirrorEarth. In the early 1830s I spent many hours in a shop that is a copy of your shop. I have every reason to suppose that my actions there were copied by the MirrorPoe who lives here. Of course you think me mad, Mr. Coale, but have a caution." Eddie paused and glanced intently around the shop. Coale turned his plain face to me, wondering. "I have it," exclaimed Eddie. "Mr. Coale, do you remember a rainy April day in eighteen thirty-two when you and Edgar Poe sat here quite alone and played a game of chess? Poe checkmated your king with a rook, a bishop, and a knight. Turning your king on its side, you said, 'Motley, Poe, but well done!' You and he lunched on bread and cheese, and in the afternoon a crate with twenty copies of Washington Irving's *The Alhambra* arrived. Poe whiled away the rest of the afternoon reading to you from it, and then you and he went out for dinner. And *this*!" Eddie pointed a triumphant finger at Coale's chest. "*This* you surely must remember! While eating an oyster, you found a large black pearl. You wear it yet!"

Smiling feebly, Coale fingered his black pearl stickpin. "That I found this pearl in an oyster is common knowledge, good sir. I grant that your account of that April day has verisimilitude. But after seventeen years..." Coale shrugged and spread his hands. "Pray be open. What is it you want of me?"

"Books!"

"And you have no money?" Coale shook his head. "Very like Edgar Poe. Very like. Which books did you want?"

"What did you think? I want *The Narrative of Arthur Gordon Pym*, the *Tales*, *The Raven*, and *Eureka*. The total cost is two dollars and fifty cents. I give you my word as a gentleman that I will repay you,"

"Your word?'

"Wait," said I, drawing out the manuscript of "The Raven." "This is worth something, is it not?"

Coale peered at the paper for a long time, then glanced up at me. "It is a forgery?"

"You are unable to tell?"

"I know Poe's hand intimately." He stepped to the front of the shop and scrutinized the papers in the light from the window. "Very plausible," he said, after a time. "If I were to deem it genuine, it could be worth three dollars. Certainly it is a famous poem, but the manuscripts of living authors fetch no excessively high price."

"Can I have another book?" asked Eddie.

"Which?" said Coale, good-humoredly entering our fantasia.

"Due to our long voyage, I am ignorant of the past twelve years of literature. Who are the best pens? Who shines? Who...who has your Poe reviewed favorably?"

"Nathaniel Hawthorne," said Coale, stepping to the rear of his store and storing our manuscript of "The Raven" in his high desk. "Mr. Poe reviewed *Twice Told Tales* so favorably in *Graham's Magazine* that he is quoted in the endpapers. I have a copy over there." He pointed to a spot near me, and I took the book down.

I opened to the endpaper and read aloud. "'The style is purity itself. Force abounds. High imagination gleams from every page. Mr. Hawthorne is a man of the truest genius.'—E. A. Poe, *Graham's Magazine*. You say we can take this book as well, Mr. Coale?"

"You both read?" marveled Coale.

"Yes, and mayhap someday I will be a writer like Mr. Poe. My name is Mason Algiers Reynolds." I gave a little bow, and Seela laughed to see me move so oddly. She had not the slightest notion of what books were or of what we were doing here.

When we got back to Jilly's, Eddie and I sat down in the parlor to read. Jilly was in excellent spirits—she'd shown her rumby to a jeweler after all, and he'd offered to trade her a sizable diamond for the unearthly gem.

"But I'm keepin what's mine!" exclaimed Jilly. "Look at you two with yo books. Regular gentlemen!" She coaxed Seela into the kitchen and chattered at her as she began to cook a dinner.

We read all the rest of that day and most of Sunday and Monday as well. As Poe had always been my favorite author, the experience was delicious for me. But for Eddie it was shattering. Here in these four volumes were the full-grown fruits of so many of the seeds his soul harbored! It seemed as if all that he'd dreamed of writing had already been accomplished…and the joy of creation, the public acclaim, and the income had gone to another man.

This other man, this MirrorPoe, had not forgotten us. He came to us at dawn Tuesday morning, rapping on our door with the head of his cane. I opened to see him there, with Jilly standing anxiously behind him. She supposed him to be an agent for a master we'd fled.

"They tole me they free," she was saying.

"Leave us," said MirrorPoe. "And do not fret. I wish only to speak with them." He stepped into our room and closed the door. He was dressed in black as before, and carried the same cane. A rich cloak rested on his shoulders. His eyes were clear and sober.

"Seela, Mason Reynolds, and…Eddie Poe," said he, looking us over with some care. "I was not entirely sure that you were real. That night on the *Pocahontas*, I was not quite well."

"You were recovering from a drinking bout," said Eddie. "There is no need to dissemble before your own double. And Mason knows me as well as anyone ever has. From your appearance I would say that you have been free of the *mania a potu* these last three days. Are you ready to start again?"

"*Mania a potu?*" said I.

"Poe Latin for drunkenness," explained my Eddie, laughing. "What did you do in Philadelphia, Mr. Poe?"

MirrorPoe gave a smile that was almost boyish. "I have been courting two rich poetesses. I am raising money to start a new magazine, *The Stylus*."

"Just the name I would choose," said Eddie. "Tell me this. Have you written any tales about Symmes's Hollow Earth?" He indicated our little library of Poe books. "So much of what I might write has already been accomplished by you. I don't remember if Mason told you that we lost twelve years going through the Hollow Earth. Though you are forty, I am still but twenty-eight. Do you know that on my first day here in MirrorBaltimore I wrote 'The Raven'? I took it to Hewitt at the *Visiter*, and he threw it in my black face. He thought me a plagiarist!"

"This…this is what drew me back," said MirrorPoe, growing pale. "You truly are my double? The story young

Reynolds told…it is quite veracious? There is an Earth and a MirrorEarth, both hollow, and the two worlds are connected by a kind of maelstrom at their centers?"

"These facts are incontestable," said Eddie. "The two Earths form a pair which enjoys an exceeding yet imperfect symmetry. For a full symmetry, *you* should have traveled to the other Earth, my home. But you did not do so." He paused, thinking. "Is there a MirrorMasonReynolds?" he asked MirrorPoe, and then pointed at me to clarify his question. "Do you know a MirrorEarth double of this rogue?"

"No…" said Poe, looking at me closely. "I know a *Jeremiah* Reynolds, promulgator of the Symmes theory. He and I once attempted some plans for outfitting a trip to the antarctic…"

I thought back to the day Jeremiah had appeared in Richmond. It was I who'd met him on the porch, and I who'd kept him there talking until Eddie came back from trying to get his marriage license. "It was Saturday, May fourteenth, in the year eighteen thirty-six," said I. They looked surprised, and I smiled modestly. "I've always had a good head for dates. That was the day when Jeremiah Reynolds brought us James Eights's plates for the counterfeit Bank of Kentucky bills. Did you counterfeit the money too, Mr. Poe?"

"Jeremiah and I missed our meeting," said MirrorPoe. "Perhaps he came by the house when I was not in. I do remember that on the following Monday, that would be May sixteenth, I got an advance from my employer Mr. White, posted bond, and married Virginia. And the next day we went to Petersburg on our honeymoon."

"You see, Mason," said Eddie. "You're the cause of it all. What do you think became of MirrorMason?"

"I think he's dead," said I. "Remember our vision? When you saw MirrorVirginia, too?"

"Poor Jeremiah," responded my Eddie, quick to change the subject. He jerked his thumb at Seela. "*Our* Jeremiah was decapitated and fed to a giant nautilus by her tribe. Mr. Poe, your *Narrative of Arthur Gordon Pym* proceeds to the very rim of the South Hole and then breaks off. I pray that you have contemplated no supplement. Tell me that you have not yet written our tale of the Hollow Earth!"

"No," said MirrorPoe. "I have not. And willingly do I cede this field to you." There was a low hubbub in Jilly's house now, as the roomers woke and shuffled off to their jobs. Arf got up, shook himself, and scratched at the door to be let out.

"What should we do next?" said I.

"Let's get drunk," said black Eddie, grinning at his white twelve-years-older self with easy, jeering intimacy. "Do you have pocket money, Mr. Poe? Some opium would be pleasant, and some good port wine. Laudanum—can we afford laudanum? What if we were to pawn your cloak?"

MirrorPoe's face took on a skulking, haunted cast—but only for a moment. Arf scratched the door once again. MirrorPoe drew himself up to his full height and scrutinized us, every inch the gentleman, his crossed hands resting on the head of his ebony cane.

"Come then, you three," said he. "Let us go to the white part of town. I shall await you in my carriage." He drew his cloak about himself and let himself out of our room, Arf hard on his heels.

"He Eddie's bro?" asked Seela. "We goin with him?" Sunday afternoon, she had begun to speak black English. With magical abruptness, our past tekelili, my tutoring, and Jilly's ministrations had taken effect at Sunday dinner. And perhaps the aura of the rumbies had helped as well. Seela's first sentence had been, "Gimme mo fried chicken!" Mr. Turkle had passed her the platter of fried chicken, and Seela had talked for the rest of the meal.

"We'll go with him," said I.

With MirrorPoe waiting for us, we hurriedly attempted to make ourselves presentable. I went down to the street to empty our slops and to fetch fresh water. A hackney carriage was waiting at the corner of the National Road. I sped back upstairs with the water, and we cleaned ourselves up.

Ten minutes later we were in the hackney with Mirror-Poe, maneuvering our way around great Conestoga wagons, each with a team of four to six horses, setting out down the National Road for the western frontier. "My trip to

Philadelphia was not in vain," said MirrorPoe. "Singularly enough, I prosper. I have collected two hundred dollars toward the founding of *The Stylus*." MirrorPoe smiled and patted Eddie on the knee. "Guess where I've put up, my dear younger self."

"The Fountain Inn?"

"Better! I have a suite at Barnum's Hotel!"

"Hallelujah." Eddie cackled. "The finest hotel in Baltimore!" He glanced down at his black hands and rough clothes. "Will they let us in?"

"For a certainty," said MirrorPoe. "You have only to pose as my slaves. I have registered myself as a Colonel Embry. Simply keep mum and follow me. Mason, you carry Arf."

Set on MirrorBaltimore's Monument Square, the Barnum City Hotel was the biggest building I'd ever seen: a full seven stories high. Our carriage clattered under the elegant, columned entrance. Keeping a respectful distance, we followed MirrorPoe inside. The doorman grinned and sang, "Yas ma'am!" as he let Seela in. With her yellow hair and yellow dress, all clean, and with her red teeth flashing against her dark skin, she was stunningly beautiful.

The rich carpeting of the lobby was thick as the grass of the Umpteen Seas. Heavy red velvet curtains hung at the sides of each of the many entranceways, and great gilt-framed mirrors ran from floor to ceiling on every available wall.

"I be glad if this where we live," said Seela, finally pleased by something on the outside of the Hollow Earth. She pointed to one of the mirrors. "Do that be another new world?"

"No, dear Seela, it is a mirror, like stiff water." I walked over to one of the mirrors with her and rapped my knuckles on it. "Not real."

"You and me?" She pointed. There we were, both of us black as the ace of spades, Seela with full lips and flattish nose, and my face very fine-featured for a dog-carrying slave. Tan-and-white old Arfie lolled at ease in my arms, his black lip-line looking particularly winsome. Behind us I could see MirrorPoe and Eddie, waiting for us by…the elevator! I'd never ridden in an elevator before. "Come, Seela."

The elevator ride was unpleasantly reminiscent of our trip through the ocean in the fried egg—but of course it was over in but a few moments. The slave who ran the elevator eyed MirrorPoe, Eddie, Seela, and me curiously.

"She yo wife?" he asked me.

"Yes," said I, proudly.

MirrorPoe's fourth-floor suite consisted of a drawing room and a bedroom, placed side by side together at the middle of the hotel's front wall. Each room had two windows looking out onto the street—so four windows in a row. Magnificent lodgings! Like the lobby, the rooms were thickly carpeted and hung with red velvet curtains, and there were several mirrors as well. As if the plush carpeting were not enough, several Oriental rugs were laid out over it. The bed itself had curtains, and the bedroom had a washroom, complete with a full-size bathtub overhung by a great petcocked tank of wash water, fresh and warm.

MirrorPoe pushed an electric bell-button, and the next minute a servant was at our door, a sympathetic though feeble-looking Negro with white hair and red livery. His name was William.

"Bring us dinner for four," said MirrorPoe. "The duck we had yesterday, is it still available? Yes? Most excellent. Duck for four and a good supply of Chateau Margaux. I think three bottles. And could you send a boy out to the chemist's for an ounce of opium? Wonderful." It was ten o'clock of a Tuesday morning.

"Oysters and champagne as well," demanded my Eddie. "Four dozen oysters and five bottles of champagne in a tub of ice. Cognac and armagnac. And amontillado."

"It shall be as you desire," rejoined MirrorPoe. "Do you hear, bell captain? And a pint of laudanum with the opium."

William recited the order as if it were as harmless as toast and tea. "So that be four dozen oysters, four duck dinner, three bottle wine, ounce of opium, five bottle champagne on ice, one bottle cognac, one bottle armagnac, one bottle amontillado, an a pint of laudanum. There be sump'n else, Colonel Embry suh?"

"Make it a quart of laudanum, Mr. Poe," said Eddie.

"As he says." MirrorPoe nodded, with that haunted, skulking air again.

"Yassuh. You speck that be all you need? Is yo servants sleepin on the seventh flo?"

"I prefer to keep them with me for the present. And let us continually settle accounts straightaway." He drew a slim sheaf of bills from his pocket and handed one to William. The bills were twenties!

"Yassuh, Colonel Embry. I bring up you change with the order straight away."

While we waited, Eddie and MirrorPoe fell into a conversation about their childhood. Arf settled himself in a corner of the bedroom. Seela and I went into the washroom and enjoyed a full bath together.

By the time we finished our bath, William had reappeared with a maid and a waiter in tow. The waiter stood with back to us, opening the oysters and arranging them on the sideboard. Meanwhile, William and the maid moved a table to the center of the room, covered it with a white linen cloth, and quickly laid out four place settings. William accepted a tip from MirrorPoe, and then he and the maid took their leave.

Thus did our long last feast begin.

15. The Conqueror Worm

"Sherry would be the thing just now," said MirrorPoe. "Before the champagne and oysters. Waiter, can you pour us four glasses of the amontillado?"

"Yes sir."

When the waiter turned from the sideboard bearing a small silver tray with four glasses, I got my first good look at him. It was Otha?!? No, no, it was *MirrorOtha*, the very image of my Otha, twelve years older and gone somewhat to fat.

"*Oo'm gowow* Otha!" exclaimed Seela. "Why you old, Otha?"

Already puzzled by the sight of a white man taking dinner with three slaves, MirrorOtha was quite dumbfounded by Seela's exclamation. Silently, he served each of us a crystal glass of amontillado sherry: first MirrorPoe, then Seela, then Eddie, then me. As I took my glass, MirrorOtha looked into my face and started back with a shock of recognition.

"Is you from Virginia?" he asked me.

"I'm Mason Reynolds," said I. "A copy of the Mason you knew."

MirrorPoe and Eddie were busy toasting each other, while Seela stared at MirrorOtha and me.

"It's MirrorOtha," I told her. "Not Otha. Like Eddie and MirrorPoe."

"You never seen me before?" Seela asked MirrorOtha.

"I sees you now," said he. "Is you slave or free? I'm free. Where you from?"

"The Hollow Earth," said Seela. She nodded toward me. "On my home flower, Mason's a slave and I'm free."

"Don't mix everything up," I told Seela, and turned to MirrorOtha. "We're both free, and Seela is my wife, and we're white, and I grew up with your double."

"Bull*shit*," muttered MirrorOtha, pushing out his lips.

I thought of a way to convince him. "Hey, Arfie," I called. "Hey, Arf!"

Arf stood up and shook himself so hard that his ears flapped against his head. I could tell that he relished the return to gravity. "Arfie! Come say hello. It's Otha!" Arf twitched his nose to taste the scent of MirrorOtha, and then, acknowledging the verisimilitude, put his legs up on MirrorOtha and whined hello.

"Do you recognize Arf?" said I. "Boon pet of yore?"

"Arf!" cried MirrorOtha. "How you get here, boy? I left you to home under the bed!"

"You have a dog like him? You have a MirrorArf?"

"Ain't no mirror about him," said MirrorOtha, rubbing Arf's head but not really looking at him. "Cept his ha'ar always shed. He can't eat nothin but mush no more. Don't know how he followed me in here..." He happened to glance down at Arf's head, which rested on his thigh as he caressed it. He gave a grunt of surprise and jerked his hand up into the air. "This ain't Arf! This dog still young!" He stepped close to me and studied my face. He was almost angry. "Stop lying and tell me where you from. I can believe that yo dog is Arf's son and I can see from your look that Marse Reynolds was yo pa. But who's yo ma? Is—is yo Ma be named Turl? Who raise you, an where?"

MirrorOtha thought I was Purly, the little "nephew" whose mother was Turl and whose father was Pa! The memory of that wretched Christmas night when Pa had raped Turl rushed back to me. I remembered how Otha had broken our new skittles game and run out to crouch crying in our empty field, and I remembered my last farewell to Otha at the Umpteen Seas. My heart gave a little jerk; it felt like a flower unfolding. I seized his hand and pressed it between mine.

"Believe me, Otha, I'm not Purly. I'm Mason Reynolds, from another world. On my way here I went through some strong light that turned me black, and now I can begin to understand what it is to be black. I'm sorry I ever thought you and your folks were slaves. I'm sorry for what Pa did to Turl that Christmas."

MirrorOtha pulled back his hand and stared at me. "You ain't Mason, cause Mason been dead since 1836. I seen him die. It were me carried him back to his pa. You don't got to tell me about no Mason Reynolds. I growed up with him, an I seen him go into the ground."

"Another amontillado, boy," called MirrorPoe to MirrorOtha. "And then quit your crow-cawing and get the oysters ready!"

"Do it yourself!" I yelled. I picked up the sherry bottle and slammed it down on the table in front of Eddie and MirrorPoe. "Go on, you two! Get drunk and go crazy, but don't tell Otha what to do!"

"Set down or leave, Purly," said MirrorOtha to me sharply. "And don't try an speak for yo elders. I'm a waiter, and I got a meal to serve."

"MirrorOtha!" exclaimed Eddie, finally noticing.

"Exactly," said I. "Don't you think he should eat with us?"

"No." Eddie poured himself and MirrorPoe another glass of sherry. "Drink your amontillado, Mason, if only as a tonic for blue devils and the mania. Remember—this is the MirrorEarth. This Otha is not our companion of yore."

Seela and I took our seats and tasted our sherry. It was fragrant and strong. The alcohol mounted immediately to Seela's head, and she began to giggle.

The table was longer than it was wide; we were seated two to a side. Eddie and Seela were across from MirrorPoe and me. MirrorPoe and I had our backs to the hall. We could see out the two windows in the drawing-room wall. A sea breeze had blown away the low clouds of dawn, and then the breeze had died, leaving a calm, sunny Tuesday mid-morning, the second day of October 1849. When I looked out the windows, I saw down into the shimmering red and yellow leaves of two maples and an elm. MirrorPoe's cane leaned in the corner. The windows were separated by an oak sideboard, which was a flat-topped waist-high cabinet with griffin legs. Seela and Eddie faced the drawing room's inside wall, which held a wall-mounted candelabrum, a door, and one of the Barnum's huge red-curtained mirrors. MirrorPoe was on my left, as was the door to the bedroom. Seela sat directly across from me.

"I'd like to hear another installment of your narrative," said MirrorPoe to me. He seemed greatly invigorated by his two drinks. "On the *Pocahontas* you told of your trip to the antarctic, of your fall through Symmes's Hole, of your time with Seela's tribe, and of your second fall to the Earth's center. Tell me more of what you found there; tell me of the Great Old Ones and of the maelstrom between the worlds."

"Did he tell you about tekelili?" said my Eddie. "All layers of the mind become as patent as the strata on a quarried cliff. So wonderful a union with the All…" His voice trailed off, and he began again. "Where did you put the opium, Mr. Poe? If we smoke a bit we'll have something very like."

"These days I prefer to eat it," said MirrorPoe, reaching into his pocket and drawing forth a dark, irregular bolus of the sticky poppy dust. He used his razor-sharp penknife to section out a slice the size and shape of a small orange segment. He divided this in two and gave half to Eddie.

"Champagne, boy!" sang MirrorPoe, and placed his opium on his tongue. I started again to protest on MirrorOtha's behalf, but before I could speak, MirrorOtha turned and glared at me, his hands busy all the while with the cork of a champagne bottle. He pushed his lips out and narrowed his eyes in a way that he had used to do when angered to the point of administering a beating to one of the other black boys. I thought it the better part of wisdom to cease badgering him for now, and to consult privily with him later.

The champagne bubbled into our fluted glasses with a stiff crackle. Neither Eddie nor MirrorPoe thought to propose a toast, but simply fell to. I raised my glass to Seela. She sniffed her glass, sipped, coughed, and began to giggle again. MirrorOtha removed the sherry bottle and glasses and brought us each eight oysters on ice. They were live and fresh, with the crisp taste of the sea. We ate them with a will.

Another glass of champagne, and now came the duck and the Margaux. There were two roast ducks on the sideboard, and MirrorOtha carved us each a red-running medallion of breast and a crisp-skinned slice of thigh. There was a dollop of currant jelly on the side of each plate, and a quivering mound of bread pudding filled with nutmeats, mushrooms, and greens. MirrorOtha brought around a sauce boat of clear gravy and anointed our plates. Then he refilled the champagne flutes and poured out four glasses of the tart, fragrant, richly red Margaux. Eddie, Seela, and I fell on the food like wolves, and MirrorPoe dined as ravenously as if he were no more accustomed to this luxury than were we.

MirrorOtha served out seconds for those who wanted it, refilled the Margaux glasses, served thirds, refilled the champagne glasses, and then went back to the oysters. When we'd quite finished dining, he cleared the plates and brought us snifters and the bottles of cognac and armagnac. Eddie and I had told about the rest of our journey; MirrorPoe and Eddie had further reminisced over their common childhood; MirrorPoe had intently and with great fascination questioned Seela over the flora and the fauna of the Hollow Earth; and I'd told of my union with Seela and of my vision of our child, to be born in late June or early July, 1850, as I reckoned MirrorEarth time.

By now, believe it or not, it was five o'clock in the afternoon, come and gone. Otha had lit the candelabrum on the wall and had placed two candles on our table. All four of us were quite thoroughly sozzled, Seela so much so that she had kicked off her shoes and lain down on the floor.

MirrorPoe called for his cane, then stood and, with patient hand, poured a heady mixture of the two liquors into three of the cut-crystal snifters.

"A pipe," cried Eddie. "Let me clear my head with a pipe, Mr. Poe."

"Not the laudanum?" said MirrorPoe coolly.

"Not yet."

"Very well." MirrorPoe went into his bedroom and returned with a small brass pipe and a thin shingle of wood. "Waiter!" called he.

"Yes sir."

"Will you sit down and share a pipe?"

"Thank you, Colonel."

MirrorOtha sat down at the head of the table between Eddie and MirrorPoe, his chair pulled a respectful distance back. While carving and trimming the ducks, he had let numerous gobbets drop Arf's way. Pleased, greasy Arf ambled over to lie at his feet.

MirrorPoe pinched a bit off his ball of opium and rolled the pinch into a little sphere. He put the spherule in the pipe and handed the pipe to Eddie. Then he broke a long splinter off the edge of the shingle and used the splinter as a taper, lighting it from the candle and holding it over Eddie's bowl. Eddie drew in air and the thick, tarry opium melted, bubbled, and began to glow ruby-red at its base. It reminded me of the Central Anomaly, as seen from the antarctic end of Symmes's Hole.

I stood up and stretched. Seela was, as I said, comfortably asleep on the thick rug. This would have been perfectly natural on the home blossom or among the Umpteen Seas, but here in the slave state of Maryland, it could prove incendiary to social mores. I urged Seela to her feet. We walked into the bedroom and I tucked her into the clean white linen of the bed, a sheet on bottom and a soft linen-covered comforter on top.

"*Oomo gooba'am*, Mason," said she, smiling sleepily up at me. "This is very nice. You get in too?"

I studied Seela's full out-turned lips, her comfortable nose, the down of blond hair on her temples, the delicate curves of her ears. Why not get in bed with her? I had no special desire to smoke opium with MirrorOtha and the Poes.

"Yes."

I pushed the door closed and undressed. Seela pulled her dress off, and now we lay naked together between sheets for the very first time.

"This is how it's supposed to be," I told Seela. "Once we're white again, we'll always live this way."

"*Gooba'am.*"

We made love for nearly an hour and then dropped into a deep sleep.

I woke sometime after midnight to the sound of laughter in the next room. My tongue felt foul and I had a thumping headache. Were those three still at it? I pulled on my trousers and opened the bedroom door to see.

The candle stubs were burning brightly. The dishes and the remains of the duck sat on the sideboard with the emptied bottles of wine and champagne. On the table were the ball of opium, greatly reduced in size, the brown medicine bottle of laudanum, nearly full, and the cognac and armagnac bottles, three-quarters empty.

Eddie, MirrorPoe, and MirrorOtha sat just where I'd left them, each with a snifter of alcohol and MirrorPoe still with his cane at his side. Eddie was in the act of lighting the opium pipe. His motions were elaborately smooth.

Skin color did not show up so clearly in the monochrome illumination of the candlelight, and as they bent together, Eddie and MirrorPoe looked more like each other than ever, with their identical high brows, small mustaches, and delicate chins. Opium smoke curled up from MirrorPoe's pipe, scenting the smoky air with yet stronger fragrance.

I put my shirt on and pulled a chair over to sit down at MirrorOtha's side. I still wanted to ask him about how MirrorMason had died and about how all the others in MirrorVirginia fared. I now realized I had no intention of going there. In the past I'd thought of taking Seela to MirrorLynchburg for a real church wedding—but the longer I walked around as a black, the less I wanted anything to do with the slave states. Or, for that matter, with churches. When I left Baltimore, I'd head north or west.

"Hello, Otha," said I. He turned slowly to gaze at me with drugged, reddened eyes. "I've already told you I'm a copy of Mason and you don't believe me, but can you tell me how your Mason died? Who shot him, and why?"

"It were the goddamn stableboy from the Liberty Hotel shot him," said MirrorOtha slowly. "Mason lost all his pa's gold to the hotel, and when he steal it back, that damn little wretch done shoot Mason in the back of his head."

The stableboy! It all came down to that one instant when the stableboy and I had fired our guns; that had been the instant when my Earth and MirrorEarth diverged. Hadn't the black god Watcher hinted at that? My linked life and death were the flaw that unlocked the symmetry of the worlds. I felt fragile as a grain of corn in a gristmill.

"Did you ever get Wawona?" I asked, just to be saying something.

MirrorOtha stared heavily at me. His body was slowly rocking back and forth. "Naw. But I'm married just the same. Married me a gal in Baltimo' after I moved up…been ten years ago. Got three kids with her and I got two more with my other gal."

"Did…did Pa set you free?"

"He died two year after Mason. And in his will he set us free. Even left some land to Luke and Turl. Wantin to make up for what he done. Luke an Turl stayed on the farm, but me, I left that shithole soon as I could."

My throat felt thick and constricted. If MirrorPa was dead, could my real Pa still live? Not likely. Pa dead, and nobody in the whole world to care for me. I tried to blink the tears out of my eyes. Eddie nudged me now, and handed me the pipe. I'd never smoked opium with him and Otha back in Norfolk, and even now, in my grief, I saw no reason for it. None of these three looked any the happier for their vice. I gave the pipe on to MirrorOtha, who smoked it down to the ash.

The three of them leaned back slackly in their chairs, staring silently at the candle flames, perhaps seeing visions. I had a raging thirst. There was no water, but I found some champagne in one of the bottles on the sideboard and filled a glass with that. Arf woke and petitioned me for a few more gobbets of duck. I fed him and ate a bit myself. With the pain of Pa's death in my heart, I was glad for Arf s company.

Finished with my snack, I was on the point of getting back in bed when suddenly Eddie spoke.

"Virginia," groaned he. "Where is Virginia?"

MirrorPoe had been sitting there still as a waxwork, but the mention of his dead wife's name set him back into motion. He pinched off a bit of opium and recharged and relit the pipe. Exhaling a blue cloud of tendrilled smoke, he breathed the names of the women he'd written of, staring into the smoke as if he saw their faces.

"Annabel Lee. Ulalume. Lenore. Eulalie. Ligeia. Morella. Eleonora. Berenice. Helen."

"Virginia," insisted Eddie. "How did your Virginia die?"

"Insolent fool," said MirrorPoe. "Have you no Virginia of your own in the false world which spawned you?"

"She is dead," said Eddie, choking on the word. "I killed her."

"You did *what!*"

"It...it was an accident. I gave her laudanum."

"Laudanum," murmured MirrorPoe, seemingly letting go the thread of the conversation. "By all means." He opened the medicine bottle that held the alcoholic tincture of opium and tipped a heavy dollop into his snifter to mingle with the liquors already present. As he raised his glass, his attention drifted back to Eddie. "What are the necklaces you wear?" asked MirrorPoe. "Are you then a savage?"

"It is not for you to know," said Eddie.

"Precious stones?" pressed MirrorPoe. "Why do you not give me one?" Suddenly, he shook all over as with a fit of the ague. "I need money for *The Stylus*, let us not forget. Perhaps you and your Mason could write up your adventures for us. Give me one of your gems, you foul child killer." He lurched forward and seized one of the necklaces.

Eddie jerked back, and the threads of the necklace parted. A white tooth fell to the table: Virginia's front tooth.

MirrorPoe cocked his head this way and that, trying to make out what he saw, all the while plucking at the threads of the necklace, which he now held. A red tooth dropped out, and then two more white ones. He picked up the first tooth, and as he studied it intently, his lips began to writhe.

"Yes," screamed Eddie, in an agony of shame. "They are Virginia's teeth. Yes, yes, I pulled them after she was dead!"

Slowly and silently, MirrorPoe rose to his feet, his eyes never wavering from Eddie's face. Now he took his cane in two hands and pulled on the handle. The sword that was hidden in the cane sang softly as it slid from its sheath. MirrorOtha was too stupefied to interfere, and I was too scared. Eddie screamed, snatched up a cloak that lay ready to hand, and rushed past MirrorPoe toward the hall door, only to stumble on an Oriental carpet and stagger against the mirror on the wall, wrapping the cloak around himself. MirrorPoe came at him with an oath.

The attack was brief indeed. MirrorPoe was frantic with every species of wild excitement and seemed to feel the energy and power of a multitude within his single arm. In a few seconds he had forced Eddie by sheer strength against the floor, and thus, getting him at his mercy, plunged his sword, with brute ferocity, repeatedly through and through Eddie's cloak.

Eddie shook all over; his legs spasmed and beat a last tattoo; and then he was dead.

MirrorPoe wiped his sword on the tablecloth and thrust it into the sheath of his cane. Uttering not a sound, he grabbed the bottle of laudanum, and hastened out of the room, leaving his cloak behind to be our Eddie's shroud.

"What *happen?*" said MirrorOtha, heavily. "What goin *on?*"

"I'm leaving," I told him. My voice was shaking. "Seela and I are clearing out of here fast."

MirrorOtha forced himself to his feet and went to kneel by Eddie. "Lord, Lord. I got to get outta here too, less they blame me!"

"Wait," said I, thinking a bit deeper. If we left the body here, then there would be an intensive search for "Colonel Embry" and his three "slaves." Seela above all would be easily found, with her red teeth and yellow hair. "Stay here, Otha, or I'll turn you in."

I pulled the bloodstained cloth off the table and went to kneel by Eddie. He lay pale and still, swathed in the cloak upon the small Oriental carpet that had tripped him. I didn't have the heart to unwrap him to see the full extent of his injuries. The deed was done. I put his broken necklace and its fateful teeth in with him and wrapped the cloak tight around his body, covering his pitiful face.

"How far is it to the ocean?" I asked MirrorOtha.

"Five block. You think we gonna carry him all that way?"

"We have to. We'll be in trouble if the murder is known."

I went and wakened Seela. Numbed by the shocking news, she dressed in silence. I tore our linen bedsheet into strips and used the strips to tie the cloak around Eddie into a tight bundle. I pulled a pillowcase over his projecting feet and tied that into place as well. Meanwhile, MirrorOtha carried a candle into the bedroom and looked through MirrorPoe's luggage for valuables. If he found any, he didn't let me know. Each of us took hold of one of the linen straps around the cloak, and then we marched out into the hall, Arf following along. MirrorOtha led us to the back stairs and, unseen, we found our way into an alley behind the hotel.

As we walked down the back streets toward the harbor, the tugging of Eddie's poor dead body traveled up my arm and into my heart. The jerking of his weight seemed almost to speak to me. For all his faults, he'd been a faithful friend, a wise teacher, and the greatest artist our generation will ever know.

We found our way out to a deserted spot along the Inner Harbor wharves, and there we stripped off Eddie's cloak, leaving his blood-stained clothes intact. He still wore one single necklace, the one with the rumby knotted into its string. None of us had the heart to steal the dead man's amulet. I tied a heavy rock to his feet, and dropped him into the sea. Arf let out a cry. As Eddie sank into the deep, I said a prayer for his tortured soul. We made a separate bundle of the cloak, the tablecloth, and the rug, along with the broken necklace of teeth. We tied a rock to the bundle, and sank that too. How piteous an end to Eddie's long journey!

MirrorOtha took his leave and hurried off toward his home. Day was just breaking, and a warm land breeze began to blow. Seela and I walked along the docks, talking and thinking. Woeful Arf stuck close to our heels. Now there was no one but us three. Seela and I sat on a bench to watch the sunrise. I found a week-old copy of *The Baltimore Sun* in a trash can by the bench and, until she tired of the game, I tried to teach Seela how to spell out the headlines.

One of the stories that caught my particular attention was about the new territory of California, which the U.S. had won from the Mexicans just a year before. There was a gold rush on in California, and people were heading out there on wagons and on ships. The port of San Francisco had grown from a mere fishing village to a city of twenty-five thousand in the last year. And there was no slavery in California. I was dead sick of slavery.

We walked back along the docks, looking at the ships. I asked a grizzled white dockworker if any of them were bound for California.

"You'd want to go to New York for that," he said. "Plenty o' clippers there. Sail around the Horn to San Francisco in less than a hundred days!"

"Do you know how much a passage costs?"

"Got the gold fever, do you, boy? A hundred dollars a head!"

My thoughts turned to the little sheaf of twenty-dollar bills in MirrorPoe's pocket. In his state of intoxication, he wouldn't get far, particularly if he were nipping at the laudanum. He would collapse somewhere around here, and be found. Not quite wanting to admit to myself what I planned, I told myself that the murder would be even less likely to be found out if MirrorPoe were no longer to resemble "Colonel Embry." The best thing for him, I reasoned, would be if I were to find him and to change clothes with him, and if I forgot to hand him the contents of his pockets—why, it was an oversight anyone could make.

Seela, Arf, and I spent the rest of the morning wandering the streets near the Barnum City Hotel. With no success, I asked for "Colonel Embry" at all the hotels and rooming houses. It would have been natural to seek the besotted MirrorPoe in a tavern, but as it happened, today was Election Day, so all the public houses had been temporarily closed or turned into polling places. By noon we were quite tired, and still had no success at all. We sat down at the edge of a stream-carved gully called Jones Falls and I thought back on yesterday's many conversations.

Up until the day when I'd appeared at *The Southern Literary Messenger*, Eddie's and the MirrorPoe's lives had been entirely the same. Yesterday they'd passed a pleasant hour or two reminiscing and marveling over their identical pasts. Across Jones Falls I could see Baltimore's great Shot Tower—a huge cylindrical brick building in which spheres of lead gunshot were made by dripping molten lead through colanders and letting it fall into tubs of water at the bottom. It was easily two hundred feet high. Eddie and MirrorPoe had spoken of the Shot Tower and of having lived near it in the early 1830s. *Wilks Street*, that was it! They'd lived in the block of Wilks Street known as Mechanics' Row, happy with Mrs. Clemm and little Virginia. I had a sudden conviction we'd find MirrorPoe there.

I found a bridge over Jones Falls and, asking directions of passersby, soon led Seela and Arf to Mechanics' Row, an L-shaped block with perhaps a score of small two- and three-story brick townhouses, each of them sharing a wall with the house next door. There was an alley that led in behind them. Leaving Seela at the entrance to the alley as a lookout, Arf and I sauntered in, staring keenly at the little houses' yards and outbuildings. Sure enough, we hadn't gone more than fifty feet before Arf singled out a disused carriage shed. A low muttering came from within. I entered to find MirrorPoe seated on the ground and wrapped in his cape. His cane and his bottle of laudanum lay beneath his limp hands on his lap.

He gave a low moan when he saw me—he thought I was Eddie. "Oh damned Imp," groaned he. "Can I never get free?"

Eddie had been my friend and this man had killed him, yet I felt no anger toward him. If it made me unhappy to think of the death of MirrorMason, how very much unhappier must it have made MirrorPoe to know he'd killed his double with a sword? He was more than halfway to suicide.

No, I was not here to punish MirrorPoe, but neither had I come to aid him. I was here to rob him—for robbery it was. While he watched in befuddled wonderment, I took off all my clothes and then pushed him onto his back and stripped him of his vestments. It was, as I say, a personal point of honor for me not to look in his pockets. Poe was slightly larger than me, which meant that getting his clothes onto me went easier than putting my clothes onto him, but in only a few minutes the deed was done. He struggled a bit, but not much—I think my actions quite stunned him by their unexpectedness.

"I do this so the authorities won't find you, Mr. Poe," said I when I was done. I'd donned his cloak as well, though I'd left him the laudanum and his cane. "It's a disguise." Still did I keep myself from feeling in his pocket. If there were two hundred dollars there, we could be on our way to San Francisco tomorrow!

"Reynolds," said he blearily, finally recognizing me. "Young Mason Reynolds. Where's Eddie gone?"

"I tied a rock to him and threw him in the sea."

MirrorPoe shuddered and raised the laudanum to his lips. He sipped a bit, and then he began to retch up clear liquid. "Are you going to leave me here in peace?" asked he when the retching stopped.

"Certainly."

"Thank you." He sipped again at his laudanum, and this time kept it down well enough to feel some of the drug's euphoric effect. "So happy," said he, pointing vaguely toward the back of one of the houses. "So long ago."

I left him then and went back out the alley. Just as I reached the end, I heard him calling for me by name: "Reynolds! Reynolds! Reynolds!" But I never turned back.

§

The end of Poe's story is public knowledge. Joseph Walker, a compositor on The Baltimore Sun, found Poe lying on the sidewalk in front of Gunner's Hall, a public house two or three blocks from where I left him. As it was Election Day, Gunner's Hall was being used as a polling place. Poe was taken to the Washington College Hospital in a state of violent delirium, which lasted from that Wednesday until Saturday, October 6. Saturday night he began again to call for "Reynolds," and Sunday morning he died, his last words being, "God help my poor soul!"

His funeral was the afternoon of Tuesday, October 9, 1849, at the Presbyterian cemetery at Fayette and Greene streets, only four blocks from Jilly Tackler's rooming house. I went to the funeral, or tried to, but one of the grave diggers called me a black bastard and chased me away—perhaps because with Poe's fine cloak on, I looked as if I were putting on airs.

And how much money did I find in Poe's pants? None. By the time I got to him, he'd already lost it all.

"And much of Madness, and more of Sin, and Horror the soul of the plot." So runs a line in one of Poe's last poems, "The Conqueror Worm." The poem tells of a "gala night within the lonesome latter years" wherein a throng of angels sit watching a play. A crawling fanged creature appears onstage and kills all the actors. For weeks after the funeral, I couldn't get the last lines of that poem out of my mind:

> Out—out are the lights—out all!
>   And, over each quivering form,
> The curtain, a funeral pall,
>   Comes down with the rush of a storm,
> And the angels, all pallid and wan,
>   Uprising, unveiling, affirm
> That the play is the tragedy, "Man,"
>   And its Hero the Conqueror Worm.

Right now as I pen these words, it's the evening of Saturday, March 2, 1850. All winter I've worked on this narrative and waited tables at Ben's Good Eats, making just enough money for our clothes and our pleasures. Seela and I are almost white enough to pass now, except for the fact that all the people who know us are used to thinking of us as Negroes. And slowly Seela's teeth have faded back to white as well. She's beautiful either way.

This week Seela and I will embark from for San Francisco on a clipper ship, the *Purple Whale* out of New York City. We'll start a new life as white people in San Francisco. Perhaps I'll find work at a newspaper.

Although Seela is nearly six months pregnant, she insists she's fit to travel. Pregnancy isn't viewed as a delicate condition among the flowerpeople tribe. We'll be in San Francisco in time for our son to be born white.

I've arranged for steerage tickets, and Arf will come with us. In the end we had to sell Seela's other rumby for the ticket money; it brought three hundred dollars from Jilly's eager jeweler. And now, before leaving, I'll entrust my manuscript to Mr. Coale at the bookstore. He says he'll try and get it published or, failing that, send it on to me in California when I have an address.

I'm excited about sailing around the Horn, and thereby nearing the South Pole once more. It's too bad this MirrorEarth doesn't have an open South Hole, because if it did, I think I'd be tempted to go back inside, back to the wonderful Hollow Earth.

Editor's Notes

EDITOR'S NOTE TO THE FIRST EDITION

Since I am guilty of the occasional science-fiction novel, I'd better make clear right away that *The Hollow Earth: The Narrative of Mason Algiers Reynolds of Virginia* is an authentic nineteenth-century manuscript and was *not* written by me. The original is available for inspection as catalog item *PS2964.S88S8 in the Edgar Allan Poe Collection of the University of Virginia in Charlottesville, Virginia. I first saw the manuscript there on March 7, 1985. It consists of 378 pages of parchment, handwritten in black ink. I have edited *The Hollow Earth* from a notarized Xerox copy of the manuscript.

I'm sure it would boost my desultory half career as an author to present *The Hollow Earth* as my own creation, but I'd be doing a big disservice to everyone. The simple fact is: Every word of *The Hollow Earth* is true, and we must all question our beliefs about the planet we live on.

My confidence in the legitimacy of *The Narrative of Mason Reynolds* grows out of the research I've done over the past five years. I've traveled to Hardware, Lynchburg, Richmond, Norfolk, and Baltimore. Every single thing I've looked into checks out completely, right down to the courthouse documents.

Simplest to confirm were the facts about E. A. Poe. In the years 1831-1833, Poe lived in Mechanics' Row on Wilks Street in Baltimore with Mrs. Clemm and Virginia, next moving to a house on Amity Street in the western part of Baltimore. From 1835 to 1836, he was editor of *The Southern Literary Messenger* in Richmond. Upon visiting the Poe shrine there, I was able to examine the marriage bond of Edgar Poe and Virginia Clemm, which is indeed dated Monday, May 16, 1836. At that time Eddie, Virginia, and Mrs. Clemm lived in a boardinghouse on Bank Street at Capitol Square. The reader can check many of these facts for him- or herself in any reliable biography of Poe. The biography I know best is Arthur Hobson Quinn's beautiful and meticulous book, *Edgar Allan Poe: A Critical Biography* (New York: Appleton-Century, 1941).

After the marriage, Mason's information about *his* Poe does not, of course, correspond to what we know of our *own* Poe, the one whom Mason calls MirrorPoe. But the information Mason gives us about our Poe from September 27, 1849, through his burial on October 9, 1849, accords perfectly with what is known. Poe *did* take a steamboat from Richmond to Baltimore on that September 27, and he *was* indeed found dying near a polling place on October 3, dressed in cheap clothes.

With respect to the last period of Poe's life, *The Hollow Earth* solves one of the riddles of Poe scholarship; Why did the dying Poe keep crying out for "Reynolds"? Till now, many had thought that Poe might be thinking of Jeremiah Reynolds, who also appears in *The Hollow Earth*. But now that we can read *The Hollow Earth*, we learn that Poe's last days in Baltimore were far, far stranger than anyone had ever imagined, and that the Reynolds he cried for was the one who'd brought him his deadly double, all the way from another world.

Who was Jeremiah Reynolds? In our own "MirrorEarth," Jeremiah Reynolds was a follower of John Cleves Symmes, Jr., of St. Louis (Missouri Territory), who on April 10, 1818, began proselytizing his doctrine of the Hollow Earth. The best surviving accounts of Symmes's ideas can be found in James McBride, *Symmes's Theory* (Morgan Lodge & Fisher, 1826), and in Adam Seaborn's novel *Symzonia, A Voyage of*

Discovery (Cincinnati: 1820). These books heap so much praise on Symmes, by the way, that I agree with Mason's suspicion that Symmes actually wrote them himself and published them under pseudonyms.

Jeremiah Reynolds was an accomplished traveler. On one of his voyages he went as far as the coast of Chile, where the mutinous crew put him and the officers off. He seems to have *walked* all the way back to the U.S. An excerpt of his journals appeared as "Mocha Dick, or, The White Whale of the Pacific," in *The Knickerbocker* in May 1839. This excerpt is thought to have been one of the inspirations for Herman Melville's *Moby Dick*, of 1851.

For us, of course, the most important thing that Jeremiah Reynolds did in his lifetime was to agitate in Congress for the funding in 1838 of America's first scientific expedition: the United States Exploring Expedition. The seal hunters of that time had penetrated far to the south but had always been stopped by a "wall of ice." As a follower of Symmes, Reynolds believed that beyond the wall lay a great hole, leading to the interior of the Hollow Earth. He was able to interest enough congressmen in this proposition to obtain funding for the expedition, as is well described in William Stanton's monograph *The Great United States Exploring Expedition of 1838-1842* (Berkeley, CA: University of California Press, 1975), and in Charles Wilkes, *Narrative of the United States Exploring Expedition* (Philadelphia: Lea & Blanchard, 1845).

Thanks to *The Narrative of Mason Reynolds*, we now know that John Cleves Symmes and Jeremiah Reynolds were right in all essentials. But yet there is a hitch. Presumably our Earth is the "MirrorEarth" of which Mason Reynolds writes. But, unlike Mason Reynolds's home Earth, our "MirrorEarth" seems to lack the South Hole and North Hole which Mason Reynolds describes.

As for the lack of any apparent South Hole in our antarctic continent—it could well be that such a hole in fact exists, but it is presently plugged up with an ice cap. Although the ice plug that Mason describes was fortuitously thin enough for his party to break through, our antarctic ice plug could well be scores of miles deep.

The question of the North Hole is more vexing. Mason reports having seen a vast vortical maelstrom at our North Pole—but all we see is an undisturbed Arctic Sea with an ice cap. Might the great maelstrom at our North Pole have died down since 1850?

And what of the undersea hole through which our heroes' saucer floated up? I find it suggestive that the hole is in the general area of the Bermuda Triangle. It is my fervent hope that the publication of *The Hollow Earth* will inspire some modern-day Jeremiah Reynolds to step forward and convince Congress to fund the construction of a deep-sea diving apparatus capable of locating the hole and retracing Mason's path.

During the end of his time in Richmond, our Poe finished work on his only novel, *The Narrative of Arthur Gordon Pym of Nantucket* (New York: J. & J. Harper, 1838). For information about the southern seas, Poe drew much of his information from Benjamin Morrell, *A Narrative of Four Voyages* (New York: J. & J. Harper, 1832). *The Narrative of Arthur Gordon Pym* tells of a journey to the very high southern latitudes and ends with a description of what could be Poe's vision of a huge South Hole in the sea: "I can liken it to nothing but a limitless cataract, rolling silently into the sea from some immense and far-distant rampart in the heaven. The gigantic curtain ranged along the whole extent of the southern horizon. It emitted no sound…. The summit of the cataract was utterly lost in the dimness and the distance. Yet we were evidently approaching it with a hideous velocity…. Many gigantic and pallidly white birds flew continuously now from beyond the veil, and their scream was the eternal *Tekeli-li!*"

I puzzled for some time over how it could have come about that Edgar Poe and Mason Reynolds seem independently to have arrived at the same word, which they write, respectively, as *Tekeli-li* and as *tekelili*. Did Poe somehow have a vision of the language of the black gods at the center of the Hollow Earth? I think a simpler explanation is possible. Before Mason actually set pen to paper on his own *Narrative*, he had already read Poe's *Narrative of Arthur Gordon Pym*. It is likely that the book influenced him in subtle ways. Never having seen the word *tekelili* written down—it was, after all, merely a sound that he had heard—it is natural that Mason might have adopted a spelling similar to that used by Poe.

I might mention that the poems and passages Mason Reynolds quotes from the works of Poe are all faithfully transcribed. He quotes the poems "To Helen," "The City in the Sea," "The Raven," and "The Conqueror Worm"; and he quotes brief passages from the stories "Berenice" and "William Wilson." All of these are attributed in the text, save for the quote from "William Wilson," which consists of the climactic paragraph, where MirrorPoe stabs Eddie. I can find no other places where Reynolds has directly plagiarized Poe for more than two or three words at a time.

Granted that all the historical facts jibe—and, yes, there really was a Cornelius Rucker—the modern reader must doubtless wonder if the physics of the Hollow Earth are plausible. Apparently so. The spindle—or the Central Anomaly, or the spherical Gate—that Mason finds at the center of the Hollow Earth is nothing other than the narrow throat of what today's cosmologists call an Einstein-Rosen bridge (ER-bridge, for short). One of the better popular accounts of such a space structure is to be found, I may say, in my own book *The Fourth Dimension* (Boston: Houghton Mifflin, 1984). Not only can an Einstein-Rosen bridge function as a kind of wormhole between the insides of two worlds, but it can also bring about the varying gravitational fields that Mason and his friends encountered on their trip from inner surface of the Rind to the Great Old Ones.

It is well known that many ER-bridges are unstable and must collapse in on themselves, effectively "pinching off" the vortical connection in question. A simple, nonrotating, uncharged ER-bridge collapses in depressingly few fractions of a second. But if an ER-bridge carries a large static or dynamic electric charge, then it is in fact stable due to the charged hyperwalls' mutual electrical repulsion.

Whence comes the charge that fills the spindle and enables it to send out the streamers of pink light? If we consider the Kerr solutions for the ER-bridge configuration, we find that if the two ends of the bridge are counterrotating, then the bridge becomes a source of electrical energy; like a dynamo or, more appropriately, like a Wimshurst machine. I first understood this refinement of the theory when examining a "plasma sphere" toy for sale in a San Francisco gimcrack shop.

In these plasma spheres, which presumably some of my readers will have seen, a fractally branching electrical discharge connects an outer sphere of doped glass with a small metal sphere at the center. To visualize the model that Mason describes, we need to suppose that, slightly displaced in the fourth dimension, there is another outer plasma sphere, whose only overlap with our sphere is the small metal sphere at the center. Set the two glass balls into opposing rotations, break the small metal sphere up into squirming Great Old Ones, and you have Mason's model.

What of the time dilation that is experienced near the Gate or Central Anomaly? The phenomenon dovetails correctly with modem astrophysical theory as well, for Kruskal has shown that a charged, rotating ER-bridge must engender exactly the time-dilation effects that Mason describes. I have carried out extensive calculations, which confirm all these harmonies to a high degree.

Although the concept of an Einstein-Rosen bridge was utterly unheard of in the nineteenth century, Mason Reynolds's descriptions make it very clear that an ER-bridge is what he has in mind. To me, this strongly confirms that *The Hollow Earth* is in no way a hoax or a fabrication by Mason Reynolds but is rather a true account of things he really experienced and saw.

What was the eventual fate of Mason Algiers Reynolds? The March 6, 1850, issue of *The Baltimore Sun* reports that the *Purple Whale* did indeed set out for San Francisco on March 3, but the July 10 edition of the same paper reveals that, tragically enough, the *Purple Whale* never made it around the Horn of South America and was presumed lost with all hands in a gale off Tierra del Fuego.

Grim news—but somehow I find it impossible to believe that Mason, Seela, and Arf could have died so simply. Surely, in the grand scheme of things. Mason's breaking of the great symmetry of the worlds must have had some higher goal.

Even in a screaming gale and a shipwreck, would not Mason's uncanny luck and ingenuity have found some way to keep him, Seela, and Arf alive? Would not the Great Old Ones, who know all, have preserved them?

I am presently continuing my investigations and would greatly appreciate information about any post-1850 manuscripts that mention, or could possibly be attributed to Mason Algiers Reynolds of Hardware, Virginia, born February 2, 1821.

—Rudy Rucker, Lynchburg, Virginia, July 26, 1986

Editor's Note to the Second Edition

A full twenty years have rolled past since I edited the first edition of Mason Reynolds's account of his incredible journey. I had hoped the publication might bring in some leads regarding the reality of the Hollow Earth. But, until quite recently, only one really substantial bit of new information came my way, this being an original drawing that somehow ended up bound into a much-repaired copy of Augustus A. Gould, *Mollusca & Shells*, (Philadelphia : C. Sherman 1852). The volume is to be found in the Wilkes Exploring Expedition collection at the Bancroft Library of the University of California at Berkeley, filed as catalog item xfQ115.W6 v.12. I owe thanks to my eccentric and difficult friend Frank Shook for pointing this out to me.

The sepia ink on vellum drawing is initialed and hand-dated "M. R. 1850." Although I was unable to obtain permission to scan the fragile original, I've sketched a replica which is accurate in all essential respects.

In viewing the sketch, understand that it depicts a cross-section of Mason's Hollow Earth, sliced from pole to pole. The lumpy outer shapes represent the Earth's crust, partly overlaid with seas. Mason's Earth has Holes at both poles, and there are several additional holes passing through its seas. The creatures within the Hollow Earth are not drawn to scale.

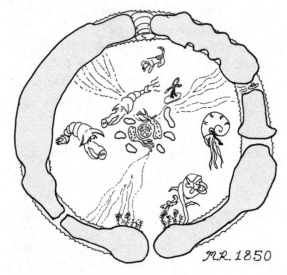

Running clockwise from the top, features to note are:

- The maelstrom at the North Hole.
- Mason's dog Arf beneath it.
- A black god riding a lightstreamer.
- A gap where an ocean runs through Earth's crust, with a tiny "fried-egg ship" floating up through it—this corresponds to the hole near Chesapeake Bay.
- A *ballula* or giant shellsquid.
- A second ocean gap, in the vicinity of the Bermuda triangle.
- A flowerperson (Seela?) on a giant flower.
- A harpy bird above the inner jungle.
- The South Hole.
- A second lightstreamer.
- Another "blue hole" gap within the sea which is meant to lie, I believe, near Tonga and Fiji.
- A pair of *koladull* or shrigs.

- A third lightstreamer, which leads in toward the center where it meets the fan of a *woomo* or giant sea cucumber.
- The center also depicts six Umpteen Seas, another *woomo*, and the sphere of the Central Anomaly, with MirrorSeas visible within.

I feel certain that this drawing could only have come from the hand of Mason Reynolds. The reader will appreciate that I was immensely relieved to find the drawing, whose dating indicates that he survived the wreck of the *Purple Whale*.

Just this week, while editing this second edition, I got some new and, I hope, reliable information. If my source is to be trusted, Mason did make a return trip to the Hollow Earth, and at least part of a manuscript about his trip exists. I won't say more until I've investigated further—which requires a trip to the Great Astrolabe Reef of Fiji.

If all goes well, I'll present new findings before another twenty years have elapsed. And if I come up blank—as is all too likely—never mind. The main thing today is that *The Hollow Earth* will be out in a fine new edition. It's an amazing adventure and, I venture to say, a subterranean classic of American literature.

—Rudy Rucker, Los Gatos, California, Sept26, 2006

EDITOR'S NOTE TO THE THIRD EDITION

I'm publishing this new edition of *The Hollow Earth* at the same time as I'm publishing Mason Reynolds's second narrative, *Return to the Hollow Earth*. I did not, as I'd hoped in 2006, find the full text for the second narrative in Fiji. The material came to me in a more roundabout way—which I describe in my editor's note at the end of *Return to the Hollow Earth*.

I've slightly revised the third edition of *The Hollow Earth* so that it fits better with the *Return to the Hollow Earth*. In particular, I included more discussion of the gems from the Hollow Earth known as rumbies—as these play a significant role in Mason's later adventures.

—Rudy Rucker, Los Gatos, California, July 4, 2018

RETURN TO THE HOLLOW EARTH

1. Cape Horn

On March 4, 1850, my wife Seela and I left Baltimore for San Francisco. Seela was nearly six months with child. We were cutting it fine, trying to reach California before the birth, but Seela was game. The Hollow Earth flowerpeople are a hardy lot.

During our five months in Baltimore, people viewed Seela and me as Negroes. We two had been crisped dark by the glow of the woomo—the huge, ancient, sea-cucumber-like beings who live at the core of the Hollow Earth. I would have preferred that we be treated as white.

Now six months had passed, and our skins had faded—but in Baltimore we were still viewed as black. This opinion was by now engraved in the locals' minds. If we wanted to be white, nothing would do but to go and make a fresh start in California.

We made our way by stagecoach from Baltimore to the wharves of New York City, and on March 9, 1850, we boarded a schooner for California, a fubsy craft called the *Purple Whale*. The other emigrants were uninterested in the past or future shades of our skin. A rough spirit of equality reigned aboard the *Purple Whale*. Many of us had tangled pasts, and all of us dreamed of golden futures.

A pilot rode aboard and guided our captain through the currents and shoals to the harbor entrance. As we neared the open Atlantic, a small pilot boat scudded to our side to pick up our guide. A final, laggard passenger was aboard the pilot boat, and he made his way up a long rope ladder to the *Purple Whale*. He was dressed in a well-cut brown suit, and he carried a small bag.

Our sails filled with wind and we scudded to sea. Seela and I leaned against the taffrail, admiring the horizon ahead and the city behind, with our faithful dog Arf at our feet.

"Wonderful," I said to Seela. "We're free."

"I feel trapped," she said, glaring at the open sea. "We're stuck on this big wooden cradle. Rock, rock, rock." She glanced around at the other passengers. "Seedy. What fool wants to dig for gold?"

During our six months together in Baltimore, Seela and I had begun speaking very openly to each other. Her English had greatly improved, although she sounded, at times, illiterate. But what of it? I had a growing sense that Seela was smarter than I'd ever be. The honeymoon was over, and the marriage was underway.

"No cradle yet," I said. "A big ship. Hull, deck, sails." I held out my arms. "Feel that clean, salty wind. Be glad!"

"You wave your arms, but you don't fly," muttered Seela. "We're stuck in this tub."

Inside our Hollow Earth, where Seela comes from, the people are weightless. Our Earth is a big egg full of air—with critters, blobby lakes, and tangles of plants drifting around on the inside. Inside our Hollow Earth, the gravity from the different parts of the Rind cancels out. Seela's tribe—the flowerpeople—they fly by making fins out of flower petals and kicking themselves through the air.

"No answer about being stuck?" said Seela, increasingly peevish.

"Fine, we can't fly," said I. "But at least we can swim."

"I don't like to swim," said Seela. "Your ocean is cold and nasty. And we're on this ship for—how long, Mason?"

"Three or four months," I replied. "The days will speed by. And in California we'll have our fresh start."

"And my baby will come," said Seela, mollified by this thought.

"The three of us," I said. "It'll be lovely."

"And when do we go home to see my folks?" probed Seela. This was a sore point. A return to the Hollow Earth loomed large in her mind.

"It's not so easy," I said with a sigh.

In principle, a hollow planet has two large holes in its shell, or *Rind*—which I prefer to capitalize. One hole at each pole. But our South Hole was clogged with a miles-deep plug of ice. There was, however, a North Hole in the form of a huge maelstrom. We'd seen it from inside the Hollow Earth. And here on the surface, Seela and I had discussed the chances of sailing or ballooning through the North Hole. But for the moment it didn't seem like a realistic prospect. Things would have been different if we still had the reckless and resourceful Edgar Allan Poe with us. But he was dead.

"I know you're thinking about that North Hole," said Seela. "But listen to me. When you brought me here from the Hollow Earth, we floated up through a hole in the bottom of the ocean. Why can't we do that again? Instead of floating up, now we sink down. Get in a waterproof box, tie on an anchor, and there we go."

"We'd need *woomo* help," I said. "We'd need some of those air-plants they gave us before. I don't see any *woomo* around just now."

"They'd come if we had enough tekelili to call them," said Seela. *Tekelili* was the Hollow Earth term for a psychic power that made one sensitive to others' thoughts. "We used to get tekelili from our rumby gems," continued Seela. "And tekelili from making love." Lately there hadn't been much love-making, what with Seela's morning-sickness, and with our anxieties about the trip to California.

"I miss making love," I said, wrapping my arms around Seela's rounded waist. "You're my magic egg. Almost ready to hatch. I bet we can still make love. I won't push hard."

Seela cast an impatient look at the other passengers on the deck. "Do it with this sad crowd around? Not likely. And, Mason, tell me you're not going to be a gold miner. I don't want a digger dungbeetle."

"I mean to be a literary man," I reassured her. "Like Eddie Poe."

"Poor Eddie," she said. Five months ago, we'd sunk his dead body into the Baltimore harbor.

Next to us, a lean, travel-worn man lounged against the rail, as if eavesdropping. He looked to be about thirty. I recognized him as the one who'd arrived aboard the pilot boat. He seemed better dressed than the other passengers, more prosperous. He drained a flask of nerve tonic, studied its label, and tossed the empty into the sea.

The traveler flashed a smile my way. "I'm Connor Machree," said he. "You're wise not to be a prospector. I have reason to believe you've got wider horizons."

"I'm Mason Reynolds, and this is Seela," said I. "I'm hoping to work for a newspaper in San Francisco. I can set type, and I write."

"Fancy plans," said the man with a laugh. "Not so dumb for a country boy." He had a Virginia accent like mine.

"Gold is what's dumb," put in Seela. "We've got better rocks where I'm from. Heavy rocks like you never seen."

"Now, that's what interests me," said Connor Machree, cocking his head. "Heavy rocks and heavy gems. Would you guide me to your homeland?"

I didn't like the abrupt turn the conversation was making. Had Machree learned of the two Hollow Earth rumby stones we'd sold in Baltimore?

"We're not miners at all," I repeated.

"Yes, yes, Mason" said he. "I heard you. You seek to work at composing and printing a newspaper. A refined, but low-paying craft." Exhaling a plume of smoke, he gestured toward the other passengers. "I wonder how many of our fellow Argonauts can read?"

"Seela and I will get along fine," I said. "We'll make a new life."

"I'll hazard you two aren't legally married," said Machree, as if wanting to goad me. "Seeing as how you're black."

"Seela is indeed my wife," I assured him. "And you have no reason to call us black. We faded white in Baltimore."

"I know that," said Machree. "I know all. You lived in Baltimore, but you were born in Virginia. I'm a Virginian as well. I'm from Lynchburg. A town you frequented. Perhaps we once met."

"You're tedious," said I, liking this man less all the time. "Be gone."

"We were married by the tekelili of the *woomo* inside the Hollow Earth," put in Seela. She loved to talk about the Hollow Earth, although few understood her meaning.

But Machree was attentive, even avid.

"The Hollow Earth," he echoed. "Your homeland, eh Seela? I've read of it, but I don't fully understand. It's a true reality? Not a tale?"

"What are you nosing for?" I asked Machree point blank. "What's your trade?"

"Assayer and jeweler," said he. "I shear golden fleece from the bleating flock. I unsnarl their wool-wrapped jewels. I mine the miners." He paused and lit a short, thin cigar. "Mark this: I seek rumby gems."

My stomach sank. I had a growing sense that this man had come aboard the *Purple Whale* expressly to meet us. Silently I shook my head.

"Machree got hold of one of our rumbies from the Hollow Earth," exclaimed the forthright Seela. "That's what he's talking about. It's clear."

"I long to enter your Hollow Earth," said Machree. "The unknown Eden where you harvested your gems, eh, Mason? The land where you found your fresh, fruitful, red-toothed Seela. Happy man thou art."

My mind in a whirl, I still declined to answer. But now Machree made his crowning revelation. "I know these things because I read your manuscript in Baltimore. *The Hollow Earth*, by Mason Reynolds."

"What!" I exclaimed, baffled and shocked.

"Indeed," said Machree. "You'd left Baltimore when I arrived. But I asked around. Everyone remembered Seela—the blonde, black woman with red teeth. I found your landlady Jilly Tackler. And her pawnbroker David Marion. And the bookseller E. J. Coale."

"That manuscript you read," I stammered. "It's a fantasia. I wrote it as if I'd traveled with Edgar Allan Poe. I'm quite a student of his work."

"*Which* Mr. Poe is the question, eh?" said Machree. "*Our* Mr. Poe died in the gutter last October. In Baltimore. As you know."

The memory of Poe's death brought with it a wave of sorrow. "I was with him," I confessed, unable to hold it in.

"In your manuscript you wrote that our Poe had a younger double," pressed Machree, staring at me, as if waiting to see what else I'd say. "Your Poe."

I felt like a cornered rat. It was past time to make a stand. "If you press further, Seela will cut your throat," I told Machree. And I meant it. Seela had her big new knife strapped to her leg beneath her skirt. She was fierce and fast. Minutes ago we'd been free—and now we were under siege.

"I won't impose any further," said Machree, taking in my words. "I'm sure your Seela remains formidable—even though her skin and her teeth have nearly faded to white. But later I hope to discuss the route into the Hollow Earth. I'd pay a handsome sum indeed, were you two to guide me." And then he was off to his cabin, strutting smoothly across the rolling deck, very sure of himself. I could hardly stand to think of such a man reading my manuscript.

"I'm saying he's got one or two of the rumbies that Jewel gave us," repeated Seela. "I can feel the tekelili."

"I traded my rumby to Jilly Tackler for our rent in Baltimore." I mused. "And we sold yours to Jilly's pawnbroker last month, to get money for the tickets. I guess Machree bought that one. I wonder what put him onto our trail."

"Our Eddie had a rumby too," mused Seela. "A third gem."

"Yes, but both the Poes are dead. We left our Eddie's rumby on him when we sank his body in the harbor. A heavy amulet on his neck."

"I should have taken it," said Seela.

"I wasn't going to do that," I said. "Maybe it helped him to the next world."

"Shrigshit on next worlds," said Seela. "Shrigshit on your stupid religions. I should have snatched Poe's rumby. Did we get good money from the pawnbroker for my rumby? Machree would have paid more. What kind of tickets do we have? First class? Take me to our cabin. I need a lie-down. This dumb wood cradle is sloshing my guts." The waves were relentless.

"It's not exactly a cabin we have," I had to tell Seela. I'd held back from explaining this before. "It's second-class steerage. That's all we could afford." I leaned closer. "You do remember that we needed money for the stagecoach from Baltimore to New York. And we bought the knife for you. And clothes. And we wanted to keep some of our money for California."

Seela herself had helped me fashion the cloth band that I now wore hidden around my waist. It had twenty Mexican silver dollars sewn inside. A pitiful sum.

"What's steerage?" Seela now asked me, poor thing.

"Let's go see!" I said feigning enthusiasm.

Most of the other passengers were already below. The dismayed Seela and I had trouble finding an unoccupied corner for ourselves. The brig's skinflint Yankee owners hadn't bothered to put in bunks—we human cargo were left to make nests for ourselves amid a tangle of sails, ropes, and bundled trade goods. Foul bilge water sloshed beneath the slats of the makeshift floor. Many of the passengers were seasick, and few were ascending to the deck. A dozen sloshing buckets held our reeking slops, and to fully perfect the hellish scene, the ship now rolled to one side, spilling every single bucket on its side. Arf nosed one of the puddles.

"I can't bear this," said Seela, on the point of tears. "It's like we're dead inside a coffin."

"Let's go over there," I urged her. "A nice pile of sails. We'll settle in and you can sleep."

"You're a shrigbrain to bring us here," cried Seela. "I want to go home."

"Gold's a-waitin!" called out a man nearby. "Californee!" He was more wistful than jolly. As scared as we.

"Go to hell, sh*thead," Seela told him. I was hoping eventually to improve the *politesse* of her speech.

"*Marry a rose—hold your nose*," said the man, baring his teeth in a fake smile. I ignored him. All of us in steerage were at our wits' ends. It was far worse than I'd imagined.

Seela and I bedded down in our canvas nest, with our one little bundle of possessions behind us, and Arf at our feet. My disheartened wife cried against my shoulder until, blessedly, we fell asleep.

Twice a day we could fetch food from the low galley on the main deck. As part of our paid passage we were entitled to sea biscuits, salt beef, and watery tea, with a noggin of lime juice every third day. Leaving the hold was a signal pleasure. Before long, Seela, Arf and I were spending most of our daylight hours on the deck. The mates discouraged the passengers from loitering topside, but Seela's bright face, lively voice, and womanly form drew the sailors and officers into our camp. They were glad to see us out and about.

The mate kept the men busy scrubbing the deck, cleaning the spars and splicing the rigging—when they weren't reefing, setting, hauling, or striking the sails. But once in a while they had time to talk. Our best friend among crew was a lithe, well-spoken, dark-skinned youth named Crispa. He was eighteen years of age to my seventeen, and a native of Baltimore.

"We're from Baltimore, too," Seela told him.

Crispa studied us closely. "I never seen neither of you before," he said.

"We're new," I said.

Crispa reached out and touched the skin of my cheek. "You black? Run away from down South?"

"I'm getting over being black," I said.

"I'm getting over being from Baltimore," said Crispa with a laugh that showed his fine, even teeth. "It's safe at sea, Mase."

"I'm gonna live in California," I said.

"I'm ready to jump ship and go off with the Crow Nation," said Crispa in a low voice. "See how it feel to be all the way free. My grandpa was an Upsaroka Indian. Some of the crew is gonna jump ship to dig gold. But diggin ain't for me."

"Me neither," I said.

"We too good," said Crispa with a laugh.

"Mason's a writer and a printer, you see," said Seela, proud of me.

"Teach me to read?" asked Crispa.

"I need to learn that too," confessed Seela. "Been meaning to ask."

So now a part of our daily chats became lessons. Somehow Crispa got me a writing slate and a squeaky slate pencil from the ship's stores. We started with A and went to Z while running south along the coast of South America. I had the two of them writing their names by the time we passed the equator.

As you may know, the seasons are reversed in the southern hemisphere. That is, down there, April, May, and June have the weather of our October, November, and December. So when we reached a latitude of 55° S in mid-April, we were surrounded by sleet and rain, with the days turning short. The tip of the Cape lay some five hundred miles to our west, and we had a long, heavy, ugly sea running against us.

For days on end we sailed into the teeth of the unrelenting west wind, tacking southwest and northwest, making slow progress against the gales and the swells. The *Purple Whale* was an ungainly old brig, formerly used for the New York to London route, and newly pressed into service for the profitable passenger run to California.

The sodden days wore on. Every so often, we'd fall off the beat of the ocean's rhythm, and our raised bow would slam against the sea with a dead, hollow sound that made me afraid. Like the boom of a clenched fist on the lid of a coffin.

As the weather grew worse, the sailors took to wearing full Cape Horn rigs: boots, long-brimmed southwester hats, and oil-cloth suits. In exchange for one of my silver dollars, Crispa equipped Seela and me with the abandoned outerwear of two youths who'd been lost at sea in earlier journeys. Nobody else wanted the outfits—sailors are loath to wear the garb of a drowned man.

Suitably clad, Seela and I continued spending most of each day on deck. And Arf was out there too, thickening his fur at a noticeable rate. The importuning Connor Machree was often on deck as well, offering sly smiles. It irked me that this man had read my manuscript of *The Hollow Earth*. He'd taken it in entirely the wrong way, as if it were a treasure map. Fool. Why did he think we'd met before? At least, for now, he was keeping his distance. I hoped to give him the slip in San Francisco.

For days blending into weeks we beat our slow way against the westerlies. One afternoon a clean-lined cutter flew past us, tacking a clever line that sliced the waves like a knife.

"It's the *Sea Witch*," Connor Machree said, edging up beside me. "Used to be an opium clipper from India to China. Now she runs rich folks and dainty geegaws to San Francisco. Gets there first with the best. Left New York a week after us." He gave me one of his lingering looks. "I would have shipped on the *Sea Witch*, if I hadn't managed to squeeze onto the *Purple Whale*." He shook his head. "That was a near thing. I rode out to you on the pilot boat, after taking an express coach from Baltimore. I'm bent on following you."

"Why is that again?" I asked, exasperated with the man.

"You and I have a history," he said, staring at me. "We fit like two gears, eh? Don't get it? Never mind for now. I've told you I want to know where you and Seela get your rumby gems." He stepped closer and rummaged in his pockets beneath his oilskin coat. "Look."

And there it was in Machree's pale hand, Seela's rumby, the one I'd sold to the pawnbroker in Baltimore. It was even lovelier than I'd remembered, the size of a small grape, quite heavy, with a subtle pattern of pentagonal facets, perpetually shifting, clearer than the finest crystal, and shattering the daylight into full-spectrum rainbows. I felt an overwhelming desire to touch and to caress it. As well as its dazzling beauty, the rumby had so strong a tekelili aura that I could nearly read my companions' thoughts.

"It's mine," said Seela, reaching for the stone. "It knows me."

"Mine," said Machree, his hard face folding into a semblance of a smile. "I bought it." He thrust the rumby back into an inner pocket.

"You know I can kill you," Seela told him. Both Machree and I were inclined to believe her. And this knowledge was, to some extent, keeping the man under control. Seela was from a far harder culture than ours.

"Don't talk that way," implored Machree. "I'd prefer that you sell me a map to the rumby mine in the Hollow Earth! Five hundred dollars. And if you guide me yourselves, I'll pay five thousand." I doubted if, even now, he grasped that the Hollow Earth is the space inside the Earth. Machree reading my manuscript was like a dog in a Latin class. I cursed the man aloud, and from the bottom of my heart. He walked away.

Dispirited by the man's ignorant machinations, I turned my attention to the passing *Sea Witch*. She was sleeker, faster and probably better-helmed than the *Purple Whale*. She had raked, back-slanting masts, a long boom, and a sharp, V-shaped hull.

"Not like our roly-poly tub," remarked Crispa, who'd joined us. But he said this too loud, and the mate set him to repairing rigging in the highest reaches of the masts for several days. Finally, on a Sunday morning, Crispa again had an hour off.

"Might could take another week more to clear the Horn," Crispa remarked to me. We were sitting with Seela and Arf on the deck behind the galley, out of the freezing wind. Overhead the spars and the rigging were coated in ice.

"What if we can't make it around the Horn at all?" asked Seela.

"There's an inland passage north of here," said Crispa. "The Strait of Magellan. But I doubt our captain could thread it. He sank a schooner off Nantucket two years back. Half the crew drowned."

"Captain didn't go down with his ship?" I asked.

"Weren't no call for that," drawled Crispa. "Captain's married to the fleet owner's daughter." He patted Arf, who'd crawled halfway onto his lap. "I admire this tattoo on your dog's belly."

"A rough fellow needled it on, last time Arf and I went to sea," said I. "Dirk Peters. An Upsaroka, come to think of it. Same as what you said about your grandpa."

"From the Crow Nation in the Great Plains," said Crispa, tracing his finger along the dotted spiral. "I can feel the tribal spirit. Good luck."

"Wasn't good luck for poor Peters," I said. "He got crushed between two icebergs."

"Let's say the luck went to Arf," said Crispa. "And let's say he's my dog too. I don't want no cold water filling my lungs."

"You're with us," I said, and Seela agreed. We saw Crispa as a fast friend. His brightness of spirit was uplifting.

"Nobody drowns inside the Hollow Earth," put in Seela, wanting to tell Crispa more about her home. "No heaviness in there. Nothing to drag you down."

"Machree always asks about the Hollow Earth," said Crispa. "And you don't tell him. Can you tell me?"

"If you can listen," said Seela. "Earth's a hollow ball. We're close to a Hollow Earth entrance right now. The iced-over South Hole. Big *woomo* sea cucumbers down inside the core. I wish one of them would snake a feeler up through some cracks. Or send a tendril through the maelstrom at the North Hole, or through a hole in the ocean floor. We'd see a *woomo* frond in front of the *Purple Whale* like a sea serpent. A branching stalk of pink light."

Crispa looked uneasy. "I don't want to hear about no sea monsters in a place like this. Let's be scanning the sky instead."

"So—how about that black cloud coming in so fast?" I said, looking upward. "It's covering us like a lid." As well as darkness, the cloud was bringing a bank of mist and a rising wind.

"Cape Horn express," said Crispa, as if calmed by the thought of a non-supernatural danger. "Our Sunday morning meeting's done, maties. I'm glad we're friends. I've got a secret to tell you by and by."

In short order, we were plowing into the heaviest seas I'd ever seen. Blasts of spume exploded off our bow. The air glittered with dancing drops. The deck was awash with seawater that ran knee-deep through the scuppers. All after-noon and all night the storm continued.

Seela and I lay below decks on our heap of sailcloth, with our arms wrapped tight around each other, and with Arf on our legs. We sang little songs by way of keeping up our courage, some songs in English, and some in Seela's native tongue. And when we ran out of songs we whimpered. And when we ran out of whimpers we prayed to the *woomo* at the heart of the Hollow Earth. And when Seela fell asleep I began working on a sequel to *The Hollow Earth* in my head. When the endless night ended and the sun peeped up, we went topside, and found the deck covered with a foot of snow.

The wind went down, the sky cleared, and all of Monday morning we tossed in frigid calm. The ocean swells were rolling, but their surfaces were glassy smooth. The *Purple Whale* bobbed like a snowy log upon a mill pond at the bottom of the world. The scene was like a fever dream—and I had an odd off-kilter sense that my written narratives were consuming me.

Adding to the scene's phantasmagoric quality, an alba-tross came floating by, asleep on the surface of the rolling sea, completely white, and with his head beneath his wing, now rising on a heavy billow, and then sliding into a hollow. Our voices and the creaking of our ship's timbers roused him. The bird opened his dark, deep-set eyes and clacked his hooked, ivory beak. The ever-present Connor Machree yelled a nervous curse at the albatross. The creature spread his enormous wings, easily ten feet across, and took flight, catching a stray ghost of breeze.

As if fanned into life by the bird, the wind returned, and this time it was favorable. Our sails bulged. For four happy days we sped toward Cape Horn.

On the eve of the fourth day the wind fell, and a fresh storm approached from the west. Its thunder was a continu-ous grumble, and its lightning sparked all along the western verge. We reefed our sails and waited through an uncanny interval of calm. The air was alive with actinic energy, and the hairs on my skin tingled.

"Look there!" cried Crispa, pointing at the rigging.

Pale coronas tipped the yardarms, and rosy flares rode the masts like candle flames. The cold fires hissed—an intricate murmur that mixed with the plash and purl of the sea.

The crew stood in a cluster, their faces lit by the eerie glow, their eyes aglint. Crispa and Seela were at my side, with Crispa cradling Arf in his arms like a baby. Arf lay on his back, as if in a gesture of surrender, with his tattoo showing dark in the uncanny light. Connor Machree was with us as well, always staring at me with that same odd look in his eyes.

The glow lifted from the ship, massing into a streamer that withdrew into the sky. Had it been a tendril from the all-knowing *woomo* within the Hollow Earth? Had it arced up from Earth's center, and through the Rind, and across the globe's surface to meet us? I felt a strong sense of tekelili from the rumby within the acquisitive Machree's inner pocket. A dense, precious, gleaming gem that was rightly ours.

"We gotta take it off him," said Seela's voice in my head, as clearly as if she'd spoken aloud.

Perhaps we would seize the rumby amid the furor of the coming storm. Perhaps Machree would fall overboard and drown. Or, if necessary, Seela could slit his throat. Machree glared at me. The tekelili was showing him the tenor of my thoughts. He moved away.

The wind rose, the rigging moaned tense chords, the sea ahead was like a colossal furrowed field. A low moon shone through the torn clouds, silvering the crests of the towering waves, and brushing glints along their hollow bellies. The sailors clewed and trimmed our sails, keeping two small rags aloft.

And then we were for it. The ranked waves came at us like attacking troops. Lest our ship roll sideways, the mate maintained a course directly into the wind, with the bow plunging madly into the tremendous seas. Each concussion buried the entire forward part of our vessel.

As if sensing the approach of doom, Crispa ignored his duties and stayed close to my side, once again clutching Arf in his arms. He, Seela and I huddled amidships near the main mast. For the ship, each individual wave required a daring and unlikely escape. Our luck would only hold for so long.

It was a freak wave that did us in, towering above the other waves like an oak above brambles, four times the height of our masts, a grim reaper of a wave, spawned in the bottomless gulfs, and risen to bring us low. At the last moment I glimpsed a leathery orange hawser, wrapping itself around our mast and straining at it, as if to tilt our deck to precisely the worst angle at which to meet the wave.

2. Shipwreck

The unfathomable mass of water broke onto the *Purple Whale*, burying us in untold tons, both fore and aft. The savage, implacable currents whirled me and my companions into the sea. And beneath the watery tumult, I heard a crunch and a crack. The ship had split in two, right across the middle where we'd stood. The pieces belched air, turned turtle, and dove for the abyss, trailing whirlpool currents that dragged us deep and deeper into the stygian gloom, perhaps a full twenty fathoms down. My ears spiked with pain, then adjusted to the depth. It was utterly dark, and the antarctic cold was astonishing. I was growing stiff and numb, but even so, I hung onto my companions by touch—to Seela, Crispa, and Arf. We'd rise together, or not at all. But I doubted we would rise.

And then, when all was lost—here came a pink streamer of divine *woomo* light. It was lifting us upward. Dimly I saw my companions. To my surprise, Connor Machree was in our midst, quite senseless, limp as a rag. Seela lunged at our foe, wriggled her hand inside his garments and emerged with— *huzzah*—her glowing rumby gem and then—*excelsior*—a second one. It was my rumby—the one I'd given our landlady Jilly Tackler for the rent. Perhaps Machree had stolen it from her. What a find! I savored the tekelili of the dense, precious gems. A rumby sense of self. *Here we are*.

Meanwhile, of course, Arf, Seela, Crispa, and I were on the very point of drowning and freezing to death —albeit in an agreeable state of tekelili from the *woomo* light and the rumbies. But we were rising, one slow fathom at a time, flailing our cold-stiffened legs against the eddies and the vortex threads of the foundered *Purple Whale*. The pink light was bearing us upward with the inert Machree.

The gleaming underside of the sea's surface was in view. A wildly squirming orange tentacle lashed through the water, stirring bubbles in its wake. It caught Seela by the ankle and tugged her up and out of sight. One, two, eight, ninety more tentacles appeared, urgent and intense, taking hold of me, Crispa, and Arf, drawing us to the roiled sea's surface with Seela.

The *woomo* light was moving away. Machree was no longer in view. Perhaps he'd sunk back into the depths. I drew in sobbing gasps of air. The tight grip of the orange tentacles was draining all force from my hands and feet. The coldness of the water and my recent exposure to the pink *woomo* light had left my skin feeling as if it were on fire.

The implacable tentacles were pulling us higher, out of the water and into the air. A menacing form bobbed above the wind-torn waves, oh no, it was a *ballula*, a giant man-eating nautilus, buoyed by a shell full of hydrogen, a carnivorous denizen of the Hollow Earth, now lifting us toward the barn-door-sized opening of its shell, a dark smooth cave whence ninety orange tentacles emerged, plus two bollard-like eyestalks, and a horribly clacking, razor-sharp beak. By the illumination of the receding *woomo* light, I could see blood upon the *ballula* beak, and a sailor's bitten-off arm and shoulder within. The remains of Machree? No, someone else. The clothing was different. Machree—he'd disappeared.

"We dead and gone to hell!" cried Crispa, bundled tight against Seela, Arf, and me by a tangle of the smooth, strong tentacles. "It gonna eat us!"

"She's not allowed to eat us!" screamed Seela. "We've got two rumbies! Rumbies have power over these beasts!" She held the heavy gems high so the *ballula*'s dead-black eyes could perceive them, with each rumby a beacon of tekelili. "Obey me, you damned shell-squid!" cried Seela. "Take us to safety! I am your ruler!" A convincing performance. I don't think I could have carried it off.

So now, rather than devouring us, the *ballula* tucked the four of us into a tangle of tentacles below her huge, parrot-style beak. I felt like a pork chop on a bed of yams—with ravening jaws overhead. Arf writhed and whimpered at my side, his eyes rolling.

The *ballula* wasn't eating us. That leathery orange hawser I'd seen before our ship sank—it had been one of these tentacles. The *ballula* had scuttled our ship, yes, and she'd eaten some of the passengers and sailors. But as for us, she was taking us…somewhere.

Through the stuttering lightning we rose, with the sinister *ballula* bearing us northwest, toward the far side of the storm, propelling herself with farting bursts from her siphon tube, and finding her way to a favorable wind. Nearly an hour passed. We four huddled together, shielded by the great shell from the rushing air, sharing our bodies' sparks of warmth, and wrapping the tentacles around us like mufflers. The stream of pink *woomo* light had long since withdrawn itself, and the weather was calm. I spotted a pair of lanterns on a three-masted schooner far below, with the ship herself visible by the light of the moon.

"The *Sea Witch*!" exclaimed Crispa. "We done caught up."

Smoothly adjusting her attitude, while blatting from her muscular siphon tube, the *ballula* swept toward the cutter like a balloonist coming to earth.

"That ship's got a big lizard on front," said Seela. Indeed, the cutter's figurehead was a carved and gilded Chinese dragon with a coiling tail, markedly fierce, and dramatically brought into relief by the moon.

And then, just like that, the *ballula*'s sticky tentacles uncurled and dropped Seela, Arf, Crispa, and me to the *Sea Witch*'s deck. We thumped down and slid along the planks. Rather than flying into the sky, the *ballula* sank into the sea and descended, leaving a stream of bubbles that slowly settled down.

Seela, Arf, Crispa, and I had come to rest at the base of the *Sea Witch*'s main mast. Stimulated by the deck beneath his feet and the smell of chickens and pigs, Arf let out an exultant bark.

"Avast!" cried a man on watch. "Boarders!"

Moments later, Seela, Crispa, and I were in the custody of a mate with a pistol, and two seamen with swords.

"Our ship went down," Seela cried. "Have mercy."

"And you swam here?" asked the mate, thrusting out his lower chin. "Tell me another. This water would stop your heart in five minutes." He was a know-it-all Yankee.

"Two albatrosses carried us," I said. "Uncommonly large." Nobody bothered answering that one.

"All right, the truth is that we're stowaways," said Seela. It helped that she was beautiful, and great with child. Even so, the mate chose to argue.

"Then where exactly have you been hid for these last seventy days at sea?"

"With the pigs," said Crispa, pointing at the pen on deck. It had a low sty with a tiny door.

"Flaming flapdoodle!" said the mate, believing the tale. "What do we do with you three and your dog? Drown you? Shove you back in with the hogs?"

"Let us ride as passengers," I suggested. "We'll pay to smooth our way," As it happened, I still had nineteen silver dollars inside the band around my waist. I kept one of dollars and offered up eighteen. Not an imposing sum by some lights, but it was enough to cheer the mate and his men. They did a three-way split. The hooting sailors danced a hornpipe jig, jingling their coins between cupped hands. The mate smiled and shook my hand.

"My name's Stearns," he said. "Welcome aboard the *Sea Witch*. I'll bunk you three in the scribbler's cabin. Hope he don't mind."

"Scribbler?" said I.

"Fancies himself a gentleman. Little fellow with a bulging brow. Very quiet in his habits. The captain enjoys him. Mr. Goarland Peale."

I broke into a convulsive grin. Seela didn't yet get the wheeze, but the shuffled letters of "Goarland Peale" told me what was afoot, farfetched though it might be.

"I'm sure Mr. Peale will take to us," I assured Stearns.

Taking pity on us now, the sailors gave us biscuits, beef, and beer, all of a much finer quality than the grub on the late, lost *Purple Whale*. Even better, they gave us wool blankets to enfold our shivering frames.

"Bunk down before the captain gets the word," the mate told us. "He takes a change easier once it's squared away. Here, this is Mr. Peale's cabin." Stearns waggled his chin and let out a thin cackle. "The high and mighty Goarland. It'll take him down a peg to share his state room with three darkies and a dog."

Darkies? Again? Staring at Seela in the lantern light, I gleaned the hard truth. The insinuating glow of the great pink *woomo* light had baked us brown once more, with even Crispa gone darker than before. Arf was of course unchanged. Always a dog.

Yes, Seela and I had enjoyed ourselves well enough as blacks in Baltimore. In some ways, life as a Negro was congenial to me, at least when white people weren't around. And Seela herself was in the habit of viewing dark skin pigment as a sign of high status. In the Hollow Earth, the dark race who lived near the center were referred to as black gods. But, even so, to set out for a white life in California, only to find myself again relegated to a low estate.

With a peremptory knock, Stearns flung open the door of a low cabin near the rear of the deck. With a bark of laughter, he bundled us in, and slammed the door behind us.

A lantern burned within. And there, pale as wax, at his ease in a soft chair, ruminating over pen and parchment, with a small pipe and a glass of claret ready to hand, was—

"Eddie!" exclaimed Seela. "You're not dead?"

"I've been expecting you," he said.

Yes, it was Eddie Poe, the Eddie who'd traveled through the Hollow Earth with me. In his soft, familiar, tenor voice he sang the altered verse of an Easter hymn.

The nine sad months are quickly sped;
He rises glorious from the dead;

All glory to your risen Ed!
Hallelujah!

"But—I saw MirrorPoe murder you!" I protested. "Your double."

"A nice piece of theater, that," said Eddie, trying to control his widening smile. "My parents were actors. From my earliest years I knew how to feign a florid death."

"But he ran his blade through and through you!" I protested. "He killed you."

"Misdirection," said Eddie. "You saw him repeatedly thrust his sword—but only through my cloak, and mostly to no effect. Admittedly the first jab nicked my side, and most convenient that was, as it unleashed blood enough for horrific effect. But I contrived to avoid my besotted enemy's ensuing pokes. For the culminating effect, I smeared gore on my face, drummed my heels and expired. The Death of Poe. You were diddled, my dear Mason, tender heart that you are."

"So, you were lying doggo while we carried you to the harbor?"

"Thou sayest it, my liege."

"But then surely you drowned! I tied a rock to your ankles and sank you into the depths."

"Not so very deep as all that. Thirty feet. A sandy bottom."

"You loosened the knot?"

"A bagatelle. I braced my ankles against the rope while you bound me. In the water, I relaxed, and the binding went slack. I swam free. And surfaced behind a fortuitously anchored yawl, waiting there until you decamped in a touching state of heartfelt grief."

"You're a devil, Eddie."

"An imp," said he. "A strayed lamb. A mage." He laid a finger against his nose and winked. "I have more to tell. As I left the harbor, I found I had a pet. She was swimming in the sea at my side, the size of a house. Reaching out a supplicating tentacle toward my fine amulet. A *ballula*. Tamed by my rumby's spell."

Eddie touched his Hollow Earth gem, nearly the size of a gooseberry, tightly wrapped in silk thread, and tied to a cord around his neck. I could sense the rumby's psychic glow across the room. Before Seela could tell Eddie about us recovering our own two rumbies, Eddie got to his feet and brought his lantern closer to us.

"Let's have a look at you. But how the devil is it that you two are black again? Hopeless bunglers."

"The pink light of the Great Old Ones," said I. "A beam of *woomo* light plumbed into the depths to save us, dragged down in the wake of our foundered ship. Twenty fathoms down. The light exalted us. And then—and then a *ballula* carried us here."

"My same *ballula* from Baltimore," said Eddie with an air of quiet pride. "I call her Cytherea. She accompanied me from Baltimore to New York. And now she's following the *Sea Witch* to California, sometimes above, and sometimes below. She jets through the sea and rides the winds. And tonight I sent her to fetch you."

"Did you tell her to sink our ship?" I demanded.

"A ghastly loss," said Eddie, as if in sorrow. He wrung his hands and furrowed his brow. "Those inhuman *ballulas*—"

"Back up," I said. "How did you know that Seela and I were on the *Purple Whale*?"

"Someone told me," said Eddie, a twinkle in his eye. "Can you guess?"

"Connor Machree," I said.

"Well reasoned, my pup. Yes, it was he. More on Machree anon."

"So far as I know he drowned," I interjected. "But pray continue."

"I learned of your departure from Machree," said Eddie. "And I booked passage aboard the speedy *Sea Witch* expecting to reach San Francisco before the *Purple Whale*. And I arranged for my Cytherea to fetch you to my ship en route."

"Why?" I asked, uneasy at the thought of Eddie Poe making all these plans for me. Wanting a distraction, I poured out a bowl of water for Arf, and settled him onto a pillow. He drank deeply and was instantly asleep.

"I want you and your Seela to help me return," said Eddie, not quite answering my question. "A second sally through the Hollow Earth—after a brief investigatory stop in San Francisco for filling out our equipage. My goal? To journey through the Anomaly at the core of the Hollow Earth—and to claim my deserved throne as dean of letters on the original Earth. May I propose a toast to my plan?"

He raised his glass of claret, and made a gesture that we were free to help ourselves. I gladly got glasses of water for Seela and me—we two were very well-salted from our ordeal. Crispa took a glass of water and a glass of wine.

"I'm for the Hollow Earth," said Seela, raising her glass. "I keep telling Mason this. He doesn't listen."

"I'll go too!" said Crispa, raising first his water, and then his wine, and draining the two glasses in a row. "If I don't find no Indians to join. I'll start out with you at least."

"Is this fellow black all the time?" Poe asked me. "Or just temporarily?"

"Black and white be bullshit in California," said Crispa. "What I heard. Fact of the matter, I'm one quarter Upsaroka Crow. But that ain't the real surprise." Crispa paused and made a bow. "I'm a woman and not a man."

As soon as Crispa said this, I understood it to be true. Her sympathy, likeability, and ready intelligence—she'd been female all along. Disguised as a man to get a berth as a sailor on a ship to California. Of course.

Thanks to the rumbies, there was enough tekelili in the room so that all these things could be readily understood. Even so, I wasn't ready to let Eddie Poe start running my life.

"You listen to me," I told him. "Right now Seela and I are going to San Francisco. With a ship this fast, we'll make landfall in two weeks. We'll feather a nest for our baby. We'll be happy. We'll settle down."

"But we don't *have* to settle," cried Seela. "With this *ballula* being Eddie's friend—he named her Cytherea? With Cytherea we can fly down through the North Hole. The great maelstrom!"

"Oh no," said I.

"Together again," said Eddie sententiously. "It is well. Tell me the tale of your past nine months, friends. I am an ear. Large and tremulous. Strike your lyres, and freely slake your thirst with wine. I've found a bit of opium in the ship's stores as well."

"Not now," said I. "Anyway, Eddie, if anyone narrates, it should be you. You could start with what you were doing with Machree."

"Not now," echoed Seela. "Eddie, lend us your bed." She used her sweetest tone. "Soft and warm. For weeks Mason and I slept on sails with slops all around. We'll take your bed, and Crispa, you get in with us. Fun. Eddie won't mind. He's a gentleman."

"When it suits me," said Eddie, with one of his thin, inwardly amused smiles. "As it happens, I'll be up all night writing. I'm mining a fresh vein of prose. Articles I can sell as when we reach San Francisco. Reports on the antics of the prospectors in the gold country."

"And you haven't even been there yet," said I, not entirely surprised.

"Genius hath its benisons," said Eddie, pouring himself a fresh glass. "Sleep well, my two lovebirds plus one, my stormy petrels, my ravens of the night. Our skewed reunion augurs well."

We three were undressing, glad to get out of our wet, cold clothes. Crispa unwrapped a cloth she'd worn tight around her chest to hide her bosom. Seela was already in the nude, her breasts full, and her belly a wondrous fertile round.

"Look at this," she said to Eddie. "Look what I got!" She could have been talking about her baby, but no, she was showing off our two recovered rumby gems, holding them up in her hands, weighing their powers. Tekelili filled the room like sunshine in a crystal vase.

"Wonderful woman!" exclaimed Eddie. "You took them from Connor Machree? —I'm sure Cytherea honored you and Mason the more for having rumbies."

"Honored?" said I. "She sank our ship,"

"Possible," said Eddie. "Probable. Unforeseen. Not what I wished. I am no fiend, Mason, no murderer."

"You've said that before. About Virginia."

"Take me as I am! An errant wanderer, a lost soul. Let us be glad the burdensome Machree has gone to the fishes. And now you sleep. I must write."

3. Brumble

The *Sea Witch* made good time on the sail north. We arrived in San Francisco at four in the afternoon on June 11, 1850, with Cytherea the *ballula* out of sight, riding air currents far overhead. Although the harbor was crowded with ships, many of them were empty. Abandoned by their crews and left at anchor, or scuttled near the shore. The mania for gold was at fever pitch.

Before we tied up to one of the long piers, the captain called the crew together and promised a bonus payment of seventy dollars apiece to those crew members who stayed with the *Sea Witch* and sailed the next leg—which was to be a run to Singapore to fetch a shipment of china, lacquered chests, and silk for the prospering citizens of San Francisco. The captain's offer went over well, and the sailors chaffed those among us, such as Crispa, who'd made remarks about setting off on their own. Crispa, by the way, was continuing her stratagem of dressing as a young man.

"I have my sketches of the gold country ready to sell," Eddie told Crispa, Seela and me as we disembarked, with Arf at our heels. "But first I need to secure a working relationship with Edward Kemble. the editor of the *Daily Alta California*. They have a steam-powered press! I wrote Kemble from New York—but, hmm, if the mail was on the *Purple Whale*, it's a dead letter, eh?"

"Don't joke," said Seela. "We had friends on that *Purple Whale*. People hoping for a change. Oh, that dark, awful water. So cold it was slow and thick." She broke off with a sound of distress, laying her hand across her belly. Although the afternoon sea air was cool and clear, Seela looked like she might faint.

Eddie turned sympathetic. "What say we lodge in the same hostelry?" He proposed. "Help me with my luggage, would you, Mason?"

Seela, Crispa and I had no possessions at all, other than our clothes and our two rumby gems, which Seela had knotted into her garments. But Eddie had a sizable trunk, containing fine clothes, camping gear, and writing supplies. Somehow Crispa and I ended up carrying it.

"Where did you get money for this kit?" I asked him.

I'd wanted to broach this subject during our two weeks together on the *Sea Witch*, but I hadn't wanted to get Eddie's dander up. Not with Seela, Crispa, and I spending nearly all our time in his cabin—lest we have to face the ship's captain. We'd lurked in Eddie's quarters, and he'd been good enough to have the cabin boys bring us food from the galley.

"I teamed with a Manhattan widow," Eddie now informed us. "A patroness of the arts, and a force among lovers of the occult. How came I to her arms? Having escaped my watery grave, I rode my *ballula* to New York, and found my way to the literary salons. My natural hunting ground." He touched the amulet at his neck. "The force of my rumby smoothed over the fact that I appeared to be a Negro. And my name, as you know, was Goarland Peale."

"And then?" Seela asked, distracted from her discomfort by the tale.

"And there I found my companion, Annabel Whistler. She admired my sensitive profile, my pensive brow. I told *la veuve* Whistler that I was the late MirrorPoe's cousin, perforce darkly incognito, due to a curious twist of fate, and that I was due to become white quite soon. She had known MirrorPoe, it seems."

"This be the longest pier ever," said Crispa, looking around. The harbor was a shallow little inlet off the bay, with remarkable thousand-foot-long wharves going out into it like sidewalks.

Ignoring the interruption, Eddie went on with his tale. "I polished several of Annabel's mystical odes and saw them into print. And I presented her with a beautifully penned copy of my appositely entitled poem, *Annabel Lee*. India ink on fine vellum. I cadged the lyrics from MirrorPoe's obituary."

"She didn't recognize the work?" I asked.

"Oh, she knew it, but I told her that MirrorPoe had in fact plagiarized it from me," said Eddie. "She doubted this, but she relished my shadowy semblance to the great man just the same. I was Annabel Whistler's inky Bohemian imp."

"Did she give you money?" put in Crispa.

"She had none," said Eddie, still walking along this endless pier. Arf has drawn ahead of us. Now and then he paused to glance back. "Annabel misled me," continued Eddie. "Her husband left a mountain of debt, and she was on the point of losing her home. She expected to put the touch on me or, failing that, to engage me as a confederate. And so it played out. Annabel and I founded an elite occult society, a mystical hoax, a confidence game. We milked our company of seekers, some two dozen strong. The Order of the Golden Frond. We recruited our first member in mid-December, 1849. Just in time to buy Christmas dinner, and coal for heating Annabel's house. All hail the Golden Frond."

"How far must we walk!" interrupted Seela, holding her enormous belly with both hands. "I need a bed. The baby's coming." I left the trunk to Crispa and Eddie now. Seela leaned against me, uncertain on her feet, and we made the last fifty yards to shore. An afternoon fog was drifting in, giving the scene a dreamlike air. Porters, wagons, and carts were all around. We were on Montgomery Street, with the city sloping up from the docks into hills.

The buildings were a hodgepodge of three-story wood frame structures, surfaced with paint, tin, or tarpaper, and seemingly all erected in the last two years. Higher up the hills, the structures gave way to canvas-sided cabins, and peaked tents. Mingled among the lodgings were shops, pot-houses, restaurants, and gambling hells, as they were called. Dogs were everywhere, and many of the men wore guns. The nearest center of activity looked to be a clamorous square some two hundred yards off.

Eddie raised his arm and summoned a shrill-voiced young porter rolling a diminutive luggage cart, a lad no older than fourteen. His name was Pip.

"Conduct my slaves and me to your city's finest hotel," Poe instructed the porter. "I understand that to be the Parker House?"

"Fine digs, if they let you in," said young Pip, looking us over. He'd loaded the trunk onto his little cart.

"On our way, then," ordered Eddie. "This *enceinte* African woman is in some distress." He glanced over at me. "Mason! Mind the dog. And you, Crispa, take up the rear."

I glared at Eddie, but, for the moment, I let it pass. After all, I'd spoken much the same way to our Otha in my Virginia days. The thing to do now was to get Seela to shelter. She was breathing in short gasps. The baby was on the way. And so we traipsed uphill, with Eddie in the lead. Seela leaned against Crispa and me, one of us on either side. Arf stuck close to our feet. And Pip handled the trunk.

The Parker House hotel was a single-story row of wooden rooms along one edge of the square I'd noticed before—Portsmouth Square. Several restaurants were on the square, and a gambling hell called the Eldorado. With the day winding down and the fog coming in, several hundred strangers were in the square—talking, making deals, and planning their evening's debauch. Pre-assembled house frames were piled in a corner of the square, as well as a mountain of lumber. Eddie made a quick foray into the lobby of the Parker House and emerged chagrined. Not only did they have no rooms for Eddie, the clerk had said something cutting.

"Puffed up mountebank," muttered Ed, and turned again to our porter Pip. "Perhaps a more Spartan style befits us. Something along the lines of a rooming house? We may, I believe, be here for as long as a week."

Pip brushed his unkempt shock of hair out of his eyes and proposed leading us to a two-story wooden rooming house that lay three blocks further up the hill. We ascended a steep narrow street, crowded with pickpockets, drunks, fancy women, speculators, and bearded miners. Not every-one was white, there were a few blacks, and more than a few coppery-skinned Mexicans, many of them speaking Spanish.

The higher we got, the more of the establishments were makeshift canvas-walled buildings with unfinished planks for their counters. The goods on sale here were in higgledy-pig-gledy piles inside and outside the shops. It was like a mad fairground, although some of the rowdies were brandishing little sacks of gold dust like weighty tobacco pouches. Inside one of the tents I glimpsed a toothless rustic betting two full ounces of gold on the turn of a faro card.

Seela's pains were rolling steadily. We pressed on. It was nearly evening.

Our goal was in sight: a brown-painted pine building with *Fashionable Rooms* inscribed upon its side. In the grasp of a particularly sharp contraction, Seela gasped and stood still, leaning against me.

Looking over her shoulder, I could see into a can-vas-walled saloon at our side, the awning painted in curlicues with the name *The Broken Harp*. Inside, a man on a stool was playing a screeching fiddle while a guffawing prospector did a jig with a plump woman in cascading skirts. Behind them was a wooden counter resting on two saw horses, and lined with bottles on top. A man with sallow skin, red hair and an uncommonly thin head tended the bar. And, sitting at the counter, dining on a steak, a bottle of ale and some whiskey on the side, was—Connor Machree, his skin burnt dark.

His eyes locked onto mine—and there could be no doubt this was he. Not a ghost. All too real. And with a knowing look on his face. He gestured, as if inviting me to come speak with him. I assumed he wanted to resume begging for guidance to the Hollow Earth. But how could he be here at all? I combed through my memories. We'd been in the polar water, amid the pink *woomo* light, and Machree seemingly comatose. Seela had gleaned the rumbies from him, and then the *ballula* tendrils had—

Pip's sharp whistle broke my train of thought. Arf nudged my leg with his head, as if wanting to herd me along. I was glad to follow our porter Pip's lead to the brown hotel that advertised Fashionable Rooms. A Mrs. Mackie ran the place. She was a sinewy lady of middle years, hard-bitten but not unkind.

Eddie told her he was Goarland Peale, and went on to introduce Seela, Crispa and me as his slaves, I stopped him dead in his tracks.

"Don't skylark," I told him. I turned to Mrs. Mackie. "This man is my cousin. Now that we've made a fortune in the gold fields, he wants to play the grandee."

"I see," said Mrs. Mackie. "I've heard of such family complications among you Southerners. And your name is?"

"I'm Mason Reynolds, and this is my wife Seela and our friend Crispa. Appearances can be deceiving. We're anything but slaves. And—can you put me in touch with a midwife? My wife has very nearly reached her term."

"Won't be the first babe born in my rooms," said Mrs. Mackie with a smile. "An auspicious event. I'll put you in a chamber on the second floor with fine view over the harbor." She paused, watching Seela wince against a wave of pain. "I can send for a midwife, but I expect the woman's busy tonight, the way things are. You'll have to make do. And I'll tell you now that I charge you an extra dollar for laundering the bedding after a birth."

"Never mind a midwife," said Crispa. "I can birth the baby. Done it six or seven times back home before I left. We had a big family."

"A boy for a midwife?" said Mrs. Mackie, doubting this.

"Crispa is a young lady," I told her. "In disguise so the sailors and miners leave her be."

"Men are ticks," said Mrs. Mackie with a shake of her head. "Bloodsucking parasites."

"Including me?" said Eddie.

"Surely not you, Cousin Goarland," said I. "And I'll leave you to settle the accounts. You can keep Arf in your room for company." And with that, Crispa and I helped Seela up the stairs, leaving Eddie to take the only other free room—which would prove to be a low-ceilinged rat-trap with a window on the alley behind the hotel.

Seela had to pause several times on the stairs. But then we were in our room, with the windows full of sky and the evening fog, warmed by the faint orange disk of the setting sun.

Seela's face was glistening with sweat. Before anything else, she stashed our two quietly glowing rumbies beneath our bed's mattress. And then she stripped off her clothes and sank onto the sheets. I bathed her face with a wet cloth from the basin. And, at Crispa's suggestion, I put some pillows behind her so she could sit up enough to see the view above the windows' half-curtains. Quite overwhelming, this ramshackle new city at dusk, a fairy kingdom in the fog, with the ghostly ships and bay and hills beyond.

"I feel like we're inside," said Seela.

"What?" I asked

"The sky and the sea are all around us. It's like we're in the Hollow Earth. And everything is singing."

"Maybe you're right about going back inside," I told her, patting her hand.

"Someone comin out of Hollow *Seela* pretty soon," said Crispa with a laugh.

Seela's water broke, and she gave a cry, more in surprise than in pain. The bed was soaked. I was ready to panic. But Crispa calmed me. As ever, our companion's features were calm and kind. She laid her hand upon Seela, and sat on a chair beside the bed, quietly coaching her through her ongoing contractions. An hour passed. And still no baby. A gong rang downstairs. The dinner bell? I realized how hungry I was.

"Go," Crispa gently urged me, divining my thoughts. "Eat. You have time."

Gratefully, I left Seela in our friend's care.

The dozen or so other lodgers were already at table. A polyglot crew. Californios, Oregonians, Australians, Chileans, and citizens from the East Coast. None of them seemed bent on going up into the gold country. They preferred, rather, to stay in San Francisco—profiting upon the gold-panners' gains. Among the company was a grocer, a bailiff, a clerk, a fireman, a security guard, and perhaps a thief or a pimp in the mix.

Eddie arrived in the dining room about the same time as me, with the inevitable Arf in tow. We two sat down beside Calvert Combs, a purveyor of mining equipment. Arf went under the table, awaiting scraps. Combs was a Yankee from Massachusetts. My feeling is that Yankees lack the innate nobility of Virginians. They're stingy, unscrupulous, and vain—not that they have anything to be vain about.

By way of greeting, Combs took the liberty of telling me I should eat in the kitchen with my dog, seeing as how I was a mulatto. And then he smirked at me, as if he'd lit off a stink bomb and was expecting me to go wild.

"I've heard that word before," I told Calvert evenly. "*Mulatto*. It doesn't apply to me, nor to my suffering wife upstairs, nor to our friend Crispa, and you're a jackass."

"Calling me a jackass, you whelp? Shall I box your ears?" Hearing the man's tone, Arf released a low growl.

"I see no point to fights," I said, maintaining an appearance of calm, although my pulse was pounding. "Why would I stand in place so a bonebrain can hit me in the face? No thank you. The way we do it in Virginia—if a fella rides you, you sneak into his room one night and cut a new mouth in his throat. Or you slip offal into his plate of stew. Or you pour lamp oil onto your man and set him on fire, next time he's passed out drunk in the street. Are you a heavy drinker, Mr. Combs?"

"It's hardly your place to play the inquisitor," snapped the Yankee.

"But do you take the point that I mislike fisticuffs?" I said. I held up my hand and studied the back of it as if I hadn't seen it lately. "I freely admit I'm the color of fine leather saddle. But this is a passing condition, eh? We'll all be skeletons, by and by. With no skin to bear the taint of tint."

Calvert stared at me in silence for the better part of a minute, with his head cocked to one side, as if he were a dog baffled by a strange sequence of sounds. And then he gave up on trying to understand and let out a laugh.

"You're welcome with the rest of this rum lot, Mason. I can't say I honestly give a damn what you are, as long as it ain't Chinese. And stay away from my stew! Ripe offal garnish—no thank you indeed!"

"Mason's wife is Chinese," put in Eddie, very quick and mocking. "She's from the utmost southern region of China. Beneath the central glacier of the Antarctic pole."

"Whatever you two say," went Calvert Combs, refilling his glass. "And welcome to the liars' club. You're fortunate you landed here. The food is toothsome—which is something of a wonder in a rooming house, eh, Mrs. Mackie?"

"Of course it's good," said Mrs. Mackie. "Why shouldn't it be? With all the cattle in the fields, and the fish and crabs in the bay. And my kitchen garden is flourishing. Salmon, steak, and corn chowder tonight, boys, with greens and sourdough bread."

I ate my fill, passing tidbits to Arf, and losing myself in the gut joy of the meal. It was only when Mrs. Mackie set to ladling out bowls of pudding that I remembered myself, or rather, remembered Seela. That faint high noise in the background—those were my wife's cries! I snatched up spoons with three bowls of pudding and thundered up the stairs. And this time Arf came with me. He didn't want to be in Eddie's room.

Seela had no appetite, but Crispa readily ate two shares of dessert. Seela's labor went on through the night. An hour before dawn Arf and I went out into the street for a break, and I found Eddie Poe out there as well, staring up the hillside at the rest of the town. San Francisco was waking to the coming day's activity.

"See the canvas sides of the tent houses, lit from the lamps within," said Eddie. "Dwellings of solid, geometric light. Living jewels. Quite wonderful."

"Travelers we," said I, drawing a measure of calm from my friend's presence.

"I've been awake all night, penning lines and smoking opium from the *Water Witch*," said Eddie. "Bliss. How fares your Seela?"

"She says she feels like she's being torn in half," I told him. "And I'm scared she'll die. Without Seela—I'd be a lost farmboy again."

"You're more than that, Mason," said Eddie. "You've begun to write. The Hollow Earth narrative that you left at Coale's bookstore in Baltimore! Do you deem it publishable?"

"How would I know?" I said. Somehow I wasn't ready to tell Eddie that Connor Machree had read my manuscript for *The Hollow Earth*. If Machree was dead, what did that matter? But, wait, wait, I'd seen the man in the Broken Harp saloon on the way to our hotel last night. Or had I? Perhaps it had been a trick of the light, or a figment brought on by fatigue. I pushed Machree from my mind.

"I would want to edit it, were I to stay," Eddie was saying, still talking about my *Hollow Earth* manuscript. "I'd amend the infelicities. I rather suspect you made verbal sallies at my expense. It's bad taste when a student slights his master."

"I see you didn't shed any vanity during your passage through the grave," said I.

"How sharper than a serpent's tooth it is to have a thankless child!" intoned Eddie. "The Bard. *Lear*, Act 1, Scene 4. Publish what you will, impudent pup. What have I to lose? I'm twice dead. In any case, the monstrous dungbeetle Rufus Griswold has had his way with my reputation. In California, we're beyond the backbiting literary mandarins of New England and Manhattan. Should I fail at my return to my proper Earth, we'll publish your *Hollow Earth* intact, and proceed to the sequel. The *Return*. It might be well for you to enhance the first volume with a map of the inner world. Who knows how far our narratives may lead—considering that *every word is true*.

"I'm certainly in need of money," said I. Arf at my feet was at ease, delicately sampling the myriad of smells threading along the waking city's air.

"Indeed," said Eddie, his eyes still playing across the glowing tents on the hillsides. "Three mouths to feed! A manly obligation. I myself—I may never be a father."

"There's still time," I said. "If you can pick a suitable woman. Not a cousin and not a widow."

"You rebuke my wayward heart?" said Eddie, raising his eyebrows. "Your impudence knows no bounds. But in my genial mood, I refrain from umbrage." He paused a minute, rocking on his heels, as if weighing my words. "Find a suitable woman? The shapely and forthright Jewel in the Hollow Earth, do you remember her? I would gladly deem her as suitable, if I were so allowed to choose." He touched the silk-wrapped amulet at his neck, as he was wont to do. "It is, after all, Jewel's gift of this rumby that has given me dominion over that *ballula* whom I call Cytherea. It may be that Jewel hopes Cytherea will carry me back to her dark embrace."

"But who sent Cytherea?" I asked.

"The *woomo*, I'm sure," said Eddie. "But who can fathom their tenebrous plans?"

A wail from Seela drifted from our room's window. Arf sat upright, pricking his ears and staring at the window. "Go to your lady, Mason," said Poe. "Taste life's joys and pains to the lees."

Our boy was born an hour later, with the rising of the sun. I wept with joy and relief. The babe had a wide mouth and strong lungs. His umbilical cord made a particularly strong impression on me. It was thick and twisty, engorged by a red artery and a blue vein, a glistening link that led from his belly into Seela's slippery birth canal. I had a vision of a garland through time, a cord from the boy to Seela, a second cord from Seela to her mother, a third cord from Seela's mother to her grandmother, back and back, a chain of navel cords, festooned with babies like cucumbers upon a vine!

Crispa and I cleaned up Seela, got new sheets, and remade the bed. Arf stayed well out of the way, lying in a corner of the room watching. Crispa settled down on an extra feather-erbed and fell asleep. Our new baby, this tiny wight, lay at Seela's breast, not suckling as yet, just nestled there, perfectly at ease, a bit wearied by his birth, his lips a quiet triangle. For a moment he regarded me with deep eyes of primordial mystery, unfocused and untrained, taking my measure. I would do. His eyelids fluttered and he slept. He was white against Seela's dark skin. I ran my hand across his body. Skin like silk, as if without pores.

"Do you need anything?" I asked Seela.

"I'm hungry," she said. I was glad to hear this. The labor was over. We were back to—well, not back to *normal*. With the baby, our lives as we'd known them were done. New pathways lay ahead.

I went downstairs with Arf, and the roomers were at table again. I received congratulations all around. As yet Eddie was not to be seen. I heaped Seela a plate of eggs, ham, bread, butter, and jam. Arf took up his station beneath the dining table. I bore Seela's plate upstairs with a mug of coffee. She ate and drank, smiling and laughing the whole time. We couldn't stop looking at our new baby. Such a miracle—that a perfectly formed human could have grown inside Seela. How does it happen? Life is a mystery, and every instant a miracle.

Seela and I chatted for a while, though I don't remember what we said. Sweet nothings. Two birds in a nest, admiring their hatchling.

"Can we call him Tuck?" I asked her.

"Tuck? That's a name?"

"My uncle's name. He was always nice to me."

"I like Brumble," said Seela. "*My* uncle's name."

"You uncle's really called Brumble?"

"His nickname. He has a deep voice." She stroked the baby's fat cheek with the tip of her finger and raised her voice as high as it would go. "Little Brumble." The baby shifted and made a wee sound. A coo. Seela gave me a sunny, guileless smile. I could only assent.

"Brumble he is," said I.

"Now let me sleep too," said Seela. "Hard night. Worth it." She smiled at the baby again.

"Don't roll on him and crush him," I cautioned her. "Sometimes on the farm, a sow will…"

"Oh, get on with you. And take your rumby. Just in case."

I pulled my fat, heavy, glinting rumby from where it rested with Seela's, beneath the mattress. It seemed to greet me. I put it in my pants pocket, leaving the companion for Seela. Silently the rumbies sang to us, happy to be in play. When Seela had time, she'd wrap them in thread, and they'd hang on our necks again.

I kissed Seela goodbye, and walked downstairs, mentally composing my narrative of the past day's events.

RUDY RUCKER

4. Roulette

Eddie was alone in the common room, with Arf at his feet, studying a newspaper and drinking coffee. "The bridegroom cometh," he said, glancing up. "The father almighty. All is well?"

"Brumble," I said, grinning like a fool. I went to Eddie and shook his hand. "You can be his godfather."

"An honor," said Eddie, miming a tip of the hat. "Brumble? An hirsute cub?"

"Soft as a rabbit," said I. "Smooth as cream. I love him already."

"Hallelujah," said Eddie, with apparent sincerity. "I envy you. Are you ready to seek employ?"

"In what sense?" Today of all days, I had no lust for going hat in hand to beg for jobs.

"The *Daily Alta California*!" said Eddie, tapping the newspaper against his hand. "Their typesetting is vile, and their writers are inarticulate. Let us hie ourselves thither and amend their ways. You recall that on the ship I concocted some fanciful reports from the gold country. I warrant they'll sell. Come to my room and we'll toff you up. You have the look of a bleary sailor on a spree."

I washed, and combed my hair, and took a clean white shirt of Eddie's. I ran upstairs to check on Seela and Brumble. They were blissfully asleep, and so was Crispa. I told Mrs. Mackie I'd be going out for an hour, and she assured me she'd watch over my precious ones.

344

"A baby boy in the house is good luck," said she.

"What of a baby girl?" asked Eddie.

"A baby of any kind is good luck," said Mrs. Mackie. "Take care of your cousin today, Goarland. His head spins." She wagged a finger at Eddie. It was as if everyone who met Eddie could tell what he was like. "No saloons!"

"A morning drinker is doomed," said Eddie.

At this point I realized there would indeed be trouble. Of course our first day in town would call for celebration. Of course Eddie would be drunk. And then, who knew?

I turned to my imp of a mentor. "Perhaps I'd better stay here with—"

But by now Eddie had bundled me into the street with Arf right behind us. It was about nine in the morning, with a fading blanket of fog at the mouth the bay, and a brightening sun above. The air was soft, fragrant, and elastic, with each breath like a sip of tonic. Far from being exhausted after the night's cavalcade of events, I felt exhilarated. Why not walk about with my dog and my friend?

"A fellow told me the *Daily Alta* office is on Montgomery Street next to the port," said Eddie gesturing past the tents, the canvas cabins, and the brightly painted wooden buildings. "We might have passed it yesterday."

From here I could see scores of ships, some at anchor, some tied to the piers of the harbor's little cove. The abandoned vessels among them were like decaying, empty houses, but the others were clean and bright in the morning sun. The trim hull of the *Water Witch* winked a hello.

"Curious town," said I, as we descended toward Portsmouth Square. "Grown up like a mushroom fairy ring. From a few hundred souls to twenty thousand in one year."

"We'll have an easy time cozening the lads at the *Daily Alta*," said Eddie. "They're rawhide Westerners, and we're men of ink and pen. They'll sign us onto the *Alta* payroll, I'll give them my gold country pieces, we'll get fat advances, we'll take the rest of the day off. And perhaps before doing any further work at all, we'll leave town. In any case we'll have established a contact for our projects to come."

"I can be the muse for you two *writers*," said a bold girl with a husky voice. As she passed, she elbowed Eddie and brushed her hip against my leg. She was about my age. "Come see me at the Broken Harp," she said. "I brim with tales of weal and woe." A few steps uphill she glanced back over her shoulder, gauging her effect. Her lips were heavily rouged, and her eyes held an unspoken question. "Ask for Ina Durivage," she said. "That's me. I need a knight." She strode on her way, leaving Eddie in an amorous tizzy.

"Little chance of *you* courting a street girl like that," he told me, almost spiteful in his tone. "Leave her to me, my boy. After we visit the newspaper offices, you'll speed back to your mother hen and your downy chick. A faithful patriarch at age seventeen, poor lad. Caught in the trap. Meanwhile I'll spend a few hours in doubling our holdings via my mathematico-logical understanding of faro and roulette. With gold pouch full, I'll assemble the equipage for our foray to the Hollow Earth." Eddie pointed toward the sky. "Our celestial chariot awaits, richly lined with mother of pearl, eh? I've rethought our schedule. I propose we set out tomorrow at dawn. I'll arrange our supplies by dusk and then, during my last night in San Francisco, I'll pay court to the antic Ina. Quite my style, this saucy coquette. Disturbed, declamatory, decadent, doomed. Even more to my taste than the dark Jewel of the Hollow Earth. And—"

"Wait," I interrupted. "You say dawn tomorrow? We can't leave so soon as all that. Not with Seela and a newborn babe."

"Seela can manage," said Eddie. "She's wild, uncorrupted, and from a truly natural world. Unencumbered by the fripperies of civilized woman and man."

"Maybe," I said. "I can talk to her about it. But, you, Eddie, you're half out of your head. If you want to travel tomorrow, you need to rest. Not sit up all night writing and smoking opium."

"Perhaps I'll be sharpening my pen in Ina's bed," said Eddie. It was quite unlike him, such a ribald remark. But I laughed just the same.

"You dog," said I, getting into my friend's reckless mood. We were on the verge of another epic journey, and ready to slip our moorings again.

As it happened, we never made it to the offices of the *Daily Alta* newspaper. Upon entering the lively Portsmouth Square, Eddie, feeling in his pocket, observed that he still had a ten-dollar gold eagle coin left from the hoard that he and the widow Whistler had amassed in New York. He reasoned aloud that, since he would be repeatedly doubling his stake at the faro table, ten dollars was as good a start as a hundred. So really there was no need to visit the *Alta* office at all.

"My mind is keen in the early morning," added Eddie, easily throwing his arm across my shoulders. "When my night of intoxicated wonder ends, I feel a jangle in my nerves. The workaday world's details slap at me like combers against a cliff. My psyche is a raddled shower of sparks. *Ergo* let us hie ourselves to the Eldorado!"

This was the moment when I again remembered my glimpse into the Broken Harp the night before. "I saw Machree in a saloon near our hotel," I blurted out. "The man we left to drown. Not a ghost. He was real. He recognized me."

"Oho," said Eddie, halting his progress. "The plot thickens." His face went blank while his powerful mind assayed the possibilities. "The *woomo* light!" he presently exclaimed. "It carried him here. And he is burned quite black?"

"Indeed," said I, wondering at Eddie's acumen. "But why would the mighty *woomo* save a conniving jeweler? Tell me all you know, and have done with playing the Sphinx."

Eddie drew a breath and began. "First of all, the jeweler Machree is my disciple. A Crozier, as I term him, in the Order of the Golden Frond, a society invented by Annabel Whistler and me, with a congregation approaching twenty. My followers call me the Tulku. He who is reborn. I've told them my tale of being stabbed and drowned and resurrected."

"It's not grand enough to be a writer?" I said.

"I'm destined for more," said Eddie. "I am the Tulku and Machree is my Crozier. He helps me tend my flock. It's hard to be sure if he fully grasps the wheeze, not that I've been overly frank with him. He's a fellow with a wide circle of friends, and a steady need of funds. Very useful."

"So you've started a religion," I said, trying to sort this out.

"Not a religion, per se. Something more like the Scottish Rite, or like Mesmerism. But with a sting. Annabel, Machree, and I have crafted a liturgy for our occult rites—and the ceremonies culminate in psychic contact with our august friends the *woomo*."

"Wait, tell me about the occult rites," said I.

"The usual bill of fare," said Eddie, with the sly smile of a jaded roué. "Wine, hashish, and copulation—to the tune of *la Whistler's* harp arpeggios and Machree's thunderous organ music. Being the Tulku, I preside."

"You preach?"

"Often I contribute a literary recitation, such as 'The Raven.' And then, with my plump and thinky rumby gem to hand, I summon the *woomo*. The mighty sea cucumbers' tendrils find their way to us from the Hollow Earth's core, and the golden fronds illuminate my rumby. The gem twitches like a sleeper ready to awake. And my followers enter a state of ecstasy."

"Do you take advantage of your subjects when they swoon?" asked I.

Eddie looked abashed. "Not always in the coarse, animal way. Even in the absence of physical touch, I can attain a sense of intimate contact with my adepts. Samples of their life essences are physically transferred from their bodies into mine. The *woomo's* subtle tendrils extract the samples from my flock, you see, and they store these living cells within my generative organs." He lowered his voice to a whisper. "I feel a growing lump within my sack. A library of human forms."

This was not a topic I cared to pursue. I moved on. "And Connor Machree wants a rumby of his own."

"All the more reason to depart at the morrow's dawn," said Eddie.

As if conjured up, the little porter boy from last night appeared before us. Pip of the unruly hair. Arf greeted him effusively, putting his feet on Pip's chest and licking his face.

"Settled in well, gentleman?" piped the boy, framing a winsome glance through his bangs. "Any errands I can help with today?"

"We're likely to go shopping for expedition supplies this afternoon," Eddie told Pip. "You might come to Mrs. Mackie's and ask for us."

"Digging in the gold country, eh?" said Pip. "Some of the tenderfeet end up like that quiz over there. A onetime Harvard student, as he used to say."

Pip directed our attention to a forty-year-old man sitting alone on the ground in a corner of the square. He was wrapped in a rough blanket, his matted hair hung across his wasted face, and his eyes glared steadily forward. He wore an expression of hopeless suffering, and he was muttering to himself.

"Traded his digging-spot for a meal," said Pip. "And then the gold came in. The man drank bad whiskey and went mad."

"How do you know?" I asked.

"He was my father," said Pip. "Not that he recognizes me anymore. Useless fool." It was sad to see so young a boy feign such hardness.

"We're not planning to dig for gold at all," I gently told Pip. "And I'm sorry about your father."

The smudged urchin made a razzing noise and skipped away. Arf followed him for a few steps, then came back to us.

"A cold, predatory child," mused Eddie. "Aged beyond his years."

"Why don't you finish telling me about Machree and the rumbies?" I said, putting Pip from my mind. "So I know what we're in for."

"Very well." Eddie steered me to one side of the square's foot traffic, and we found a perch on the mound of unsold house frames I'd noticed before. Their owner, a little man in a dark suit, fixed us with a watchful eye.

"The sum that Machree offered for my personal rumby, although largish, was unconvincing," Eddie continued. "I told Machree I would prefer to sell him advice on how to obtain a rumby of his *own*. Machree acceded, and in return, I instructed him to seek out Mason Reynolds and his woman

Seela in Baltimore. I assumed you two were still there, and
that a physical description of Seela might suffice. She hides
not her light beneath a bushel. Machree boarded a stagecoach
for Baltimore. This was on the first of March."

"Go on," I said.

"Machree arrived in Baltimore on March the fifth, only
to learn that you two had departed for New York on March
the fourth. Machree stole or purchased your two rumbies
in Baltimore, and he learned that you meant to ship to San
Francisco aboard the *Purple Whale*. I gleaned these details
via a note from Machree which I received in Manhattan on
March the ninth. By the time I got the note, you and Machree
were on the high seas. I resolved to follow. I didn't want you
and Seela at my covetous disciple's mercy."

"That is, you didn't want to miss out on what we did."

"If you will. I thought you and Seela might soon bolt for
the Hollow Earth. And I, too, wanted to revisit that eldritch
landscape or, better yet, pass fully through it and return to
the Edenic Earth from which I came."

"A method in your madness," said I. "Continue."

"I boarded the *Water Witch*, a faster ship than the *Purple
Whale*. And I bid Cytherea to follow along. And, soon after
my ship had rounded the Horn, I petitioned my good *ballula*
to ferry you and Seela from your ship to mine. In this wise
we three would arrive in San Francisco before Machree.
We'd have time to see the city, to garner supplies, and then
to embark upon our return to the Hollow Earth without that
venal, tiresome man in tow. That was my plan."

"But the *woomo* saved Machree," said he. "And he got
here before us."

"Refined and devious are the sea cucumbers of the
Hollow Earth," said Eddie, shaking his head in bemuse-
ment. "They sped Machree northward like a signal upon a
telegraph wire."

"And again I ask *why*. Why do the *woomo* help first you,
and then Machree?"

"Are we in court, Mason? Are you taking a deposition?"
Eddie shrugged. "Perhaps the *woomo* value the tuneless,
yawping hymns of the Order of the Golden Frond, paeans

composed by Machree himself. Perhaps my cult is no hoax at all? *Nescio.* I do not know. For now, our task is to raise a grubstake for a return to the Hollow Earth. An expeditious departure is of growing urgency, with the tedious Machree on the scene."

The owner of the stack of house frames had been studiously eavesdropping. But our tale made little sense to him. Weary of Eddie's opaque farrago, the merchant nudged us on our way. Miners, swindlers, speculators, and vaqueros were streaming past, everyone talking at once. I roused Arf, then stood and turned slowly around, staring into the corners and recesses of the square.

"No sign of Machree," I said.

"It may be that he's engaged cat's-paws to watch for us," said Eddie, with a touch of unease. "The man is devious. Thanks to the *woomo*, he's had nearly a month here to lay snares." He fondled his weighty rumby gem, which he wore, as always, in an intricate wrapping of silk threads upon a cord around his neck. "I sense that you have your own rumby to hand?"

"I do."

"It is well," said Eddie. "This doubles our power of tekelili. And Seela's stone?"

"It's with her. Under our mattress. Do you think Crispa might steal it? Should I go back to our room?"

"And miss our impending financial coup?" said Eddie. "Seela, Brumble, and Crispa can wait. Grant me an hour of your time, my boy. Accompany me into the Eldorado, San Francisco's premier gambling hell. We'll perform lucrative legerdemain."

"How so?"

"We'll use our rumby tekelili for exchanging signs, for remote viewing, and mayhap to engage the hylozoic inner soul of the roulette wheel. Tekelili has untapped potency, Mason. Mind pervades matter." Meaning to offer a demonstration, Eddie fell silent and stared at me while the crowd continued swirling past.

The rumby in my pocket gave a shudder and a shake. Very faintly I heard Eddie's smooth voice in my head, asking if I could hear him. I nodded, and now Eddie sent an image. I saw a playing card, a ten of diamonds, very clear, hanging in the air. I named the card aloud.

"To victory!" said Ed, and we marched into the Eldorado. The doorman, or bouncer, refused to let Arf inside, but I persuaded the dog to lie quietly on the ground outside the door. What with my rumby, and with all that Arf and I had been through in the Hollow Earth, he did at times seem to understand what I wanted him to do.

The Eldorado's outer walls were rough wood, but the inside was sumptuous. The so-called hell was a single, large, high room. A row of fluted columns ran down the middle, with a massive, polished redwood bar along one side. The games dominated on the floor—tables for the card games faro and monte, a pair of elegantly clicking roulette wheels, and three spinning chuck-a-luck bird-cages with dice within. Eddie told me that chuck-a-luck was for greenhorns.

"We'll build a stake at faro, and make a killing at roulette," he told me.

Worn-out gamblers and languid women relaxed on the cushioned and gilded furniture. The room was illuminated by dangling crystal chandeliers, with no frank rays of sunlight allowed. Mirrors, China silk hangings, and paintings of nude women adorned the walls. I'd hardly ever seen paintings before.

Before starting at the tables, Eddie approached the bar. A comely girl in a close-fitting black silk dress awaited us. Her slender fingers were adorned with rings.

"My cousin and I would rather fancy a pick-me-up," Eddie told her. "May I charge it on account, my dear…"

"Persephone," said the smiling maiden, with a modest air. "No credit here. Open your poke and I'll take a pinch of gold dust. That's the rate for idlers."

"I, ah, have a coin," said Eddie. "But I'm loath to cut into it. I'll let Dame Fortuna make the change."

He strode over to a nearby faro table, and set down his ten-dollar gold eagle on a layout that showed each rank of card, from Ace to King. Eddie bet on the ten. The dealer brandished a card holder, known as a *shoe*, and dealt out cards in pairs. The members of each pair signaled a losing number and a winning number. Presently ten was anointed as a winning number. Barely containing his nervous glee, Eddie rejoined me at the bar, with his gold eagle and a trimmed-down gold doubloon in hand.

"Now cake and brandy for two," he told the girl with the rings, setting his mangled doubloon on the bar.

"It's on the house," said Persephone, waving off the coin. "As long as you keep playing." She gave a low laugh. "Maybe you'll hit big, maybe we'll take all."

The sweets were of a kind I'd never had before: square little iced cakes that Eddie termed *petits fours*, glancing to see if the alluring Persephone marked his command of French. But she didn't seem to care.

As Eddie and I stood there, enjoying our cake and brandy, he watched the faro game, intently eyeing the dealer's shoe of cards. At a given moment, he strode over and put his two coins on the Jack. Moments later he'd won again. Four gold coins now: two eagles, a doubloon, and a guilder. He gave me the two eagles.

The rumby in my pocket warmed. I saw a Queen card in the air. An image from Eddie. I myself was unable to see into the dealer's deck, but Eddie was in a high state of psychic clarity. I bet on the Queen, and I won on the next pair of cards from the shoe. In short order we'd amassed a hundred and ten dollars.

"Now for the roulette," Eddie said to me as we leaned against the bar, gloating over our eleven gold coins. "I'll imbibe another small brandy before I explain the plan."

"Are you sure you should keep drinking?" I asked him.

"Frightened farm boy," said he. Eddie could turn ugly very fast.

"Drinks on the house," repeated Persephone, her voice sweet.

Stepping aside to let Eddie take his pleasure, I carried a scrap of cake to Arf, lying by the wall just outside the entrance. And then back inside for me. It was nearly noon, and the Eldorado was filling up. Across the big room a young boy was lighting a full-sized cigar, an odd and unwholesome apparition. As the tousled child exhaled a great plume of smoke, I realized it was our porter once again, little Pip. Catching me looking at him, he mimed a salute and made his way over, attempting a swagger in his walk.

"Do you have a mother?" I asked him. "Does she know you're here? Does she know your Pa's gone mad?"

Speaking of family matters, about which I knew so little, I was suffused with a pang of shame. Why was I with Eddie in a gambling hell and not with Seela and Brumble?

"Pa's nuts, Ma's dead, and I don't need coddling," said Pip, closing down the topic. "You working gaffs?"

"Gaffs?"

"Gambling tricks," said Eddie, gliding over from the bar with a plume of alcohol on his breath. "The boy imagines we're sharpers." Daintily Eddie nibbled a pink *petit four*. "Currants with cream," he reported.

"If you ain't miners, you gotta be sharpers," said Pip.

"Never mind what we are," I said, misliking the intentness of the boy's glittering eyes. He was like a shrill, predatory insect. My fatigue and my glass of brandy were getting to me. "Get away from us," I snapped. "You're a jinx."

Pip sneered, blew another cloud of smoke, and headed over to cozen a drunken miner at the chuck-a-luck dice. No doubt Pip hoped to pick the man's pocket. It was a sorry class of people in here.

"I want to leave," I told Eddie. "It's too much. I need to be with Seela."

"Wait!" he hissed. "We're at the climax. One single turn on Fortuna's wheel. I'll bet our stake. We have a hundred and ten—well, no, a hundred, as I tipped Persephone. You'll stand as close to the wheel as possible. Hold your rumby in your hand, and focus the full power of your tekelili on the number we bet."

"Which number?" I asked, intrigued by Eddie's plan.

"A deeper wrinkle here," said Eddie. "*The wheel will tell us.* We'll work together—you, the wheel, and me. It pays thirty to one. We'll win three thousand dollars."

"It is well," said I. "And God help me, Eddie, once we win, we'll leave immediately, with no more drinks, and no more bets, or I'll bash your noggin in." I rapped a knuckle against his pale, bulging brow, and gave him a shake. "Do you hear me, you demonic charlatan?"

"The nest is best," crooned Eddie, as if addled from his drinks. "Back to the hen and chick for you, eh? But first we peck!"

I slipped my bare hand into my pocket. I held my fat dense rumby, and merged into its tekelili. The gem tingled against my skin, as if barbed like a burr. Colors flowed up my arm and into my eyes. Meanwhile Eddie laid his left hand across his silk-wrapped, neck-worn amulet, in conversation with his own gem.

Unexpectedly I heard a squeaky woman's voice in my head. "Twenty-three," she said. The voice of the wheel, and who knows how I heard it. Via tekelili, I shared the number with Eddie, and I heard his silent hosanna.

Eddie slapped our really rather pitifully small pile of coins onto the roulette layout. The croupier spun the horizontal wheel, and whirled a little white ball into the encircling bowl. The ball clattered against the slots and danced. Red, black, red, red, black. I fixed my eyes on the red twenty-three, and Eddie did the same. I could feel our tekelili power. Impossibly fine tendrils veined the air around us.

The red slot of the twenty three was like a polar maelstrom drawing in the tiny traveler that was the ball, or like a sun pulling down a moon, or a serpent swallowing a mouse, or a tornado pulling us into its eye. *Click, clatter, click,* and a low exclamation from those around us. We'd won three thousand dollars.

The croupier told us that the Eldorado gold was worth twenty dollars an ounce, and, with some prodding, he paid us our winnings in the form of fifteen ounces of glittering dust. Nearly a pound! I had the man bag it into two deerskin pouches, approximately equal in size, one for Ed, and one for me.

For a wonder, Eddie was willing to leave the gambling den. I think, like me, he was feeling skittish about Connor Machree. We made our way into Portsmouth Square, a little stunned by the intensity of the pure sunlight. Arf was right at our heels, sniffing us to see if we'd brought food from inside.

"I'm coming with you gents," said the barmaid Persephone, appearing beside us, and twining her arm around Eddie's waist. "I've worked enough today. I can get us a private dining room at the Delmonico. Entrance in back. We'll have a spree." Delmonico was a fancy restaurant just across the square. But I doubted we'd be getting any food if we followed Persephone there.

"Guard your pocket," I warned Eddie, and he pushed Persephone away.

"You're mistaking me for an entirely different class of person," Eddie told her, always glad for a chance to tell some thumpers. "My cousin Mason and I are tending to his wife and their newborn baby. We only came out for diapers and clabber. We entered the Eldorado by mistake—Mason here thought it was a church. He's quite pious, you know. As for the roulette, well, twenty-three was Grandmother's birthday. We're grateful for her holy blessing. But we have no lust for low jinks. Do mark that I already tipped you. Sojourn on, young woman, and may the Light be with you."

"You sober up fast, don't you?" said Persephone with disgust. She turned on her heel and flounced back into the Eldorado. Eddie pulled out his poke of gold, loosed the rawhide around the pouch, and stared in, as if wanting to confirm it was real.

"Stop that," I told him. "People are looking. Some thief is going to jostle you."

"Indeed," said Eddie, gathering his wits and pocketing his gold. "Up the hill to Mrs. Mackie's. And to Mason's wee chickabiddy. You named him—what was it?"

"Gramble, I think," said I, that single shot of bandy still buzzing in my ears. "Or, no, it was Brumble." How could I forget my son's name? Tears started into my eyes at the thought of his tiny fuzzed head. And somehow the sight of Arf's kind, liquid eyes with his mobile, sympathetic eyebrows was like a knife in my heart. I had to bring my life into order.

Taking tight hold of Eddie's arm, I swept him up the hill toward the hotel. I had a bad moment as we passed that cloth-walled saloon, the Broken Harp. The girl who'd approached us this morning—Ina—she was in there conning a miner who had precisely half of his teeth missing. The left half. Standing behind the counter with a dour expression was the thin-headed red-haired man I'd seen before. Inevitably Ina's eye caught mine, and she gave me a beckoning wave.

"That's where I saw Connor Machree," I told Eddie.

"Looking to find him?" shrilled a voice just behind us. "Want me to bring him to your room?"

Naturally it was Pip. "What does it take to get rid of you?" I cried.

"Gold," said he. "I've got a ready sack. In my spare time, I gather specks of dust off the streets. But *you're* giving me a full ounce."

I leaned back and lifted my foot, preparing to kick him, and before I knew it I'd fallen heavily onto the muddy street. Pip had shoved me off balance. The little boy was a tiger. He was on me, trying to work his hand into my pocket, meaning to steal my pouch of gold, robbing me in the full light of day. Arf snarled and nipped at Pip, but the covetous urchin thrust the dog aside.

Eddie, never one for physical fisticuffs, called for help from the patrons of the Broken Harp. The thin, cold-looking proprietor of the Broken Harp was watching us, but he made no move to interfere

"That's the boy, Pip," urged the streetwise Ina, standing in the opening that was the saloon's door. "Hold them tight. Machree's coming out from our room."

Hearing this, Eddie turned to start uphill, but Pip hooked one of his feet around Eddie's ankle, sending him to the ground as well. At this point, Arf got a really good bite into Pip's calf, and the boy yelped. And then Machree was standing over us, still dressed in his brown suit. His skin was as dark as my old companion Otha's had ever been. He looked more peaceful than before.

"The sorcerer and his apprentice," said Machree exaggerating his Virginia drawl. "Simmer down, Pip, leave them be." He turned his attention to my companion. "The boy's like a pond leech, eh, Eddie?"

"You know full well my name is Goarland Peale," said Eddie. "I'm the Tulku of the Order of the Golden Frond, and you've had the privilege to assist me as the order's Crozier."

"Come now, Edgar Allan Poe," said Machree putting on a jovial air. "Hasn't this ruffian Mason told you I read his full manuscript in the back room of E. J. Coale's bookstore in Baltimore? *The Hollow Earth*, or, *The Narrative of Mason Algiers Reynolds of Virginia*. I know the whole story. You can't bamboozle me. I'm traveling with you to the Hollow Earth, and that's that. I'm meant to be a part of your dodgy schemes."

"Perhaps," said Eddie, as if thinking this over.

I got free of Pip, rose to my feet, and addressed Machree myself. "Why don't you ask the *woomo* to carry you to the Hollow Earth on a tendril of light? Like they did for you when the Purple Whale sank. You don't need us, and we don't need you. Go it alone."

"We're having a forthright honest conversation now?" said Machree. "High time. Yes, a *woomo* ray bore me to San Francisco. Evidently the Great Old Ones see value in me. But I wouldn't know how to ask them to carry me onward to the Hollow Earth. Especially not with my rumbies stolen by you and that—"

"Mason, Seela, and I are planning to ride in my *ballula*," interrupted Eddie. "Cytherea. Didn't you see her rescuing Mason and Seela at sea?"

"I wasn't seeing anything," said Machree, all traces of a smile gone. "I'd been robbed and left to drown. At least Seela had done me the kindness of not slitting my gullet."

"Find your *own* rumby in the Hollow Earth," I told Machree.

"If Eddie lets me come," said Machree.

"I propose we meet at our hotel tomorrow morning," said Eddie. "Crack of dawn."

"You should give Seela and the baby a little more time," I told Eddie again.

"And I told you not to fret," said Eddie. He turned to Machree. "My plan is to make my way back to my original Earth and to resume my literary career. And it's now crossed my mind that you might do well as my literary agent over there. You're hard-scrabble enough to make me rich. And bully enough to fend off my fiendish literary foe Rufus Griswold." Poe glanced over at me. "Don't be envious, Mason. You're not low enough for the job."

"Flattery greases no skids, Mr. Poe," said Machree. "And hear me when I say I'm coming with you right now, and I'll be sleeping in your room."

"I'm coming too!" put in Pip.

"No," said Eddie, Machree, and I—fully united on this one point. "You're not."

"Ounce of gold?" wheedled Pip.

"Hold out your pouch," said I, and I tipped over some dust.

"What about me?" called Ina, emotion welling in her voice. "Machree's been cadging space in my room for three weeks. Promising the stars and the moon. And as romantic as Saturn and the cinders. And meanwhile the villain Cruickshank, I mean that worm-headed man behind the bar, with his red hair and dead heart—he collects a procurer's fee from men like Machree, and still he says I owe him money. I'm a prisoner here, boys, a crushed rose. I once had hopes to enter high society—now dashed. Step forward and save me, Mason and Eddie!"

"Watch your tongue or you're back in the street," said Cruickshank from behind the bar.

"Help yourself to some of Pip's gold dust," Machree coldly advised Ina. "I'm leaving your orbit now."

"Bedbug," said Ina. "Whinger. Leech."

Pitying Ina, and admiring her fine, high invective, I gave Pip a supplemental tablespoon of gold, taking care lest Arf snuffle it up with his wet, probing nose. "Share this with your friend," I told Pip.

"Can Ina and me help you shop for supplies?" petitioned the boy.

"*On verra*," said Eddie, fixing Ina with an inquisitive eye. Clearly she fascinated him. "One will see."

And with that, Eddie, Machree, Arf, and I broke free of Pip and Ina, making our way up the hill to Mrs. Mackie's hotel.

5. Cytherea

I ran up the steps to our room, and there they were, Seela and Brumble, awake now, with Seela holding Brumble to her breast, the baby sweetly content, intent as a little animal, making the tiniest of grunts and sighs, and occasionally jerking his arms. A rich entertainment. Seela had found an open nightshirt to keep her shoulders warm.

"My darlings," I said.

"Brumble doesn't know how to nurse," said Seela, staring down at the baby, and smoothing his fine hair with a finger.

"Takes a couple of tries to start," put in Crispa, who was still there.

Arf pushed into the room and ate some scraps off a plate of Seela's on the floor. Lunchtime had come and gone. I wasn't hungry myself, not after the petits fours at the Eldorado.

"I won a lot of gold," I told Seela, showing her my pouch of dust. "Over a thousand dollars. Eddie won too."

"You didn't get a job?" said Seela. A wifely question. Not that her heart was in the role.

"This is the Gold Rush," said I. "If you're sharp, there's no need for work."

"Gold," echoed Seela, shaking her head. "So how did you win your sparkly dust?"

"We guessed a number on a turning wheel," I said.

"Did you and Eddie find a way to cheat?" asked Crispa. Aboard the *Water Witch*, I'd regaled her with my tale of Eddie and I counterfeiting Bank of Kentucky bills in Virginia.

"Sure we cheated," I said. "We put tekelili pressure on the ball. And it worked."

"Will the gamblers come after you?" asked Crispa.

"No," I said. "They don't know what we did. Even so, we might be leaving soon. Eddie's about to outfit us for an expedition."

"Oh yes!" exclaimed Seela, sitting up in the bed. "We're going to the Hollow Earth?"

"I think we should wait a week or two until you and Brumble are quite strong," I said. "But yes, we'll ride Eddie's *ballula* through the North Hole. He's pushing to go tomorrow, but I told him that's—"

"Tomorrow is fine!" said Seela, stretching out her arms, and kicking her legs beneath the sheet. "I'm a tough, wild flowerperson from the Hollow Earth. I've already been out of bed. My muscles are fine, and I'm not bleeding."

"What about Brumble?"

"He'll be in my arms."

"Can I hold him for a minute?"

Brumble's limbs were tiny, and his skin slack, as if he needed inflating. His gums were starkly bare, his nose like two holes, and his eyes cloudy. The bones on the top of his skull hadn't yet grown together, although the warm skin felt tough.

I put the tip of my finger into his mouth, and he sucked on it with some force. I tested the thickness of his cheek muscles between my finger and thumb. Impressively powerful. He'd be fine. I held him against my shoulder, cupping the back of his head with my hand. His smell was intimate and warm. Our little baby, fully formed.

Meanwhile Crispa had run downstairs to talk to Eddie about the trip. She wanted to be sure that she too was going along, even if only for part of the way.

Seela was smiling at me and the baby, taking us in.

"Well?" she said.

"Wonderful," I said. "And you grew him in your stomach."

"And now I'm my own right size again. And we can show him to my people in the Hollow Earth."

"But—really leave tomorrow?" I said, looking down at Brumble. He was asleep, with his little face closed up like a bud. I sat down beside Seela on the bed, and we laid Brumble on the sheet between us, taking in his infinitesimal changes—a pout, a dimple, a wince, a wiggle of the finger. Still deeply weary from last night, we laid ourselves flat, still staring at the baby, then fell asleep with him between us.

It was nearly dusk when we woke. We'd slept the afternoon through. Brumble was mewling, waving his little arms in a disorganized way, and mixing in yawns, hiccups, and single sneezes.

"Hello, tiny," sang Seela. She drew him to her bared breast, and this time he latched on, and, how wonderful, began to nurse, with a stream of minute grunts and swallows. Pale milk was visible at the verges of his lips.

Someone downstairs was calling my name. It was Connor Machree.

"What?" said I, upon rising from the bed, opening our door, and leaning into the stairwell.

"It's your friend Eddie Poe. I took a nap after lunch. I had a wonderful dream of the *woomo*. And now Eddie and Crispa have been gone three hours with Pip and Ina. Do you think Eddie imagines he can give us the slip?" Machree's face was a dim, anxious oval.

I checked in my pocket, and my pouch of gold was intact. It wasn't likely the light-fingered Poe would have left it in place if he was skipping out. "Don't worry," I called to Machree. "Eddie will be loading his magic seashell during the night. I reckon he'll come for us at dawn. You can depend on Seela and me."

"Would that were true," said Machree in a low tone. I was getting the impression that his ride in the *woomo* light had changed more than his skin. He seemed meeker now, more inclined to accept that he was a pawn or a cog—a bit player in the ever-expanding machinations of the *woomo*. As was I.

"Just wait in Eddie's room," I advised Machree.

"You and I are paradox incarnate," said Machree, staring up at me. "A fulcrum to pry the Earths in two. The axle of fate's turning wheel."

I had no idea what he meant by this—nor did I want to. I closed our door.

"You told Machree that he can depend on us?" said Seela. "Who even said he can come along on our trip?"

"Eddie said," I said. "Turns out Machree is Eddie's—I don't know—deacon? In a religion that Eddie made up. The Order of the Golden Frond. And Eddie's like their pope. Or no, he's the Tulku? They worship the *woomo.*"

"I want us to get away from Eddie when we're in the Hollow Earth," said Seela. "I've never liked him, not really." She got out of bed and stood with Brumble against her shoulder, gently patting his back. Across the bay, another sunset was coming down.

"A fresh adventure tomorrow," said I. "It never stops."

"Changes mean you're alive," said Seela. "If we're going on a trip with those rascals I want to hang our rumbies safe upon our necks again." She paused for a moment in thought, caressing Brumble all the while. "Fetch a spool of thick, strong thread from Mrs. Mackie or, better, ask for two spools of contrasting colors. So that the amulets look well."

Machree was nowhere to be seen when I went down to get the thread. Remembering Eddie's advice to draw a map of the Hollow Earth to go with my manuscript, I managed to cadge a pen and a sheet of vellum paper from Mrs. Mackie as well as the thread. Tomorrow our party would set out aboard the redoubtable Cytherea, but I'd leave my map in our room, in the hope it might someday accompany a published edition of *The Hollow Earth*.

Back in our room, I began drawing, enjoying myself with the task, and Seela set to work with the threads. I went down again an hour later to have my dinner, and to fetch a full plate and a flagon of ale for Seela. It's well known that beer is a specific for nursing mothers. Before long, my little map was done, and we two were wearing our heavy, wrapped-up rumbies on our necks again. Seela was very nimble with her fingers. I signed my map "M.R. 1850."

As night fell, we lit a candle and sat admiring the baby some more, with Seela nursing him whenever he took the whim, and with me fetching us further food and drink from the hotel kitchen's larder as needed. Eddie and Crispa were out all night. Seela and I slept, the baby woke us, we slept again, the baby woke us, we slept again—and so it went till dawn. Busy Earth, busy Sun, busy Seela, busy Mason, busy Brumble.

In the dawn's cottony glow, we sat up in our bed with the baby. Fog blanketed the city. The hidden sunrise's radiance lent the mist a warm tone. I couldn't see the next building over, so thick was the haze. But, closer than that, above the street, something was moving, a dim bulk the size of a hot-air balloon, with an inchoate filigree of faint tendrils below. Arf began barking. The shadowy curves flexed, grew, came into clarity, and reached toward us, fastening onto our window frame.

"It's Cytherea!" cried Seela. "Eddie and his *ballula*." She jumped to her feet and moved nimbly around the room, gathering her few garments, with Brumble in the crook of her arm. "Quick, Mason," she urged, opening the window sash. "We'll climb aboard."

The edge of the huge floating nautilus shell clattered against the outside wall. The shell's opening was fully twenty-five feet across, and the shell itself was a spiralled disk some seventy-five feet in diameter. Quite properly large. The hydrogen-filled shell could lift a heavy load. I peered into the queasy mass of twisting orange tentacles. Amid them were Eddie, Crispa, and, yes, Connor Machree, a mixture of greed and terror on his face.

Arf was growing hoarse. I nudged him and demanded silence. He pointed his dark nose at me, his eyes expressive. He was panting from excitement. He didn't like this at all.

"You go out the window," I told Arf, making a gesture. "It's safe. We're all coming. Same *ballula* as before." Grudgingly Arf hitched up his back legs and balanced on the window sill. He gave me another heartfelt stare. Crispa called sweetly to him from her nest amid the tentacles. Arf hopped over.

Seela went next, with some clothes under one arm, and with tiny Brumble in the other. She was wearing the nightshirt and a pair of pants, and—like me—her rumby on her neck. I meant to help Seela over the windowsill, but she exited on her own, with quick agility, springing into the *ballula's* open shell, graceful as a dancer, even now. The baby made a gurgling yodel. I followed Seela close behind.

Some early risers in the street had noticed the great hovering ammonoid. A young woman, calling out. A boy's voice as well. A cart was rolling by, and it was hard to hear them. And the fog was so dense that I couldn't make out their forms. Presumably they could see our huge shell's outline against the brightening sky. Now I heard a man's voice as well, blurred from a full night of drinking, angrily berating the woman.

I settled myself onto the heap of tentacles. Rather than being slimy, they were dry, and a bit adhesive. Cytherea was responsive enough to sculpt me a comfortable perch.

"Crew accounted for, and our vessel equipped," said Eddie, as if dictating a captain's log. He sounded well pleased with himself. "Our stores lie deeper in the shell, Mason. All is well. But—Ina's not in your room? I'd told her to—"

Below us in the fog, the man and woman were quarrelling, and now a sudden gunshot cracked. A bullet ripped through the air nearby. Cytherea wasn't one to flee a fight. She lashed down with a fifty-foot-long tendril and pulled it back with the tip wrapped around the struggling shape of—the desperate Ina Durivage. Streamers of saliva poured from the *ballula's* foul beak as she drew the woman closer, preparing, perhaps to bite off her head. Ina's cries and curses were fierce beyond all imagining.

"Halt!" cried Eddie, and Seela echoed him, very queenly in tone, and holding her hand against the dreaming rumby at her neck. Her and Eddie's grape-sized gems emitted pulses of psychic energy that caused the *ballula* to—set Ina down beside us. Though quite out of breath now, she looked well pleased.

The unseen man in the befogged street hollered something coarse and stupid. It was of course the slaving Cruickshank, the owner of the Broken Harp pothouse. A second gunshot boomed. This time the bullet ricocheted off the edge of the *ballula's* shell, knocking loose a chip. If this murderous, drunken procurer were to puncture the main body of Cytherea's shell, the hydrogen would rush out and our trip would be done.

The unseen boy in the street cried out to us. Pip.

"I conjure thee to rise," Eddie coolly said to Cytherea. He stared portentously into one of the *ballula's* great black eyes, and the eye stared back, wobbling on its short stalk.

"Do as Eddie says," I chimed in. "Rise!" I could feel the tekelili power of my own rumby at my neck, and, ever so faintly, I could feel the fabric of the *ballula's* crude mind. It was a meager consciousness, a taut web of hunger and rage.

Piqued at being ordered about, Cythera flew upwards so abruptly that I might have tumbled out backwards from the shell if Ina hadn't wrapped her arms around my midriff.

"Who *are* you?" Seela demanded of Ina. She didn't like seeing me in the embrace of this sly, loose woman of the Gold Rush streets.

"A lost lamb," said Ina. "A poetess. A man trap. And now, I hope, your friend."

"Miss Ina Durivage is from a fine New Orleans family," put in Eddie. "A free spirit, and not without literary skills. She's told me that she came to San Francisco with her journalist father, and when *père* Durivage died in an affair of honor, Ina befriended the homeless boy Pip—and they made common cause. Crispa and I spent last night with Ina and Pip, roaming the streets, assembling our equip."

"And sharing some sweet moments *à deux*," added Ina.

"I only rejoice that Pip didn't come aboard," said Machree. "Ina is much more to my humor."

"But you're not to *my* humor," huffed Ina. "I decree an end to your addled and impotent flirtations, Machree. Eddie Poe is my liberator!"

"And not I?" I sallied, so piqued was I by Ina's reckless, worldly demeanor.

"*Not* you," said Seela, and handed me our baby. Brumble was crying. Perhaps the rapid ascent had pained his wee ears.

"Indeed," said I, coming to my senses.

We'd reached the limits of the fog. The golden lamp of our Sun greeted us in our pearly chariot, the rush of light as palpable as a kiss. Peaks and mountain ranges projected from the cloud cover, with redwood forests upon the hills.

Further inland lay slopes dotted with oaks, and open fields, already sere and yellow, though it was but June.

We had six adults in our party: me, Eddie, Seela, Crispa, Machree, and Ina Durivage—with the addition of Brumble and Arf. A thousand-pound load at the very least. This meant that our full weight was well over a ton, taking into account the mass of the *ballula* herself, along with whatever casks, bales, tarpaulins, and crates Eddie had stowed at the base of her tentacles. I marveled that the lifting power of the hydrogen in Cythera's chambered shell was sufficient to keep us aloft.

How were we to reach the North Hole? This is where Cytherea's siphon came into play. It was a tube the size of a culvert, muscular yet flexible, nestled amid her tentacles. Rhythmically and repeatedly, the *ballula* drew in air, then forced it back out in a whistling stream, driving us forward. Her shell was well-adapted to this motion, and we made good speed, a forward progress enhanced by a favorable current that Cytherea located within the sky's sea of air.

Ina was full of questions. She'd had no plan of coming on the trip, but now she was excited at the prospect. Taking pleasure in the young woman's attentions, Eddie filled her in on the story of the Hollow Earth, and the Order of the Golden Frond, and our plans to descend through the North Hole. And, almost in passing, he told Ina that he was the younger double of the famous and recently deceased Edgar Allan Poe. A double from another world.

Connor Machree got in on the conversation as well. Having read my manuscript for *The Hollow Earth*, and having travelled to San Francisco aboard a tendril of *woomo* light, he had some sense of what we were in for. He did his best to clarify Eddie's extravagant claims.

But Ina kept thinking they were bragging, or speaking in jest. "Our Earth is like an egg or a womb?" she said. "What would be hatching inside? Baby suns? Come now, Mister Fake Edgar Allan Poe. Where are we *really* going? I hope it's New York."

"You'd cut a fine figure on Broadway," said Eddie. "And we'll get there when I publish my next book. But first we'll visit the brilliantly illuminated interior of our orb, eh, Mason?"

"Through the throat of the giant maelstrom," said I, projecting more confidence than I felt. "We saw it from inside the Hollow Earth."

"You were really and truly inside?" asked Ina, looking uneasy.

"Yes," said Seela. "The Hollow Earth is my home. And I've seen the North Hole maelstrom from below."

"Will it make a noise?" asked Ina.

"A low, unending moan," said Eddie, enjoying Ina's consternation. "The aggrieved groan of a fallen angel."

We progressed steadily northward and perhaps a bit to the east, with a landscape of mountains, forests, and plains unrolling below. Eddie rooted amid the stores in the depths of the shell, and produced a joint of ham, a roast chicken, some loaves of bread, several bottles of ale, and even a relatively intact chocolate cake. We feasted at leisure, wondering at the scope of the journey we'd begun.

"Never seen so much empty land," said Crispa, peering down at the lakes and prairies. "This is where grandpa come from. I can feel it." She was perched between Seela and me.

As she'd told us aboard the *Purple Whale*, Crispa had been raised in poverty by freed slaves in Baltimore. And her grandfather had been a Crow Indian. "How long ago was it you left home?" I asked her. "I forget."

"Five years," said Crispa. "I stove out a man's brains with a brick. He forced himself on me. A month later he did it again. And then I wouldn't stand it no more." She paused for effect. "Maybe I should have scalped him."

"Were you punished?" asked Seela.

"Would have been, but I run away," said Crispa. "Cut my hair, dressed like a boy and went to sea."

"None of the other sailors noticed?" I asked her.

"If they did, we generally made common cause," said Crispa. "And any skunk who put the muscle on me, well, pretty soon some rigging snapped and he'd fall in the drink and drown."

"Crispa's my kind of woman," said Seela. She smiled and dandled Brumble. "Your nanny's as bad as your ma," she crooned.

"Don't count on me to be nanny much more," said Crispa, lying on her belly the better to stare at the lands below. "I done told you I have a hankering to be an Upsaroka like grandpa. And I think I see a Crow camp down below. Teepees and smoke and, yeah, they got horses. They riding after buffalo. I rode a horse once in Baltimore."

"Will you join the Crow as a woman or a man?" I asked. "If you're a woman, you might not get to ride."

"People have a way of comin round to my way of doing things," said Crispa, undaunted. "If I want to ride, they'll let me."

"What about the Hollow Earth?" I asked.

"Don't like Eddie's talk about that giant whirlpool," said Crispa. "A sailor don't like hearin that at all. I'd just as soon this big farting shell set me down here right now."

As if responding to Crispa's words, the *ballula* began descending. Surprised, I used my rumby power to dip into Cytherea's crude mind, and learned it wasn't Crispa's plans that motivated Cytherea. She was hungry, ravenous, and bent on tearing into one of those bison that the Upsaroka were hunting.

We came in at a shallow angle, gliding above the wooly, thundering herd, with the shell side of the *ballula* first, her tentacles trailing, and the hiss of her siphon slowing down.

At the sight of Cytherea, the Upsaroka horses shied and galloped away. And the buffalo were in a frenzy of fear. Cytherea lashed out her tentacles, nearly knocking us off our perches in her shell. With quick, skillful movements, the *ballula* lassoed three of the bison, catching them round their bellies, and she forced extra tentacles down their throats to block off their air. Minutes later the three dead bison were jouncing along in the flying nautilus's wake. The survivors drummed away.

Cytherea drew one of the bison to her great clacking beak. Blood gushed over us as she consumed the creature, which may have weighed a ton. I was inclined to abandon my nest in the *ballula*'s shell while the great shellsquid fed, but Eddie and Seela held me back.

"She might make a precipitate departure," cautioned Eddie. "It would be unfortunate to sacrifice your great journey to a squeamish sense of propriety." Half his face was covered in hot bison blood, but he didn't seem to mind. Eddie, after all, had a taste for the ghastly. For her part, Ina was laughing steadily, as if at a loss for any other response. Machree, who seemed to be losing his nerve, was at the rear of our chamber, huddling against the curved mother-of-pearl that walled off the hydrogen-filled lifting chambers. Arf, of course, was scavenging scraps.

Crispa shook my hand and hopped down from the edge of the *ballula* shell to the prairie grass. "I'm sayin farewell," said she. "God speed, Mason, Seela, Eddie, and Ina. You're good people." She couldn't bring herself to say the same to Machree.

"Here's a Bowie knife for you," said Eddie, extracting the large blade from his supplies. "I've savored your company, Crispa."

"I'm gonna tell the Upsaroka I killed one of these buffalo myself," she responded, glad to have the big knife.

Casting aside the cracked-open skull of the first bison, the slobbering Cytherea tore into a second beast. Making efficient use of her dark, raspy tongue, she ate the brain, liver, heart, and kidneys, as well as the fatty muscles of the bison's hump—and then she cast the gory, rag-doll remains aside and—fully satiated—left the intact third bison to serve as Crispa's trophy. Crispa slit this dead animal's throat so that it would bleed out, and she struck a pose with one foot on the wooly creature's haunch.

The *ballula* adjusted the hidden rear parts of her body so as to increase the volume of the hydrogen chambers. And then, with her heavily taxed digestive system in loud percolation, we lifted off.

As we rose, a hail of arrows bounced off the great shell. Fortunately the aperture of our unprotected compartment was facing away from the Upsaroka tribe. And, even more fortunately, the easily-angered Cytherea chose not to launch a retaliatory attack. She was ready for a nap.

Soon we were hundreds of feet above the prairie. Looking down, I rejoiced to see Crispa making friends with the natives. No doubt they were impressed by her knife and by her self-possessed demeanor. I sensed that she wouldn't have to pretend to be a man. She'd be in a class of her own. A woman from the sky.

Meanwhile, having maneuvered her great shell into a highly favorable air stream, Cytherea cleaned the blood and gore from our quarters with quick motions of her feelers, then let her eyes grow dull, slackened all but two of her tentacles, and fell asleep, her siphon faintly whistling. Her still-active pair of tentacles extended to a length of a hundred feet in our wake. These graceful swaying limbs bore small steering-paddles on their ends—it seemed Cytherea could reflexively guide her path as she slumbered.

The northbound river of air swept us along at a fine rate, exceeding that of a clipper ship or even of a locomotive. The western prairies gave way to lakelands, to forests, to mountains, to tundra. Still Cytherea snored. The day was wearing on.

I nestled with Seela and gloated over our darling Brumble. He began fitfully wailing.

"He's cold," said Seela, pressing him between her breasts. "And I'm hungry."

Eddie and I broke out more food, and Machree passed around furs and blankets. We'd drifted high above the clouds, which extended below us on every side, a bumpy field of white, lit by the afternoon sun, bright into the preternaturally blue sky. We'd been underway for perhaps nine hours.

"I still don't grasp where we're going," said Ina. "Or how long it will take."

"Ten or fifteen more hours," said Eddie. "And then we'll begin a descent through a hole in the sea. The North Hole."

"It'll be night time," said Seela. "Dark."

"The arctic sun never sets in June," said Eddie.

"Will it be dark on the inside?" asked Ina. "Inside that Hollow Earth?"

"*Lux aeterna*," said Eddie. "Perpetual light."

"Because we'll be dead?" said Ina with a nervous giggle.

"Light from the *woomo*," said Eddie. "You'll see."

Another couple of hours went by. Ina told us a bit more about her childhood. Her father Joseph Durivage had been a journalist for the New Orleans *Picayune*, and, upon the death of his wife, he'd travelled overland to San Francisco with Ina, his sole child, passing through Mexico and Death Valley en route.

"And then he died in a duel," concluded Ina. "I was watching. A girl of fourteen. At dawn on the ocean beach. It was horrible."

"Last night you said it was an affair of honor?" said Eddie.

"Oh, what does that phrase even mean?" said Ina. "It's whitewash on a putrid grave. My father was murdered. One of the seconds who assisted at the duel told me father's pistol held no lead." She stared into the distance, her face working.

"What wretch did this?" asked Eddie.

"You can't guess?" said Ina. "Cruickshank the saloon owner. A procurer. A land speculator. A thief. Father revealed in the *California Alta* newspaper that Cruickshank was selling lots that lay below the tide line."

"Cruickshank a murderer," mused Eddie. "But how came he to enslave you?"

"Cruickshank forged a will assigning the custody of my father's child to him. So great is this man's baseness. It was me he sought."

"And not as a wife?" I said.

"As a low woman to buy and sell," said Ina with peculiar relish.

"Had I but told Cytherea to kill him," said Eddie.

"Indeed," said Ina.

"But you're well out of that now," said Eddie.

"Indeed," said Ina once again, batting her great eyes at Eddie.

"Enough of this dumb-show," interrupted Seela. "Play the waif for Eddie, my girl, but—mark you this—leave my Mason clear of your plans."

"Indeed," said Ina yet again, and unleashed one of her odd laughs, a ululating tone that rose into high chirps. A crafty, unstable adventuress, well-matched to Eddie Poe.

Some gaps had formed in the blanket of clouds beneath us. Far, far below, a cold gray ocean glinted in the dusky light of the low sun. We'd floated north beyond all of Canada and were embarking across the Arctic Sea with its irregular jumble of icy, barren isles.

"The air's as cold as it was off Cape Horn," grumbled Machree, who'd been studiously silent as Ina told her tale. "Ask the *woomo* to send a ray to warm us, Eddie. I miss their light. Or might this cold-blooded shellsquid find a way to kindle some heat?"

"I'd advise letting her sleep," Eddie told Machree. "When Cytherea wakes, she's in a foul temper, and…peckish. She might eat one of us who lacks a rumby—and that would be Ina or you. Or she might dive down to kill another kind of animal."

"A buffalo like before?" said Ina. "There's no more land."

"A walrus," I suggested. "A dolphin."

"I don't want to go in that water!" cried Seela.

"Let Cytherea sleep," repeated Eddie.

As the sated *ballula* dreamt, she continued guiding our path with the spade-like tips of her long tentacles. The hours went by. I did a little mental work on my projected second narrative—*The Return to the Hollow Earth*. Midnight came and went, but even so it wasn't dark. Finding a spool of twine amid Eddie's supplies, Seela took the time to weave sturdier coverings for the dense rumbies owned by Eddie, her and me—encasing our thread-wrapped stones with decorative, sailor-like knots that hung upon our necklaces. Machree and Ina watched with a certain envy, although Machree was confident he'd find his own rumbies within the Hollow Earth.

As the air grew colder, we sat closer together, snacking and chatting. Everyone was being nice to Brumble, even Ina and Machree. Seela made a little hat for Brumble by cutting off the tip of a loaf of sourdough bread and tearing out most of the bread from within the tip's crust. The cap fit nicely on the boy, cushiony and resilient, and it stayed on tight.

In our unease about this journey, the baby became a source of cheer. Seela began showing him off to Ina—whom she'd by now befriended after all—showing off Brumble by holding him up like a doll or a puppet and pretending to speak for him, using a high squeaky voice to utter odd words from the Hollow Earth flowerpeople's tongue.

"*Flaxxon moompf grooble*," said Seela, and Ina gaily mimicked her.

Brumble was—well, the boy was less than two days old, so it would have been unfair to expect any reasoned response. His unfocused eyes glinted, and the little O of his mouth opened and closed. Perhaps he was ready again to nurse? Seela hugged him against her bare breast.

At this point I noticed the sound of the North Hole. It was much as Eddie had predicted, a dirge-like drone with deep bass overtones. I felt the more profound tones as vibrations in my belly and chest. Cytherea's shell was delicately vibrating in concert with the low song as well. The *ballula* awoke with a shudder of her tentacles. It was about three in the morning, but, as I say, the sun remained above the horizon.

In silent unity, Eddie, Seela, and I used the tekelili power of our rumby gems to project a sense of purposeful calm into our outlandish bearer's mind. She hungered, yes, but not so very keenly. The bison meat was still working its way through her body. She extended her eyestalks, and changed the angle of her shell, taking the measure of the strange zone ahead.

Eddie lay slouched in the rear part of the shell with Machree and Arf. He'd brought some of his opium along, and the two men had been smoking. Eddie gazed at me with a dreamy smile on his face.

"Let me describe what you see," he intoned. "The near edge of the vast Hole is like a depression in the horizon, bounded by a white band of foam. Above the depression is a sea of mist, dotted with thunderheads and penetrated by antic tendrils of *woomo* light. Beyond the clouds is the obsidian slope of the maelstrom's far rim—like a giant cataract rolling into the sea. And yet further is the open Arctic ocean, the true horizon, and the polar sky. Surely you discern these things, Mason and Ina? Seela?"

"I see it," said Seela. "We're going home. *Volivorco gooba'am*, Brumble."

I saw the pattern too, but for the moment Ina and Machree were baffled. The hole was so large that it required a flip of mental perspective to perceive it as a single thing. The width of maelstrom matched, I believe, the breadth of my native Virginia, that is, it was two hundred miles across.

We were a few thousand feet above the Arctic Sea, and some hundred miles from the edge of the Hole. The atmosphere around the North Hole was whirling as strongly as the sea below, drawing us closer and swirling us in a convergent spiral. The ocean's surface was beginning to tilt, as if we were nearing a waterfall.

"We're going to die," said Ina. "Why couldn't you crackpots have left me alone?"

"You begged us to save you," I said. "You said Cruickshank shot your pa and made you a wagtail."

"And if I said that then, does it mean this is better? I think not. But here we are. Whirling down the drain." Ina unleashed her reckless laugh. Somehow the sound heartened me—like a war whoop. Better to laugh than to cry.

6. Maelstrom

Steering us with her siphon and her long tentacles, Cytherea rode the spiraling winds ever closer to the Pole. We were close to the ocean's surface, and below the level of the scattered thunder clouds, like dark islands in the air. The low sun's rays sliced beneath the clouds, sending glints across the water.

Round and round we swirled. The ocean slanted in an ever-steepening curve, and somewhere up ahead it disappeared from view, presumably plummeting into the open throat of the planetary maelstrom, the great North Hole, its entrance as yet hidden from us.

Unsteady pink streamers of *woomo* light were dancing up through whirlpool's core. Occasionally a pink tendril would play over our faces, taking our measure and approvingly caressing us—setting my hairs on end and further darkening my skin.

And then, at last, we could see down through the Hole. We were as motes of dust amid this vast tableau, sweeping headlong into an abyss, lit by the *woomo* streamers and by the polar summer sun. Our helical descent began.

Ina had joined Machree and Arf in the furthest recess of our vestibule in the *ballula's* shell. For his part, Eddie was now with Seela and me at the shell's edge. Having traveled through Earth's South Hole a year and a half earlier, Eddie and I weren't overly dismayed by the North Hole, even though this hole was the throat of a vast maelstrom. I might also add that Eddie was bolstering his courage with repeated puffs from his opium pipe, periodically striking sparks from a silver tinderbox.

Seela seemed at her ease. She'd grown up amid the vast and untrammeled landscape within the Hollow Earth. Eddie liked to call Seela's homeland *Htrae*, that is, *Earth* spelled backwards, and he said he was writing a heroic epic about it, composing the work in his head—much in the same fashion I was mentally composing my *Return to the Hollow Earth*.

In any case, for Seela, the North Hole was a familiar feature of the inner world's vault, and it was a handy passageway that would lead us closer to the great flower where her tribe lived. But now she said something troubling.

"I hope the empress ant will stay in her place," said she.

"What do you mean?" I asked, feeling a pulse of fear.

"The creature who lives in the water around the maelstrom," said Seela. "She swims in a circle to keep it swirling. I'm sure she won't notice us. She's too big. And don't tell Eddie about her. He's always so quick to lose his head."

"But—"

"Hush." Seela turned away from me, focusing on Brumble.

Wanting at least to reassure myself that Cytherea could navigate the throat of the maelstrom, I used the power of the rumby stone at my neck to look into the *ballula's* primitive mind. She seemed fully confident about our route—perhaps she'd even traveled it before. And as an amphibious being, she had no misgivings about possibly ending up underwater. If the chaotic winds drove us against the twisting waters of the maelstrom's wall, and if the hungry currents were to tear loose Cytherea's passengers and her cargo—well, that was no great matter for her. And if, indeed, we humans drowned, we'd no longer be bossing the *ballula* with our rumbies. And then the *ballula* would eat us. Unless the empress ant got to us first.

With a supreme effort of will, I closed down my conscious thoughts and focused my attention on the wavering song of the whirlpool, letting the subtly shaded tone take over my mind. I was part of the chant, and it was part of me. We'd been en route for a full day. Bemused and torpid, I stared at the sparkling funnel that enclosed us on every side. My mouth was slack and half open. My chin was slick with drool. I drowsed.

"Hey, you," said Seela, waking me with a nudge. Once again she handed me our baby. Brumble was like a talisman— in important ways more powerful than a rumby gem. As I took hold of his little body I returned to conscious thought. I nestled him in the crook of my arm, and let him suck the tip of my finger. So tiny, this wight, and so focused upon the task of staying alive. Such a wonder to see the awkward motions of his stubby limbs. One of the *woomo* tendrils rose through the maelstrom, licked against us, and was gone.

"I can see through the hole," cried Eddie. Indeed we could now see the glow of the Hollow Earth's pink-lit interior. The airy whirlwind within the maelstrom was sweeping us in narrowing circles. The sun-glinted water walls were very nearly vertical by now, and the open throat below us was not much wider than a mile—which was tight enough to provoke unease, but spacious enough for a viewport.

Evidently the whirlpool's spindle opened out again below the center—in the manner of a double funnel. And for this reason we couldn't see the maelstrom's lower walls from here. We saw the Hollow Earth's seas and lands, its mighty jungles, its Umpteen Seas, its flying shrigs, and the giant *woomo* at its core.

"I'm looking for flowers," said Seela. She meant the immense sunflowers growing upon the Hollow Earth's inner surface. Her original home had been the surface of a flower like this. She took Brumble back from me, and gently held his little cheek against hers. "See, baby, see?"

It could well be that Seela meant to settle permanently into the Hollow Earth with Brumble. And if she stayed— whither I? Might I live in the Hollow Earth for the rest of my days? Or return to San Francisco with Arf? Or—somehow take up with Ina?

I glanced over at that quirky woman. Intrigued by our talk of seeing into the Hollow Earth, she was making her way forward to join us. I was taken by the negligent grace of her motions, and by the mixture of irony and intelligence on her face. Might I win her away from Eddie? But how could I entertain such a faithless thought? Seela was my everything, no?

Machree followed on Ina's heels, and now the five of us were together at the lip of Cytherea's shell, with Brumble in Seela's arms, and Arf wedged between my feet. As our *ballula* descended into the maelstrom's central throat, her shell began rocking more strongly than before. I used my rumby tekelili to petition Cytherea to brace us in place by wrapping tentacles around our waists. With Eddie and Seela reinforcing my psychic admonition, the *ballula* obliged.

The winds at the maelstrom's core were turbulent, but the waters of the walls were not so much rough as they were *ropy*. That is, the surface was as glassy as in the upper regions, and lit by the summer sun, but in this central zone, the flows were so intense that the water was corrugated or gnarled, with striated bulges angling down through the hole. Even relative to the hole's mile-wide aperture, the ridges of water were quite substantial, several hundreds of yards high, like folds in a giant's handkerchief, or like ridges in a titanic twist of dough, with the crests winding around the throat of this, our upper funnel, and flowing to the surface of the as yet unseen funnel below. A mighty streamer of *woomo* light came flickering through. Inconceivably great forces were in play.

Seela, Machree, and I exchanged glances, silently sharing memories of the *Purple Whale* foundering off Cape Horn. No, the North Hole wasn't a savage riot of monstrous waves. But perhaps it was, in its own way, even more sinister.

Blatting her siphon, Cytherea caught hold of a rogue air current that carried us to the still eye of the tornado-like whirlwind within the maelstrom's constricted throat. In relative calm we drifted down along the central axis of the hole. On every side of us were the bulging, clear ridgelines of water upon the maelstrom's wall. The flexed, embossed currents wriggled from side to side, like rivulets of rain on a windowpane.

So powerfully urgent were the water flows that we saw no hint of foam. Lit by the *woomo* streamers and by the polar sun, the pellucid waters were like a mass of molten glass. As we passed through the narrowest part of the neck, we saw something within the transparent sea, a glowing leviathan in rhythmic motion—

"Behold!" cried Ina, extending a pale, elegant arm, and leaning her body against Eddie's. Actually, her arm wasn't pale anymore. The *woomo* light had taken its usual effect. To all appearances, Ina was now a mulatto. But that didn't seem to faze her. She smiled up at dusky Eddie. "Does the monster mean to devour us, my dear?"

"That's the empress ant I was talking about," said Seela, as if this were an ordinary thing. "The creature who spins the whirlpool at the North Hole. She's swims in a circle. We call her Jormungo."

"Like the fabled Ourobouros," exclaimed Eddie. "The great world snake who bites his tail."

"Jormungo is an *ant*," repeated Seela. "She has wings, six legs, and a stinger on her rear, With twitchy antennae, and crushing jaws on her head, She's nested here for centuries. Slowly, slowly, she's hatching her royal eggs."

Stepping away from Ina, Eddie leaned out from our flying shell, hungry for a better view of the prodigious beast. And then, unsatisfied with that—and in an act of extreme recklessness he bade Cytherea to grasp him with a tentacle tip and to dangle him in the empty air. Never would Eddie have done this if he hadn't been smoking opium. Normally he had a morbid fear of heights, and a deathly terror of falling.

But now, here he was jiggling at the end of a fifty-foot *ballula* tentacle, waving his arms and holding forth on the wonders of what he saw. Arf stood at the edge of our shell, furiously barking—not that we could hear either him or Eddie over the noise of the maelstrom, which at this point had reached a stunning pitch. It was as if we were inside an alpine horn sounding a deep, solemn, sustained blast.

And what of the empress ant Jormungo? She was relatively narrow, and a bit over three miles long, wrapping all the way around the maelstrom's throat. Like any ant, she was segmented into head, thorax and gaster. Her great head was like a long-stretched African mask. She had great, faceted eyes, and narrow wings half a mile long. Her surfaces were a dark iridescent purple with touches of green. And her segments were but two hundred yards across. A very slender ant indeed. Even so, her six legs were active and strong, with feet like great oars.

The ant lay sideways in the water around the maelstrom's hole, positioned like a bracelet, with her legs pointed inward. As I say, she was bent into a full circle, and with her vast toothy mandibles clamped onto the base of her onyx stinger. She was continually beating her legs and sculling the water with her veined wings. By dint of these dogged, obsessive motions the empress ant kept the whirlpool spinning.

Why? Perhaps she did it to irrigate the dozen large, golden eggs adhering to the underside of her dark belly.

Initially I supposed that our tiny presences made little impression on the empress ant. I focused on the rumby at my throat and felt for the ant's vibrations. Her mind was ancient, vast, and flickering with activity. Like a city that burns but never collapses. I seemed to see a vast round coliseum, filled with galleries and radial rooms, and within each room was a lambent yellow flame, and the flames held dark central spots that were astral eyes. Jormungo was watching us after all.

And then we were through the maelstrom's throat, with the lower funnel opening up around us, and the wondrous high arch of the Hollow Earth in view, and the central *woomo* firing off light streamers as if in greeting. Eddie was at my side, gesticulating and cheering, both of us well-lodged in Cytherea's tentacles.

At this point I want to remind you of an aspect of the Hollow Earth that is little known. The naive expectation is that inside the Hollow Earth one will walk around on the inner surface with one's head pointing toward the center of the planet. But no less a man than Isaac Newton has proved this is not the case. Within a hollow shell one feels no gravitational force whatsoever. At all points within the shell, the mass of the shell above one's head counteracts the attraction from the shell beneath. You don't walk upon the inner surface of a Hollow Earth. You drift about within a great sphere of air.

This entails, perforce, that when you fall down a vertical passageway through the Hollow Earth's Rind, your speed lessens as you near the tunnel's lower terminus. You coast to a stop.

And thus our *ballula's* rate of fall diminished as we moved downward through the lower funnel of the maelstrom, traversing the two or three hundred miles that separated us from the inner surface of the Hollow Earth. In order to aid our progress, Cytherea was steadily jetting her siphon. By now it was perhaps nine in the morning in San Francisco time. I'd gone a whole day with but one hour of sleep. Not that I could possibly think of sleeping just now.

It was helpful that the winds and waters in this lower zone of the maelstrom were spiraling in the same direction as in upper zone—and were thereby flowing out from the maelstrom toward the inner surface of the Rind.

We passed our time in conversation, raising our voices to be heard above the whistle of the siphon and the maelstrom's waning drone. Eddie was pointing out features of the Hollow Earth to Ina and Machree. And Seela was exclaiming over the clumps of her race's sunflowers that she claimed she saw. She insisted she could even see the home flower where she was born, not far from the South Hole.

"You can't see the South Hole from here," I told her. Our view to the antipodal side was occluded by the busy center of the Hollow Earth, that is, by the jiggling jewels of the weightless Umpteen Seas, by the light streamers flowing out of the mighty *woomo*, and by the warped space of the Central Anomaly at the core.

"I see past the center well enough." said Seela. "Look at the sea by the edge of the southern jungle. *That's* where my home flower is."

"Even if you do see that spot, remember that your home flower isn't actually here," I told Seela. "You grew up on the other side of the Anomaly. You came from inside Earth. We're inside MirrorEarth."

We'd talked about this before. But Seela didn't want to understand. Yet again I told her that the Hollow Earth comprises two globes called Earth and MirrorEarth, each with its own hollow world inside, and that the two hollow planets are connected via a Gate within their shared Central Anomaly. Seela brushed my tidy logic aside.

"Jibber jabber yak wak," she said. "Backwards, upside-down, inside-out. Maybe the flower on this side is different, and maybe it's the same. I wonder if Yurgen is here. I wonder if he misses me."

I tensed. Yurgen had been Seela's suitor when I first met her on her home flower. A slender musician with great cachet among the flowerpeople—he played an instrument called a reverb tube, and his music put his listeners into a trance. Superficially a charming man, he was in fact sly and unkind. That's why Seela had chosen me over him. And it helped that I was exotic. I'd carried her off to a new world.

But maybe now Seela was tired of me? Or, more char-itably, just tired. She'd given birth to our baby, and the next day she'd rushed into this mad journey. I brought to mind how much in love we'd been, lying on our bed looking at Brumble, and that was only the day before yesterday. I soft-ened my heart and gave Seela a kiss.

"How would you get all the way to the south?" broke in Ina, taking an interest in our discussion. "All the way to the other side of this—Hollow Earth? Our planet is truly a big empty ball? So very peculiar."

"Phantasmagoric," said I. "Mind boggling."

"I'm flummoxed," said Ina, as fond of words as I. "Non-plussed. Bowled over. And to think that the Hollow Earth has always been here, and that none of us ever knew. What are the people like?"

"Like me, some of them," said Seela, looking down at herself. "Except whiter. And the ones in the middle are darker. We call them the black gods. You'll like the black gods, Ina. They're jolly. They live with giant floating lakes all around. They make love."

"We're going there?" asked Ina.

"Eddie's wish," said Seela. "And it's handy for Mason and me as well. The easiest way to cross the space of the Hollow Earth is to drift inward to the Umpteen Seas—and to ride a lightstream back out."

"Fine with me," said I. "But I don't want to go near that hungry Gate inside the Anomaly. Eddie can do that on his own. I'm happy to stay out here in MirrorEarth. We'll pick up some rumby gems, have some new adventures I can write about, and then back to San Francisco. We'll be happy there, Seela. I'll write for the paper, and publish *The Hollow Earth* and the *Return to the Hollow Earth*. We'll have more children. We'll build ourselves a little house."

"They know the editor at the *California Alta* newspaper," put in Ina. "Thanks to my father. Perhaps I can help you get in there, Mason."

"I thought you were going through the Gate with Eddie," said Seela.

"We'll see," said Ina airily.

"Yes, we will see," said Seela, getting angry again. "We'll see that you leave Mason alone. And, Mason, don't be too sure that I'm going back outside the Hollow Earth again. I like it better in here."

"We'll see," I said. So many wills around me, and everyone pulling a different way. I looked at little Brumble in my arms, and to myself I was wondering if, should Seela refuse to return to San Francisco, she might let me take our son. Seemed unlikely. He was the dearest thing I'd ever seen.

And now Eddie had to stick his oar in. "I'm going the whole hog," he reaffirmed. "I'll pass through the central Gate to old Earth, and there I'll resume my proper career. Starting with the publication of my masterwork *Htrae*. My versified travel account that will take its place beside Homer's *Odyssey*."

"Everyone back on Earth will be a lot older than when you left," I said. "We lost twelve years going through that Gate the first time, Eddie. We were like bees in slow honey, with the world spinning round. That'll happen again on the way back."

"I snap my fingers!" exclaimed the defiant Eddie. "I bite my thumb. Your cavils mean nothing, Mason. They'll marvel at me on old Earth. I'm still in my early thirties, and my erstwhile rivals will be fifty years old and more." He raised a finger for emphasis. "The old Earth shall be mine. With no vile MirrorPoe to usurp me. I brim with tales, I creak with logic, I jingle with poesy."

"Fine talk," I said, somehow goaded to provoke Eddie. "You'll drink brandy, smoke opium, and copy out the MirrorPoe's works from the MirrorEarth anthology."

"Fiddle-dee-dee," said Eddie. "I abandoned that fusty tome in Mrs. Mackie's hotel. You say I shall be a besotted voluptuary and plagiarize stale tales? Nay, my friend. I'll spin fine new fantasias. And, unlike the debauched MirrorPoe, I'll moderate my vice."

"When does the moderation start?" I shot back. "You were smoking opium ten minutes ago."

"Insolent pup!" cried Poe. "I'll create an oeuvre like none has ever seen."

"How very audacious," said Ina, hanging on Eddie's arm. "Go it, my dear! And, yes, I'll come with you to the old Earth and be your muse."

"I'm with you too," Machree told Poe. "I'll be your agent, as you say."

"My epic *Htrae* will far surpass Mason's feeble tome *The Hollow Earth*," said Eddie, casting a frown at me.

"You dream in vain," said I, roused by the prospect of competing with the notorious Poe. "To cap my initial narrative, I'll scribe the sequel. *Return to the Hollow Earth*. I'm already working on it."

And by this I meant, as I've mentioned, that I'd begun formulating a clear account of our current trip in my mind— fixing the order of the events and working out felicitous phrasing for key scenes. I found this a soothing, meditative process. It felt as if I were speaking aloud to an unseen listener.

"You fancy yourself to be Poe's equal?" scoffed Machree. He gave me a piercing stare. "I'm your true rival, Mason. Our deaths ratified the split between Earth and MirrorEarth."

"What do you mean by that?" I asked, caught by surprise, and roiled by a sick feeling.

"Ask the *woomo*," said Machree shortly. "But enough of ontological cosmogony. At root, I'm a jeweler with a lust for rumbies. Can we simply discuss my hope to inaugurate trade between Earth and Hollow Earth?"

For the moment, none of us cared to reply. The wondrous Hollow Earth was slanting up on every side of us, fabulous beyond imagining. By now the waters of the maelstrom's wide opening were nearly level with surface of the inner sea's surface. The accompanying whirlwind had died to a caressing breeze that wafted us along.

Branching and swaying streamers of pink light were continually illuminating the Hollow Earth's open space. The seas and continents upon the great Rind were like images on a map, although with contours quite different from those of the familiar Earth. The oceans were a fine shade of aquamarine, with occasional dark blue patches that betokened benthic depths that ran through to the outer Earth. Wrinkled mountain ranges wandered across the continents, with deserts, grasslands, and, above all, jungles. I saw no signs of human cities or roads.

The vast atmosphere held mighty flocks of flying beasts—leathery birds with enormous beaks balanced by crests on the backs of their heads, the penguin-shaped carnivorous fowl called harpies, jeweled hummingbirds the size of fists, and, shades of Cape Horn, gliding albatrosses. In the far distance were *ballula* shellfish like Cythera. And a miles-long flock of shrigs was gathered nearby, several thousand of them—wheeling in the air, roaring, farting, perching, feeding, mating.

We were just off the coast of a Hollow Earth landmass. Its jungled shore adjoined a ring of titanic cliffs surrounding an immense volcanic butte. The cliffs were honeycombed with enormous caves. And this was where the shrigs made their nests.

These creatures would have been entirely comical, were they not a bit fearsome as well. A shrig's form is that of an immense boar's head mounted on a body curved and sectioned like that of a shrimp. The younger ones are the size of airborne cows, and the grizzled patriarchs and matriarchs have the heft of hovering frigate ships, perhaps a hundred and fifty feet long.

Normally the shrigs feed on offal, whatever they can find, and they spend much of their time near the core of the Hollow Earth, where debris tends to gather. But when they wished to mate and to produce young, they gathered around the towering mesa nearby. Beating their flat tails and twitching their foolish, tiny legs, the shrigs were engaged in a ponderous social gavotte, moving from cave to cave, inquisitively sniffing each other, flirting with slaps of their tails, confabulating via grunts and squeals, and then inevitably copulating—a singular sight, richly enhanced by the participants' triumphant bellowing. To behold twenty or a hundred shrigs in rut—it was a staggering and, I blush to confess, at times an erotically stimulating spectacle, although I freely grant that the great beasts are ungainly and unclean.

The mouths along the shrigs' mighty pig-snouts were lipless and toothless, giving the effect of a knowing smile. But, as I well knew, the normally placid shrigs could become savage when confronted by their arch-enemy and occasional prey: *ballula* shellsquid such as Cytherea, within whom we were rather conspicuously on display.

For the moment, the shrigs were a safe distance away, and fully preoccupied with their own activities. It bears mentioning that these animals are profoundly unintelligent.

Meanwhile Cytherea was doing her best to make landfall at some distance from the sky-darkening swarm, and I was glad for her caution. A trio of smallish, newly-fledged shrigs, were flying about nearby, and I could sense that Cytherea, being hungry as usual, would have liked to devour them. But even her crude intellect could grasp that, were she to follow her passions, she would suffer for it.

At this point we noticed something moving in the clear waters of the sea.

"I hope that's not the ant's husband," said Seela.

"Why do you say such a thing?" I cried.

"Everyone knows about the ants," said Seela. "The empress in the maelstrom, Jormungo, she doesn't have time to forage. Her special worker, or husband, or prince consort—we call him Fafnir—he swims around this region and gathers food. He's as big as her. And he can fly like Jormungo. He's fast and strong."

"He eats shrigs?" I asked.

"And how. His legs are hollow. He sucks the juices from their bodies.

"Does he eat *woomo* too?"

"No, no, the royal ants are friends of the *woomo*. Partners. They're not like those farmer ants. The pale, creamy ones. The farmer ants want to eat the *woomo*, but they never get a chance. They're not much bigger than dogs. They'd probably eat a person if they had a chance."

"We shouldn't be here!" I said.

"No," agreed Seela. "Only a shrig would be stupid enough to nest near the North Hole. But I didn't want to warn you. I wanted us to come through."

For now we didn't see the empress ant's husband. The nearby moving life in the sea turned out to be a pod of whales. They began leaping out of the water, and hanging for a rather long time in the low-gravity air, wriggling their bodies as if for pure joy. Perhaps they were simply shaking off parasites, but I had a rumby sense that they were happy, and I mentioned this to the others. Observing the square cut of the disporting animals' brows, Eddie said they were sperm whales.

Frustrated over not having attacked the baby shrigs, the ravening Cytherea unleashed her native savagery. With an unbelievably rapid motion, the shellsquid jetted forward and splatted against the muscular body of a disporting whale—who was nearly three times her size. Scattering most of our supplies into the air, Cytherea stretched out her tentacles to their full extent, wrapping them around the midriff of the whale. And then she began digging her great beak into the top of his head, perhaps meaning to break it open and feed upon the hundreds of gallons of waxy spermaceti oil therein.

We five passengers held fast to the bases of the mad *ballula's* tentacles, hoping only to stay aboard. It was much as we'd done when Cytherea slew the buffalo. I pressed baby Brumble against my chest, Arf was cowering by my feet, and Seela was screaming, with Machree chiming in. Ina Durivage was again laughing in that half-mad manner she had, while Eddie had his eyes squeezed shut, and was perhaps trying

to send calming rumby tekelili into Cytherea's tiny brain—
something I was too distracted to even attempt.

Blood and water spray splashed across us, and now came
the retaliation. The whale beat his tail and flippers against
the air, twisted his body, blasted steam from his spout, and
tossed off Cytherea. Before the *ballula* could try to jet away,
the enraged cetacean had seized her shell in his great toothed
jaws. A resonant crunch, a high whistle of escaping hydrogen
gas, and now our flying charioteer was a twitching tangle
of orange flesh, with scraps of her shattered shell drifting
weightlessly in the brilliant sea. Cytherea's body muscles
were clenched in pain.

The whale, despite a shallow gash on the top of his head,
was fully intact. He devoured the unfortunate Cythera with
two snaps of his long, saw-toothed jaws. And then he fixed us
with a baleful glare from a high-mounted and by no means
jolly eye, quite black, and the size of a cantaloupe.

What the whale beheld was of little interest to him—five
adult humans, a baby, and a dog, ineffectually wallowing in the
aquamarine waters. With a contemptuous spout of mist, he
turned flukes and dove deep into the sea—possibly heading
back to the Arctic Sea and the upper exit of the North Hole.
His fellows followed in his wake.

As I've said, at the surface of the Hollow Earth's inner sea,
we were in a zone of neutral gravity, with no forces pulling
us up or down. As a result of our sea battle, jiggly globs of
water hung suspended all across the surface, and the surface
itself was pocked with divots where water had been scooped
out. Slowly the liquid's natural flows were smoothing the
dents over.

But not everything that rose came falling back. Indeed,
most of the casks and bundles which Eddie had brought along
were suspended in the air, and were very gradually rising
higher. As I've mentioned before, once something moved far
enough away from the Rind, a gentle and secondary attraction
from the core's Anomaly came into play.

The sea's shore was perhaps two miles off, a muddy overgrown bank with a labyrinth of thickets and vines dangling
upward—or rather *inward*—toward the core. The jungle

extended inward for something like thirty miles, an over-whelming and formidable sight.

Balanced at this precise neutral zone, there were no forces dragging me into the depths or, for that matter into the sky. But I had an intense fear of drowning and, even more, I was exceedingly concerned about Brumble. Steadily I fluttered my legs, keeping myself upright, but not leaping wholly out of the sea and into the empty air. I kept the lower part of my body submerged, and held the baby well above the surface in my two hands. The newborn was flexing his legs and arms, and making little noises, as if warming up for a crying jag. He didn't feel safe, and he wanted his mother. I very much wanted her as well. She was a hundred yards off, although I had no real hope of swimming that distance without the use of my arms.

But soon Seela was at my side. She'd scavenged a large, curved fragment of Cytherea's shell, serviceable as a dinghy, and she was wielding a thin fragment of shell as a paddle. With great relief, I handed Brumble over to her. The exasperated baby made a spluttering noise, then settled against Seela's breast, softly grunting as he nursed. Not wanting to risk overturning Seela's coracle, I floated at its side, kicking my legs to propel us toward the overgrown shore of the promontory with the shrig's great rookery. As it happened, the current around the outer edge of the maelstrom was sweeping us in that general direction.

Beating his legs and with snout held high, Arf was very nearly managing to walk on the water. I set him into the shell with Seela. Naturally he insisted on rising to his feet and giving his body several heartfelt shakes—a process which, in this weightless zone, sent him tumbling into Seela, who scolded him severely. But she was laughing at the same time, so happy was she to have the precious Brumble in her arms. I lay on my back in the water and swam along at the floating shell-fragment's side, now and then nudging or tugging it to keep it with me. As we went along, I managed to rub my face and body with my hands, cleaning off some of the gore from the slain buffalo, the wounded whale, and the destroyed *ballula*.

What of the others? Eddie, Machree, and Ina were bunched together, making for landfall, lying on their stomachs and stroking their arms against the sea like oars, thereby gliding across the surface of the water, much as I was doing. Machree was less dexterous than the other two, and he was lagging behind, and even calling out that he might drown, not that this was especially likely.

The pink light of a *woomo* tendril fell across us, illuminating a zone several hundred yards wide. Did the *woomo* mean to carry us to safety? The light streamer focused, grew brighter and—lifted up Connor Machree alone, bearing him into the sky and toward the Hollow Earth's core.

"See you laaaaater," the illuminated figure called down to us, his voice rising as if in ecstasy.

"Go to blazes!" shrieked Ina. "*Damn* you, Machree! Why is this low worm exalted?"

What was it Machree had said to me back in San Francisco? "*You and I are paradox incarnate. The axle of fate's turning wheel.*" He'd also said that he'd encountered me in Lynchburg, Virginia—the town where my first journey to the Hollow Earth had begun.

In a flash, I finally saw who Machree was—as clearly as if a stroke of lightning had illuminated a beclouded landscape. My revelation took the form of a syllogism.

- On Earth, Mason killed the stableboy.
- On MirrorEarth, the MirrorStableboy killed MirrorMason.
- Therefore Machree is the MirrorStableboy.

I didn't bother trying to explain this to the others, nor did I share my further line of logic—which seemed to explain why the *woomo* were aiding Machree in his journey to the core.

- Having both Mason and Machree on MirrorEarth is an imbalance.
- The *woomo* are intent on keeping the worlds in balance.
- Mason intends to remain on MirrorEarth.

- Therefore the *woomo* wish to move Machree to Earth.

QED, as graybeard Euclid might say. *Quod erat demonstrandum.* I'm not as ignorant as city slickers think. As a boy, I studied a copy of Euclid's *Elements* on rainy winter days, lying on the plank floor by the fire in Pa's cabin. And I'd perused a Latin primer as well. Not to mention the *Southern Literary Messenger*, replete with Eddie Poe's essays and tales.

But, as often happens in the heady realm of pure reason, one of my assumptions was wrong, as were the ensuing deductions. The *woomo* cared nothing about my specious notions of balance between the worlds. The *woomo* were helping Machree because they wanted him to fetch rumbies from the Hollow Earth and to ferry them to the surface.

Why? Read on.

7. Ants

I sculled along, swimming on my back beside Seela in her shell boat, with my bone-deep exhaustion like a bag of sand inside my chest. I focused my attention on my senses to keep from nodding off.

Any droplet of water which rose more than about six feet would keep on falling inward toward the center. Just as it had been when we'd come through the South Hole on our first expedition. And those valuable bundled provisions that Eddie had brought along—they were fairly high in the air by now, and not coming back. A pair of large shrigs were in fact feeding on this equipage, engulfing whole barrels and bales with their blandly pleased snouts, while guiding themselves through the air with thunderous farts and with flicks of their flattened tails. A few dozen shrigbirds fluttered around the shrigs, hopping onto them and pecking up parasites as the opportunity arose, the shrigbirds a bit like terns.

I kept worrying about the purplish-green royal ant called Fafnir—but saw no sign of him as yet. In any case, I had a simpler problem to occupy my mind: I didn't want Seela and me to fall into the sky. If we did, we might tumble for four days before reaching the Umpteen Seas at the core. The distance to Earth's center from the Rind is three thousand miles. What with our bodies' drag against the air, the gentle effect of the core's pull wouldn't bring our speed to much more than thirty miles per hour. Which meant a hundred hours of falling—about four days.

On my first trip to the Hollow Earth, I'd fallen to the core while riding upon a sunflower blossom the size of a city. The great mass of the flower had allowed it to plow through the air like a dreadnought, reaching a terminal velocity of something like a hundred miles per hour. That fall had taken only thirty hours. But on our own it would be longer.

Seela and I wouldn't starve to death or die of thirst during a four-day fall—provided we brought along fruit, a supply of dried meat, and some leaf-wrapped water globs. And even if we fell without supplies, we might make it. But there was another problem. Adrift in the vasty volume of the Hollow Earth, we'd be easy prey.

A wide range of creatures ply the fecund Hollow Earth's sky. The low-flying harpy birds, the spear-billed leather-wings, the ravenous *ballula*, and floating colonies of pale, irritable farmer ants.

When Seela and I reached the water's edge, we were glad the shore was overgrown with mangroves—leafy shrubs that rested on tall, branching, stilt-like roots. We could hold onto them. I wedged my feet into the sandy mud—lest I accidently drift upward—and I helped Seela to step out of her makeshift shell boat, with Brumble in her arms. Immediately Arf set to rooting in the undergrowth.

The mangroves grew much taller here than on the islands I'd seen during my sea journeys on Earth's outer surface. In here, everything grew high. Mounting up beyond the mangroves was every manner of tree and vine, and through a gap caused by a spit of rock, I could glimpse the monumental butte, nearly a mile high, with the cliff-dwellings of the shrigs, and the populous, ever-shifting flock of them, trailed by the shrigbirds who fed upon their parasites. It's hard to judge such a thing, but Eddie suggested there might be seven thousand of the shrigs. I was very glad they weren't man-eaters.

Little purple crabs perched upon the mangrove roots. They had long feelers and asymmetrical claws, and, when disturbed, they were quick to spring down to the ground. I wished I wasn't barefoot. I'd shed my shoes in the *ballula*, and, as I say, at this point everything we'd carried was lost—although, yes, Seela, Eddie, and I still had our dense and potent rumby stones wrapped in threads and twine upon our necklaces.

"Welcome home," said Seela, as if to herself. She dimpled and took a bow—which sent her drifting up a few feet to some overarching mangrove roots above us. "Now, dear husband," she continued, addressing me from on high. "Now you'll help me travel to the opposite pole."

"Is it so important to see Yurgen again?" I asked, staring up at her.

"That boy means nothing to me," said Seela. "I only want to show Brumble to my parents."

"I thought you said you don't know who your father was. And that your mother left your home flower to join a different tribe."

"Why are you cross with me, Mason? We have a new baby!"

Right around then, one of the little crabs pinched my toe. I screamed, leapt, banged my head on a thick air-root, and yelled a curse. A funnel-shaped leaf tipped a bobbling glob of water onto my head. I had to use both hands to get the water off my face. Low comedy. Seela laughed merrily. I had a distinct feeling she'd used her rumby tekelili to guide the crab my way.

"Look at Daddy!" Seela cooed to the dozing Brumble, who was floating next to her in the air. "Daddy gets red. *Big* old crab."

"Here we come," called Ina's voice from afar. She and Eddie were some distance down the shore. Eddie had shown her how to swing weightlessly through the low branches of the mangroves. A minute later our two companions were at our side.

"Our goodies are gone!" said Ina. "Into the sky and eaten by shrigs. It's bad."

"We'll forage food and drink easily enough," said I. "The Hollow Earth is a land of plenty." Balls of water shone in the misty jungle ahead of us. Fruits like grapes dangled from a nearby vine, with fist-sized berries on a branch just beyond. Slugs writhed upon the trunks, and quick, bright-eyed creatures peeked from behind branches.

More of those fledgling shrigs were snouting at the mud. They were not unlike black, hairy pigs, save that they had no legs, and their bodies were ridged into segments which tapered to a horizontal shrimp-tail.

One of their number, about the same size as me, was busying himself less than fifty feet away. He seemed to have found a dead fish, or perhaps even a piece of the unfortunate Cytherea. Or maybe it was a tangle of decayed seaweed. In any case the shrig threw back his head, convulsively gumming down his fodder with his toothless jaws.

"Slaughter him for us, savage Seela," said Eddie. "Roast shrig meat is toothsome. And it dries to make an excellent pemmican."

"But what of the shrig's mother?" asked Ina. "They're fierce when protecting their young, one would suppose."

"The grown shrigs can't see us down here amid the trees," said Eddie. "And the little one won't have time to squeal. Pretend you want to feed it, Seela. Lure it close and slit its throat. There's the girl. Mason will mind the baby. I see that you have your knife."

Indeed, both Seela and I had thought to strap our knives against our legs. But she demurred. "Shrigs disgust me," said she. "That one you want me to butcher, he has manure crusts all over his body. What I want to eat is flower-leather. *Gooba'am.*"

"Why not roast a bird?" proposed Ina, cocking her head. "I hear some in the jungle. One of them's very loud. *Awk-kwawk?*"

"That's a harpy," said Seela. "They're killers. And they taste horrible. You don't want to deal with them."

"Fruit would suit me very well," said I. "Let's eat something easy, and then sleep. No intricate preparations. I'm at my rope's end. After we sleep, I'll show you how to fish in the water globs, Ina, and we'll roast them, and we can take the measure of this congeries of shrigs. I suppose we can ride one to the center. Either get one to swallow us, or mount its back and hang onto the bristles."

"It's best to *glue* yourself on," said Seela. "If needs be. There's a cactus in the jungle with a juice you can use. Pancake cactus, it has no thorns. But I worry about riding a shrig with Brumble along. The shrigs have lice as big as turtles. That's what those shrigbirds are eating."

"I'll squash the lice," said Ina. "I'm good at that. From living in Cruikshank's foul den."

"Mason, Brumble, Arf, and I won't be riding with you and Eddie," Seela informed her. "We'll ride straight to my flower. You two should pick an especially stinky shrig for your ride to the Umpteen Seas. Stinky shrig, stinky Ina, stinky Eddie."

"I thought we were friends now!" exclaimed Ina, a little hurt.

"I don't like the way you smile at Mason," said Seela.

"You and I will do as you say," I told Seela, meaning to mollify her. "We'll fly straight to your flower with the baby. And perhaps we'll see Eddie and Ina again later on."

I was trembling with exhaustion, and I wanted peace. Certainly I had no lust to remind Seela yet again that her true home was inside *Earth* and that we were now, strictly speaking, inside *MirrorEarth*. But perhaps a village on some mirorflower on this side would be much the same as her home. At this point I didn't care.

Nor did I have the spunk to tell my companions of the great insights I'd had about Machree and me, that is (a) Machree and I had murdered copies of each other, and (b) the *woomo* wanted Machree to travel from MirrorEarth to Earth in order to promote balance. If I told these things to the others, they'd go blank (Ina), or deny (Seela), or attempt to pick holes in my crystalline logic (Eddie).

But now, thinking of Eddie's possible attacks, my convictions regarding balance began leaking away. By now any precise balance between the worlds was an impossibility. MirrorEarth's Eddie Poe was dead, but our old Earth's Eddie Poe was not only alive, but here with me in person. And forget not the vexed nexus when I killed the stableboy on Earth and, simultaneously, the MirrorStableboy on MirrorEarth killed MirrorMe.

A long-forgotten image came to mind. When I'd been running away from the stable in Lynchburg—I'd envisioned a fat worm with tendrils reaching out to me, and I'd nearly stumbled. Was it not obvious that the worm had been a *woomo*, witnessing my transition via tekelili?

Any notion of balance was a delusion, a will o' the wisp, and I was foolish to even think of it. We were deep into the authorial ink indeed. But who was writing the plot?

I followed the others, worming our way a deeper into the jungle and a bit further from the Rind, avoiding the winged lizards and the pale, haughty ants—Seela said these were a species distinct from the royal ants or the farmer ants. The jungle, as I may have mentioned, extended inward for thirty miles, not that we could see anything like that distance while in the thick of it.

We passed a long, twisty branch with exceedingly long thorns upon it. Seela pointed them out to me, and said the flowerpeople word for "rapier." Indeed, I remembered having Seela's folk use these spikes as weapons. I wondered if they'd greet us gently, if and when we reached the mirrorflower.

Preferring to think of something else, I feverishly returned to my delusional speculations about the *woomo's* plans. Might it be that the *woomo* would want to *retroactively* repair the broken balance? Was that even possible? What if they killed Eddie, Machree, and me? And what of Seela's MirrorEarth double, the MirrorSeela whom we'd surely encounter before long. Food for thought.

In the distance, the randy shrigs were rutting on the cliffs. Their thunderous wheenks were a paean in praise of physical love, which had the effect of shunting my mental focus from abstract ruminations about cosmic balance, and toward dreamy visions of making love to Seela and Mirror Seela at the same time.

Seela nudged me, and I realized that, thanks to rumby tekelili, she knew what I was thinking. She didn't mind. Everything was fine. We were free of the dangerous *ballula*, and at large in this Edenic natural world. We were Adam, Eve, and Brumble—and soon we'd have a MirrorEve as well. Surely everything would work out.

We entered a clear region amid great trees. Arf emerged from a thicket with a fish in his jaws. He hadn't forgotten the tricks he'd learned on our first trip through the Hollow Earth.

"You see?" I told Ina as Arf wolfed down his catch. "It'll be easy here."

"A melon for now," said Poe, rapping a perfectly round green orb against a branch. It split it two, revealing creamy orange flesh like that of a cantaloupe. I cut the two halves into slices with my knife and passed them around. The *woomo* light tendrils flickered among the trees, rising around us in a pleasant maze.

"Let's sleep here," said Seela, pointing out a stack of four or five large shelf-mushrooms on the titanic trunk of an oak. We settled in as if in bunk beds, with Eddie and Ina between an upper pair of shelves, and Seela, Brumble, and I between a lower pair.

There was no such thing as night inside the Hollow Earth—the light tendrils never stopped. But on our fungal shelves we felt safe from drifting off. With the baby between Seela and me, there was, of course no question of us two sleeping *well*. We made it through some six or seven hours—with two feedings of the baby along the way—and then my own hunger pangs compelled me to rise.

While the others slept on, Arf and I managed to catch six stubby-finned fish from a glob of water some twenty feet across. He swam about in the middle, herding the fish to the surface, and I stabbed them as they flopped onto branches, meaning to scuttle away. Extracting the sleeping Eddie's tinderbox from his coat, I got a little fire going inside a dry hollow spot in our tree trunk, and by the time the others awoke, we were able to breakfast on two roast fish apiece, complemented by melon and some banana-like fruits that Seela found.

In the near-zero gravity of this zone, the fire's smoke tended to linger, and the flames oozed around rather than flickering. I'd learned that as long as I occasionally fanned a Hollow Earth fire, it could stay alive for a day or more. But in this damp jungle there was little risk of a runaway forest fire.

A great hubbub emerged from the shrig colony, hardly visible beyond the jungle leaves. I left our fire slowly smoldering inside its hollow, and we four bounced a quarter mile through the jungle—where it ended beside the bare rocky foothills that mounted to the shrigs' cliffs. We were four adults in number with Brumble in Seela's arms, and Arf making his own way. From our new vantage point I could see an enormous hole in the center of the slightly slanting butte—which was, I now realized, a volcanic vent, no longer flowing with lava but, rather, being used as a passageway by—the second giant ant whom Seela had been telling me about.

"Fafnir," she said, satisfied to have her suspicions confirmed. "Jormungo's husband. He's coming out. Look at his wings."

The narrow ant was, like his spouse, over three miles long and some two hundred yards wide. His iridescent form writhed against the sky—a narrow-bodied silhouette, with elegant wings and six devilishly lively legs in play. The royal ant's L-shaped antennae were like pennants, and the great joints of his tripartite body hinged wildly back and forth. He was vital as a flame. The twitching legs were several hundred feet long, and he was using them to skewer shrigs.

Once he'd impaled a shrig with a leg, the victim would begin sagging and dwindling—Fafnir's legs served as hollow feeding-tubes and, vampire-like, he was draining the juices of his prey. Periodically he'd bend himself double and tear at the wizened, folded-up husks of those shrigs he'd impaled upon his energetic limbs. He was dark as night and very shiny, with sheens of purple and green. The colors were continually shifting with his body's nimble play.

Directing my inner sight through the lens of my rumby stone, I picked up a somewhat confused sense of the consort ant's personality. Like Jormungo, Fafnir had a chaotic psyche, seething like a cauldron or like a storm at sea, crowded with patterns that merged and parted like the dust devils on an arid field. I was unable to decide if Fafnir was aware of me as an individual.

Meanwhile the thousands of clumsy, flying shrimp-pigs whirled in a storm, wildly roaring, striving to find safety in the center of their herd or, less successfully, to fly off on their own.

As I mentioned in my first narrative, when a shrig wants to travel a long distance, it uses an explosive means of propulsion, that is, it sets afire the thunderous gasses that emerge from its anus, in effect flying upon the propulsion of a burning fart. But several of the large shrigs attempting this ruse were brought down by the male ant. He was exceedingly nimble and very cunning in his moves, far more so than the bumbling, dimwitted shrigs.

We beheld, in short, a scene of great carnage. By the time that Fafnir the royal ant had eaten his fill, he'd consumed a hundred shrigs or more. And even then he granted his prey no surcease. Continuing with his same finicky urgency as before, he skewered a hundred more shrigs upon his pointed, hollow limbs. But these he did not drain dry. These were to be carried intact to his mate.

With deft twitches of his shiny, translucent wings, Fafnir headed back into his gore-stained tunnel, bringing a fresh meal to his wife Jormungo, that is, to the undulating, three-mile-long empress ant whom we'd seen nested in the sea, endlessly swimming her circuit in the waters around the throat of the North Hole's great maelstrom, with her slowly-maturing gold eggs aligned upon her belly.

As if goaded into blood lust by Fafnir's onslaught, a platoon of four harpy birds dove at us, meaning to tear apart our flesh. I'm proud to say that I dispatched the first harpy by plunging my long knife into the beast's heart. Ina sheltered baby Brumble in her arms while Seela slew a second harpy. And then, squawking with baffled fury, the other two harpies turned tail and flew to a sinister bare-limbed tree half a mile from our perch.

We eased back into the jungle a bit, but not so far that we couldn't keep watching the show.

"Quite a death toll for so early in the day," said Ina, passing Brumble back to me. "Those poor shrigs. I wish I had some brandy."

Eddie sighed. "The cask is gone. My opium as well. And Fafnir has indeed frayed my nerves. I'll be glad when we can hop a shrig and fly to the Umpteen Seas. The center's steady play of *woomo* light is a salubrious tonic."

Not that there was much chance of Eddie and Ina mounting a shrig just now. Although Fafnir had retreated from sight, the blimp-like shrigs were highly agitated. They wheeled and roared, chorusing their dismay. Looking higher up, I could see a haze of shrig dung drifting into the sky.

"How often does Fafnir come here?" I asked Seela.

"He eats every day," she said.

"Our native guide is well versed," observed Eddie.

Seela turned to Eddie. "As I told Mason, all the people in the Hollow Earth know about Fafnir and Jormungo," said she. "But I didn't like to mention it before our trip. Especially not mention it to a coward like you, Eddie Poe. And, you see, we came through fine. Perhaps tomorrow we'll ride a pair of shrigs away from here. It might be best to do it just after Fafnir feeds again. When the shrigs are giddy and stunned."

"I'm not a coward," said Eddie, fastening on that word. "I'm merely rational."

"I'm not leaving until we kill that cruel giant ant!" cried Ina. "It's the least we can do. Eddie can find a way to do it. He's so clever."

"It will be so," said Eddie, wanting to play the hero in Ina's eyes. "We'll right the wrong, my lady, and slay the dragon. What say you to *that*, doubting Seela?"

"I *can* think of a way to attack Fafnir," she said. "But I'm not sure it's wise. Why kill a glorious and iridescent, royal ant for the sake of some stupid, manure-coated shrigs? We have a legend that the royal ants hollowed out this great space. And they split it in two."

"What a story!" I exclaimed. "Why didn't you tell me?"

"Well, I never fully understood the legend before," responded Seela. "But now that I've been to the surface, I understand that our world is a hollow ball. Who hollowed it out? The royal ants! Listen to the legend. At the dawn of time, Jormungo and her babies were inside an apple, eating and eating, and shitting into a crack in the air in the middle of the apple. Jormungo made the apple hollow, and the crack in the air was still here. They put so much shit into the crack that it pried the apple into two apples. And that's why the Earth is hollow, and that's why there's an Earth and a MirrorEarth." Seela smiled. "See?"

Ina wasn't listening, or wasn't understanding.

"I do so love those shrigs," she crooned. "They're jolly and gay. They make me feel like a happy girl again. We have to save them from Fafnir."

"And then what happens?" I said to Ina. I was still holding Brumble against my shoulder. He was half asleep. "If we kill Fafnir, who feeds Jormungo? Seela says Jormungo is the empress ant, and the ants made the shape of our world. Weren't you listening? The royal ants are like gods."

"The wild, ignorant legends of Seela's tribe mean nothing," said Eddie. Knowing him, I think he was annoyed he hadn't come up with Seela's speculations first. "Let the widowed Jormungo seine algae, shrimp, and kelpweed from the sea she swirls," he continued in a lofty tone. "The great insect's fate is not our concern."

"I'm quite sure Eddie is right," said Seela with a sly, demure smile. She gave me a calculating look as she reached some internal decision. "Very well then. We'll cut off Fafnir's head. Tomorrow morning. All we need to do is find a thread vine. In fact I saw one near our camp. And we'll gather some pancake cactuses as well. For gluing us to the shrigs when we leave."

My bloodthirsty Amazon tucked our baby against her breast. And then our group swung through the branches, vines, and water globs to the safety of our shelf-mushroom bunks. Arf appeared in our wake. My little fire was still glowing in its hollow branch.

"That one there," said Seela, pointing to a snaky vine with purple, mouse-ear leaves. It ran along the giant tree with the shelf-mushrooms, and inward toward the core. "We'll need three hundred yards of it, Mason, and we'll use a torch to cut it."

"No knife?" said I.

"You can't cut this vine," said Seela. "The thread—the strand running along the vine's center—it's unbreakable. But you can burn it in two."

"I want to catch fish," put in Ina, uninterested in the practical details of the Herculean task that she had set in motion. For whatever reason, Seela was intent on carrying it out. Even though, to me, it seemed a reckless whim.

"I'll show you how to fish," Eddie told Ina. "It's best if we shed our clothes. Does modesty forbid?"

"My modesty's gone," said Ina, preening. "Quashed by the slaving saloon-keeper Cruikshank, murderer of my Pa." I was beginning to have doubts about Ina's veracity. I felt she was acting a role—in this case, playing the orphan in need of rescue by a heroic male such as Eddie Poe.

Perhaps Eddie sensed this too, but was enjoying himself, casting aside his usual somberness and breaking into a smile. Moments later his and Ina's clothes were floating in the air, and the two were splashing in a nearby water glob the size of a church. Arf joined them. My eyes were drawn to the quick motions of Ina's pale brown limbs.

"Mason!" said Seela, demanding my attention. "Make a torch."

I broke a short length of dead branch off a tree, and stuck the end into the glowing nest of embers in the trunk. Using a leafy branch, I fanned the fire into renewed life, and now one end of my branch was alight. A torch. I waved it in the air, admiring the odd motions of the low-gravity flame.

"Now you burn a gap," said Seela, leading me to the smooth vine with the purple leaves.

The thread vine was turgid with sap, and not corky or pithy at all. I set to charring it through. As I reached the center of the vine a vein of some odd substance emitted a percussive crack, propelling a shower of sparks from the torch. I'd burned the thread through. I paused to rest, letting the torch hang all but weightless in the air at some distance from me. Due to the listless flow of air currents here, the heat of the torch was somewhat burdensome.

Seela had the avid Brumble at her breast. Eddie and Ina were laughing in the water. I didn't like to stare at them, but it seemed possible that they were making love, or trying to, although I recalled my Uncle Tuck's claim that a man can't do the deed while underwater. I had, in point of fact, successfully accomplished this feat with Seela in the Umpteen Seas last year. It's a matter of using rapid motion, which provides sufficient warmth to preserve love's tender glow. Of course I'd been a lively sixteen years, unlike Eddie Poe, now doddering into his twenty-ninth. Given the opportunity, I'd be glad to try the trick again. But not with Seela still on the mend from delivering herself of Brumble—had it been three days ago? Surely I'd need to wait a month until—

Seela's lips were moving. "Are you deaf?" she was saying. "I'm telling you to climb up three hundred yards, burn through the vine up there, and pull the whole length back down. I can't do it for you. You can see I'm busy with Brumble."

Indeed. A dutiful husband I, aged seventeen. Ina and that old coot Eddie continued disporting themselves, but never mind. I hopped along to a point three hundred yards further inward on the tree—really quite some distance—and then I burned another gap, and then, bracing myself against nearby branches, pulled the vine's rootlets away from the tree, freeing up a flexible, three-hundred-yard segment which I coiled into a massive ring of loops. I lugged the unwieldy load back with some effort and presented it to my wife.

"Now hold the baby," said she.

I'd been feeling a bit put upon, but my heart melted anew as I beheld our tiny folded flower-bud of a baby. I wondered at his little yawns and at the sweetly random twitches of his legs and arms. I settled him against me and he slept.

Meanwhile Seela had unsheathed the large knife that she still wore strapped to her leg. Taking the vine, she whittled away some of the vine's outer rind near one end, exposing the all-but-invisible thread that ran along its central axis. She worked on the other end of the vine as well, as if fashioning a handle at each end. The three-hundred-yard thread that ran along the center of the vine was still under cover—Seela said it was too dangerously sharp to uncover right away.

"We'll yank the thread loose tomorrow," she told me. With a small sideways motion of one handle, she showed me that, if we pulled in the right direction, the hidden thread could cut its way out of the sheathing vine.

"We'll stretch the thread across Fafnir's burrow?" I said.

"Yes. You and I will be hovering there, Mason. We'll each hold a handle, and we'll pull the cutting-thread taut between us, and when Fafnir sticks his head out of the tunnel—*zack*."

She swept her free hand across her throat and lolled her head to one side. As if she'd been guillotined.

"Ghastly," I said. "This is madness, Seela. Who am I to kill so magical a beast? It's not my place. I know nothing of the Hollow Earth."

"Maybe those royal ants have been awaiting a jolt," said Seela. "Expecting an attack for scores of years. Or for centuries. That's in the legend too. Our onslaught will mark the day of their children's birth. All in accordance with an ancient rhythm that's known to everyone except you and your surface-dwelling friends, Mason. Known throughout the Hollow Earth." Her smile was sly, enigmatic, mocking.

"I can't tell if you're teasing me," I complained. "I never know what's going on." I was a little worn-down by Seela. She'd been wildly unpredictable for the last few days—although I freely grant she had good reason. How strange it must be to have a child emerge from your body.

We heard laughter from Eddie, and a burst of merry song from Ina. "Come join us, Mason," she called, sweetening her voice.

"So, yes, we'll go attack the giant ant for Ina," said Seela, hardening her tone. "You can't keep your eyes off her. It excites you that she says she's a fallen woman, a little lost bird with a broken wing. Liar. She's grabbing for you with her nasty, dirty claws! Just when I need you the most."

Falling silent now, Seela tethered our looped coil of vine to a branch, stripped off her clothes, and leapt from the branch were we stood, arrowing thirty or forty feet through the leaves and into the great ball of water where the other two swam. From Seela's expression, you might have thought she was going to kill them.

Brumble remained behind, hanging in the air beside me. I scooped him up and set to gathering fruit, talking to the baby as we moved around.

The day went slowly, with the four of us chatting, eating fruit and fish, and poking twigs at the beetles and the alert, pale beige ants who came lolloping by. These weren't the farmer ants that Seela had talked about, these fellows were a lesser breed, less than two inches long. But it wouldn't do to try and hold one. They were quick to nip with their jaws, and they had sharp stingers on their rears.

Eddie, who was in a talkative mood, reprised a published story of his about a balloon journey to the Moon. Not that, in my opinion, Eddie's jejune hoaxing tale, which I'd read several years ago, could hold a candle to the journey we were presently on, nor did it compare, in my estimation, to my narrative, *The Hollow Earth*, which was penned, I might remind you, while I was still but seventeen years of age. So which of us two was the genius?

When I posed this question to Eddie, he told me I was a vainglorious dunderhead, and he retreated to the back of his shelf-mushroom bunk, where he busied himself with a parchment-like leaf, a thorn pen, and the ink of a crushed berry. Perhaps he was outlining his epic poem *Htrae*. Not that I'd actually heard or seen a single line of it.

The mood improved when Seela undertook the task of outfitting us with the air-kicking fins that she and her tribe called *pulpuls*. Seela had found some good-sized flowers higher up in the jungle, blooms like large chrysanthemums, and their individual petals had hollow bases that you could stick your feet through, as if into boots. Using her steel knife, Seela trimmed off the main bodies of the petals, creating shapes like paddles, and making little slits for securing the tips of our toes. And now we had rather efficient airfins. Eddie and I already knew how to beat our way through the air with these *pulpuls*, and the lithe Ina was quick to learn. Laughing as she worked, Seela even put some wee *pulpuls* on Arf, something she hadn't thought of doing on our last trip through.

We played tag for a while, in and around the glens and passages of the jungle, with Brumble reacting to the goings-on with fitful grimaces, kicks of his legs, and blinks of his eyes.

Arf got overly curious about the beige ants and trailed them to their colony a hundred yards off, a swarm of them living inside a great hollow tree. The dog snouted open a hole in the bark, revealing masses of the large, feisty, and territorial ants, all of them intent on repelling his attack. They nipped and stung him more than a few times, but, thanks to his doggie *pulpul* fins, he managed to escape them, and returned alone to our little camp. I took off his fins, and he settled into our bunk to lick his paws.

By now my little spat with Seela had faded away. I was doing my best to make it clear to her, by words and by deeds, that she, and no other, was my life's great love. Eddie, too, was back on good terms with me. He'd managed to write a poem on that leaf, and he read it to us with gusto. I showered him with praise. The poem was called "The Haunted Palace." The theme was, as would be customary for Eddie, a great mansion that falls under a curse. The last stanza sticks in my mind.

> And travellers now within that valley,
> Through the red-litten windows see
> Vast forms, that move fantastically
> To a discordant melody;
> While, like a rapid, ghastly river,
> Through the pale door
> A hideous throng rush out forever,
> And laugh — but smile no more.

"You're worried about the giant royal ants?" I said to Eddie, noticing the bit about something ghastly rushing through a door. "Just remember—it's Seela and me that will be going up against them."

"We'll tend Brumble," said Ina.

As if rehearsing tomorrow's ambush of the consort ant—Seela managed to behead a winged snake. I roasted the meat in my fire pit, which remained aglow. The serpent's flesh proved more than acceptable. It was whitish and dense, with a taste of butter and mint. We licked our fingers when we were done.

At no point did it ever get any darker here, but eventually we deemed it time to lie down and get another night's worth of sleep. Seela dropped off almost immediately. I lay awake for some time, engaged in my daily process of placing my memories in order, in preparation for eventually writing my *Return to the Hollow Earth*. More strongly than ever, I had a sense that some unseen higher being was recording my thoughts, lest my labors be lost. Would that it were so. And then I too slept, although not continuously. Every few hours

Brumble would rouse Seela so he could nurse, and oftentimes I'd awaken for a spell as well. Everything about Brumble and Seela interested me.

The animals of the Hollow Earth had their own rhythms, alternating between sleep and activity all day long. We woke with the shrigbirds chirruping and the shrigs placidly calling each to each. The slow-witted giants showed no sign of anticipating the deadly Fafnir's daily visit.

Our party breakfasted on fruit, augmented by a seedpod that had something like the stimulating effect of coffee. We four made our way to the jungle's far edge, where Seela and I parked Brumble and Arf with Eddie and Ina. Kicking ourselves into the air, Seela and I unrolled the thread vine and then, with a twitch of the handles, let the central thread cut its way out. The husk drifted into the sky. The thread itself was essentially invisible, but to test it out, Seela and I kicked our way along the edge of the jungle with the thread stretched tight between us—as if we were clearing the edge of a road.

We sliced shrubs, vines, and branches of trees, avoiding those hefty, pinching beige ants that could appear out of nowhere. I felt no tugging from the thread. It was as if the jungle plants were phantoms of the air. Urging me on, Seela kicked her way to the inner, jungle side of a five-mile-high breadfruit tree. I kept pace with her, passing the diamond-patterned trunk on its outer side. At contact, I again felt no reaction from the thread, even though the titan of the forest was soon cut in two. It seemed likely the vine's thread could cleave the ant Fafnir's chitinous head from his body.

Urged ever so slowly by the faint gravity, the miles-high crown of the breadfruit tree drifted free of the jungle and into the sky. A flock of shrigs gathered to feed on it, going after its lumpy fruits and lobed foliage.

Seela and I continued kicking our fins, traversing the two-mile gap between the towering jungle and the opening of the tunnel in the top of the butte. On the way, a party of inexperienced young shrigs mistook us for drifting food and flew toward us. I don't think they'd ever seen live humans before. With a skillful kick of her *pulpuls*, Seela adjusted our trajectories so that our wire cut the leading shrig in half, from nose to tail, like a small loaf of bread being cut along its length for a catfish sandwich at the side of the James River. A great fart rushed out and shrig dung scattered, along with gouts of the straw-yellow fluid that serves shrigs as blood.

The other shrigs in the party shied away from us—and began feeding on their companion's remains, starting with sniffs and nibbles, and progressing to gobbles and gulps. Shrigs are inelegant to the highest degree.

Seela and I passed on, directing our kicks to keep us at a steady distance from the Rind, studiously avoiding the fate of falling into the sky. As always in the near-free-fall conditions of the Hollow Earth, there were no particular directions that one felt compelled to call down or up. The words in and out were consistently more useful here—*in* meaning toward the center, and *out* meaning toward the Rind. Whether we flew with our bellies facing in or out was a matter of indifference, although, all in all, it seemed more useful to fly with our eyes facing the Rind.

Approaching the great volcanic butte, we could see into the caves wherein the shrigs nested. Inflated mothers bobbled against the ceilings of the caves, with baby shrigs nursing upon them from below. To Seela and I, the shriglets' grunts and squeals seemed harmonious, and even cozy. The chirping shrigbirds were everywhere, continually grooming their hosts. I glanced back at the tangled green wall of the jungle. I could make out the tiny figures of Eddie and Ina minding Brumble, although the baby himself was too small to see.

Unlike the fledgling shrigs who'd thought to try eating us, the adult shrigs let us pass. The mature beasts had a sense that humans were best left alone, just as we humans know not to disturb wasps.

And so Seela and I progressed, passing along the lumps and ridges of ancient lava that sloped to the lip of the butte. We flew with each of us holding one end of the cutting-string, and with the string stretched taut between us, lest a stray loop or bight sever a limb. So we were three hundred yards apart. The air was calm and relatively quiet, save for the steady background mooing and wheenking of the shrigs, and, with the help of our rumby tekelili, it was just barely possible to converse.

"You're truly set on doing this?" I called to Seela.

"A lark," she sang back. "I like change."

"But you don't like change enough to stay in San Francisco," I said.

"Live in the present," admonished Seela. "Today we cut off Fafnir's head."

"Are you quite assured the string can do it?" I said. "Perhaps the royal ants are like hammered steel—or some yet starker alloy. Not like soft shrigs."

"Let's test our thread's power," said Seela.

Just outward from us was a spire of petrified lava—shaped like the pile of mud that a crawfish makes outside its hole in the bottom of a stream. Seela said the lava was of an adamantine hardness, indeed it may have been composed of the preternaturally dense minerals that lie at the Rind's core. Keeping an eye on each other, Seela and I rose outward and swept along on either side of the spire.

Again I felt no vibration, no tremor, and no slowing in the thread. Silently it moved through the tower of lava, which was easily fifty feet wide. Slowly, the severed, stony tip drifted free of the base, and inward toward the Hollow Earth's core.

"Fafnir is doomed," declaimed Seela as we alit atop the great vent. We took our positions on either side of the great ant's tunnel.

8. Tallulah

So there we were, Seela and I, hanging head-down from a volcanic vent upon the Earth's inner surface, hanging like bats on the ceiling of a cave, but not a dark, small cave, no, this was a pastel planetary "cave" filled with flickering pink light streamers from the *woomo* sea cucumbers at the Hollow Earth's core, the great inner surface patterned with continents and wonderful blue seas. If I flipped my mental sense of perspective, we weren't hanging head-down, no, we were standing up. Or projecting out to the side. In any case, we had our feet wedged into cracks of the lava so we didn't drift into the sky.

The consort ant's crawl-hole was some three hundred yards across, just the length of our thread. Although the royal ants were three miles long, they were only two hundred yards wide, so he'd slide smoothly from the hole. Seela and I had positioned ourselves on diametrically opposite points of the rim of the hole, and we had our deadly-sharp vine thread pulled taut.

The simplest idea was that, as Fafnir scrambled out of his hole, he might ram into the thread and immediately split his head in two. Like a meat cleaver hitting him in the forehead. The other idea was if he came out wholly on one side of the thread, Seela would jump free and kick her fins, sweeping the thread across the opening, thus guillotining the ant.

Why were we doing this? It had started as a peevish request by Ina, and then Eddie had advocated for it, if only to make himself seem big, and then, for whatever veiled personal reasons, Seela had said we'd get it done. As for me, I'd simply been drawn along.

My faint rumby contacts with the ants Jormungo and Fafnir had shown me that these beings weren't anything like the bovine shrigs. The royal ants had complex and, for me, barely comprehensible inner lives. Seela said they'd hollowed out the Earth. Were, then, the royal ants not worthy of worship?

I'd decided I was not going to slaughter Fafnir. Far from holding the thread taut, I was going to yank it out of Fafnir's way when he appeared. I held this thought deep in my mind, lest Seela see it via our tenuous rumby link.

I felt a vibration in the adamantine stone of the volcanic vent, and I heard a faint, echoing roar. A joyful sound, a riotous squawk from, as Seela had it, one of our world's creators.

Fafnir's psyche was like a bonfire, an inner roar, the consuming pyre of a thousand saints—albeit saints who enjoy killing and eating shrigs. Amid the turmoil, I sensed Fafnir's love of his wife Jormungo, and his exultation that, at long last, her brooding upon her eggs was coming to term. I found it passing odd that Seela and I had arrived on this particular day. Odd or—as Seela had seemed suggest—fated.

Yes, I repeated to myself, Fafnir must live. As a new father, I felt full sympathy for the giant ant. Nothing must spoil his joy at the hatching of his wife's eggs.

At my first sight of the tips of Fafnir's gleaming purple-black mandibles, I pulled my feet free and kicked away from the tunnel's entrance. But—oh no!—the cunning Seela had anticipated my move. She was kicking *her* limbs as well, moving in precisely the opposite direction from me, so that our stretched thread was rotating above the tunnel's hole like a great compass needle—rather than being yanked to the side.

In order to save Fafnir, I might simply have released my hold upon the thread, but I was leery so to do, dreading a disastrous encounter between my body and the deadly-sharp line. But now these considerations became moot. Fafnir rammed into our stretched thread with his long, massive head and the effect upon him was—nil.

I wasn't entirely surprised that the ant's armor had a hardness and a solidity unknown among Earth's normal creatures. Why not? This was, after all, a being from the dawn of time.

Perhaps by way of teaching us a lesson, Fafnir gave our vine string an abrupt yank. The handles were torn from my grasp and from Seela's. The thread coiled invisibly into the surrounding air. My luck held, and no bight of the freed line happened to decapitate me. With all his surfaces and protuberances intact, Fafnir shook out his long wings and flew free of the butte.

Although Seela and I were tiny relative to the leviathan, we were aglow with our rumby tekelili. *And* we were the ones who'd been holding the vine thread. Fafnir marked us with a flash of his eyes—but for now he let us be. He had larger plans.

Moving in elegant swoops, the flying purplish-green ant impaled a succession of a hundred or more shrigs upon his fearsome legs, draining their bodies rapidly as his own body swelled. The spectacle was similar to his attack the day before—but with ten times the noise. Fafnir's grainy cries were like the harsh caws of a bird of prey. And now, unfathomably, the exultant royal ant began beaming a brilliant red ray from the great stinger at his rear—directing the blinding, needle-like beam inward toward the basking *woomo* at the core of the Hollow Earth.

Inevitably the ray and the distant clamor attracted the attention, and perhaps the opprobrium, of the *woomo*. A dense, burning streamer of light focused upon Fafnir's flickering form, following his gyrations with barely a lag. The impaled and drained bodies of the shrigs were crisped into ashes. Fafnir's body glowed first red, then yellow, and then white. But he didn't seem to mind. Indeed, he seemed to be enjoying himself. He flapped his illuminated wings; he danced like a bonfire. His cries grew louder, more harmonious, more jubilant. And he continued goading the distant *woomo* with his tail-stinger's red beam.

Drawn by her husband's clamorous cries, Jormungo now made her appearance, wriggling out of the volcanic tunnel upon the butte and buzzing free. All the while, Seela and I were frantically kicking our airfins, wanting to make our way back to the shelter of the jungle.

A particularly bright *woomo* beam played across Seela and me, lingering rather longer than was comfortable, perhaps even for a full two minutes, and in that time, Seela and I were once again cured to a total ebony blackness, which was seemingly to be my recurrent fate for the rest of my days. The good news was that the light stream moved away from us before we were roasted like pigs or kindled into flame.

The *woomo* had homed in their primary target by now, and their intolerably intense light streamers were playing across the white-hot Fafnir from one end to the other, over and over. But, as I say, the light seemed to do the ant no harm. Remember that—if Seela was to be believed—Fafnir and Jormungo were primeval, nearly god-like creatures, capable of hollowing out a planet and splitting space in two. For beings like these, the heat of a *woomo* light beam might even be agreeable. Perhaps the *woomo* knew this. Perhaps they were not in fact trying to kill the royal ant. Perhaps they were caressing him.

Jormungo flew to Fafnir and seized him in a full-body embrace, never flinching from his heat, and indeed, writhing against him as if in ecstatic transport, their flame-like bodies as one. And as they embraced, Fafnir shared with her the steaming vapors of his ingested shrig juice. The two of them caromed off the surface of the Rind. With joyful twitches and snaps of their shimmering bodies and wings, Jormungo and Fafnir propelled themselves across the lava fields, past the jungle, and into the aquamarine sea, sending up a dense explosion of steam, which was quickly followed by a dozen loud reports, as if from the detonation of twelve bombs. The eggs? Events were unfolding very rapidly indeed.

The cloud of steam had developed into a great bank of fog, which put an end to the efficacy of the *woomo* light beams. All around us the shrigs were bellowing in the expanding mist. No longer could I see our way to the jungle. But Seela took hold of my hand, and led me with unerring instinct, guided in part, I suppose, by the tekelili of Eddie's rumby. As soon

415

as we reached our friends amid the branches and vines, Seela seized baby Brumble. And I took hold of Arf.

"What have you done?" Ina demanded in a petulant tone. "You shouldn't have stirred up the giant ants like that. And now you're blacker than ever. I spoke in jest when I said to kill Fafnir. What madness have you unleashed?"

I could sense Seela's strong emotions. She'd gone beyond disliking Ina. She despised her. And so she favored the woman with no response.

"We're leaving," Seela said to Eddie. "Mason, Brumble, Arf and I are riding a shrig to my flower."

"We'll await you at the Umpteen Seas," said Eddie. "But only for a time. Before I return to my ancestral home."

"Mason and I will stay on my flower forever," said Seela. I didn't agree with this plan, but my wife was in no mood to be contradicted.

Off in the nearby sea, the pair of royal ants were excitedly chirping. It was perhaps like an operatic duet. Not that I'd ever heard an opera.

"I don't want to go to any Umpteen Seas," wailed Ina. "Nor go to some other Earth. I want to go home to San Francisco."

"This remains your choice," said Eddie. "But first I pray you accompany me to the Hollow Earth's core. It's like a waking dream, Ina, a sublunary paradise with heavy teke-lili. The black gods—they're beyond compare for flash and fancy. You'll bid farewell to me—and I'll journey on through the Central Anomaly, perhaps with Machree for company, if he's not too busy harvesting rumbies. And, Ina, if you will it, the *woomo* can send you back to your California, perhaps aboard a fried-egg flying disk. Seela may well stay on her dull flower with her pup. But I ween the young Mason will accompany you to San Francisco. He'll be overdue for a new woman—and a seaport spree."

I chose to ignore Eddie's divisive and impolite badinage. A beam of *woomo* light was playing across the befogged jungle. I wondered if they were looking for us. Two great, lost shrigs were mooing nearby, with their shrigbirds fluttering around them.

"Quickly now," Seela said to me, smearing her dark hands and feet with sap from one of those thornless pancake cactuses. They were common around here. "Do as I do. This plant-taffy can glue you to the back of a shrig. We'll use our rumbies to direct our shrig to my flower. The shrigs stink, and they have lice, but they'll do. We need to get out of here now. Come, Mason."

Without a word for Eddie or Ina, Seela was kicking away from the jungle. She had Brumble in her arms, the baby's face a spot of white against his black mother. I had no choice but to follow. I bid godspeed to Ina and Eddie, crushed a fat lobe of cactus, smeared the juice onto my arms and legs, and followed in Seela's wake, towing Arf by a small vine tendril I'd tied to one of his feet.

The shrig that Seela and I found was a big one, a female, subdued by Fafnir's rampage, not to mention the thunderous explosions of the eggs and the sudden blanket of mist. Seela and I infiltrated the shrig's psyche with our rumby tekelili, and she allowed us to land upon her bristly hide. Kneeling on her back and deploying our sticky sap, we fixed our positions, with Seela cradling Brumble in the crook of one arm, and me holding Arf as if he were my son. Using her rumby tekelili, Seela ordered the flying shrimp-pig to rocket us away.

The shrig—her name was Tallulah—responded with a grumbling groan and, for the moment, took no action. But I had a sense that, on the whole, the shrig didn't mind having us guide her getaway. By now she'd already spawned and released her season's quota of fry, and surely she was ready to leave—particularly with Fafnir and Jormungo on a rampage.

What Tallulah didn't as yet grasp was that Seela would be directing her toward the South Hole, rather than toward the Hollow Earth's core. In the mist and the low gravity, navigation was tricky. Especially for a shrig.

Seela repeated her order, and now Tallulah fired up her rocket. That is, she began leaking out a steady stream of fart which she set alight—by striking a spark with a pair of flint stones that she carried at all times in the prehensile tissues near her anus. And then we were on our way, leaving the shrigbirds behind.

417

Looking back, I saw that Eddie and Ina had imitated our actions. They'd boarded the other shrig, glued themselves down, and their shrig was rocketing toward the Hollow Earth's core. I waved farewell. Presumably they'd find Machree already at the Umpteen Seas.

Our initial velocity was not so great as to prevent Seela and me from getting a good view of what the giant ants were up to. The cloud of fog had drifted away from the sea. Below us, Fafnir and Jormungo were cavorting in the water—with the dozen newly hatched royal ants at their side. Fafnir was no longer directing his red beam of light at the *woomo*, and the *woomo* had suspended their rays as well.

The newborn ants were like their parents—but in a juvenile stage—ten yards long, with bright eyes, and with paddle wings. Their dark skins scattered highlights of purple and green, reminding me of the emperor staghorn beetles I'd seen on our manure pile in Hardware, Virginia. They had little bumps where their legs would so grow, and as yet they had no mandibles. But they were alert and they could fly, moving about like gnats, albeit gnats three times the size of cows.

The sea here had been circling the great maelstrom that ran in from the North Pole. But the maelstrom's swirl was dying—for the empress ant Jormungo was no longer at the great whirlpool's throat, and was no longer driving its rotation by her swimming. As a result, the passageway through the central hole was narrowing fast.

Somehow I hadn't anticipated this. But Seela had. She flashed me a fierce grin, a mixture of passion and possessiveness.

"You won't get away so easy now, Mason Reynolds! You'll stay with me in my cozy flower home."

I was speechless. Surely, if I tried, I might find a way to float up through hundreds of miles of cold, black sea. But ballooning through back the North Hole would have been so much simpler.

At this point the North Hole's throat was still just barely open. Did the family of royal ants mean to fly through it? Outwards from the core they flapped, rising in a helix, entering deeper and deeper into the narrowing strait, the two adults and the twelve juveniles. They moved with startling speed, and then—*thip, thip*—the parent and eleven of the children dove into the maelstrom's sidewall, just below the throat.

"Why did they do that?" I asked Seela.

"They'll paddle sideways to get into the middle layers of the Rind. People say that's where the royal ants have their big nest."

And just about then the maelstrom's throat pinched shut. The North Hole was gone. It remained only for the vast dimple in the sea to rebound.

I studied the last of the twelve royal ant juveniles—a restive dot just short of the maelstrom's closed-off throat. Changing his vector of motion, he was arcing away from the Rind, as if heading inward toward the Hollow Earth's core. I wondered what kind of reception the *woomo* would give him.

Meanwhile Seela was exhorting our shrig Tallulah to blast herself away from the Rind. And with good reason. As I say, once the maelstrom's throat closed over, the seawaters were due to rebound. For a single still moment a great aqueous dimple covered the hole where the whirlpool's mouth had been. But then, due to water's natural tendency to smooth itself, the surface began tautening toward us. With a certain physical exuberance, the onrushing mass of water overshot its mark, and rose high above the aquamarine surface of the inner sea—becoming, for a few moments, a continent of water thirty miles high, and thereby submerging the nearby jungle, as well as the cliffs with the nests of the shrigs, and indeed rising so far that this domed sea came nearly within touching distance of the rocketing Tallulah. Whether the rogue ant juvenile escaped the flood, I did not see.

As the sea settled back, damping herself with a series of dwindling oscillations, we continued on our way. Seela and I had seated ourselves just behind the shrig's large head, which shielded us from the wind of our rapid passage. I tied Arf's leash to an especially large shrig bristle, lest he drift away. Seela and I took the glue off our hands and sat in place with spots of glue holding our rear ends in place.

"Tell me more about the ants," I said.

"The story is that every thousand years, Jormungo hatches a clutch of royal ants to help start a new colony on

419

another world. The *woomo* like it when the empress ant is brooding over her eggs and keeping a North Hole maelstrom open. Makes it easier to send out their tendrils. But now that won't happen for a while." She leaned over and gave me a kiss. "You were right, wanting to save Fafnir."

"Why didn't you admit that before?" I asked.

"Well, I did think it would be fun to get Jormungo excited," said Seela. "Give her a jolt. I was hoping she'd go ahead and hatch her eggs. And I wanted to see the maelstrom close." She smiled. "For the reason I told you."

"You're a sly one," I said

"I mean to keep you," said Seela. "You suit me well." She kissed me. I liked her with the dark skin.

"And what about that one juvenile royal ant who got away?" I said after a bit.

"Supposedly whenever they hatch a royal litter, they send one of the juveniles to visit with the *woomo* at the core. To tell them it's time for what they call a Bloom. That's when they send some *woomo* and some royal ants out together. Inside a couple of those fried egg ships. To colonize a new world. I'm not exactly sure about the details."

"The *woomo* and the royal ants are partners?"

Seela laughed. "Like you and me. I'm the *woomo* and you're the ant."

"I'll bite you," I said. "I'll pinch you hard!"

"I'll zap you! I'll sting you with my fronds!"

We got into an inconclusive amorous tussle, then burst into laughter and let the hours pass. As so often happened in these new days, Brumble was the focus of our attention.

"Four days old," said Seela. "I think he's opening his eyes a little more."

"He doesn't really see me," I said. "But maybe he sees you."

"He knows your voice," said Seela. "He waves his arms."

Arf pressed forward and licked Brumble on the face.

"Baby's bath," said Seela. "Keep an eye out for shrig lice, Mason." She pointed along Tallulah's hide. "There! Like a crab. See? It matches the shrig's skin. If it bites Brumble, I'll kill you."

"Can you calm down?" I said. "You've got everything you wanted. We're back inside the Hollow Earth, the North Hole is closed, and we're flying to your mirrorflower. Just you and me and Arf and Brumble. With Eddie and Ina and Machree out of the picture."

"That's all fine, but we don't have food, which *does* bother me," said Seela, taking herself seriously. "Now be a man, Mason, and kill that shrig louse before it gets the baby!"

I caught hold of the shrig louse and pulled. It came loose from the shrig's hide, leaving a dribble of pale yellow shrig blood. The louse didn't look at all like food. I snapped it in half and tossed it into the wind. I felt something like the ghost of a thank-you. From Tallulah? Perhaps the shrigs had an inner mental life after all. Probing back, I seemed to hear a steady note of song. As if the shrig were singing to herself as she flew, content with her task, meditatively moving on.

We were getting ever further from the curved Rind as Tallulah continued her route across the Hollow Earth's great round cavity—and toward the environs of the South Hole. Our path was very nearly a diameter or, more precisely, a chord of the sphere.

"Let's cuddle now," said Seela, her mood changing once again.

"You mean have sex?"

"Maybe," she said. "But no poking. I'm as sore as if I fell down a flight of stairs in Mrs. Mackie's rooming-house. Another reason it's better in the Hollow Earth. No stairs." She smiled at me as if expecting something.

"You were talking about cuddling," I said, feeling my way. "And then I said sex, and you said no poking, and now?"

"I'm saying we're tired, but we can, you know, kiss and touch, To help us bounce back."

"Like the sea from the maelstrom hole."

"The mount of love," said Seela, cheerfully bucking her pelvis. She still had Brumble curled in her right arm. "You don't see any shrig lice, do you?"

"Nary a one," said I, smearing some of the cactus glue onto the backs of my black shoulders and gluing myself flat on my back. "Have at me, Seela. Play me like a fiddle."

"A country tussle," she said, her face suddenly very close to mine. "Like with Yurgen. On the flower. When I was a virgin girl and he was the pied piper."

Clumsily we spent our passion, dozed off, and then I woke to Brumble crying. My shirt was wet with Seela's milk. This was the same white shirt of Eddie's that I'd taken from his room at Mrs. Mackie's hotel in San Francisco a week or so before. And my pants were still the same gray twill. Both garments were much stained by travel, and by our encounters with the Hollow Earth's outlandish inhabitants.

The better part of another day had passed. We were in an empty zone, midway between the Rind and the core, headed south rather than inward, with Tallulah making for a green spot of jungle beside the sea at the South Hole, this being where Seela's mirrorflower lay. Tallulah's flame still burned, but her gas supply was dwindling. Her inner song was wavering. She needed a meal.

I myself was hungry as well, and thirsty too. Thanks to the wild chaos brought on by Fafnir and Jormungo, Seela and I hadn't been thinking clearly when we'd left. We hadn't even thought to bring a water glob, let alone a supply of fruit.

But now fate smiled upon us again.

"Look," said Seela pointing ahead to a shoal of curious shapes—fuzzy blimps, whirling pods with whip-like tails, and long green chains of green sausages, tangled around like vines. The blimps, pods, and sausages glowed. The blimps were the size of Tallulah, the sausages were the size of my arm, and the pods were somewhere in between. There were a lot of these critters—or were they plants? They were heaped up like a tangled mound of garbage, and managing not to fall inward toward the Hollow Earth's core, thanks to the beating fuzz on the blimps, the thrashing tails on the pods, and the sparkling bubbles within the sausages.

"Brobdingnagian cryptozoa?" I said, drawing fine words from my *Southern Literary Messenger* store of learning. I meant that these creatures seemed like overgrown versions of the tiny plants and animals that scuttle about beneath the debris of a forest floor.

"Brob *what*?" said Seela, laughing. "This is an antfarm, tended by farmer ants. They're mean and creamy-white. They're a reasonable size. They grow these things you see: ant-sheep, ant-pigs, and ant-plants. Poach as much as you want, but don't let the farmer ants catch you."

"What exactly do you mean when you say the ants are a reasonable size?".

"Like big dogs."

"I don't see any of them."

"They're hiding on the other side of all this junk," said Seela. "They're scared of Tallulah. But soon they'll rush in for an attack. We have to eat fast The ant-plant sausages are especially good. Look at our shrig go."

Tallulah had focused on a tangle of those green sausages, and she was harvesting bushels of them with her open mouth. Periodically she'd pause to crunch her catch, bursting the sausages, releasing the verdant, effervescent slime within. Tallulah grunted with pleasure as she gulped down her questionable cud.

Seela leaned out from our perch on Tallulah's back to snag a foot-long ant-plant sausage herself. Nimbly Seela sliced it across the middle, popping something at its center. The sausage stopped glowing and went limp. Seela handed me half—like a floppy goblet. I lapped and sipped at the foamy ichor within, spilling out dancing droplets for Arf to snap from the air. The slime was grassy, but sweet, with a slight pungency, and bearing an odd tingle. The goo slid readily down my throat, slaking my thirst and restoring my energy. I snagged a second ant-plant sausage and then a third. A capital form of alimentation.

"Now for meat," said Seela, brandishing her blade. "A hunk of that sky-whipping guy's tail. We call that an ant-pig. The tail's a special treat."

Although none of the ant-sheep or ant-pigs had eyes, they were aware of our bulky shrig's progress—I suppose they were alerted by our smells, our jostling, our sound vibrations, and perhaps our psychic emanations. The blimp-like ant-sheep in particular were tracking us rather closely. They were glorious creatures, illuminated from within, with rainbow highlights shimmering along their cilia, and they had colorful globules of food and fat and water within their gelatinous flesh.

"Are those brains in the middle of these things?" I asked Seela. Each of the whirling ant-pigs and fat ant-sheep had a round, flickering mass at the core of its translucent body.

"Those are stomachs," said Seela. " It's not just the ant farmers you have to worry about—their livestock is dangerous too. If one of those critters happens to wrap itself around you, it'll start in on digesting you right away."

And with that, Seela set off on the hunt. Her intended prey was a whip-tailed ant-pig, and she was steering our shrig its way. Sensing our approach, the creature beat its flagellum, spinning its body like a top, and caroming off whatever came in contact. Seela rose to her feet, checked her airfins, and handed Brumble over to me. Choosing her moment with care, Seela plunged into a void amid the bustling population of the antfarm, kicking her legs to speed her way. With no solid matter nearby, I feared Seela's sally might go badly awry, with her missing her mark, losing her fins, and endlessly tumbling inward toward the Hollow Earth's core.

But Seela had precisely timed her leap so that her body would interrupt the sweep of the targeted ant-pig's tail. Seizing this thick, ropy strand in one hand, Seela slashed off a three-foot segment of the tip. And then she held the still-twitching bit of tail at such an angle that it propelled her back to our shrig. Cradling Brumble in one arm, I used my free hand to catch hold of Seela's leg.

She glued herself to our shrig again, and held up her prize, that is, a severed length of the tail. After some diminishing shudders, the tail-tip fell still. Seela cut off a bit and began eating it, all the while grinning at me and exaggerating her chomps.

"Try it, Mason. We're masters of the Hollow Earth. Conquerors of the antfarm. And remember to eat fast. Those farmer ants are gonna come after us any minute."

I accepted a piece of her odd, fibrous catch, whatever it really was. The substance was very chewy, like aged pemmican, with what I would call an off or a "high" taste, like spoiled meat. Its tingling juices had the property of numbing my lips and tongue. I spit out what was in my mouth, and gave the rest of my portion to Arf. Of course the dog loved this offal, and he begged Seela for more.

Stunned by Seela's abrupt attack, the ant-pig was moving crookedly. Again I had a sense of contact with Tallulah the shrig's mind. Her energy was mounting like a wave. She sensed an opportunity. As Tallulah's mental activation peaked, she executed a great wallowing lunge, and seized the narrow end of the ant-pig with her toothless but powerful jaws. The glowing ant-pig failed to spin free. Tallulah burst a hole in its hide—and slurped down perhaps a hundred gallons of the wounded creature's gelatinous body mass. But then the ant-pig's central digestive organ came slopping out along with the slime. The stomach—if that's what it was—glowed an angry yellow-white.

Emitting a sharp squeal, Tallulah backed off. The odd, hot sphere from within the dying ant-pig flew past us and collided with one of the fuzzy, fat, ant-sheep. In a transition that I found hard to understand, the glittering ant-sheep widened itself at one end and engulfed the stomach-ball—which united itself with the other glowing core that was already present in the ant-sheep's core. Like two whirlpools merging into one.

Meanwhile Tallulah was bellowing in triumph, celebrating her kill and her escape. Swept into a close sympathy with my new friend, I raised my voice with hers, twisting my cries into mad squeals.

"What is *wrong* with you?" said Seela.

At this point about a dozen pale white, dog-sized ants came after us—some of them winged like Jormungo, and all of them clacking their jaws and wielding their stingers. One of them bit Tallulah in the ass, and another one stung her. The beleaguered shrig's roars turned to wild, screeching wheenks.

"Flame on!" steady Seela ordered the shrig, and we were off again, riding a burning plume of fart.

I, for one, was weary of death-matches with fantastical beasts. To my relief the rest of the trip to Seela's mirrorflower went smoothly. Tallulah got into her meditative inner hum. Seela nursed Brumble, then napped again. The sated Arf was sleeping as well. And I sat awake, watching for shrig lice, and killing seven of them. I felt a bump of approval from Tallulah with each one. The attack of the farmer ants had set the lice to crawling up Tallulah's body toward her head.

As we approached the sea and jungle near the South Hole. I squinted my eyes, hoping to make out some pinpricks of color along the jungle's edge—these would be the flowers where Seela's folk and their rivals lived. And one particular yellow flower would be the mirrorflower we sought, that is, the twin to the home flower where Seela had been raised and where I'd won her love.

Despite my reluctance to settle on this mirrorflower for good, I was looking forward to the visit. I liked the flower-people. And after the wild twists of the last few days, I was ripe for a rest.

Perhaps in a week, with energy renewed and terror sub-dued, I'd find my way to the Hollow Earth's core, there to bid farewell to Eddie before he and Machree passed onward through the great Gate or Central Anomaly, bound for the old Earth where Eddie and I had been born

My feverish thoughts returned to my fantasies about balancing the two worlds. Machree would go, and I would stay. Admittedly, he and I had already broken the two worlds' balance with our crisscrossed acts of murder. But perhaps it was important for the two of us to live on opposite sides? Probably not. The more basic truth was that I misliked Machree, and I wanted him to go.

And what of Seela and MirrorSeela? What if I coaxed both of them into the core with me? And then I'd talk Seela into travelling through the Rind and back to the surface of MirrorEarth with me. Was there any chance I could bring MirrorSeela to San Francisco with us as well? San Francisco would be better for us than, god forbid, the South. Thanks to the intense *woomo* light at the Hollow Earth's core, Seela and I would be even blacker than now, and MirrorSeela would be black as well. And we'd remain black for half a year or more.

But how exactly would we pass out through the Rind? The South Hole of this MirrorEarth was plugged by ice, and its North Hole maelstrom was gone—thanks in part to our own actions. *Oh la*—fate would provide. I felt strangely happy. My plans were all nonsense anyway. I could only watch the adventure unfold. I spooned against dear Seela's side, and fell asleep yet again.

I woke to the sound of Seela's voice comforting Brumble, followed by a heavy thump echoing through the gassy body of our shrig. Tallulah had landed against an enormous sunflower blossom, a curved, patterned surface, easily two miles across, yellow in the middle, with gently waving white petals around the rim, with a large glittering glob of water resting delicately upon the center, and with smaller globs twinkling all around.

"How did you find it?" I asked Seela.

"It was easy," said she. "It's almost as if Tallulah knew the way."

The flower was affixed to an enormous stalk that wound out from a fantastical jungle that was, once again, thirty miles high, with vine upon bush upon fungus upon waterglob upon tree upon moss upon stone.

Seela was holding Brumble and fluttering her finned feet, gliding off Tallulah's back and onto the flower. Arf had already landed. The flower faced the Rind, which meant that the Hollow Earth's gentle inward pull tended to hold us to the flower's face, albeit very weakly.

Before joining the other two, I drew upon my growing sense of empathy with Tallulah. "You go hide!" I told her, using images rather than words. I added a scene of the shrig eating wildly for days. "Food in the jungle," I said aloud. "And then we fly to the *woomo*."

Seela was good enough to support me. "Do as Mason says," she thought to the shrig. "Wait until we call." Even though Seela yearned—or thought she yearned—to settle down upon this flower, she was wise to the ways of the world, and she appreciated the value of having an exit.

I fluttered clear of the beast's grubby hide and came to rest upon the springy, sweet-smelling, two-mile-wide surface of the flower.

With a fart and a joyful roar, Tallulah flew off into the staggeringly huge tangle of the southern jungle. Like Seela,

I had a sense the shrig had been here before. Yes, I had a growing rapport with the shrig—potentiated by my rumby tekelili—and she knew that I wanted her to stay. But her primary motivation may have been that she knew this jungle, and she wanted to forage. From where we rested, I could spot at least ten species of fruit upon the tangled vines and trees.

Shrigs had an ability to take on weight very rapidly, and if Tallulah really went at it, she might increase her size by as much as a third in the course of a single gluttonous week. And this would please her well. A shrig's status was strictly dependent upon its heft.

"Look!" cried Seela, pointing past the great ball of water that rested in the blossom's center. "Here they come."

A pair of flowerpeople were flying toward us across the broad, yellow surface of the flower, a man and a woman, with the woman in front and the man behind, the two of them kicking their legs against their airfins, and carrying long, sharp thorns.

9. MirrorSeela

The two who came to meet us were MirrorSeela and MirrorYurgen. A coincidence? More likely it was an inevitability—and yet another of the slightly-off-kilter harmonies between Earth and MirrorEarth. After my first visit to the Hollow Earth. Seela and I had emerged on the surface of MirrorEarth with Eddie Poe in our company—and almost immediately we'd met the MirrorPoe. Opposites attract, and ever the twain shall meet.

MirrorSeela had never seen me before. And initially she didn't seem to recognize her young double Seela. Seela and I were, after all, completely black again, thanks to our exposure to intense *woomo* light during the scene with the royal ants and the shrigs.

For their part, MirrorSeela and MirrorYurgen were creamy white. MirrorSeela's stomach was a bit soft, and the muscles on her legs were hard. Her green/brown eyes were the same. Her skin was slightly oily, and somehow very comfortable looking, like the leather of a cherished deerskin glove—although that simile is neither chivalrous nor fully apt, for the demeanor of the MirrorSeela was by no means that of an old glove. Indeed, with her rapier at the ready, she looked capable of killing the two of us on the spot. I longed to touch her before I died.

MirrorYurgen was keeping most of his body behind MirrorSeela's. I recalled that Yurgen was, if not a coward, exceedingly meticulous about his safety. I was surprised he'd come out to meet us with MirrorSeela. Probably she'd made him.

"Don't you recognize me?" Seela called to MirrorSeela. She spoke of course in the language of flowerpeople, rather than in English. But after my earlier time on Seela's flower, I knew a bit of the native tongue.

"Why should I know you?" replied MirrorSeela. "You're black gods who flew here on a shrig, and now the shrig is hiding in the jungle. We've seen her here before. Tallulah, no? What do you want? Are you here to loot?"

"Would I bring my baby on a raid?" exclaimed Seela. "And you should know me because I'm you, *blaga'am*. But twelve years younger." She propelled herself closer to her double. "My man is Mason. Our baby's name is Brumble, and he's five days old. Our dog is Arf."

"*Dog?*" echoed MirrorYurgen, missing the gist of the message and focusing on the unfamiliar word. They had no dogs in the Hollow Earth. "Does he bite?"

Seela's old suitor wasn't aging well—a front tooth was missing, his hands trembled, and his once luxuriant hair was thin. He was like the glove that you throw away, the one with its finger-tips worn off. Seela didn't bother answering his question. Her attention was focused on her double.

"*Gooba'am*," said MirrorSeela very slowly. She lowered her rapier. "How is it so, my twin sister? How are you young?"

"Your world is a mirror of ours," I told MirrorSeela. "Twelve years twinkled past as we came through."

"You're pretty," MirrorYurgen told Seela. "I like you black."

"Ah, dear Yurgen," said Seela, flirting. "Do you still charm the tribe with the reverb tube? I remember our golden days. Before I left with Mason."

"Tell us why you've come," interrupted MirrorSeela.

"I missed my home," said Seela quite simply. "Is old Ogger still alive?"

"Gone," said MirrorYurgen. "He fell asleep in the open, and a *ballula* ate him. How he screamed."

"We'll bring you to the village square as guests," MirrorSeela told us. We'll celebrate. MirrorYurgen will play the reverberator tube, and we'll all eat *juube* and get to know each other." She gave me a look.

"I wonder—I wonder if we'll make love?" I found myself saying. MirrorSeela laughed gently, as if approving an answer by a slow student, and my Seela herself tittered in amusement.

"The four of us!" cried MirrorYurgen

I hadn't been including this broken-down bard in my daydreams. I had a sudden, demented impulse to dart forward and plunge the blade of my knife into his gut. As if sensing and forestalling this possibility, Seela spoke up, her voice mild and controlled.

"It's pleasant to imagine such idylls, but remember I just gave birth. I'm sore."

"Of course," said MirrorSeela. "Men imagine there's a rush to have sex, but there isn't." She tucked her rapier into a sheath upon her back, and fluttered forward to have a closer look at Brumble, who was nursing at Seela's breast. Mirror-Yurgen moved a bit further back.

"Such a baby it is," said MirrorSeela. "So sweet. So white against your skin."

"The *woomo* light cooked Mason and me yesterday," said Seela. "And just then Brumble was in the arms of two friends."

With domesticity entering the picture, my simple-minded, lust-maddened wish to kill MirrorYurgen was fading away. He and I even exchanged a look of mutual sympathy. There wasn't going to be an full-on orgy anytime soon, and we were sad about that.

"You don't have children?" Seela was asking MirrorSeela.

"She's barren," called MirrorYurgen, quick to place the blame on his partner.

"The problem is you," snapped MirrorSeela. "You waste your force on *juube*. And you put what's left into your resonator tube. With me you're often limp."

"No man truly knows what gets a woman with child," protested MirrorYurgen. "Perhaps it's the *woomo* light, or what the woman eats, or the sting of an airshrimp. There's no call to take me to task."

"I'd forgotten," Seela said to MirrorSeela in a low tone. "Forgotten how stupid the men on this flower are. That's why I left with Mason. How quickly the mind makes the past sweet. I shouldn't have returned."

"I'll leave with you if I can," murmured MirrorSeela. "On your friend, Tallulah the shrig. She's eating in the jungle as usual. I see the trees shaking from here."

"Depend on us, sister," said Seela. "But first a night of rest." She detached Brumble from her breast, fastened up her blouse, and shot a smoldering look at MirrorYurgen, as if testing her powers.

"Seela and I have an extra chamber you can use," said the musician, fluttering his fins.

"There may be some fun for you yet," Seela told him, parting her lips and waggling her tongue. She hadn't acted like this in Baltimore! But now she was back home. I didn't have it in me to be jealous. The situation was too fantastical and absurd. Foremost in my mind was the fact that we two would be sharing a dwelling with the potentially pliant MirrorSeela—and never mind what MirrorYurgen did.

"Let's eat, drink, and fly to the village," I proposed.

The great flower's surface was tiled into hexagonal cells, like on a common sunflower, except these cells were about thirty feet across. Each cell had a hole in the middle, with a more-or-less empty chamber beneath. A ring of stubby, yellow growths surrounded each hole. I suppose you could call these petals, although they were nothing like the large white true petals around the flower's outer rim.

I used my knife to harvest a handful of these secondary petals and offered them around. Tender flowerleather. Seela ate with gusto, very pleased to be tasting this staple again. For their part, MirrorSeela and MirrorYurgen weren't hungry—but they were fascinated by the sharpness of my steel knife. They'd never seen one before. The flowerpeople lived like cavemen.

There happened to be a waist-high glob of water trapped in the middle of the next cell, and Seela and I drank deeply from it. And then we sat down to rest with MirrorSeela and MirrorYurgen. I dandled tiny Brumble on my lap, letting him suck the tip of my finger. Arf nosed about, snapping at the shiny beetles that came buzzing by.

Around this time, MirrorSeela sensed the import of the tight-wrapped amulets that Seela and I wore at our necks.

"I had a rumby myself," she exclaimed.

"How would *you* get one?" asked Seela, doubting her. "Rumbies come from beyond the Umpteen Seas. There aren't any down here on this…this old flower." She was losing her enthusiasm for being here.

"The *woomo* sent me the rumby," said MirrorSeela, drawing herself up. I could tell this had been one of the great events of her circumscribed life. "I was dizzy with *juube*, staring into the sky. A beam of light swooped down like a bird, this way, that way, coming straight to me. The light was carrying a rumby for me. I held it in my hand like a little plum. It was heavy. It gave me tekelili. It was alive." Absorbed in her memory, MirrorSeela clasped her hands against her chest.

"Where's the rumby now?" asked Seela.

"You'll see," said MirrorSeela, her tone exalted.

And then MirrorYurgen turned to me and asked if he might borrow my knife. Weighing my options, I handed him the blade. He accepted it with a graceful bow, then squeezed down through the hole at our cell's center. After about five minutes he popped back out, bearing a *juube* bean the size of a roast turkey. Such beans were the unripe seeds of this great flower. Moving with purpose and agility, MirrorYurgen carved up half the bean like a watermelon.

I well knew the intoxicating effects of these dripping chunks, and I partook very sparingly. This was not the time to lose my edge. Seela and MirrorSeela each had but one slice as well. We'd be facing the whole tribe soon.

But MirrorYurgen exercised no restraint. He wolfed down three, four and then five hearty slices of *juube* and began to laugh, to sing, and to howl into the sky, as if trying to bounce an echo off the planetary Rind. To complete his performance, he removed his breechcloth and showed us his member. An unprepossessing sight.

"My Yurgen is difficult," said MirrorSeela, shaking her head. "But he's an angel on the reverberator tube. His great skill. You'll hear him later. It's concert night."

"But—" began Seela, and broke off. MirrorYurgen was crawling on all fours and pressing his nose up against Arf's.

"The tribe honors him still," said MirrorSeela. "And this makes him useful to me. His status shields me from low, importunate men. I pick who I want. Come now, let's kick fins to the village."

"But—" said Seela again.

"We'll leave Yurgen here," said MirrorSeela. "He'll find his way back for the concert. Or drift into the sky. Or be eaten by a *ballula*. Like Ogger. I pick bad men for sex."

"You did it with *Ogger*?" said Seela with a laugh. "I never—"

"You were lucky," said MirrorSeela. "You left the flower young. I stayed and I got bored. And I hoped Ogger might get me with child."

"Even if he was your father?" said Seela.

"He said he wasn't," said MirrorSeela

"Perhaps Mason can help," said Seela lightly. "He bursts with seed."

MirrorSeela gave me an appraising glance, then drew close and kissed Seela on her mouth, long and deep and leisurely. Seela seemed to enjoy it.

I was standing there holding the baby, Arf was nudging me with his nose, and MirrorYurgen was lying inert on his back. My brain—and other parts of me—were about to explode. Have I mentioned that I was seventeen?

The women broke apart, breathing hard. MirrorSeela spoke. "In a few days we we'll all be leaving together on Tallulah, yes Seela dear?"

"Perhaps," said Seela. "Look at Mason. So excited."

The women laughed at me, and then the three of us kicked our way across the pleasant-smelling expanse of flower. But before we left, I retrieved my knife from MirrorYurgen. In the air, I held Brumble, and MirrorSeela carried Arf, making much of him, and holding him out in the air as if he were flying on his own.

"Stop here!" called MirrorSeela as we came to the truly enormous glob of water that rested upon the great flower's center. "We'll swim."

Held together by the tension of its surface, the glassy button slanted up on all sides from where it lightly touched the flower. Seela and I were once again ripe for a bath—what with the cactus glue, the ichor from the smashed shrig lice, the slime of the primeval ant-plant sausages—and our bodies' own secretions. We would have liked to swim together, but Seela didn't feel comfortable leaving Brumble alone with MirrorSeela who, after all, had no children of her own, and might possibly wish to steal our baby. So first the two women swam together, and then I swam with Arf.

I can't say that I'd often seen truly clear water in Virginia. Muddiness was the norm. The floating ponds and lakes of the Hollow Earth were nothing like. Think of distilled corn whiskey in a clear glass. Or air that is a liquid that wets your skin. The view from inside the mirrorflower's great central lake: stupendous.

Arf and I swam within a living lens, with the pulsing pink-lit Hollow Earth on every side—its vast skies rich with life, its Rind embossed with seas and jungles, the warped mystery of the Central Anomaly like a navel at the core. The water blob itself was populated by legged fish, schools of them like glittering scarves, darting and veering, and occasionally leaping through the water's membrane, crawling across the flower, and finding their way back in. Arf tried in vain to catch one.

Seela had once said you can't drown while swimming in the Hollow Earth, but if you're a blockhead you can. Your weight isn't dragging you into the depths, but, contrariwise, your buoyancy isn't lifting you to the surface. When short on air, you need to swim to the edge. But, having been here before, Arf and I knew this. Beating our legs, we dove and surfaced again and again, rejoicing.

As a practical matter, the clean water was most welcome upon my soiled and crusted skin. Of course I stayed black just the same. Not that being black was in any way a burden here. As I've mentioned, the flowerpeople referred to the *woomo*-blackened natives of the Umpteen Seas as gods. When I left the pool, MirrorSeela again eyed me with approval.

Carrying Brumble and Arf in our arms, the two Seelas and I kicked onward to the cleared-out hexagon that was the commons of the local tribe. This clearing was at the flower's far edge. A pair of guards flew out to meet us, with rapiers and shell knives at the ready. Their names were Kurt and Kong. Tough characters with ragged beards, well-known to MirrorSeela, but not her friends. They accompanied us to the village green, which was a spot where the flowers' yellow cells had been torn away, leaving bare the blossom's verdant lower layer. Open-doored cells surrounded the clearing—these were the dwellings of the tribe.

Twenty or thirty locals appeared: men, women, and children, with handsome faces and well-formed limbs, lightly dressed in breechcloths and tunics of leaves, petals, and soft bark. The flowerpeople were keen on meeting us, initially taking us for black gods. When I told them we were from somewhere yet further away, beyond the sky, and on the other side of the Rind—that made us only the more intriguing. They marveled that I spoke their tongue, and even more did they wonder to see that my Seela was a young, dark double of theirs.

Just as when I'd visited Seela's original home flower, Arf was the great sensation. Everyone wanted to pet his fur and, in the manner of the flowerpeople, to lick his nose. The noble hound suffered their ministrations with dignity. In return, they fed him scraps of dried fish and meat.

I'd expected, or rather dreaded, that we'd have to face a ruler of some kind, perhaps a peevish queen who might, on a whim, ordain our execution. But the leader, or icon, or mascot, or god of this tribe was something odder than that.

"Look," said Seela, pointing past the flowerpeople. Something bulged over there, metallic and shiny.

"A fried egg craft!" I exclaimed. Seela and I had seen one before, and I'd based my name for it on its shape, that is, the fried egg was a disk-shaped object some forty feet across, with a central dome fifteen feet in diameter. And I knew by now that the locals called it a *veem*. Its dome was a cabin with a big window, two small portholes, and a door that was presently closed.

"It's the very same one," said Seela as we kicked toward it. She was right. I recognized the hieroglyphs and the pattern of holes upon its rim. The very same fried egg that Seela, Eddie and I had fished out of the Umpteen Seas about a year ago—a year, that is, of my own body's time.

The fried egg, or *veem*, was inscribed with symbols upon its flat rim and upon the inner walls of its cabin. Having studied these pictographs, we'd determined that the fried egg was an alien space craft which had brought the *woomo*—and us humans—to this, our Hollow Earth.

When we'd first found the fried egg, we'd been intent on making our way back to the outer surface of the Hollow Earth. And so Eddie, Seela, and I had settled into the domed cabin with Arf, and we'd prevailed upon a helpful *woomo* named Uxa to hurl us across the Hollow Earth's inner sky, thus landing us in an ocean upon the inner side of the Rind. Eddie had then contrived to close the fried egg's door and, buoyed by the air in the cabin, the craft had wobbled up through the sea, emerging in the Chesapeake Bay. When we debarked, we'd left the door open, and the *veem* sank, presumably all the way back to the surface of very sea that arched up across the inner Rind. And now here it was on this flower, and we were next to it. Once again, causes and effects were intertwining.

"I see something inside it," said Seela peering through the *veem's* window. "Like a big soft yam lying on the floor. A larva or grub worm or a slug."

I would have liked to go inside, but the fried egg's door was closed, and I felt uneasy about trying to open it.

"That's a baby *woomo* asleep in there," said MirrorSeela, joining us. "Her name is Nyoo. We worship her."

So the flowerpeople had a queen of sorts after all. But—a *woomo*?

"Tallulah dragged the *veem* here last year," added MirrorSeela. "Your shrig friend. The *veem* was Tallulah's gift to us so that Karl and Kong don't hunt her while she feeds in the jungle. She brought the *veem*, yes, and after a few days I took the notion to put my rumby inside the *veem*. The rumby was talking to me about it, not with words. With tekelili. I put my rumby in the *veem*, and at first—nothing. But then, a day later, a ray of light came from the *woomo* in the sky. It went inside the *veem* and tickled my rumby."

Seela nodded, enthralled. "The rumby hatched?"

"A baby *woomo*," said MirrorSeela. "Little Nyoo. Thanks to me. Look. She makes pink light." She rapped the hilt of her shell knife against the fried egg's window. The little shape inside writhed, then lifted one end. The end was puckered. Nyoo the *woomo* flexed her body and pushed out a—branching tree of flesh. Like soft coral, or like fungus, and the branches were flexing, and they had fronds at the ends. A faint glow formed along the branches, a pale pink aura, and then came a steady stream of pink light, smooth as milk pouring from a pitcher, flowing from the *woomo* and playing across the inner walls' hieroglyphs, and the cabin's silvery surfaces, and the broken-off control upon the panel within the fried egg. The beam focused, then lanced out through the glass of the fried egg's window, etching a bright line across the Hollow Earth's sky. The flowerpeople cheered, but with an undertone of awe or even fear.

"*Nyoo!*" they cried. "*Gooba'am Nyoo!*"

"We're the only flowerpeople whose queen is a *woomo*," said MirrorSeela with pride.

"Was your old queen called Quaihlaihle?" I asked.

"Yes," answered MirrorSeela. "She wanted to forbid me from putting my rumby inside the *veem*. She wanted Kurt and Kong to stop me. My rumby called Tallulah, and Tallulah ate the queen."

"I thought shrigs don't eat people," I said.

"Tallulah did anyway. Kurt and Kong say it's another reason they should eat Tallulah."

"Lots of eating," I said to Seela in English. "Not safe here."

"Don't you let Brumble out of sight," said Seela, also in English. The baby was crying in her arms. He was hungry and he didn't like the rough, jumbled noise of the crowd. "You watch over Brumble even when you start rutting on MirrorSeela."

"Who says I'll do that?"

438

"You don't fool me one bit, Mason Reynolds. You're slobbering over MirrorSeela, jaded old prick-pocket that she is." This was similar to the line of attack Seela had taken regarding Ina. "Not that I mind," continued Seela, throwing in a heartbroken shrug. "It's fine, I'm sure. I'm in no shape for sex. So it's natural for you to run after any woman who crooks her finger. It's a knife in my heart, yes, but I'll grin and pretend I'm wanton too. You're a man, and—"

"Should we just leave right now?" I interrupted. "I don't care about MirrorSeela. You're the one for me, Seela. Always. Should I call Tallulah for a ride?"

"Too tired." said Seela mustering a weak smile of triumph. She held tiny Brumble against her shoulder, patting him. "Let's go into that grabby hag MirrorSeela's cell and rest."

MirrorSeela was watching us, not quite sure what we were saying, but surely catching the drift. But she was in fact a much kinder person than Seela was making her out to be. She led us to her apartment—which was two adjacent flower cells off the main square—and she made us comfortable. And then she went back out with Arf, wanting to show him off to her friends.

Seela and I refreshed ourselves with water, flowerleather and dried eel, and I told her I loved her, and made much of her, and agreed that men are worthless. And then we talked a little about the fried egg and the *woomo*, not coming to any real conclusions. We were too tired to work out any plans. As we talked, Seela nursed Brumble to satiation, and then we lay down and napped on the soft floor, with our arms around each other and dear baby Brumble in between.

By the way, I realize it sounds as if we were sleeping very often, but events were coming at us in an unrelenting torrent, and we needed to rest when we could. Also keep in mind that there's no night inside the Hollow Earth, and that most of the denizens alternate between sleeping and waking in short cycles.

We woke to the sound of MirrorSeela and MirrorYurgen arguing. He'd snapped out of his *juube* trance and had made his way back to the apartment, shaky and disheveled. MirrorSeela was helping him to clean himself and to don freshly-picked petals. His mood was very much worse than before. Noticing I was awake, he scowled at me with hatred. And then he went outside. A murmur mixed with cheers rose among the flowerpeople. Several hundred of them had gathered.

"I'll introduce you to the tribe," MirrorSeela told us. "And then Yurgen will play. Depending what he does, you might not want to stay here very long." MirrorSeela paused. "And I just might leave with you." She smiled ingratiatingly, as if hoping for approval. Seeing this worn woman in her moment of uncertainty, my heart went out to her.

I could sense that Seela wasn't quite happy with this, but she wasn't fully against the prospect either. MirrorSeela was, after all, her twin.

Are you quite sure you can summon Tallulah?" was all Seela said..

Laying my hand upon my dense, plump, living rumby I communed with its tekelili. Somehow the mind of a dreaming, unborn *woomo* was embodied within this curious gem. How strange. The rumby's tekelili was indeed so intense that I could reach all the way to Tallulah, off in the jungle nearby.

As I made contact, it struck me that the shrig wasn't anything like so stupid as I'd imagined. Gluttonous, clumsy, comical—but not dumb. She was devouring greasy pods that resembled varicolored bananas, although maybe they were something else. Her gut swelled with fart, but she was holding in the gas. Building up her supply. She sensed my tekelili, and wordlessly she told me she was ready to come at any time. She knew about the unborn *woomo* within my fat rumby gem. She'd known all along. Sensing a coming crisis, I urged her to begin her approach, and to hide herself beneath the underside of the flower.

Meanwhile Seela and I followed MirrorSeela out of her living-quarters, with Seela nursing Brumble at her breast. The windows of the fried egg were dark again. Nyoo the *woomo* slumbered. But the village green was lit with the unceasing warm-summer-afternoon glow of the Hollow Earth. The crowd stared at us, eyes bright, very curious, and hopping into the air, the better to see us. The mood was cheerful, with many of them holding slices of *juube*.

Someone had fastened a long, hollow plant stem so that it sloped from the flower's upper surface down to the village green. Its smaller end was tied to a branch protruding from the ground. MirrorYurgen stood beside it, at the ready, with Kurt and Kong poised behind him, as if guarding his back.

MirrorSeela took Seela's free hand, and my hand, holding them high. She spoke briefly to the crowd, saying she was glad to have us here, that Seela was her double, and that this was another a sign of divine *woomo* favor toward their tribe.

"*Ahnaa bogbog Ma'aassong lamalama Seela gloloo Brumble. Nicabange nansi A'arf! Doolango emthonjeni womculo. Jjanjee woomo? Thul'ulale sini lindile. Gooba'am!*"

The crowd roared. A dirty-faced little boy named Peepy handed me some chunks of *juube*. A voluptuous woman pressed herself against my right side, ignoring Seela on my left. A man smiled at Seela and offered her bright bits of shell. Old people cooed at Brumble. Arf perched at our feet, looking around with interest.

And then MirrorYurgen's music began. The reverb tube had a taut shrigskin membrane across its small end, and MirrorYurgen sang into a small hole in the center of this hide. Evidently there was another such drumhead across the wide end of the tube, some hundred feet off. MirrorYurgen's voice resonated inside the great tube, building up layers, with the sounds overlapping and forming beats, reminding me of crisscross waves in a current. He chanted and crooned a tune that meandered up and down a half-note at a time. It reminded me of an Oriental dirge I'd heard a Malay sailor play on a flute during his companion's burial at sea. As amplified by the reverberating tube, the effect of MirrorYurgen's song was entrancing, and even hypnotic.

The crowd was in a festive mood. Everyone was smiling at us, and at each other. The flowerpeople swayed in a slow dance, and those who were intoxicated by *juube* were caressing each other. The guardsmen Kurt and Kong were fixated upon MirrorYurgen, utterly absorbed by his performance, staring at him from only a few inches away.

But things were turning sour. Each time MirrorYurgen paused to grab a breath, he glared over at me, shooting daggers with his eyes. He was jealous about the budding relationship I had with his MirrorSeela. And, more than that, he wanted my Seela for his own.

With the consummate craft of a mature artist, MirrorYurgen began weaving his emotions into his performance. Harsh tones entered his stream of song, and his changes in pitch were abrupt, driving away any sense of comfort. Were the flowerpeople regarding me in a less friendly way than before? Yes. The woman who'd been rubbing me with her breasts now favored me with a sharp elbow to the kidney. The *juube*-bearing urchin Peepsy pulled Arf's tail. The man who'd been admiring Seela took rough hold of her shoulder, as if meaning to violate her. With a quick kick, Seela knocked the oaf off balance, and then stunned him with a knee to his head. He withdrew, bleeding from his nose. But more enemies waited. And Brumble was crying very loud.

MirrorYurgen had a gloating, saturnine air—like a cruel jester at a feast where his rival is to be slain. His music surged and throbbed. Kurt and Kong detached themselves from MirrorYurgen and began pushing through the crowd, coming my way. They carried barbed spears much longer than the rapiers they'd borne before. Somehow the baby *woomo* in the fried egg was still asleep. The windows of the *veem* remained dark.

"Call Tallulah!" MirrorSeela urged me in her tongue. "And remember that I'm leaving with you."

"It is well," said Seela. "Hurry, Mason."

No need to tell me. I was already putting my full energy into my tekelili summoning of the shrig. Here she was, bumbling through the ruff of white petals at the flower's edge, rising like a bloated moon.

Seela, MirrorSeela, and I were already wearing our pulpul airfins. It was a simple thing to hop into the air, and kick toward the edge of the flower where the baby *woomo* slumbered within the dark fried egg. MirrorYurgen's ugly, angry music was raging. The flowerpeople were out for our blood—reaching toward us and hollering imprecations. A few were airborne like us, and we managed to dodge them, but here came the formidable Kurt and Kong, hefting their weapons. Did they mean to kill us outright?

With no pause in their motion, the two guards used throwing sticks to hurl their barbed lances our way. Time seemed to stop. I noticed that the spears had long cords unwinding from their ends. Harpoons. Rather than striking Seela and me, they flew past us—and sank deep into the fatty abdomen of dear Tallulah.

Wheenk!

My tekelili told me that the wounded shrig was about to flee upon a flaming jet of fart. But in that instant Kong had already hauled himself over to her, and had slashed open Tallulah's belly with a broadsword made of *ballula* shell. The shrig's store of gas blatted ineffectually into the air, spreading a sad, miasmal stench across the village green. Mirror Yurgen's music had come to a stop.

In this silent moment of dismay, the two women and I landed upon the rim of the fried egg, me carrying Arf, and Seela bearing Brumble. I executed a carefully reasoned-out gesture that Eddie Poe had taught me—a looping sweep of my hand across the outer surface of the domed cabin. My move worked—the door opened. And once we were inside, I used the reverse of Eddie's move to close the hatch behind us, blocking out Kurt and Kong.

As the two bandits pounded against the *veem*, Nyoo the baby *woomo* awoke and filled the chamber with intense pink light. Taking a quick look around, I recognized the same features as before. This *veem* was of an incalculable antiquity, tens of thousands of years in age. It had a stubby, broken stand that might once have supported a seat, and the brackets on the wall might have held bunks. Undoubtedly it had been an airship. The inside of the cabin wasn't a full hemisphere, for a section of it was walled off by a bulkhead. Eddie had said there must be a stove of some kind in there to produce the aethereal lifting gas that allowed the fried egg to fly. Friezes and cartouches of pictograms and hieroglyphs were embossed upon into the cabin's dully shining walls like tattoos upon skin.

The walls were smooth and luminous. Not metal. Too soft for that. The embossed images on the walls showed the cucumber-like bodies of the *woomo*, and their branching fans, and fried-egg craft, and some figures that were surely ants, women, and men. The ants, *woomo* and the humans had traveled together to Earth in the primordial past, long before the dawn of known history.

Kurt was bashing at the fried egg's front window with a stone axe. Seela and MirrorSeela were emphatically pointing this out to me. What to do? We needed to nudge the *veem* off the edge of the village green so that it could drift into the sky, thence falling inward to the core.

Again I put myself into tekelili contact with Tallulah. Kong had cut her throat, and her ichor was leaking out in wobbly globules. The poor beast had entered her death flurry; she was flopping spasmodically upon the village green. Some of the flowerpeople were already in the act of butchering her, carving off hunks of her tasty meat whenever she was momentarily still. Her mind was a contracting vision of the world, dark around the edges and bright at its core.

"Please push us," I beseeched the shrig, using images rather than words. "Set us free. Push the *veem*."

The good Tallulah gave one last snap of her great tail. Our ancient fried egg craft skidded across the surface of the village green and we were in free fall. On our way to the core.

10. Fwopsy

A rabble of flowerpeople came after us, wanting to drag our craft back to the village green. But their combined forces were insufficient to divert the stately path of our craft. And with the fried egg craft's door closed, we were secure from personal attack. Arf was barking and Brumble was crying, with the noise reverberating within the stuffy confines of our hull.

Slowly the *veem* was gaining velocity. The miles-thick wall of jungle was drifting past. Even so, the mirrorflowerpeople persisted in their attempts to save their prize. Urged on by MirrorYurgen's blasts on the great reverb tube, our pursuers tied vines to the holes in our craft's rim. With Kurt barking commands, they began kicking their air fins in regular rhythm—with disconcerting effect. Our progress slowed and halted. Kurt redoubled his cries. Slowly, slowly we began moving back toward the Rind and the mirrorflower. Eventually we'd have to open the fried egg's door for air. And then Kurt, Kong, and MirrorYurgen would kill me.

"Help," I silently implored our *woomo*. She'd filled our *veem* with a tekelili far stronger than what a rudimentary rumby could produce. Her mind was alight with energy, and she was excited about traveling to the core. But perhaps she didn't realize what was happening. I bent my will to projecting my emotions into her. "You need to save us."

The *woomo* responded with an outward rush of thought.

Sparks leapt from the outer rim of the fried egg, severing the attached vines, and scorching the hands of the importunate flowerpeople. Had the sparks come from the *woomo*, or from the *veem* itself? Hard to say. Cursing and yelling, the pirates fell away. Once more our craft began gaining speed. Mirror-Yurgen's plangent honks faded away.

Inside the freely falling fried egg, Seela, MirrorSeela, Arf, Brumble, Nyoo, and I were as if weightless. We had no tendency to settle upon any particular area of the cabin's dimly shining walls. To my eyes, by the way, the walls seemed increasingly like patterned skin. Could it be possible that the *veem* was alive?

Seela produced a strand of woven bark and fastened Brumble's foot to her wrist, lest he somehow drift away. And then I opened the door so we could have fresh air. Our motion was producing a stiff breeze. Arf knew to stay back lest he be whirled out. I noticed also that Arf kept a healthy distance from Nyoo. I don't think he liked *woomo*.

Nyoo damped down her pink glow, but by now MirrorSeela was as black as Seela and me. We all agreed the pigmentation looked well on her. We drifted at our ease, watching the Rind move away. Seela nursed Brumble and then, after a fit of hiccups, he fell asleep, floating in the air beside her. Meanwhile MirrorSeela and I were eying each other with admiration.

"But no, you're not going to poke your member into me," said told me via tekelili. Unwelcome news.

"Thank you," Seela said to MirrorSeela.

"You're my sister," MirrorSeela told her. "You're me. And that's why it means nothing if you and I kiss."

"But—but what about me helping you have a baby?" I asked MirrorSeela, playing the only card I had.

"There's plenty of men at the Umpteen Seas," said Seela tartly.

"I don't want a man," said MirrorSeela. "Just a drop of seed. I need a rest from men." She and Seela burst into laughter at this sally.

I didn't mind their teasing. I was with two women and we were on a wonderful journey. Seela and I had a healthy baby, and in a few weeks Seela and I would be making love again. Moreover, my intense tekelili contact with the two Seelas felt satisfyingly erotic. I had a constant sense that I was merging with them. Not quite like sex, but for now I was content.

I noticed that, by means of occasional twitches of its rim, our *veem* was keeping itself on an even keel. Was the airship awaking from an eons-long slumber?

In any case, rather than spinning, tumbling or, worse, swooping back and forth like a feather, we were slicing through the air edge-on. This meant that our drag was low. I hazarded a guess that we were going sixty miles per hour. Which meant we'd reach the center after fifty hours of falling. Two days.

And so we sat and chatted, savoring the intimacy of our close tekelili contact. Intermittently we dozed, or saw to Brumble's needs. Arf had his snout pointed up, continually sniffing this strange sky's airs.

As always, I delighted in the joyous curving sweep of the Hollow Earth's inner Rind—not to mention the pink streamers. the jungles and seas, the scattered clouds, the dotted flocks of flying beasts, and the odd, lensing quality of the space at the core. And with Nyoo the *woomo* aboard as our ally, I wasn't much worried about carnivorous shell-squids and the like.

But there was a problem. Stupidly enough, Seela and I had once again set out upon a long sky journey with no food or water. Food wasn't crucial—I expected us to reach the core in another day. But we did need water, particularly with Seela nursing.

Again I let my psyche mingle with our *woomo's* mind. Nyoo had a sense of pride about ushering two outer-world sojourners to the Hollow Earth's core, a nd she was pondering the friezes of glyphs that covered our rounded cabin's walls. I studied the images with her. Certainly there were images of *veem* craft—most of them round, rather than like hemispherical fried eggs. Within the craft I saw, as I mentioned before, images of *woomo* and humans and ants."

"The humans are natural pilots," said Nyoo. "I think you could do it."

"When?" I asked.

I could tell that Nyoo had some specific mission in mind, but she wouldn't share the details. The Central Anomaly was involved. I earnestly hoped I wouldn't have to go back in there.

Getting back to basics, I did my best to make Nyoo aware that we were thirsty. The little creature gave me no direct answer. Instead she crawled across the floor like a foraging sea-slug, and thrust her stubby snout into the wind rushing past our open door. She aimed a narrow pink streamer toward the core and wobbled it.

Apparently she was calling to her relatives. A thick tendril of light came our way. The forking stream of radiance reached into our vessel and played across our faces, as if getting to know us. I felt the vast calm of the Great Old Ones at Earth's core, and I had a sense of being surrounded by choral song. A spare, crooked epigram entered my mind.

> The past not now
> The future not yet
> Between two nots
> Is

Well and good, but now the fat light stream flicked out to the Rind and back, thereby fetching several hundred gallons of water into our fried egg's chamber, the water in a single mass that engulfed my legs and sloshed over the heads and shoulders of the two Seelas.

We flailed our limbs, sputtering and shrieking, more glad than frightened. The water split into juddering globs that repeatedly divided and rejoined as they danced around us—like miniature versions of the Umpteen Seas at the Hollow Earth's core.

Brumble, who'd been momentarily submerged, was in a paroxysm of fury. Arf was lapping at the globs, slaking his thirst. Seela held Brumble against her shoulder with one arm, while using her free hand to scoop water into her mouth. I gulped down a pint that I gathered with both hands, and then I took the outraged Brumble from Seela so she drink faster.

In a few minutes the bulk of the water had jounced out the door, with a only few blobs still inside the fried egg. During the inundation, Nyoo the *woomo* had used her bumpy skin to cling to the floor near the door. And now she was on the move again, creeping back to the cabin's center. She waved a cheerful tendril at me.

"Thank you," said I, bowing to the far-fetched creature.

"I hope you didn't ask for food," said Seela. "Who knows what they'd bring. How much longer will we fall?"

"Maybe twenty hours," said I.

"I *do* want food," said MirrorSeela.

No sooner said than done. Nyoo the *woomo* angled a jagged beam out the door, and the fat light stream from the core returned. Again it twitched out to the Rind—and our cabin was cluttered with those multicolored banana-like objects I'd seen Tallulah devouring in the jungle beside the mirrorflower.

The objects within the colored rinds had a redolent, meaty quality. They weren't bananas, they were pupae from some unknown insect. The pupae were oily, with a bitter quality beneath their cloying sweetness. But we ate our fill just the same. And I was quite sure I saw several of the meaty things being swallowed by slits in the *veem's* floor.

Dazed and stupefied by our unwise repast, we slept. I had a dream of sex with the two Seelas, and I awoke in a state of excitement. As it happened, MirrorSeela was in fact fondling me in an intimate manner. Amused and titillated by the game, my Seela was kissing her elder double. Floating in the air beside us, Brumble dozed.

Seeing my eyes open, the two women withdrew, and feigned an air of primness—smirking at me withal. Was their teasing an idle pastime, or did it mean more? Light-headed with lust, I brazenly finished what their lubricious play had begun. The Seelas caressed each other as they watched. I asked no more. I was seventeen, and this was heaven enow. As my sweet spasm subsided, MirrorSeela used a fingertip to ensure that a bit of my seed made its way to her womb. I was glad.

In a calm mood of exaltation, we ate some more of those bright-skinned insect pupae, and scavenged up the last few floating globs of water. Meanwhile we were passing through a zone of feeding shrigs. They tended to gather fifteen miles out from the Umpteen Seas, scavenging the slowly drifting debris of the entire Hollow Earth. They feared to go very much further in, as the black gods were so fond of hunting them for leather and meat.

A couple of the shrigs nosed at us, but Seela and I, as well as the more powerful Nyoo, used our tekelili to project images of shrig-friendliness and of inedibility. MirrorSeela was in a tizzy, but our efforts were sufficient to ward off the languid flying pigs. There were, after all, many other things to eat here—corpses, offal, and the rich debris of the jungles—all of them freely adrift. The Hollow Earth's inward attraction died out in this zone,

Carried onward by inertia, we slowly coasted through the last dozen miles, closing in on the Umpteen Seas. At any given time there were between a dozen and a score of these miles-long bodies of water—they were continually merging and breaking apart. Once again I had a fond memory of how in the summers on the farm, Otha and I would throw buckets of water into the air and delight at the water's jiggles. I wondered how Otha was doing.

Beyond the Umpteen Seas was the inner zone where the ancient *woomos* lived—arranged upon the surface of that invisible and impalpable sphere known as the Central Anomaly or the Gate—the very throat of the tunnel between MirrorEarth and Earth.

Unceasing streams of pink light flowed from the *woomo* tendrils. The tekelili in the air was intense—my two Seelas' minds were warm and clear, and even Brumble's and Arf's thoughts were manifest—not that they were thinking much. I savored the comfortable joy of this heavenly zone.

I peered inward, hoping to spot some of the black gods, or even Eddie Poe and Ina. But now came an interruption.

It was that juvenile royal ant whom we'd seen hatched at the North Hole—the one who'd flown inward toward the core, rather than following the others into the sea. I recognized his psychic vibrations. He was some twelve feet long now, with a flattened round head, a tapering torso, and a plump gaster bulge at the rear. Although he had antennae, he still lacked mandibles, and his up-curved mouth was like a melon-slice cut from his head, which gave him a cheerful air. His faceted eyes were the size of dinner plates, and his skin was a rich and reflective purplish-green with an iridescent sheen. As before, his legs were still just two rows of bumps. And he had the stubby wings, and a nascent spike at his rear. He hovered by our *veem*, peering in through our craft's door at Nyoo.

Seela had said the royal ants and the *woomo* were partners. Yet I'd seen Fafnir and the *woomo* blasting intense rays at each other. So I was half-expecting a fight. But Nyoo seemed pleased to see the juvenile royal ant. The two of them had a rapid, wordless, tekelili conversation which, in its rough outlines, I might represent as follows.

Ant: I'm Skolder. You ride with humans—why?
Woomo: I'm Nyoo. We aim to gather rumbies for a Bloom.
Ant: It's past time for a Bloom.
Woomo: We need to awaken the *veem*. The one called Eddie Poe will help.
Ant: I will aid with my zap. Charge me.
Woomo: Will you eat me if I come close to you?
Ant: I have as yet no pinchers, Nyoo.

Nyoo bid us a temporary farewell, and flew out of our door. As if stimulated by the presence of the ant, the *woomo* swelled abruptly in size, growing into a warty sea cucumber some twenty feet long. The ant narrowed his shape by pressing his wings against himself and tightening the bulges of his body. Nyoo widened one of her ends, and formed a cylindrical cavity. The ant slipped into Nyoo's body like a spit into a chicken, like a sausage into a bun, like a dagger into a sheath.

Given my erotic byplay with the Seelas, I naturally took the *woomo*-ant union to be in some way sexual—but the coupling was, rather, a way for Nyoo to infuse Skolder with an extremely high electrical charge. The *woomo* were prodigious sources of electrical fluid. And, with their separated thorax and gaster, the royal ants could behave like Leyden jars, or like Volta's galvanic piles, that is, they could store a titanic reservoir of electrical fluid for an abrupt release.

As Nyoo was charging up the ant, her numinous tekelili aura reached a critical state. And for a moment, I accessed a higher level of knowledge.

- The flying fried eggs, or *veem*, are alive.
- Ants, humans, *woomo*, and *veem* work together in a symbiosis.
- Our Hollow Earth bears our four races on a journey through the stars
- Occasionally the four races send a colony to another world. This is a Bloom.
- The *veem* craft bear the colonists across space during a Bloom.
- The humans pilot and speed the *veem*.
- The royal ants hollow out the colony world for the *woomo*.
- The *woomo* orchestrate the evolution of the colony world, and guide its travels.

It was as I'd been groping in a night landscape—now illuminated by a bolt of lightning. I'd already gotten some hints regarding the nature of the Bloom, and the role of the royal ants. But the full truth had been eluding me.

I stood slack-jawed, staring out the fried egg's door, in a state of exaltation, dazed by the psychic intensity of Nyoo's tekelili, and doing my best to note the details of my revelation for inclusion in this narrative you read, *Return to the Hollow Earth*.

The two curious creatures pinwheeled away, their tekelili voices raised in silent song. They passed behind the nearest of the Umpteen Seas and vanished for a time. Meanwhile our fried egg ship had drifted to a full stop. This was the terminal zone—a gutter in space, if you will, a resting place before the inmost core. I hoped we'd find Eddie Poe here.

The nearest of the Umpteen Seas was wobbling as if it might soon engulf us. For me this was not a disturbing prospect. The miles-long, floating lakes had clean, sparkling water and edible fish. And this one contained a substantial island at its other end. We could kick our way to this bit of land with our airfins or *pulpuls*. But MirrorSeela was alarmed.

"We're fine," Seela reassured her. Like me, she'd been to the core before. "The black gods will greet us." Her voice rose. "Look! Here they come."

Two well-formed black gods were approaching, a man and woman, both of them riding the polished scraps of *ballula* shell that they called lightboards. If you positioned your lightboard along the edge of a *woomo's* great pink streamer, you could ride the wake of heated air that surrounded the tube of light. One of the black gods looked familiar. I'd known her as Shrighunter on the other side of the Central Anomaly. Presumably this was her MirrorEarth double.

And the man—he was more than familiar, he was the first friend of my youth, my companion on my initial trip to the Hollow Earth, the beloved equal whom I'd left at the core when I traveled on to MirrorEarth, and a kinsman of sorts—in that we shared a common half-brother.

"Otha!" cried I, my voice cracking.

"Mase!" called Otha, gliding up to us and stopping his motion with a kick of his shrig-leather *pulpul*. "You done rode back on this old fried egg? With *two* Seelas? And, looky here, it's Arf and a baby!"

"We call him Brumble," said Seela. "It's fine to see you, Otha. You didn't get old. Not like my twin MirrorSeela."

"Are both you women doing the juicy with Mason?" asked Otha, never one to stand on ceremony.

"Not exactly," I said. "Not in the ways I'd like."

"The ways *we* like," said MirrorSeela, touching her belly. "Mason is useful."

"Tell us how you got to this side of the Gate," Seela said to Otha.

"I come through it same as you. Lookin to find my woman. Shrighunter. We two was bundled tight. She disappeared on a hunt, Mason, and I missed her so hard, I pushed through that *woomo* Gate to see if she might be here. Watcher said naw, the two sides are mostly the same, but that ain't true, not since you and me and Eddie Poe come to stir it up. And

I *did* get Shrighunter back, see? She didn't know me none, but I worked my mojo, same as before."

"So this is *MirrorShrighunter* you're with," I primly said.

"Ain't no mirror about her," said Otha. "Go on and introduce yourself to the new Shrighunter, brother Mason."

Otha was right, it would be petifogging pedantry to Mirror-modify the name of each familiar black god we found. Suffice it to say that the Mirror versions were substantially like the ones we'd met on the Central Anomaly's other side. Shrighunter, Watcher, Jewel, Smoker, Offerer—I soon encountered versions of them all.

Thanks to tekelili, I was quickly fast friends with the new Shrighunter. She enjoyed the sampler of Otha-memories that I offered her, and she laughed at my story of the time Otha had inadvertently exploded a shrig—by slitting open its gassy gut while its butt-flame was lit.

"That story ain't funny no more, Mase," interjected Otha. "Might could be that's how the old Shrighunter died. She'd borrowed my steel knife."

I felt the pang of Otha's grief. But even so, we were soon in a festive mood—especially after he told me that, yes, Eddie Poe, Ina, and Connor Machree were already here. We found them on the large island at the end of the nearby Umpteen Sea—it was a popular gathering spot for the black gods. We met amid cheers, with greetings all around.

"You rode up on a *woomo* ray of light?" Seela asked Machree, still miffed about the jeweler's special treatment. Smugly he nodded.

The island was mostly above water just now, and coated with wiry grass and little white flowers. We'd contrived to tow our fried egg after us, and we fastened it to tufts of grass with a woven rope. I hadn't forgotten Nyoo's suggestion that we might somehow restore the fried egg or *veem* to a fully living status. That new ant Skolder might help, now that Nyoo had fed him such a powerful charge. And perhaps Eddie could do something. On our first trip, Eddie had spent days and weeks studying the *veem's* hieroglyphs.

The black gods Smoker and Watcher were here, and Jewel would soon arrive. Because Seela, Eddie, and I had lost a dozen years during our passage through the Gate on our first journey, these versions of our black god friends were older than the originals—but I hardly noticed.

Remember that, due to the salutatory effect of so much tekelili, the black gods have lifespans of three hundred years. In the face of that, a decade does little to change their appearance. Time's passage had, however, left stronger traces on the less than happy MirrorSeela. But here in the cheerful company of the black gods, she already seemed more bright and youthful.

Smoker, as always, had a wicker basket filled with choice bits of dried meats—shrig meat, fish filets, and chunks of the small sea creatures who nestled in the island's tangled grasses. He was sedulously offering his treats to MirrorSeela, and she was favoring him with warm smiles. I should mention, by the way, that the black gods were using tekelili to talk with us, and their lips didn't move when they spoke.

"Hallelujah!" exclaimed Eddie. "We stand united at the heart of eternity!"

"With the changes never done," said old Watcher.

Let me mention again that, even though the speech of the black gods was silent tekelili, I tended to hear their words as if spoken in a black accent similar to Otha's. In Otha's opinion, this indicated that black people were in fact the original, and higher, race of humans on Earth, and that their modes of speech were more correct, and to be preferred.

"Changes because of *us*?" pert Ina replied to Watcher's remark. She was nestled against Eddie's side. Ever the coquette, she threw back her head and poured out a merry laugh. "And we're just black people from California," she added—by now all of us were indeed dark-skinned. Ina focused a bright eye on me. "Looks like our Mason fished up an extra Seela!"

"Seela's older twin," I said.

"Bedazzling," said Smoker. "A ripe flowerperson. You liking it here, Seela the elder?"

"Leave out the *elder*," said MirrorSeela, extending her arms as if taking in her surroundings. "This is stunning. Vast.

Everything is everywhere. And the tekelili—so rich and strong. I know exactly what you're thinking, Smoker."

"Do it suit you?

"Well, I *am* in need of a man," said MirrorSeela, contradicting what she'd said to me in the in the fried egg. Perhaps Smoker looked to be a better long-term prospect. "I left my partner," MirrorSeela continued, and then paused, as if looking down into herself. "And, and I may be with child."

"Fast work by our Mason," trilled Ina. "Too bad young Seela has claimed him. The boy is *such* a catch!"

"Am *I* not a catch?" said Eddie, inclining his head toward his saucy flirt. "Or am I, rather, an aging, inky, half-mad scribbler?"

"Our raw nation's literary master," said Ina. "The true Edgar Allan Poe. And you've brought me to this paradise. Huzzah, my dear. I taste and savor your mind, Edgar. I'd do well at declaiming your poems onstage. You and I could go on tour. You'd manage me, under your cognomen of Goarland Peale—and I'd perform. I'm a very quick study."

"A cunning hoax," said Eddie slowly, thinking this over. "A way to make a living—short of undertaking a second passage through the uncanny Gate between worlds. The closer it is, the more I dread it."

"I fear that Central Anomaly too," said Ina.

"What say you and I return to the MirrorEarth," Poe said to Ina.

"I'll return with you two," put in Machree. "Bringing my load of rumbies."

"Don't interrupt," said Eddie. "I'm telling Ina that I see a way for us to capitalize on the vulgar notion that Edgar Allan Poe is dead." He pressed the back of his hand to his forehead, like an actor recounting a vision. "I see Ina Durivage on stage, performing Poe's posthumous work—a clairvoyant Ina, sensitive to spirit voices from the other world! First-rate flimflam. And in this wise I can decant my versified epic *Htrae* into the public ear. By Deadgar Ailing Pro." He smiled, but his expression was resolved. "I jest not."

"Very fine," said Ina, assimilating the plan. "We'll go back home together, yes. And avoid that spooky Gate. We'll—we'll get up subscriptions for our performances. Your epic, you call it *Htrae?*"

"*Earth* spelled backwards," I told Ina. "Eddie talks about it all the time. Not that I've read or heard any of it."

"I compose in my head," said Eddie, turning haughty. "Like the bards Dante and Homer. The oral tradition, where rhymes and iambs house the words. Each night I form verses in my head, and the recording angels bear them away."

Grandiose though Eddie's words were, and much as I doubted he was in fact working on his project, his underlying notion resonated with me. Lacking time or the facilities to write out a draft of *Return to the Hollow Earth*, I really had been drafting my narrative in my head.

In the near distance the bulky *woomo* creatures lolled, stretching their tendrils. They were positioned upon the oddly glowing sphere that was the Gate, or Central Anomaly, the improbable nexus which links the hearts of the two Hollow Earths. The *woomo* had a way of steadily rolling their bodies like roasts on spits, and thereby sweeping their tendrils between the worlds. Faint images of the Umpteen Seas on the other side could be glimpsed between the warty bodies of the *woomo*. Like Eddie, I had little desire to venture in there again.

"It's tolerable in there," put in Watcher, alert to my thoughts. "A fountain of youth. I can slip by fifty years in a flash."

"Skipping twelve years is enough, huh, Mase?" said Otha.

"And I went through as fast as I could," said I.

Machree cleared his throat. He wasn't quite following our discussion. By way of changing the subject, he addressed a question to the statuesque Shrighunter. "With regard to your Great Old Ones—the *woomo?* Are they friendly?"

"I expect so," said Shrighunter, a bit wary of Machree. "If they weren't friendly, we'd be dead."

"Good," said Machree. "My belief is that the *woomo* want me to gather jewels and to bring them to the Earth's surface. I'm speaking of rumby gems? The *woomo* saved me from a shipwreck, and carried me to this core—to be close to the gems. But I'm not clear if I need to pay the *woomo* for them—or what I *could* in fact pay."

"Listen at him," said Shrighunter. "The man thinks he's makin deals with the *woomo*."

"The *woomo* aren't shopkeepers," put in Watcher. "If they want something, they take it. If they want to give something, they do."

"They'll give me rumbies for free?" pressed Machree.

"It's time that all of you know that rumbies are *woomo* eggs," burst in MirrorSeela.

I think Watcher already knew this, but the other black gods were surprised.

"*Woomo eggs!*" sang out Jewel, who'd recently arrived to perch herself next to Otha. "Why didn't nobody tell me? How you find that out, Seela elder?"

"A *woomo* tendril handed me a fat rumby, down on my flower by the Rind, and then it hatched," said MirrorSeela. "Hatched inside this beat-up old thing that we rode here in." She nodded toward the ancient craft we'd tied to the grasses.

"*La no*," exclaimed Jewel in wonder. "Can't hardly believe it."

Jewel's role among the black gods was to collect rumbies, to weave them into little nets upon string necklaces, and to supply them to her companions. It was Jewel who'd given Eddie, Seela, and me our rumbies last year—or, rather, the gift had come from Jewel's counterpart, who lived on the other side of the Central Anomaly.

That other Jewel was, as Eddie had already confided to me, a woman greatly to his liking. And presumably his feelings for this Jewel were much the same. But he was containing any signs of passion. Firstly, this Jewel had never seen him before and might not even find him attractive. Secondly, Eddie was now in the web of the eccentric Ina. Thirdly, nothing seemed important beside MirrorSeela's stunning news.

"A jewel that's an egg," mused Eddie. "A flame within the gem. A chorus of reflections. A crystalline library, with *woomo* wisdom woven in place."

"All along I thought them rumbies were *refined turds*," said Jewel with a cackle. "Squoze down outta the *woomos'* guts, and with a touch of tekelili in them. Eggs? An egg's supposed to be soft and juicy"

Oblivious to the import of this revelation, Machree turned the conversation to his practical concerns. "Do you think we can ride that broken-down fried-egg airship back to the surface? Collect the rumbies and float up through that column of water that fills the North Hole."

"No more maelstrom in the Hole?" asked Otha.

"You didn't notice?" said Watcher. "Mason and Seela ruined it. They chased off the royal ants."

"My fault," said Ina. "I talk too much." She turned to Seela. "And I'm sorry for being unkind to you, Seela. We need to stick together, we women. I've been a little fool."

"Agreed," said Seela with a slight smile. "And do you promise to leave my Mason alone?"

"I don't want him!" said Ina, doing her all to sound sincere. And maybe she was. "It's Eddie I've set my cap for."

"Wise choice," said Poe.

"It may have been *woomo* tekelili that led you to provoke the royal ants," Watcher told Ina. "By way of bringing on the Bloom. Wheels within wheels."

"It don't matter if the maelstrom's flooded," persisted Machree, dumb as a post. "I tell you, that old fried egg will float."

"You're a bonehead," Seela told him. "Don't you understand that *the rumbies are woomo eggs*? Nobody wants to buy fake gems that hatch into giant sea cucumber gods. And what happens to Earth's surface when we have all those *woomo* flopping around? They might eat everything, or set fires, or dig holes."

"Not my lookout," came Machree's quick response. "Not if I been paid in cash."

Maybe he was teasing. We were all a little giddy here, bathed in the heavy tekelili.

"A shrewd man is our jeweler Machree," said Eddie. "I wish I had his acumen."

"That little *woomo* that we hatched," I put in. "She thinks you can fix our *veem*, Eddie. Bring it back to life. I don't think the *woomo* can do it alone."

Eddie cleared his throat, drew back his shoulders, and puffed himself up. "Yes, I may well be more adept at ratiocination than the Great Old Ones. They dream through the millennia in a mystic glow, fanning fronds of divine light. But to fix a watch, or to analyze a chess-playing machine, or to resurrect an ancient alien—yes, such tasks are best left to a man like me."

"And to a woman like me," put in Ina. "I see the *veem* patterns in your mind, Eddie. And, if you please, I have a more efficacious touch than you. You're a man of words. I stop not at words—I'm a woman of craft."

Arf was rooting in the grass, and he pulled out a small, ordinary sea cucumber, also known as a trepang or *bêche de mer*. It was about the size of a squash, green and warty, with dark purple striations. It had retracted its tendrils in fear. It was leaking water from both ends. Arf held it for a moment his jaws, considering it, and then he dropped it.

"Is that a baby *woomo*?" asked Machree.

"No, no," said Watcher. "Those things in the grass are no-account, low-down, shirt-tail cousins of the Great Old Ones. They're not full *woomo* anymore than a mouse is a man."

"Watcher's right," said MirrorSeela. "When my rumby egg hatched, it was a Great-Old-One kind of *woomo* right away. Not a sad little bag."

Smoker took the trepang from between Arf's feet and used his shell knife to slit it open along its length. Via tekelili, I'd felt the creature's tiny, pitiful spark of life wink out.

"More meat to dry!" said Smoker, scraping out the slimy innards, and stashing the body in his basket.

"I want to see that new baby *woomo* you done hatched out," Jewel told MirrorSeela. "Where's it at?"

As if beckoned by our thoughts, Nyoo came sailing around from the other side of the floating sea and landed on the island at MirrorSeela's side. She readjusted her size—perhaps by flexing or slackening her internal tissues—and now she was the size of a small dog. Her juvenile royal ant friend Skolder was with her, looking a bit more adult than before, dark and glistening, with the beginnings of mandibles at the corners of his mouth.

Nyoo bent one end upwards. The tip had a hole in it like a letter O. She was talking to Eddie—by means of silent tekelili. I could of course hear her too.

"You'll help us fix the *veem*," Nyoo was saying to Eddie. "The Old Ones say you know how. You're smart. You learned from the pictures on the *veem*. You tell me what the *veem* needs, and I can grow it with my light."

"Light into matter," said Eddie. "A sorcerer's dream."

"I'm the wand," said Nyoo. "You're the wizard, Eddie Poe."

"But what are you after?" Eddie asked.

"We *woomo* have been waiting for thousands of years for our next Bloom. And we haven't been able to do it because only two *veem* remain. One *veem* is in hiding, and this one is inert. We need to resurrect it. But none of us *woomo* has the right turn of mind to do it."

"And if I help?" said Eddie. "What then?"

"A new Bloom," said Nyoo. "Three *veem*, some royal ants, a hundred rumbies, and an Adam and Eve. Upon this reed, a new world can blossom."

"Resurrect this fried egg to start with," echoed Eddie. "Yes."

He reached out and touched Nyoo's sparkling hide. The *woomo* gave him a friendly shock. Due to tekelili, the rest of us could precisely calibrate the strength of the stimulus—a pleasant tickle.

By the way, how many of us were present? I make it sixteen. Thirteen humans: me, Seela, Brumble, Arf, MirrorSeela, Smoker, Otha, Shrighunter, Eddie, Ina, Machree, Jewel, and Watcher. And three others: Nyoo, Skolder, and the fried egg. Assuming it was fair to count the *veem* as a conscious being. And, as we soon saw, it was.

Holding Nyoo under one arm like a lapdog, Eddie hopped onto the shiny rim of the fried egg and went into the cabin. Aiming the *woomo's* tip like a hose, Eddie let its light play across the interior—guiding the *woomo* energy with his nimble and responsive mind, and taking into account Ina's clean concepts of design.

The broken column before the control panel grew like the stalk of a plant. A tulip-like seat formed on the tube's crown. It was mounted on a swivel, so that, whichever way the craft turned, a pilot could sit at any angle desired. Next, Eddie, Ina and the *woomo* healed the broken stub upon the control panel. The restored control was simplicity itself: a protruding rod with a spherical bulb on the end. A pilot had only sit in the chair and waggle the knob.

With Eddie and Nyoo's attention, the ship's weathered friezes of hieroglyphs grew bright with colors, and the symbols themselves seemed to twitch. The rim and dome flexed into more pleasing curves. But I had a sense that the cabin's rear walled-off section required a special infusion of energy.

Skolder the juvenile royal ant slipped his rear stinger beneath the base of the *veem* and released a staggeringly powerful jolt. The fried egg pulsed like a beating heart. A jagged gout of light zig-zagged out from a particular *woomo* in the Central Anomaly. Via tekelili, I recognized this *woomo* as my friend Uxa. Her energies haloed the fried egg in a radiance so great that the craft grew dark with light.

The grasses beneath the fried egg caught fire. The agile Shrighunter jumped into our Umpteen Sea and guided her lightboard into a tight circle, sluicing up a roostertail that doused the conflagration amid smoke and steam. And when Uxa turned off her torrent of light, the fried egg was fully healed and actively alive. I could sense her psyche via tekelili. Her aura had a distinctly feminine tinge.

"Gweetings," said the fried egg, actually speaking aloud. She spoke by vibrating her skin. Her lisping voice was like the soft quacking of a baby duck. "I'm weady to fly far," said she. "But first I need more to eat."

"She needs lifting salts for her hidden stove," Eddie opined. Even now he remained under the illusion that the fried egg's method of flight would be the same as that of a hot air balloon.

"Completely wong," quacked the fried egg.

"What's your name?" Ina asked her.

"Fwopsy," said the fried egg.

"How is it that you speak English?" I asked.

"I wearn fast," said Fwopsy. "I'm smart. I wearned English by weading your minds with tekelili."

"Most excellent," said Ina. "Can you take us for a ride, dear Fwopsy? Now that clever Eddie and clever Ina fixed you?"

"Hold off on that," called Otha. "The black gods come first. Fwopsy is spang new, and we gonna be the ones to show her around."

The fire had burned away the ropes that had tethered Fwopsy to the grass. She pirouetted, displaying herself. And then she held her door open for Otha, Smoker, Shrighunter, Jewel, and Watcher to come aboard. They fit comfortably, with Jewel in the chair, and the others standing. Before Seela, MirrorSeela, Eddie, Ina, Machree or I could protest, Fwopsy closed her door and dove into the depths of the miles-wide floating sea, with Nyoo and Skolder in her wake.

Eddie, Seela, and I looked at each other and smiled. This was shaping up to be a hell of a run.

11. Uxa

Fwopsy and the black gods flew looping paths through and around our Umpteen Sea, with an excursion toward the Central Anomaly and back. From my viewpoint, the lively ship seemed to slow down as she edged into the beginning of the *woomo* zone. The *woomo* welcomed her with still more light. I myself hoped I wouldn't be going into the Anomaly at all. I wanted to get Seela and our baby back to the San Francisco of 1850.

While we waited for Fwopsy to return, hummingbirds were picking at the dried-meat basket that Smoker had left. They were little birds, filling the air with pert cheeps, their bodies blue with red throats, but their bills—I now noticed for the first time—their bills had rows of tiny, sharp teeth. I wondered if they drank blood. An abandoned ant-farmer tangle from the inner sky was drifting our way, with its twirling, slightly menacing livestock. Pterodactyls were feeding on them. Further out, a dozen *ballula* hovered. I felt unsafe.

One of the other Umpteen seas was approaching ours. The two great lakes were wildly bobbling, almost as if they were eager to meet. *Oops*, the second Umpteen Sea merged with ours, and a forty-foot-high wave came barreling across our sea's ropy, dimpled surface. The moving mountain submerged our island, of course. We had to use our *pulpuls* to kick ourselves into the air with, once again, great worries about our tiny, week-old Brumble, whom Seela held struggling against her breast. As when doused before, the little fellow began roaring with pique. And the flesh-eating humming-birds were near.

"I want a street I can stand on!" Ina yelled at Eddie. "I want a house with a roof! I don't want everything around me to be alive!"

"First we get the rumbies," insisted Machree.

Seela and MirrorSeela were calm. The hummingbirds and pterodactyls dispersed. The untended antfarm had been devoured. We hovered now amid random spawned-off ponds of water, with a lovely aurora of *woomo* light behind us, a peaceful herd of shrigs separating us from the *ballula*, and the great Rind arching in the background.

"*You* shouldn't have come to the Hollow Earth at all," MirrorSeela told Ina. "It's beautiful here in the core. I'm going to seduce Smoker, and he'll partner up with me. I can tell he's game."

"I'm glad for you," said Seela, looking down at Brumble, who'd calmly started nursing again. "Do you really think you're pregnant, big-sister Seela?"

"With all this tekelili, I can see into myself," said MirrorSeela. "It's like I'm made of clear water. Yes, I'm going to bear Mason's second son."

At some level I already knew this—but hearing it aloud was disorienting. What a responsibility! How could I live up to it? Or, more frankly, how could I escape? But I'd been raised a Virginian, and I did my best to play the gent.

"I'm deeply honored," I told MirrorSeela. "And I'll ask you again: are—are you sure you don't want to come to the surface with us? I'd be proud to help you with the boy."

"Smoker will be a good father," said MirrorSeela. "The Umpteen Seas are a good place to raise the boy."

Seela laughed a bit ruefully. "Having a baby is harder than you think."

"Why is Fwopsy moving so slow?" interrupted the fretful Ina, staring in at the core.

"It's like in Washington Irving's tale about a man named Rip Van Winkle," said Eddie. "Rip goes for a stroll in the mountains, and he meets some dwarves. He drinks genever gin with them and plays nine-pins, and he takes a nap. When he awakes, twenty years have passed. For all those twenty years, Rip was slow." Eddie gave one of his inward smiles.

"Nine-pins?" said Ina, utterly at a loss. "What are you talking about?"

"Never mind, my lady, our gilded coach arrives." And, yes, Fwopsy was swooping our way, with Nyoo and Skolder still in her wake. The carefree black gods tumbled out, talking and laughing. It was our turn.

Eddie took the single swiveled seat at the control panel of the fried egg. Machree and Ina stood behind him with Seela. In this low gravity, it was no great effort to stand. I hesitated outside with Arf for a moment, saying goodbye to Otha.

"I guess you'll stay on here," I said.

"How they treatin black people in the United States these days?" countered Otha.

"It's hard," I said. "And I'll have to go through it all over again. The *woomo* light's made me dark again."

"But you'll fade to white after a year," said Otha. "Not like me."

"I take your point, Otha. But it's not so bad in California."

"How bout if you went back to Lynchburg to look up our younger brother Purly?" Otha asked. Purly was the offspring of my father and of Otha's mother. A blood link. Otha and I had known Purly, growing up, but not well. He'd lived in town, and we'd lived on the farm.

"Would *you* go to Lynchburg?" I asked.

"Naw." Otha cracked a slight smile. "Not even for *Purly*." He'd always been a little put out over how fond of Purly his mother was. And, of course, angry at Pa for having forced himself on his mother.

"The MirrorEarth Otha lives in Baltimore," I told Otha, by way of changing the topic. "Twelve years older than us. Gray hair. Married to a woman called Juicita. And he's got a copy of Arf."

"Arf and Juicita? MirrorOtha livin well. What he do?"

"He's a waiter in a fancy hotel. Eddie Poe and I smoked opium with him."

"Like old times," said Otha, shaking his head. "I don't need none of that white mess no more. Doin good here with the tekelili and Shrighunter and the *woomo*. Hell, Mase, I'm a black god."

"Their king," I said, meaning it. We hugged.

Arf and I got into the fried egg to join the others. I truly hoped we'd go speeding outward toward the Rind—but Fwopsy was in the process of telling us that she wasn't done with her affairs here. This was fine with the low, grasping Machree. His only thoughts were of collecting rumbies.

"I'll ride with you," said Nyoo, darting into the fried egg ship with us. "I'll help with those rumbies."

"How about you?" Fwopsy asked Skolder

"I come indeed," said Skolder via tekelili. His voice in my head was scratchy. "The rumby hunt is needful for the Bloom. To this end I sought out Nyoo, dear Fwopsy, and it is for the Bloom we roused you. We'll gather rumbies, find your mate, and fly to Earth's surface where the rumbies shall be cellared until the time is ripe. I will wait by the rumbies for decades or even centuries, in full vigilance, intent that my fellow royal ants will be on hand when the Bloom is finally achieved." Skolder did a mid-air pirouette, and buzzed in through Fwopsy's door.

Fwopsy closed her door. With her body fully restored, she was generating a steady supply of air. Nearly weightless, Ina and I bounced along on the floor and leaned our backs against the wall. Seela came to join us. I put my arm around Seela, and held Brumble in my lap. Arf lay at our feet, keeping his distance from Nyoo. Eddie, still perched in the single chair, had grasped the protruding knob upon Fwopsy's panel, and was moving it with no apparent effect. Machree was leaning over Eddie's shoulder talking to him about where they might best find rumbies. Nyoo the *woomo* lay quietly in a corner, with Skolder at her side.

With a sinking heart I watched as we headed in toward the Central Anomaly. Behind us were the Umpteen Seas, spread out like a flock of blobby, wayward sheep. Due to the Anomaly's spacewarp, as we progressed, the zone of the Seas looked increasingly flat, as did the innermost zone of the Anomaly, which was the Gate itself. About sixty of the Great Old Ones were on the surface of the Gate.

My paramount concern was how many years we were going to lose by approaching the Gate. By way of distracting myself, I studied Fwopsy's refurbished interior. The friezes were much clearer than before. Now that I was beginning to know what to look for, I could distinctly make out images of spherical *veem* craft, one of them holding *woomo*, one with humans inside, and one containing ants. The royal ants, I now understood, would be the ones to hollow out the colony world targeted by the Bloom.

Another glyph caught my eye. This one showed a *woomo* with a series of chambers inside her body. Curled inside the cavities were figures like human babies. Tiny babies ripening in *woomo* wombs. How deep did the *woomo*-human partnership go? Nyoo wasn't saying.

Meanwhile Eddie was still playing pilot—waggling the stubby lever on the control panel. It didn't matter. Fwopsy was taking us exactly where she wanted to. Deeper into the damned Anomaly. We were hovering about half a mile from the Great Old Ones. Fwopsy was flexing her body and Nyoo was humming a high, thin tune. Fwopsy was slowly rotating. Her window framed a view of the Umpteen Seas above. They were speeding around like the balls on a billiard table and, being water, they were merging and splitting at a furious rate.

"What's going on?" asked Ina uneasily.

"Time is molasses in here," Eddie told her. "The closer we get to the center, the slower our time goes. It's like being drugged, or almost dead, eh?"

"Maybe it would be more apposite to say time is *faster* in here," said I. I was all nerves, and in a mood for quarrel. "Last time through, we spent five minutes here, and we found we'd hopped from 1838 to 1850. We'd travelled twelve years in five minutes. We weren't slow, we were *fast*."

Eddie shook his head. "Don't try to cogitate, Mason. Not your forte. We were *slow*. Consider this: we only managed to nibble through five minutes, while the others gobbled down twelve years. Look out there at the Umpteen Seas leaping. They're fast, and we're slow, stretched, molasses."

Knowing I was defeated, I didn't give Eddie the satisfaction of a response.

"Where are the rumbies?" demanded the obsessed Machree. "Open your door, Fwopsy, so we'll be ready to scoop them up. Fly in closer to Uxa."

"You'd piss away twenty years for twenty dollars," I told Machree. "You pig-blind fool." I gave Machree a rough shove. Fwopsy had by now opened her door for the rumbies, and Machree very nearly lost his footing and fell out.

Taking my side, Seela jeered at the jeweler. "We should squeeze you out like the big fat turd you are," said she.

We were sinking ever deeper into the Anomaly. Beneath us, the *woomo* Uxa looked as big as San Francisco, and very nearly as hilly, with great warty mesas on her primeval integument. Via tekelili she told us she was ripe with rumbies. Expatiating on this, Uxa showed me a vision that was in accordance with my eight-point revelation from Nyoo, and with the evidence of the *veem* glyph frieze.

Uxa's rumbies were to spawn into *woomo*—and the *woomo* would fly into space aboard a flotilla of three *veem* ships, one of the ships piloted by a woman and a man. Human lovers had the power to *push*, or to *yearn*—and therewith to hop across the void of space in the blink of an eye. Uxa expressed this last point with a physical sensation of Seela and I becoming a tunnel in space. As if, impossibly, I were to crawl down Seela's throat while she crawled down mine.

The plan felt like a fever dream in a fairy tale. I feared it much.

Meanwhile, rumbies were exuding from puckers in Uxa's flesh. A slow, heavy shower of them, dropping like ripe cherries. The living gems were calling each to each, excited to be on the loose—*I'm here, I'm here, I'm here.* Fwopsy drifted closer.

"Hurry and finish," I urged the *veem*. "Scoop them up!"

"Get weady," said Fwopsy. She cupped her edge like a shovel and funneled a drift of rumbies in through her open door. Three or four dozen of the dense, thumb-sized, gemlike eggs were bouncing inside our cabin, caroming off the walls. Their bright tekelili was like the cries of schoolchildren. Machree was snatching them from the air and stuffing them inside his shirt. Nyoo was doing her best to catch some with her tendrils. Skolder the juvenile royal ant was holding down a few of them with his body. Eddie and Ina were grabbing them too.

"Oh no!" screamed Seela. She was pointing away from the core and out through Fwopsy's front viewport. The Umpteen Seas were jiggling at pell-mell pace that was nightmarish to behold. We were losing months like the ticks of a clock.

"That's enough rumbies!" I cried. "We have to leave!" I flung myself at Fwopsy's door and executed the gesture for closing it. The portal closed. Dozens more of unharvested rumbies pattered against our hull.

"Damn you!" yelled Machree, punching me in the stomach. I doubled over from the blow. "Open the door again," Machree ordered Fwopsy. The *veem* acceded to his request.

A fresh clutch of rumbies bounded through the door, drawn by little Nyoo's mental force. I was still working to catch my breath. Eddie was sedulously stuffing the excited rumby eggs into his trousers. He'd tucked the cuffs of his pants into his socks to stop the gems from tumbling out. By now he and Machree must have collected more than a hundred of them.

Ina was berating Machree, but Seela's anger at the man was truly incendiary. My Hollow Earth wife! Handing Brumble to Ina for safe-keeping, Seela curved her fingers like talons, and clawed Machree's face—digging into his flesh and drawing blood.

Machree bellowed, seized Brumble from Ina, and threw our frightened, mewling infant out the open door. I had no choice but to go after the baby, and loyal Arf came after me, and then Machree threw Seela out after the three of us. And—I was grateful to see—Nyoo the *woomo* came out with us too. But Skolder the princeling royal ant stayed aboard. The fate of the rumbies was his prime interest.

Whether in response to a command from Machree, or a word from Eddie, or by her own decision—Fwopsy closed her door and left the *woomo* zone. Her apparent speed grew faster and faster, and by the time she passed the zone of the Umpteen Seas, she was a blur.

Unbelievable. Seela, Brumble, Arf and I had been abandoned here with Nyoo. And the little *woomo* had no clear plan of how to save us. I was beginning to doubt entirely that the *woomo* were all-knowing gods. Perhaps they were but strange alien creatures, albeit with high intelligence, an ability to read minds, and a curious power of extending their bodies via thousands-of-miles-long pink fronds. But divinities? No.

Floundering and at a loss, Seela and I kicked our legs, beating our *pulpul* fins against the air, hoping to work our way back to the Umpteen Seas. But we weren't strong enough to escape the unpleasantly potent attraction toward the core. We tumbled and sank—coming to rest upon one of the cupped mesas atop Uxa's hide, with Nyoo at our side. Nyoo was delighted to be in physical contact with a full-grown *woomo* such as Uxa—indeed, she was more than delighted, she was entranced, and her mind damped down to a steady glow of bliss.

I huddled wretchedly there with Seela, the two of us taking in our surroundings with frightened eyes. Although we were too shocked to talk, we were joined in tekelili, We cradled Arf and Brumble between us. Despite having been tossed around like a ball, Brumble was calmly snuggled against Seela's breast. Arf was unhappy. He didn't like *woomo*, and they were all around.

Beyond the jostling haze of the Umpteen Seas lay the distant Rind and, how frightful, I could see the seasonal light of passing summers, pulsing through the water-filled window of the North Hole. Years rushing by.

The mountainous bodies of the fifty or sixty *woomo* were on every side, great warty barrels, bedizened with suckers, puckers, and subbranching fans, steadily rolling, spreading their tendrils toward one Earth and then the other. Their steady, stately motion carried Seela and me through the Gate into the old Earth's zone, then back through the Gate to the MirrorEarth's side. From my point of view the outer world dissolved into a haze each time we moved through the plane of the Gate. We were fortunate to have Uxa's momentum carrying us through.

Uxa's vast, slow tekelili was all around, and she allowed me to visualize her race's cosmic journey. The *woomo* were bound for an impossibly huge space spindle at the heart of the starry disk we call the Milky Way. I could see the spindle in my mind's eye, a perpetual fountain of souls, rising like a Jacob's ladder to a transcendental heaven of flowers that folded in upon themselves, and opened again, eternally new, forever old, unceasingly singing the higher-dimensional music of the spheres.

By now we'd lost at least a century of ordinary time. What kind of city would we find—if we ever made it back to San Francisco? My past was utterly lost, but yet I was happy, sitting here with my Seela, the two of us secure on Uxa's rough skin, and with our baby and our dog between us.

The oceanic flows of *woomo* tekelili lulled me into a trance, and, forgetful of all around me, I once again set to work putting my narrative of my trip into order. All along it had been as if I were writing my *Return to the Hollow Earth* in my head, starting with the journey upon the *Purple Whale* and ending, for now, with an interlude at the center of the Hollow Earth. All along I'd imagined that some celestial being was remembering my thoughts—and now I realized my recording angel was Uxa.

Yes, Uxa was sedulously absorbing my narrative—although her purpose was as yet unclear. Did she mean to create the book for me? Was she on the point of transmitting my words to some distant human scribe? No matter. A calming phrase echoed in my head. *All will be well, and all will be well, and all manner of things will be well.*

With a start, I noticed someone standing ten feet away from us. It was Watcher. Somehow he'd made his way inward to us, and he'd touched down unnoticed. He raised a hand in greeting, and his voice spoke in my head.

"It's gettin on toward time to go," said he.

"How long?" I asked him. "How long have we been here?"

"One and a half centuries of Earth years," said Watcher. "And you'll lose a few more years on the way out."

"We're missing everything!" cried Seela, very upset.

"Don't matter none," said the weathered black god. "Everything's always the same. I like it in here."

"How's Otha?" I asked.

"He's passed on. He only lived a hundred and sixty years. Not long for a black god, but of course he wasn't actually born at the core. His wife's still alive, Shrighunter. Our man Otha died a great-great-grandfather. He had a good life."

"What about my sister?" Seela asked, her voice breaking. "The other Seela. Is she alive? Did she have her son?"

"The other Seela's still shakin'," said Watcher. "She named her baby Bramble—to match your Brumble. Bramble looks like you, Mason, according to the people who remember you. Bramble's in the middle of his second century, with children and grandchildren of his own."

"Lives gone in a wink," said Seela with a sigh. "As if they're nothing."

The thought of meeting my aged son and his grandchildren gave me gooseflesh—and not in a good way. I didn't want to go back to the Umpteen Seas at all.

"Get us out of here," I implored Watcher.

"Fwopsy will arrive directly," he said. "She expects to meet Duggie here. That's who you been waiting for. It took all this time for the *woomo* to find him."

"Who's Duggie?" I asked.

"A *veem* like Fwopsy," Watcher told me. "What you call a fried egg? You saw Duggie when you fell through the South Hole on the old Earth. Uxa went sifting through your memories, and finally she spotted your Duggie hit. You the key to it all, Mason. You and Seela gonna be Adam and Eve. Uxa's bringin Duggie here. Show Mason his memory, Uxa."

In a flash I saw the scene.

Eddie, Otha, and I have fallen through the ice cap that covered the South Hole. We dropped hundreds of miles, with shattered bergs of ice tumbling after us, melting as they fell. Looking up, I see what I take to be a metal ball emerging from a cracked mountain of ice. Or no, not a ball—half a ball, with a rim. Maybe it isn't metal. It reminds me of a great, shiny, fried egg—frozen and still. It disappears into the dim, drizzling mist.

"Hail Uxa," said I.

"Here they come," cried Seela. "Fwopsy and Duggie!"

Two *veem* craft were approaching, one from Earth and one from MirrorEarth, speeding toward us at a furious pace, one on each side of the Gate.

The fried egg on our side was Fwopsy. As Fwopsy drew closer, her motion seemed to slow. Her voice was silent for now, but I could hear her thoughts via tekelili. She hadn't fully abandoned us. She'd had a two part plan.

The first part involved carrying Poe and the hundred or so rumbies to the year 1860. The second part involved working with the *woomo* to find a mate for herself—however long the search might take. Meanwhile she'd stored Seela and me here in slow time. We'd be part of the Bloom. The puzzle-pieces were coming together.

Duggie was on the other side of the Gate. Fwopsy's intended mate, revived from his frozen trance by the *woomo*. He too was shaped like a dome joined to a disk but, unlike Fwopsy, he generally flew with his dome on the downward side. That is, if Fwopsy resembled an igloo on an ice floe, Duggie had the form of a lid resting upon a bowl. He slowed down to a crawl as he inched through the Gate. But as he rose toward us, his time-stream came into synchronization with ours, as Fwopsy's had already done.

Seela was like as a coiled spring, itching for escape. Baby Brumble watched us with us with sweet, wise eyes.

"Now," said Seela. "Now we can go."

"Take these," Uxa thought to us. Raising a delicately branched tendril, she handed me three—scarves? Finely-textured, greenish-beige rectangles of a textile akin to woolen felt. But slippery. They were made of matted *woomo* fronds.

"Thank you," I said, too preoccupied with escape to ask what the scarves were for.

Finally returning to activity, the little *woomo* Nyoo lifted herself off the surface of Uxa and flexed her warty body. "It's been lovely here," she intoned.

"Are you coming with us?" I asked her.

"Indeed," she said. "I'm tasked to orchestrate the Bloom. The great migration."

"You can do what you want," I said. "Me, I'm planning to settling back down on Earth."

"*All will be well*," said Nyoo, echoing Uxa's slogan, but not really accepting my answer.

Seela and I kicked our *pulpul* fins. She carried Brumble, and I bore Arf. What with the deep tekelili, I could understand my dog's inner mentations—simple but sincere. Unease about the *woomo*, curiosity about their vinegary smell, a fondness for Bumble, a wish to lick my face—which he now did. Seela and I fluttered toward Fwopsy with Nyoo floating after us. We were like marooned sailors swimming for a dory just off their desert island.

Somehow Fwopsy was a bit too far. Or perhaps the pull of the Central Anomaly was a shade too great. We weren't going to make it. Watcher floated along at our sides, somehow without having to kick his legs. He was savoring the adventure, but not offering aid. Nor was Nyoo of any help. She was back in her tekelili trance.

I prayed with all my heart—and finally picked up an answer. A psychic message from Duggie, the other *veem*. A competent creature, poised to act.

"No problem!" quoth he.

Moving in unison, Duggie and Fwopsy positioned themselves above and below us, with Fwopsy like a dome above us, and Duggie like a cup beneath us. Both dome and cup were sealed off by flat disks. To complete their coup, the two *veem* opened large round holes in the flat disks that had hidden their interiors. The *veem* were now like a matched pair of cupped hands, poised to trap six moths.

"Do it!!" called Watcher. The *veem* clapped together, dome joining cup, with the rims of their two disks merging to one. Their hemispherical cabins were conjoined into a sphere with an inner ledge like a circular balcony. Watcher, Seela, Brumble, Arf, Nyoo, and I were within. As usual, Arf was avoiding Nyoo—and I could sense he was glad to be away from Uxa.

The doubled cabin had six windows, two doors, and two control panels, each with a single swivel seat. The seats grew from the narrow ledge that ran along the spherical cabin's equator—with Fwopsy's seat oriented upward, and Duggie's seat downward. As I've mentioned, the seats were on swivels, so that the pilots could position their bodies as they pleased. And each pilot would be holding one of those ball-tipped controls. And, finally there was a flattish, closed-off volume along one side of the inner sphere. Eddie had once imagined that "lifting salts" were in there, but more likely the space held internal organs.

In any case, a lovely winding frieze of symbols covered the conjoined walls. The parade of hieroglyphs spiraled outward from the apex of one dome, wound along the central ledge, then spiraled inward to the apex of the second dome. It seemed as if one of the two depicted histories was the continuation of the other, not that—to speak truthfully—I was sure which direction represented the forward flow of time.

I should mention that the word *veem* is used in three ways. Firstly, it can refer to a single fried-egg-style aircraft, like Fwopsy. Secondly, it can be viewed as a plural form, akin to the words *deer* or *woomo*. Thus one can speak of a pair of *veem*. Thirdly, we can use *veem* to refer to a conjoined pair of the individual craft. Thus: Fwopsy was a *veem*, Fwopsy and Duggie began as separate *veem*, and after they joined themselves together they were a higher sort of *veem*.

Duggie was chatting away, his tenor voice filling the cabin. He'd managed to pick up English too. He was a livelier character than Fwopsy. A rowdy, you might say. And with a Southern accent instead of a lisp.

"We're ripe to mate!" exulted the *veem*. "I'm back from cold storage. Fwopsy and me gonna hatch out some *larvae*! We the last two *veem* on your two Earths! All our children flew away during the last Bloom."

"I'm not weady," demurred Fwopsy. "Not till we're on the outside—where we can welease our wittle ones wight away. We don't want our warvae settling on the walls inside our cabin."

"You right," said Duggie. "And we don't want no sessile ufological saucerian larvae taking root on our human guests neither."

"Where do you get those odd words?" inquired Watcher. "They're unfamiliar to me."

"When Uxa's ray woke me up under the South Pole, I tanked up on radio talk from today's Earth," said Duggie. "It's a new world up there! Get up to speed, old coot."

By now we'd escaped the Central Anomaly and were heading into the zone of the Umpteen Seas. Once again the floating lakes were wobbling at a reasonable rate. We'd rejoined Earth's quotidian flow of time.

"You left us in there too long?" I told Fwopsy. "We've lost—"

"Over a hundwed and sixty years," said Fwopsy. "Watcher told you why. Didn't you wisten? It took that wong to find Duggie."

"It's still hard to believe you'd do that to us," I muttered.

"Go ahead and drop me off here," the dignified Watcher now told the pair of *veem*. "Any place around the Seas is good. My folks will find me."

I turned to Seela. "You don't want to visit with the black gods again, do you? After all this time?"

Seela shook her head. "Too much," said she. "Let's go back to California and see what happens there. We've still got our own lives to live."

"Yes, we do," said I, liking the prospect. I had a mental image of a cozy little house with children in the yard, a garden, me writing at my desk, and Seela with a jewelry studio.

12. Twenty Eighteen

The trip went quickly. This time it wasn't a matter of passively floating up though the ocean in the all-but-lifeless hulk of a long-abandoned fried egg. Instead we were aboard a coupled pair of fully functional *veem*. Their powers of flight were extreme.

In less than an hour, we'd sped from the core to the Rind, and then upward through the seawater and the icepack of the MirrorEarth's now frozen-over North Hole. A half hour after that, we were hovering high above San Francisco. The setting sun gilded the ocean and bay.

It was odd to be dealing with weight again. Relative to the Earth's pull, Fwopsy was right side up, and Duggie was upside down. We were looking out through the *veem* viewports while standing on the inner surface of Duggie's inverted dome.

"What are those shapes?" said Seela, peering through one of Duggie's windows at the city. "All angles and lines. Buildings like teeth. Streets so smooth. A park like a green tongue. San Francisco is huge."

"And see the bridges," I said, uneasily studying the busy bay. "And the cranes and ships."

"Flying machines too," said Seela, her voice rising as she pointed at one of Fwopsy's windows. "Look out Duggie!"

Our *veem* ship twitched to one side, and a nasty metal aircraft screamed past. A hateful, violent thing, intent on doing us harm. Seen from below, it was shaped like a cross.

Our paired fried eggs picked up speed so fast that we fell on our butts. Seconds later, we were low over a beach town down the coast. It had a harbor and a river, and looked to be a more manageable size. The town had paved roads running along its cliffs, with shiny closed-up wagons speeding along them. Alive like our *veem*? Machines powered by steam? I noticed some people playing in the waves—riding boards like the black gods had done inside the Hollow Earth. But the people here were riding water, rather than flows of light.

"This is Santa Cwuz," said Fwopsy's voice, vibrating from the cabin walls. Santa Cruz had been a tiny fishing village when we'd sailed to San Francisco in 1850.

"Why's everything so strange?" I complained, knowing the answer, but wanting the words to be said.

"It's the year twenty eighteen," intoned Duggie. "Long wait since the last Bloom. That was in the year ten twenty, as I do recall. Fwopsy and I been zonked out ever since. We the only two *veem* left. It's time to feed and breed."

Twenty eighteen. Numbly I revolved the numbers in my head, trying to make sense of them—and wondering if Seela and I could fit in here.

Once again, a savage, flying metal cross flew at us.

"Quick," said Nyoo to our *veem*. "Let me out. I'll get them off your trail."

In the blink of an eye, the door irised open, Nyoo sped out, and the door closed. Nyoo flew straight at the angry metal cross, then cut to the side, leading the clumsy thing on a frantic upward arc.

Meanwhile Fwopsy and Duggie dove into the sea beside a long wharf. Moving rapidly beneath the surface, the *veem* sped some miles further south, and found shelter in a deeply shaded crack within a precipitous ocean trench. We lurked there, where no spy rays could pry. Full night fell.

It was utterly dark inside the paired fried eggs, and cold. Brumble didn't like it at all. He was crying inconsolably. And Arf was endlessly barking, as if he'd lost his mind.

"Put us ashore," Seela begged the *veem* craft. "It's enough now."

"Seela's right," came Duggie's voice inside the gloomy cabin. "Those crazy killers who were chasing us are gone."

"We'll take you to Big Sur," said Fwopsy. "The wumbies are in a tweasure chest in a secwet cave. Machwee and I put them there after we took Eddie and Ina to San Fwancisco. Skolder is watching them."

"We gonna spawn in that cave?" asked Duggie.

"Yes, dear *veem*," said Fwopsy. "That's the whole idea. We make our babies. And the wumbies there are weady to hatch into *woomo*. And we have Mason and Seela for Adam and Eve. Time for the Bwoom!"

So we rose out of the ocean and flew yet further to the south, reaching the coastal district known as Big Sur. Even after a century and a half, this was in large part a wild, uninhabited land, with few lights. The moon was up, the sky was clear, and no bullying, metal flying machines were in view. Nor, for now, was Nyoo anywhere to be seen.

"Do you know the exact date?" I asked Fwopsy.

"March 24, 2018," she said.

"So I missed my birthday," I remarked. "That was on February 2." Not much of a reaction from Seela. The flowerpeople were barely aware of the passing years, and they had no reckoning of months and days. Seela was staring at the rolling sea and the hills of Big Sur, lit by the fat moon.

"I'm going to start saying I'm eighteen," I told little Brumble, whom I had against my shoulder. I loved the smooth, warm skin of his silky head. "Right, baby? Papa's all done being seventeen. It was a short year, but a busy one."

Brumble made a single hiccup, which I took to be agreement.

We skimmed across the moon-silvered waves and rose fifty yards up a sheer coastal cliff. And here was an isolated grassy meadow, perched amid the rock faces like a shelf. Our double fried egg nestled into the inky shadows of a grove of gnarled cypress trees, hard against a steep ragged wall of stone, complete with the steaming pool of a hot spring. *This is how it's supposed to be in California*, thought I. I was glad not to be in one of those cold and overbuilt new towns we'd seen.

"The cave's over here," Fwopsy told Duggie. "Away from the hot spwing. We'll dig now."

Although the shadowed meadow seemed to meet the dry part of the cliff quite seamlessly, Fwopsy and Duggie rooted at the soil with their shared, flexible rim, scattering dirt, and shoving boulders aside, with some of the rocks rolling across the meadow and off the cliff into the foaming sea.

Soon they'd opened a low tunnel that did indeed lead into a cave, a largish one, as big as the nave of a church. Once we were inside, the two *veem* lit up. Fwopsy, who was still on top, glowed pale yellow, and Duggie shone vegetable green. Seela and I were still sealed inside them. We watched through the viewports as the conjoined *veem* settled in. I noticed a time-worn treasure chest against the cave's wall. This must be the box that Fwopsy said was full of rumbies. And I glimpsed stealthy, moving forms at the far, low end of the cave. But then the shapes retreated into deeper gloom.

"We'll hatch new *veem* to make a wittle fweet," Fwopsy lisped to Seela and me.

"What's a *fweet*?" I had to ask.

"She means *fleet*," said Duggie. "A fleet of three *veem* balls. Each of them will be a pair of our fried-egg hatchlings."

"Why does Fwopsy have to lisp like that?" asked Seela, annoyed. "If you two are so smart, why can't she talk right?'

"She thinks what she does is funny," said Duggie. "I think so too."

"Can you let us out now?" I said, really very tired of these *veem*. "I don't want to be inside you anymore."

"Just a minute," said Duggie. "We can't open our doors until we spawn. Are you ready, Fwopsy?"

"Weady, my love. I've waited ten thousand years."

The *veem* trembled at a rising rate. Duggie grunted and Fwopsy squeaked. A scent of musk and cinnamon filled the air. Then all was still.

"We done it!" said Duggie after a bit, his voice gone husky. "I'm woke and I'm lit and I squirted."

The air of our cabin was befogged by drifts of eggs and milt, with lucky larvae forming apace. This round space was alive with tiny, writhing *veem* fry.

"Look at them sparkle," added Duggie, his voice low in awe. "Feel the fizz."

"You should be bweathing through Uxa's scarves wight now," Fwopsy cautioned us, her voice languid. "The ones she gave you?"

"Don't want no flying saucer barnacles in your wind-pipes!" whispered Duggie.

"Flying saucers, yes," faintly echoed Fwopsy. "That's what the men in those fwying metal things were calling us. Even though Duggie and I together are like a ball and not like a fwied egg."

I wrapped one of Uxa's scarves across Brumble's nose and mouth, and covered the lower part of my own face. Seela donned a scarf too. Wise Arf curled up on the floor and stuck his snout into the fur of his belly.

My skin itched at the thought of baby *veem* settling onto me like limpets fastening themselves to a tide-washed rock. But now, thank heavens, Fwopsy and Duggie had finally opened their doors, and their spawn was drifting out.

As the verminous exodus abated, Seela, Brumble, Arf, and I disembarked as well. The cave's inner walls were cool, dry, smooth. Hundreds of the *veem* larvae were alighting on the stone. Each hatchling carried a slight spark of conscious-ness—I could track their locations via a trickle of tekelili from Fwopsy and Duggie. But the vast majority of the tiny new *veem* were dying. Only a very few of them would flourish and take root.

And there was something more daunting than this. The two parent saucers, Fwopsy and Duggie—their tekelili was fading. They'd fallen away from each other, breaking their embrace, no longer joined as one. Their flexing bodies were beginning to stiffen and dry. They were, if not dying, doing something very like. A final pulse of thought came from Fwopsy.

"A ten thousand year nap," she said. "Good wuck to you two." The *veem* dropped senseless to the dusty, stone floor. Their bodies had gone dark. The only light in the cave was a faint ray of moonlight angling in the door.

Seela and I stood there for a moment, taking it in.

"I liked them," she said.

"Even though Fwopsy left us at the core?" I said.

"I liked their voices," said Seela. "And their beautiful designs."

"Fwopsy says they'll be back some day," I said.

"We won't be here," said Seela.

We could hear things moving in the rear of the cave. Creepy. We made our way outside. It was wonderful in the salty, fresh, cool night air. There wasn't much of a wind.

The mouth of the cave was dark, but the moon highlighted the cliff and the seaward branches of the low trees. Mist drifted from the hot spring. Its shallow pool would be a good source of warmth against the March night.

Seela stripped off her travel-stained pants and shirt and seated herself in the pool, submerged to her waist. I quickly disrobed and joined her, then took hold of Brumble and rinsed his little body. He gaped, gurgled, sneezed, and kicked his legs like a crawfish snapping his tail. He liked the warm water. Arf came into the pool as well, picking his way slowly and carefully, with much suspicious sniffing.

When had I last bathed? Less than a day ago, by one reckoning. Or over a hundred and sixty-seven years ago, by another.

"We can stay by the spring all night," said Seela.

"Or we could go in the cave," I said.

"I don't like the scuttling," said she.

"Maybe it's something friendly," I said.

"Maybe it's something that bites."

"I wish we'd brought food," I said. "Why don't we ever remember that?"

"Trust fate," said Seela. "It's brought us this far." Raising her voice she yelled aloud, just in case there might actually be something friendly in the cave. "Bring us food!"

I could see my darling by the moonlight. Thanks to our massive doses of *woomo* light, our skins were deeply black. And Brumble was black too.

"Starting at our society's low end again," I said. "I'm tired of it."

"Why do you care?" said Seela, discerning my import. "I like dark skin. It's better."

"Not in Virginia or in Baltimore," I said.

"I've never been to Virginia," said Seela. "But you and I did fine in Baltimore. We had more fun than those pinched, anxious whites. We were free, and newlyweds, and we had no baby to worry about, and we made love all the time. And now we're in California."

"California twenty eighteen," I said.

"That's a year number?" said Seela. "You used to say eighteen fifty. I don't like numbers. The flowerpeople don't use them."

"I know," I said, putting my arm around her. Smooth, wet, warm. Brumble between us, very darling, even though he hadn't yet learned to smile. "Real things are better than numbers," I agreed. "Warmer and rounder. With colors and smells."

"Maybe you can find a job on a newspaper," said Seela. "Like you planned."

"If people will read me," I said. "I'm from the days of yore. I'll be judged quaint and skew, a pompous relic."

"Write simple," said Seela. "Learn new words. Like Duggie was doing. *I'm lit.* I liked when he said that. We'll fit in. We're sly rats. Stop worrying!"

"I'll soak my head," I said, passing Brumble to Seela so I could lie back in the water. It was good being submerged, in a primeval puddle unchanged for centuries. Me, my wife, and our baby. After a while the wife poked me and I sat up.

"You're rude," she said. "You didn't ask what I plan to do."

"Tell me now," I said. "I'm sorry. What will you do in this new world?"

"Necklaces," said Seela. "Jewelry. What I've always done. You called them money nets? I'll weave doodads onto wires and threads."

"*Doodads,*" I echoed. I'd never heard that before.

"A modern word," said Seela. "Duggie's tekelili was full of them. I can't believe he came back to life for about one day and now he's already gone."

"Harsh," I said. "That's a Duggie word, too."

"Remember how in Baltimore I traded one of my money nets for a ham, and one for a dress, and one for twelve pieces of fried chicken? Jewelry."

"Sly rat," I fondly said. "Did you notice the treasure chest in there? Fwopsy said the chest is full of rumbies, right? And the rumbies are *woomo* eggs, awaiting the great Bloom."

"I know all that," said Seela. "And I hope the Bloom's a flop. The rumbies were brought here by Eddie and Machree and Ina, and those three are vile parasitic shrig-fleas, and I hate them. They left you and me at the Hollow Earth's core to die."

"But we didn't die," I said, meaning to calm her emotions. "Sure, I hate Machree too, but Ina's our friend, and Eddie—well, he's Eddie. I'm surprised the rumbies all ended up in the trunk. I thought Machree wanted to sell them."

Seela shrugged. "Maybe they're *not* in the trunk. Or maybe Machree didn't get his way. Do you think he and Eddie and Ina are still around?"

"I think they got back here a hundred and fifty years before we did," I said.

"Numbers are shit," Seela reminded me. "Numbers are numb."

"We were in the slow time longer than they were," I said, rephrasing my thought. "And while we were in the slow time, they rushed through the years in fast time. I'm pretty sure they're dead."

"Well—you can never be sure about Eddie," said Seela. "He's a weasel."

I had to agree. "We saw him stabbed and drowned in Baltimore," I recalled. "And then he was back. Drinking claret in a stateroom on the *Water Witch*."

Seela shook her head and dropped the topic. She scooped more warm water onto Brumble, then raised her voice and called out again to whatever helpful-elf-type beings might conceivably be rustling at the back of the cave.

"*Bring us food!*" she yelled.

Moonlight glinted off a shape at the mouth of the cave. A low creature, moving daintily as if on tiptoe, walking backwards with his head lowered, dragging something—was it a magic cougar bringing us the haunch of a slain deer? No, larger than a cougar. The being glistened in shades of purple and green.

"A royal ant!" exclaimed Seela. "With ant-plant sausages!"

Arf was barking furiously. Ignoring him, the large ant deposited a pair of plump, foot-long, ant-plant sausages beside our pool. Raising his head, he clacked his great jaws at Arf, enjoining the dog to be silent. I picked up a touch of the ant's tekelili.

He was none other than Skolder—the royal ant princeling who'd hatched near the North Hole, and whom we'd encountered near the core of the Hollow Earth. He was a century and a half older now, and perhaps not yet his full adult size, but decently large, the size of a horse, albeit a horse with six very short legs. Formidable.

"Remember me?" came Skolder's scratchy tekelili voice in my head.

"We do," said Seela. "You ditched us at the core."

"Is that all you two ever talk about?" said Skolder. "Here you are. Be happy. I've been waiting by the rumbies with my family, to make sure we get in on the Bloom. Riding off on those flying saucers to a new world. And you two are supposed to be Adam and Eve."

"No we're not," said Seela. "I'm not going."

"Perhaps your man harbors thoughts you choose to ignore," said Skolder in our heads.

"Go away," said Seela. "Stupid, overgrown ant. I'd like to crush you under my heel."

Skolder chirped something unintelligible and returned to the cave.

"I hate when others say they know things about you that I don't know," Seela said to me. "All of them sneaking and reading our minds. Are you going to leave on those saucers or not?"

"Can't we just eat? Quarrelling is so hard."

"Yes," said Seela.

We cut the sausages in half and set to. They were like the ones we'd eaten on the hovering ant farm within the Hollow Earth—brimming with a bubbly, tasty jelly that went down as fast as I could swallow. Delicious and marvelously restorative. I'd been aching all over, but soon I felt fine

Seela and I lounged beside the warm pool with Uxa's *woomo* scarves wrapped around us, and with Brumble between us. We felt comfortable and at ease. And, at least for now, I felt I'd stay with Seela forever. We'd sleep out here tonight, and tomorrow we'd find our way to one of the settlements north of here, perhaps to a town smaller than the ungainly sprawl of twenty eighteen San Francisco.

But the unresolved question remained. "We don't really have to fly off in one of those *veem* ships, do we?" Seela asked.

At one level I did want to travel on and on, finding ever newer wonders. I was born for adventure. But—now I had Seela and Brumble. So maybe I'd stay. In any case, for now it was easiest to say what Seela wanted to hear.

"I've had enough of the *woomo* and the *veem* and the royal ants," I told her. "It's as you said. We're ready for a life of our own." Using my rumby tekelili, I went so far as to show her my vision of us three in a rustic cottage—without revealing my thought that our home might be on the new colony world, rather than on Earth. I was hoping to have it both ways at once.

"Yes," murmured Seela, taking in the superficial lineaments of my vision. "A cabin like that. And with a cow." She cuddled against me and we fell asleep.

I was awakened by a thud or a splat. It was early morning, with the rising sun gilding the foggy sea. Our cliffside meadow was damp with dew, and still in the shadow of the Big Sur coastal range. Lying next to us was—Nyoo. She'd plopped down out of the sky, quite unharmed. She was full of energy and raring to go. Meanwhile Seela and Brumble were still asleep.

As I've mentioned, Nyoo was a tubular creature of variable size. Just now she was about three feet long, with branching fleshy fronds on either end, and with warts and suckers along her striped green-and-black body—very like a sea cucumber. She had no eyes—she saw solely by the power of tekelili.

"Mason!" came her lively voice in my head. "Are you ready? You'll need to round up Eddie and Ina and the rumbies for the Bloom. We'll have at least six good new fried eggs turning ripe on the cave walls in a few days. And Fwopsy said the rumbies are in a treasure chest in the cave." All this came in the form of impulses and emotions rather then as images and words.

"Do you know that Fwopsy and Duggie are dead?" I asked.

"In hibernation," corrected Nyoo, evoking a drifty sense of how Fwopsy had been when she was an inert hulk amid the Umpteen Seas. "Never mind them. Those newborn saucers will carry you away!" A sense of the cave's six baby fried-egg saucers clapping together in pairs to make three big sphere saucers.

"Seela doesn't want to go in a saucer," I told Nyoo. "I'm not sure I'm going to help any more with the Bloom. I might be finished."

"Nonsense. Look at everything we've done for you." Nyoo expressed this with a kinetic sense of my arms being laden with gifts, followed by a sense of me kneeling in gratitude.

"*Everything you've done?*" I cried. "Like throwing us a hundred and sixty seven years into the future? I'm supposed to be glad about that?"

"Thanks to me you had the opportunity to mate with Seela and MirrorSeela at the same time," said Nyoo, casting this sentiment into a transfixing erotic scene. "I know this was important to you."

"It didn't happen that way at all. You saw what it was like. You were there."

Nyoo sent a thought indicating her disinterest in the fine points of human words, or in the niceties of human courtship. She expressed this via a montage of humans speaking in barks, squeals, and grunts while twisting their bodies into shameless, unnatural displays. Done with this topic, she viscerally prodded me to accompany her into the cave. It was hard to gainsay a *woomo*'s direct order. I acquiesced.

"What—what's happening?" said Seela, awakened by the aethereal vibrations of my teeping with Nyoo. She sat up with her beautiful hair mussed. Brumble wormed his bald little head against her, opening and closing his mouth.

"I'm taking Nyoo to see the rumbies and the baby *veem*," I said, already on my feet and donning my clothes—the stained gray pants and the dirty white shirt. It occurred to me that Nyoo might not know that Skolder the royal ant was still here. I did my best to suppress this thought. If I knew something that Nyoo didn't, it might somehow help me to get free of her demands.

"Wait till I'm done feeding the baby," said Seela, who sensed that I was uneasy. "I want to come with you. Just in case you need help." With or without rumby tekelili, we two had grown so intimate that Seela was aware of my faintest ruminations. But Nyoo wasn't so perceptive. Perhaps the vaunted *woomo* weren't as knowledgeable as I'd once supposed.

So Nyoo and I waited till Seela and Brumble were ready. Rather than leaving Brumble on his own on the cliff, Seela brought him along on her shoulder, quietly hiccupping. And naturally Arf came too. He was curious about whether we'd find food in the cave.

Pink energies flickered from Nyoo's feelers and she levitated into the air. She drifted through the mouth of the cave, with us following after.

Fwopsy and Duggie lay dark and still on the floor. Nyoo played her pink rays across their gleaming hides. "We'll haul them to the core," she told me, or rather showed me. By the light of Nyoo's rays, I saw that precisely six of the newly spawned fried eggs had successfully taken root on the cave's walls. They were the size of dinner plates, or even serving platters.

The little treasure chest sat by the wall, dark with age, a box of stained wood with wrought iron fittings along its edges, and with a heavy brass padlock in its tarnished hasp.

I heard a shrill chirp. Skolder was watching us from a position high up on a cave wall to our left. Incredible that a creature the size of a horse could lodge himself there. He had strong legs and highly adhesive feet.

"Caution!" said Skolder, communicating via a mixture of tekelili, antennae twitches, and mandible clicks. "The chest of rumbies—it's not as it seems."

"Stand back," advised Nyoo, confidently aglow. Fwopsy had assured us the rumbies were here, and that's what Nyoo believed—to the point of ignoring her old friend Skolder's warning.

Nyoo tilted her stubby body and directed a zap of energy at the lock. It sprang open and fell to the ground. Skolder chirped another warning. Finally sensing something might be amiss, Nyoo urged or, rather, commanded me to open the trunk myself.

"Don't do it," called Seela. She was standing with Brumble in the cave's mouth, a shapely silhouette against the brightening Big Sur day.

Despite the warnings, I gingerly pulled upwards on the chest's convex lid. As I say, Nyoo's tekelili gave the *woomo* a certain power over me. And, boy that I still was, I was unable to resist the lure of a treasure chest. I'd expected some resistance from the lid, but the hinged top flew open in a rush, clacking against the cave's wall. Pale, shining, smudged surfaces seethed within. Nyoo emitted a silent cry of alarm and turned to flee.

But she was too slow.

Dozens, nay scores, of dog-sized white ants rushed from the open trunk, which had a slyly tunneled hole in place of its base. Farmer ants. They roiled out like pale smoke from a fire. They were the size of dogs, cunning, vicious, quick on their feet, and capable of leaping halfway across the cave in one go.

Nyoo extended a tendril and sent some rapid zaps of light at the pale ants—to no avail. The creatures' dirty-looking white bodies were highly reflective, and *woomo* beams bounced away. Faster than it takes to tell, six or seven of the farmer ants had hold of Nyoo, tearing at the *woomo* with their jaws, and repeatedly thrusting their stingers into the alien sea cucumber's flesh.

Nyoo dropped to the dusty floor. Two dozen of the pale ants were upon her. A few seconds later our friend the *woomo* was gone—entirely consumed by the savage, ravenous, farmer ants—leaving behind nothing more than a damp spot of ichor upon the ground. The *woomo* were, in the end, as vulnerable as me. It was only the intoxicating force of their tekelili that had made me deem them immortal gods. I felt lost and sad.

Still on the wall, Skolder the princeling royal ant creaked an audible sound like a dirge. Faintly luminous, the pale farmer ants stood in a phalanx, watching Seela and me. Somehow I had a feeling they weren't quite sure what manner of beings Seela and Brumble were. Maybe Seela's rumby vibrations were throwing them off, or maybe they'd never seen a human baby before. Skolder grew an intense beam of light from his stinger and played it across the eyes of the farmer ants. They stood their ground.

"I once told my friend Nyoo that I savored her," said Skolder's voice in my head. "These brutal, low-caste, farmer ants take such a thought in too crude a way. They've lurked here for years, patiently wanting to devour some *woomo* at the time of the Bloom. My royal ant siblings and cousins are in a nest nearby. We have a young empress in waiting, and I am to be her consort. We'll ride together to the new world. It is for you two to finish the preparations for the Bloom. My kin and I will block the farmer ants from claiming all the room. Go to fetch Eddie and Ina. And find the rumbies. The rumbies are no longer here." And with that, big Skolder wriggled into a hole in the upper left corner of the cave.

Still at the mouth of the cave, Seela spoke. "I've always heard there's nothing a farmer ant would rather do than eat a *woomo*. And I said it's like the way we women control you men. Remember, Mason? We joked about this in happier times. I'm like a *woomo*, you're like an ant."

The pale, whitish farmer ants studied us with their unreadable eyes. Were they going to set upon us? Unlike Skolder and his royal tribe, the farmer ants had no tekelili at all. Their antennae waggled up and down, and they were chirping. *Skritch skzz skritch.* I made my way to Seela's side.

"I know I'm terrible, but I kind of loved how the farmer ants ate Nyoo," said Seela. "So juicy. I was half-expecting it. All along I had a feeling they might be hiding in the chest."

"How did you know?" I asked.

"Well, first of all, when we saw Skolder bring the ant-plant sausages last night, I figured there had to be farmer ants around. The royal ants and the farmer ants—they fight with each other, but often they're neighbors as well. And, second of all, if the rumbies were put here a hundred and forty years ago, it figures that by now someone would have stolen them. So why not have farmer ants waiting in the treasure chest. Surprise, Nyoo!" She laughed again.

"Do you think the farmer ants carried the rumbies down to their nest?"

"Hoarding rumbies would fit with them being obsessed with eating *woomo*," said Seela. "After all, the rumbies are *woomo* eggs. Those greedy, mindless, low-caste, white ants might sit and wait for years for a rumby egg to hatch—just so they can gobble down a newborn *woomo*. But the shiny purple-green royal ants like Skolder—they understand about cooperation. You heard what he said. He's angling to get himself and his empress ant wife onto a *veem* ship of the Bloom. Even though the Bloom is probably screwed."

"This is getting so complicated," I complained.

"Let's get out of here," urged Seela. "Before any rumbies hatch, and before the ants start a war, and before those saucers on the wall wake up."

"Nyoo and Skolder said that it was up to me to find Eddie and Ina and the rumbies," I told Seela. "I feel like I owe the *woomo* that much."

"*You owe the woomo?* Why, exactly?"

I groped for an answer. "I—I mean, the *woomo* are like gods. They're always sending out tendrils to do things for us. And both the times we were at the core they helped us get through."

"They're using us," said Seela. "They shuttle us back and forth—between Earth and MirrorEarth, between the inside and the outside, and along they way they kept us in storage at the core for over a hundred years—and it's all just to help their precious Bloom. We're supposed to pilot the ships? And hatch a new race? Fuck the *woomo*, Mason. Fuck the Bloom. It's not going to work. Face facts."

"I still feel like I should try to find Eddie," I stubbornly said. But part of me was wondering if Seela were right. Had I become a *woomo* slave? No, no, I was a free agent. A young hero. Born for adventure.

"How the hell would you find Eddie?" pressed Seela. "By now he's been dead for years and years, no? He came up here much earlier than us. You're going to dig up his corpse? It's not up to you to make the Bloom happen, Mason. And we're *not* going on those saucers, right?"

"I guess not," I said, just to shut her up. Would you think me a traitor if I admitted I was already wondering if there might be a way to settle Seela in Santa Cruz—seen from the air, the town looked more congenial than San Francisco. Maybe I should leave Seela there, and ride a saucer to an entirely different world on my own? I was in complete inner turmoil.

Dressed in our dirty clothes, and with Seela carrying Brumble in the *woomo*-woven scarf she'd tied across one shoulder, Seela and I made our way up the jagged cliff, hoping to find a road. Somewhere along the way we'd lost our shoes, but that only made the climb easier.

Blessedly it was a pleasant, sunny day, as can happen any day of the year in California. As we'd flown the last part of our trip in darkness, I'd unthinkingly supposed that the road, if there was one, would be a dirt track, as it might have been in 1850.

We started hearing traffic when we were a hundred feet below the top. A growing hiss, a percussive roar, and then a hiss that faded away. Over and over again. Looking along the coast we could see bits of the dark gray road. Shiny wagons sped along it, rolling on smooth, black wheels. These were the things we heard. I felt no spark of life from them. They were machines. Were people inside them?

The slope leveled out, and we made our way onto a patch of red and yellow gravel. And there was the dark gray road, very solid, as if baked from a slurry of tar, mortar and stones. For the moment none of the glossy, enclosed wagons were in sight.

"Which way do we go?" asked Seela, who even now was a bit unfamiliar with how we oriented ourselves on Earth's outer surface.

"There," said I, pointing to the left. "Up the coast. North to Santa Cruz." I'd fixed on that town as our goal. Although I'd heard little mention of it on the *Water Witch* or during our brief time in San Francisco, I liked the look of it from the air.

One of those smooth, shiny wagons was approaching, heading north to south. Seela and I stood well back from the road and watched it pass. It was large, with tinted windows all around, and I could clearly see a man and a woman within. The entire rear area of the wagon was unoccupied. The man and the woman wore spectacles with dark lenses. Seela waved to the couple, but they offered no response. If anything, they seemed to avert their gaze.

"Let's stand on the other side of the road," I suggested. "If we can hail one of the wagons it might carry us to Santa Cruz. That's better than walking all the way."

We stood by the road for perhaps two hours, every now and then walking a bit further toward the north. The walking wasn't easy with our bare feet. Certainly some of the drivers saw us, but none of them wanted to stop, nor did they smile. To the contrary, many of them scowled, and one white man, riding as a passenger, stuck his arm out his window as if shaking his fist, but with his middle finger extended. I'd seen sailors use this sign to express disrespect.

"You were right," Seela said to me, shaking her head. "It's hard to be black in America. The whites fear us and hate us."

"Some of them are kind," I said. "In time someone will stop."

It was another two hours till we got our ride, shortly after noon. The sun was high and hot, despite the steady ocean breeze. The wagon that stopped was boxy and dirty, with worn green paint. The driver was an energetic, copper-skinned woman in yellow-lensed glasses, with a bearded brown man sitting next to her wearing darker glasses. I could see another man and woman in back, and a pair of small children.

"*Andale*," called the woman at the wheel in a friendly tone. "We got room. Don't stand with your *niño* in the sun. Look at him, *que lindo*. A little flower bud."

A side door on the wagon slid open. The door was made of metal and it clanged. After the noon sun, it seemed dark in the car. It smelled good on the whole, like food, mostly, although there was an undertone of diapers.

Our saviors were mostly talking Spanish, although they did know some English. I was pleased to realize that the tekelili of our rumbies gave Seela and me some slight ability to speak Spanish ourselves. Our new friends said they were from Mexico, living and working in Santa Cruz, and that they were returning from a trip they'd made down the coast to visit some relatives who worked on a ranch. I communicated to them that we wanted to go to Santa Cruz, and they said they'd take us all the way.

The woman driving was named Aida. She had dark, wavy hair, a noble, straight nose, and a bulky body. She was the boss, a big talker and a flirt. She beamed a few smoldering looks my way, as if testing my reactions.

"*Muy caliente*," said her husband Hector, after the second of stocky Aida's fierce, tooth-baring smiles. He laughed and nudged her, not taking this byplay seriously. "You be a proper old lady, Aida, for the sake of little Tomás."

Tomás was Hector and Aida's son, a two-year-old, wriggling in a little chair next to Maya, who was the wife of Hector's brother Rafaelo, and the mother of Frida, who was one, and was seated in another tiny chair. Our speeding wagon had three padded benches, with Seela, Brumble, Arf, and me in the middle one, along with Tomás in his chair. To make room for us, Rafaelo and Maya had moved onto the rear-most bench next to Frida. Maya wore a lacy black blouse, with buttons in it so she could easily nurse Frida. Rafaelo wore a fancy shirt with a scalloped section on the shoulders, and snaps on the pockets. He had a thick, black ponytail as long as Maya's.

It was confusing to be with so many people, but even more, it was unsettling to be flying along this narrow gray road at an unheard of speed, with other shiny wagons racing toward us, very nearly colliding with us and then roaring past. The road ran along the rising and falling edges of the cliffs, with the aquamarine Big Sur ocean throwing wild spume from the rocks below. Seela clutched Brumble tight.

Aida was an extremely inattentive driver, constantly talking, and using one hand to hold a type of small cigar with white paper wrapping. She had a round steering wheel, and a control with a handle on top, a bit like the single control on the panel of a fried egg saucer. Every minute she would turn almost completely around to assess the impact of her jokes, admonitions, and sallies upon us in the rear. All the while, furious blasts of music issued from the van's control panel—massed horns, accordions, and lamenting voices, raised in expressive arcs of Mexican song.

Seela looked at me goggle-eyed, sharing my anxiety. Rafaelo offered us something to drink, that is, he handed us two oddly lightweight little cans, very smooth-skinned, and with sharp edges around a hole in the top. I was thirsty, but I couldn't quite see the trick of how to drink from the can, nor was I sure the contents would be salubrious. I spilled a bit of the stuff onto the palm of my hand, then sniffed and licked it, sending the ponytailed Maya into gales of laughter.

Having determined that my can held thin, bitter beer—which they called Tecate *cerveza*—I tried to drink it, but I spilled most of my first mouthful onto my chin and my filthy shirt. Seeing my embarrassment, Rafaelo slowly raised his own can to his mouth, with his eyes fixed on mine, as if demonstrating a physical principle to a child, and then took a long drink, with his prominent Adam's apple wagging. Hector laughed. I think they assumed we were primitive villagers, which wasn't so far off the mark. No matter. Seela and I successfully emulated Rafaelo, and the beer was indeed welcome.

I'd been so anxious about getting a ride that I'd hardly noticed how thirsty and hungry I was, but now I could gainsay my hunger no more.

"Food *por favor*?" I inquired.

"*Tamales*," said Maya.

With an auspicious rustle, she extracted larval shapes from a box on the floor—corn husks wrapped around cornmeal patties with shredded pork in the middle, a food not wholly unlike things I'd eaten in Virginia. Gratefully, Seela and I ate several tamales, and Arf got one too, nearly choking on it, as he insisted on swallowing the thing in one gulp. Brumble began to nurse. Little Tomás watched in fascination.

"You coming north from Belize?" Hector asked, pointing at Seela and me. "Long trip."

"*Si*," I said, glad to have a ready explanation for our origin. We were to be impoverished immigrants from, I surmised, a country called Belize. But Seela felt the need to correct Hector.

"We're from the Hollow Earth," she said. "*La Tierra Hueca.*" Why did she have to make things so hard? But it was fine.

"*Fantastico*," Rafaelo said, as if he'd heard of the Hollow Earth. And with that, we let the topic go. Seela and I were destitute non-white immigrants, we spoke a little Spanish, we were their guests, and that was enough.

And so we traveled on, past the intense ink-blue sea, the round green hills, and the dry red rocks. Seela made much of little Frida and Tomás, and the Mexicans showered kindnesses upon Brumble. They kept asking Seela to say his name again, as her pronunciation made them laugh.

Houses and business establishments began appearing beside the road, low flimsy structures with large windows. Metal wagons like ours were stationed in front of them, like hitched horses. The wagons were called cars and trucks. They were everywhere. We saw very few people on foot. The pedestrians carried small rectangular objects that they stared at all the time. They seemed dazed. They wore bright clothes, with colored shoes. On their heads they had skullcaps with projecting bills.

The road widened to hold more cars and trucks, racing in both directions at insane speeds. Large green signs with instructions appeared on poles beside the roads, and on mighty horizontal bars overhead. The road's surface had changed to featureless gray stone with lines painted on it. Other roads crossed over our road by way of improbably huge viaducts that roared with echoes. Poles lined the roads, bearing sets of black wires.

A town slid by on our left, and another on our right, each of them a congeries of dun, shoddy houses, with low, sloping roofs. Unaccountable gargantuan stores were amid the houses, with short, meaningless words written large upon their sides. People teemed in and out of the stores like swarming gnats. We passed a crooked hotel by the sea, as ugly and unornamented as the homes.

The flow of cars grew heavier as we approached Santa Cruz, and the drivers more agitated. Continually our car blasted strident music that sounded sad even when it was supposed to be merry. I felt desperate and lost. Seela and I held hands and silently comforted each other via tekelili. Still more beige buildings flew by, with their crude blank walls and moronic signs. The future was horrible. We were marooned in a shoddy, overcrowded hell.

The ocean appeared again on our left. The high cliffs were gone. I glimpsed boats. Aida veered off the busy highway into a quieter street. Blessedly she slowed down. It was late afternoon. I saw a woman walking a tiny dog on a red leather leash. The woman's dark hair was dyed in stripes of yellow. She was staring at one of those shiny rectangular items in her hand.

"You get out here now?" Aida asked us.

"I don't know," said Seela, nearly in tears. "We don't know what we're doing at all. I'm scared."

"We'll be fine," I said, manfully taking Brumble on my shoulder. "Thanks for the ride."

"You don't got papers, do you?" said kind Rafaelo. "We're the same. You can stay with us."

"*Bene*," I said, shaky with relief.

"Only for a short time," said Aida, casting a stern look over her shoulder.

"Month, two month, three month," said the mellow Hector.

"And you find work," Aida told me. "Put money in the pot."

"Yes, yes," said Seela. "We will. Thank you, oh, thank you."

"And Mason can tell me about the *Tierra Hueca*," said Rafaelo. To some extent he was joking, but I could also sense true curiosity.

13. Impostor

So our Mexican friends brought us to the small, rented house that they shared, low and tan, in the sandy flats near the mouth of a small river, and near a fantastical outdoor amusement park that Maya called the Boardwalk. A great wheel in the park was turning, and small carts with people were rolling along a high track. A tower with lever arms was swinging people in the air. I'd never seen such large machines.

"It's open?" I asked Maya, wanting to go over there and explore—as if I hadn't had thrills enough this week, and as if I wasn't totally disgusted with the clangor of twenty eighteen. But, remember, I was seventeen, and the idea of a pleasure park had some appeal. But wait, I'd decided to start saying I was eighteen, as my February 2, 2018, birthday had been last month. On the other hand, I'd skipped over nine months, along with those 167 years, so—

"Yes, the Boardwalk's open today," said Maya, interrupting my number thoughts. "Sunday. Not on work days. And it closes in an hour. So never mind. Look at our house."

"You sleep here," said Hector, pointing to a large open shed adjoining their house. A stable for cars, I supposed. But they called it a garage. A well-used mattress lay on the floor at the back of the car stable. The walls were of an odd kind of wood, exceedingly thin, as if pressed flat by rollers. A lifeless machine stood near the front of the stable. It had two great rubber wheels, like those on a car, and an oily engine of some kind between the wheels. Shiny, opulent white fenders shielded the wheels. A seat cushion rested above a teardrop-shaped tank, with a pillion cushion behind. Presumably two people could sit astride the cushions and ride. It seemed very dangerous and impractical. To make the machine still odder, it had a one-wheeled pod attached to the right side, an open passenger compartment with its own small windshield and a cushion on the floor. Its wheel, too, had a curved white fender.

"My sidecar motorcycle," said Hector. "I got this rig from my cousin cause the engine *no mas* run. I dream I fix it."

"I can help," I said, wanting to make myself agreeable. My friends had resurrected a comatose flying saucer. Maybe I could do the same for a broken motorcycle.

"Let's go in and chill," said Maya, leading the way.

The first miracle was that Aida pushed a switch on the wall, and the room was filled with light. From a fixture on the ceiling. Gas? No, the light came from a small, frosted glass bulb that seemed to have a tiny sun inside it.

"E-lec-tri-ci-ty," said Maya, laughing at my expression. "*Tu sabe?*"

The house had virtually no furniture, just a lumpy divan, a mattress in each of the two bedrooms, a spindly table, and six diverse folding chairs made of lightweight metal tubes and with woven straps of a material I'd never seen.

The second miracle was that the house had water running from metal fixtures—and hot water as well, not to mention an indoor water-filled bowl in place of an outhouse. Seela and I flushed it five or ten times in a row, fascinated to see the vortex go spiraling down, carrying the little mock boats of tissue that we set upon it for drama.

One would have expected a house like this to very lavishly furnished, but the inside walls lacked cornices or framed paintings. In lieu of this, the blank walls were decorated with crude, hand-made representations of rattlesnakes, cactuses, stone gods, and what must have been a Mexican flag. "I make these," said Maya with pride. "The landlady don't know."

"Will she throw you out?" I asked.

"Hard to evict someone in Santa Cruz," said Rafaelo. "Even us illegals."

"What are the chairs made of?" I asked. "Those flat straps."

"This *vato* is from nowhere," said mother Aida, eyeing me. "You lived in a hut and pounded a log and ate bananas in Belize, Mason?"

"I myself lived on a flower," said Seela, always one for circling back to her origins. "In the Hollow Earth."

"*Loco*," said Hector.

"Plastic," Rafaelo said to me, running his hand along the yellow straps on one of the chairs. "Everywhere. Not plant, not leather, not metal. From factories in China. Our coats and shoes—plastic too. Everywhere. Like Spiderman."

"I don't like plastic," said Seela decisively.

"Don't matter," said Maya. "You in California, baby. Look here, everybody. I got still more tamales!"

We sat in the plastic chairs and ate the rest of the food. Arf got a tamale too. The beer was gone, so we drank water. In plastic cups. Tomás toddled around, and Frida crawled, the two of them accepting scraps of tamale from their parents. Tomás liked to wrap his arms around Frida and pick her up, and then she'd yell in rage. Excited by the sound of other kids, Brumble waved his arms and gurgled. And then Seela nursed him while Maya nursed Frida, who was by now nearly weaned.

The Mexicans told us about their jobs. Aida was a maid at a nearby place named the Clearlight Court Motel. Hector worked at a small restaurant called Los Trancos Taco Bar. Rafaelo was a cleaner in a building in downtown Santa Cruz. And Maya sold jewelry in a craft shop called Sparkle Wow.

"Some of them like to hire illegals and pay us under the table," said Aida. I didn't know what she meant by this. Were Seela and I illegals?

"You can work at Sparkle Wow with me," Maya was telling Seela.

"That's good," said Seela, brightening. "I can make jewelry for them."

"If Josh lets you," said Maya with a shrug. "He's the owner. Thinks he knows a lot. I painted a mural on his garage, but he didn't pay me none. He's one who takes advantage of illegals. He makes a lot of the stuff he sells. And he likes the girls. So we've got that good old pussy power on our side."

"Charming turn of phrase," I said, feeling uneasy.

"What about a job for you, Mason?" said Aida.

"I'd like to write," I said. "For a newspaper."

Aida guffawed. "A barefoot illegal from Belize, and you want a job like that?"

"My English is excellent," I said. "My penmanship is very fine."

"So let Mason try," said Rafaelo. "A new voice, *verdad*? The building where I clean, the newspaper office is there. The *Good Times*. I bring you there tomorrow, Mason, and you push in and talk *excelente* and you ask to write for them. People are crazy in Santa Cruz. The editor might say yes."

"*Si, si*, but Mason still needs shoes," said Aida. "You got so much shoes, Rafaelo. Give shoes to him."

"Air Jordan," said Rafaelo. "Twenty fifteen model. Very sharp for you, Mason."

"And take clothes from our heaps!" said Hector, waving his hand toward the mounds on the floor and at the stuffed double closet by the front door. "For *donnas y hombres*. Mason and Seela. Pick coats for sleep in garage."

Rafaelo's shoes fit me. They were huge and red. Seela selected tight, lime green pants, a blouse with large purple flowers, a puffy pale blue plastic jacket, and some furry pink slippers that were almost like shoes. I got a black sweatshirt, that is, a long-sleeved shirt with no buttons and no collar, and a matching pair of black sweatpants, plus a puffy plastic silver jacket similar to Seela's. Also a black cap with a bill, and the number forty-nine on the cap.

As the early sunset wound down, Hector, Rafaelo, Seela and I kicked around a yellow plastic ball in the front of the house. It was a game of sorts, with the idea being to kick the ball into the stable where we were to sleep. Arf sleepily watched us from our mattress, where he'd already settled in.

Afterwards Hector played the trumpet—wielding his long, thin horn with some skill. Maya and Rafaelo sang along, and then Aida joined, and then Seela and I, feeling our way through the Spanish lyrics. The music sounded better live than from the control panel of a car. We sang for a long time.

Hector and Aida went to bed with little Tomás, and Maya lay down with little Frida at her breast, and after that, Rafaelo showed me and Seela his great treasure, a piece of black glass that showed moving images of monsters fighting women and men. At first I thought the creatures were alive inside the device—perhaps via a woomo trick of space and time—but they were only pictures. The toy also emitted the sounds of roars, shouts and explosions.

"I dream someday I'll build games like this," Rafaelo told us with a faraway look. "If I can learn the tricks."

"You could make a game about the *Tierra Hueca*," I speculated. "Maybe the woomo can help."

Rafaelo continued playing with his toy, which quickly grew tedious for Seela and me. We bundled up and went to lie on our mattress with Brumble. He sneezed once and yawned. We had one of the *woomo* shawls wrapped around him. I'd worried the mattress might be damp, but it was dry, and we went to sleep right away.

At some point during the night Uxa woke me. It started as a dream. I saw a crooked ray of pink light creep in through our stable's open door—and lay hair-thin fronds across my body, with special attention to my spine and the back of my neck.

I sat bolt upright on the mattress, looking around, and, yes, I was seeing the pink main branch of the ray. It was subtler in color than in my dream, but it was real, and Uxa was wordlessly speaking to me. She showed me an image of myself on a pedestal, haloed in glory, a mighty avatar, an idol of the human race. A lure for my vanity. Lest I dream of escape, Uxa added a motion sequence image that showed how her tendrils had been tracking Seela and me ever since our sojourn upon the slick, rubbery mesas of her body at the Gate.

Thanks to the loss of the Big Sur rumbies, the Bloom wasn't going to work. The *woomo* could of course transport more rumbies to the surface. But, for whatever reason, they wanted me to be involved. And I couldn't tell how.

Did Uxa want me to drive the pugnacious farmer ants from the Big Sur cave? Was I to recruit a corps of human volunteers for the Bloom? Was I on a quest for Eddie Poe and the missing rumbies?

Uxa wasn't one to reveal her long-range plans—if she had any. Perhaps she lived only in the now. She urged me to my feet, and showed me an image of myself fixing the engine of Hector's motorcycle.

My hands were glowing. I was a channel for Uxa's *woomo* energy. I rose to my feet. Seela and Brumble continued sleeping, but Arf got up to watch. Just to test my powers, I touched my forefinger to his nose—and his fur puffed out like dandelion fluff. He gave me an accusing look, then backed away and shook himself, settling his hair into place.

I walked quietly to the sidecar motorcycle, which rested at the car stable's entrance like a stilled insect. The three-quarters-full moon was in the west, sending glints off the fuel tank of the three-wheeled machine. My mind filled with diagrams of the motorcycle's odd engine, and of the toothy gears it wore upon the axle of its rear wheel. Yes, I knew how to put this particular type of engine into working order. Whence came the knowing? Uxa showed an image of a dexterous motorcycle groom, sleeping with his tattooed wife in a low home not so far away. Within easy reach of *woomo* tekelili.

Playing on my longing for renown, Uxa fed me a blasphemous image of myself in the role of a robed Messiah, raising a dead man by the laying on of hands. The corpse was Hector's motorcycle. I stepped forward. Jagged fronds grew from my fingertips and fed into the oily crannies of the engine's innards. White hot sparks sputtered within. I had a sense of things merging and dividing. And then—Uxa's will was accomplished. I cried out in a loud voice.

"Rise, Lazarus, and sin no more!"

Understand that I said this in jest. I've never had much truck with religion. But I'd read the Bible back on the farm, and I liked the language and the strange tales. Giddy with exultation, I sat atop the motorcycle, twisted the grips on its steering bar, and used my foot to pump a sturdy lever on the thing's side. The engine popped and roared. Arf watched these things in wonder and kept them in his heart.

"The fuck you doin? Turn it off!"

It was Rafaelo, sleepily peering from the side door that led into the garage. Uxa had released her hold over me, but even so, I knew how to kill the engine. The sudden silence was deafening.

"I fixed it," I told Rafaelo, getting off my seat.

"How?" said he, greatly doubting me.

"Secrets of the Hollow Earth. Giant sea cucumbers. Crooked rays of light."

"What you smokin, dog? Go to sleep. I'll take you to my job tomorrow. Crack of early."

I woke to the sound of the motorcycle, farting and growling, its voice rising to a snarl. Hector sat astride it, turning the grip on the handle, greatly pleased.

"Aida!" he called. "We ride to work!"

She appeared in the garage, with very little paint on her face, wearing plain blue clothes, her hair in a bun, and her body the shape of a potato—ready for her day as a maid at the Clearlight Court Motel. She'd parked their son Tomás with an old lady next door.

"*Que pasa?*" she asked.

"Mason fixed the motorcycle," said Rafaelo.

"Mason da man!" yelled Hector, beaming at me. "*Bueno, amigo.*"

Aida blew me a juicy kiss, put a hand on Hector's shoulder and, rather than sitting in the low sidecar, swung her leg over the pillion cushion and wrapped her arms around proud Hector's waist. "*Andale.*"

With a concussive roar, the creamy white sidecar motorcycle pulled onto the street and sped away.

Arf barked, by way of punctuation. Brumble wailed. Seela sat up. "You did something?" she asked me.

"I'm the man," I told her.

"We gotta go to my building now," Rafaelo told me. "And, Seela, you can go with Maya when she wakes up."

"Fine," said Seela drinking some water and lying back down with Brumble. She was still tired. "Good luck, Mason."

We were close to downtown Santa Cruz, so Rafaelo and I walked. Today he was wearing a long-sleeved dark-red shirt with white shoulders. Black piping separated the shoulder yoke from the lower part. After his own fashion, Rafaelo was a well-dressed man.

I looked around the streets with interest, avidly taking them in. It was nicer to be on foot than in a car. As we crossed a busy street, Rafaelo stopped at a brightly colored food shop with large windows and thin walls. The shop's name was written in yellow letters in dozens of places on the walls, and on the plastic clothes of the employees, but somehow the name didn't stick in my mind. They had music inside the shop. Rafaelo bought us coffee and paper-wrapped buns with ham and scrambled eggs in the middle. Very welcome. The coffee was in paper cups.

Then we entered an older part of the town, with normal-looking buildings of brick and stone, although the street-level shop fronts were almost entirely glass. Signs were everywhere, with big, screaming letters. I couldn't understand what some of the shops sold. The short words on the signs didn't always make sense.

Fog shrouded the sky, and the sounds were muted. I noticed three people riding on velocipedes—metal frames with spoked wheels that they turned by pressing levers with their feet. Rafaelo called them bicycles. I'd once seen an engraving of a Parisian velocipede in the *Southern Literary Messenger*, but I'd never seen one in person.

The women wore their hair loose or in ponytails, and hardly anyone had a proper hat—just those foolish billed caps like the one on my head. Over and over I muttered the year number to myself. *Twenty eighteen.* Surely I was in a different world, but the people seemed, in their essence, much the same as in eighteen fifty. Beggars, ladies, men of the world, dunderheads, poets, merchants, termagants, coquettes—all the usual types were here. A surprise and a relief.

I hoped Seela was getting along well with Maya. And that they'd tethered Arf at the house. And that Maya's boss didn't mind that Seela would be bringing Brumble to work. Maya had said she often brought Frida, at least for part of the day, although sometimes she'd leave her with the old lady who was watching Tomás.

Rafael's building was a pile of granite, several stories high. We went in by a back door, where Rafael changed into a drab work uniform of beige pants and shirt. And then he equipped himself with a rolling bucket, a rolling trashcan, and a cart with rags and mops. His first task of the day would be to swab and polish the building's six bathrooms. I felt disheartened that that my clever, personable friend was relegated to so humble a role—in part because he lacked proper papers. Surely he sensed my feelings, and was himself in some measure abashed, but he covered it over with his fine good humor.

"You help me, Mason, and we work our way to the top, and you meet the big man at the *Good Times* newspaper."

Six bathrooms later, Rafaelo ushered me into the offices of the *Good Times*. A woman named Janelle greeted us. She wore black pants and a flowing blue blouse with white dots. Her face was sensual and a bit rough-skinned, with a layer of oily beige paint, and with her lips colored very red. This was, as I'd already noticed on Aida yesterday, an ordinary practice in the year twenty eighteen.

Janelle knew Rafaelo, and she seemed to find him attractive.

"*Hola,*" said he. "My homie Mason wants to talk to the boss."

"About?" Janelle was looking me over—black-skinned in my black sweatpants and sweatshirt, with my puffy silver coat, my enormous red shoes, and a billed hat with the number forty-nine. It struck me, in this fraught moment, that the forty-nine might be a symbol for that epochal California Gold Rush year.

"Mason's a writer," Rafaelo was saying. "He has a story about someplace weird."

"Weird is good," said Janelle agreeably. "And Noah's not especially busy right now. All he does before lunch is read email."

The editor Noah Blanker was relaxed and genial. He wore a silky shirt the like of which I'd never seen—it was pale blue with pink and green spirals and an enormous floppy collar. He spoke very slowly, almost as if he were talking in his sleep, but this was a conversational stratagem. His eyes were alert. He invited me to tell him my idea for a story, then leaned back in his chair and listened, beginning to smile as I went on.

I outlined the narrative of my first trip to the Hollow Earth. This was easy for me, given that only about four months of my personal time had elapsed since I'd finished writing *The Hollow Earth*, my book-length manuscript about my trip—which manuscript I'd foolishly left with E. J. Coale in Baltimore, 1850. But I digress. Quickly I told Noah Blanker of my trip to the antarctic with Poe, our fall through the South Hole, our encounter with the *woomo* at the Hollow Earth's core, and our return through an ocean hole in the Rind near Baltimore.

"Awesome rap," said Noah when I finally paused. "Like a happy dream. But it has nothing to do with Santa Cruz."

"I could mention that living flying saucers from the Hollow Earth have recently spawned babies in a Big Sur cave," I blithely said. As I spoke, I felt an unpleasant twinge in my spine, as if to say: *Don't talk about that.* Uxa was still watching me.

Noah Blanker was shaking his head. "No saucers," said he. "The Hollow Earth is enough. Think harder, Mason. Find a local hook, and I'll run your piece day after tomorrow. I need two thousand words."

"I—I've never counted words," I said, a little confused.

"You can learn," drawled Blanker. "You're a bright kid." He paused, studying me. "I do have one question. You talk like a white guy in a historical movie. But you look black, you're dressed like you're homeless, and it's our Latino custodian Rafaelo who brought you in. How do the pieces fit?"

"May I speak without artifice?" I said.

"Lay it on me, dude." How curiously this man spoke!

"My Hollow Earth narratives are veridical," I said. "And I am in fact white. I was burned black by the light of the *woomo* at the Hollow Earth's core. I'm from the Virginia of 1850. I lost over a century and a half in an eddy of slow time."

"The *woomo*," said Noah Blanker with a bark of laughter. "I love how you stay in character. Maybe you can turn your routine into a book." He paused, thinking. "Find the damn hook and write your piece by tomorrow morning. Tuesday. Our weekly issue comes out on Wednesday. And we've got a two-thousand-word hole. Tracy Ting was writing a piece on this year's surf scene, but then she took off for Tonga with a pro surfer she met."

"Will you pay me?"

"Peanuts," said Blanker. "A hundred bucks. But if your story works out, you can do a sequel next month and I'll pay you two hundred for that one. But, remember: you've gotta find a local hook."

"You mention surfing," I slowly said. "I believe I saw surfing on Saturday. People stand on lozenge-shaped boards and slide down the faces of ocean waves."

"You got *that* right, spaceman."

"In the Hollow Earth, we use lozenges of ballula shell to coast upon the heated air around giant moving streams of light. We call these lozenges lightboards. And the rays are from the *woomo*."

"Lightsurfing!" exclaimed Noah Blanker. "Perfect. Love, love, love those *woomo*. Your title is *Lightsurfing the Hollow Earth*. Now go write the rest."

"Might I petition for a partial advance payment of my fee?"

Blanker chuckled. I think he relished his recklessness in trusting me. "Here's two twenties," he said, handing them across the desk. My heart sang.

I went downstairs and found Rafaelo buffing a hallway floor.

"Noah Blanker is buying a story about the Hollow Earth!" I exulted. "It'll be in the *Good Times* on Wednesday."

"No way!" said Rafaelo. "You're magic, Mason. You fix Hector's motorcycle and you sell a story to a white newspaper. You gonna program my Hollow Earth videogame too?"

"Not today," I said. "I need to draft my narrative."

"Buy a pad of paper and a pen. There's a store right down the street. Palace Art. Then you go sit somewhere. A coffee shop, or the library."

"A library? That would be wonderful. I've never seen one."

"It's somewhere near here. I don't know exactly. You got money for the pen and paper?"

"Noah Blanker gave me forty dollars," I said, showing him my bills. "I get sixty more when the article comes out."

"*Fantastico.* You the goose who lay the golden egg! We'll buy us *carnitas* meat and a case of *cerveza* for tonight, *si?* Case is twenty-four cans."

"*Bueno.* But should I go and see if Seela and Brumble are safe before I start writing?"

"They'll be at Sparkle Wow with Maya till five. You go to the library, *vato.* Settle in. Then come meet me here at five."

"*Adios,*" I said.

It was difficult for me to purchase the paper and the pen. Even opening the store's swinging glass door was a problem, and then I had no idea what a pen might look like here, nor how it would work, nor how a notebook of blank paper might be packaged. A kind young clerk came to my aid, a woman not much older than me. She wore a name tag that that read Shelly.

I completed the purchase, watching attentively as Shelly blinked numbers onto a glass rectangle and extracted change from a rolling drawer that was set into a chunk of machinery. Wanting to impress Shelly, I said I was going to the library to write an article about the Hollow Earth for the *Good Times* weekly newspaper.

"That's nice," said Shelly, her neutral smile flattening into a tense line. She thought I was a liar or a madman. She pitied and feared me. As she gave me directions to the library, her voice was a cold monotone.

One of the librarian ladies was leery of me as well. This was a Mary Bisby, who sat at a counter near the door. I felt she disliked my presence because my clothes were shabby and my skin was dark—and I told myself that white attitudes toward blacks hadn't changed much since eighteen fifty. This said, after I'd worked quietly for an hour, Mary Bisby switched to giving me approving nods. In her eyes I was bettering myself.

And so I wrote away in my notebook, using a fine hand so Noah Blanker would find my submission pleasant to read. "Lightsurfers of the Hollow Earth," yes. I remembered my original *Hollow Earth* narrative very vividly, and I was able to quote key phrases from it, which helped me compose at a rapid pace.

Even more—and this is a bit hard to explain—I had by now a sense that I'd already written the bulk of my new narrative *Return to the Hollow Earth*. Admittedly I hadn't yet scribed any of it in pen and ink. But, as I've mentioned, I'd been composing it in my head during the past three or four months of lived time. And all along I'd had a tekelili sense that I was somehow dictating my narrative to an unseen being. And while we were becalmed at the core of the Hollow Earth, I'd realized that my listener was in fact Uxa. The great *woomo* had a record of my whole composition thus far. It struck me that Uxa might here and now be prevailing upon some third party to commit my narrative to paper. Someone in California twenty eighteen. I did enjoy doing the writing myself, but having an astral secretary would certainly be handy.

But just now I was on my own, writing the old-fashioned way, leaning over blank paper pages and inscribing letters with my peculiar futuristic pen. Every now and then my fingers would cramp, and I'd wander among the shelves and look at the books. What a treasure trove! The art, science, history, and literature of my lost hundred and sixty seven years were ranged here for my education and delectation. If Seela and I were to settle in Santa Cruz, I would read hundreds of these books.

As I continued writing in my notebook, I felt the same creative ecstasy as when I'd written out my *Hollow Earth* manuscript, and I vaingloriously thought to myself that really I had no need to read other people's books, nor did I need further schooling. What with my unparalled adventures, and with the metaphysical illuminations I'd experienced amid the *woomo* at the Hollow Earth's core, and with my mental vision of *Return to the Hollow Earth* nearly done—with all this in hand, I was a genius complete—an author on a par with Eddie Poe. I grinned as I wrote.

By the time it occurred to me to estimate my count of words, I found I'd amassed six thousand. I flipped through my pages, X-ing out blocks of text and condensing the more florid descriptions. And then I had it down to three thousand words. That would do. I still needed to make a fair copy of what I had, but by now the sun was sinking, and the large, humming clock on the wall said it was nearly five, so I went to meet Rafaelo.

He changed back into his handsome clothes, and we had a fine fiesta at their home. Seela was in a good mood. Josh at Sparkle Wow had not only been pleasant to Seela, he'd allowed her to create two of her networked necklaces of wires and geegaws, and one of them had already sold. Seela liked Josh, and she matter-of-factly told me she could make him fall in love with her.

"Why do you say that?" I cried. "To make me jealous?"

"I'm going to find a way to stay here," said Seela. "Even if you're crazy enough to fly off in a *veem*. I can tell you're thinking about it. You don't fool me one bit."

"Let's wait and see what happens," I said, a little put out. "Don't you go jumping into bed with that man right away. Relationships work a little differently here than they did among your Hollow Earth flower tribe."

"No they don't," said Seela, turning sly and worldly. "They're just the same." Impudently she extended her forefinger and pushed it in and out of a loop she made with the thumb and forefinger of her other hand. "See?"

"If we split up, who keeps Brumble?" I asked.

"Let's wait and see what happens," said Seela, smugly echoing me. She dandled the baby on her lap. Our shared treasure.

I sat up late and made my fair copy of my condensed article, working by the light of our Mexican hosts' wondrous lightbulb.

Tuesday morning I gave Noah Blanker my article, and he took a photo of me to run with it. I spent the rest of Tuesday walking around town with Arf and Brumble while Seela worked at Sparkle Wow. I even managed to buy a sandwich and bring it in to Seela when it was time for her to nurse the baby. The new necklace-nets she was making were glorious. I didn't get a chance to size up her boss Josh. He hadn't come in for work yet.

My article was to appear in the *Good Times* with a photo of me on Wednesday morning. By the time I rose on Wednesday, Rafaelo had gone to work. I left Brumble with Seela and walked over to Noah Blanker's office with Arf. I planned to get my copy of the paper, and to claim the sixty dollars they still owed me. Arf ran to Rafaelo on the bottom floor and I went upstairs. Noah's assistant Janelle wasn't at the front desk. Peering out from his office, Noah waved me in.

He was frowning. He'd just spoken to the assiduous Mary Bisby, the librarian who on Monday had observed me writing my article in her common room. La Bisby had noticed my picture next my article this morning. Doubting my honesty, she'd canvassed her shelves for an alternate source of my material. And, oh woe, she'd found a narrative entitled *The Hollow Earth*, and attributed to a local author named Rudy Rucker.

In a trice, the spiteful Bisby had convinced herself that my "Lightsurfing the Hollow Earth" was copied from Rucker's volume—and she'd hastened to pour her poison into Noah Blanker's ear. I was a plagiarist.

"It's not plagiarism," I told Noah after he'd explained this to me. "I myself wrote *The Hollow Earth*. In 1850. It's my account of what actually happened. My name is in the book, Mason Reynolds. It's abundantly clear. Somehow my manuscript found its way to Rucker's hands. You may say he's the author, but he's only the editor."

"Doubling down on your lies, eh?" said Noah, his expression stern. "You're a plagiarist *and* an imposter. Not only did you copy from the book, you claim you're a character from it. *Mason Reynolds*. What a total crock of shit."

"You'll withdraw my article?"

"Too late for that," said Noah with a shrug. "The paper's in stacks in shops and on street corners all over town. I'll run an apology next week." His eyes were sad. "Too bad it worked out this way, Mason. Or whatever your name is. I'd thought this would be fun."

"Can I have my sixty dollars now?"

He glared, then fished out his wallet. "Obviously you need it." He handed me three twenties. "Now beat it. We're done."

As I rose to my feet, Noah's assistant Janelle came into the office, sipping a cup of coffee she'd bought herself. "Oh, good, Mason's still here. I wasn't sure. I got a written message for you this morning, Mason. This skungy street person brought it to the office."

"Can I see the note?" I asked. "Who's it from?"

"You don't have to help him," Noah told Janelle. "He's a con-man. The librarian says he copied his article. And he's not even Mason Reynolds."

"He's still kind of cute," said Janelle. "I like how he always wears the same clothes." She was making fun of me, a little bit.

"Like that guy in AC/DC," said Noah, his gloom slightly lifting. "The one who always wore the schoolboy uniform? Angus? I saw AC/DC play at the Cow Palace when I was in the eleventh grade. It was the absolute high point of my life. The women in the audience, Janelle. Beyond all dreams."

"Old much?" said Janelle.

Would I ever learn to banter like the overlords of twenty eighteen? "Did you save the piece of paper?" I pressed Janelle. "With the message?"

"I think so," she said carelessly. "Somewhere on my desk. It's cuckoo jive-talk and it's signed Edgar Allan Poe. Supposedly Poe wants you to meet him at the Evergreen Cemetery. Oh, and he needs clothes."

For a moment Noah looked intrigued. But then he shook his head. "I'm guessing our young author wrote the message himself," he said. "And he had one of his skeevy pals bring it to you. Step lively, *Mason*. Don't let the door hit you in the ass on the way out." Janelle and I exited.

In the front office, Janelle handed me my message—it was handwritten in dark pencil on a thick, dirty scrap of paper, yellow with age. The writing was unmistakably Eddie's—as was the style and, above all, the content.

> Greetings Mason. It is I, the penitent Poe. Ina and I have lain in wait for one hundred and forty one years

515

while Fwopsy sought her mate. The rumbies are ours. Their forces have preserved us like royal pharaohs. And the villain Machree is no more. Roused by *woomo* tekelili, Ina and I hail your and your lady's advent, o new Adam and Eve, o scions of the Bloom. Ina and I sit amid foul, unclean shrouds, windings, and cerements in the Evergreen Cemetery dell. Bring us raiment and, in the name of God, bring cake and brandy. Make haste, I beseech you. With heartfelt rue, Edgar Allan Poe / Goarland Peale

Pure Eddie. Keeping a straight face, I repressed a shout of joy, and shoved the scrap into my pocket. "Stuff and nonsense," I muttered to Janelle. "But, yes, I'll go. I have, as you may surmise, little else on my agenda. Can you direct me to the Evergreen Cemetery?"

"Sure," said Janelle, glancing over at Noah's closed door. "But you really do need to leave. I've hardly ever seen Noah so mad. And there is zero chance of him buying another article from you. You need to internalize that."

Janelle conjured an image onto the glass screen she had on her desk. The glowing map made little sense to me. Janelle pecked at a row of keys. A white plastic box beside her desk whirred, then spit out a warm, typeset sheet of paper with walking instructions. Janelle said it wouldn't take me more than a half an hour.

"But maybe you should wait for night?" she added with a puckish smile. "I mean, for meeting ghosts in a graveyard?"

"I don't believe in ghosts," I said, trying to salvage some dignity. "I'm a rational man."

"Of course you are," said Janelle, holding her lips tight, lest she laugh in my face.

14. Reunion

I'd risen so late that by the time I left the *Good Times* office it was nearly noon. To my relief, Rafaelo was willing to accompany me and Arf to the cemetery. I was very uneasy about what I might find. Rafaelo replaced his dull dun work uniform with his bright, joyful clothes, and he walked across town with me, eating an extra egg sandwich he had along. Today he wore black leather pants with shiny medallions along the outer seams, and a red and gray shirt with piping, pearl buttons, and embroidered dots and whorls. Atop his head he sported a stiff, white straw hat with a brim.

Using my new money, we purchased two used sweatsuits, a bottle of brandy, and a small chocolate cake. Rafaelo got a packet of those thin white paper cigars as well. Cigarettes. He offered me one. It made me cough, and dizzied me in a pleasant way.

"Pop the cap," said Rafaelo, pointing at the brandy bottle, with cigarette smoke drifting from his lips like liquid. "I'm not goin back to work today at all."

"Very well," I said. We each drank a slug. More coughing, more dizziness. I felt calm.

We crossed a wide road roaring with cars. A subtle system of colored lights indicated when we could cross. I had to bend over and lead the uneasy Arf by the scruff of his neck lest he run off.

On the other side of the road was a gravel pit, and some flimsy, beige stores with big windows. We kept walking, and came to a field with white lines on it, and then to a steep, sodden hill covered with enormous trees. Redwoods. A low iron fence ran along the bottom of the hill, with tilted, mossy gravestones and funerary monuments within. I saw two pale, bedraggled figures seated on a low cement wall beneath an immense laurel tree. I could smell them from across the street, rank and wild. Arf sniffed deeply at the air, tasting the intricacies of the high, thin reek.

"That's your friends?" Rafaelo asked me. "They look *malo*."

Eddie tried to call to us, but his voice was so wispy I couldn't make it out. And he could barely wave his hand. He was dirty and naked, with a flattish silver box beside him, a box the size of a thick book.

"Mason," husked Ina, her voice very rough. Her hair hung down, long and lank. "You're still young. What year is it?"

"Twenty eighteen," said I,

"Don't know what that means," said Ina, very wretched. "The sun—still here. Pale and lost." She dropped her head and her shoulders shook. She was sobbing. Poor, poor thing. Her skin had turned as white as the flesh of a mushroom. She was clad in greasy scraps of shroud from the tomb.

I made my way up the low stone stairs to where she and Eddie sat, and I offered Ina a pink Goodwill sweatsuit. She waved it off.

"I need to bathe," said she. "I'm foul."

"There's a hose," said Rafaelo. "I'll get it." Quickly he had water running through a rubber tube from a metal fixture like I'd seen in their house. A faucet.

Ina drank, then played the stream across herself and Eddie. The two of them rubbed their bodies, groaning with relief, showering water across their eyes, mouths, noses, and ears; gargling and spitting, washing their crotches and armpits and feet and hair. The wet grass sparkled; the drops twinkled against the sharp, sour green.

"Thank you, old friend," croaked Eddie, accepting the yellow sweatsuit I had for him. He rubbed himself with it, then pulled it on. His hair, like Ina's, was nasty, dank, and disturbingly long. His fingernails had grown out and curled over. He had a scraggly beard. He was the very image of a creature from his tales—a ghoul, a revenant, an undead corpse. He sensed me thinking this, and he smiled a bit, as if pleased to be so theatrically ghastly.

For whatever reason, we had a fair amount of tekelili here. Oh, of course—I now sensed that Eddies' rounded silver box was full of rumbies, close to a hundred of them, clacking against each other like massive marbles.

He reached out for the bottle of brandy. I uncapped it and he deeply drank. Taking out a pocket knife, Rafaelo cut slices of our cake. Ina snatched a piece, wolfed it down, then ate a second and a third, willfully smearing chocolate icing across her deathly pale face. She drank of the brandy as well—we all did. We shared a communion of spirits and cake.

"You two were buried here?" I said. "How did you emerge?

"Wormed through the tree," said Eddie, making an intricate, expressive gesture that encompassed the towering bay laurel in whose shade we sat. It had a hole in its bole, as if from rot. Fluttering his fingers, Eddie indicated that they'd crawled up through the tree's roots and into its hollow base, having started in—and this I saw via tekelili—a bronze double casket that lay six feet below the sun-splashed grass. I stepped over to read the inscription on the ornate free-standing gravestone. Their names were in bas-relief ovals amid stone ivy leaves.

INA DURIVAGE OF LOUISIANA
DIED JAN 19, 1877.
AGED 33 YEARS

<--->

GOARLAND PEALE, A BOSTONIAN
DIED JAN 19, 1877.
AGED 44 YEARS

<--->

"WHAT LAUGHING HEART HAS DIED IN VAIN"

"You copied the epitaph from my stone?" I exclaimed. "The grave of MirrorMason in Lynchburg, Virginia. He was shot by the MirrorEarth stableboy?"

"I'm aware of this," said Eddie. "I draw upon what comes to hand. When I designed this stone, you were present in my mind. I knew we'd see you when we rose."

"By what route did you enter the grave?"

"The burghers termed it *misadventure*," said Eddie. "Meaning suicide, presumably by laudanum. In truth we benumbed ourselves with the tekelili of our mass of rumbies, and we entered a state of life-in-death. I paid an undertaker in advance to see that we were interred intact in a shared bronze casket—which contained a secret sliding door of my own design."

"Your purposes are opaque, my liege."

"We hoped to be part of the Bloom," said Eddie, pausing to hawk up phlegm, and then to drink more brandy. "And we knew it would be a long wait. When we left you and returned to the Earth's surface, the year was 1862. Fwopsy dropped Ina and me in San Francisco, and proceeded onward with Machree and the rumbies, we knew not where."

"Did you see Machree again?"

"We saw him fifteen years later, said Ina. "More on that anon. Eddie and I spent the intervening years as performers. I treaded the boards as a spiritualist trance-speaker, declaiming poems and tales that I purported to channel from that lost literary titan, Edgar Allan Poe."

"And I posed as Ina's stout, fusty, clean-shaven, bespectacled manager, Goarland Peale," said Eddie. "I sat near the stage and fed her my words via tekelili. An efficacious diddle. But I tired of the work. It's dull, pleasing dullards."

"It's thanks to me that we worked our hoax for as long as we did," said Ina. "We carried it to London and Berlin, to Tokyo, Sydney, and Honolulu. During the seasons when Eddie was having his vapors and doldrums, I'd spout fresh bluster on my own. It's easy to beat a drum, once you find the stick." She rested a cool gaze upon Eddie. "I'm your equal, Goarland Peale."

"The vixen is a virago," said Eddie fondly. "An elfin Xanthippe."

Incongruously, Ina giggled. "We should have published a book of my verse. *Happy Poe*."

"And we could have included *Htrae*," said Eddie. "My blank-verse epic of the Hollow Earth. I formulated great swatches of it, Mason, and Ina declaimed them to the crowds."

"But he never wrote down a single word of it," said Ina. "Too bad. And then came the climax."

"We took possession of the long-lost rumbies—and murdered Connor Machree," said Eddie, drinking yet again from the brandy bottle. "He reappeared and sent us to a Big Sur cave to fetch the rumbies where he'd hidden them. Ina and I very nearly died in the process. We were set upon by vile white farmer ants who'd recently infested the cave. Machree himself was scared to go, you understand. I managed to throw the attacking ants into a trance, Ina and I carried the rumbies back to Santa Cruz. And then Machree made as if to claim them from us by force. Ina cozened him into bed, as if for old time's sake—and she slit his throat from ear to ear."

"Well done," said I, gladdened by the death of my stableboy rival.

"With the rumbies in our possession, our role in the coming Bloom was assured," said Ina. "Una told us this via tekelili. She said we had only to await the advent of Mason and Seela."

"But now loomed the noose," said Eddie. "Our murder was in no wise a perfect crime."

"And thus arrived in the year eighteen seventy-seven our season of hibernation," said Ina, pausing to drink more water from the steadily running hose. "And there in the double-sized bronze casket we lay. Awaiting Adam and Eve."

"Here am I," said I, smiling at my friends' tangled tale.

"But where is Seela?" asked Ina. "And the baby Brumble—is he well?"

"In the pink," I responded. "He's aged less than a week since you last saw him. He and Seela are nearby with Rafaelo's wife."

Eddie had managed to light one of Rafaelo's cigarettes. "Fine tobacco, my friend," said he. "Are you quite in Mason's confidence? Do you know of the Hollow Earth?"

"He tells me something about it," said Rafaelo. "The *Tierra Hueca*. Mason say maybe I can write a video game."

"A game, eh?" said Eddie, not at all grasping Rafaelo's point. His attention turned to the cheap, worn, yellow sweatsuit we'd given him. "Is this customary garb in the year twenty eighteen?"

"For poor people," said Rafaelo, laughing. He flicked a finger against the colorfully stitched collar of his shirt. "You have money, Eddie Poe? You want to buy sharp clothes like me?"

"I have magical, living gems," said Eddie, rattling his silver box. A thudding came from within. "The eggs of gods. Would you like to see?"

"Don't spill them," snapped Ina. "You're already drunk." She glanced at me. "That's the worst thing about Eddie. Over and over. I'm so tired of men. Do summon Seela, Mason. And tell her to bring scissors. We'll cut our nails and hair. And if she brings a razor I'll shave Eddie's beard."

"Or mayhap you'll slit my throat," said Eddie, narrowing his eyes in a manner meant to be jocose. But the grimace only made him look befuddled.

With a sudden gesture, Ina snatched the still half-full brandy bottle from Eddie and shattered it against their gravestone. Arf yelped in surprise.

For a moment nobody said anything, and then Ina spoke again, making her voice very calm, as if she were in full command of the situation, even though she was barefoot, emaciated, and quite pathetic. To all appearances, Ina and Eddie were homeless, unhealthy vagrants—like the others I'd already seen around Santa Cruz.

"Eat more cake," Ina was saying to Eddie. "The chocolate will bring you back. And smoke more of Rafaelo's tobacco." She turned to us. "For god's sake, get Seela."

"I can phone my wife Maya to bring her," said Rafaelo. "Maya can bring Seela here on the sidecar motorcycle. Hector left it at home."

We three relics from the past watched as Rafaelo produced one of those glassy black rectangles from his pocket. So-called phones, for speaking across distances. And supposedly these phones were in some sense smart as well. Rafaelo poked his and it lit up. He talked into it in Spanish, then returned it to his pocket. He smiled at us.

"In ten, fifteen minutes they come," he said. "Maya brings Seela and Brumble and our little Frida too. Also some cola and *hamburguesas*. *No mas* alcohol. We chilling."

Accepting that the brandy was gone, Eddie let the hose water run steadily into one side of his mouth, slopping out of the other side, as if rinsing himself out. He paused now and then to swallow water, and to retch. And then he ate some cake. Slowly the light of intelligence was returning to his eyes.

We sat on in silence for a time, watching a bluejay hop around on the grass, springy on his legs, pecking at the bright bits of broken glass. Crows cawed overhead, and a faint breeze rustled in the leaves. High afternoon fog was drifting in from the sea, dimming the sky.

Once in a while someone would drive by—a small truck with garbage in the back, a dirty sedan, a bigger truck carrying a machine. I wondered if the police might come. I'd seen a police car yesterday, and Rafaelo had warned me about it, as if telling a new fish about a shark. The police cars were black on the bottom and white on top. They might not like our looks. A Mexican in a fancy shirt, a black man in a sweatsuit (me), a dog, and two decrepit beggars. The five us sitting on the wall in the sun in an abandoned graveyard. Harmless and low. But bullies homed in on people like us. I'd seen that in the South.

A roar and a beep broke my foreboding mood. It was Maya aboard the white motorcycle, with Seela in the sidecar. Brumble and Frida were squeezed into the sidecar with Seela, perched side-by-side in a special little baby-carrier in front of Seela. A cute pair of human larvae. Maya hopped off and helped her passengers out of the sidecar. Frida was quacking in excitement. She wore a one-piece yellow terry suit with a zipper, and Brumble had a similar outfit in white with stripes of red. He looked very trim. They came to us, with Seela carrying Brumble. Maya was toting some rustling paper bags that she'd had behind Seela in the sidecar. How hale and normal these four looked.

"Eddie and Ina?" called Seela. "It's you? You've lain in the ground for all these years?"

"I'm sorry we abandoned you at the core," said Ina right away.

"We'll discuss that later," said Seela, overcome with pity for Ina just now. She rested her hand on Ina's shoulder. "You poor woman. Look at you. You buried yourself? Eddie Poe's idea, I'm sure."

"What an unalloyed joy it is to encounter Seela," put in Eddie, defensive and sarcastic. "My great admirer."

Seela shrugged this off. "Never a thought of reform, eh, you wretch? But this is no time to scold you, brought so low. Meet our friend Maya and her daughter Frida."

Maya was cautiously polite to Eddie and Ina—clearly she took them for derelicts who, for whatever reason, Rafaelo and I had taken under our wing. But she had a great reservoir of empathy. She drew out a comb and a pair of scissors, briskly snipping the scissors in the air. Frida danced around in excitement.

"Let's clean you up," Maya told Eddie and Ina. "Who goes first?"

"Me," said Ina, bowing her head. "These lank corpse strands—ghastly. Trim it down to a few inches, Maya. You're very kind."

The haircut only took a few minutes. And then Maya washed Ina's head with soap she'd filched from her workplace's bathroom. Eddie came under Seela's ministrations next. She had not in fact brought a razor, but she used her scissors to minimize Eddie's nasty beard, and to trim his mustache to seemly size. And then she dried their heads with paper towels. Our friends didn't look *good*, but they no longer looked dead. Keep in mind that, in terms of actual, lived, non-casket years, Ina and Eddie were aged but thirty-three and forty-four.

"*Fabuloso*," said Rafaelo. "We gotta fatten you up, Eddie and Ina. You look like beef jerky." He smiled down at Frida. "You want to eat too?"

And so we set upon the food that Maya had bought. Fried fingers of potato, and hamburgers, that is, ground beef on buns with a red paste called ketchup. Eddie and Ina slavered and ate. And, as always, Arf got some too.

As we sipped our fizzy, sweet drinks, I explained the situation to Seela.

"Were you awake all that time in the casket?" she then asked Eddie.

"In a stupor," said he. "Pleasant enough. Cellared like tubers, we were. And the worms never came."

"Eddie was clever about our casket's design," said Ina. "He's a good man. Except when he's not."

His spirits rising again, Eddie struck a pose and declaimed a variation on the hymnal verse he'd used when we'd found him restored to life aboard the *Water Witch*.

> *Seven score years are quickly sped;*
> *He rises glorious from the dead;*
> *All glory to our risen Ed!*
> *Hallelujah!*

"Alleluia to me too," said Ina, consuming a bit more chocolate cake. A heartening touch of pink had appeared on her cheeks. "Do tell, Mason old chum. Has Fwopsy mated? Is the Bloom time come? I hope Uxa didn't rouse us in vain."

"Fwopsy found a mate, yes," I said. "Duggie. They spawned baby saucers in that Big Sur cave. The new *veem* craft will carry an expedition of people, *woomo*, and Earth ants—to colonize a new world. The only remaining problem was the missing rumby eggs."

"I just knew Eddie had stolen them," said Seela.

"Ina and I guarded them in fiduciary trust!" said Eddie. "As our reward, we'll emigrate to a new world with the ships of the Bloom!"

"I suppose so," said I, not quite sure how I felt about the immanence of the Bloom. "Supposedly the royal ants can convert a solid colony planet into a construct like our doubled Hollow Earth."

"I have a rather interesting theory about this," said Eddie.

"No theories from you," Ina told Eddie. "You're half in the bag." She glanced over at Seela and me. "The man has no tolerance for spirits. Especially today, when we're so starved down. Drink more soda, Eddie."

"As Mason says, the royal ants hollow out a planet for the *woomo*," continued Eddie, wagging a bony finger. "And then—they pry the hollow planet's space into two sheets. Like Earth and MirrorEarth. With a Gate of warped space between. A Central Anomaly that forms a proper nest for the *woomo*. I have deduced this with crystalline logic. I am in no way addled, nor subject to fits."

Eddie's speculations were, so far as I know, largely correct. And they dovetailed well with the myths of Seela's tribe. But Ina didn't want to hear about this. She silenced Eddie and turned her attention to Seela.

"Are you two ready?" she asked. "To be the new Adam and Eve? That's how it's supposed to be."

"We don't want to go," said Seela. "We want to settle down here with Brumble. On a little farm."

"With a cow," I added, smiling at Seela to make her happy. But deep down I was thinking that when the saucers left I'd be aboard.

"You and Eddie should go in the saucers instead of us," Seela was telling Ina.

"Perhaps we can be the ship pilots, but we're not fit to be Adam and Eve," said Ina, running her thin hands across her raddled face. "Cain and Lilith is what we are."

"We'll get better," croaked Eddie. "Inside a *woomo* womb."

"I'd fancy that," said Ina. "Looking as we do now, one might expect we'd spawn a skewed, unwholesome world. Like Earth before the Flood. Or worse. I don't know that I can even bear one child. Eddie never quickened me during our fifteen years together."

"I brim with life essences," said Eddie. "I house multitudes. I will be the Abraham of a new race. Mason knows what I mean, eh? The fruits of the Order of the Golden Frond. I have a third testicle."

Wearing a fixed, embarrassed smile, Ina made no attempt to explain. "Perhaps it might work if the four of us went on the *veem* together," she said. "And perhaps you can bring your nice new friends, Mason. Mayhap this is the Great Architect's will."

As I've mentioned, I mistrust religious talk—even after the wonders I've seen. "Did you see God while you were in the grave?" I challenged Ina. "Or an angel host?"

"I saw Uxa," said Ina. "And the shared *woomo* mind—and the Earth's mind, and the mind of the Sun, and the one great Mind beyond. Is the Mind the same as God? Might we view the planets and the stars as angels? But never fear, you fractious young freethinker, I saw no Jehovah, no Moses, no Jesus, no Buddha, no Allah, nor any others of that tedious, manly ilk."

"I quite liked being dead," put in Eddie. "The years flew by—like they must have done for you at the Earth's core, Mason."

"Let's talk about that now," said Seela, a flush of anger rising to her cheeks. "Why didn't you stop Fwopsy from marooning us? I heard her story about needing all this time to find her mate Duggie, but even so—"

"Blame Machree," came Eddie's quick response. "He was the one who threw Brumble out the door. And he was the one who didn't want to let you back in."

"Ina says she cut Machree's throat," I told Seela.

"Such a rush of blood," said Ina, with her pert and hardened air.

"I'm sure you had reason to hate Machree," Seela said to Ina. "In San Francisco he presumed to buy you from a procurer."

"It was nothing so legalistic as all that," said Ina, coolly. "I don't mind sex. No, I didn't kill Machree for that."

"So you killed him for abandoning us at the core!" exclaimed Seela. "That's what I need to hear! Vengeance done."

The contrary Ina didn't want to agree. "Truth is, I killed Machree over the rumbies. We already told this to your husband."

Eddie hefted his heavy silver box and raised the lid, careful not to spill the contents. And then he peeped inside, wearing an expression of senile gloating that made Rafaelo laugh. Again I assumed Eddie meant his display as comedic mime, but in his current state, it was hard to be sure.

"And now comes the Bloom," said Seela in a weary tone. She gave me a frank, searching look. "Are you with them, Mason? Or with me?"

And that's when the police car showed up—black and white, with a single driver, a youngish white man, not particularly zealous, but in any case intent on evicting us from the cemetery.

"Hi guys," he said, walking over from his car. "We got a complaint. You'll have to take your picnic somewhere else. There's a homeless shelter just two blocks away. Can you walk that far? Anyone need a ride? How about you, sir? Where did you get that silver box?" He directed these last questions to Eddie Poe. The scent of brandy was strong in the air.

"The question to hand being what or why?" said Eddie, temporizing. None of us wanted to get into the grilled-off rear seat of the policeman's car.

"I don't suppose you have ID?" said the policeman. "Never mind. I'm not going to ask if you're illegal. Sanctuary city and all that. All I want is for you to pick up your trash and move along." He studied Arf, baby Brumble, little Frida, and the shiny sidecar motorcycle. Complicating factors. "Whose trike is that?"

"Belongs to my brother-in-law," said Maya, flashing her best smile. "We using it today. And, yes, I have a driver's license, no *problema*. I brought my friend Seela and her baby and my little girl here for a picnic. We all old friends. We can leave." Rafaelo, working quickly, had already packed up our debris.

Brumble chose this moment to pitch a fit, unleashing howls, heartbroken sobs, and desperate gasps—with his face red and wet, his toothless mouth wide open, and his tongue folded double. Seela dandled and rocked him to no avail. It wasn't time to nurse him—she'd done that only a few minutes ago.

"You the father?" said the policeman, focusing on me. I sensed he didn't like that Seela, Brumble, and I were black. "Yes."

"Do you and the mother have a home? Is the infant receiving proper care?"

"We've only just arrived here," I said.

"I'd like to take you and your family to the shelter down the road," said the policeman. "One of their counselors can talk to you and your wife, and we'll see about getting the infant into the system."

"We're none of your business," challenged Eddie. "Mason and I are from a mirror world, and Seela's from the Hollow Earth."

"You're going to the shelter too, Grandpa," the policeman said to Eddie. "I want the four of you in my car. And the silver box. And the dog. He's going to the pound." The policeman glanced over at Ina, Rafaelo, Maya, and Frida. "The rest of you can go. You've got a place to stay?"

"We have an apartment," said Rafaelo quickly. "We have jobs. And this thin lady, we take care of her too."

"So pile onto your trike and vamoose."

But now yet another vehicle was at the curb—a small, dark green car, dense-looking, shaped like a quick bug. The door flew open, and a lively, white-haired man extracted himself, fairly bursting with glee. He spotted me and waved.

"Mason!" he cried. "Mason Reynolds! I'm Rudy Rucker."

15. Rudy

Old Rudy strode up to me and shook my hand. He seemed to know exactly what was going on. And he wanted to tell me all of it at once.

"I knew you'd come to Santa Cruz," said Rudy. "So I drove over today, and right away I saw your story in the *Good Times*, and of course I went by their office. The woman said to look for you in this cemetery, and here you are. And you're still black. What a trip. And, oh my god, there's Poe and Ina. They look so *gnarly*. Hi Eddie! So *insane* that you buried yourself in a bronze casket for a hundred and forty years. You're *nuts*! I love it! Glad to see you've got your box. And here's Seela and Brumble? So wonderful to meet you, Seela. You're gorgeous. I know it's hard when your baby cries like that." He drew out a handkerchief, dried Brumble's face, and cooed to him in a high voice. "Did the policeman scare you? Do you need a new di-di? Can I hold him, Seela? Maybe he'll be so surprised that he stops."

Seela glanced at me, and I nodded, and she handed the baby to Rudy. Brumble emitted a single, shocked squall, and then settled down into hiccups, resting his head on Rudy's shoulder.

"And there's Rafaelo and Maya with little Frida," old Rudy continued. "Hi, guys. Thanks for helping my friends. Every detail is in place, it's perfect."

Finally I found my voice. "How do you know all this?" I asked. "I understand that you edited *The Hollow Earth*—so of course you'd know my history. But the new things—how do you know them?"

"I've been writing your next book for you, Mason, I've been working on it for nearly a year. The writing's never been easier. At first I said the Muse was helping me. But I now I can see the words are coming from you. Long-distance tekelili, radiating from Uxa at the Hollow Earth's core! I've been transcribing the second narrative of Mason Algiers Reynolds—direct from the source. I'm your astral amanuensis. Ever heard that word? It's like secretary, but more high-tone." Rudy smiled, cupped his hands beside his mouth and boomed, "*Return to the Hollow Earth!* Right? That's what I've been writing, okay? It's really happening, and we're in the story, and it's all around. I can't believe it." He leaned over to pet the dog. "And here's good old Arf. Hi, Arfie."

The policeman watched Rudy's performance with some uncertainty. To all appearances Rudy was a respectable, well-off man, nicely dressed in an argyle sweater, well-spoken, and with a good car. The fact that Rudy was greeting me so effusively was surely a point in my favor. Even though he was, to some extent, raving like a maniac. But extravagant outbursts were perhaps common in Santa Cruz.

Rudy turned and addressed the policeman on our behalf. "Mason's an old friend," he said. "I'd be glad to give him and his family and their dog a place to stay."

"Where would you take them?" asked the policeman. "To the homeless shelter?"

"They're welcome to stay at my house," said Rudy. "I'm happy to take care of them until they get things set up—if I can talk my wife into it. We live over the hill, in Los Gatos."

"Fine with me," said the policeman. "And what about this addled elder gent who likes to run his mouth? Possibly in possession of stolen property?" He meant Poe. "You going to take him too? Otherwise I'll put him in the tank at the shelter."

"Leave Mr. Poe with me." said Rudy. "We'll work things out. That box is definitely his. Believe it or not, Eddie's a famous writer."

"Believe it or not, I've got other shit to do," said the policeman. He gave us a last look. "If I see any of you in this graveyard again, you're going to jail. For reals." Therewith he got into his car and ponderously rolled away.

"What now?" Seela said to me. "You're getting yourself in deeper all the time, Mason. And I want to back away."

"I have to talk to Rudy," I said. "He's nearly finished writing my next book. I want to see what he's done."

"You two do what you like," put in Rudy. "You're the characters. I'm just the scribe."

"Let's go to our house to talk things over," proposed Maya.

So some of us piled into Rudy's car and the rest of us got onto the trike, and we drove a mile to the Mexicans' beige, flimsy house, with its walls half an inch thick. Hector and Aida were still at work. I showed Ina and Eddie the light switches and the faucets, and they liked them exceedingly. Eddie started formulating explanations, more and more like his old self, while keeping a tight grip on his box of rumbies. Maya dug up more shoes—she herself had as big a stash as Rafaelo did. Seela nursed Brumble, and Maya nursed Frida, then gave her a teething biscuit. We were ready to talk about what to do next.

But we didn't get a chance to talk right away—because Seela's rumby hatched. The way it happened was that a zigzag ray of *woomo* light meandered through the open window, and alit upon the string-wrapped bulge on Seela's necklace. The rumby. The heavy gem gave a silent tekelili cry, burst its wrappings, dropped to the floor, and—*behold*—it was a wriggling *woomo* that started out the size of a thumb, then grew to the size of a summer squash, and then, in a sudden rush, expanded into a great tubular form that ran from one side of the living-room to the other, plump and warty, bulking as high as my chest. Everyone was yelling and upset. Arf was barking furiously. He was backing toward the door with the hair on his hackles erect.

Meanwhile I'd quietly tuned in on the new arrival's tekelili.

"She says she's Uxa's daughter," I told the others. "Don't be scared. Her name is Lux."

Lux's bumps were flat on the top, a bit like suckers, and her hide was mottled in shades of green. Lux's powerful teke-lili was throbbing like a barroom band with a rowdy crowd. Very nearly overwhelming. Lux was communicating with us via feelings of motion rather than via images and words. And her message? She was going to carry us to the saucer cave in Big Sur, with some of us inside her, and some on her back like riders on a flying dragon.

Arf wasn't going to be riding on any *woomo*. Seela didn't like the idea either, and Rafaelo and Maya were very dubious as well. Eddie and Ina were all for it—this was the reason they'd taken their tortuous route to the year twenty eighteen. And I—I too was intrigued. What an adventure it would be, after all, to travel to a new planet as a part of the *woomo* Bloom.

"I'll ride to Big Sur," said old Rudy. "But no further. I need to stay here and publish your book, Mason."

A thought crossed my mind. "Will you share the money with Seela and me?"

"Sure," said Rudy. "You guys can have half of the money for the new Hollow Earth book, and I'll give you some of whatever I got for the first one. It's hard to remember exactly how much I made. I can look it up. Not a huge amount."

"Your books don't sell well?"

"They do okay, but they don't hit big," said Rudy. "Science fiction fans think I'm too literary, and the mandarins pretend I don't exist. I joke, I'm dirty, I use math, I hate the pig, and I'm old."

"What of me?" interrupted Eddie Poe. "How goes my literary career?"

"You're a titan," said Rudy. "Millions of books. Tens of millions."

"More than Nathaniel Hawthorne?" Eddie wanted to know.

"Way, way more," said Rudy. "Hawthorne's in the pantheon, sure. But really he's just for English profs. He never learned how to make it nasty and crazy like Poe. You're the king, Eddie. A demigod."

"Why are you three talking about *books*?" interrupted Seela. "And meanwhile this enormous rubbery *woomo* is about to kidnap us!"

Rudy cackled at this. "We're writers," he said. "What do you expect? Just give us another second, and then we'll let our tale's hair-raising climax kick in. Mason, I don't want to build up too much hope, but it's just possible our new book could score. I mean—it's a fucking masterpiece! Of course I always think that. But this could be the one. I'll publish it along with a reprint of our first Hollow Earth book.

"By Mason Reynolds," said I. "Put that on the cover."

Rudy shook his head. "I've developed a following over the years. If my name is on the cover, we're guaranteed to sell at least a thousand copies. And it could take off from there. And of course I'll write an Editor's Note where I say the book's really written by Mason Reynolds, and that he fed it to me via *woomo* tekelili." Rudy smiled. "Everyone will believe *that*!"

"I should get credit too," put in Eddie.

"Like you need it, you glory-hog," said Rudy, flaring up. "Give us a chance."

"My glory will be magnified beyond your ken when I engender a new human race," said Eddie. "My scrotum holds a thousand life essences, you see. Donated by the adherents of the Order of the Golden Frond, and by unwitting passers-by. My third testicle. Not unlike a third eye."

"This gets better all the time," said Rudy, taking Eddie's remark in stride. It was as if he'd set aside all belief in ordinary reality—and was glad so to do.

"Donated?" said I.

"I believe I mentioned this to you once before," resumed Eddie. "*Woomo* rays extracted cell clusters from the donors and tingled them into my sack for safe-keeping."

"Tingled?"

"Slipped them through the meatus, then guided them along the urethra, across the seminal vesicle, and through the vas deferens," Eddie said, assuming a professorial air.

"Sounds like a tour of ancient Rome," jested Rudy, then made a calming gesture. "Don't be mad at me, Eddie. What you did is a good idea. You'll avoid the genetic bottleneck.

The dreaded founder effect." Rudy glanced over at me. "With only a few adults in a new Eden, one needs a source of exogamy to avoid incest—lest the population be poxed by recessive genes." I didn't recognize all the phrases, but I grasped the import.

"Inbreeding is ill," summarized Eddie. "Outbreeding is well. I have the seeds for a thousand new babies." Departing from his usual refined manner, he patted his crotch. "Some are from members of the Order of the Golden Frond. And some were *woomo*-plucked from worthy candidates we happened to see. A pensive brow, a noble countenance and—*whisk*—into Eddie's sack! No races barred."

"Who'll grow all those babies?" asked Rudy. "You can't ask proud women like Seela and Maya to serve as brood mares."

"We'll use *woomo* wombs," said Eddie. "A *woomo* can form an entirely efficacious uterus within her flesh, complete with umbilical cord and placenta, you see. A womb indeed, warmed by the *woomo's* glow." Triumphantly he raised his silver box of rumbies and rattled it. "I'll supply not only the seeds, but the *woomo* as well!"

"Zounds!" exclaimed Rudy, getting into the spirit.

Looking back, it seems hard to believe that Rudy, Eddie, and I took the time to have this conversation—what with Lux the *woomo* newly arrived in the room. As Seela had already pointed out, and was just now pointing out again, I should be discussing Lux's declared intention to rush us to the saucer cave in Big Sur. But perhaps my conversation with Rudy and Eddie didn't take as long as it seems in written form. After all, thanks to Lux, we were in intense tekelili contact, and our remarks may have been in silent psychic form. A quick flutter of sense and emotion.

In any case, Seela now had her hands on my shoulders. She was shaking me, and in fact screaming into my face.

"I don't want to fly off in those saucers!"

With a sudden motion she pressed Brumble into my arms. "You can take the baby, fine, but you can't take me. I'll stay here alone. I'll settle in with Josh, the Sparkle Wow jeweler. He says that he loves me. He'll marry me if I want.

But he'd prefer not to have another man's child on his hands."
She was crying as she said this, and her hands kept flying out
to caress the sleeping Brumble's hairless pate.

My chest felt hollow. My mouth was dry and it was hard
to talk. "Seela— "

"You can't stop me!" she interrupted, glaring at me even
as she wept. "I'm leaving you and leaving that, that noisy,
greedy baby who nobody wants. I'm not following you into
a *veem*. You made me leave my flower, you made me leave the
Hollow Earth, and now you want me to fly into the horrible
empty sky, and, no, no, no, I won't do it!"

With that, Seela turned and ran out the little house's
door, sobbing as if her heart would break, and with her thin
shoulders shaking. And still Brumble slept.

"Branch point," said Rudy at my side. "Which fork do
you take?"

I was stung by Seela's assertion that she would settle in
with that Josh character. And shocked that she was willing
to abandon Brumble. Our baby unwanted? Never! Most of
all, I grieved to see Seela in such a state. Poor, dear woman.
Arf looked up at me, uncertain.

"Go with Seela," I told him. "Be her friend." Perhaps
it was due to his dislike of *woomo*, but this was one of those
rare times when Arf obeyed a command. He took off after
Seela without looking back.

I recalled the time in Richmond that Arf had left me for
Otha. I'd been fifteen. With the ongoing rush of events, that
felt like half a lifetime ago, but it was only three years. I saw
no sign of the turmoil abating. And I liked that. But—what
of Seela's dream of a farm by a river with a cow? How could
I so coldly set myself against her heart's desire?

"You'll be fine," said the opportunistic Ina, replacing
Rudy by my side. She ran her wizened hand across my cheek.
She was about as alluring as moldy scarecrow. "Lux is going to
restore Eddie and me on the way to Big Sur," she continued.
"We'll crawl inside her and marinate in her smeel. Like babies
in the womb. I heard Eddie telling you about *woomo* wombs.
The *woomo* will make Eddie and me beautiful again. Fresh.

Turgid. Pert. We'll travel with you on the saucer. I'll be your lover. I'll teach you tricks. What fun we'll have."

"Smeel?"

"That's what we call Lux's divine *woomo* body nectar," said Ina. "I'll be lissome, I tell you, *virgo intacta*. Just wait and see. Eddie and I will be capital company. And you'll have Maya to chivvy with as well. I warrant you'll bed her."

"Be cool," Maya said to Ina. "I'm bringing my husband Rafaelo."

"You two are coming in the saucer to another world?" I asked Maya. "On your own free will? You understand what it's about?"

"We want to very much," said Rafaelo. "No more working for white people. You know what I mean, Mason. You're *negro*. They don't treat us good. This new world, it can be beautiful. Better than a videogame."

"Yes," I assented. "The *woomo* will pick a good planet. They want us to be at ease. We'll all fit. The humans, the *woomo*, the flying saucers, and the big ants."

"Ants?" said Maya. "I didn't hear nothing about ants."

"You won't notice them much," I said. "When we land, the ants will go underground, digging out space for the *woomo*. And prying the new planet in two. Into a world and a mirrorworld. To make room for the dirt they dig out from inside. Never mind. We'll live on the outside with meadows and seas and flowers and trees. We'll have children of our own, and Eddie will hatch extra babies from the *woomo*. Nobody has to marry a cousin."

Rafaelo was holding Frida against his shoulder, and I was holding Brumble. "Maybe some day our two kids—who knows?" he said, "But, you, *vato*, you need to bring your own wife for this trip. I don't want you hanging round my back door. You find Seela and beg her on your knees to come with you. You're *loco* to lose that girl."

"I—I don't know," I said. It would be cruel—and probably impossible—to force Seela to come. Yes, I'd be desperately lonely, making the trip without her. But if I didn't leave on the saucer, I might regret it for the rest of my life. I was born for adventure, wasn't I? At least I'd have Brumble with me.

And Seela would have Arf. Rafaelo was still glaring at me. "I won't bother Maya," I humbly promised him.

"As if that's up to you two," said Maya. "We'll go to Sur now and see what we see."

Meanwhile the sea cucumber Lux had opened a hole in her side.

"Heal me!" cried Ina. She shed her pink sweatsuit and scooted in, feet first. It looked dark and wet in there—one could indeed say it was like a womb. Certainly it was more welcoming than a bronze casket six feet underground. A tube dangled from the side of Lux's inner wall.

"You too, Eddie," sang Ina before fitting the tube to her navel. And then Lux opened a womb for Poe as well. Leaning on my shoulder, he too removed his sweat clothes, and I helped him in. He took his place in there, with his heavy box of rumbies clasped against his bony, naked chest.

"I hope this works," I said, showing Eddie his umbilical cord.

"A new man," said Eddie. "A nam wen." Playing with words even now, in such low estate, my worn old friend. I prayed for his restoration—but prayed to whom? To the great Mind, I suppose.

Lux sealed in Ina and Eddie. Rudy, Maya, Rafaelo, and I remained—plus the two children—Brumble in my arms, and Frida in Rafaelo's. Maya ran and filled a big laundry bag with assorted clothes. And I managed to replace my sweat pants with a pair of the blue denim trousers called jeans.

And then the *woomo* narrowed herself and wormed between our legs, cupping herself against our bottoms so that we four adults were, in effect, sitting on saddles atop a warty, eyeless, fronded slug. Lux wriggled out the door of Maya's house and sprang into the air before any of us could manage to jump free, not that any of us did want to jump free. We were drawn by the magnitude of the impending adventure, and we were a bit under the sway of Lux's tekelili.

Minutes later we were five hundred feet high in the air, cruising southward along the California coast. It was late afternoon, and clouds were piled on the horizon, with the low sun turning orange. Despite the chill, we were comfortable, as Lux was exuding a gold glow that covered our bodies and sent sparks off our fingertips. Perhaps the halos made us hard to see—in any case, no military planes were taking notice of us today, nor, for that matter, had the neighbors raised an outcry.

Rudy sat in front, then me with Brumble, then Maya with her laundry bag, and Rafaelo in the rear with Frida. I felt sadly alone. In truth, I barely knew these people. Seela was the one I knew. And we'd parted. I imagined her dear face before me, sad and uncertain, and imagined the sound of her voice: *"Is the little one well?"*

Brumble was still asleep. He had an enviable ability to ignore his surroundings. And he'd nursed his fill before Seela left. Kind Maya would surely nurse him when he woke. I studied the little slits of Brumble's closed eyes, and his tiny pursed mouth. Was it in any way reasonable to load this little fellow onto a flying saucer to another world? Could I really leave his birth mother behind?

As we angled down from the sky toward Big Sur, I noticed low buildings and a chapel atop a nearby hill. They faded from view as Lux bore us lower. We landed unobserved upon the same tiny, mid-cliff ledge-meadow as before—with the hot spring, the cave, and the stand of twisted pines.

Dusk was coming on; the air was calm. Brumble awoke, crying plaintively and without relent. As I'd hoped, Maya took him over.

"The saucers in there?" said Rafaelo, pointing at the dark mouth of the cave. "You sure this is on the up and up, Mason?"

"It should be fine," I said, hoping this was true. "I should tell you that the saucers aren't metal machines. They're alive."

"You've talked to them?"

"Not these new ones. They just got hatched. Maybe they'll fly out and say hello. Maybe we don't have to go inside the cave."

Meanwhile Lux was flexing her body. She kinked the region where Eddie and Ina were ensconced, and then—*behold*—the two of them slid onto the ground like new-foaled colts. Wet, gasping, and wholly restored—supple, clean-featured, bright-eyed, and all their wits about them.

"*Ecce homo*," said the nude Eddie, striking a pose with his heavy box of rumbies held firm in his hand. "Behold the man."

Gracefully Ina took Eddie's hand. "Husband mine," said she, setting aside her designs on me, at least for now.

Rudy, Maya, Rafaelo, and I cheered, and for a few minutes we five chattered excitedly about the transformation. For the first time since Eddie's and Ina's emergence from the grave, it seemed possible to me that they were indeed capable of being a new Adam and Eve.

After so much tekelili with the *woomo*, I'd developed a sense of duty to their cause, and a conviction that it was up to me to make their Bloom work. And perhaps I was drawn by the romantic pathos of being doomed to leave for a new world. But that was nonsense. With Eddie and Ina in fine fettle—I didn't really have to go.

My thoughts were interrupted by a section of the cliff exploding outward—some fifty feet to the left of the cave's door. Lit by the rays of the sinking sun, rocks avalanched toward the inky sea, clattering and overtaking each other. Furious, jointed forms struggled amid the dust cloud within the cliff's ragged new hole.

The combatants were, of course, oversized ants—Skolder and his cow-sized royal companions versus the nasty, creamy, dog-sized farmer ants. A large and very graceful purplish-green form was fighting at Skolder's side. Presumably this was his betrothed, the empress ant for the intended colony world. Peering deeper into the seething fracas, I perceived that the creamy ants had a queen of their own. She was demonically ripping the heads off any royal ants she could reach. Not that she had much hope of victory, for Skolder and his empress were slicing through the farmer ant troops like scythes reaping grain.

Maya was jabbering in fear, but Rafaelo was incongruously seized by mirth. Perhaps the myrmicine struggle reminded him of a jolly scene in his beloved videogames. Rudy and I, who had a fuller understanding of what was taking pace, called out encouragement to Skolder. Meanwhile Eddie and Ina sat to one side amid the gnarled pines, quietly talking about their upcoming plans. The weighted silver box of rumbies rested on the ground between them.

The focus of ants' battle progressed into hidden subterranean passageways. For a time, showers of pebbles continued emerging from the newly opened hole in the cliff. And all this while, our helpful *woomo* companion Lux was darting out rays and tendrils to deflect any wayward stones that came our way. Slowly the signs of the ant war abated. We felt a few more irregular shudders, and a final shiver of ripples patterned our hot spring's pool. I was relieved that the densely grown stand of pines had held our perch intact. I sensed that the royal ants had all but annihilated their farmer ant foes.

"For sure I'm not going in that cave," said Rafaelo.

"I can't stand ants," repeated Maya.

"Our three *veem* craft will float out," I said. "Royal ants will be in the first one. And then we'll hatch Eddie's box of rumbies to make *woomo*, and they'll go aboard the second craft. And the third one—well that's for people."

"I don't like this," said Rafaelo. The sun was down. The sky was a fading gray.

"Good news," announced Ina, rejoining us. "Lux just told Eddie and me that I'm pregnant."

"Capital," said I, relieved that fertilizing Ina was no longer a task I might be called upon to perform.

"Eddie did it!" exulted Ina. "It's finally clicked. The *woomo*—while Eddie and I were inside her, she mated us. My egg and Eddie's sperm. We're going to have a girl, says Lux. The princess of New Eden."

"Who she gonna marry?" asked Maya, homing in on the central difficulty with our understaffed colonization plan.

"She can share Mason's Brumble with your Frida!" said Ina, as if this fully solved the problem.

"And what about the next generation after that?" I ventured. "And what if Maya and Rafaelo and Brumble and Frida and I don't come along at all?"

"Maya don't like those ants," ventured Rafaelo.

"We don't need you shirkers and your children," snapped Eddie Poe. "Watch. I have powers beyond compare. I'll sire all the babies we need—and they'll have fresh heritage. Help me, Lux!"

Lux directed a branching ray of light upon the wrapped rumby amulet at Eddie's throat, haloing it in a shower of sparks. The enclosing twine burned away, and on the way to the ground the jewel morphed into a *woomo* slug. She sat at Eddie's feet, with one alert tip lifted into the air.

"I dub thee Lenore," said Eddie, still naked.

He knelt over the newly hatched *woomo* Lenore, running his fingertips along the tiny sea cucumber's hide. Lenore pressed back against Eddie, as if enjoying the petting. Continually she grew in size. Her upper surface began to smooth itself—and to flow. She was spreading like batter on a griddle.

"Oh no," said I, sensing what was coming.

"Gnarly," said Rudy. He had an inkling too. After all, he'd already transcribed the bulk of the *Return to the Hollow Earth*.

Lenore formed her body into a low platform like a bed. Embossed upon her was a simulacrum of a pale, female figure—as still and lifeless as a marble effigy recumbent upon a tomb. Eddie stared, fascinated, his eyes burning, his lips pressed tight together.

"It's Virginia?" murmured old Rudy.

And, yes, the form was the very imago of Eddie's lost child bride, Virginia Clemm. With a shriek, the unclothed poet threw himself upon the phantasmal form—and furiously copulated with the *woomo*. A repellent sight indeed.

Rudy giggled. "Exogamous children," said he. "Straight from the sack. Poe's third ball."

"*So* nasty," said Maya.

"We're bailing," declared Rafaelo. "You too, Mason?"

"Yes," I said. "Me too." Saying this, I felt a flush of happiness. All was not lost. I could still be with Seela—if she'd have me back.

"We'll find a ride to Santa Cruz," said old Rudy. "But first let's watch the Bloom."

16. Farewell

"Too much for you?" Eddie said to me when he was done. His tone was exultant and even haughty, so sure of himself was our Poe.

"Find yourself some clothes in Maya's laundry bag," I suggested. "You and Ina both."

"What a stolid burgher you've become," said Eddie. "So far, and no further, my would-be rake? It'll be paradise in the world I'm to engender. I'll be the Tulku, and you can be my Crozier. Like Machree was."

"Leave Mason alone," said Ina. "He wants to be with Seela. I don't blame him. He wants his own life."

"And you, Ina?" said I. "You're content with the *woomo* plan?"

"Perhaps I seek doom," she lightly said. "That may explain the paths I choose. But let's be sunny. I am indeed fond of Eddie. I'll welcome the clarity of a new world. Farewell to the muck and the ruck. And, yes, restored by our *woomo* Lux, I am indeed fit to be Eve."

While Ina spoke, she was rooting in Maya's laundry bag, and now she produced a pair of outfits. Red jeans and a blue frock for her, a white shirt and a black business suit for Eddie. And of course, bright athletic shoes for both of them.

"Time to hatch our rumbies!" said Eddie, once he and Ina were clad. "Help me, Lux and Lenore."

With a conjuror's flair, Eddie lifted the lid from the silver box and skimmed the lid across our meadow. It arced over the edge and downward to the rumbling sea. By now the daylight was nearly gone. Careful not to spill the contents, Eddie laid his open box on the ground beside the hot spring's steaming pool, then stepped well back. The box held eighty or so rumbies. They were excited—they glowed a bit, and a silent hubbub of their tekelili filled the air.

Lux and Lenore set to work, sending branching tendrils into the bustling rumby box. I laid a protective hand across the rumby amulet I still wore at my neck. I was concerned that it, too, might be impelled to hatch. I had an inchoate plan to hatch it later on, privily, and that my personal *woomo* would then help me and Seela on our way. Surely we two did have a future path together, Seela and I, despite that vile interloper, Josh the jeweler of Sparkle Wow. To keep my amulet safer, I took it off my neck and shoved it deep into my jeans pocket.

The eggs were hatching one by one, each of them with a pop or a hiss or a squeal. Each new-hatched *woomo* wormed out of the box and into the pool of the spring, stretching itself, sucking in water, spurting it out, nudging the others, and steadily increasing in size. The air thrilled with the auras of four score new minds, keen for adventure. Lux began advising them about the trip.

At this point the first of the three spherical *veem* craft pushed out the cave, forcing its way, enlarging the cave's mouth to ten and then twenty yards wide, excavating masses of dirt and stone on either side. This first *veem* glowed with lavender light, and was laden with young royal ants. A wondrous sight. But the craft's exit from the cave had set off yet another avalanche. Just on the other side of the cave, great blocks of stone were coming loose and tobogganing downhill.

"Come sit with us," called Eddie, perched with Ina atop the hovering *woomo* Lenore.

Uneasy though I was about my footing, I was loath to join them. For all I knew, Eddie would whisk me into one of the *veem* craft, and I'd be headed into deep space against my will. Scanning across the face of increasingly the unstable cliff, I spotted a damp, upward path to the right. It held a flowing rivulet, and was choked with grasses, bushes and moss.

"Let's go!" I shouted to Rafaelo, Maya, and Rudy.

Slipping and panting, we four wended our way up the muddy path. Rafaelo carried Frida, and I held Brumble. Off to the left the roar of the landslide grew. The ground shuddered hideously. At one point I fell. I had trouble regaining my footing, what with the bawling Brumble in my arms. Maya and Rudy lifted me up, their hands firm and kind.

Venturing a quick glance over my shoulder, I saw the spherical *veem* ship of ants hovering in mid-air, at an altitude lower than my position on the cliff, but not all that far. The craft was a good forty-five feet across, very nearly spherical, with a Saturn-like rim, and with the *veem* skin stretched so tight that I cold see the green and purple armor of the royal ants within. None of the pale farmer ants had been allowed to join the mission.

A second ship now appeared—a lambent, copper-colored orb, thirty feet across. It took up a position directly above where the ants' *veem* ship hovered. It was approximately level with where I stood. Our eighty newly hatched *woomo* flew up from the hot spring's pool and began wriggling in through the saucer's two open doors. Lux—the *woomo* from Seela's amulet—flew up with them, reducing herself to their scale.

At this point the alien sea cucumbers were about the size of human legs, intricately whorled with rubbery warts, and each of them glowing in its own unique shade. The lustrous light-emitting tendrils of the individual *woomo* were continually in motion, limning a choreography that etched an intricate tracery against the night. Added to this exquisite visual beauty was the intense tekelili I felt from these joyous, youthful beings, destined to live for millennia, and reveling at the inception of their great quest.

I'd experienced the tekelili force of a *woomo* swarm twice before—both times at the core of the Hollow Earth. But to be with this new generation of Great Old Ones at their earliest flowering, and to be witnessing the scene amid the magical, unparalleled beauty of Big Sur...the experience struck me even more profoundly than before. My soul brimmed and overflowed, like a wineglass in a waterfall.

Nevertheless, a part of my attention stayed fixed upon the quaking mire beneath my feet, and upon our struggle up the cliff. Some extra ants were on the cliff with us—both royal ants and surviving farmer ants. These were resentful, disappointed individuals who'd failed to secure passage aboard the ant *veem*. The ants were snapping at each other, and their mandibles made percussive clicks. Blessedly they had no interest in us. Their goal was only to find passageways to the remains of their nests within the ruined cliff.

"Here's the top!" called Rudy. I saw him as a silhouette against a clear sky brightened by a sea of stars. The waning moon had yet to rise. And then I was at Rudy's side. We'd reached the patch of gravel by the road. No cars were coming by. I was glad for that.

Rudy, Rafaelo, Maya, and I stood at the brow of the cliff, catching our breath and nursing our bruises. The avalanche had abated. Our footing was stable. Out past the face of the cliff hovered the large pale purple craft of the ants, and above that the medium-sized coppery sphere of the *woomo*. Meanwhile Eddie and Ina sat upon the airborne *woomo* Lenore—awaiting the appearance of the third *veem* craft, the one that would carry the humans.

Ever the showman, Eddie called out one of his Latin mottos: "*Aude sapere*," meaning, "Dare to know." A fitting phrase for this protean man of changes, undaunted by risk, seemingly indestructible. I was glad to hear the power and energy in his voice. I prayed that he and Ina would prosper and thrive upon their new world, peculiar though Eddie's methods were.

If I haven't made it fully clear: I loved Eddie from the start, and I will admire him till I die.

The third and final *veem* craft pushed free of the rubble around the collapsed cave. This *veem* ship was of a golden hue, and its flesh had the crystalline pellucidity of a jellyfish. The sphere was comfortably small, little more than fifteen feet across. It rose to a level precisely even with the top of the cliff, and not all that far away from us. I could see into it quite well.

The golden *veem* was canted back with its two viewports facing the sky. Eddie and Ina made their way inside it, and their *woomo* Lenore darted down to join her fellows in the copper-colored craft.

Eddie took one of the pilot's seats, and Ina the other. They leaned back, recumbent, with their heads pointing away from each other—staring up through their view ports at the starry heavens. With the moon still down, the ghostly stream of the Milky Way was clear to see. Somewhere out there was the next planet the *woomo* would colonize.

Eddie and Ina took hold of their rudimentary *veem* controls—those simple knobs on sticks—and instigated a process that would complete the Bloom.

I heard a low hum, and the brightness of the gold sphere increased. A circuit of energy was building. Eddie glanced over at me. I could clearly see the expression of his face. He raised his dark eyebrows, as if asking if I was sure I didn't want to come. There was still time. I shook my head no.

He shrugged and smiled. An actinic glow flowed from his sphere to the ball of the *woomo*, and thence to the ship of the ants, spilling down like a cataract. Aroused by the influx, the royal ants thrust their stingers from their ship's doors and darted rays at the craft of the *woomo*. In turn the *woomo* swathed Eddie's *veem* with crackling sparks of tekelili energy. Continuing the cycle, Eddie sent fresh energies cascading down and, once again, the lower spheres sent aethereal forces up.

As the iterated interplay intensified, the *veem* craft were drawn into contact with each other. With showers of sparks they welded themselves together at their points of tangency, producing a stack of three spheres, intensely humming with a rising pitch.

"Too loud!" cried Maya, covering her ears.

She was right—the sound was hurting my head or, worse, boring into my brain. The singing of the conjoined spheres slid up beyond the range of human ears. Arf wouldn't have liked it.

In concert with the sound, a halo was expanding outward from the three *veem*, a luminous hollow shell that rushed towards us and passed through my body as if I were air or glass. The touch set my hairs on end.

All around us the hollow shell was inflating itself, hungrily racing in every direction, above and below, soon enclosing the land, the sea, and even the stars above. A pregnant pause. A colossal clap of thunder made the welkin ring.

The shell of pale light rushed back in upon us, like a ring of breakers in a phosphorescent sea—or, rather, like the walls of a collapsing room. Again the shell passed through my body as if I were naught. It condensed into a bright, egg-like globule located above the three welded-together *veem*. It gleamed like a star above a snowman.

Flexing with arcane, eldritch energy, the egg roughened its surface and grew a single porcupine quill. Taking careful aim, the egg hurled the luminous lance above the damp, rounded hills, and high into the star-besprent firmament, leaving a hair-thin trail of light in its wake. Tekelili told me that the lance was aimed at the most promising world that the scouting shell had found.

Again a pause. No sound from the sky, the stars, the *veem*, or the pale egg. A sudden flash glared at the heavens' zenith. I held my breath, expecting a boom, but, no, I'd heard the thunder a minute ago—*before* the flash. The deep structures of length and duration were baffled by the Bloom's wild play.

A jointed arm of light reached down from the heavens and placed a spindly fingertip upon the egg. And, behold, a space tunnel opened directly above Eddie's and Ina's *veem*.

This higher-dimensional Gate was much like the one at the heart of the Central Anomaly. And, as it happened, the new tunnel led, not to a mirrored copy of Earth, but to the *woomo*'s next colony planet, very far away.

I could see through the tunnel. A sunny prospect of verdant meadows, with stubby reddish-brown creatures in the fields. Cows? Not exactly. I yearned to visit this new Eden, and sorrowed that I would not.

The linked gold, copper, and lavender *veem* craft rose smoothly toward the Gate, seeming to shrink into the distance, yet without moving very far. And then—they were on the other side, with the green field and the not-quite-cows. Eddie, Ina, the *woomo*, and the ants—all of them were on the other side. The Gate shrank back to an egg, and to a white dot. It shivered and winked out.

The *woomo's* intoxicating aura of tekelili was gone, as was the musky energy of Eddie and Ina. The only tekelili I still had was a faint pulse from the rumby in my pocket. The Bloom was done. The ocean waves splashed on as before. I felt homely and dull. My life was but a common thing.

§

Rudy, Rafaelo, Maya, and I talked things over for a bit. We felt disoriented by the rapid changes. The time was perhaps nine pm. Our location was so remote that Rudy's pocket phone didn't work.

"There's a monastery on the hill," said Rudy. "A hermitage. I've been there before. Nice people. Maybe we can pay one of them to give us a ride."

"Is it a long walk?" asked Maya.

"An hour," said Rudy. "Up a side road."

And so we set off, arcing back and forth with the road's bends. The tardy, gibbous moon rose. The timeless sea glinted like hammered bronze. Images of my long journey flitted through my mind.

The bateau trip down the James River from Lynchburg to Richmond. My meeting with Poe in his newspaper office. The packet boat to Norfolk, and then the clipper ship *Wasp* to Antarctica. The balloon trip with Eddie and Otha to the South Pole. The collapse of the ice cap, and the fall through the Earth's Rind. The journey across the Hollow Earth jungle to Seela's flower. My union with Seela. Our fall to the central zone of the black gods. Finding Fwopsy the fried egg. Uxa the *woomo* skimming us through the Central Anomaly and to the inner surface of MirrorEarth. The bobbling drift up through the Chesapeake Bay. The boat ride to Baltimore. The seeming deaths of Poe and MirrorPoe. Settling in with Seela like newlyweds. Our shipboard passage to the Horn, and the foundering of the *Purple Whale*. Our rescue by the flying ballula. Finding the revived Poe aboard the *Water Witch*. The birth of Brumble in San Francisco. The flight to the North Pole aboard Cytherea. Our passage through the neck of the vast maelstrom. The herd of shrigs, and the encounter with the royal ants. Riding Tallulah to MirrorSeela's flower. Recovering Fwopsy the fried egg, with the newly hatched *woomo* Nyoo inside her. MirrorYurgen and his horn. Drifting once more to the Hollow Earth's core. Dallying with MirrorSeela along the way. Bringing Fwopsy to life. Our strangely ecstatic century-and-a-half sojourn upon Uxa at the Anomaly. Flying with Fwopsy to the cave in Big Sur. Our ride with the Mexicans to Santa Cruz. Poe and Ina risen from the grave. Meeting old Rudy. Breaking with Seela. Riding Lux the *woomo* to the cave at Big Sur. Eddie's departure for the new Eden. Here I was.

"What you thinking about?" said Rafaelo at my side. I could see his face quite clearly in the light of the moon.

"I'm lost," said I. "Out of place."

"I hear that," said Rafaelo. "I don't know how long we can stay in Cruz. So many Mexicans getting deported these days."

"I'd like to leave Santa Cruz," I said. "Too crowded. Seela and I were going to look for some land." A thought struck me. "Would you and Maya want to come along? Move out into the country. Or to an island?"

"We're ready for anything," put in Maya. "But it's hard to travel with no green card and no passport."

"First we'll get back to Cruz," said Rafaelo. "And then Mason finds Seela. And then—*quién sabe.*"

Onward we walked. The cracked old road leveled out and we passed some pines. I kept glancing at the sky, as if expecting to see Eddie's new world up there.

Finally we came to the hermitage, and managed to find a monk on watch, a calm, gentle young man who seemed amused by the story we told him, not that our tale contained any actual facts. In any case, the monk readily accepted that something remarkable had happened to us—he'd seen the odd lights in the sky, and it may have been that he'd felt the tekelili touch of the massed *woomo*. His name was Brother Nguyen.

He agreed to use the monastery's van to ferry us up to Santa Cruz immediately, and for a reasonable sum. And that was that.

Weary, drained and sorrowful, I dozed for most of drive. It was perhaps one am when we reached Aida and Hector's house. Having found only the briefest of notes from Maya, they'd been wondering where we were, or if we were coming back at all,

I'd hoped that Seela might be there, but she wasn't. Evidently she was spending the night with Josh. I had an urge to run over to Josh's house and rouse them, but Maya held me back.

"Josh is flaky," she said. "Loses his temper. You need to be strong when you go in there for the showdown, Mason. And it's better for you if Seela has a whole night to think it over. So she gets sick of Josh and starts missing Brumble."

"You're on my side?" I asked Maya.

"I'm on Seela's side," she said. "And you're a better catch than Josh. He's a jerk. Bossy. He says he's PC, but he rips off his workers when he can. Lie down and sleep, Mason. What a crazy *loco* day. Those big wriggly slugs? And that nut Eddie humping one of them? And the giant ants who made a frikkin avalanche? *Hayzooz Christo.* I'm glad we didn't go in no flying saucers."

Not wanting to leave yet, old Rudy took Seela's place on the mattress at my side, with Brumble between us, which wasn't much to Brumble's liking. He yawned, sneezed, and had a fit of hiccups. The night passed like a waking dream, with me repeatedly having to carry Brumble to Maya and petition that she nurse. I was going to have to learn about bottle feeding, but blundering around a strange house in the moonlight at three am was not the time. Finally Maya just let me leave Brumble in her bed.

And then at last the sun came up, not that I could directly see it, what with the whole town shrouded in white fog, but at least it was bright out, and I could stop pretending to sleep. And go get Seela.

Josh's house was within walking distance. It was another of those flat, beige boxes in the poor part of town. The shades were down and the lights were out—no surprise, as it was only six am. I stood outside the house for fifteen minutes, looking things over and waiting to hear a sound. Josh had a nice-looking mural on the closed garage door—a flowing image of sparkling stones, waves, goddesses, and the like—and I remembered Maya saying that she'd painted it. It was a little like the murals she'd put on walls of their rented house.

One of the window curtains of the house twitched, and I saw the quick flash of Seela's eyes. A moment later she was standing on the concrete stoop outside the front door. She was barefoot, with tangled hair, and wearing a long T-shirt as a nightgown. She seemed conditionally glad to see me.

"What are *you* doing here?" she asked, holding back a smile.

The ice in my heart melted. Any doubts about staying were gone. I held out my arms and Seela came to me, her body wonderfully warm and familiar against mine. "I need you," I said.

"Where's Brumble?"

"With Maya. They didn't leave on the saucers either. It was just Eddie and Ina. He was being too—"

"Too Eddie," said Seela, with a soft giggle. "And, Mason, we can always go back into the Hollow Earth, if life here is too tame. But, you know, I'm starting to think the outside is interesting."

"I hate how crowded it is in twenty eighteen," I said.

"Maybe we'll go somewhere out of the way. Virginia?"

"Oh god, no. I'm not going back there after all this. And with black skin? We—we could go to a South Seas island."

"I bet Rudy can tell us about one. And, don't forget, he's going to give us money. For your books! I can set up a little shop on the island and make necklaces to sell."

"And I'll buy a boat," said I, getting into the vision. "I'll take up diving. I saw a dive shop here. People wear tanks on their backs and breathe underwater. I could be a guide. You'll like diving too. It'll feel like flying around inside the Hollow Earth."

The beige house's door opened again, and here was Josh. He was a bit taller than me, in his twenties, with long, braided hair and a tidy beard. I sized up his strength. Could I beat him in a fight? I didn't like that he was holding a hammer.

"I'm Mason Reynolds," said I. "Seela's husband. We two are getting back together."

"Not so fast," said Josh. "Seela told me you deserted her. And suddenly you're back? This woman needs personal time to process her feelings, Mason. I'm giving her a safe space. You show up at six am—that's an invasion. It's stalking. I'm asking you to leave. Otherwise I have to call the police."

"The police!" I exclaimed, anger flooding my veins. "You should be glad I don't thrash you. You ridiculous popinjay. Come on, Seela. Get your clothes and we'll go back to Maya's."

"You need to watch yourself," Josh told me, his tenor voice rising. "I happen to know that you and Seela and Maya and Rafaelo are illegals. I think it's totally cool that Santa Cruz is a sanctuary city, but sometimes we have to draw a line. You people are guests here, Mason, and you have to mind your manners." He was tapping his hammer against the palm of his other hand.

"What's the dumbshow with the hammer?" I said, stepping closer to him. "Go ahead and fetch your clothes, Seela. We're clearing out."

Seela slipped past Josh into the house.

"I'm seeing some mental health issues with you as well," said Josh, increasingly strident. "Seela was telling me about this fantasy life you two share. The Earth is hollow, and you've been inside? You need treatment, Mason, and so does she. We're talking fugue state and psychotic break. You're ripe for a 5150—and that means involuntary commitment. If you're man enough to walk away, Mason, I'll nurture Seela like a stray dog. Otherwise—"

Right on cue, Arf pushed the door open with his nose and slipped outside to join us. He smiled at me in that way he had, letting his pink tongue loll from his open mouth. Seela was right behind him.

"I'm ready, Mason!" said Seela, her voice bright.

Josh put his hand on Seela's shoulder. "If you think this is going to be over as easily as all that—"

"It *is* over," I said, shoving Josh's hand aside.

Josh began talking very fast, his voice even higher than before, his eyes a bit blank. He raised his hammer into the air.

Was I supposed to knock him down? And wrest the hammer from his hand? Not my usual style—but once again Uxa the *woomo* came to my aid.

A zig zag line etched its way down from the low, pearly mist—and plunged into my brooding rumby amulet, which was once again on my neck. This was the last of the rumbies. It sang a silent tekelili note—and hatched. The new *woomo's* name was Ned. Most of the *woomo* were female, but Ned was a *woomo* boy.

Initially Ned resembled a yellow banana slug, three or four inches long, clinging to my black sweatshirt. His sudden arrival gave Josh pause. And then, of course, Ned began to grow. Within thirty seconds, he was three feet long, hovering in the air between Josh and me. Arf yelped in displeasure.

As for Josh—he was scared shitless. His stopped playing the madman and scooted away from me. Just for the joy of it, Ned zapped Josh's hammer with a galvanic shock. The hammer clattered to the concrete stoop. Josh went in his house and bolted the door.

"Hooray!" said Seela. "The mighty Mason and his gallant *woomo* steed!"

Not wanting to attract undue attention, I stuffed he great sausage of a *woomo* inside my sweatshirt and tucked the shirt in around my waist. Basking in the pleasant glow of Ned's tekelili, Seela and I walked back to Maya's place with Arf at our heels.

"Quick work!" said Rudy, meeting us at the door. He tapped his head. "I'm all up to date. I'm ready to write your last chapter."

"How does the chapter end?" I asked.

I freed Ned from my shirt and he hovered in the air. Arf balefully watched the *woomo* from behind the couch. Seela was exclaiming over Brumble and rocking him her arms. She paused to glance over at Rudy.

"I know how it ends," she told Rudy. "You tell us the name of a nice island and we go there."

"I like Micronesia," said the white-haired Rudy. "I went there on a dive trip with my brother a few years back. This one particular island—Pohnpei. It's perfect. Even better than Fiji."

"We'll go there," said Seela.

"We want to come too," said Rafaelo.

"I'm not sure they invited us," said Maya.

"Mason did," said Rafaelo. "On the hike up to the monastery."

"Sure, let's all go," said Seela. "We'll stick together. None of us is white. At least not now."

"I think Hector and I stay here," said Aida. "We like to be near Mexico."

"I wonder if Ned can get American passports for all of you guys," said Rudy. "That would make things easier."

No sooner said than done. Thanks to his vast tekelili, the newly-hatched Ned was already cognizant of our government's intricate workings. He sent out a tendril, almost too thin to see, and a moment later, eight blank US passports dropped to the floor. Moving with stunning speed, Ned successively personalized a passport for each of us, even for the children. His delicate fronds tattooed our personal information onto the passports, along with color photos of us. And he sprayed on some slime to cover his additions with a shiny, official-looking gloss of faint stars.

"Be sure to copy their personal info to the chips," Rudy told Ned.

"What are chips?" I asked.

"You'll learn," said Rudy. "They're everywhere in twenty eighteen. Like lice. There's one inside the back cover of each passport."

"I have a chip in here," put in Rafaelo, holding up the black glass rectangle he used for his games. "You still gonna help me code my *Tierra Hueca* game, Mason?"

"Not directly," I said. "The trick will be to have a *woomo* help you. Uxa helped me fix Hector's motorcycle—by finding the skill in a mechanic's brain. You'll want to ask Uxa or Ned to ferret out the know-how you need. Or maybe you could study books."

"There's a two-year college in Pohnpei," put in Rudy. "It's always good to get more education."

"Me, I might do that," said Maya. "Learn business math."

"No school for me," said Rafaelo. "I'll just ask the *woomo*. We'll go back and forth, try this and try that. I'll be the game designer, see, and the *woomo* will be my coders."

"Listen at him," said Maya.

While we'd been talking, Ned had finished the passports. Beautiful work, utterly convincing, at least to me, not that I'd ever seen a passport before. Rudy said they'd work. Aida, Hector, Maya, Rafaelo, Frida, Seela, Brumble, and me—all of us were free to travel anywhere we liked.

"And you won't need special permission to settle in Pohnpei," said Rudy. "Last I heard, with a U.S. passport, you can stay there as long as you like."

Rather than planning for Pohnpei, Aida and Hector were talking about taking a road trip to visit their relations in Mexico. But Maya and Rafaelo were packing for the move. At nine am, Rudy went over to the Wells Fargo bank and extracted what he deemed to be a fair sum for my share of our two Hollow Earth books.

"Kind of hurts to give you this much," he said, handing me a sheaf of a hundred hundred-dollar bills. "But *The Hollow Earth* did pretty well, and I'm thinking *Return to the Hollow Earth* might do better."

Counting the bills, I privately wondered why Rudy hadn't given me more.

"Very kind," said Seela, giving the old man a kiss on the cheek. "Thank you. And how do we get to Pohnpei?"

"I guess you could take a plane," said Rudy. "Kind of expensive, though, with two couples and two kids."

Ned had been lolling on the floor, drawing in unseen energies and steadily getting larger. He was twenty feet long, and still growing. To fit in the room, he'd curled up one end. He broke in on our conversation with a burst of tekelili. His message came as a kinetic sense of us lying on his back and arrowing across the sky, with his *woomo* aura shielding us from the frigid air. More or less like the way Lux had flown us from Santa Cruz to Big Sur.

"Can we trust Ned?" Seela asked. "What if he ships us off to Eddie's new Eden? Or carries us back inside the Hollow Earth?"

Ned reassured us that he and his race were exceedingly grateful to Seela and me for helping to bring about the Bloom. He would most certainly take us to Pohnpei. He expansively added that he would remain in Pohnpei as our backup, and for as long as we liked. A few years—or even a century—didn't mean much to a *woomo*.

So now everything was resolved. Ned stretched himself out in the house's front yard. Rafaelo, Maya, Seela, and I began loading on the luggage and the kids. A couple of neighbors were watching. They had no idea what was going on. And even if they talked, it didn't seem likely anyone would listen to them. All of us were poor. We didn't matter.

I'd thought Seela and I would be able to coax Arf onto Ned's back, but the dog was highly recalcitrant. Rather than growling or actively fighting us, he lowered himself onto his belly, made himself flat, and whimpered, with his expression bereft and piteous. He just didn't like *woomo*.

"I'll take care of him," said Rudy, hunkering down beside Arf and stroking his fur. "I used to have a dog like this, a long time ago. Will you come live with me and my wife, Arfie? We have a sunny front deck and a grassy back yard. You'll get table scraps. And I'll give you a flea collar." Rudy paused, thinking. "Oh, I just remembered something. They eat dogs on Pohnpei! All the more reason to stay with me."

Arf stuck his snout in Rudy's face and took a deep sniff, then rose to his feet and stood at the old writer's side. The man and the dog were in agreement.

"You'll finish my book?" I asked Rudy.

"I've got everything I need," he said. "I'll mail you a printed draft. We can stay in touch by email."

"What's email?"

"Maya and Rafaelo know. Good luck out there, Mason. I'm glad we met. It's a dream come true."

§

We took our places atop Ned. The *woomo* had fashioned shallow depressions for us. And Rafaelo had thought to pack drinks and food. We rose into the air, bound for Micronesia. Ned amped up his aura, and we were invisible.

Although the trip took over twelve hours, it was pleasant enough. Our money and our passports ensured us a cordial welcome in Kolonia—a sleepy, tree-shaded settlement of six thousand. It's the main town of Pohnpei. We rented a tree-shaded home made of concrete and logs, with a corrugated tin roof, a long porch, and an open-sided pavilion for cooking and eating, cooled by the breeze from the sea.

Maya and Seela are opening a jewelry stand. Rafaelo and I are starting a dive business with the guy next door. And I'm doing some writing for the local paper. Our *woomo* Ned has taken up residence in a local reef, and we visit him from time to time. Rafaelo is making progress on his *Tierra Hueca* game. They don't have cows on Pohnpei—but I got us some chickens, and we're thinking about a pig.

Rudy mailed me his draft of *Return to the Hollow Earth*, and it reads as if I wrote it myself. I didn't find much of anything to change. Tekelili is amazing.

I used to dream of a literary career. But getting to know Eddie Poe took the bloom off that rose—as did Rudy's inability to sell our book to a commercial publisher who would actually pay us some money. He's printing the narrative himself, for what little that's worth. And he says nobody believes my story is true. To hell with them all.

We're starting to make friends in Pohnpei. Brumble has learned to lie on his stomach and lift his head. Maya calls it tummy time. Frida is almost talking. It's beautiful here—the flowers, the birds, the rain, the fruit, the fish, the waves, the faces. It's almost as good as the Hollow Earth.

And Ned is out there in the reef.

Editor's Note

In 1990, I edited Mason Reynolds's 1850 manuscript, *The Hollow Earth*, and I saw it into publication. *The Hollow Earth* ends with Mason and his wife Seela setting off for California aboard a clipper ship, the *Purple Whale*. Newspaper records of the time report that the *Purple Whale* sank off Cape Horn with no survivors.

For years I've wondered if Mason and Seela might somehow have made their way to California anyway—and whether they ever revisited the Hollow Earth.

In 2006, one of my woman readers emailed me that, while on a dive trip to Fiji, she'd spent a passionate night with a man named Alan Poague, who showed her an unfinished manuscript attributed to Mason Reynolds and entitled *Return to the Hollow Earth*.

By way of researching this, my wife and I took a cruise on a liveaboard dive boat in Fiji—great fun. In a village on one of the smaller islands, I met this Alan Poague, a Californian who'd gone native in the islands. A raffish and engaging man, he played a steel guitar in the lounge of an inn that catered to divers and surfers. I told him my story, and he readily showed me the manuscript pages that he'd shown the woman diver who'd emailed me.

Poague said he was familiar with my edition of *The Hollow Earth*, and that his manuscript was by Mason Reynolds as well. How so? Supposedly the words had come to Poague in a *kava* trance, that is, in a waking dream brought on by an intoxicating local plant. He'd typed the text without really having to think about it. He'd produced eleven pages this way, and then the flow had stopped, or he'd gotten distracted—and he'd moved onto other projects. He was now assembling a diving guidebook for the Great Astrolabe Reef. And he dreamed of writing a New Age work based on his notions of the thought-processes of the *woomo*. I made a copy of Poague's eleven pages and we returned home.

Ten years later, in April, 2017. I began having lucid dreams involving the Hollow Earth—in particular I was sensing the mind of the giant *woomo* whom Mason called Uxa. Uxa was extending her tendrils from the core, worming them through volcanic vents and ocean-floor holes. Upon reaching me, Uxa's fronds wrapped my body in a net of pale gold. Using this connection, the Great Old One was speaking to me—not in words nor in images, but via certain physical sensations. She was making my fingers twitch.

I had no writing project that April. Sitting at my computer keyboard one morning, I turned my thoughts to my dreams of Uxa. As I thought of her, my fingers began to move. Suddenly I realized that Uxa wanted me to type the second narrative of Mason Reynolds.

I knew this in the same non-verbal way that I might know the workings of a mathematical proof. Mason had written *Return to the Hollow Earth* in his head, Uxa had read his mind, and now she was using me to put Mason's words to paper. She'd tried earlier to use Alan Poague of Fiji for her scribe, but he hadn't had the patience. But now, with me already having edited *The Hollow Earth*, Uxa had found someone who would see the project through.

Smiling to myself, I unleashed my fingers and let the story flow. As my tekelili connection to Uxa sharpened, I began mentally hearing the words I wrote, and inwardly seeing the scenes I described.

The strange, intense transmission lasted several hours, and when I was done, I'd typed the first six pages of *Return to the Hollow Earth*. The next day I typed five more. I compared what I had to my copy of the Alan Poague manuscript. The two texts were word for word the same.

For a week nothing more came. I lost hope. Perhaps I'd unwittingly memorized Poague's manuscript and had merely retyped it. Perhaps there was no Uxa. Perhaps I was a doddering, self-deluded, borderline-senile old man. A writer at the end of his rope.

But then, *bam*, Uxa linked into me for three days in a row—and I was well into the second chapter. My joy mounted, and in the coming months my confidence steadily grow. I didn't like telling my wife or my friends exactly what I was up to. I just said I was working on a sequel to *The Hollow Earth*, and that I had no outline at all, and that I was depending entirely on the muse. My scribing continued, off and on, for nearly a year. Nobody paid me much mind. Writing is what I do.

On March 24, 2018, things got stranger. According to what I was transcribing in the pages of *Return to the Hollow Earth*, Mason had arrived that day in Big Sur! No longer was he a fictional or a historical figure. He was here and now, just down the coast from my Los Gatos home. A day later, I found myself typing that Mason and his family had moved in with four undocumented Latinos in the Beach Flats neighborhood of Santa Cruz. Should I go and meet him? I didn't quite dare.

How had Mason jumped so far forward in time? I had only to study the pages I'd written. Mason had spent over a hundred and sixty seven years stranded with the *woomo* Uxa in the slow time zone at the Hollow Earth's core. Evidently it was near the end of that stay when Uxa began using her tekelili to send out Mason's narrative for transcription. First she'd tried it with Alan Poague, and then she'd turned to me. And then Mason had escaped the slow time zone and he'd ridden to Big Sur in a live flying saucer made of two *veem*. And, now, even with Mason so far away from the Earth's core, Uxa was still picking up his mental narrative—and transmitting the updates to me.

On March 28, 2018, I found myself writing that Mason had sold an article to a Santa Cruz newspaper called *Good Times*, and that his article was appearing that day. I'd been leery of seeking him out, but this pushed me over the edge. I got in my car and drove to the *Good Times* editorial office in Santa Cruz, and asked where I could find Mason Reynolds. A young woman told me to check the crumbling old Evergreen Cemetery.

I hurried there—and I found Mason, along with his wife Seela, their baby Brumble, Mason's new friends Maya and Rafaelo, plus an inquisitive policeman, and none other than the recently resurrected Edgar Allan Poe, accompanied by his wife Ina. I felt like I was going crazy.

But yet, everything remained, in some ways, ordinary. Mason already knew that I'd edited and published his manuscript of the *Hollow Earth*, and he was interested in discussing this. He and his friends were on the point of being in trouble with the police, and I was able to talk our way past the problem.

And—Edgar Allan Poe? Was I really meeting Poe? It certainly seemed so, not that he was in good shape, having spent well over a century buried in a bronze casket, and then having immediately gotten drunk. But you know all this if you've read *Return to the Hollow Earth*. Mason describes these scenes better than I. He's a born writer, a natural.

Having grown used to the fluent, assured tone of Mason's two narratives, I was startled to see how young he was in person. Eighteen years old, or not quite that. He was dark-skinned from the *woomo* light, with the features of a slender, white, Southern boy, and with, of course, something of a Virginia accent. He was very articulate, and with a rich vocabulary. His speech had a leisurely pace that matched his origin in slower times. His eyes were quick, animated, and perhaps a bit haunted.

Seela was dark brown, with thin lips and a delicate nose, resembling the Melanesian women of Fiji. She was beautiful and lively, with a sharp tongue. Clearly she loved Mason and Brumble. The moment of her parting with them was very painful, and their reunion a joy.

Mason and Seela didn't like our present day world, and Mason himself was a bit let down that he hadn't traveled onward through that dubious tunnel in space with Eddie Poe. I was glad to give Mason and Seela some money—although he thinks it should have been more. I hope I did well in suggesting they move to Pohnpei. And I'm glad to have inherited their dog. Arf is good company, with deep wisdom in his eyes.

In my excitement, I didn't think to take any photos of Mason, nor of the epic scenes at Big Sur. But Arf is here in the flesh. As I like to tell people, "If you don't believe the Hollow Earth is real, come visit me and you can see the dog!"

As I write this, he's lying in a patch of sun, thumping his tail against the floor. Good dog. Arf is my proof that the Earth is hollow.

I'm no longer getting any tekelili updates from Uxa. Perhaps, from the *woomo* point of view, my mission is done—not that I'm certain what was the purpose of my mission. Perhaps Mason's two narratives are meant to prepare our society for an eventual merger with the civilizations of the Hollow Earth? The *woomo* take a long view.

I don't have any contact information for Mason, but I do have Rafaelo's email address. A couple of months ago I mailed a paper printout of my draft of *Return to the Hollow Earth* to Mason in care of General Delivery at Pohnpei. Rafaelo emailed me Mason's response, and this comprises the brief closing section of the book's final chapter. I've heard nothing more since then.

Judging from Mason's ending to the book, I think he's angry about his book being published with so little fanfare—and that he blames me. And never mind that I spent a year writing his book for him, and gave him ten thousand dollars! A slicker promoter might have found a way to package Mason's adventures into a best-seller. A wiser editor might not insist—in the face of universal derision—that Mason's two books are literally true.

The public is wary of nuts—and this category unfairly includes believers in the doctrine of the Hollow Earth. But Mason and I are right. As he puts it—*to hell with them all*. What matters is that we've managed to publish the truth, and nobody stopped us.

As a final point, note that definitive proofs of the Hollow Earth doctrine are in the offing. Eventually the passageways at the poles will reopen. As the Antarctic ice melts, the cap across the South Hole will crumble. And, as ice vanishes from the Arctic and the speed of the polar jet stream increases, the pre-1850 North Hole maelstrom will reemerge.

And then Mason Reynolds will be granted his just place in the Pantheon of great explorers!

One final note. In 2021, I removed offensive uses of racial epithets from *The Hollow Earth & Return to the Hollow Earth*. The 2021 edition supersedes all earlier combined or separate versions of the narratives.

—Rudy Rucker, Los Gatos, California
July 4, 2018 and May 29, 2021

Acknowledgements

Although it seemed obvious to me—and to those around me—that the public would welcome a new Hollow Earth novel, I could find no commercial publisher who agreed.

So I turned once again to Kickstarter to crowd-source my funding, and it worked well. I raised enough money to make it feasible to publish *Return to the Hollow Earth*, along with a new edition of *The Hollow Earth*. Heartfelt thanks to my supporters!

Here's a list of their chosen names, alphabetized by their first letters.

@ofeenah, Adam Browne, Adrian Magni, AgentKaz, Al Billings, Alan Robson, Albert Henry Tyson, Alex McLaren, Alexander Pappajohn, Alexander the Drake, Allen Tollin, Allen Varney, Andrew Binder, Andrew Gordon White, Andrew Ward, Aris Alissandrakis, Arthur Murphy, Beat Suter, Benet Devereux, Benjamin H Henry, Bob Hearn, Bob Schoenholtz, Brian Anderson, Brian Dysart, Cameron Cooper, Carlos Pascual, Carrie G, Chad Bowden, Chris McLaren, Chuck Ivy, Chuck Shotton, Cliff Winnig, Collin Bennett, DaddyChurchill, Dan P, Daniel Rubin, Daniele A. Gewurz, Dave Bouvier, Dave Holets, David Chatterjee, David H. Adler, David Kirkpatrick, David Rains, David Schutt, Derek Bosch, Don and Harriet, Don Tardiff, Doug Bissell, Dwayne Plain, Eamon John Carrig, Ed Kirkland, Edward Marr, Eibo Thieme, Eli Tishberg, Elijah Wendell Cauley and Benjamin Harry Cauley, eorojas@gmail.com, Eric Wollesen, Erik Sowa, Fraser Lovatt, Gaia Maffini Mazzei,

Gara Gaines, George Bendo & Hedvig Bartha, Grat Crabtree, Greg Deocampo, Gregory Scheckler, Hiroyuki OGINO, https://twitter.com/cixelsyd, Ian Chung, Iggy Utah, Jayson Lorenzen, Jeffrey Ferrell, Jeremy W, Jerry Bonnell, Jim Anderson, Joe Sislow, Joel Ward, John, John C Monroe, John Kohler, John R Donald, John T. Baldwin, John Winkelman, Jon, Jon Cook, Jon Hamlow, Jon Kimmich, Jon Nebenfuhr, Josh Cooper, Julia Grillmayr, Karl W. Reinsch, Karl-Arthur Arlamovsky, kath odonnell, Kevin J. "Womzilla" Maroney, Kevin Wehner, Lee Fisher, Leland Poague, lord of anti-slack, Luke Gutzwiller, Mark Anderson, Mark Chatinsky, Mark L Cohen, Martin, Matthew Cox, Maxim Jakubowski, Mayer Brenner, Michael Becker, Michael W, Michail Sarigiannidis, Moshe Feder, None, Norbert Bruckner, Patrick Shettlesworth, Philip Rubin, Rafael Fajardo, Rafael Laguna de la Vera, Raja Thiagarajan, Ramon Cahenzli, Rebecca :), Richard J. Ohnemus, Richie O'Hara-Beamand, RJ Moore, rob alley, Robert Guffey, Rod Bartlett, Ronald Pottol, Ronan Waide, Ross Presser, Roy Berman, Sandor Silverman, Sandy McAuley, Scott and Annabelle Call, Scott G Lewis, Scott Lazerus, Seanstoppable, Stefan Schmiedl, Steve Hirst, The Hackers Conference, Theron Trowbridge, Thom Slattery, Thomas Gideon, Tim Conkling, Tim Gruchy, Timothy Lee Russell, Timothy M. Maroney, Todd Ellner, Todd Fincannon, Tom M, Tom Velebny, Walter F. Croft, William Sked, Yaro Godziumakha, and Yoshimichi Furusawa.

Thanks also to those backers who chose not to be listed here. And thanks to Michael Troutman and my wife Sylvia, who proofread my final manuscript. And thanks to John Douglas, who published the first edition of *The Hollow Earth*, and to Chris Roberson, who published the second.

In closing, I'll remind you of my website for the Hollow Earth novels of Mason Reynolds.

www.rudyrucker.com/thehollowearth

Yours in full *woomo* tekelili.

—Rudy Rucker, Los Gatos, California
   July 4, 2018 and May 29, 2021

12/21 Ingram 17.95 ✓

...on can be obtained
...com

1

9 781940 948355